Deathworld One

On all sides the earth was buckling, cracking, as more loops of the underground thing forced its way into the light. Safety lay ahead. Only in front of it rose an arch of dirt encrusted clay.

Jason stood, frozen. Even the smoke in the sky hung unmoving. The highstanding loop of alien life was before him, every detail piercingly clear. Thick as a man, ribbed and grey as old bark. Tendrils projected from all parts of it, twisting lengths that writhed slowly with snake-like life. Shaped like a plant, yet with the motions of an animal....

Deathworld Two

There was a flickering in the darkness, a wavering light coming toward them. Jason could not speak, but he heard Mikah cry out for help. The light came nearer, some kind of flare or torch....

It was like a nightmare. It wasn't a man but a thing that held the flare. A thing of sharp angles, fang-faced and horrible. It had a clubbed extremity with which it clubbed down Mikah, and then the creature turned toward Jason....

Deathworld Three

As the band of men turned to follow Temuchin, the standard-bearer passed in front of Jason's cage. His pole was topped with a human skull and Jason saw that the banner itself was made up of string after string of human thumbs, mummified and dry, knotted together on thongs.

"Wait!" Jason shouted at their retreating backs. "You can't just do this—"

A squad of soldiers surrounded his cage. Jason cowered back as the entire cage swung up on creaking hinges, and he clutched at the bars as the soldiers reached for him....

Berkley books by Harry Harrison

THE ADVENTURES OF THE STAINLESS STEEL RAT
THE DEATHWORLD TRILOGY

THE
DEATHWORLD
TRILOGY
Three Novels
HARRY HARRISON

Ⓑ®
BERKLEY BOOKS, NEW YORK

THE DEATHWORLD TRILOGY

A Berkley Book / published by arrangement with
the author

PRINTING HISTORY
Berkley edition / February 1976
Twelfth printing / July 1983

ISBN: 0-425-06827-7

CONTENTS

THE
DEATHWORLD
TRILOGY

DEATHWORLD

For JOAN

1

With a gentle sigh the service tube dropped a message capsule into the receiving cup. The attention bell chimed once and was silent. Jason dinAlt stared at the harmless capsule as though it were a ticking bomb.

Something was going wrong. He felt a hard knot of tension form inside of him. This was no routine service memo or hotel communication, but a sealed personal message. Yet he knew no one on this planet, having arrived by spacer less than eight hours earlier. Since even his name was new—dating back to the last time he had changed ships—there could be no personal messages. Yet here one was.

Stripping the seal with his thumbnail, he took the top off. The recorder in the pencil-sized capsule gave the taped voice a tinny sound, with no clues as to the speaker.

"Kerk Pyrrus would like to see Jason dinAlt. I'm waiting in the lobby."

It was wrong, yet it couldn't be avoided. Chances were that the man was harmless. A salesman perhaps, or a case of mistaken identity. Nevertheless Jason carefully positioned his gun behind a pillow on the couch, with the safety off. There was no way to predict how these things would turn out. He signaled the desk to send the visitor up. When the door opened, Jason was slumped down on a corner of the couch, sipping from a tall glass.

A retired wrestler. That was Jason's first thought when the man came through the door. Kerk Pyrrus was a grey-haired rock of a man, his body apparently chiseled out of flat slabs of muscle. His grey clothes were so conservative they were almost a uniform. Strapped to his forearm was a rugged and much-worn holster, a gun muzzle peering blankly from it.

"You're dinAlt the gambler," the stranger said bluntly. "I have a proposition for you."

Jason looked across the top of his glass, letting his mind play with the probabilities. This was either the police or the competition—and

3

he wanted nothing to do with either. He had to know a lot more before he became involved in any deals.

"Sorry, friend," Jason smiled. "But you have the wrong party. Like to oblige, but my gambling always seems to help the casinos more than myself. So you see . . ."

"Let's not play games with each other," Kerk broke in with a chesty rumble. "You're dinAlt and you're Bohel as well. If you want more names, I'll mention Mahaut's Planet, the Nebula Casino and plenty more. I have a proposition that will benefit both of us, and you had better listen to it."

None of the names caused the slightest change in Jason's half-smile. But his body was tensely alert. This musclebound stranger knew things he had no right to know. It was time to change the subject.

"That's quite a gun you have there," Jason said. "But guns make me nervous. I'd appreciate it if you took it off."

Kerk scowled down at the gun, as if he were seeing it for the first time. "No, I never take it off." He seemed mildly annoyed by the suggestion.

The testing period was over. Jason needed the upper hand if he was to get out of this one alive. As he leaned forward to put his drink on the table, his other hand fell naturally behind the pillow. He was touching the gun butt when he said, "I'm afraid I'll have to insist. I always feel a little uncomfortable around people who are armed." He kept talking to distract attention while he pulled out his gun. Fast and smooth.

He could have been moving in slow motion for all the difference it made. Kerk Pyrrus stood dead still while the gun came out, while it swung in his direction. Not until the very last instant did he act. When he did, the motion wasn't visible. First his gun was in the arm-holster—then it was aimed between Jason's eyes. It was an ugly, heavy weapon with a pitted front orifice that showed plenty of use.

Jason knew if he swung his own weapon up a fraction of an inch more he would be dead. He dropped his arm carefully, angry at himself for trying to substitute violence for thought. Kerk flipped his own gun back into the holster with the same ease he had drawn it.

"Enough of that now," Kerk said. "Let's get down to business."

Jason reached out and downed a large mouthful from his glass, bridling his temper. He was fast with a gun—his life had depended on it more than once—and this was the first time he had ever been outdrawn. It was the offhand, unimportant manner it had been done that irritated him.

"I'm not prepared to do business," he said acidly. "I've come to Cassylia for a vacation, get away from work."

"Let's not fool each other, dinAlt," Kerk said impatiently. "You've never worked at an honest job in your entire life. You're a professional gambler and that's why I'm here to see you."

Jason forced down his anger and threw the gun to the other end of the couch so he wouldn't be tempted to commit suicide. He had been so sure that no one knew him on Cassylia and had been looking forward to a big kill at the Casino. He would worry about that later. This wrestler type seemed to know all the answers. Let him plot the course for awhile and see where it led.

"All right, what do you want."

Kerk dropped into a chair that creaked ominously under his weight, and dug an envelope out of one pocket. He flipped through it quickly and dropped a handful of gleaming Galactic Exchange Notes onto the table. Jason glanced at them—then sat up suddenly.

"What are they—forgeries?" he asked, holding one up to the light.

"They're real enough," Kerk told him, "I picked them up at the bank. Exactly twenty-seven bills—or twenty-seven million credits. I want you to use them as a bankroll when you go to the Casino tonight. Gamble with them and win."

They looked real enough—and they could be checked. Jason fingered them thoughtfully while he examined the other man.

"I don't know what you have in mind," he said. "But you realize I can't make any guarantees. I gamble—but I don't always win."

"You gamble—and you win when you want to," Kerk said grimly. "We looked into that quite carefully before I came to you."

"If you mean to say that I cheat . . ." Carefully, Jason grabbed his temper again and held it down. There was no future in getting annoyed.

Kerk continued in the same level voice, ignoring Jason's growing anger. "Maybe you don't call it cheating, frankly I don't care. As far as I'm concerned, you could have your sleeves lined with aces and electromagnets in your toes. As long as you win. I'm not here to discuss moral points with you. I said I had a proposition.

"We have worked hard for that money—but it still isn't enough. To be precise, we need three billion credits. The only way to get that sum is by gambling. With these twenty-seven million as bankroll."

"And what do I get out of it?" Jason asked the question coolly, as if any bit of the fantastic proposition made sense.

"Everything above the three billion you can keep, that should be fair enough. You're not risking your own money, but you stand to make enough to keep you for life if you win."

"And if I lose?"

Kerk thought for a moment, not liking the taste of the idea. "Yes, there is the chance you might lose. I hadn't thought about that."

He reached a decision. "If you lose—well, I suppose that is just a risk we will have to take. Though I think I would kill you then. The ones who died to get the twenty-seven million deserve at least that." He said it quietly, without malice, and it was more of a considered decision than a threat.

Stamping to his feet, Jason refilled his glass and offered one to Kerk who took it with a nod of thanks. He paced back and forth, unable to sit. The whole proposition made him angry, yet at the same time had a fatal fascination. He was a gambler and this talk was like the sight of drugs to an addict.

Stopping suddenly, he realized that his mind had been made up for some time. Win or lose—live or die—how could he say no to the chance to gamble with money like that! He turned suddenly and jabbed his finger at the big man in the chair.

"I'll do it—you probably knew I would from the time you came in here. There are some terms of my own, though. I want to know who you are, and who *they* are you keep talking about. And where did the money come from—is it stolen?"

Kerk drained his own glass and pushed it away from him.

"Stolen money? No, quite the opposite. Two years' work mining and refining ore to get it. It was mined on Pyrrus and sold here on Cassylia. You can check on that very easily. I sold it. I'm the Pyrric ambassador to this planet." He smiled at the thought. "Not that that means much, I'm ambassador to at least six other planets as well. Comes in handy when you want to do business."

Jason looked at the muscular man with his grey hair and worn, military-cut clothes, and decided not to laugh. You heard of strange things out in the frontier planets and every word could be true. He had never heard of Pyrrus either, thought that didn't mean anything. There were over thirty thousand known planets in the inhabited universe.

"I'll check on what you have told me," Jason said. "If it's true we can do business. Call me tomorrow. . . ."

"No," Kerk said. "The money has to be won tonight. I've already issued a check for this twenty-seven million; it will bounce as high as the Pleiades unless we deposit the money in the morning, so that's our time limit."

With each moment, the whole affair became more fantastic—and more intriguing for Jason. He looked at his watch. There was still enough time to find out if Kerk was lying or not.

"All right, we'll do it tonight," he said. "Only I'll have to have one of those bills to verify."

Kerk stood up to go. "Take them all, I won't be seeing you again until after you've won. I'll be at the Casino, of course, but don't recognize me. It would be much better if they didn't know where your money was coming from or how much you had."

Then he was gone, after a bone-crushing handclasp that closed on Jason's hand like vise jaws. Jason was alone with the money. Fanning the bills out like a hand of cards, he stared at their sepia-and-gold faces, trying to get the reality through his head. Twenty-seven million credits. What was to stop him from just walking out the door with them and vanishing. Nothing really, except his own sense of honor.

Kerk Pyrrus, the man with the same last name as the planet he came from, was the universe's biggest fool. Or he knew just what he was doing. From the way the interview had gone, the latter seemed the best bet.

"He *knows* I would much rather gamble with the money than steal it," he said wryly.

Slipping a small gun into his waistband holster and pocketing the money, he went out.

2

The robot teller at the bank just pinged with electronic shock when he presented one of the bills and flashed a panel that directed him to see Vice President Wain. Wain was a smooth customer who bugged his eyes and lost some of his tan when he saw the sheaf of bills.

"You—wish to deposit these with us?" he asked while his fingers unconsciously stroked them.

"Not today," Jason said. "They were paid to me as a debt. Would you please check that they are authentic and change them. I'd like five hundred thousand credit notes."

Both of his inner chest pockets were packed tight when he left the bank. The bills were good and he felt like a walking mint. This was the first time in his entire life that carrying a large sum of money made him uncomfortable. Waving to a passing helicab, he went directly to the Casino where he knew he would be safe. For awhile.

Cassylia Casino was the playspot of the nearby cluster of star systems. It was the first time Jason had seen it, though he knew its type well. He had spent most of his adult life in casinos like this on other worlds. The décor differed but they were always the same. Gambling and socialites in public—and behind the scenes all the private vice you could afford. Theoretically no-limit games, but that was true only up to a certain point. When the house was really hurt, the honest games stopped being square and the big winner had to watch his step very carefully. These were the odds Jason dinAlt had played against countless times before. He was wary but not very concerned.

The dining room was almost empty and the majordomo quickly rushed to the side of the stranger in the richly cut clothes. Jason was lean and dark and moved with a positive, self-assured manner. More like the owner of inherited wealth than a professional gambler. This appearance was important and he cultivated it. The cuisine looked good and the cellar turned out to be wonderful. He had a professional and enthusiastic talk with the wine steward while waiting for the soup, then settled down to enjoy his meal.

He ate leisurely and the large dining room was filled before he was through. Watching the entertainment over a long cigar killed some more time. When he finally went to the gaming rooms, they were filled and active.

Moving slowly around the room, he dropped a few thousand credits. He scarcely noticed how he played, giving more attention to the feel of the games. The play all seemed honest and none of the equipment was rigged. That could be changed very quickly, he realized. Usually it wasn't necessary; house percentage was enough to assure a profit.

Once he saw Kerk out of the corner of his eye, but he paid him no attention. The ambassador was losing small sums steadily at seven-and-silver and seemed to be impatient. Probably waiting for Jason to begin playing seriously. He smiled and strolled on slowly.

Jason settled on the dice table as he usually did. It was the surest way to make small winnings. *And if I feel it tonight, I can clean this casino out!* That was his secret, the power that won for him steadily—and every once in awhile enabled him to make a killing and move on quickly before the hired thugs came to get the money back.

The dice reached him and he threw an eight the hard way. Betting was light and he didn't push himself, just kept away from the sevens. He made the point and passed a natural. Then he crapped out and the dice moved on.

Sitting there, making small automatic bets while the dice went around the table, he thought about the power. *Funny, after all the years of work, we still don't know much about* psi. *They can train people a bit, and improve skills a bit—but that's all.*

He was feeling strong tonight, he knew that the money in his pocket gave him the extra lift that sometimes helped him break through. With his eyes half closed he picked up the dice—and let his mind gently caress the pattern of sunken dots. Then they shot out of his hand and he stared at a seven.

It was there.

Stronger than he had felt it in years. The stiff weight of the million credits had done it. The world all around was sharp-cut and clear and the dice were completely in his control. He knew to the tenth credit how much the other players had in their wallets and was aware of the cards in the hands of the players behind him.

Slowly, carefully, he built up the stakes.

There was no effort to the dice; they rolled and sat up like trained dogs. Jason took his time and concentrated on the psychology of the players and the stickman. It took almost two hours to build his money on the table to seven hundred thousand credits. Then he caught the stickman signaling they had a heavy winner. He waited until the hard-eyed man strolled over to watch the game, then he breathed on the dice, bet all his table stakes—and blew it all with a single roll. The houseman smiled happily, the stickman relaxed—and, out of the corner of his eye, Jason saw Kerk turning a dark purple.

Sweating, pale, his hand trembling ever so slightly, Jason opened the front of his jacket and pulled out one of the envelopes of new bills. Breaking the seal with his finger, he dropped two of them on the table.

"Could we have a no-limit game," he asked. "I'd like to—win back some of my money."

The stickman had trouble controlling his smile now, he glanced across at the houseman who nodded a quick *yes*. They had a sucker and they meant to clean him. He had been playing from his wallet all evening, now he was cracking into a sealed envelope to try for what he had lost. A thick envelope, too, and probably not his money. Not that the house cared in the least. To them money had no loyalties. The play went on with the Casino in a very relaxed mood.

Which was just the way Jason wanted it. He needed to get as deep into them as he could before someone realized *they* might be on the losing end. The rough stuff would start and he wanted to put it off as long as possible. It would be hard to win smoothly then—and his *psi* power might go as quickly as it had come. That had happened before.

He was playing against the house now, the two other players were obvious shills, and a crowd had jammed solidly around to watch. After losing and winning a bit, he hit a streak of naturals and his pile of gold chips tottered higher and higher. There was nearly a billion there, he estimated roughly. The dice were still falling true, though he was soaked with sweat from the effort. Betting the entire stack of chips, he reached for the dice. The stickman reached faster and hooked them away.

"House calls for new dice," he said flatly.

Jason straightened up and wiped his hands, glad of the instant's relief. This was the third time the house had changed dice to try and break his winning streak. It was their privilege. The hard-eyed Casino man opened his wallet as he had done before and drew out a pair at random. Stripping off their plastic cover, he threw them the length of the table to Jason. They came up a natural seven and Jason smiled.

When he scooped them up, the smile slowly faded. The dice were transparent, finely made, even weighted on all sides—and crooked.

The pigment on the dots of five sides of each die was some heavy metal compound, probably lead. The sixth side was a ferric compound. They would roll true unless they hit a magnetic field—which meant the entire surface of the table could be magnetized. He could never have spotted the difference if he hadn't *looked* at the dice with his mind. But what could he do about it?

Shaking them slowly, he glanced quickly around the table. There was what he needed. An ashtray with a magnet in its base to hold it to the metal edge of the table. Jason stopped shaking the dice and looked at them quizzically, then reached over and grabbed the ashtray. He dropped the base against his hand.

As he lifted the ashtray, there was a concerted gasp from all sides. The dice were sticking there, upside down, boxcars showing.

"Are these what you call honest dice?" he asked.

The man who had thrown out the dice reached quickly for his hip pocket. Jason was the only one who saw what happened next. He was watching that hand closely, his own fingers near his gun butt.

As the man dived into his pocket, a hand reached out of the crowd behind him. From its square-cut size, it could have belonged to only one person. The thick thumb and index finger clamped swiftly around the houseman's wrist, then they were gone. The man screamed shrilly and held up his arm, his hand dangling limp as a glove from the broken wrist bones.

With his flank well protected, Jason could go on with the game. "The old dice, if you don't mind," he said quietly.

Dazedly the stickman pushed them over. Jason shook quickly and rolled. Before they hit the table, he realized he couldn't control them—the transient *psi* power had gone.

End over end they turned. And faced up seven.

Counting the chips as they were pushed over to him, he added up a bit under two billion credits. They would be winning that much if he left the game now—but it wasn't the three billion that Kerk needed. Well, it would have to be enough. As he reached for the chips he caught Kerk's eye across the table and the other man shook his head in a steady *no*.

"Let it ride," Jason said wearily, "one more roll."

He breathed on the dice, polished them on his cuff, and wondered how he had ever gotten into this spot. Billions riding on a pair of dice. That was as much as the annual income of some planets. The only thing that made it possible to have stakes like that was the fact that the planetary government had a controlling interest in the Casino. He shook as long as he could, reaching for the control that wasn't there—then let fly.

Everything else had stopped in the Casino and people were standing on tables and chairs to watch. There wasn't a sound from that large crowd. The dice bounced back from the board with a clatter loud in the silence and tumbled over the cloth.

A five and a one. Six. He still had to make his point. Scooping up the dice, Jason talked to them, mumbled the ancient oaths that brought luck and threw again.

It took five throws before he made the six.

The crowd echoed his sigh and their voices rose quickly. He wanted to stop, take a deep breath, but he knew he couldn't. Winning the money was only part of the job—they now had to get away with it. It had to look casual. A waiter was passing with a tray of drinks. Jason stopped him and tucked a one hundred credit note in his pocket.

"Drinks are on me," he shouted while he pried the tray out of the waiter's hands. Well-wishers cleared the filled glasses away quickly and Jason piled the chips onto the tray. They more than loaded it, but Kerk appeared that moment with a second tray.

"I'll be glad to help you sir, if you will permit me," he said.

Jason looked at him and laughed permission. It was the first time he had a clear look at Kerk in the Casino. He was wearing loose, purple evening pajamas over what must have been a false stomach. The sleeves were long and baggy so he looked fat rather than muscular. It was a simple but effective disguise.

Carefully carrying the loaded trays, surrounded by a crowd of excited patrons, they made their way to the cashier's window. The manager himself was there, wearing a forced grin. Even the grin faded when he counted the chips.

"Could you come back in the morning," he said, "I'm afraid we don't have that kind of money on hand."

"What's the matter," Kerk shouted, "trying to get out of paying him? You took *my* money easy enough when I lost—it works both ways!"

The onlookers, always happy to see the house lose, growled their disagreement. Jason finished the matter in a loud voice.

"I'll be reasonable. Give me what cash you have and I'll take a check for the balance."

There was no way out. Under the watchful eye of the gleeful crowd, the manager packed an envelope with bills and wrote a check. Jason took a quick glimpse at it, then stuffed it into an inside pocket. With the envelope under one arm, he followed Kerk toward the door.

Because of the onlookers, there was no trouble in the main room, but just as they reached the side entrance two men moved in, blocking their way.

"Just a moment," one said. He never finished the sentence. Kerk walked into them without slowing and they bounced away like tenpins. Then Kerk and Jason were out of the building and walking fast.

"Into the parking lot," Kerk said. "I have a car there."

When they rounded the corner, there was a car bearing down on them. Before Jason could get his gun clear of the holster, Kerk was in front of him. His arm came up and his big ugly gun burst through the cloth of his sleeve and jumped into his hand. A single shot killed the driver and the car swerved and crashed. The other two men in the car died coming out of the door, their guns dropping from their hands.

After that they had no trouble. Kerk drove at top speed away from the Casino, the torn sleeve of his pajamas whipping in the breeze, giving glimpses of the big gun back in the holster.

"When you get the chance," Jason said, "you'll have to show me how that trick holster works."

"When we get the chance," Kerk answered as he dived the car into the city access tube.

3

The building they stopped at was one of the finer residences in Cassylia. As they had driven, Jason counted the money and separated his share. Almost sixteen million credits. It still didn't seem quite real. When they got out in front of the building, he gave Kerk the rest.

"Here's your three billion. Don't think it was easy," he said.

"It could have been worse," was his only answer.

The recorded voice scratched in the speaker over the door.

"Sire Ellus has retired for the night, would you please call again in the morning. All appointments are made in advan————"

The voice broke off as Kerk pushed the door open. He did it almost effortlessly with the flat of his hand. As they went in, Jason looked at the remnants of torn and twisted metal that hung in the lock and wondered again about his companion.

Strength—more than physical strength—he's like an elemental force. I have the feeling that nothing can stop him.

It made him angry—and at the same time fascinated him. He didn't want out of the deal until he found out more about Kerk and his planet. And "they" who had died for the money he gambled.

Sire Ellus was old, balding and angry, not at all used to having his rest disturbed. His complaints stopped suddenly when Kerk threw the money down on the table.

"Is the ship being loaded yet, Ellus? Here's the balance due." Ellus only fumbled the bills for a moment before he could answer Kerk's question.

"The ship—but, of course. We began loading when you gave us the deposit. You'll have to excuse my confusion; this is a little irregular. We never handle transactions of this size in cash."

"That's the way I like to do business," Kerk answered him.

"I've canceled the deposit, this is the total sum. Now how about a receipt."

Ellus had made out the receipt before his senses returned. He held it tightly while he looked uncomfortably at the three billion spread out before him.

"Wait—I can't take it now, you'll have to return in the morning, to the bank. In normal business fashion," Ellus decided firmly.

Kerk reached over and gently drew the paper out of Ellus' hand.

"Thanks for the receipt," he said. "I won't be here in the morning so this will be satisfactory. And if you're worried about the money, I suggest you get in touch with some of your plant guards or private police. You'll feel a lot safer."

When they left through the shattered door, Ellus was frantically dialing numbers on his screen. Kerk answered Jason's next question before he could ask it.

"I imagine you would like to live to spend that money in your pocket, so I've booked us two seats on an interplanetary ship." He glanced at the car clock. "It leaves in about two hours so we have plenty of time. I'm hungry, let's find a restaurant. I hope you have nothing at the hotel worth going back for. It would be a little difficult."

"Nothing worth getting killed for," Jason said. "Now where can we go to eat? There are a few questions I would like to ask you."

They circled carefully down to the transport levels until they were sure they hadn't been followed. Kerk nosed the car into a shadowed loading dock where they abandoned it.

"We can always get another car," he said, "and they probably have this one spotted. Let's walk back to the freightway, I saw a restaurant there as we came by."

Dark and looming shapes of overland freight carriers filled the parking lot. They picked their way around the man-high wheels and into the hot and noisy restaurant. The drivers and early morning workers took no notice of them as they found a booth in the back and dialed a meal.

Kerk chiseled a chunk of meat off the slab in front of him and popped it cheerfully into his mouth. "Ask your questions," he said. "I'm feeling much better already."

"What's in this ship you arranged for tonight? What kind of cargo was I risking my neck for?"

"I thought you were risking your neck for money," Kerk said dryly. "But be assured it was in a good cause. That cargo means the survival of a world. Guns, ammunition, mines, explosives and such."

Jason choked over a mouthful of food. "Gun-running! What are you doing, financing a private war? And how can you talk about survival with a lethal cargo like that? Don't try and tell me they have a peaceful use. Who are you killing?"

Most of the big man's humor had vanished: he had that grim look Jason well knew.

"Yes, peaceful would be the right word. Because that is basically all we want. Just to live in peace. And it is not *who* are we killing—it is *what* we are killing."

Jason pushed his plate away with an angry gesture. "You're talking in riddles," he said. "What you say has no meaning."

"It has meaning enough," Kerk told him. "But only on one planet in the universe. Just how much do you know about Pyrrus?"

"Absolutely nothing."

For a moment Kerk sat wrapped in memory, scowling distantly. Then he went on.

"Mankind doesn't belong on Pyrrus—yet has been there for almost three hundred years now. The age expectancy of my people is sixteen years. Of course most adults live beyond that, but the high child mortality brings the average down.

"It is everything that a humanoid world should not be. The gravity is nearly twice earth normal. The temperature can vary daily from arctic to tropic. The climate—well you have to experience it to believe it. Like nothing you've seen anywhere else in the galaxy."

"I'm frightened," Jason said dryly. "What do you have, methane or chlorine reactions? I've been down on planets like that—"

Kerk slammed his hand down hard on the table. The dishes bounced and the tablelegs creaked. "Laboratory reactions!" he growled. "They look great on a bench—but what happens when you have a world filled with those compounds? In an eye-wink of galactic time all the violence is locked up in nice, stable compounds. The atmosphere may be poisonous for an oxygen breather, but taken by itself it's as harmless as weak beer.

"There is only one setup that is pure poison as a planetary atmosphere. Plenty of H_2O, the most universal solvent you can find, plus free oxygen to work on—"

"Water and oxygen!" Jason broke in. "You mean Earth—or a planet like Cassylia here? That's preposterous."

"Not at all. Because you were born in this kind of environment, you accept it as right and natural. You take it for granted that metals corrode, coastlines change, and storms interfere with communication. These are normal occurrences on oxygen-water worlds. On Pyrrus these conditions are carried to the nth degree.

"The planet has an axial tilt of almost 42°, so there is a tremendous range of temperature from season to season. This is one of the prime causes of a constantly changing icecap. The weather generated by this is spectacular to say the least."

"If that's all," Jason said, "I don't see why . . ."

"That's *not* all—it's barely the beginning. The open seas perform the dual destructive function of supplying water vapor to keep the weather going, and building up gigantic tides. Pyrrus' two satellites, Samas and Bessos, combine at times to pull the oceans up into thirty meter tides. And until you've seen one of these tides lap over into an active volcano you've seen nothing.

"Heavy elements are what brought us to Pyrrus—and these same elements keep the planet at a volcanic boil. There have been at least thirteen supernovas in the immediate stellar neighborhood. Heavy elements can be found on most of their planets of course— as well as completely unbreathable atmospheres. Long-term timing and exploitation can't be done by anything but a self-sustaining colony. Which meant Pyrrus, where the radioactive elements are locked in the planetary core, surrounded by a shell of lighter ones. While this allows for the atmosphere men need, it also provides unceasing volcanic activity as the molten plasma forces its way to the surface."

For the first time, Jason was silent. Trying to imagine what life could be like on a planet constantly at war with itself.

"I've saved the best for last," Kerk said with grim humor. "Now that you have an idea of what the environment is like—think of the kind of life forms that would populate it. I doubt if there is one off-world specie that would live a minute. Plants and animals on Pyrrus are *tough*. They fight the world and they fight each other. Hundreds of thousands of years of genetic weeding-out have produced things that would give even an electronic brain nightmares. Armor-plated, poisonous, claw-tipped and fanged-mouthed. That describes everything that walks, flaps or just sits and grows. Ever see a plant with teeth—that bite? I don't think you want to. You'd have to be on Pyrrus and that means you would be dead within seconds of leaving the ship. Even I'll have to take a refresher course before I'll be able to go outside the landing buildings. The unending war for survival keeps the life forms competing and changing. Death is simple, but the ways of dealing it too numerous to list."

Unhappiness rode like a weight on Kerk's broad shoulders. After long moments of thought, he moved visibly to shake it off. Returning his attention to his food and mopping the gravy from his plate, he voiced part of his feelings.

"I suppose there is no logical reason why we should stay and fight this endless war. Except that Pyrrus is our home." The last piece of gravy-soaked bread vanished and he waved the empty fork at Jason.

"Be happy you're an off-worlder and will never have to see it."

"That's where you're wrong," Jason said as calmly as he could. "You see, I'm going back with you."

4

"Don't talk stupidly," Kerk said as he punched for a duplicate order of steak. "There are much simpler ways of committing suicide. Don't you realize that you're a millionaire now? With what you have in your pocket, you can relax the rest of your life on the pleasure planets. Pyrrus is a death world, not a sightseeing spot for jaded tourists. I cannot permit you to return with me."

Gamblers who lose their tempers don't last long. Jason was angry now. Yet it showed only in a negative way. In the lack of expression on his face and the calmness of his voice.

"Don't tell me what I can or cannot do, Kerk Pyrrus. You're a big man with a fast gun—but that doesn't make you my keeper. All you can do is stop me from going back on your ship. But I can easily afford to get there another way. And don't try to tell me I want to go to Pyrrus for sightseeing when you have no idea of my real reasons."

Jason didn't even try to explain his reasons, they were only half realized and too personal. The more he traveled, the more things looked the same to him. The old, civilized planets sank into a drab similarity. Frontier worlds all had the crude sameness of temporary camps in a forest. Not that the galactic worlds bored him. It was just that he had found their limitations—yet had never found his own. Until he met Kerk he had acknowledged no man his superior, or even his equal. This was more than egotism. It was facing facts. Now he was forced to face the fact that there was a whole world of people who might be superior to him. Jason could never rest content until he had been there and seen for himself. Even if he died in the attempt.

None of this could be told to Kerk. There were other reasons he would understand better.

"You're not thinking ahead when you prevent me from going to Pyrrus," Jason said. "I'll not mention any moral debt you owe me for winning that money you needed. But what about the next time? If you needed that much lethal goods once, you'll probably need it again some day. Wouldn't it be better to have me on hand—old tried and true—than dreaming up some new and possibly unreliable scheme?"

Kerk chewed pensively on the second serving of steak. "That makes sense. And I must admit I hadn't thought of it before. Staying alive day by day is enough trouble. So we tend to face emergencies as they arrive and let the dim future take care of itself. You can come. I hope you will still be alive when we need you. As Pyrran ambassador to a lot of places I officially invite you to our planet. All expenses paid. On the condition you obey completely all our instructions regarding your personal safety."

"Conditions accepted," Jason said. And wondered why he was so cheerful about signing his own death warrant.

Kerk was shoveling his way through his third dessert when his alarm watch gave a tiny hum. He dropped his fork instantly and stood up. "Time to go," he said. "We're on schedule now." While Jason scrambled to his feet, he jammed coins into the meter until the *paid* light came on. Then they were out the door and walking fast.

Jason wasn't at all surprised when they came on a public escalator just behind the restaurant. He was beginning to realize that since leaving the casino their every move had been carefully planned and timed. Without a doubt, the alarm was out and the entire planet being searched for them. Yet so far they hadn't noticed the slightest sign of pursuit. This wasn't the first time Jason had to move just one jump ahead of the authorities—but it was the first time he had let someone else lead him by the hand while he did it. He had to smile at his own automatic agreement. He had been a loner for so many years that he found a certain inverse pleasure in following someone else.

"Hurry up," Kerk growled after a quick glance at his watch. He set a steady, killing pace up the escalator steps. They went up five levels that way—without seeing another person—before Kerk relented and let the escalator do the work.

Jason prided himself on keeping in condition. But the sudden climb, after the sleepless night, left him panting heavily and soaked with sweat. Kerk, cool of forehead and breathing normally, didn't show the slightest sign that he had been running.

They were at the second motor level when Kerk stepped off the slowly rising steps and waved Jason after him. As they came through the exit to the street a car pulled up to the curb in front of them. Jason had enough sense not to reach for his gun. At the exact moment they reached the car, the driver opened the door and stepped out. Kerk passed him a slip of paper without saying a word and slipped in behind the wheel. There was just time for Jason to jump in before the car pulled away. The entire transfer had taken less than three seconds.

There had been only a glimpse of the driver in the dim light, but Jason had recognized him. Of course he had never seen the man before, but after knowing Kerk he couldn't mistake the compact strength of a native Pyrran.

"That was the receipt from Ellus you gave him," Jason said.

"Of course. That takes care of the ship and the cargo. They'll be off-planet and safely away before the Casino check is traced to Ellus. So now let's look after ourselves. I'll explain the plan in detail so there will be no slip-ups on your part. I'll go through the whole thing once and if there are any questions you'll ask them only when I'm finished."

The tones of command were so automatic that Jason found himself listening in quiet obedience. Though one part of his mind wanted him to smile at the quick assumption of his incompetence.

Kerk swung the car into the steady line of traffic heading out of the city to the spaceport. He drove easily while he talked.

"There is a search on in the city, but we're well ahead of that. I'm sure the Cassylians don't want to advertise their bad sportsmanship, so there won't be anything as crude as a roadblock. But the port will be crawling with every agent they have. They know once the money gets off-planet, it is gone forever. When we make a break for it they will be sure we still have the cash. So there will be no trouble with the munition ship getting clear."

Jason sounded a little shocked. "You mean you're setting us up as clay pigeons to cover the takeoff of the ship."

"You could put it that way. But since we have to get off-planet anyway, there is no harm in using our escape as a smokescreen. Now shut up until I've finished, like I told you. One more interruption and I dump you by the road."

Jason was sure he would. He listened intently—and quietly—as Kerk repeated word for word what he had said before, then continued.

"The official car gate will probably be wide open with the traffic through it. And a lot of the agents will be in plain clothes. We might even get onto the field without being recognized, though I doubt it. It is of no importance. We will drive through the gate and to the takeoff pad. The *Pride of Darkhan*, for which we hold tickets, will be sounding its two-minute siren and unhooking the gangway. By the time we get to our seats, the ship will take off."

"That's all very fine," Jason said. "But what will the guards be doing all this time?"

"Shooting at us and each other. We will take advantage of the confusion to get aboard."

This answer did nothing to settle Jason's mind, but he let it slide for the moment. "All right, say we *do* get aboard. Why don't they just prevent takeoff until we have been dragged out and stood against a wall?"

Kerk spared him a contemptuous glance before he returned his eyes to the road. "I said the ship was the *Pride of Darkhan*. If you had studied this system at all, you would know what that means. Cassylia and Darkhan are sister planets and rivals in every way. It has been less than two centuries since they fought an intrasystem war that almost destroyed both of them. Now they exist in an armed-to-the-teeth neutrality that neither dare violate. The moment we set foot aboard the ship we are on Darkhan territory. There is no extradition agreement between the planets. Cassylia may want us—but not badly enough to start another war."

That was all the explanation there was time for. Kerk swung the car out of the rush of traffic and onto a bridge marked *Official Cars Only*. Jason had a feeling of nakedness as they rolled under the harsh port lights toward the guarded gate ahead.

It was closed.

Another car approached the gate from the inside and Kerk slowed their car to a crawl. One of the guards talked to the driver of the car inside the port, then waved to the gate attendant. The barrier gate began to swing inward and Kerk jammed down on the accelerator.

Everything happened at once. The turbine howled, the spinning tires screeched on the road and the car crashed open the gate. Jason had a vanishing glimpse of the open-mouthed guards, then they were skidding around the corner of a building. A few shots popped after them, but none came close.

Driving with one hand, Kerk reached under the dash and pulled out a gun that was the twin of the monster strapped to his arm. "Use this instead of your own," he said. "Rocket-propelled explosive slugs. Make a great bang. Don't bother shooting at anyone—I'll take care of that. Just stir up a little action and make them keep their distance. Like this."

He fired a single, snap shot out the side window and passed the gun to Jason almost before the slug hit. An empty truck blew up with a roar, raining pieces on the cars around and sending their drivers fleeing in panic.

After that it was a nightmare ride through a madhouse. Kerk drove with an apparent contempt for violent death. Other cars followed them and were lost in wheel-raising turns. They careened almost the full length of the field, leaving a trail of smoking chaos.

Then the pursuit was all behind them and the only thing ahead was the slim spire of the *Pride of Darkhan.*

The *Pride* was surrounded by a strong wire fence as suited the begrudged status of her planetary origin. The gate was closed and guarded by soldiers with leveled guns, waiting for a shot at the approaching car. Kerk made no attempt to come near them. Instead he fed the last reserves of power to the car and headed for the fence. "Cover your face," he shouted.

Jason put his arms in front of his head just as they hit.

Torn metal screamed, the fence buckled, wrapped itself around the car, but did not break. Jason flew off the seat and into the padded dash. By the time Kerk had the warped door open, he realized that the ride was over. Kerk must have seen the spin of his eyeballs because he didn't talk, just pulled Jason out and threw him onto the hood of the ruined car.

"Climb over the buckled wire and make a run for the ship," he shouted.

If there was any doubt what he meant, he set Jason an example of fine roadwork. It was inconceivable that someone of his bulk could run so fast, yet he did. He moved more like a charging tank than a man. Jason shook the fog from his head and worked up some speed himself. Nevertheless, he was barely halfway to the ship when Kerk hit the gangway. It was already unhooked from the ship, but the shocked attendants stopped rolling it away as the big man bounded up the steps.

At the top he turned and fired at the soldiers who were charging in through the open gate. They dropped, crawled, and returned his fire. Very few shot at Jason's running form.

The scene in front of Jason cranked over in slow motion. Kerk standing at the top of the ramp, coolly returning the fire that splashed all about. He could have found safety in an instant through the open port behind him. The only reason he stayed there was to cover Jason.

"Thanks," Jason managed to gasp as he made the last few steps up the gangway, jumped the gap and collapsed inside the ship.

"You're perfectly welcome," Kerk said as he joined him, waving his gun to cool it off.

A grim-jawed ship's officer stood back out of range of fire from the ground and looked them both up and down. "And just what the hell is going on here," he growled.

Kerk tested the barrel with a wet thumb, then let the gun slide back into its holster. "We are law-abiding citizens of a different system who have committed no criminal acts. The savages of Cassylia are too barbarous for civilized company. Therefore we are going to Darkhan—here are our tickets—in whose sovereign territory I believe we are at this moment." This last was added for the benefit of the Cassylian officer who had just stumbled to the top of the gangway and was raising his gun.

The soldier couldn't be blamed. He saw these badly wanted criminals getting away. Aboard a Darkhan ship as well. Anger got the best of him and he brought his gun up.

"Come out of there, you scum! You're not escaping that easily. Come out slow with your hands up or I'll blast you . . ."

It was a frozen moment of time that stretched and stretched without breaking. The pistol covered Kerk and Jason. Neither of them attempted to reach for their own guns.

The gun twitched a bit as the ship's officer moved, then steadied back on the two men. The Darkhan spaceman hadn't gone far, just a pace across the lock. This was enough to bring him next to a red box set flush with the wall. With a single, swift gesture, he flipped up the cover and poised his thumb over the button inside. When he smiled, his lips peeled back to show all of his teeth. He had made up his mind, and it was the arrogance of the Cassylian officer that had been the deciding factor.

"Fire a single shot into Darkhan territory and I press this button," he shouted. "And you know what this button does—every one of your ships has them as well. Commit a hostile act against this ship and *someone* will press a button. Every control rod will be blown out of the ship's pile at that instant and half your filthy city will go up in the explosion." His smile was chiseled on his face and there was no doubt he would do what he said. "Go ahead, fire. I think I would enjoy pressing this."

The takeoff siren was hooting now, the *close lock* light blinking an angry message from the bridge. Like four actors in a grim drama, they faced each other an instant more.

Then the Cassylian officer, growling with unvoiceable, frustrated anger, turned and leaped back to the steps.

"All passengers board ship. Forty-five seconds to takeoff. Clear the port." The ship's officer slammed shut the cover of the box and locked it as he talked. There was barely time to make the acceleration couches before the *Pride of Darkhan* cleared the ground.

5

Once the ship was in orbit, the captain sent for Jason and Kerk. Kerk took the floor and was completely frank about the previous night's activities. The only fact of importance he left out was Jason's background as a professional gambler. He drew a beautiful picture of two lucky strangers whom the evil forces of Cassylia wanted to deprive of their gambling profits. All this fitted perfectly the captain's preconceptions of Cassylia. In the end, he congratulated his officer on the correctness of his actions and began the preparation of a long report to his government. He gave the two men his best wishes as well as the liberty of the ship.

It was a short trip. Jason barely had time to catch up on his sleep before they grounded on Darkhan. Being without luggage, they were the first ones through customs. They left the shed just in time to see another ship landing in a distant pit. Kerk stopped to watch it and Jason followed his gaze. It was a grey, scarred ship. With the stubby lines of a freighter—but sporting as many large guns as a cruiser.

"Yours, of course," Jason said.

Kerk nodded and started toward the ship. One of the locks opened as they came up but no one appeared. Instead a remote-release folding ladder rattled down to the ground. Kerk swarmed up it and Jason followed glumly. Somehow, he felt, this was overdoing the no-frills-and-nonsense attitude.

Jason was catching on to Pyrran ways, though. The reception aboard ship for the ambassador was just what he expected. Nothing.

Kerk closed the lock himself and they found couches as the takeoff horn sounded. The main jets roared and acceleration smashed down on Jason.

It didn't stop. Instead it grew stronger, squeezing the air out of his lungs and the sight from his eyes. He screamed but couldn't hear his own voice through the roaring in his ears. Mercifully he blacked out.

When consciousness returned the ship was at zero-G. Jason kept his eyes closed and let the pain seep out of his body. Kerk spoke suddenly; he was standing next to the couch.

"My fault, Meta, I should have told you we had a one-G passenger aboard. You might have eased up a bit on your usual bone-breaking takeoff."

"It doesn't seem to have harmed him much—but what's he doing here?"

Jason felt mild surprise that the second voice was a girl's. But he wasn't interested enough to go to the trouble of opening his sore eyes.

"Going to Pyrrus. I tried to talk him out of it, of course, but I couldn't change his mind. It's a shame, too, I would like to have done more for him. He's the one who got the money for us."

"Oh, that's awful," the girl said. Jason wondered why it was *awful.* It didn't make sense to his groggy mind. "It would have been much better if he stayed on Darkhan," the girl continued. "He's very nice looking. I think it's a shame he has to die."

That was too much for Jason. He pried one eye open, then the other. The voice belonged to a girl of about twenty-one who was standing next to the bed, gazing down at Jason. She was beautiful.

Jason's eyes opened wider as he realized she was *very* beautiful —with the kind of beauty he had never found on the planets in the center of the galaxy. The women he had known all ran to pale skin, hollow shoulders, grey faces covered with tints and dyes. They were the product of centuries of breeding weaknesses back into the race, as the advance of medicine kept alive more and more nonsurvival types.

This girl was the direct opposite in every way. She was the product of survival on Pyrrus. The heavy gravity that produced bulging muscles in men, brought out firm strength in strap-like female muscles. She had the taut figure of a goddess, tanned skin and perfectly formed face. Her hair, which was cut short, circled her head with a golden crown. The only unfeminine thing about her was the gun she wore in a bulky forearm holster. When she saw

Jason's eyes open she smiled at him. Her teeth were as even and as white as he had expected.

"I'm Meta, pilot of this ship. And you must be—"

"Jason dinAlt. That was a lousy takeoff, Meta."

"I'm really very sorry," she laughed. "But being born on a two-G planet makes you a little immune to acceleration. I save fuel too, with the synergy curve—"

Kerk gave a noncommittal grunt. "Come along, Meta, we'll take a look at the cargo. Some of the new stuff will plug the gaps in the perimeter."

"Oh, yes," she said, almost clapping her hands with happiness. "I read the specs, they're simply wonderful."

Like a schoolgirl with a new dress. Or a box of candy. That's a great attitude to have toward bombs and flamethrowers. Jason smiled wryly at the thought as he groaned off the couch. The two Pyrrans had gone and he pulled himself painfully through the door after them.

It took him a long time to find his way to the hold. The ship was big and apparently empty of crew. Jason finally found a man sleeping in one of the brightly lit cabins. He recognized him as the driver who had turned the car over to them on Cassylia. The man, who had been sleeping soundly a moment before, opened his eyes as soon as Jason drifted into the room. He was wide awake.

"How do I get to the cargo hold?" Jason asked.

The other told him, closed his eyes and went instantly back to sleep before Jason could even say thanks.

In the hold, Kerk and Meta had opened some of the crates and were chortling with joy over their lethal contents. Meta, a pressure cannister in her arms, turned to Jason as he came through the door.

"Just look at this," she said. "This powder in here—why you can eat it like dirt, with less harm. Yet it is instantly deadly to all forms of vegetable life. . . ." She stopped suddenly as she realized Jason didn't share her extreme pleasure. "I'm sorry. Only I forgot for a moment there that you weren't a Pyrran. So you don't really understand, do you?"

Before he could answer, the PA speaker called her name.

"Jump time," she said. "Come with me to the bridge while I do the equations. We can talk there. I know so little about any place except Pyrrus that I have a million questions to ask."

Jason followed her to the bridge where she relieved the duty officer and began taking readings for the jump setting. She looked out of place among the machines, a sturdy but supple figure in a simple, one-piece shipsuit. Yet there was no denying the efficiency with which she went about her job.

"Meta, aren't you a little young to be the pilot of an interstellar ship?"

"Am I?" She thought for a second. "I really don't know how old pilots are supposed to be. I have been piloting for about three years now and I'm almost twenty. Is that younger than usual?"

Jason opened his mouth—then laughed. "I suppose that all depends on what planet you're from. Some places you would have trouble getting licensed. But I'll bet things are different on Pyrrus. By their standards you must rank as an old lady."

"Now you're making a joke," Meta said serenely as she fed a figure into the calculator. "I've seen old ladies on some planets. They are wrinkled and have grey hair. I don't know how old they are, I asked one but she wouldn't tell me her age. But I'm sure they must be older than anyone on Pyrrus, no one looks like that there."

"I don't mean old that way." Jason groped for the right word. "Not old—but grown-up, mature. An adult."

"Everyone is grown-up," she answered. "At least soon after they leave the wards. And they do that when they're six. My first child is grown-up, and the second one would be too, only he's dead. So I *surely* must be."

That seemed to settle the question for her, though Jason's thoughts jumped with the alien concepts and background, inherent behind her words.

Meta punched in the last setting, and the course tape began to chunk out of the case. She turned her attention back to Jason. "I'm glad you're aboard this trip, though I am sorry you are going to Pyrrus. But we'll have lots of time to talk and there are so many things I want to find out. About other planets. And why people go around acting the way they do. Not at all like home where you *know* why people are doing things all the time." She frowned over the tape for a moment, then turned her attention back to Jason. "What is your home planet like?"

One after another the usual lies he told people came to his lips, and were pushed away. Why bother lying to a girl who really didn't care if you were serf or noble? To her there were only two kinds of people in the galaxy. Pyrrans, and the rest. For the first time since he had fled from Porgorstorsaand, he found himself telling someone the truth of his origin.

"My home planet? Just about the stuffiest, dullest, dead-end in the universe. You can't believe the destructive decay of a planet that is mainly agrarian, caste-conscious and completely satisfied with its own boring existence. Not only is there no change—but no one *wants* change. My father was a farmer, so I should have been a farmer too—if I had listened to the advice of my betters. It was unthinkable, as well as forbidden for me to do anything else. And everything I wanted to do was against the law. I was fifteen before I learned to read—out of a book stolen from a noble school. After that there was no turning back. By the time I stowed away aboard an off-world freighter at nineteen I must have broken every law on the planet. Happily. Leaving home for me was just like getting out of prison."

Meta shook her head at the thought. "I just can't imagine a place like that. But I'm sure I wouldn't like it there."

"I'm sure you wouldn't," Jason smiled. "So once I was in space, with no law-abiding talents or skills, I just wandered into one thing and another. In this age of technology, I was completely out of place. Oh, I suppose I could have done well in some army, but I'm not so good at taking orders. Whenever I gambled I did well, so little by little I just drifted into it. People are the same everywhere, so I manage to make out very well wherever I end up."

"I know what you mean about people being alike, but they are so *different*," she said. "I'm not being clear at all, am I? What I mean is that at home I know what people will do and why they do it at the same time. People on all the other planets do act alike, as you said, yet I have very much trouble understanding why. For instance, I like to try the local food when we set down on a planet, and if there is time I always do. There are bars and restaurants near every spaceport so I go there. And I always have trouble with the men. They want to buy me drinks, hold my hand."

"Well a single girl in those port joints has to expect a certain amount of interest from the men."

"Oh, I know that," she said. "What I don't understand is why they don't listen when I tell them I am not interested and to go away. They just laugh and pull up a chair, usually. But I have found that one thing works wherever I am. I tell them if they don't stop bothering me I'll break their arm."

"Does that stop them?" Jason asked.

"No, of course not. But after I break their arm they go away. And the others don't bother me either. It's a lot of fuss to go through and the food is usually awful."

Jason didn't laugh. Particularly when he realized that this girl *could* break the arm of any spaceport thug in the galaxy. She was a strange mixture of naïveté and strength, unlike anyone he had ever met before. Once again he realized that he *had* to visit the planet that produced people like her and Kerk.

"Tell me about Pyrrus," he asked. "Why is it that you and Kerk assume automatically that I will drop dead as soon as I land? What is the planet like?"

All the warmth was gone from her face now. "I can't tell you. You will have to see for yourself. I know that much after visiting some of the other worlds. Pyrrus is like nothing you galaxy people have ever experienced. You won't really believe it until it is too late. Will you promise me something?"

"No," he answered. "At least not until after I hear what it is and decide."

"Don't leave the ship when we land. You should be safe enough aboard, and I'll be flying a cargo out within a few weeks."

"I'll promise nothing of the sort. I'll leave when I want to leave." Jason knew there was undoubtedly a reason for her words, but he resented her automatic superiority.

Meta finished the jump settings without another word. There was a tension in the room that prevented them both from talking.

It was the next shipday before he saw her again, then it was completely by accident. She was in the astrogation dome when he entered, looking up at the spark-filled blackness of the jump sky. For the first time he saw her off duty, wearing something other than a shipsuit. This was a thin and softly shining robe that clung to her body.

She smiled at him. "The stars are so wonderful. Come see." Jason stood close to her, looking up. The oddly geometric patterns of the jump sky were familiar to him, yet they still had the power to draw him forward. Even more so now. Meta's presence made a disturbing difference in the dark silence of the dome. Her tilted head almost rested on his shoulder, the crown of her hair eclipsing part of the sky, the smell of it soft in his nostrils.

Almost without thought his arms went around her, aware of the warm firmness of her flesh beneath the thin robe. She did not resent it, for she covered his hands with hers.

"You're smiling," she said. "You like the stars too."

"Very much," he answered. "But more than that. I remembered the story you told me. Do you want to break my arm, Meta?"

"Of course not," she said very seriously, then smiled back. "I like you, Jason. Even though you're not a Pyrran, I like you very much. And I've been so lonely."

When she looked up at him, he kissed her. She returned the kiss with a passion that had no shame or false modesty.

"My cabin is just down this corridor," she said.

6

After that they were together constantly. When Meta was on duty he brought her meals to the bridge and they talked. Jason learned little more about her world since, by unspoken agreement, they didn't discuss it. He talked of the many planets he had visited and the people he had known. She was an appreciative listener and the time went quickly by. They enjoyed each other's company and it was a wonderful trip.

Then it ended.

There were fourteen people aboard the ship, yet Jason had never seen more than two or three at a time. There was a fixed rotation of duties that they followed in the ship's operation. When not on duty, the Pyrrans minded their own business in an intense and self-sufficient manner. Only when the ship came out of jump and the PA barked *assembly* did they all get together.

Kerk was giving orders for the landing and questions were snapped back and forth. It was all technical and Jason didn't bother following it. It was the attitude of the Pyrrans that drew his attention. Their talk tended to be faster now as were their motions. They were like soldiers preparing for battle.

Their sameness struck Jason for the first time. Not that they looked alike or did the same things. It was the *way* they moved and reacted that caused the striking similarity. They were like great, stalking cats. Walking fast, tense and ready to spring at all times, their eyes never still for an instant.

Jason tried to talk to Meta after the meeting, but she was almost a stranger. She answered in monosyllables and her eyes never met his, just brushed over them and went on. There was nothing he could really say, so she moved to leave. He started to put his hand out to stop her—then thought better of it. There would be other times to talk.

Kerk was the only one who took any notice of him—and then only to order him to an acceleration couch.

Meta's landings were infinitely worse than her takeoffs. At least

when she landed on Pyrrus. There were sudden acceleration surges
in every direction. At one point there was a free fall that seemed
endless. There were loud thuds against the hull that shook the
framework of the ship. It was more like a battle than a landing and
Jason wondered how much truth there was in that.

When the ship finally landed, Jason didn't even know it. The
constant two-G's felt like deceleration. Only the descending moan
of the ship's engines convinced him they were down. Unbuckling
the straps and sitting up was an effort.

Two-G's don't seem that bad. At first. Walking required the
same exertion as would carrying a man of his own weight on his
shoulders. When Jason lifted his arm to unlatch the door it was as
heavy as two arms. He shuffled slowly toward the main lock.

They were all there ahead of him, two of the men rolling transparent cylinders from a nearby room. From their obvious weight and
the way they clanged when they bumped, Jason knew they were
made of transparent metal. He couldn't conceive any possible use
for them. Empty cylinders a meter in diameter, longer than a man.
One end solid, the other hinged and sealed. It wasn't until Kerk spun
the sealing wheel and opened one of them that their use became
apparent.

"Get in," Kerk said. "When you're locked inside, you'll be
carried out of the ship."

"Thank you, no," Jason told him. "I have no particular desire to
make a spectacular landing on your planet sealed up like a packaged
sausage."

"Don't be a fool," was Kerk's snapped answer. "We're all
going out in these tubes. We've been away too long to risk the
surface without reorientation."

Jason did feel a little foolish as he saw the others getting into
tubes. He picked the nearest one, slid into it feet first, and pulled the
lid closed. When he tightened the wheel in the center, it squeezed
down against a flexible seal. Within a minute the CO_2 content in the
closed cylinder went up and an air regenerator at the bottom
hummed into life.

Kerk was the last one in. He checked the seals on all the other
tubes first, then jabbed the airlock override release. As it started
cycling, he quickly sealed himself in the remaining cylinder. Both
inner and outer locks ground slowly open and dim light filtered in
through sheets of falling rain.

For Jason, the whole thing seemed an anticlimax. All this preparation for absolutely nothing. Long, impatient minutes passed
before a lift truck appeared driven by a Pyrran. He loaded the

cylinders onto his truck like so much dead cargo. Jason had the misfortune to be buried at the bottom of the pile so could see absolutely nothing when they drove outside.

It wasn't until the man-carrying cylinders had been dumped in a metal-walled room, that Jason saw his first native Pyrran life.

The lift truck driver was swinging a thick outer door shut when something flew in through the entrance and struck against the far wall. Jason's eye was caught by the motion; he looked to see what it was when it dropped straight down toward his face.

Forgetful of the metal cylinder wall, he flinched away. The creature struck the transparent metal and clung to it. Jason had the perfect opportunity to examine it in every detail.

It was almost too horrible to be believable. As though it were a bearer of death stripped to the very essentials. A mouth that split the head in two, rows of teeth, serrated and pointed. Leathery, claw-tipped wings, longer claws on the limbs that tore at the metal wall.

Terror rose up in Jason as he saw that the claws were tearing gouges in the transparent metal. Wherever the creature's saliva touched, the metal clouded and chipped under the assault of the teeth.

Logic said these were just scratches on the thick tube. They couldn't matter. But blind, unreasoning fear sent Jason curling away as far as he could. Shrinking inside himself, seeking escape.

Only when the flying creature began dissolving did he realize the nature of the room outside. Sprays of steaming liquid came from all sides, raining down until the cylinders were covered. After one last clash of its jaws, the Pyrran animal was washed off and carried away. The liquid drained away through the floor and a second and third shower followed.

While the solutions were being pumped away, Jason fought to bring his emotions into line. He was surprised at himself. No matter how frightful the creature had been, he couldn't understand the fear it could generate through the wall of the sealed tube. His reaction was all out of proportion to the cause. Even with the creature destroyed and washed out of sight, it took all of his will power to steady his nerves and bring his breathing back to normal.

Meta walked by outside and he realized the sterilization process was finished. He opened his own tube and climbed wearily out. Meta and the others had gone by this time and only a hawk-faced stranger remained, waiting for him.

"I'm Brucco, in charge of adaptation clinic. Kerk told me who you were. I'm sorry you're here. Now come along, I want some blood samples."

"Now I feel right at home," Jason said. "The old Pyrran hospitality." Brucco only grunted and stamped out. Jason followed him down a bare corridor into a sterile lab.

The double gravity was tiring, a constant drag on sore muscles. While Brucco ran tests on the blood sample, Jason rested. He had almost dozed off into a painful sleep when Brucco returned with a tray of bottles and hypodermic needles.

"Amazing," he announced. "Not an antibody in your serum that would be of any use on this planet. I have a batch of antigens here that will make you sick as a beast for at least a day. Take off your shirt."

"Have you done this often?" Jason asked. "I mean juice up an out-lander so he can enjoy the pleasures of your world?"

Brucco jabbed in a needle that felt like it grated on the bone. "Not often at all. Last time was years ago. A half-dozen researchers from some institute, willing to pay well for the chance to study the local life forms. We didn't say no. Always need more galaxy currency."

Jason was already beginning to feel lightheaded from the shots. "How many of them lived?" he mumbled vaguely.

"One. We got him off in time. Made them pay in advance, of course."

At first Jason thought the Pyrran was joking. Then he remembered they had very little interest in humor of any kind. If one half of what Meta and Kerk had told him was true, six-to-one odds weren't bad at all.

There was a bed in the next room and Brucco helped him to it. Jason felt drugged and probably was. He fell into a deep sleep and into the dream.

Fear and hatred. Mixed in equal parts and washed over him red hot. If this was a dream, he never wanted to sleep again. If it wasn't a dream, he wanted to die. He tried to fight up against it, but only sank in more deeply. There was no beginning and no end to the fear and no way to escape.

When consciousness returned, Jason could remember no detail of the nightmare. Just the fear remained. He was soaked with sweat and ached in every muscle. It must have been the massive dose of shots, he finally decided, that and the brutal gravity. That didn't take the taste of fear out of his mouth, though.

Brucco stuck his head in the door then and looked Jason up and down. "Thought you were dead," he said. "Slept the clock around. Don't move, I'll get something to pick you up."

The pickup was in the form of another needle and a glassful of evil-looking fluid. It settled his thirst, but made him painfully aware of a gnawing hunger.

"Want to eat?" Brucco asked. "I'll bet you do. I've speeded up your metabolism so you'll build muscle faster. Only way you'll ever beat the gravity. Give you quite an appetite for awhile though."

Brucco ate at the same time and Jason had a chance to ask some questions. "When do I get a chance to look around your fascinating planet? So far this trip has been about as interesting as a jail term."

"Relax and enjoy your food. Probably be months before you're able to go outside. If at all."

Jason felt his jaw hanging and closed it with a snap. "Could you possibly tell me why?"

"Of course. You will have to go through the same training course that our children take. It takes them six years. Of course, it's their first six years of life. So you might think that you, as an adult, could learn faster. Then again, they have the advantage of heredity. All I can say is you'll go outside these sealed buildings when you're ready."

Brucco had finished eating while he talked, and sat staring at Jason's bare arms with growing disgust. "The first thing we want to get you is a gun," he said. "It gives me a sick feeling to see someone without one."

Of course Brucco wore his own gun continually, even within the sealed buildings.

"Every gun is fitted to its owner and would be useless on anyone else," Brucco said. "I'll show you why." He led Jason to an armory jammed with deadly weapons. "Put your arm in this while I make the adjustments."

It was a box-like machine with a pistol grip on the side. Jason clutched the grip and rested his elbow on a metal loop. Brucco fixed pointers that touched his arm, then copied the results from the meters. Reading the figures from his list, he selected various components from bins and quickly assembled a power holster and gun. With the holster strapped to his forearm and the gun in his hand, Jason noticed for the first time they were connected by a flexible cable. The gun fitted his hand perfectly.

"This is the secret of the power holster," Brucco said, tapping the flexible cable. "It is perfectly loose while you are using the weapon. But when you want it returned to the holster—" Brucco made an adjustment and the cable became a stiff rod that whipped the gun from Jason's hand and suspended it in midair.

"Then the return." The rod cable whirred and snapped the gun back into the holster. "The drawing action is the opposite of this, of course."

"A great gadget," Jason said. "But how *do* I draw? Do I whistle or something for the gun to pop out?"

"No, it is not sonic control," Brucco answered with a sober face. "It is much more precise than that. Here, take your left hand and grasp an imaginary gunbutt. Tense your trigger finger. Do you notice the pattern of the tendons in the wrist? Sensitive actuators touch the tendons in your right wrist. They ignore all patterns except the one that says *hand ready to receive gun*. After a time the mechanism becomes completely automatic. When you want the gun, it is in your hand. When you don't, it is in the holster."

Jason made grasping motions with his right hand, crooked his index finger. There was a sudden, smashing pain against his hand and a loud roar. The gun was in his hand—half the fingers were numb—and smoke curled up from the barrel.

"Of course, there are only blank charges in the gun until you learn control. Guns are *always* loaded. There is no safety. Notice the lack of a trigger guard. That enables you to bend your trigger finger a slight bit more when drawing so the gun will fire the instant it touches your hand."

It was without doubt the most murderous weapon Jason had ever handled, as well as being the hardest to manage. Working against the muscle burning ache of high gravity, he fought to control the devilish device. It had an infuriating way of vanishing into the holster just as he was about to pull the trigger. Even worse was the tendency to leap out before he was quite ready. The gun went to the position where his hand should be. If the fingers weren't correctly placed, they were crashed aside. Jason only stopped the practice when his entire hand was one livid bruise.

Complete mastery would come with time, but he could already understand why the Pyrrans never removed their guns. It would be like removing a part of your own body. The movement of gun from holster to hand was too fast for him to detect. It was certainly faster than the neutral current that shaped the hand into the gun-holding position. For all apparent purposes it was like having a lightning bolt in your fingertip. Point the finger and *blamm*, there's the explosion.

Brucco had left Jason to practice alone. When his aching hand could take no more, he stopped and headed back toward his own quarters. Turning a corner, he had a quick glimpse of a familiar figure going away from him.

"Meta! Wait for a second! I want to talk to you."

She turned impatiently as he shuffled up, going as fast as he could in the doubled gravity. Everything about her seemed different from the girl he had known on the ship. Heavy boots came as high as he knees, her figure was lost in bulky coveralls of some metallic fabric. The trim waist was bulged out by a belt of cannisters. Her very expression was coldly distant.

"I've missed you," he said. "I hadn't realized you were in this building." He reached for her hand but she moved it out of his reach.

"What is it you want?" she asked.

"What is it I want!" he echoed with barely concealed anger. "This is Jason, remember me? We're friends. It *is* allowed for friends to talk without 'wanting' anything."

"What happened on the ship has nothing to do with what happens on Pyrrus." She started forward impatiently as she talked. "I have finished my reconditioning and must return to work. You'll be staying here in the sealed buildings so I won't be seeing you."

"Why don't you say with the rest of the children—that's what your tone implies. And don't try walking out, there are some things we have to settle first—"

Jason made the mistake of putting out his hand to stop her. He didn't really know what happened next. One instant he was standing—the next he sprawled suddenly on the floor. His shoulder was badly bruised, and Meta had vanished down the corridor.

Limping back to his own room, he muttered curses under his breath. Dropping onto his rock-hard bed, he tried to remember the reasons that had brought him here in the first place. And weighed them against the perpetual torture of the gravity, the fear-filled dreams it inspired, the automatic contempt of these people for any outsider. He quickly checked the growing tendency to feel sorry for himself. By Pyrran standards, he *was* soft and helpless. If he wanted them to think any better of him, he would have to change a good deal.

He sank into a fatigue-drugged sleep then, that was broken only by the screaming fear of his dreams.

7

In the morning, Jason awoke with a bad headache and the feeling he had never been to sleep. As he took some of the carefully portioned stimulants that Brucco had given him, he wondered again about the combination of factors that filled his sleep with such horror.

"Eat quickly," Brucco told him when they met in the dining room. "I can no longer spare you time for individual instruction. You will join the regular classes and take the prescribed courses. Only come to me if there is some special problem that the instructors or trainers can't handle."

The classes, as Jason should have expected, were composed of stern-faced little children. With their compact bodies and no-nonsense mannerisms, they were recognizably Pyrran. But they were still children enough to consider it very funny to have an adult in their classes. Jammed behind one of the tiny desks, the redfaced Jason did not think it was much of a joke.

All resemblance to a normal school ended with the physical form of the classroom. For one thing, every child—no matter how small—packed a gun. And the courses were all involved with survival. The only possible grade in a curriculum like this was 100 per cent and students stayed with a lesson until they had mastered it perfectly. No courses were offered in the normal scholastic subjects. Presumably these were studied after the child graduated survival school and could face the world alone. Which was a logical and coldblooded way of looking at things. In fact, logical and coldblooded could describe any Pyrran activity.

Most of the morning was spent on the operation of one of the medikits that strapped around the waist. This was an infection and poison analyzer that was pressed over a puncture wound. If any toxins were present, the antidote was automatically injected on the site. Simple in operation but incredibly complex in construction. Since all Pyrrans serviced their own equipment—you could then only blame yourself if it failed—they had to learn the construction and repair of all the devices. Jason did much better than the child students, though the effort exhausted him.

In the afternoon, he had his first experience with a training machine. His instructor was a twelve-year-old boy, whose cold voice didn't conceal his contempt for the soft off-worlder.

"All the training machines are physical duplicates of the real surface of the planet, corrected constantly as the life forms change. The only difference between them is the varying degree of deadliness. This first machine you will use is of course the one infants are put into—"

"You're too kind," Jason murmured. "Your flattery overwhelms me." The instructor continued, taking no notice of the interruption.

"—infants are put into it as soon as they can crawl. It is real in substance, though completely deactivated."

Training machine was the wrong word, Jason realized as they entered through the thick door. This was a chunk of the outside world duplicated in an immense chamber. It took very little suspension of reality for him to forget the painted ceiling and artificial sun high above and imagine himself outdoors at last. The scene *seemed* peaceful enough. Though clouds banking on the horizon threatened a violent Pyrran storm.

"You must wander around and examine things," the instructor told Jason. "Whenever you touch something with your hand, you will be told about it. Like this . . ."

The boy bent over and pushed his finger against a blade of the soft grass that covered the ground. Immediately a voice barked from hidden speakers.

"Poison grass. Boots to be worn at all times."

Jason kneeled and examined the grass. The blade was tipped with a hard, shiny hook. He realized with a start that every single blade of grass was the same. The soft green lawn was a carpet of death. As he straightened up, he glimpsed something under a broad-leafed plant. A crouching, scale-covered animal, whose tapered head terminated in a long spike.

"What's *that* in the bottom of my garden?" he asked. "You certainly give the babies pleasant playmates." Jason turned and realized he was talking to the air; the instructor was gone. He shrugged and petted the scaly monstrosity.

"Horndevil," the impersonal voice said from midair. "Clothing and shoes no protection. Kill it."

A sharp *crack* shattered the silence as Jason's gun went off. The horndevil fell over on its side, keyed to react to the blank charge.

"Well—I *am* learning," Jason said, and the thought pleased him. The words *kill it* had been used by Brucco while teaching him to use the gun. Their stimulus had reached an unconscious level. He was aware of wanting to shoot only after he had heard the shot. His respect for Pyrran training techniques went up.

Jason spent a thoroughly unpleasant afternoon wandering in the child's garden of horror. Death was everywhere. While all the time the disembodied voice gave him stern advice in simple language. So he could do unto, rather than being done in. He had never realized that violent death could come in so many repulsive forms. *Everything* here was deadly to man—from the smallest insect to the largest plant.

Such singleness of purpose seemed completely unnatural. Why was this planet so alien to human life? He made a mental note to ask Brucco. Meanwhile he tried to find one life form that wasn't out for his blood. He didn't succeed. After a long search, he found the only thing that when touched didn't elicit deadly advice. This was a chunk of rock that projected from a meadow of poison grass. Jason sat on it with a friendly feeling and pulled his feet up. An oasis of peace. Some minutes passed while he rested his gravity-weary body.

"ROTFUNGUS! DO NOT TOUCH!"

The voice blasted at twice its normal volume and Jason leaped as if he had been shot. The gun was in his hand, nosing about for a target. Only when he bent over and looked closely at the rock where he had been sitting, did he understand. There were flaky grey patches that hadn't been there when he sat down.

"Oh, you tricky devils!" he shouted at the machine. "How many kids have you frightened off that rock after they thought they had found a little peace!" He resented the snide bit of conditioning, but respected it at the same time. Pyrrans learned very early in life that there was no safety on this planet—except that which they provided for themselves.

While he was learning about Pyrrus, he was gaining new insight into the Pyrrans as well.

8

Days turned into weeks in the school, cut off from the world outside. Jason almost became proud of his ability to deal with death. He recognized all the animals and plants in the nursery room and had been promoted to a trainer where the beasts made sluggish charges at him. His gun picked off the attackers with dull regularity. The constant, daily classes were beginning to bore him as well.

Though the gravity still dragged at him, his muscles were making great efforts to adjust. After the daily classes, he no longer collapsed immediately into bed. Only the nightmares became worse. He had finally mentioned them to Brucco, who mixed up a sleeping potion that took away most of their effect. The dreams were still there, but Jason was only vaguely aware of them upon awakening.

By the time Jason had mastered all the gadgetry that kept the Pyrrans alive, he had graduated to a most realistic trainer that was only a hairsbreadth away from the real thing. The difference was just in quality. The insect poisons caused swelling and pain instead of instant death. Animals could cause bruises and tear flesh, but stopped short of ripping off limbs. You couldn't get killed in this trainer, but could certainly come very close to it.

Jason wandered through this large and rambling jungle with the rest of the five-year-olds. There was something a bit humorous, yet sad, about their unchildlike grimness. Though they still might laugh in their quarters, they realized there was no laughing outside. To them survival was linked up with social acceptance and desirability. In this way Pyrrus was a simple black-and-white society. To prove your value to yourself and your world, you only had to stay alive. This had great importance in racial survival, but had very stultifying effects on individual personality. Children were turned into like-faced killers, always on the alert to deal out death.

Some of the children graduated into the outside world and others took their places. Jason watched this process for awhile before he realized that all of those from the original group he had entered with were gone. That same day he looked up the chief of the adaptation center.

"Brucco," Jason asked, "how long do you plan to keep me in this kindergarten shooting gallery?"

"You're not being 'kept' here," Brucco told him in his usual irritated tone. "You will be here until you qualify for the outside."

"Which I have a funny feeling will be never. I can now field strip and reassemble every one of your blasted gadgets in the dark. I am a dead shot with this cannon. At this present moment, if I had to, I could write a book on the Complete Flora and Fauna of Pyrrus, and How to Kill It. Perhaps I don't do as well as my six-year-old companions. But I have a hunch I do about as good a job now as I ever will. Is that true?"

Brucco squirmed with the effort to be evasive, yet didn't succeed. "I think, that is, you know you weren't born here, and . . ."

"Come, come," Jason said with glee. "A straight-faced old Pyrran like you shouldn't try to lie to one of the weaker races that specialize in that sort of thing. It goes without saying that I'll always be sluggish with this gravity, as well as having other inborn handicaps. I admit that. We're not talking about that now. The question is, Will I improve with more training, or have I reached a peak of my own *development* now?"

Brucco sweated. "With the passage of time there will be improvement, of course. . . ."

"Sly devil!" Jason waggled a finger at him. "Yes or no, now. Will I improve *now* by more training *now*?"

"No," Brucco said and still looked troubled. Jason sized him up like a poker hand.

"Now let's think about that. I won't improve, yet I'm still stuck here. That's no accident. So you must have been ordered to keep me here. And from what I have seen of this planet, admittedly very little, I would say that Kerk ordered you to keep me here. Is that right?"

"He was only doing it for your own sake," Brucco explained. "Trying to keep you alive."

"The truth is out," Jason said. "So let us now forget about it. I didn't come here to shoot robots with your offspring. So please show me the street door. Or is there a graduating ceremony first? Speeches, handing out school pins, sabers overhead. . . ."

"Nothing like that," Brucco snapped. "I don't see how a grown man like you can talk such nonsense all the time. There is none of that, of course. Only some final work in the partial survival chamber. That is a compound that connects with the outside—really is a part of the outside—except the most violent life forms are excluded. And even some of those manage to find their way in once in awhile.''

"When do I go?" Jason shot the question.

"Tomorrow morning. Get a good night's sleep first. You'll need it.''

There was one bit of ceremony attendant with the graduation. When Jason came into his office in the morning, Brucco slid a heavy gunclip across the table.

"These are live bullets," he said. "I'm sure you'll be needing them. After this your gun will always be loaded."

They came up to a heavy airlock, the only locked door Jason had seen in the center. While Brucco unlocked it and threw the bolts, a sober-faced eight-year-old with a bandaged leg limped up.

"This is Grif," Brucco said. "He will stay with you, wherever you go, from now on."

"My personal bodyguard?" Jason asked, looking down at the stocky child who barely reached his waist.

"You might call him that." Brucco swung the door open. "Grif tangled with a sawbird, so he won't be able to do any real work for awhile. You yourself admitted that you will never be able to equal a Pyrran, so you should be glad of a little protection."

"Always a kind word, that's you, Brucco," Jason said. He bent over and shook hands with the boy. Even the eight-year-olds had a bone-crushing grip.

The two of them entered the lock and Brucco swung the inner door shut behind them. As soon as it was sealed, the outer door opened automatically. It was only partly open when Grif's gun blasted twice. Then they stepped out onto the surface of Pyrrus, over the smoking body of one of its animals. Very symbolic, Jason thought. He was also bothered by the realization that not only hadn't he thought to look for something coming in, but he couldn't even identify the beast from its charred remains. He glanced around carefully, hoping he would be able to fire first next time.

This was an unfulfilled hope. The few beasts that came their way were always seen first by the boy. After an hour of this, Jason was so irritated that he blasted an evil-looking thorn plant out of existence. He hoped that Grif wouldn't look too closely at it. Of course the boy did.

"That plant wasn't close. It is stupid to waste good ammunition on a plant," Grif said.

There was no real trouble during the day. Jason ended by being bored, though soaked by the frequent rainstorms. If Grif was capable of carrying on a conversation, he didn't show it. All Jason's gambits failed. The following day went the same way. On the third day, Brucco appeared and looked Jason carefully up and down.

"I don't like to say it, but I suppose you are as ready to leave now as you ever will be. Change the virus filter noseplugs every day. Always check boots for tears and metal-cloth suiting for rips. Medikit supplies renewed once a week."

"And wipe my nose and wear my galoshes. Anything else?" Jason asked.

Brucco started to say something, then changed his mind. "Nothing that you shouldn't know well by now. Keep alert. And . . . good luck." He followed up the words with a crushing handshake that was totally unexpected. As soon as the numbness left Jason's hand, he and Grif went out through the large entrance lock.

9

Real as they had been, the training chambers had not prepared him for the surface of Pyrrus. There was the basic similarity, of course. The feel of the poison grass underfoot and the erratic flight of a stingwing in the last instant before Grif blasted it. But these were scarcely noticeable in the crash of the elements around him.

A heavy rain was falling, more like a sheet of water than individual drops. Gusts of wind tore at it, hurling the deluge into his face. He wiped his eyes clear and could barely make out the conical forms of two volcanoes on the horizon, vomiting out clouds of smoke and flame. The reflection of this inferno was a sullen redness on the clouds that raced by in banks above them.

There was a rattle on his hard hat and something bounced off to splash to the ground. He bent over and picked up a hailstone as thick as his thumb. A sudden flurry of hail hammered painfully at his back and neck; he straightened hurriedly.

As quickly as it started, the storm was over. The sun burned down, melting the hailstones and sending curls of steam up from the wet street. Jason sweated inside his armored clothing. Yet before they had gone a block, it was raining again and he shook with chill.

Grif trudged steadily along, indifferent either to the weather or the volcanoes that rumbled on the horizon and shook the ground beneath their feet. Jason tried to ignore his discomfort and match the boy's pace.

The walk was a depressing one. The heavy, squat buildings loomed greyly through the rain, more than half of them in ruins. They walked on a pedestrian way in the middle of the street. The occasional armored trucks went by on both sides of them. The midstreet sidewalk puzzled Jason until Grif blasted something that hurtled out of a ruined building toward them. The central location gave them some chance to see what was coming. Suddenly Jason was very tired.

"I suppose there wouldn't be anything like a taxi on this planet," he asked.

Grif just stared and frowned. It was obvious he had never even heard the word before. So they just trudged on, the boy holding himself back to Jason's slogging pace. Within half an hour, they had seen all he wanted to see.

"Grif, this city of yours is sure down at the heels. I hope the other ones are in better shape."

"I don't know what you mean talking about heels. But there are no other cities. Some mining camps that can't be located inside the perimeter. But no other cities."

This surprised Jason. He had always visualized the planet with more than one city. There were a *lot* of things he didn't know about Pyrrus, he realized suddenly. All of his efforts since landing had been taken up with the survival studies. There were a number of questions he wanted to ask—but of somebody other than his grouchy eight-year-old bodyguard. There was one person who would be best equipped to tell him what he wanted to know.

"Do you know Kerk?" he asked the boy. "Apparently he's your ambassador to a lot of places but his last name—"

"Sure, everybody knows Kerk. But he's busy, you shouldn't see him."

Jason shook a finger at him. "Minder of my body you may be. But minder of my soul you are not. What do you say I call the shots and you go along to shoot the monsters. Okay?"

They took shelter from a sudden storm of fist-sized hailstones. Then, with ill grace, Grif led the way to one of the larger, central buildings. There were more people here and some of them even glanced at Jason for a minute, before turning back to their business. Jason dragged himself up two flights of stairs before they reached a door marked COORDINATION AND SUPPLY.

"Kerk in here?" Jason asked.

"Sure," the boy told him. "He's in charge."

"Fine. Now you get a nice cold drink or your lunch or something, and meet me back here in a couple of hours. I imagine Kerk can do as good a job of looking after me as you can."

The boy stood doubtfully for a few seconds, then turned away. Jason wiped off some more sweat and pushed through the door.

There were a handful of people in the office beyond. None of them looked up at Jason or asked his business. Everything has a purpose on Pyrrus. If he came there, he must have had a good reason. No one would ever think to ask him what he wanted. Jason, used to the petty officialdom of a thousand worlds, waited for a few moments before he understood. There was only one other door to the room, in the far wall. He shuffled over and opened it.

Kerk looked up from a desk strewed with papers and ledgers. "I was wondering when you would show up," he said.

"A lot sooner if you hadn't prevented it," Jason told him as he dropped wearily into a chair. "It finally dawned on me that I could spend the rest of my life in your bloodthirsty nursery school if I didn't do something about it. So here I am."

"Ready to return to the 'civilized' worlds, now that you've seen enough of Pyrrus?"

"I am not," Jason said. "And I'm getting very tired of everyone telling me to leave. I'm beginning to think that you and the rest of the Pyrrans are trying to hide something."

Kerk smiled at the thought. "What could we have to hide? I doubt if any planet has as simple and one-directional an existence as ours."

"If that's true, then you certainly wouldn't mind answering a few direct questions about Pyrrus, would you?"

Kerk started to protest, then laughed. "Well done. I should know better by now than to argue with you. What do you want to know?"

Jason tried to find a comfortable position on the hard chair, then gave up. "What's the population of your planet?" he asked.

For a second Kerk hesitated, then said, "Roughly thirty thousand. That's not very much for a planet that has been settled this long, but the reason for that is obvious."

"All right, population thirty thousand," Jason said. "Now how about surface control of your planet? I was surprised to find out that this city within its protective wall—the perimeter—is the only one on the planet. Let's not consider the mining camps, since they are obviously just extensions of the city. Would you say then that you people control more or less of the planet's surface than you did in the past?''

Kerk picked up a length of steel pipe from the desk that he used as a paperweight and toyed with it as he thought. The thick steel bent like rubber at his touch as he concentrated on his answer.

"That's hard to say offhand. There must be records of that sort of thing, though I wouldn't know where to find them. It depends on so many factors. . . .''

"Let's forget that for now then," Jason said. "I have another question that's really more relevant. Wouldn't you say that the population of Pyrrus is declining steadily, year after year?''

There was a sharp clang as the pipe struck the wall. Then Kerk was standing over Jason, his hands extended toward the smaller man, his face flushed and angry.

"Don't ever say that!'' he roared. "Don't let me ever hear you say that again!''

Jason sat as quietly as he could, talking slowly and picking out each word with care. His life hung in the balance.

"Don't get angry, Kerk. I meant no harm. I'm on your side, remember? I can talk to you because you've seen much more of the universe than the Pyrrans who have never left the planet. You are used to discussing things. You know that words are just symbols. We can talk and know you don't have to lose your temper over mere words. . . .''

Kerk slowly lowered his arms and stepped away. Then he turned and poured himself a glass of water from a bottle on the desk. He kept his back turned to Jason while he drank.

Very little of the sweat that Jason wiped from his sopping face was caused by the heat in the room.

"I'm—sorry I lost my temper," Kerk said, dropping heavily into his chair. "Doesn't usually happen. Been working hard lately, must have got my temper on edge." He made no mention of what Jason had said.

"Happens to all of us," Jason told him. "I won't begin to describe the condition my nerves were in when I hit this planet. I'm finally forced to admit that everything you said about Pyrrus is true. It is the most deadly spot in the system. And only native-born Pyrrans could possibly survive here. I can manage to fumble along a bit after my training, but I know I would never stand a chance on my own. You probably know I have an eight-year-old as a bodyguard. Gives a good idea of my real status here.''

Anger suppressed, Kerk was back in control of himself now. His eyes narrowed in thought. "Surprises me to hear you say that.

Never thought I would hear you admit that anyone could be bette
than you at anything. Isn't that why you came here? To prove tha
you were as good as any native-born Pyrran?''

"Score one for your side," Jason admitted. ''I didn't think
showed that much. And I'm glad to see your mind isn't as mus
clebound as your body. Yes, I'll admit that was probably my mai
reason for coming, that and curiosity.''

Kerk was following his own train of thought and puzzled where
was leading him. ''You came here to prove that you were as good a
any native-born Pyrran. Yet now you admit that any eight-year-ol
can outdraw you. That just doesn't stack up with what I knew abou
you. If you give with one hand, you must be taking back with th
other. In what way do you still feel your natural superiority?'' H
asked it lightly, yet there was weight of tension behind his words.

Jason thought a long time before answering.

'I'll tell you,'' he finally said. ''But don't snap my neck for i
I'm gambling that your civilized mind can control your reflexe
Because I have to talk about things that are strictly taboo on Pyrrus.

''In your people's eyes I'm a weakling because I come fron
off-world. Realize, though, that this is also my strength. I can se
things that are hidden from you by long association. You know, th
old business of not being able to see the forest for the trees in th
way.''

Kerk nodded agreement and Jason went on. ''To continue th
analogy further, I landed from an airship, and at first all I *could* se
was the forest. To me certain facts are obvious. I think that yo
people know them too, only you keep your thoughts carefull
repressed. They are hidden thoughts that are completely taboo. I'
going to tell you the biggest one of these secret thoughts and hop
you can control yourself well enough not to kill me.''

Kerk's great hands tightened on the arms of the chair, the onl
sign he had heard. Jason spoke quietly, but his words penetrated a
smoothly and easily as a lancet probing into a brain.

''I think human beings are losing the war on Pyrrus. Afte
hundreds of years of occupation this is the only city on the planet—
and it is half in ruins. As if it once had a larger population. That stun
we pulled off to get the shipload of war materials *was* a stunt. I
might not have worked. And if it hadn't, what would have happene
to the city? You people are walking on the crumbling rim of
volcano and you won't admit it.''

Every muscle in Kerk's body was rigid as he sat stiffly in th
chair, his face dotted with tiny beads of sweat. The slightest pus

too far and he would explode. Jason searched for a way to lessen some of the tension.

"I don't enjoy telling you these things. I'm doing it because I'm sure you know them already. You can't face these facts because you would then have to admit that all this fighting and killing is for absolutely no purpose. If your population is dropping steadily, then your fight is nothing but a particularly bloody form of racial suicide. You could leave this planet, but that would be admitting defeat. And I'm sure Pyrrans prefer death to defeat."

When Kerk half-rose from his chair Jason stood too, shouting his words through the other man's fog of anger.

"I'm trying to help you—do you understand that? Wipe the hypocrisy out of your mind, it's destroying you. Right now you would rather kill me than admit consciously that you are fighting an already lost battle. This isn't a real war, just a disastrous treating of symptoms. Like cutting off cancerous fingers one by one. The only result might be ultimate defeat. You won't allow yourself to realize that. That's why you would rather kill me than hear me speak the unspeakable."

Kerk was out of his seat now, hanging over Jason like a tower of death, about to fall. Held up only by the force of Jason's words.

"You must begin to face reality. All you can see is everlasting war. You must begin to realize that you can treat the *causes* of this war and end it forever!"

The meaning penetrated, the shock of the words draining away Kerk's anger. He dropped back into the chair, an almost ludicrous expression on his face. "What the devil do you mean? You sound like a bloody Grubber!"

Jason didn't ask what a Grubber was, but he filed the name.

"You're talking nonsense," Kerk said. "This is just an alien world that must be battled. The causes are self-obvious facts of existence."

"No, they're not," Jason insisted. "Consider for a second. When you are away for any length of time from this planet, you must take a refresher course. To see how things have changed for the worse while you were gone. Well that's a linear progression. If things get worse when you extend into the future, then they have to get better if you extend into the past. It is also good theory—though I don't know if the facts will bear me out—to say that if you extend it far enough into the past you will reach a time when mankind and Pyrrus were not at war with each other."

Kerk was beyond speech now, only capable of sitting and listening while Jason drove home the blows of inescapable logic.

"There is evidence to support this theory. Even you will admi
that I, if I am no match for Pyrran life, am surely well versed in it
And all Pyrran flora and fauna I've seen have one thing in common
They're not functional. *None* of their immense armory of weapon
is used against each other. Their toxins don't seem to operate
against Pyrran life. They are good only for dispensing death t
Homo sapiens. And *that* is a physical impossibility. In the thre
hundred years that men have been on this planet, the life form
couldn't have naturally adapted in this manner."

"But they *have* done it!" Kerk bellowed.

"You are so right," Jason told him calmly. "And if they have
done it, there must be some agency at work. Operating how, I hav
no idea. But something has caused the life on Pyrrus to declare war
and I'd like to find out what that something is. What was the
dominant life form here when your ancestors landed?"

"I'm sure I wouldn't know," Kerk said. "You're not sug
gesting, are you, that there are sentient beings on Pyrrus other than
those of human descent? Creatures who are organizing the planet t
battle us?"

"I'm not suggesting it—you are. That means you're getting the
idea. I have no idea what caused this change, but I would sure like t
find out. Then see if it can be changed back. Nothing promised, o
course. You'll agree, though, that it is worth investigating."

Fist smacking into his palm, his heavy footsteps shaking the
building, Kerk paced back and forth the length of the room. He wa
at war with himself. New ideas fought old beliefs. It was s
sudden—and so hard not to believe.

Without asking permission, Jason helped himself to some chille
water from the bottle and sank back into the chair, exhausted
Something whizzed in through the open window, tearing a hole i
the protective screen. Kerk blasted it without changing stride
without even knowing he had done it.

The decision didn't take long. Geared to swift activity, the bi
Pyrran found it impossible not to decide quickly. The pacing
stopped and he looked steadily at Jason.

"I don't say you have convinced me, but I find it impossible t
find a ready answer to your arguments. So until I do, we will have t
operate as if they are true. Now what do you plan to do, what *ca*
you do?"

Jason ticked the points off on his fingers. "One, I'll need a place
to live and work that is well protected. So instead of spending m
energies on just remaining alive I can devote some study to thi

project. Two, I want someone to help me—and act as a bodyguard at the same time. And someone, please, with a little more scope of interest than my present watchdog. I would suggest Meta as the person most suited for this job.''

"Meta?" Kerk was surprised. "She's a space pilot and defense screen operator; what good could she possibly be on a project like this?''

"The most good possible. She has had experience on other worlds and can shift her point of view—at least a bit. And she must know as much about this planet as any other educated adult and can answer any questions I ask." Jason smiled. "In addition to which she is an attractive girl, whose company I enjoy."

Kerk grunted. "I was wondering if you would get around to mentioning that last reason. The others make sense, though, so I'm not going to argue. I'll round up a replacement for her and have Meta sent here. There are plenty of sealed buildings you can use."

After talking to one of the assistants from the outer office, Kerk made some calls on the screen. The correct orders were quickly issued. Jason watched it all with interest.

"Pardon me for asking," he finally said. "But are you the dictator of this planet? You just snap your fingers and they all jump."

"I suppose it looks that way," Kerk admitted. "But that is just an illusion. No one is in complete charge on Pyrrus, neither is there anything resembling a democratic system. After all, our total population is about the size of an army division. Everyone does the job they are best qualified for. Various activities are separated into departments with the most qualified person in charge. I run Coordination and Supply, which is about the loosest category. We fill in the gaps between departments and handle procuring from off-planet.''

Meta came in and talked to Kerk. She completely ignored Jason's presence. "I was relieved and sent here," she said. "What is it? Change in flight schedule?"

"You might call it that," Kerk said. "As of now you are dismissed from all your old assignments and assigned to a new department. Investigation and Research. That tired-looking fellow there is your department head."

"A sense of humor," Jason said. "The only native-born one on Pyrrus. Congratulations, there's hope for the planet yet."

Meta glanced back and forth between them. "I don't understand. I can't believe it. I mean a new department—why?" She was nervous and upset.

"I'm sorry," Kerk said. "I didn't mean to be cruel. I thought perhaps you might feel more at ease. What I said was true. Jason has a way—or may have a way—to be of immense value to Pyrrus. Will you help him?"

Meta had her composure back. And a little anger. "Do I have to? Is that an order? You know I have work to do. I'm sure you will realize it is more important than something a person from *off-planet* might imagine. He can't really understand . . ."

"Yes. It's an order." The snap was back in Kerk's voice. Meta flushed at the tone.

"Perhaps I can explain," Jason broke in. "After all, the whole thing is my idea. But first I would like your cooperation. Will you take the clip out of your gun and give it to Kerk?"

Meta looked frightened, but Kerk nodded in solemn agreement. "Just for a few minutes, Meta. I have my gun so you will be safe here. I think I know what Jason has in mind, and from personal experience I'm afraid he is right."

Reluctantly Meta passed over the clip and cleared the charge in the gun's chamber. Only then did Jason explain.

"I have a theory about life on Pyrrus, and I'm afraid I'll have to shatter some illusions when I explain. To begin with, the fact must be admitted that your people are slowly losing the war here and will eventually be destroyed. . . ."

Before he was half through the sentence, Meta's gun was directed between his eyes and she was wildly snapping the trigger. There was only hatred and revulsion in her expression. It was the most terrible thought in the world for her. That this war they all devoted their lives to was already lost.

Kerk took her by the shoulders and sat her in his chair, before anything worse happened. It took some time before she could calm down enough to listen to Jason's words. It is not easy to have destroyed the carefully built up rationalizations of a lifetime. Only the fact that she had seen something of other worlds enabled her to listen at all.

The light of unreason was still in her eyes when he had finished, telling her the things he and Kerk had discussed. She sat tensely, pushed forward against Kerk's hands, as if they were the only things that stopped her from leaping at Jason.

"Maybe that is too much to assimilate at one sitting," Jason said. "So let's put it in simpler terms. I believe we can find a reason for this unrelenting hatred of humans. Perhaps we don't smell right. Maybe I'll find an essence of crushed Pyrran bugs that will render us immune when we rub it in. I don't know yet. But whatever the results, we *must* make the investigation. Kerk agrees with me on that."

Meta looked at Kerk and he nodded agreement. Her shoulders slumped in sudden defeat. She whispered the words.

"I—can't say I agree, or even understand all that you said. But I'll help you. If Kerk thinks that it is the right thing."

"I do," he said. "Now, do you want the clip back for your gun? Not planning to take any more shots as Jason?"

"That was foolish of me," she said coldly while she reloaded the gun. "I don't need a gun. If I had to kill him, I could do it with my bare hands."

"I love you too," Jason smiled at her. "Are you ready to go now?"

"Of course." She brushed a fluffy curl of hair into place. "First we'll find a place where you can stay. I'll take care of that. After that, the work of the new department is up to you."

10

They walked downstairs in a frigid silence. In the street, Meta blasted a stingbird that couldn't possibly have attacked them. There was an angry pleasure in the act. Jason decided not to chide her about wasting ammo. Better the bird than him.

There were empty rooms in one of the computer buildings. These were completely sealed to keep stray animal life out of the delicate machinery. While Meta checked a bedroll out of stores, Jason painfully dragged a desk, table and chairs in from a nearby empty office. When she returned with a pneumatic bed, he instantly dropped on it with a grateful sigh. Her lip curled a bit at his obvious weakness.

"Get used to the sight," he said. "I intend to do as much of my work as I can, while maintaining a horizontal position. You will be my strong right arm. And right now, Right Arm, I wish you could scare me up something to eat. I also intend to do most of my eating in the previously mentioned prone condition."

Snorting with disgust, Meta stamped out. While she was gone,

Jason chewed the end of a stylus thoughtfully, then made some careful notes.

After they had finished the almost tasteless meal, he began the search.

"Meta, where can I find historical records of Pyrrus? Any and all information about the early days of the settlers on this planet."

"I've never heard of anything like that. I really don't know. . . ."

"But there has to be something—*somewhere*," he insisted. "Even if your present day culture devotes all of its time and energies to survival, you can be sure it wasn't always that way. All the time it was developing, people were keeping records, making notes. Now where do we look? Do you have a library here?"

"Of course," she said. "We have an excellent technical library. But I'm sure there wouldn't be any of *that* sort of thing there."

Trying not to groan, Jason stood up. "Let me be the judge of that. Just lead the way."

Operation of the library was completely automatic. A projected index gave the call number for any text that had to be consulted. The tape was delivered to the charge desk thirty seconds after the number had been punched. Returned tapes were dropped through a hopper and refiled automatically. The mechanism worked smoothly.

"Wonderful," Jason said, pushing away from the index. "A tribute to technological ingenuity. Only it contains nothing of any value to us. Just reams of textbooks."

"What *else* should be in a library?" Meta sounded sincerely puzzled.

Jason started to explain, then changed his mind. "Later we will go into that," he said. "Much later. Now we have to find a lead. Is it possible that there are any tapes—or even printed books—that aren't filed through this machine?"

"It seems unlikely, but we could ask Poli. He lives here somewhere and is in charge of the library. Filing new books and tending the machinery."

The single door into the rear of the building was locked, and no amount of pounding could rouse the caretaker.

"If he's alive, this should do it," Jason said. He pressed the out-of-order button on the control panel. It had the desired effect. Within five minutes, the door opened and Poli dragged himself through it.

Death usually came swiftly on Pyrrus. If wounds slowed a man down, the ever-ready forces of destruction quickly finished the job. Poli was the exception to this rule. Whatever had attacked him originally had done an efficient job. Most of the lower part of his face was gone. His left arm was curled and useless. The damage to his body and legs had left him with the bare capability to stumble from one spot to the next.

Yet he still had one good arm as well as his eyesight. He could work in the library and relieve a fully fit man. How long he had been dragging the useless husk of a body around the building, no one knew. In spite of the pain that filled his red-rimmed, moist eyes, he had stayed alive. Growing old, older than any other Pyrran Jason had seen. He tottered forward and turned off the alarm that had called him.

When Jason started to explain, the old man took no notice. Only after the librarian had rummaged a hearing aid out of his clothes, did Jason realize he was deaf as well. Jason explained again what he searched for. Poli nodded and printed his answer on a tablet.

there are many old books—in the storerooms below

Most of the building was taken up by the robot filing and sorting apparatus. They moved slowly through the banks of machinery, following the crippled librarian to a barred door in the rear. He pointed to it. While Jason and Meta fought to open the age-encrusted bars, he wrote another note on his tablet.

not opened for many years. rats

Jason and Meta's guns appeared reflexively in their hands as they read the message. Jason finished opening the door by himself. The two native Pyrrans stood facing the opening gap. It was well they did. Jason could never have handled what came through that door.

He didn't even open it for himself. Their sounds at the door must have attracted all the vermin in the lower part of the building. Jason had thrown the last bolt and was starting to pull on the handle—when the door was *pushed* open from the other side.

Open the gateway to hell and see what comes out. Meta and Poli stood shoulder to shoulder firing into the mass of loathsomeness that boiled through the door. Jason jumped to one side and picked off the occasional animal that came his way. The destruction seemed to go on forever.

Long minutes passed before the last clawed beast made its death rush. Meta and Poli waited expectantly for more; they were happily excited by this chance to deal destruction. Jason felt a little sick after the silent ferocious attack. A ferocity that the Pyrrans reflected. He

saw a scratch on Meta's face where one of the beasts had caught her.
She seemed oblivious to it.

Pulling out his medikit, Jason circled the piled bodies. Something
stirred in their midst and a crashing shot plowed into it. Then he
reached the girl and pushed the analyzer probes against the scratch.
The machine clicked and Meta jumped as the antitoxin needle
stabbed down. She realized for the first time what Jason was doing.

"Thank you. I didn't notice," she said. "There were so many of
them and they came out so fast."

Poli had a powerful battery lamp and, by unspoken agreement,
Jason carried it. Crippled though he was, the old man was still a
Pyrran when it came to handling a gun. They slowly made their way
down the refuse-laden stairs.

"What a stench!" Jason grimaced. "Without these filter plugs in
my nose, I think the smell alone would kill me."

Something hurled itself into the beam of light and a shot stopped
it in midair. The rats had been there a long time and resented the
intrusion.

At the foot of the stairs they looked around. There *had* been
books and records there at one time. They had been systematically
chewed, eaten and destroyed for decades.

"I like the care you take with your old books," Jason said
disgustedly. "Remind me not to loan you any."

"They could have been of no importance," Meta said coolly,
"or they would be filed correctly in the library upstairs."

Jason wandered gloomily through the rooms. Nothing remained
of any value. Fragments and scraps of writing and printing. Never
enough in one spot to bother collecting. With the toe of one armored
boot, he kicked angrily at a pile of debris, ready to give up the
search. There was a glint of rusty metal under the dirt.

"Hold this!" He gave the light to Meta and, forgetting the danger
for a moment, began scratching aside the rubble. A flat metal box
with a dial lock built into it was revealed.

"Why that's a log box!" Meta said, surprised.

"That's what I thought," Jason said. "And if it is—we may be in
luck after all."

11

Resealing the cellar, they carried the box back to Jason's new office. Only after spraying with decontaminant did they examine it closely. Meta picked out engraved letters on the lid.

"S.T. POLLUX VICTORY—that must be the name of the spacer this log came from. But I don't recognize the class, or whatever it is the initials *S.T.* stand for."

"Stellar Transport," Jason told her, as he tried the lock mechanism. "I've heard of them but I've never seen one. They were built during the last wave of galactic expansion. Really nothing more than gigantic metal containers, put together in space. After they were loaded with people, machinery and supplies, they would be towed to whatever planetary system had been chosen. These same tugs and one-shot rockets would brake the S.T.'s in for a landing. Then leave them there. The hull was a ready source of metal and the colonists could start right in building their new world. And they were *big.* All of them held at least fifty thousand people."

Only after he said it, did he realize the significance of his words. Meta's deadly stare drove it home. There were now less people on Pyrrus than had been in the original settlement.

And human population, without rigid birth controls, usually increased geometrically. Jason remembered Meta's itchy trigger finger.

"But we can't be sure how many people were aboard this one," he said hurriedly. "Or even if this is the log of the ship that settled Pyrrus. Can you find something to pry this open with? The lock is corroded into a single lump."

Meta took her anger out on the box. Her fingers managed to force a gap between lid and bottom. She wrenched at it. Rusty metal screeched and tore. The lid came off in her hands and a heavy book thudded to the table.

The cover legend destroyed all doubt.

LOG OF S.T. POLLUX VICTORY. OUTWARD BOUND— SETANI TO PYRRUS. 55,000 SETTLERS ABOARD.

Meta couldn't argue now. She stood behind Jason with tight-clenched fists and read over his shoulder as he turned the brittle, yellowed pages. He quickly skipped through the opening part that covered the sailing preparations and trip out. Only when he had reached the actual landing did he start reading slowly. The impact of the ancient words leaped out at him.

"Here it is!" Jason shouted. "Proof positive that we're on the right trail. Even *you* will have to admit that. Read it, right here."

. . . second day since the tugs left, we are completely on our own now. The settlers still haven't grown used to this planet, though we have orientation talks every night. As well as the morale agents who I have working twenty hours a day. I suppose I really can't blame the people, they all lived in the underways of Setani and I doubt if they saw the sun once a year. This planet has weather with a vengeance, worse than anything I've seen on a hundred other planets. Was I wrong during the original planning stages not to insist on settlers from one of the agrarian worlds? People who could handle the outdoors. These citified Setanians are afraid to go out in the rain. But of course they have adapted completely to their native 1.5 gravity so the 2 gee here doesn't bother them much. That was the factor that decided us. Anyway, too late now to do anything about it. Or about the unending cycle of rain, snow, hail, hurricanes and sucn. Answer will be to start the mines going, sell the metals and build completely enclosed cities.

The only thing on this forsaken planet that isn't actually against us are the animals. A few large predators at first, but the guards made short work of them. The rest of the wild life leaves us alone. Glad of that! They have been fighting for existence so long that I have never seen a more deadly looking collection. Even the little rodents no bigger than a man's hand are armored like tanks. . . .

"I don't believe a word of it," Meta broke in. "That can't be Pyrrus he's writing about. . . ." Her words died away as Jason wordlessly pointed to the title on the cover.

He continued scanning the pages, flipping them quickly. A sentence caught his eye and he stopped. Jamming his finger against the place, he read aloud.

"*. . . and troubles keep piling up. First Har Palo with his theory that the vulcanism is so close to the surface that the ground keeps warm, and the crops grow so well. Even if he is right—what can we do? We must be self-dependent if we intend to survive. And now this other thing. It seems that the forest fire drove a lot of new species our way. Animals, insects and even birds have attacked the people. (Note for Har: check if possible seasonal migration might* explain attacks.) There have been fourteen deaths from wounds and poisoning. We'll have to enforce the rules for insect lotion at all times. And, I suppose, build some kind of perimeter defense to keep the larger beasts out of the camp.''

"This is a beginning," Jason said. "At least now we are aware of the real nature of the battle we're engaged in. It doesn't make Pyrrus any easier to handle, or make the life forms less dangerous, to know that they were once better disposed toward mankind. All this does is point the way. Something took the peaceful life forms, shook them up, and turned this planet into one big deathtrap for mankind. That *something* is what I want to uncover.''

12

Further reading of the log produced no new evidence. There was a good deal more information about the early animal and plant life and how deadly they were, as well as the first defenses against them. Interesting historically, but of no use whatsoever in countering the menace. The captain apparently never thought that life forms were altering on Pyrrus, believing instead that dangerous beasts were being discovered. He never lived to change his mind. The last entry in the log, less than two months after the first attack, was very brief. And in a different handwriting.

Captain Kurkowski died today, of poisoning following an insect bite. His death is greatly mourned.

The "why" of the planetary revulsion had yet to be uncovered.

"Kerk must see this book," Jason said. "He should have some idea of the progress being made. Can we get transportation—or do we walk to city hall?''

"Walk, of course," Meta said.

"Then you bring the book. At two-G's I find it very hard to be a gentleman and carry the packages.''

They had just entered Kerk's outer office when a shrill screaming burst out of the phone screen. It took Jason a moment to realize that it was a mechanical signal, not a human voice.

"What is it?" he asked.

Kerk burst through the door and headed for the street entrance. Everyone else in the office was going the same way. Meta looked confused, leaning toward the door, then looking back at Jason.

"What does it mean? Can't you tell me?" He shook her arm.

"Sector alarm. A major breakthrough of some kind at the perimeter. Everyone but other perimeter guards has to answer."

"Well go then," he said. "Don't worry about me. I'll be all right."

His words acted like a trigger release. Meta's gun was in her hand and she was gone before he had finished speaking. Jason sat down wearily in the deserted office.

The unnatural silence in the building began to get on his nerves. He shifted his chair over to the phone screen and switched it on to *receive.* The screen exploded with color and sound. At first Jason could make no sense of it at all. Just a confused jumble of faces and voices. It was a multichannel set designed for military use. A number of images were carried on the screen at one time, rows of heads or hazy backgrounds where the user had left the field of view. Many of the heads were talking at the same time and the babble of their voices made no sense whatsoever.

After examining the controls and making a few experiments, Jason began to understand the operation. Though all stations were on the screen at all times, their audio channels could be controlled. In that way, two, three or more stations could be hooked together in a linkup. They would be in round-robin communication with each other, yet never out of contact with the other stations.

Identification between voice and sound was automatic. Whenever one of the pictured images spoke, the image would glow red. By trial and error, Jason brought in the audio for the stations he wanted and tried to follow the course of the attack.

Very quickly he realized this was something out of the ordinary. In some way, no one made it clear, a section of the perimeter had been broken through and emergency defenses had to be thrown up to encapsulate it. Kerk seemed to be in charge, at least he was the only one with an override transmitter. He used it for general commands. The many, tiny images faded and his face appeared on top of them, filling the entire screen.

"All perimeter stations sent 25 per cent of your complement to Area 12."

The small images reappeared and the babble increased, red lights flickering from face to face.

"—abandon the first floor, acid bombs can't reach."

"If we hold we'll be cut off, but salient is past us on the west flank. Request support."

"DON'T, MERVV—IT'S USELESS!"

". . . and the napalm tanks are almost gone. Orders?"

"The truck is still there, get it to the supply warehouse, you'll find replacements—"

Out of the welter of talk, only the last two fragments made any sense. Jason had noticed the signs below when he came in. The first two floors of the building below him were jammed with military supplies. This was his chance to get into the act.

Just sitting and watching was frustrating. Particularly when it was a desperate emergency. He didn't overvalue his worth, but he was sure there was always room for another gun.

By the time he had dragged himself down to the street level, a turbotruck had slammed to a stop in front of the loading platform. Two Pyrrans were rolling out drums of napalm with a reckless disregard for their own safety. Jason didn't dare enter that maelstrom of rolling metal. He found he could be of use tugging the heavy drums into position on the truck while the others rolled them up. They accepted his aid without acknowledgment.

It was exhausting, sweaty work, hauling the leaden drums into place against the heavy gravity. After a minute, Jason worked by touch through a red haze of hammering blood. He realized the job was done only when the truck suddenly leaped forward and he was thrown to the floor. He lay there, his chest heaving. As the driver hurled the heavy vehicle along, all Jason could do was bounce around in the bottom. He could see well enough, but was still gasping for breath when they braked at the fighting zone.

To Jason, it was a scene of incredible confusion. Guns firing, flames, men and women running on all sides. The napalm drums were unloaded without his help and the truck vanished for more. Jason leaned against a wall of a half-destroyed building and tried to get his bearings. It was impossible. There seemed to be a great number of small animals; he killed two that attacked him. Other than that he couldn't determine the nature of the battle.

A Pyrran, tan face white with pain and exertion, stumbled up. His right arm, wet with raw flesh and dripping blood, hung limply at his side. It was covered with freshly applied surgical foam. He held his gun in his left hand, a stump of control cable dangling from it. Jason thought the man was looking for medical aid. He couldn't have been more wrong.

Clenching the gun in his teeth, the Pyrran clutched a barrel of napalm with his good hand and hurled it over on its side. Then, with the gun once more in his hand, he began to roll the drum along the ground with his feet. It was slow, cumbersome work, but he was still in the fight.

Jason pushed through the hurrying crowd and bent over the drum. "Let me do it," he said. "You can cover us both with your gun."

The man wiped the sweat from his eyes with the back of his arm and blinked at Jason. He seemed to recognize him. When he smiled it was a grimace of pain, empty of humor. "Do that. I can still shoot. Two half men—maybe we equal one whole." Jason was laboring too hard to even notice the insult.

An explosion had blasted a raw pit in the street ahead. Two people were at the bottom, digging it even deeper with shovels. The whole thing seemed meaningless. Just as Jason and the wounded man rolled up the drum, the diggers leaped out of the excavation and began shooting down into its depths. One of them turned, a young girl, barely in her teens.

"Praise Perimeter!" she breathed. "They found the napalm. One of the new horrors is breaking through to Ward Area 13, we just found it." Even as she talked she swiveled the drum around, kicked the easy-off plug, and began dumping the gelid contents into the hole. When half of it had gurgled down, she kicked the drum itself in. Her companion pulled a flare from his belt, lit it, and threw it after the drum.

"Back quick. They don't like heat," he said.

This was putting it mildly. The napalm caught, tongues of flame and roiling, greasy smoke climbing up to the sky. Under Jason's feet the earth shifted and moved. *Something* black and long stirred in the heart of the flame, then arched up into the sky over their heads. In the midst of the searing heat, it still moved with alien, jolting motions. It was immense, at least two meters thick and with no indication of its length. The flames didn't stop it, just annoyed it.

Jason had some idea of the thing's length as the street cracked and buckled for fifty meters on each side of the pit. Great loops of the creature began to emerge from the ground. He fired his gun, as did the others. Not that it seemed to have any effect. More and more people were appearing, armed with a variety of weapons. Flame-throwers and grenades seemed to be the most effective.

"*Clear the area, we're going to saturate it. Fall back.*"

The voice was so loud it jarred Jason's ear. He turned and recognized Kerk, who had arrived with truckloads of equipment. He had a power speaker on his back, the mike hung in front of his lips. His amplified voice brought an instant reaction from the crowd. They began to move.

There was still doubt in Jason's mind what to do. Clear the area? But what area? He started toward Kerk, before he realized that the rest of the Pyrrans were going in the opposite direction. Even under two gravities, they *moved*.

Jason had a naked feeling of being alone on the stage. He was in the center of the street, and the others had vanished. No one remained. Except the wounded man Jason had helped. He stumbled toward Jason, waving his good arm. Jason couldn't understand what he said. Kerk was shouting orders again from one of the trucks. They had started to move too. The urgency struck home and Jason started to run.

It was too late. On all sides the earth was buckling, cracking, as more loops of the underground thing forced its way into the light. Satety lay ahead. Only in front of it rose an arch of dirt encrusted grey.

There are seconds of time that seem to last an eternity. A moment of subjective time that is grabbed and stretched to an infinite distance. This was one of those moments. Jason stood, frozen. Even the smoke in the sky hung unmoving. The high-standing loop of alien life was before him, every detail piercingly clear.

Thick as a man, ribbed and grey as old bark. Tendrils projected from all parts of it, pallid and twisting lengths that writhed slowly with snake-like life. Shaped like a plant, yet with the motions of an animal. And cracking, splitting. This was the worst.

Seams and openings appeared. Splintering, gaping mouths that vomited out a horde of pallid animals. Jason heard their shriekings, shrill yet remote. He saw the needle-like teeth that lined their jaws.

The paralysis of the unknown held him there. He should have died. Kerk was thundering at him through the power speaker, others were firing into the attacking creature. Jason knew nothing.

Then he was shot forward, pushed by a rock-hard shoulder. The wounded man was still there, trying to get Jason clear. Gun clenched in his jaws, he dragged Jason along with his good arm. Toward the creature. The others stopped firing. They saw his plan and it was a good one.

A loop of the thing arched into the air, leaving an opening between its body and the ground. The wounded Pyrran planted his feet and tightened his muscles. One-handed, with a single thrust, he picked Jason off the ground and sent him hurtling under the living arch. Moving tendrils brushed fire along his face, then he was through, rolling over and over on the ground. The wounded Pyrran leaped after him.

It was too late. There had been a chance for one person to get out. The Pyrran could have done it easily—instead he had pushed Jason first. The thing was aware of movement when Jason brushed its tendrils. It dropped and caught the wounded man under its weight. He vanished from sight as the tendrils wrapped around him and the animals swarmed over. His trigger must have pulled back to full automatic because the gun kept firing a long time after he should have been dead.

Jason crawled. Some of the fanged animals ran toward him, but were shot. He knew nothing about this. Then rude hands grabbed him up and pulled him forward. He slammed into the side of a truck and Kerk's face was in front of his, flushed and angry. One of the giant fists closed on the front of Jason's clothes and he was lifted off his feet, shaken like a limp bag of rags. He offered no protest and could not have even if Kerk had killed him.

When he was thrown to the ground, someone picked him up and slid him into the back of the truck. He did not lose consciousness as the truck bounced away, yet he could not move. In a moment the fatigue would go away and he would sit up. That was all he was, just a little tired. Even as he thought this, he passed out.

13

"Just like old times," Jason said when Brucco came into the room with a tray of food. Without a word Brucco served Jason and the wounded men in the other beds, then left. "Thanks," Jason called after his retreating back.

A joke, a twist of a grin, like it always was. Sure. But even as he grinned and his lips shaped a joke, Jason felt them like a veneer on the outside. Something plastered on with a life of its own. Inside he was numb and immovable. His body was stiff as his eyes still watched that arch of alien flesh descend and smother the one-armed Pyrran with its million burning fingers.

He could feel himself under the arch. After all, hadn't the

wounded man taken his place? He finished the meal without realizing that he ate.

Ever since that morning, when he had recovered consciousness, it had been like this. He knew that he should have died out there in that battle-torn street. *His* life should have been snuffed out, for making the mistake of thinking that he could actually help the battling Pyrrans. Instead of being underfoot and in the way. If it hadn't been for Jason, the man with the wounded arm would have been brought here to the safety of the reorientation buildings. He knew he was lying in the bed that belonged to that man.

The man who had given his life for Jason's.

The man whose name he didn't even know.

There were drugs in the food and they made him sleep. The medicated pads soaked the pain and rawness out of the burns where the tentacles had seared his face. When he awoke the second time, his touch with reality had been restored.

A man had died so he could live. Jason faced the fact. He couldn't restore that life, no matter how much he wanted to. What he could do was make the man's death worthwhile. If it can be said that any death was worthwhile. . . . He forced his thoughts from that track.

Jason knew what he had to do. His work was even more important now. If he could solve the riddle of this deadly world, he could repay in part the debt he owed.

Sitting up made his head spin and he held to the edge of the bed until it slowed down. The others in the room ignored him as he slowly and painfully dragged on his clothes. Brucco came in, saw what he was doing, and left again without a word.

Dressing took a long time, but it was finally done. When Jason finally left the room he found Kerk waiting there for him.

"Kerk, I want to tell you. . . ."

"Tell me *nothing!*" The thunder of Kerk's voice bounced back from the ceiling and walls. "I'm telling *you*. I'll tell you once and that will be the end of it. You're not wanted on Pyrrus, Jason dinAlt, neither you nor your precious off-world schemes are wanted here. I let you convince me once with your twisted tongue. Helped you at the expense of more important work. I should have known what the result of your 'logic' would be. Now I've seen. Welf died so you could live. He was twice the man you will ever be."

"Welf? Was that his name?" Jason asked stumblingly. "I didn't know. . . ."

"You didn't even know." Kerk's lips pulled back from his teeth in a grimace of disgust. "You didn't even know his name—yet he died that you might continue your miserable existence." Kerk spat, as if the words gave a vile flavor to his speech, and stamped toward the exit lock. Almost as an afterthought, he turned back to Jason.

"You'll stay here in the sealed buildings until the ship returns in two weeks. Then you will leave this planet and never come back. If you do I'll kill you instantly. With pleasure." He started through the lock.

"Wait," Jason shouted. "You can't decide like that. You haven't even seen the evidence I've uncovered. Ask Meta—" The lock thumped shut and Kerk was gone.

The whole thing was just too stupid. Anger began to replace the futile despair of a moment before. He was being treated like an irresponsible child, the importance of his discovery of the log completely ignored.

Jason turned and saw for the first time that Brucco was standing there. "Did you hear that?" Jason asked him.

"Yes. And I quite agree. You can consider yourself lucky."

"Lucky!" Jason was the angry one now. "Lucky to be treated like a moronic child, with contempt for everything I do—"

"I said lucky," Brucco snapped. "Welf was Kerk's only surviving son. Kerk had high hopes for him, was training him to take his place eventually." He turned to leave but Jason called after him.

"Wait. I'm sorry about Welf. I can't be any sorrier knowing that he was Kerk's son. But at least it explains why Kerk is so quick to throw me out—as well as the evidence I have uncovered. The log of the ship . . ."

"I know, I've seen it," Brucco interrupted. "Meta brought it in. Very interesting historical document."

"That's all you can see it as, an historical document? The significance of the planetary change escapes you?"

"It doesn't escape me," Brucco answered briefly. "But I cannot see that it has any relevancy today. The past is unchangeable and we must fight in the present. That is enough to occupy all our energies."

The pressure of futility built up inside Jason, fighting for a way to burst free. Wherever he turned, there was only indifference.

"You're an intelligent man, Brucco—yet you can see no further than the tip of your own nose. I suppose it is inevitable. You and the rest of the Pyrrans are supermen by Earth standards. Tough, ruthless, unbeatable, fast on the draw. Drop you anywhere and you land on your feet. You would make perfect Texas Rangers, Canadian Mounties, Venus Swamp Patrolmen—any of the mythical frontier fighters of the past. And I think that's where you really belong. In the past. On Pyrrus, mankind has been pushed to the limit of adaptability in muscle and reflex. And it's a dead end. Brain was the thing that dragged mankind out of the caves and started him on his way to the stars. When we start thinking with our muscles again we are on our way right back to those caves. Isn't that what you Pyrrans are? A bunch of cavemen hitting animals on the head with stone axes. Do you ever stop to think why you are here? What you are doing? Where you are going?"

Jason had to stop; he was exhausted and gasping for breath. Brucco rubbed his chin in thought. "Caves?" he asked. "Of course we don't live in caves or use stone clubs. I don't understand your point at all."

It was impossible to be angry, or even exasperated. Jason started to answer, then laughed instead. A very humorless laugh. He was too tired to argue anymore. He kept running into this same stone wall with all the Pyrrans. Theirs was a logic of the moment. The past and future unchangeable, unknowable—and uninteresting. "How is the perimeter battle going?" he asked finally, wanting to change the subject.

"Finished. Or in the last stages at least." Brucco was enthusiastic as he showed Jason stereos of the attackers. He did not notice Jason's repressed shudder.

"This was the most serious breakthrough in years, but we caught it in time. I hate to think what would have happened if they hadn't been detected for a few weeks more."

"What are those things?" Jason asked. "Giant snakes of some kind?"

"Don't be absurd," Brucco snorted. He tapped the stereo with his thumbnail. "Roots. That's all. Greatly modified, but still roots. They came in under the perimeter barrier, much deeper than anything we've had before. Not a real threat in themselves as they have very little mobility. Die soon after being cut. The danger came from their being used as access tunnels. They're bored through and through with animal runs, and two or three species of beasts live in a sort of symbiosis inside. Now we know what they are we can watch for them. The danger was they could have completely undermined the perimeter and come in from all sides at once. Not much we could have done then."

The edge of destruction. Living on the lip of a volcano. The Pyrrans took satisfaction from any day that passed without total annihilation. There seemed no way to change their attitude. Jason let the conversation die there. He picked up the log of the *Pollux Victory* from Brucco's quarters and carried it back to his room. The wounded Pyrrans there ignored him as he dropped onto the bed and opened the book to the first page.

For two days he did not leave his quarters. The wounded men were soon gone and he had the room to himself. Page by page he went through the log, until he knew every detail of the settlement of Pyrrus. His notes and cross-references piled up. He made an accurate map of the original settlement, superimposed over a modern one. They didn't match at all.

It was a dead end. With one map held over the other, what he had suspected was painfully clear. The descriptions of terrain and physical features in the log were accurate enough. The city had obviously been moved since the first landing. Whatever records had been kept would be in the library—and he had exhausted that source. Anything else would have been left behind and long since destroyed.

Rain lashed against the thick window above his head, lit suddenly by a flare of lightning. The unseen volcanoes were active again, vibrating the floor with their rumblings deep in the earth.

The shadow of defeat pressed heavily down on Jason. Rounding his shoulders and darkening, even more, the overcast day.

14

Jason spent one depressed day lying on his bunk counting rivets, forcing himself to accept defeat. Kerk's order that he was not to leave the sealed building tied his hands completely. He felt himself close to the answer—but he was never going to get it.

One day of defeat was all he could take. Kerk's attitude was completely emotional, untempered by the slightest touch of logic. This fact kept driving home until Jason could no longer ignore it. Emotional reasoning was something he had learned to mistrust early in life. He couldn't agree with Kerk in the slightest—which meant he had to utilize the ten remaining days to solve the problem. If it meant disobeying Kerk, it would still have to be done.

He grabbed up his noteplate with a new enthusiasm. His first sources of information had been used up, but there must be others. Chewing the scriber and thinking hard, he slowly built up a list of other possibilities. Any idea, no matter how wild, was put down. When the plate was filled, he wiped the long shots and impossibles —such as consulting off-world historical records. This was a Pyrran problem and had to be settled on this planet or not at all.

The list worked down to two probables. Either old records, notebooks or diaries that individual Pyrrans might have in their possession, or verbal histories that had been passed down the generations by word of mouth. The first choice seemed to be the most probable and he acted on it at once. After a careful check of his medikit and gun, he went to see Brucco.

"What's new and deadly in the world since I left?" he asked.

Brucco glared at him. "You can't go out, Kerk has forbidden it."

"Did he put you in charge of guarding me to see if I obeyed?" Jason's voice was quiet and cold.

Brucco rubbed his jaw and frowned in thought. Finally he just shrugged. "No, I'm not guarding you—nor dc I want the job. As far as I know, this is between you and Kerk and it can stay that way. Leave whenever you want. And get yourself killed quietly someplace so there will be an end to the trouble you cause once and for all."

"I like you too," Jason said. "Now brief me on the wildlife."

The only new mutation that routine precautions wouldn't take care of was a slate-colored lizard that spit a fast nerve poison with deadly accuracy. Death took place in seconds if the saliva touched any bare skin. The lizards had to be looked out for, and shot before they came within range. An hour of lizard-blasting in a training chamber made him proficient in the exact procedure.

Jason left the sealed buildings quietly and no one saw him go. He followed the map to the nearest barracks, shuffling tiredly through the dusty streets. It was a hot, quiet afternoon, broken only by rumblings from the distance, and the occasional crack of his gun.

It was cool inside the thick-walled barracks building, and he collapsed onto a bench until the sweat dried and his heart stopped pounding. Then he went to the nearest recreation room to start his search.

Before it began, it was finished. None of the Pyrrans kept old artifacts of any kind and thought the whole idea was very funny. After the twentieth negative answer, Jason was ready to admit defeat in this line of investigation. There was as much chance of meeting a Pyrran with old documents as finding a bundle of Grandfather's letters in a soldier's kit bag.

This left a single possibility—verbal histories. Again Jason questioned with the same lack of results. The fun had worn off the game for the Pyrrans and they were beginning to growl. Jason stopped while he was still in one piece. The commissary served him a meal that tasted like plastic paste and wood pulp. He ate it quickly, then sat brooding over the empty tray, hating to admit to another dead end. Who could supply him with answers? All the people he had talked to were so young. They had no interest or patience for storytelling. That was an old folks' hobby—and there were no oldsters on Pyrrus.

With one exception that he knew of, the librarian, Poli. It was a possibility. A man who worked with records and books might have an interest in some of the older ones. He might even remember reading volumes now destroyed. A very slim lead, indeed, but one that had to be pursued.

Walking to the library almost killed Jason. The torrential rains made the footing bad, and in the dim light it was hard to see what was coming. A snapper came in close enough to take out a chunk of flesh before he could blast it. The antitoxin made him dizzy and he lost some blood before he could get the wound dressed. He reached the library, exhausted and angry.

Poli was working on the guts of one of the catalogue machines. He didn't stop until Jason had tapped him on the shoulder. Switching on his hearing aid, the Pyrran stood quietly, crippled and bent, waiting for Jason to talk.

"Have you any old papers or letters that you have kept for your personal use?"

A shake of the head, *no*.

"What about stories—you know, about great things that have happened in the past, that someone might have told you when you were young?" Negative.

Results negative. Every question was answered by a shake of Poli's head, and very soon the old man grew irritated and pointed to the work he hadn't finished.

"Yes, I know you have work to do," Jason said. "But this is important." Poli shook his head an angry *no* and reached to turn off his hearing aid. Jason groped for a question that might get a more positive answer. There was something tugging at his mind, a word he had heard and made a note of, to be investigated later. Something that Kerk had said. . . .

"That's it!" It was right there—on the tip of his tongue. "Just a second, Poli, just one more question. What is a 'grubber'? Have you ever seen one or know what they do, or where they can be found?"

The words were cut off as Poli whirled and lashed the back of his good arm into Jason's face. Though the man was aged and crippled, the blow almost fractured Jason's jaw, sending him sliding across the floor. Through a daze, he saw Poli hobbling toward him, making thick bubbling noises in his ruined throat, what remained of his face twisted and working with anger.

This was no time for diplomacy. Moving as fast as he could, with the high-G, foot-slapping shuffle, Jason headed for the sealed door. He was no match for any Pyrran in hand-to-hand combat, young and small or old and crippled. The door banged open, as he went through, and barely closed in Poli's face.

Outside the rain had turned to snow and Jason trudged wearily through the slush, rubbing his sore jaw and turning over the only fact he had. *Grubber* was a key—but to what? And who did he dare ask for more information? Kerk was the man he had talked to best, but not anymore. That left only Meta as a possible source. He wanted to see her at once, but sudden exhaustion swept through him. It took all of his strength to stumble back to the school buildings.

In the morning he ate and left early. There was only a week left. It was impossible to hurry and he cursed as he dragged his double-weight body to the assignment center. Meta was on night perimeter duty and should be back to her quarters soon. He shuffled over there and was lying on her bunk when she came in.

"Get out," she said in a flat voice. "Or do I throw you out?"

"Patience, please," he said as he sat up. "Just resting here until you came back. I have a single question, and if you will answer it for me I'll go and stop bothering you."

"What is it?" she asked, tapping her foot with impatience. But there was also a touch of curiosity in her voice. Jason thought carefully before he spoke.

"Now try not to shoot me. You know I'm an off-worlder with a big mouth, and you have heard me say some awful things without taking a shot at me. Now I have another one. Will you please show your superiority to the other people of the galaxy by holding your temper and not reducing me to component atoms."

Her only answer was a tap of the foot, so he took a deep breath and plunged in.

"What is a 'grubber'?"

For a long moment she was quiet, unmoving. Then she looked at him with disgust. "You do find the most repulsive topics."

"That may be so," he said, "but it still doesn't answer my question."

"It's . . . well, the sort of thing people just don't talk about."

"I do," he assured her.

"Well I *don't!* It's the most disgusting thing in the world, and that's all I'm going to say. Talk to Krannon, but not to me." She had him by the arm while she talked and he was half dragged to the hall. The door slammed behind him and he muttered *"Lady-wrestler"* under his voice. His anger ebbed away as he realized that she had given him a clue in spite of herself. Next step, find out who or what Krannon was.

Assignment center listed a man named Krannon and gave his shift number and work location. It was close by and Jason walked there. A large, cubical, windowless building, with the single word FOOD next to each of the sealed entrances. The small entrance he went through was a series of automatic chambers that cycled him through ultrasonics, ultraviolet, antibio spray, rotating brushes and three final rinses. He was finally admitted, damper but much cleaner, to the central area. Men and robots were stacking crates and he asked one of the men for Krannon. The man looked up and down coldly and spat on his shoes before answering.

Krannon worked in a large storage bay by himself. He was a stocky man in patched coveralls whose only expression was one of intense gloom. When Jason came in he stopped hauling bales and sat down on the nearest one. The lines of unhappiness were cut into his face and seemed to grow deeper while Jason explained what he was after. All the talk of ancient history on Pyrrus bored him as well and he yawned openly. When Jason finished, he yawned again and didn't even bother to answer him.

Jason waited a moment, then asked again, "I said do you have any old books, papers, records or that sort of thing?"

"You sure picked the right guy to bother, off-worlder," was his only answer. "After talking to me you're going to have nothing but trouble."

"Why is that?" Jason asked.

"Why?" For the first time, he was animated with something besides grief. "I'll tell you why! I made one mistake once, just one, and I get a life sentence. For life—how would you like that. Just me alone, being by myself all the time. Even taking orders from the grubbers."

Jason controlled himself, keeping the elation out of his voice. "Grubbers? What are grubbers?"

The enormity of the question stopped Krannon; it seemed impossible that there could be a man alive who had never heard of grubbers. Happiness lifted some of the gloom from his face as he realized that he had a captive audience who would listen to his troubles.

"Grubbers are traitors—that's what they are. Traitors to the human race and they ought to be wiped out. Living in the jungle. The things they do with the animals. . . ."

"You mean they're people—Pyrrans like yourself?" Jason broke in.

"Not like *me*, mister. Don't make that mistake again if you want to go on living. Maybe I dozed off on guard once so I got stuck with this job. That doesn't mean I like it or like them. They stink, really stink, and if it wasn't for the food we get from them they'd all be dead tomorrow. That's the kind of killing job I could really put my heart into."

"If they supply you with food, you must give them something in return?"

"Trade goods, beads, knives, the usual things. Supply sends them over in cartons and I take care of the delivery."

"How?" Jason asked.

"By armored truck to the delivery site. Then I go back later to pick up the food they've left in exchange."

"Can I go with you on the next delivery?"

Krannon frowned over the idea for a minute. "Yeah, I suppose it's all right if you're stupid enough to come. You can help me load. They're between harvests now, so the next trip won't be for eight days. . . ."

"But that's after the ship leaves—it'll be too late. Can't you go earlier?"

"Don't tell me your troubles, mister," Krannon grumbled, climbing to his feet. "That's when I go and the date's not changing for you."

Jason realized he had got as much out of the man as was possible for one session. He started for the door, then turned.

"One thing," he asked. "Just what do these savages—the grubbers—look like?"

"How do I know!" Krannon snapped. "I trade with them, I don't make love to them. If I ever saw one, I'd shoot him down on the spot." He flexed his fingers and his gun jumped in and out of his hand as he said it. Jason quietly let himself out.

Lying on his bunk, resting his gravity-weary body, he searched for a way to get Krannon to change the delivery date. His millions of credits were worthless on this world without currency. If the man couldn't be convinced, he had to be bribed. With what? Jason's eyes touched the locker where his off-world clothing still hung, and he had an idea.

It was morning before he could return to the food warehouse—and one day closer to his deadline. Krannon didn't bother to look up from his work when Jason came in.

"Do you want this?" Jason asked, handing the outcast a flat gold case inset with a single large diamond. Krannon grunted and turned it over in his hands.

"A toy," he said. "What is it good for?"

"Well, when you press this button you get a light." A flame appeared through a hole in the top. Krannon started to hand it back.

"What do I need a little fire for. Here, keep it."

"Wait a second," Jason said. "That's not all it does. When you press the jewel in the center, one of these comes out." A black pellet the size of his fingernail dropped into his palm. "A grenade, made of solid ulranite. Just squeeze it hard and throw. Three seconds later it explodes with enough force to blast open this building."

This time Krannon almost smiled as he reached for the case. Destructive and death-dealing weapons are like candy to a Pyrran. While he looked at it, Jason made his offer.

"The case and bombs are yours if you move the date of your next delivery up to tomorrow—and let me go with you."

"Be here at 0500," Krannon said. "We leave early."

15

The truck rumbled up to the perimeter gate and stopped. Krannon waved to the guards through the front window, then closed a metal shield over it. When the gates swung open the truck—really a giant armored tank—ground slowly forward. There was a second gate beyond the first, that did not open until the interior one was closed. Jason looked through the second driver's periscope as the outer gate lifted. Automatic flamethrowers flared through the opening, cutting off only when the truck reached them. A scorched area ringed the gate; beyond that the jungle began. Unconsciously Jason shrank back in his seat.

All the plants and animals he had seen only specimens of, existed here in profusion. Thorn-ringed branches and vines laced themselves into a solid mat, through which the wildlife swarmed. A fury of sound hurled at them, thuds and scratchings rang on the armor. Krannon laughed and closed the switch that electrified the outer grid. The scratchings died away as the beasts completed the circuit to the grounded hull.

It was slow speed, low-gear work tearing through the jungle. Krannon had his face buried in the periscope mask and silently fought the controls. With each mile, the going seemed to get better, until he finally swung up the periscope and opened the window armor. The jungle was still thick and deadly, but nothing like the area immediately around the perimeter. It appeared as if most of the lethal powers of Pyrrus were concentrated in the single area around the settlement. Why? Jason asked himself. Why this intense and directed planetary hatred?

The motors died and Krannon stood up, stretching. "We're here," he said. "Let's unload."

There was bare rock around the truck, a rounded hillock that projected from the jungle, too smooth and steep for vegetation to get a hold. Krannon opened the cargo hatches and they pushed out the boxes and crates. When they finished Jason slumped down, exhausted, onto the pile.

"Get back in, we're leaving," Krannon said.

"You are, I'm staying right here."

Krannon looked at him coldly. "Get in the truck or I'll kill you. No one stays out here. For one thing you couldn't live an hour alone. But worse than that the grubbers would get you. Kill you at once, of course, but that's not important. But you have equipment that we can't allow into their hands. You want to see a grubber with a gun?"

While the Pyrran talked, Jason's thoughts had rushed ahead. He hoped that Krannon was as thick of head as he was of reflex.

Jason looked at the trees, let his gaze move up through the thick branches. Though Krannon was still talking, he was automatically aware of Jason's attention. When Jason's eyes widened and his gun jumped into his hand, Krannon's own gun appeared and he turned in the same direction.

"There—in the top!" Jason shouted and fired into the tangle of branches. Krannon fired too. As soon as he did, Jason hurled himself backward, curled into a ball, rolling down the inclined rock. The shots had covered the sounds of his movements, and before Krannon could turn back the gravity had dragged him down the rock into the thick foliage. Crashing branches slapped at him, but slowed his fall. When he stopped moving, he was lost in the tangle. Krannon's shots came too late to hit him.

Lying there, tired and bruised, Jason heard the Pyrran cursing him out. He stamped around on the rock, fired a few shots, but knew better than to enter the trees. Finally he gave up and went back to the truck. The motor gunned into life and the treads clanked and scraped down the rock and back into the jungle. There were muted rumblings and crashes that slowly died away.

Then Jason was alone.

Up until that instant he hadn't realized quite how alone he would be. Surrounded by nothing but death, the truck already vanished from sight. He had to force down an overwhelming desire to run after it. What was done was done.

This was a long chance to take, but it was the only way to contact the grubbers. They were savages, but still they had come from human stock. And they hadn't sunk so low as to stop the barter with the civilized Pyrrans. He had to contact them, befriend them. Find out how they had managed to live safely on this madhouse world.

If there had been another way to lick the problem he would have taken it; he didn't relish the role of martyred hero. But Kerk and his deadline had forced his hand. The contact had to be made fast and this was the only way.

There was no telling where the savages were, or how soon they would arrive. If the woods weren't too lethal, he could hide there, pick his time to approach them. If they found him among the supplies, they might skewer him on the spot with a typical Pyrran reflex.

Walking wearily, he approached the line of trees. Something moved on a branch, but vanished as he came near. None of the plants near a thick-trunked tree looked poisonous, so he slipped behind it. There was nothing deadly in sight and it surprised him. He let his body relax a bit, leaning against the rough bark.

Something soft and choking fell over his head; his body was seized in a steel grip. The more he struggled, the tighter it held him until the blood thundered in his ears and his lungs screamed for air.

Only when he grew limp did the pressure let up. His first panic ebbed a little when he realized that it wasn't an animal that attacked him. He knew nothing about the grubbers, but they were human so he still had a chance.

His arms and legs were tied, the power holster ripped from his arm. He felt strangely naked without it. The powerful hands grabbed him again and he was hurled into the air, to fall face down across something warm and soft. Fear pressed in again for it was a large animal of some kind. And all Pyrran animals were deadly.

When the animal moved off, carrying him, panic was replaced by a feeling of mounting elation. The grubbers had managed to work out a truce of some kind with at least one form of animal life. He had to find out how. If he could get that secret—and get it back to the city—it would justify all his work and pain. It might even justify Welf's death if the age-old war could be slowed or stopped.

Jason's tightly bound hands hurt terribly at first, but grew numb with the circulation shut off. The jolting ride continued endlessly; he had no way of measuring time. A rainfall soaked him, then he felt his clothes steaming as the sun came out.

The ride was finally over. He was pulled from the animal's back and dumped down. His arms dropped free as someone loosed the bindings. The returning circulation soaked him in pain as he lay there, struggling to move. When his hands finally obeyed him, he lifted them to his face and stripped away the covering, a sack of thick fur. Light blinded him as he sucked in breath after breath of clean air.

Blinking against the glare, he looked around. He was lying on a floor of crude planking, the setting sun shining into his eyes through the doorless entrance of the building. There was a ploughed field outside, stretching down the curve of hill to the edge of the jungle. It was too dark to see much inside the hut.

Something blocked the light of the doorway, a tall animal-like figure. On second look Jason realized it was a man with long hair and thick beard. He was dressed in furs; even his legs were wrapped in fur leggings. His eyes were fixed on his captive, while one hand fondled an axe that hung from his waist.

"Who're you? What y'want?" the bearded man asked suddenly.

Jason picked his words slowly, wondering if this savage had the same hairtrigger temper as the city dwellers.

"My name is Jason. I come in peace. I want to be your friend. . . ."

"Lies!" the man grunted, and pulled the axe from his belt. "Junkman tricks. I saw y'hide. Wait to kill me. Kill you first." He tested the edge of the blade with a horny thumb, then raised it.

"Wait!" Jason said desperately. "You don't understand."

The axe swung down.

"I'm from off-world and—"

A solid thunk shook him as the axe buried itself in the wood next to his head. At the last instant, the man had twitched it aside. He grabbed the front of Jason's clothes and pulled him up until their faces touched.

"S'true?" he shouted. "Y'from off-world?" His hand opened and Jason dropped back before he could answer. The savage jumped over him, toward the dim rear of the hut.

"Rhes must know of this," he said as he fumbled with something on the wall. Light sprang out.

All Jason could do was stare. The hairy, fur-covered savage was operating a communicator. The calloused, dirt-encrusted fingers deftly snapped open the circuits, dialed a number.

16

It made no sense. Jason tried to reconcile the modern machine with the barbarian and couldn't. Who was he calling? The existence of one communicator meant there was at least another. Was Rhes a person or a thing?

With a mental effort, he grabbed hold of his thoughts and braked them to a stop. There was something new here, factors he hadn't counted on. He kept reassuring himself there was an explanation for everything, once you had your facts straight.

Jason closed his eyes, shutting out the glaring rays of the sun where it cut through the treetops, and reconsidered his facts. They separated evenly into two classes: those he had observed for himself, and those he had learned from the city dwellers. This last class of "facts" he would hold, to see if they fitted with what he learned. There was a good chance that most, or all, of them would prove false.

"Get up," the voice jarred into his thoughts. "W're leaving."

His legs were still numb and hardly usable. The bearded man snorted in disgust and hauled him to his feet, propping him against the outer wall. Jason clutched the knobby bark of the logs when he was left alone. He looked around, soaking up impressions.

It was the first time he had been on a farm since he had run away from home. A different world with a different ecology, but the imilarity was apparent enough to him. A new-sown field stretched lown the hill in front of the shack. Ploughed by a good farmer. Even, well-cast furrows that followed the contour of the slope. Another, larger log building was next to this one, probably a barn.

There was a snuffling sound behind him and Jason turned quick- y—and froze. His hand called for the missing gun and his finger ightened down on a trigger that wasn't there.

It had come out of the jungle and padded up quietly behind him. It ad six thick legs with clawed feet that dug into the ground. The wo-meter-long body was covered with matted yellow-and-black ur, all except the skull and shoulders. These were covered with verlapping horny plates. Jason could see all this because the beast vas that close.

He waited to die.

The mouth opened, a frog-like division of the hairless skull, evealing double rows of jagged teeth.

"Here, Fido," the bearded man said, coming up behind Jason nd snapping his fingers at the same time. The thing bounded orward, brushing past the dazed Jason, and rubbed his head against he man's leg. "Nice doggie," the man said, his fingers scratching inder the edge of the carapace where it joined the flesh.

The bearded man had brought two of the riding animals out of the arn, saddled and bridled. Jason barely noticed the details of mooth skin and long legs as he swung up on one. His feet were uickly lashed to the stirrups. When they started, the skull-headed east followed them.

"Nice doggie!" Jason said, and for no reason started to laugh. The bearded man turned and scowled at him until he was quiet.

By the time they entered the jungle, it was dark. It was impossible o see under the thick foliage, and they used no lights. The animals eemed to know the way. There were scraping noises and shrill calls rom the jungle around them, but it didn't bother Jason too much. 'erhaps the automatic manner in which the other man undertook the ourney reassured him. Or the presence of the "dog" that he felt ather than saw. The trip was a long one, but not too uncomfortable.

The regular motion of the animal and his fatigue overcame Jason nd he dozed into a fitful sleep, waking with a start each time he lumped forward. In the end, he slept sitting up in the saddle. Hours assed this way, until he opened his eyes and saw a square of light efore them. The trip was over.

His legs were stiff and galled with saddle sores. After his feet vere untied, getting down was an effort and he almost fell. A door pened and Jason went in. It took his eyes some moments to get

used to the light, until he could make out the man on the bed befor
him.

"Come over here and sit down." The voice was full and stron,
accustomed to command. The body was that of an invalid.
blanket covered him to the waist, above that the flesh was sick
white, spotted with red nodules, and hung loosely over the bone
There seemed to be nothing left of the man except skin and skeleto

"Not very nice," the man on the bed said, "but I've grown use
to it." His tone changed abruptly. "Naxa said you were fro
off-world. If that true?"

Jason nodded yes, and his answer stirred the living skeleton
life. The head lifted from the pillow and the red-rimmed eyes soug
his with a desperate intensity.

"My name is Rhes and I'm a . . . grubber. Will you help me?"

Jason wondered at the intensity of Rhes's question, all out
proportion to the simple content of its meaning. Yet he could see r
reason to give anything other than the first and obvious answer th
sprang to his lips.

"Of course I'll help you, in whatever way I can. As long as
involves no injury to anyone else. What do you want?"

The sick man's head had fallen back limply, exhausted, as Jas
talked. But the fire still burned in the eyes.

"Feel assured—I want to injure no others," Rhes said. "Qui
the opposite. As you see, I am suffering from a disease that o
remedies will not stop. Within a few more days I will be dead. No
I have seen . . . the city people . . . using a device, they press
over a wound or an animal bite. Do you have one of the.
machines?"

"That sounds like a description of the medikit." Jason touch
the button at his waist that dropped the medikit into his hand. "
have mine here. It analyzes and treats most . . ."

"Would you use it on me?" Rhes broke in, his voice sudden.
urgent.

"I'm sorry," Jason said. "I should have realized." He steppe
forward and pressed the machine over one of the inflamed areas
Rhes's chest. The operation light came on and the thin shaft of th
analyzer probe slid down. When it withdrew the device humme
then clicked three times as three separate hypodermic needl
lanced into the skin. Then the light went out.

"Is that all?" Rhes asked, as he watched Jason stow the medik
back in his belt.

Jason nodded, then looked up and noticed the wet marks of tea on the sick man's face. Rhes became aware at the same time and brushed at them angrily.

"When a man is sick," he growled, "the body and all its senses become traitor. I don't think I have cried since I was a child—but you must realize it's not myself I'm crying for. It's the untold thousands of my people who have died for lack of that little device you treat so casually."

"Surely you have medicines, doctors of your own?"

"Herb doctors and witch doctors," Rhes said, consigning them all to oblivion with a chop of his hand. "The few hard working and honest men are hampered by the fact that the faith healers can usually cure better than their strongest potion."

The talking had tired Rhes. He stopped suddenly and closed his eyes. On his chest, the inflamed areas were already losing their angry color as the injections took effect. Jason glanced around the room, looking for clues to the mystery of these people.

Floor and walls were made of wood lengths fitted together, free of paint or decoration. They looked simple and crude, fit only for the savages he had expected to meet. Or were they crude? The wood had a sweeping, flame-like grain. When he bent close he saw that wax had been rubbed over the wood to bring out this pattern. Was this the act of savages—or of artistic men seeking to make the most of simple materials? The final effect was far superior to the drab-paint and riveted-steel rooms of the city dwelling Pyrrans. Wasn't it true that both ends of the artistic scale were dominated by simplicity? The untutored aborigine made a simple expression of a clear idea, and created beauty. At the other extreme, the sophisticated critic rejected overelaboration and decoration and sought the truthful clarity of uncluttered art. At which end of the scale was he looking now?

These men were savages, he had been told that. They dressed in furs and spoke a slurred and broken language, at least Naxa did. Rhes admitted he preferred faith healers to doctors. But, if all this were true, where did the communicator fit into the picture? Or the glowing ceiling that illuminated the room with a soft light?

Rhes opened his eyes and stared at Jason, as if seeing him for the first time. "Who are you?" he asked. "And what are you doing here?"

There was a cold menace in his words and Jason understood why. The city Pyrrans hated the "grubbers" and, without a doubt, the feeling was mutual. Naxa's axe had proved that. Naxa had entered silently while they talked, and stood with his fingers touching the haft of this same axe. Jason knew his life was still in jeopardy, until he gave an answer that satisfied these men.

He couldn't tell the truth. If they once suspected he was spying among them to aid the city people, it would be the end. Nevertheless, he had to be free to talk about the survival problem.

The answer hit him as soon as he had stated the problem. All this had only taken an instant to consider, as he turned back to face the invalid, and he answered at once. Trying to keep his voice normal and unconcerned.

"I'm Jason dinAlt, an ecologist, so you see I have the best reasons in the universe for visiting this planet—"

"What is an ecologist?" Rhes broke in. There was nothing in his voice to indicate whether he meant the question seriously, or as a trap. All traces of the ease of their earlier conversation was gone; his voice had the deadliness of a stingwing's poison. Jason chose his words carefully.

"Simply stated, it is that branch of biology that considers the relations between organisms and their environment. How climatic and other factors affect the life forms, and how the life forms in turn affect each other and the environment." That much Jason knew was true—but he really knew very little more about the subject, so he moved on quickly.

"I heard reports of this planet, and finally came here to study it first-hand. I did what work I could in the shelter of the city, but it wasn't enough. The people there think I'm crazy, but they finally agreed to let me make a trip out here."

"What arrangements have been made for your return?" Naxa snapped.

"None," Jason told him. "They seemed quite sure that I would be killed instantly and had no hope of me coming back. They refused to let me go on my own and I had to break away."

This answer seemed to satisfy Rhes and his face cracked into a mirthless smile. "They would think that, those junkmen. Can't move a meter outside their walls without an armor-plated machine big as a barn. What did they tell you about us?"

Again Jason knew a lot depended on his answer. This time he thought carefully before speaking.

"Well, perhaps I'll get that axe in the back of my neck for saying this—but I have to be honest. You must know what they think. They told me you were filthy and ignorant savages—who smelled. And you—well, had curious customs you practiced with the animals. In exchange for food, they traded you beads and knives. . . ."

Both Pyrrans broke into a convulsion of laughter at this. Rhes stopped soon, from weakness, but Naxa laughed himself into a coughing fit and had to splash water over his head from a gourd jug.

"That I believe well enough," Rhes said. "It sounds like the stupidity they would talk. Those people know nothing of the world they live in. I hope the rest of what you said is true, but even if it is not, you are welcome here. You are from off-world, that I know. No junkman would have lifted a finger to save my life. You are the first off-worlder my people have ever known and for that you are doubly welcome. We will help you in any way we can. My arm is your arm."

These last words had a ritual sound to them and, when Jason repeated them, Naxa nodded at the correctness of this. At the same time, Jason felt that they were more than empty ritual. Interdependence meant survival on Pyrrus, and he knew that these people stood together to the death against the mortal dangers around them. He hoped the ritual would include him in that protective sphere.

"That is enough for tonight," Rhes said. "The spotted sickness has weakened me, and your medicine has turned me to jelly. You will stay here, Jason. There is a blanket, but no bed, at least for now."

Enthusiasm had carried Jason this far, making him forget the two-G exertions of the long day. Now fatigue hit him a physical blow. He had dim memories of refusing food and rolling in the blanket on the floor. After that, oblivion.

17

Every square inch of his body ached where the doubled gravity had pressed his flesh to the unyielding wood of the floor. His eyes were gummy and his mouth was filled with an indescribable taste that came off in chunks. Sitting up was an effort and he had to stifle a groan as his joints cracked.

"Good day, Jason," Rhes called from the bed. "If I didn't believe in medicine so strongly, I would be tempted to say there is a miracle in your machine that has cured me overnight."

There was no doubt that he was on the mend. The inflamed

patches had vanished and the burning light was gone from his eyes. He sat, propped up on the bed, watching the morning sun melt the night's hailstorm into the fields.

"There's meat in the cabinet there," he said, "and either water or visk to drink."

The visk proved to be a distilled beverage of extraordinary potency that instantly cleared the fog from Jason's brain, though it did leave a slight ringing in his ears. And the meat was a tenderly smoked joint, the best food he had tasted since leaving Darkhan. Taken together, they restored his faith in life and the future. He lowered his glass with a relaxed sigh and looked around.

With the pressures of immediate survival and exhaustion removed, his thoughts returned automatically to his problem. What were these people really like—and how had they managed to survive in the deadly wilderness? In the city he had been told they were savages. Yet there was a carefully tended and repaired communicator on the wall. And by the door a crossbow that fired machined metal bolts; he could see the tool marks still visible on their shanks. The one thing he needed was more information. He could start by getting rid of some of his misinformation.

"Rhes, you laughed when I told you what the city people said, about trading you trinkets for food? What do they really trade you?"

"Anything within certain limits," Rhes said. "Small manufactured items, such as electronic components for our communicators. Rustless alloys we can't make in our forges, cutting tools, atomic-electric converters that produce power from any radioactive element. Things like that. Within reason they'll trade anything we ask that isn't on the forbidden list. They need the food badly."

"And the items on the forbidden list—?"

"Weapons of course, or anything that might be made into a powerful weapon. They know we make gunpowder so we can't get anything like large casting or seamless tubing we could make into heavy gun barrels. We drill our own rifle barrels by hand, though the crossbow is quiet and faster in the jungle. Then they don't like us to know very much, so the only reading matter that gets to us are tech maintenance manuals, empty of basic theory.

"The last banned category you know about—medicine. This is the one thing I cannot understand, that makes me burn with hatred with every death they might have prevented."

"I know their reasons," Jason said.

"Then tell me, because I can think of none."

"Survival—it's just that simple. I doubt if you realize it, but they have a decreasing population. It is just a matter of years before they will be gone. Whereas your people at least must have a stable—if not slightly growing population—to have existed without their mechanical protections. So in the city they hate you and are jealous of you at the same time. If they gave you medicine and you prospered, you would be winning the battle they have lost. I imagine they tolerate you as a necessary evil, to supply them with food, otherwise they wish you were all dead.''

"It makes sense," Rhes growled, slamming his fist against the bed. "The kind of twisted logic you expect from junkmen. They use us to feed them, give us the absolute minimum in return, and at the same time cut us off from the knowledge that will get us out of this hand to mouth existence. Worse, far worse, they cut us off from the stars and the rest of mankind.'' The hatred on his face was so strong that Jason unconsciously drew back.

'Do you think we are savages here, Jason? We act and look like animals because we have to fight for existence on an animal level. Yet we know about the stars. In that chest over there, sealed in metal, are over thirty books, all we have. Fiction most of them, with some history and general science thrown in. Enough to keep alive the stories of the settlement here and the rest of the universe outside. We see the ships land in the city and we know that up there are worlds we can only dream about and never see. Do you wonder that we hate these beasts that call themselves men, and would destroy them in an instant if we could? They are right to keep weapons from us—for sure as the sun rises in the morning we would kill them to a man if we were able, and take over the things they have withheld from us.''

It was a harsh condemnation, but essentially a truthful one. At least from the point of view of the outsiders. Jason didn't try to explain to the angry man that the city Pyrrans looked on their attitude as being the only possible and logical one. "How did this battle between your two groups ever come about?" he asked.

"I don't know," Rhes said, "I've thought about it many times, but there are no records of that period. We do know that we are all descended from colonists who arrived at the same time. Somewhere, at some time, the two groups separated. Perhaps it was a war, I've read about them in the books. I have a partial theory, though I can't prove it, that it was the location of the city.''

"Location—I don't understand.''

"Well, you know the junkmen, and you've seen where their city is. They managed to put it right in the middle of the most savage spot on this planet. You know they don't care about any living thing except themselves; shoot and kill is their only logic. So they wouldn't consider where to build their city, and managed to build it in the stupidest spot imaginable. I'm sure my ancestors saw how foolish this was and tried to tell them so. That would be reason enough for a war, wouldn't it?''

"It might have been—if that's really what happened," Jason said. "But I think you have the problem turned backward. It's a war between native Pyrran life and humans, each fighting to destroy the other. The life forms change continually, seeking that final destruction of the invader.''

"Your theory is even wilder than mine," Rhes said. "That's not true at all. I admit that life isn't too easy on this planet—if what I have read in the books about other planets is true—but it doesn't change. You have to be fast on your feet and keep your eyes open for anything bigger than you, but you can survive. Anyway, it doesn't really matter why. The junkmen always look for trouble and I'm happy to see that they have enough.''

Jason didn't try to press the point. The effort of forcing Rhes to change his basic attitudes wasn't worth it—even if possible. He hadn't succeeded in convincing anyone in the city of the lethal mutations even when they could observe all the facts. Rhes could still supply information though.

"I suppose it's not important who started the battle," Jason said for the other man's benefit, not meaning a word of it. "But you'll have to agree that the city people are permanently at war with all the local life. Your people, though, have managed to befriend at least two species that I have seen. Do you have any idea how this was done?''

"Naxa will be here in a minute," Rhes said, pointing to the door, "as soon as he's taken care of the animals. Ask him. He's the best talker we have.''

"Talker?" Jason asked. "I had the opposite idea about him. He didn't talk much, and what he did say was, well—a little hard to understand at times.''

"Not that kind of talking," Rhes broke in impatiently. "The talkers look after the animals. They train the dogs and doryms, and the better ones like Naxa are always trying to work with other beasts. They dress crudely, but they have to. I've heard them say that the animals don't like chemicals, metal or tanned leather, so they wear untanned furs for the most part. But don't let the dirt fool you, it has nothing to do with his intelligence.''

"Doryms? Are those your carrying beasts—the kind we rode coming here?''

Rhes nodded. "Doryms are more than pack animals, they're really a little bit of everything. The large males pull the plows and other machines, while the younger animals are used for meat. If you want to know more, ask Naxa, you'll find him in the barn."

"I'd like to do that," Jason said, standing up. "Only I feel undressed without my gun—"

"Take it, by all means, it's in that chest by the door. Only watch out what you shoot around here."

Naxa was in the rear of the barn, filing down one of the spade-like toenails of a dorym. It was a strange scene. The fur-dressed man with the great beast—and the contrast of a beryllium-copper file and electro-luminescent plates lighting the work. The dorym opened its nostrils and pulled away when Jason entered. Naxa patted its neck and talked softly until it quieted and stood still, shivering slightly.

Something stirred in Jason's mind, with the feeling of a long unused muscle being stressed. A hauntingly familiar sensation.

"Good morning," Jason said. Naxa grunted something and went back to his filing. Watching him for a few minutes, Jason tried to analyze this new feeling. It itched and slipped aside when he reached for it, escaping him. Whatever it was, it had started when Naxa had talked to the dorym.

"Could you call one of the dogs in here, Naxa? I'd like to see one closer up."

Without raising his head from his work, Naxa gave a low whistle. Jason was sure it couldn't have been heard outside of the barn. Yet within a minute one of the Pyrran dogs slipped quietly in. The talker rubbed the beast's head, mumbling to it, while the animal looked intently into his eyes.

The dog became restless when Naxa turned back to work on the dorym. It prowled around the barn, sniffing, then moved quickly toward the open door. Jason called it back.

At least he meant to call it. At the last moment he said nothing. Nothing aloud. On sudden impulse he kept his mouth closed—only he called the dog with his mind. Thinking the words *Come here*, directing the impulse at the animal with all the force and direction he had ever used to manipulate dice. As he did it, he realized it had been a long time since he had even considered using his *psi* powers.

The dog stopped and turned back toward him.

It hesitated, looking at Naxa, then walked over to Jason.

Seen this closely, the beast was a nightmare hound. The hairless protective plates, tiny red-rimmed eyes, and countless, saliva-dripping teeth did little to inspire confidence. Yet Jason felt no fear. There was a rapport between man and animal that was understood.

Without conscious thought, he reached out and scratched the dog along the back, where he knew it itched.

"Di'nt know y're a talker," Naxa said. As he watched them, there was friendship in his voice for the first time.

"I didn't know either—until just now," Jason said. He looked into the eyes of the animal before him, scratched the ridged and ugly back, and began to understand.

The talkers must have well-developed *psi* facilities, that was obvious now. There is no barrier of race or alien form when two creatures share each other's emotions. Empathy first, so there would be no hatred or fear. After that direct communication. The talkers might have been the ones who first broke through the barrier of hatred on Pyrrus and learned to live with the native life. Others could have followed their example—this might explain how the community of "grubbers" had been formed.

Now that he was concentrating on it, Jason was aware of the soft flow of thoughts around him. The consciousness of the dorym was matched by other like patterns from the rear of the barn. He knew without going outside that more of the big beasts were in the field back there.

"This is all new to me," Jason said. "Have you ever thought about it, Naxa? What does it feel like to be a talker? I mean, do you *know* why it is you can get the animals to obey you while other people have no luck at all?"

Thinking of this sort troubled Naxa. He ran his fingers through his thick hair and scowled as he answered. "Nev'r thought about it. Just do it. Just get t'know the beast real good, then y'can guess what they're going t'do. That's all."

It was obvious that Naxa had never thought about the origin of his ability to control the animals. And if he hadn't, probably no one else had. They had no reason to. They simply accepted the powers of talkers as one of the facts of life.

Ideas slipped toward each other in his mind, like the pieces of a puzzle joining together. He had told Kerk that the native life of Pyrrus had joined in battle against mankind, he didn't know why. Well, he still didn't know why, but he was getting an idea of the "how."

"About how far are we from the city?" Jason asked. "Do you have an idea how long it would take us to get there by dorym?"

"Half day there—half back. Why? Y'want to go?"

"I don't want to get into the city, not yet. But I would like to get close to it," Jason told him.

"See what Rhes says," was Naxa's answer.

Rhes granted instant permission without asking any questions. They saddled up and left at once, in order to complete the round trip before dark.

They had been traveling less than an hour before Jason knew they were going in the direction of the city. With each minute, the feeling grew stronger. Naxa was aware of it, too, stirring in the saddle with unvoiced feelings. They had to keep touching and reassuring their mounts which were growing skittish and restless.

"This is far enough," Jason said. Naxa gratefully pulled to a stop.

The wordless thought beat through Jason's mind, filling it. He could feel it on all sides—only much stronger ahead of them in the direction of the unseen city. Naxa and the doryms reacted in the same way, restlessly uncomfortable, not knowing the cause.

One thing was obvious now. The Pyrran animals were sensitive to *psi* radiation—probably the plants and lower life forms as well. Perhaps they communicated by it, since they obeyed the men who had a strong control of it. And in this area was a wash of *psi* radiation such as he had never experienced before. Though his personal talents specialized in psychokinesis—the mental control of inanimate matter—he was still sensitive to most mental phenomena. Watching a sports event, he had many times felt the unanimous accord of many minds expressing the same thought. What he felt now was like that.

Only terribly different. A crowd exulted at some success on the field, or groaned at a failure. The feeling fluxed and changed as the game progressed. Here the wash of thought was unending, strong and frightening. It didn't translate into words very well. It was part hatred, part fear—and all destruction.

"KILL THE ENEMY" was as close as Jason could express it. But it was more than that. An unending river of mental outrage and death.

"Let's go back now," he said, suddenly battered and sickened by the feelings he had let wash through him. As they started the return trip, he began to understand things.

His sudden unspeakable fear when the Pyrran animal had attacked him that first day on the planet. And his recurrent nightmares that had never completely ceased, even with drugs. Both of these were his reaction to the hatred directed at the city. Though for some reason he hadn't felt it directly up until now, enough had reached through to him to get a strong emotional reaction.

Rhes was asleep when they got back and Jason couldn't talk to him until morning. In spite of his fatigue from the trip, he stayed awake late into the night, going over in his mind the discoveries of the day. Could he tell Rhes what he had found out? Not very well. If he did that, he would have to explain the importance of his discovery and what he meant to use it for. Nothing that aided the city dwellers would appeal to Rhes in the slightest. Best to say nothing until the entire affair was over.

18

After breakfast, he told Rhes that he wanted to return to the city.

"Then you have seen enough of our barbarian world, and wish to go back to your friends. To help them wipe us out perhaps?" Rhes said it lightly, but there was a touch of cold malice behind his words.

"I hope you don't really think that," Jason told him. "You must realize that the opposite is true. I would like to see this civil war ended and your people getting all the benefits of science and medicine that have been withheld. I'll do everything I can to bring that about."

"They'll never change," Rhes said gloomily, "so don't waste your time. But there is one thing you must do, for your protection and ours. Don't admit, or even hint, that you've talked to any grubbers!"

"Why not?"

"Why not—! Suffering death, are you that simple! They will do anything to see that we don't rise too high, and would much prefer to see us all dead. Do you think they would hesitate to kill you if they as much as suspected you had contacted us? They realize—even if you don't—that you can singlehandedly alter the entire pattern of power on this planet. The ordinary junkman may think of us as being only one step above the animals, but the leaders don't. They know what we need and what we want. They could probably guess just what it is I am going to ask you.

"Help us, Jason dinAlt. Get back among those human pigs and lie. Say you never talked to us, that you hid in the forest and we attacked you and you had to shoot to save yourself. We'll supply some recent corpses to make the part of your story sound good.

Make them believe you and, even after you think you have them convinced, keep on acting the part because they will be watching you. Then tell them you have finished your work and are ready to leave. Get safely off Pyrrus, to another planet, and I promise you anything in the universe. Whatever you want you shall have. Power, money—*anything*.

"This is a rich planet. The junkmen mine and sell the metal, but we could do it much better. Bring a spaceship back here and land anywhere on this continent. We have no cities, but our people have farms everywhere, they will find you. We will then have commerce, trade—on our own. This is what we all want and we will work hard for it. And *you* will have done it. Whatever you want, we will give. That is a promise and we do not break our promises."

The intensity and magnitude of what he described rocked Jason. He knew that Rhes spoke the truth and the entire resources of the planet would be his; if he did as asked. For one second he was tempted, savoring the thought of what it would be like. Then came realization that it would be a half answer, and a poor one at that. If these people had the strength they wanted, their first act would be the attempted destruction of the city men. The result would be bloody civil war that would probably destroy them both. Rhes's answer was a good one—but only half an answer.

Jason had to find a better solution. One that would stop *all* the fighting on this planet and allow the two groups of humans to live in peace.

"I will do nothing to injure your people, Rhes—and everything in my power to aid them," Jason said.

This half answer satisfied Rhes, who could see only one interpretation of it. He spent the rest of the morning on the communicator, arranging for the food supplies that were being brought to the trading site.

"The supplies are ready and we have sent the signal," he said. "The truck will be here tomorrow and you will be waiting for it. Everything is arranged as I told you. You'll leave now with Naxa. You must reach the meeting spot before the trucks."

19

"Trucks almost here. Y'know what to do?" Naxa asked.

Jason nodded, and looked again at the dead man. Some beast had torn his arm off and he had bled to death. The severed arm had been tied into the shirt sleeve, so from a distance it looked normal. Seen close up, this limp arm, plus the white skin and shocked expression on the face, gave Jason an unhappy sensation. He liked to see his corpses safely buried. However he could understand its importance today.

"Here they're. Wait until his back's turned," Naxa whispered.

The armored truck had three powered trailers in tow this time. The train ground up the rock slope and whined to a stop. Krannon climbed out of the cab and looked carefully around before opening up the trailers. He had a lift robot along to help him with the loading.

"Now!" Naxa hissed.

Jason burst into the clearing, running, shouting Krannon's name. There was a crackling behind him as two of the hidden men hurled the corpse through the foliage after him. He turned and fired without stopping, setting the thing afire in midair.

There was the crack of another gun as Krannon fired; his shot jarred the twice-dead corpse before it hit the ground. Then he was lying prone, firing into the trees behind the running Jason.

Just as Jason reached the truck, there was a whirring in the air and hot pain ripped into his back, throwing him to the ground. He looked around as Krannon dragged him through the door, and saw the metal shaft of a crossbow bolt sticking out of his shoulder.

"Lucky," the Pyrran said. "An inch lower would have got your heart. I warned you about those grubbers. You're lucky to get off with only this." He lay next to the door and snapped shots into the now quiet wood.

Taking out the bolt hurt much more than it had going in. Jason cursed the pain as Krannon put on a dressing, and admired the singleness of purpose of the people who had shot him. They had risked his life to make his escape look real. And also risked the chance that he might turn against them after being shot. They did a job completely and thoroughly and he cursed them for their efficiency.

Krannon climbed warily out of the truck, after Jason was bandaged. Finishing the loading quickly, he started the train of trailers back toward the city. Jason had an anti-pain shot and dozed off as soon as they started.

While he slept, Krannon must have radioed ahead, because Kerk was waiting when they arrived. As soon as the truck entered the perimeter, he threw open the door and dragged Jason out. The bandage pulled and Jason felt the wound tear open. He ground his teeth together; Kerk would not have the satisfaction of hearing him cry out.

"I told you to stay in the buildings until the ship left. Why did you leave? Why did you go outside? You talked to the grubbers—didn't you?"

"I didn't talk to—anyone." Jason managed to get the words out. "They tried to take me, I shot two—hid out until the trucks came back."

"Got another one then," Krannon said. "I saw it. Good shooting. Think I got some too. Let him go, Kerk, they shot him in the back before he could reach the truck."

That's enough explanations, Jason thought to himself. *Don't overdo it. Let him make up his mind later. Now's the time to change the subject. There's one thing that will get his mind off the grubbers.*

"I've been fighting your war for you, Kerk, while you stayed safely inside the perimeter." Jason leaned back against the side of the truck as the other loosened his grip. "I've found out what your battle with this planet is really about—and how you can win it. Now let me sit down and I'll tell you."

More Pyrrans had come up while they talked. None of them moved now. Like Kerk, they stood frozen, looking at Jason. When Kerk talked, he spoke for all of them.

"What do you mean?"

"Just what I said. Pyrrus is fighting you—actively and consciously. Get far enough out from this city and you can feel the waves of hatred that are directed at it. No, that's wrong—you can't because you've grown up with it. But I can, and so could anyone else with any sort of *psi* sensitivity. There is a message of war being beamed against you constantly. The life forms of this planet are *psi*-sensitive, and respond to that order. They attack and change and mutate for your destruction. And they'll keep on doing so until you are all dead. Unless you can stop the war."

"How?" Kerk snapped the word and every face echoed the question.

"By finding whoever or whatever is sending that message. The life forms that attack you have no reasoning intelligence. They are being ordered to do so. I think I know how to find the source of these orders. After that, it will be a matter of getting across a message, asking for a truce and an eventual end to all hostilities."

A dead silence followed his words as the Pyrrans tried to comprehend the ideas. Kerk moved first, waving them all away.

"Go back to your work. This is my responsibility and I'll take care of it. As soon as I find out what truth there is here—if any—I'll make a complete report." The people drifted away silently, looking back as they went.

20

"From the beginning now," Kerk said. "And leave out nothing."

"There is very little more that I can add to the physical facts. I saw the animals, understood the message. I even experimented with some of them and they reacted to my mental commands. What I must do now is track down the source of the orders that keep this war going.

"I'll tell you something that I have never told anyone else. I'm not only lucky at gambling. I have enough *psi* ability to alter probability in my favor. It's an erratic ability that I have tried to improve for obvious reasons. During the past ten years I managed to study at all of the centers that do *psi* research. Compared to other fields of knowledge it is amazing how little they know. Basic *psi* talents can be improved by practice, and some machines have been devised that act as *psi*onic amplifiers. One of these, used correctly, is a very good directional indicator."

"You want to build this machine?" Kerk asked.

"Exactly. Build it and take it outside the city in the ship. Any signal strong enough to keep this centuries-old battle going should be strong enough to track down. I'll follow it, contact the creatures who are sending it, and try to find out why they are doing it. I assume you'll go along with any reasonable plan that will end this war?"

"Anything reasonable," Kerk said coldly. "How long will it take you to build this machine?"

"Just a few days, if you have all the parts here," Jason told him.

"Then do it. I'm canceling the flight that's leaving now and I'll keep the ship here, ready to go. When the machine is built, I want you to track the signal and report back to me."

"Agreed," Jason said, standing up. "As soon as I have this hole in my back looked at, I'll draw up a list of things needed."

A grim, unsmiling man named Skop was assigned to Jason as a combination guide and guard. He took his job very seriously, and it didn't take Jason long to realize that he was a prisoner-at-large. Kerk had accepted his story, but that was no guarantee that he believed it. At a single word from him, the guard could turn executioner.

The chill thought hit Jason that undoubtedly this was what would eventually happen. Whether Kerk accepted the story or not, he couldn't afford to take a chance. As long as there was the slightest possibility Jason had contacted the grubbers, he could not be allowed to leave the planet alive. The woods people were being simple if they thought a plan this obvious might succeed. Or had they just gambled on the very long chance it might work? *They* certainly had nothing to lose by it.

Only half of Jason's mind was occupied with the work as he drew up a list of materials he would need for the *psi*onic direction finder. His thoughts plodded in tight circles, searching for a way out that didn't exist. He was too deeply involved now to just leave. Kerk would see to that. Unless he could find a way to end the war and settle the grubber question, he was marooned on Pyrrus for life. A very short life.

When the list was ready, he called Supply. With a few substitutions, everything he might possibly need was in stock, and would be sent over. Skop sank into an apparent doze in his chair and Jason, his head propped against the pull of gravity by one arm, began a working sketch of his machine.

Jason looked up suddenly, aware of the silence. He could hear machinery in the building and voices in the hall outside. What kind of silence then—?

Mental silence. He had been so preoccupied since his return to the city that he hadn't noticed the complete lack of any kind of *psi* sensation. The constant wash of animal reactions was missing, as was the vague tactile awareness of his PK. With sudden realization, he remembered that it was always this way inside the city.

He tried to listen with his mind—and stopped almost before he began. There was a constant press of thought about him that he was made aware of when he reached out. It was like being in a vessel far beneath the ocean, with your hand on the door that held back the frightening pressure. Touching the door, without opening it, you could feel the stresses, the power pushing in and waiting to crush you. It was this way with the *psi* pressure in the city. The unvoiced hate-filled screams of Pyrrus would instantly destroy any mind that received them. Some function of his brain acted as a *psi* circuit breaker, shutting off awareness before his mind could be blasted. There was just enough leak-through to keep him aware of the pressure—and supply the raw materials for his constant nightmares.

There was only one fringe benefit. The lack of thought pressure made it easier for him to concentrate. In spite of his fatigue, the diagram developed swiftly.

Meta arrived late that afternoon, bringing the parts he had ordered. She slid the long box onto the workbench, started to speak, but changed her mind and said nothing. Jason looked up at her and smiled.

"Confused?" he asked.

"I don't know what you mean," she said. "I'm not confused. Just annoyed. The regular trip has been canceled and our supply schedule will be thrown off for months to come. And instead of piloting or perimeter assignment all I am allowed to do is stand around and wait for you. Then take some silly flight following your directions. Do you wonder that I'm annoyed?"

Jason carefully set the parts out on the chassis before he spoke. "As I said, you're confused. I can point out how you're confused— which will make you even more confused. A temptation that I frankly find hard to resist."

She looked across the bench at him, frowning, one finger unconsciously curling and uncurling a short lock of hair. Jason liked her this way. As a Pyrran operating at full blast, she had as much personality as a gear in a machine. Once out of that pattern she reminded him more of the girl he had known on that first flight to Pyrrus. He wondered if it was possible to really get across to her what he meant.

"I'm not being insulting when I say 'confused,' Meta. With your background you couldn't be any other way. You have an insular personality. Admittedly, Pyrrus is an unusual island with a lot of high-power problems that you are an expert at solving. That doesn't make it any less of an island. When you face a cosmopolitan problem, you are confused. Or even worse, when your island problems are put into a bigger context. That's like playing your own game, only having the rules change constantly as you go along."

"You're talking nonsense," she snapped at him. "Pyrrus isn't an island and battling for survival is definitely not a game."

"I'm sorry," he said. "I was using a figure of speech, and a badly chosen one at that. Let's put the problem on more concrete terms. Take an example. Suppose I were to tell you that over there, hanging from the doorframe, was a stingwing—"

Meta's gun was pointing at the door before he finished the last word. There was a crash as the guard's chair went over. He had jumped from a half-doze to full alertness in an instant, his gun also searching the doorframe.

"That was just an example," Jason said. "There's really nothing there." The guard's gun vanished and he scowled a look of contempt at Jason, as he righted the chair and dropped into it.

"You both have proved yourself capable of handling a Pyrran problem," Jason continued. "But what if I said that there is a thing hanging from the doorframe that *looks* like a stingwing, but is really a kind of large insect that spins a fine silk that can be used to weave clothes?"

The guard glared from under his thick eyebrows at the empty doorframe, his gun whined part way out, then snapped back into the holster. He growled something inaudible at Jason, then stamped into the outer room, slamming the door behind him. Meta frowned in concentration and looked puzzled.

"It couldn't be anything except a stingwing," she finally said. "Nothing else could possibly look like that. And even if it didn't spin silk, it would bite if you got near, so you would have to kill it." She smiled with satisfaction at the indestructible logic of her answer.

"Wrong again," Jason said. "I just described the mimic-spinner that lives on Stover's Planet. It imitates the most violent forms of life there, does such a good job that it has no need for other defenses. It'll sit quietly on your hand and spin for you by the yard. If I dropped a shipload of them here on Pyrrus, you never could be sure when to shoot, could you?"

"But they are not here now," Meta insisted.

"Yet they could be quite easily. And if they were, all the rules of your game would change. Getting the idea now? There are some fixed laws and rules in the galaxy—but they're not the ones you live by. Your rule is war unending with the local life. I want to step outside your rule book and end that war. Wouldn't you like that? Wouldn't you like an existence that was more than just an endless battle for survival? A life with a chance for happiness, love, music, art—all the enjoyable things you have never had the time for.''

All the Pyrran sternness was gone from her face as she listened to what he said, letting herself follow these alien concepts. He had put his hand out automatically as he talked, and had taken hers. It was warm and her pulse fast to his touch.

Meta suddenly became conscious of his hand and snapped hers away, rising to her feet at the same time. As she started blindly toward the door, Jason's voice snapped after her.

"The guard, Skop, ran away because he didn't want to lose his precious two-value logic. It's all he has. But you've seen other parts of the galaxy, Meta, you know there is a lot more to life than kill-and-be-killed on Pyrrus. You feel it is true, even if you won't admit it."

She turned and ran out the door.

Jason looked after her, his hand scraping the bristle on his chin thoughtfully. "Meta, I have the faint hope that the woman is winning over the Pyrran. I think that I saw—perhaps for the first time in the history of this bloody, wartorn city—a tear in one of its citizen's eyes."

21

"Drop that equipment and Kerk will undoubtedly pull both your arms off," Jason said. "He's over there now, looking as sorry as possible that I ever talked him into this."

Skop cursed under the bulky mass of the *psi* detector, passing it up to Meta who waited in the open port of the spaceship. Jason supervised the loading and blasted all the local life that came to investigate. Horndevils were thick this morning and he shot four of them. He was last aboard and closed the lock behind him.

"Where are you going to install it?" Meta asked.

"You tell me," Jason said. "I need a spot for the antenna where there will be no dense metal in front of the bowl to interfere with the signal. Thin plastic will do or, if worst comes to worst, I can mount it outside the hull with a remote drive."

"You may have to," she said. "The hull is an unbroken unit; we do all viewing by screen and instruments. I don't think—wait—there is one place that might do."

She led the way to a bulge in the hull that marked one of the lifeboats. They went in through the always-open lock, Skop struggling after them with the apparatus.

"These lifeboards are half buried in the ship," Meta explained. "They have transparent front ports covered by friction shields that withdraw automatically when the boat is launched."

"Can we pull back the shields now?"

"I think so," she said. She traced the launching circuits to a junction box and opened the lid. When she closed the shield relay manually, the heavy plates slipped back into the hull. There was a clear view, since most of the viewport projected beyond the parent ship.

"Perfect," Jason said. "I'll set up here. Now how do I talk to you in the ship?"

"Right here," she said. "There's a pretuned setting on this communicator. Don't touch anything else—and particularly not this switch." She pointed to a large pull-handle set square into the center of the control board. "Emergency launching. Two seconds after that is pulled, the lifeboat is shot free. And it so happens this boat has no fuel."

"Hands off for sure," Jason said. "Now have Husky there run me in a line with ship's power and I'll get this stuff set up."

The detector was simple, though the tuning had to be precise. A dish-shaped antenna pulled in the signal for the delicately balanced detector. There was a sharp falloff on both sides of the input so direction could be precisely determined. The resulting signal was fed to an amplifier stage. Unlike the electronic components of the first stage, this one was drawn in symbols on white paper. Carefully glued-on input and output leads ran to it.

When everything was ready and clamped into place, Jason nodded to Meta's image on the screen. "Take her up—and easy, please. None of your nine-G specials. Go into a slow circle around the perimeter, until I tell you differently."

Under steady power the ship lifted and grabbed for altitude, then eased into its circular course. They made five circuits of the city before Jason shook his head.

"The thing seems to be working fine, but we're getting too much noise from all the local life. Get thirty kilometers out from the city and start a new circuit."

The results were better this time. A powerful signal came from the direction of the city, confined to less than a degree of arc. With the antenna fixed at a right angle to the direction of the ship's flight, the signal was fairly constant. Meta rotated the ship on its main axis, until Jason's lifeboat was directly below.

"Going fine now," he said. "Just hold your controls as they are and keep the nose from drifting."

After making a careful mark on the setting circle, Jason turned the receiving antenna through 180° of arc. As the ship kept to its circle, he made a slow collecting sweep of any signals beamed at the city. They were halfway around before he got a new signal.

It was there all right, narrow but strong. Just to be sure, he let the ship complete two more sweeps, and he noted the direction on the gyrocompass each time. They coincided. The third time around he called to Meta.

"Get ready for a full right turn, or whatever you call it. I think I have our bearing. Get ready—*now*."

It was a slow turn and Jason never lost the signal. A few times it wavered, but he brought it back on. When the compass settled down, Meta pushed on more power.

They set their course toward the native Pyrrans.

An hour's flight at close to top atmospheric speed brought no change. Meta complained, but Jason kept her on course. The signal never varied and was slowly picking up strength. They crossed the chain of volcanoes that marked the continental limits, the ship bucking in the fierce thermals. Once the shore was behind and they were over water, Skop joined Meta in grumbling. He kept his turret spinning, but there was very little to shoot at this far from land.

When the islands came over the horizon, the signal began to dip.

"Slow now," Jason called. "Those islands ahead look like our source!"

A continent had been here once, floating on Pyrrus's liquid core. Pressures changed, land masses shifted, and the continent had sunk beneath the ocean. All that was left now of the teeming life of that land mass was confined to a chain of islands, once the mountain peaks of the highest range of mountains. These islands, whose sheer sides rose straight from the water, held the last inhabitants of the lost continent. The weeded-out descendants of the victors of uncountable violent contests. Here lived the oldest native Pyrrans.

"Come in lower," Jason signaled, "toward that large peak. The signals seem to originate there."

They swooped low over the mountain, but nothing was visible other than the trees and sunblasted rock.

The pain almost took Jason's head off. A blast of hatred that drove through the amplifier and into his skull. He tore off the phones and clutched his skull between his hands. Through watering eyes, he saw the black cloud of flying beasts hurtle up from the trees below. He had a single glimpse of the hillside beyond before Meta blasted power to the engines and the ship leaped away.

"We've found them!" Her fierce exultation faded as she saw Jason through the communicator. "Are you all right? What happened?"

"Feel . . . burned out. . . . I've felt a *psi* blast before, but nothing like that! I had a glimpse of an opening, looked like a cave mouth, just before the blast hit. Seemed to come from there."

"Lie down," Meta said. "I'll get you back as fast as I can. I'm calling ahead to Kerk. He has to know what happened."

A group of men were waiting in the landing station when they came down. They stormed out as soon as the ship touched, shielding their faces from the still-hot tubes. Kerk burst in as soon as the port was cracked, peering around until he spotted Jason stretched out on an acceleration couch.

"Is it true?" he barked. "You've traced the alien criminals who started this war?"

"Slow, man, slow," Jason said. "I've traced the source of the *psi* message that keeps your war going. I've found no evidence as to who started this war, and certainly wouldn't go so far as to call them criminals. . . ."

"I'm tired of your word play," Kerk broke in. "You've found these creatures and their location has been marked."

"On the chart," Meta said, "I could fly there blindfolded."

"Fine, fine," Kerk said, rubbing his hands together so hard they could hear the harsh rasp of the calluses. "It takes a real effort to grasp the idea that, after all these centuries, the war might be coming to an end. But it's possible now. Instead of simply killing off these self-renewing legions of the damned that attack us, we can get to the leaders. Search them out, carry the war to them for a change—and blast their stain from the face of this planet!"

"Nothing of the sort!" Jason said, sitting up with an effort. "Nothing doing! Since I came to this planet I have been knocked around, and risked my life ten times over. Do you think I have done this just to satisfy your bloodthirsty ambitions? It's peace I'm after—not destruction. You promised to contact these creatures, attempt to negotiate with them. Aren't you a man of honor who keeps his word?''

"I'll ignore the insult—though I'd have killed you for it at any other time," Kerk said. "You've been of great service to our people, we are not ashamed to acknowledge an honest debt. At the same time, do not accuse me of breaking promises that I never made. I recall my exact words. I promised to go along with any reasonable plan that would end this war. That is just what I intend to do. Your plan to negotiate a peace is not reasonable. Therefore we are going to destroy the enemy.''

"Think first," Jason called after Kerk, who had turned to leave. "What is wrong with trying negotiation or an armistice? Then, if that fails, you can try your way."

The compartment was getting crowded as other Pyrrans pushed in. Kerk, almost to the door, turned back to face Jason.

"I'll tell you what's wrong with armistice," he said. "It's a coward's way out, that's what it is. It's all right for you to suggest it, you're from off-world and don't know any better. But do you honestly think I could entertain such a defeatist notion for one instant? When I speak, I speak not only for myself, but for all of us here. We don't mind fighting, and we know how to do it. We know that if this war was over, we could build a better world here. At the same time, if we have the choice of continued war or a cowardly peace—*we vote for war*. This war will only be over when the enemy is utterly destroyed!''

The listening Pyrrans murmured in agreement, and Jason had to shout to be heard above them. "That's really wonderful. I bet you even think it's original. But don't you hear all that cheering off-stage? Those are the spirits of every saber-rattling sonofabitch that ever plugged for noble war. They even recognize the old slogan. We're on the side of light, and the enemy is a creature of darkness. And it doesn't matter a damn if the other side is saying the same thing. You've still got the same old words that have been killing people since the birth of the human race. A 'cowardly peace,' that's a good one. Peace means not being at war, not fighting. How can you have a cowardly not-fighting. What are you trying to hide with this semantic confusion? Your real reasons? I can't blame you for being ashamed of them—I would be. Why don't you just come out and say you are keeping the war going because you enjoy killing?

Seeing things die makes you and your murderers happy, and you want to make them happier still!''

There was a sensed but unvoiced pressure in the silence. They waited for Kerk to speak. He was white-faced with anger, held tightly under control.

"You're right, Jason. We like to kill. And we're going to kill. Everything on this planet that ever fought us is going to die. We're going to enjoy doing it very much."

He turned and left while the weight of his words still hung in the air. The rest followed, talking excitedly. Jason slumped back on the couch, exhausted and defeated.

When he looked up they were gone—all except Meta. She had the same look of bloodthirsty elation as the others, but it drained away when she glanced at him.

"What about it, Meta?" he snapped. "No doubts? Do you think that destruction is the only way to end this war?"

"I don't know," she said. "I can't be sure. For the first time in my life, I find myself with more than one answer to the same question."

"Congratulations," he said bitterly. "It's a sign of growing up."

22

Jason stood to one side and watched the deadly cargo being loaded into the hold of the ship. The Pyrrans were in good humor as they stowed away riot guns, grenades and gas bombs. When the back-pack atom bomb was put aboard, one of them broke into a marching song, and the others picked it up. Maybe they were happy, but the approaching carnage only filled Jason with an intense gloom. He felt that somehow he was a traitor to life. Perhaps the life form he had found needed destroying—and perhaps it didn't. Without making the slightest attempt at conciliation, destruction would be plain murder.

Kerk came out of the operations building and the starter pumps could be heard whining inside the ship. They would leave within minutes. Jason forced himself into a foot-dragging rush and met Kerk halfway to the ship.

"I'm coming with you, Kerk. You owe me at least that much for finding them."

Kerk hesitated, not liking the idea. "This is an operational mission," he said. "No room for observers, and the extra weight . . . And it's too late to stop us, Jason, you know that."

"You Pyrrans are the worst liars in the universe," Jason said. "We both know the ship can lift ten times the amount it's carrying today. Now, do you let me come, or forbid me without reason at all?"

"Get aboard," Kerk said. "But keep out of the way or you'll get trampled."

This time, with a definite destination ahead, the flight was much faster. Meta took the ship into the stratosphere, in a high ballistic arc that ended at the islands. Kerk was in the copilot's seat, Jason sat behind them where he could watch the screens. The landing party, twenty-five volunteers, were in the hold below with the weapons. All the screens in the ship were switched to the forward viewer. They watched the green island appear and swell, then vanish behind the flames of the braking rockets. Jockeying the ship carefully, Meta brought it down on a flat shelf near the cave mouth.

Jason was ready this time for the blast of mental hatred—but it still hurt. The gunners laughed and killed gleefully as every animal on the island closed in on the ship. They were slaughtered by the thousands, and still more came.

"Do you have to do this?" Jason asked. "It's murder, carnage, just butchering those beasts like that."

"Self-defense," Kerk said. "They attack us and they get killed. What could be simpler. Now shut up or I'll throw you out there with them."

It was a half an hour before the gunfire slackened. Animals still attacked them, but the mass assaults seemed to be over. Kerk spoke into the intercom.

"Landing party away—and watch your step. They know we're here and will make it as hot as they can. Take the bomb into that cave and see how far back it runs. We can always blast them from the air, but it'll do no good if they're dug into solid rock. Keep your screen open, leave the bomb and pull back at once if I tell you to. Now move."

The men swarmed down the ladders and formed into open battle formation. They were soon under attack, but the beasts were picked off before they could get close. It didn't take long for the man at point to reach the cave. He had his pickup trained in front of him, and the watchers in the ship followed the advance.

"Big cave," Kerk grunted. "Slants back and down. What I was afraid of. Bomb dropped on that would just close it up. With no guarantee that anything sealed in it couldn't eventually get out. We'll have to see how far down it goes."

There was enough heat in the cave now to use the infrared filters. The rock walls stood out harshly black and white as the advance continued.

"No signs of life since entering the cave," the officer reported. "Gnawed bones at the entrance and some bat droppings. It looks like a natural cave—so far."

Step by step the advance continued, slowly as it went. Insensitive as the Pyrrans were to *psi* pressure, even they were aware of the blast of hatred being continuously leveled at them. Jason, back in the ship, had a headache that slowly grew worse instead of better.

"Watch out!" Kerk shouted, staring at the screen with horror.

The cave was filled from wall to wall with pallid, eyeless animals. They poured from tiny side passages and seemed to literally emerge from the ground. Their front ranks dissolved in flame, but more kept pressing in. On the screen the watchers in the ship saw the cave spin dizzily as the operator fell. Pale bodies washed up and concealed the lens.

"Close ranks—flamethrowers and gas!" Kerk bellowed into the mike.

Less than half of the men were alive after the first attack. The survivors, protected by the flamethrowers, set off the gas grenades. Their sealed battle armor protected them while the section of cave filled with gas. Someone dug through the bodies of their attackers and found the pickup.

"Leave the bomb there and withdraw," Kerk ordered. "We've had enough losses already."

A different man stared out of the screen. The officer was dead. "Sorry, sir," he said, "but it will be just as easy to push ahead as back as long as the gas grenades hold out. We're too close now to pull back."

"That's an order," Kerk shouted, but the man was gone from the screen and the advance continued.

Jason's fingers hurt where he had them clamped to the chair arm. He pulled them loose and massaged them. On the screen the black-and-white cave flowed steadily toward them. Minute after minute went by this way. Each time the animals attacked again, a few more gas grenades were used up.

"Something ahead—looks different," the panting voice cracked from the speaker. The narrow cave slowly opened out into a gigantic chamber, so large the roof and far walls were lost in the distance.

"What are those?" Kerk asked. "Get a searchlight over to the right there."

The picture on the screen was fuzzy and hard to see now, dimmed by the layers of rock in between. Details couldn't be made out clearly, but it was obvious this was something unusual.

"Never saw—anything quite like them before," the speaker said. "Look like big plants of some kind, ten meters tall at least— yet they're moving. Those branches, tentacles or whatever they are, keep pointing toward us and I get the darkest feeling in my head. . . ."

"Blast one, see what happens," Kerk said.

The gun fired and at the same instant an intensified wave of mental hatred rolled over the men, dropping them to the ground. They rolled in pain, blacked out and unable to think or fight the underground beasts that poured over them in renewed attack.

In the ship, far above, Jason felt the shock to his mind and wondered how the men below could have lived through it. The others in the control room had been hit by it as well. Kerk pounded on the frame of the screen and shouted to the unhearing men below.

"Pull back, come back. . . ."

It was too late. The men only stirred slightly as the victorious Pyrran animals washed over them, clawing for the joints in their armor. Only one man moved, standing up and beating the creatures away with his bare hands. He stumbled a few feet and bent over the writhing mass below him. With a heave of his shoulders, he pulled another man up. The man was dead but his shoulder pack was still strapped to his back. Bloody fingers fumbled at the pack, then both men were washed back under the wave of death.

"That was the bomb!" Kerk shouted to Meta. "If he didn't change the setting, it's still on ten-second minimum. Get out of here!"

Jason had just time to fall back on the acceleration couch before the rockets blasted. The pressure leaned on him and kept mounting. Vision blacked out but he didn't lose consciousness. Air screamed across the hull, then the sound stopped as they left the atmosphere behind.

Just as Meta cut the power, a glare of white light burst from the screens. They turned back instantly as the hull pickups burned out. She switched filters into place, then pressed the button that rotated new pickups into position.

Far below, in the boiling sea, a climbing cloud of mushroom-shaped flame filled the spot where the island had been seconds before. The three of them looked at it, silent and unmoving. Kerk recovered first.

"Head for home, Meta, and get operations on the screen. Twenty-five men dead, but they did their job. They knocked out those beasts—whatever they were—and ended the war. I can't think of a better way for a man to die."

Meta set the orbit, then called operations.

"Trouble getting through," she said. "I have a robot landing beam response, but no one is answering the call."

A man appeared on the empty screen. He was beaded with sweat and had a harried look in his eyes. "Kerk," he said, "is that you? Get the ship back here at once. We need her firepower at the perimeter. All blazes broke loose a minute ago, a general attack from every side, worse than I've ever seen."

"What do you mean?" Kerk stammered in unbelief. "The war is over. We blasted them, destroyed their headquarters completely."

"The war is going like it never has gone before," the other snapped back. "I don't know what you did, but it stirred up the stewpot of hell here. Now stop talking and get the ship back!"

Kerk turned slowly to face Jason, his face pulled back in a look of raw animal savagery.

"You! You did it! I should have killed you the first time I saw you. I wanted to, now I know I was right. You've been like a plague since you came here, sowing death in every direction. I knew you were wrong, yet I let your twisted words convince me. And look what has happened. First you killed Welf. Then you murdered those men in the cave. Now this attack on the perimeter—all who die there, you will have killed!"

Kerk advanced on Jason, step by slow step, hatred twisting his features. Jason backed away until he could retreat no further, his shoulders against the chart case. Kerk's hand lashed out, not a fighting blow, but an open slap. Though Jason rolled with it, it still battered him and stretched him full length on the floor. His arm was against the chart case, his fingers near the sealed tubes that held the jump matrices.

Jason seized one of the heavy tubes with both hands and pulled it out. He swung it with all his strength into Kerk's face. It broke the skin on his cheekbone and forehead and blood ran from the cuts. But it didn't slow or stop the big man in the slightest. His smile held no mercy as he reached down and dragged Jason to his feet.

"Fight back," he said, "I will have that much more pleasure as I kill you." He drew back the granite fist that would tear Jason's head from his shoulders.

"Go ahead," Jason said and stopped struggling. "Kill me. You can do it easily. Only don't call it justice. Welf died to save me. But the men on the island died because of your stupidity. I wanted peace and you wanted war. Now you have it. Kill me to soothe your conscience, because the truth is something you can't face up to."

With a bellow of rage, Kerk drove the piledriver fist down.

Meta grabbed the arm in both her hands and hung on, pulling it aside before the blow could land. The three of them fell together, half crushing Jason.

"Don't do it," she screamed. "Jason didn't want those men to go down there. That was your idea. You can't kill him for that!"

Kerk, exploding with rage, was past hearing. He turned his attention to Meta, tearing her from him. She was a woman and her supple strength was meager compared to his great muscles. But she was a Pyrran woman and she did what no off-worlder could. She slowed him for a moment, stopped the fury of his attack until he could rip her hands loose and throw her aside. It didn't take him long to do this, but it was just time enough for Jason to get to the door.

Jason stumbled through and jammed shut the lock behind him. A split second after he had driven the bolt home, Kerk's weight plunged into the door. The metal screamed and bent, giving way. One hinge was torn loose and the other held only by a shred of metal. It would go down on the next blow.

Jason wasn't waiting for that. He hadn't stayed to see if the door would stop the raging Pyrran. No door on the ship could stop him. Fast as possible, Jason went down the gangway. There was no safety on the ship, which meant he had to get off it. The lifeboat deck was just ahead.

Ever since first seeing them, he had given a lot of thought to the lifeboats. Though he hadn't looked ahead to this situation, he knew a time might come when he would need transportation of his own. The lifeboats had seemed to be the best bet, except that Meta had told him they had no fuel. She had been right in one thing: the boat he had been in had empty tanks, he had checked. There were five other boats, though, that he hadn't examined. He had wondered about the idea of useless lifeboats and come to what he hoped was a correct conclusion.

This spaceship was the only one the Pyrrans had. Meta had told him once that they always had planned to buy another ship, but never did. Some other necessary war expense managed to come up first. One ship was really enough for their uses. The only difficulty lay in the fact they had to keep that ship in operation or the Pyrran city was dead. Without supplies they would be wiped out in a few months. Therefore the ship's crew couldn't conceive of abandoning their ship. No matter what kind of trouble she got into, they couldn't leave her. When the ship died, so did their world.

With this kind of thinking, there was no need to keep the lifeboasts fueled. Not all of them, at least. Though it stood to reason at least one of them held fuel for short flights that would have been wasteful for the parent ship. At this point, Jason's chain of logic grew weak. Too many "ifs." *If* they used the lifeboats at all, one of them should be fueled. *If* they did, it would be fueled now. And *if* it were fueled—which one of the six would it be? Jason had no time to go looking. He had to be right the first time.

His reasoning had supplied him with an answer, the last of a long line of suppositions. If a boat were fueled, it should be the nearest to the control cabin. The one he was diving toward now. His life depended on this string of guesses.

Behind him the door went down with a crash. Kerk bellowed and leaped. Jason hurled himself through the lifeboat port with the nearest thing to a run he could manage under the doubled gravity. With both hands he grabbed the emergency launching handle and pulled down.

An alarm bell rang and the port slammed shut, literally in Kerk's face. Only his Pyrran reflexes saved him from being smashed by it.

Solid fuel launchers exploded and blasted the lifeboat clear of the parent ship. Their brief acceleration slammed Jason to the deck, then he floated as the boat went into free fall. The main-drive rockets didn't fire.

In that moment Jason learned what it was like to know he was dead. Without fuel the boat would drop into the jungle below, falling like a rock and blasting apart when it hit. There was no way out.

Then the rockets caught, roared, and he dropped to the deck, bruising his nose. He sat up, rubbing it and grinning. There was fuel in the tanks—the delay in starting had only been part of the launching cycle, giving the lifeboat time to fall clear of the ship. Now to get it under control. He pulled himself into the pilot's seat.

The altimeter had fed information to the autopilot, leveling the boat off parallel to the ground. Like all lifeboat controls these were childishly simple, designed to be used by novices in an emergency. The autopilot could not be shut off; it rode along with the manual controls, tempering foolish piloting. Jason hauled the control wheel into a tight turn and the autopilot gentled it to a soft curve.

Through the port, he could see the big ship blaring fire in a much tighter turn. Jason didn't know who was flying it or what they had in mind—he took no chances. Jamming the wheel forward into a dive, he cursed as they eased into a gentle drop. The larger ship had no such restrictions. It changed course with a violent maneuver and dived on him. The forward turret fired and an explosion at the stern rocked the little boat. This either knocked out the autopilot or shocked it into submission. The slow drop turned into a power dive and the jungle billowed up.

Jason pulled the wheel back into his gut and there was just time to get his arms in front of his face before they hit.

Thundering rockets and cracking trees ended in a great splash. Silence followed and the smoke drifted away. High above, the spaceship circled hesitantly. Dropping a bit as if wanting to go down and investigate. Then rising again as the urgent message for aid came from the city. Loyalty won and she turned and spewed fire toward home.

23

Tree branches had broken the lifeboat's fall, the bow rockets had burned out in emergency blast, and the swamp had cushioned the landing a bit. It was still a crash. The battered cylinder sank slowly into the stagnant water and thin mud of the swamp. The bow was well under before Jason managed to kick open the emergency hatch in the waist.

There was no way of knowing how long it would take for the boat to go under, and Jason was in no condition to ponder the situation. Battered and bloody, he had just enough drive left to get himself out. Wading and falling, he made his way to firmer land, sitting down heavily as soon as he found something that would support him.

Behind him, the lifeboat burbled and sank under the water. Bubbles of trapped air kept rising for awhile, then stopped. The water stilled and, except for the broken branches and trees, there was no sign that a ship had ever come this way.

Insects whined across the swamp, and the only sound that broke the quiet of the woods beyond was the cruel scream of an animal pulling down its dinner. When that had echoed away in tiny waves of sound everything was silent.

Jason pulled himself out of the half trance with an effort. His body felt like it had been through a meat grinder, and it was almost impossible to think with the fog in his head. After minutes of deliberation, he figured out that the medikit was what he needed. The easy-off snap was very difficult and the button release didn't work. He finally twisted his arm around until it was under the orifice and pressed the entire unit down. It buzzed industriously; though he couldn't feel the needles, he guessed it had worked. His sight spun dizzily for awhile then cleared. Pain-killers went to work and he slowly came out of the dark cloud that had enveloped his brain since the crash.

Reason returned and loneliness rode along with it. He was without food, friendless, surrounded by the hostile forces of an alien planet. There was a rising panic that started deep inside of him, that took concentrated effort to hold down.

"Think Jason, don't emote." He said it aloud to reassure himself, but was instantly sorry, because his voice sounded weak in the emptiness, with a ragged edge of hysteria to it. Something caught in his throat and he coughed to clear it, spitting out blood. Looking at the red stain, he was suddenly angry. Hating this deadly planet and the incredible stupidity of the people who lived on it. Cursing out loud was better and his voice didn't sound as weak now. He ended up shouting and shaking his fist at nothing in particular, but it helped. The anger washed away the fear and brought him back to reality.

Sitting on the ground felt good now. The sun was warm and when he leaned back he could almost forget the unending burden of doubled gravity. Anger had carried away fear, rest erased fatigue. From somewhere in the back of his mind, there popped up the old platitude: *Where there's life, there's hope.* He grimaced at the triteness of the words, at the same time realizing that a basic truth lurked there.

Count his assets. Well battered, but still alive. None of the bruises seemed very important, and no bones were broken. His gun was still working, it dipped in and out of the power holster as he thought about it. Pyrrans made rugged equipment. The medikit was operating as well. If he kept his senses, managed to walk in a fairly straight line and could live off the land, there was a fair chance he might make it back to the city. What kind of a reception would be

waiting for him there was a different matter altogether. He woul
find that out after he arrived. Getting there had first priority.

On the debit side there stood the planet Pyrrus. Strength-sappin
gravity, murderous weather, and violent animals. Could he sur
vive? As if to add emphasis to his thoughts, the sky darkened ove
and rain hissed into the forest, marching toward him. Jason scram
bled to his feet and took a bearing before the rain closed dow
visibility. A jagged chain of mountains stood dimly on the horizons
he remembered crossing them on the flight out. They would do as
first goal. After he had reached them, he would worry about the nex
leg of the journey.

Leaves and dirt flew before the wind in quick gusts, then the rai
washed over him. Soaked, chilled, already bone-tired, he pitted th
tottering strength of his legs against the planet of death.

When nightfall came, it was still raining. There was no way o
being sure of the direction, and no point in going on. If that wasn'
enough, Jason was on the ragged edge of exhaustion. It was going t
be a wet night. All the trees were thick-boled and slippery; h
couldn't have climbed them on a one-G world. The sheltered spot
that he investigated, under fallen trees and beneath thick bushes
were just as wet as the rest of the forest. In the end he curled up or
the leeward side of a tree, and fell asleep, shivering, with the wate
dripping off him.

The rain stopped around midnight and the temperature fell sharp
ly. Jason woke sluggishly from a dream in which he was bein
frozen to death, to find it was almost true. Fine snow was siftin
through the trees, powdering the ground and drifting against him
The cold bit into his flesh, and when he sneezed it hurt his chest. Hi
aching and numb body only wanted rest, but the spark of reason tha
remained in him forced him to his feet. If he lay down now he woul
die. Holding one hand against the tree so he wouldn't fall, he begar
to trudge around it. Step after shuffling step, around and around
until the terrible cold eased a bit and he could stop shivering
Fatigue crawled up him like a muffling, grey blanket. He kept or
walking, half the time with his eyes closed, opening them only
when he fell and had to climb painfully to his feet again.

The sun burned away the snow clouds at dawn. Jason leaned
against his tree and blinked up at the sky with sore eyes. The groun
was white in all directions, except around the tree where his stum
bling feet had churned a circle of black mud. His back against the
smooth trunk, Jason sank slowly down to the ground, letting the sur
soak into him.

Exhaustion had him light-headed, and his lips were cracked fror thirst. Almost continuous coughing tore at his chest with fingers of fire. Though the sun was still low, it was hot already, burning his skin dry. Dry and hot.

It wasn't right. This thought kept nagging at his brain until he admitted it. Turned it over and over and looked at it from all sides. What wasn't right? The way he felt.

Pneumonia. He had all the symptoms.

His dry lips cracked and blood moistened them when he smiled. He had avoided all the animal perils of Pyrrus, all the big carnivores and poisonous reptiles, only to be laid low by the smallest beast of them all. Well, he had the remedy for this one too. Rolling up his sleeve with shaking fingers, he pressed the mouth of the medikit to his bare arm. It clicked and began to drone an angry whine. That meant something, he knew, but he just couldn't remember what. Holding it up he saw that one of the hypodermics was projecting halfway from its socket. Of course. It was empty of whatever antibiotic the analyzer had called for. It needed refilling.

Jason hurled the thing away with a curse, and it splashed into a pool and was gone. End of medicine, end of medikit, end of Jason dinAlt. Singlehanded battler against the perils of deathworld. Stronghearted stranger who could do as well as the natives. It had taken him all of one day on his own to get his death warrant signed.

A choking growl echoed behind him. He turned, dropped and fired in the same motion. It was all over before his conscious mind was aware it had happened. Pyrran training had conditioned his reflexes on the precortical level. Jason gaped at the ugly beast dying not a meter from him and realized he had been trained well.

His first reaction was unhappiness that he had killed one of the grubber dogs. When he looked closer he realized this animal was slightly different in markings, size and temper. Though most of its forequarters were blown away, blood pumping out in drying spurts, it kept trying to reach Jason. Before the eyes glazed with death, it had struggled its way almost to his feet.

It wasn't quite a grubber dog, though chances were it was a wild relative. Bearing the same relation as dog to wolf. He wondered if there were any other resemblances between wolves and this dead beast. Did they hunt in packs too?

As soon as the thought hit him he looked up—not a moment too soon. The great forms were drifting through the trees, closing in on him. When he shot two, the others snarled with rage and sank back into the forest. They didn't leave. Instead of being frightened by the deaths, they grew even more enraged.

Jason sat with his back to the tree and waited until they came close

before he picked them off. With each shot and dying scream, the
outraged survivors howled the louder. Some of them fought when
they met, venting their rage. One stood on his hind legs and raked
great strips of bark from a tree. Jason aimed a shot at it, but he was
too far away to hit.

There were advantages to having a fever, he realized. Logically
he knew he would live only to sunset, or until his gun was empty.
Yet the fact didn't bother him greatly. Nothing really mattered. He
slumped, relaxed completely, only raising his arm to fire, then
letting it drop again. Every few minutes he had to move to look in
back of the tree, and kill any of them that were stalking him in the
blind spot. He wished dimly that he were leaning against a smaller
tree, but it wasn't worth the effort to go to one.

Sometime in the afternoon, he fired his last shot. It killed an
animal he had allowed to get close. He had noticed he was missing
the longer shots. The beast snarled and dropped; the others that were
close pulled back and howled in sympathy. One of them exposed
himself and Jason pulled the trigger.

There was only a slight click. He tried again, in case it was just a
misfire, but there was still only the click. The gun was empty, as
was the square clip pouch at his belt. There were vague memories of
reloading, though he couldn't remember how many times he had
done it.

This, then, was the end. They had all been right, Pyrrus was a
match for him. Though they shouldn't talk. It would kill them all in
the end too. Pyrrans never died in bed. Old Pyrrans never died, they
just got et.

Now that he didn't have to force himself to stay alert and hold the
gun, the fever took hold. He wanted to sleep and he knew it would
be a long sleep. His eyes were almost closed as he watched the wary
carnivores slip closer to him. The first one crept close enough to
spring; he could see the muscles tensing in its leg.

It leaped. Whirling in midair and falling before it reached him.
Blood ran from its gaping mouth and the short shaft of metal
projected from the side of his head.

The two men walked out of the brush and looked down at him.
Their mere presence seemed to have been enough for the carnivores, because they had all vanished.

Grubbers. He had been in such a hurry to reach the city that he
had forgotten about the grubbers. It was good that they were here
and Jason was very glad they had come. He couldn't talk very well,
so he smiled to thank them. But this hurt his lips too much so he
went to sleep.

24

For a strange length of time after that, there were only hazy patches of memory that impressed themselves on Jason. A sense of movement and large beasts around him. Walls, woodsmoke, the murmur of voices. None of it meant very much and he was too tired to care. It was easier and much better just to let go.

"About time," Rhes said. "A couple more days lying there like that and we would have buried you, even if you were still breathing."

Jason blinked at him, trying to focus the face that swam above him. He finally recognized Rhes, and wanted to answer him. But talking only brought on a spell of body-wracking coughing. Someone held a cup to his lips and sweet fluid trickled down his throat. He rested, then tried again.

"How long have I been here?" The voice was thin and sounded far away. Jason had trouble recognizing it for his own.

"Eight days. And why didn't you listen when I talked to you?" Rhes said.

"You should have stayed near the ship when you crashed. Didn't you remember what I said about coming down anywhere on this continent? No matter, too late to worry about that. Next time listen to what I say. Our people moved fast and reached the site of the wreck before dark. They found the broken trees and the spot where the ship had sunk, and at first thought whoever had been in it had drowned. Then one of the dogs found your trail, but lost it again in the swamps during the night. They had a fine time with the mud and the snow and didn't have any luck at all in finding the spoor again. By the next afternoon they were ready to send for more help when they heard your firing. Just made it, from what I hear. Lucky one of them was a talker and could tell the wild dogs to clear out. Would have had to kill them all otherwise, and that's not healthy."

"Thanks for saving my neck," Jason said. "That was closer than

I like to come. What happened after? I was sure I was done for, I remember that much. Diagnosed all the symptoms of pneumonia. Guaranteed fatal in my condition without treatment. Looks like you were wrong when you said most of your remedies were useless—they seemed to work well on me."

His voice died off as Rhes shook his head in a slow *no*, lines of worry sharp-cut into his face. Jason looked around and saw Naxa and another man. They had the same deeply unhappy expressions as Rhes.

"What is it?" Jason asked, feeling the trouble. "If your remedies didn't work—what did? Not my medikit. That was empty. I remember losing it or throwing it away."

"You were dying," Rhes said slowly. "We couldn't cure you. Only a junkman medicine machine could do that. We got one from the driver of the food truck."

"But how?" Jason asked, dazed. "You told me the city forbids you medicine. He wouldn't give you his own medikit. Not unless he was . . ."

Rhes nodded and finished the sentence. "Dead. Of course he was dead. I killed him myself, with a great deal of pleasure."

This hit Jason hard. He sagged against the pillows and thought of all those who had died since he had come to Pyrrus. The men who had died to save him, died so he could live, died because of his ideas. It was a burden of guilt that he couldn't bear to think about. Would it stop with Krannon—or would the city people try to avenge his death?

"Don't you realize what that means!" he gasped out the words. "Krannon's death will turn the city against you. There'll be no more supplies. They'll attack you when they can, kill your people . . ."

"Of course we know that!" Rhes leaned forward, his voice hoarse and intense. "It wasn't an easy decision to come to. We have always had a trading agreement with the junkmen. The trading trucks were inviolate. This was our last and only link to the galaxy outside the eventual hope of contacting them."

"Yet you broke that link to save me—why?"

"Only you can answer the question completely. There was a great attack on the city and we saw their walls broken, they had to be moved back at one place. At the same time the spaceship was over the ocean, dropping bombs of some kind—the flash was reported. Then the ship returned and *you* left it in a smaller ship. They fired at you but didn't kill you. The little ship wasn't destroyed either; we are starting to raise it now. What does it all mean? We have no way of telling. We only knew it was something vitally important. You were alive, but would obviously die before you could talk. The small ship might be repaired to fly; perhaps that was your plan and that is why you stole it for us. We *couldn't* let you die, not even if it meant all-out war with the city. The situation was explained to all of our people who could be reached by screen and they voted to save you. I killed the junkman for his medicine, then rode two doryms to death to get here in time.

"Now tell us—what does it mean? What is your plan? How will it help us?"

Guilt leaned on Jason and stifled his mouth. A fragment of an ancient legend cut across his mind, about the jona who wrecked the spacer so all in it died, yet he lived. Was that he? Had he wrecked a world? Could he dare admit to these people that he had taken the lifeboat only to save his own life?

The three Pyrrans leaned forward, waiting for his words. Jason closed his eyes so he wouldn't see their faces. What could he tell them? If he admitted the truth, they would undoubtedly kill him on the spot, considering it only justice. He wasn't fearful for his own life anymore, but if he died the other deaths would all have been in vain. And there still was a way to end this planetary war. All the facts were available now, it was just a matter of putting them together. If only he wasn't so tired, he would see the solution. It was right there, lurking around a corner in his brain, waiting to be dragged out.

There was the sudden sound of heavy feet stamping outside the cabin, and a man's muffled shouting. No one except Jason seemed to notice. They were too intent on his answer. He groped in his mind, but couldn't find words to explain. Whatever he did, he couldn't admit the truth now. If he died all hope died. He had to lie to gain time, then find the correct solution that seemed so tantaliz-ingly near. Yet he was too tired even to phrase a plausible lie.

The sound of the door bursting open crashed through the stillness of the room. A gnarled, stubby man stood there, his anger-red face set off by a full white beard.

"Everyone deaf?" he snarled. "I ride all night and shout my lungs out and you just squat here like a bunch a' egg-hatching birds. Get out! Quake! A big quake on the way!"

They were all standing now, shouting questions. Rhes's voice cut through the uproar. "Hananas! How much time do we have?"

"Time! Who knows about time!" the greybeard cursed. "Get out or you're dead, s'all I know."

No one stopped to argue now. There was a furious rush and within a minute Jason was being strapped into a litter on one of the doryms. "What's happening?" he asked the man who was tying him into place.

"Earthquake coming," he answered, his fingers busy with the knots. "Hananas is the best quakeman we have. He always knows before a quake is going to happen. If the word can be passed quick enough we get away. Quakemen always know, say they can feel them coming." He jerked the last knot tight and was gone.

Night came as they were starting, the red of sunset matched by a surly scarlet glow in the northern sky. There was a distant rumbling, more felt than heard, and the ground stirred underfoot. The doryms hurried into a shambling run without being prodded. They splashed through a swamp and on the other side Hananas changed their course abruptly. A little later, when the southern sky exploded, Jason knew why. Flames lit the scene brightly, ashes sifted down and hot lumps of rock crashed into the trees. They steamed when they hit, and if it hadn't been for the earlier rain they would have been faced with a forest fire as well.

Something large loomed up next to the line of march, and when they crossed an open space Jason looked at it in the reflected light from the sky.

"Rhes—" he choked, pointing. Rhes, riding next to him, looked at the great beast, shaggy body and twisted horns as high as their shoulders, then looked away. He wasn't frightened or apparently even interested. Jason looked around then and began to understand.

All of the fleeing animals made no sound, that's why he hadn't noticed them before. But on both sides dark forms ran between the trees. Some he recognized, most of them he didn't. For a few minutes a pack of wild dogs ran near them, even mingling with the domesticated dogs. No notice was taken. Flying things flapped by overhead. Under the greater threat of the volcanoes all other battles were forgotten. Life respected life. A herd of fat, pig-like beasts with curling tusks blundered through the line. The doryms slowed, picking their steps carefully so they wouldn't step on them. Smaller animals sometimes clung to the backs of the bigger ones, riding untouched awhile, before they leaped off.

Pounded mercilessly by the jarring litter, Jason fell wearily into a light sleep. It was shot through with dreams of the rushing animals, hurrying on forever in silence. With his eyes open or shut, he saw the same endless stream of beasts.

It all meant something and he frowned as he tried to think what. Animals running, Pyrran animals.

He sat bolt upright suddenly, twisting in his litter, wide awake and staring down in comprehension.

"What is it?" Rhes asked, swinging his dorym in close.

"Go on," Jason said. "Get us out of this, and get us out safely. I know how your people can get what they want, end the war now. There *is* a way, and I know how it can be done."

25

There were few coherent memories of the ride. Some things stood out sharply like the spaceship-sized lump of burning scoria that had plunged into a lake near them, showering the line with hot drops of water. But mostly it was just a seemingly endless ride, with Jason still too weak to care much about it. By dawn the danger area was behind them and the march had slowed to a walk. The animals had vanished as the quake was left behind, going their own ways, still in silent armistice.

The peace of mutually shared danger was over; Jason found that out when they stopped to rest and eat. He and Rhes went to sit on the soft grass, near a fallen tree. A wild dog had arrived there first. It lay under the log, muscles tensed, the ruddy morning light striking a red glint from its eyes. Rhes faced it, not three meters away, without moving a muscle. He made no attempt to reach one of his weapons or to call for help. Jason stood still as well, hoping the Pyrran knew what he was doing.

With no warning at all the dog sprang straight at them. Jason fell backward as Rhes pushed him aside. The Pyrran dropped at the same time—only now his hand held the long knife, yanked from the sheath strapped to his thigh. With unseen speed the knife came up, the dog twisted in midair, trying to bite it. Instead it sank in behind the dog's forelegs, the beast's own weight tearing a deadly gaping wound the length of its body. It was still alive when it hit the ground, but Rhes was astraddle it, pulling back the bony-plated head to cut the soft throat underneath.

The Pyrran carefully cleaned his knife on the dead animal's fur, then returned it to the sheath. "They're usually no trouble," he said quietly, "but it was excited. Probably lost the rest of the pack in the quake." His actions were the direct opposite of the city Pyrrans. He

had not looked for trouble nor started the fight. Instead he ha
avoided it as long as he could. But when the beast charged, it ha
been neatly and efficiently dispatched. Now, instead of gloatin
over his victory, he seemed troubled over an unnecessary death

It made sense. Everything on Pyrrus made sense. Now he knev
how the deadly planetary battle had started—and he knew how i
could be ended. All the deaths had *not* been in vain. Each one ha
helped him along the road a little more toward the final destination
There was just one final thing to be done.

Rhes was watching him now and he knew they shared the sam
thoughts. "Explain yourself," Rhes said. "What did you mea
when you said we could wipe out the junkmen and get ou
freedom?"

Jason didn't bother to correct the misquote; it was best the
consider him a hundred percent on their side.

"Get the others together and I'll tell you. I particularly want t
see Naxa and any other talkers who are here."

They gathered quickly when the word was passed. All of then
knew that the junkman had been killed to save this off-worlder, tha
their hope of salvation lay with him. Jason looked at the crowd o
faces turned toward him and reached for the right words to tell then
what had to be done. It didn't help to know that many of them woul
be killed doing it.

"We all want to see an end to the war here on Pyrrus. There is a
way, but it will cost human lives. Some of you may die doing it.
think the price is worth it, because success will bring you everythin
you have ever wanted." He looked around at the tense, waitin
circle.

"We are going to invade the city, break through the perimeter.
know how it can be done. . . ."

A mutter of sound spread across the crowd. Some of them looke
excited, happy with the thought of killing their hereditary enemies
Others stared at Jason as if he were mad. A few were dazed at th
magnitude of the thought, this carrying of the battle to the strong
hold of the heavily armed enemy. They quieted when Jason raise
his hand.

"I know it sounds impossible," he said. "But let me explain
Something must be done—and now is the time to do it. The situatio
can only get worse from now on. The city Pyrr . . . the junkmen ca
get along without your food, their concentrates taste awful but the
sustain life. But they are going to turn against you in every way the
can. No more metals for your tools or replacements for you
electronic equipment. Their hatred will probably make them see

out your farms and destroy them from the ship. All of this won't be comfortable—and there will be worse to come. In the city they are losing their war against this planet. Each year there are less of them, and some day they will all be dead. Knowing how they feel, I am sure they will destroy their ship first, and the entire planet as well, if that is possible."

"How can we stop them?" someone called out.

"By hitting *now,*" Jason answered. "I know all the details of the city and I know how the defenses are set up. Their perimeter is designed to protect them from animal life, but we could break through it if we were really determined."

"What good would that do?" Rhes snapped. "We crack the perimeter and they draw back—then counterattack in force. How can we stand against their weapons?"

"We won't have to. Their spaceport touches the perimeter, and I know the exact spot where the ship stands. That is the place where we will break through. There is no formal guard on the ship and only a few people in the area. We will capture the ship. Whether we can fly it or not is unimportant. Who controls the ship controls Pyrrus. Once there we threaten to destroy it if they don't meet our terms. They have the choice of mass suicide or cooperation. I hope they have the brains to cooperate."

His words shocked them into silence for an instant, then they surged into a wave of sound. There was no agreement, just excitement, and Rhes finally brought them to order.

"Quiet!" he shouted. "Wait until Jason finishes before you decide. We still haven't heard how this proposed invasion is to be accomplished."

"The plan I have depends on the talkers," Jason said. "Is Naxa there?" He waited until the fur-wrapped man had pushed to the front. "I want to know more about the talkers, Naxa. I know you can speak to doryms and the dogs here—but what about the wild animals? Can you make them do what you want?"

"They're animals—course we can talk t' them. Th' more talkers, th' more power. Make 'em do just what we want."

"Then the attack will work," Jason said excitedly. "Could you get your talkers all on one side of the city—the opposite side from the spaceport—and stir the animals up? Make them attack the perimeter?"

"Could we!" Naxa shouted, carried away by the idea. "We'd bring in animals from all over, start th' biggest attack they ev'r saw!"

"Then that's it. Your talkers will launch the attack on the far side of the perimeter. If you keep out of sight, the guards will have no idea that it is anything more than an animal attack. I've seen how they work. As an attack mounts, they call for reserves inside the city and drain men away from the other parts of the perimeter. At the height of the battle, when they have all their forces committed across the city, I'll lead the attack that will break through and capture the ship. That's the plan and it's going to work."

Jason sat down then, half fell down, drained of strength. He lay and listened as the debate went back and forth, Rhes ordering it and keeping it going. Difficulties were raised and eliminated. No one could find a basic fault with the plan. There were plenty of flaws in it, things that might go wrong, but Jason didn't mention them. These people wanted his idea to work and they were going to make it work.

It finally broke up and they moved away. Rhes came over to Jason.

"The basics are settled," he said. "All here are in agreement. They are spreading the word by messenger to all the talkers. The talkers are the heart of the attack, and the more we have, the better it will go off. We don't dare use the screens to call them; there is a good chance that the junkmen can intercept our messages. It will take five days before we are ready to go ahead."

"I'll need all of that time if I'm to be any good," Jason said. "Now let's get some rest."

26

"It's a strange feeling," Jason said. "I've never really seen the perimeter from this side before. Ugly is about the only word for it."

He lay on his stomach next to Rhes, looking through a screen of leaves, downhill toward the perimeter. They were both wrapped in heavy furs, in spite of the midday heat, with thick leggings and leather gauntlets to protect their hands. The gravity and the heat were already making Jason dizzy, but he forced himself to ignore this.

Ahead, on the far side of a burnt corridor, stood the perimeter. A high wall, of varying height and texture, seemingly made of all the odds and ends in the world. It was impossible to tell what it had originally been constructed of. Generations of attackers had bruised, broken, and undermined it. Repairs had been quickly made, patches thrust roughly into place and fixed there. Crude masonry crumbled and gave way to a rat's nest of woven timbers. This overlapped a length of pitted metal, large plates riveted together. Even this metal had been eaten through and bursting sandbags spilled out of a jagged hole. Over the surface of the wall detector wires and charged cables looped and hung. At odd intervals automatic flamethrowers thrust their nozzles over the parapet above and swept the base of the wall clear of any life that might have come close.

"Those flame things can cause us trouble," Rhes said. "That one covers the area where you want to break in."

"It'll be no problem," Jason assured him. "It may look like it is firing a random pattern, but it's really not. It varies a simple sweep just enough to fool an animal, but was never meant to keep men out. Look for yourself. It fires at regularly repeated two, four, three and one minute intervals."

They crawled back to the hollow where Naxa and the others waited for them. There were only thirty men in the party. What they had to do could only be done with a fast, light force. Their strongest weapon was surprise. Once that was gone their other weapons wouldn't hold out for seconds against the city guns. Everyone looked uncomfortable in the fur and leather wrappings, and some of the men had loosened them to cool off.

"Wrap up," Jason ordered. "None of you have been this close to the perimeter before and you don't understand how deadly it is here. Naxa is keeping the larger animals away and you all can handle the smaller ones. That isn't the danger. Every thorn is poisoned, and even the blades of grass carry a deadly sting. Watch out for insects of any kind and once we start moving breathe only through the wet cloths."

"He's right," Naxa snorted. "N'ver been closer 'n this m'self. Death, death up by that wall. Do like 'e says."

They could only wait then, honing down already needlesharp crossbow bolts, and glancing up at the slowly moving sun. Only Naxa didn't share the unrest. He sat, eyes unfocused, feeling the movement of animal life in the jungle around them.

"On the way," he said. "Biggest thing I 'ver heard. Not a beast 'tween here and the mountains, ain't howlin' 'is lungs out, runnin' toward the city."

Jason was aware of part of it. A tension in the air and a wave of intensified anger and hatred. It would work, he knew, if they could only keep the attack confined to a small area. The talkers had seemed sure of it. They had stalked out quietly that morning, a thin line of ragged men, moving in a mental sweep that would round up the Pyrran life and send it charging against the city.

"They hit!" Naxa said suddenly.

The men were on their feet now, staring in the direction of the city. Jason had felt the twist in his gut as the attack had been driven home, and knew that this was it. There was the sound of shots and a heavy booming far away. Thin streamers of smoke began to blow above the treetops.

"Let's get into position," Rhes said.

Around them the jungle howled with an echo of hatred. The half-sentient plants writhed and the air was thick with small flying things. Naxa sweated and mumbled as he turned back the animals that crashed toward them. By the time they reached the last screen of foliage before the burned-out area, they had lost four men. One had been stung by an insect; Jason got the medikit to him in time but he was so sick he had to turn back. The other three were bitten or scratched and treatment came too late. Their swollen, twisted bodies were left behind on the trail.

"Dam' beasts hurt m' head," Naxa muttered. "When we go in?"

"Not yet," Rhes said. "We wait for the signal."

One of the men carried the radio. He set it down carefully, then threw the aerial over a branch. The set was shielded so no radiation leaked out to give them away. It was turned on, but only a hiss of atmospheric static came from the speaker.

"We could have timed it. . . ." Rhes said.

"No, we couldn't," Jason told him. "Not accurately. We want to hit that wall at the height of the attack, when our chances are best. Even if they hear the message it won't mean a thing to them inside. And a few minutes later it won't matter."

The sound from the speaker changed. A voice spoke a short sentence, then cut off.

"Bring me three barrels of flour."

"Let's go," Rhes urged as he started forward.

"Wait," Jason said, taking him by the arm. "I'm timing the flamethrower. It's due in . . . *there!*" A blast of fire sprayed the ground, then turned off. "We have four minutes to the next one—we hit the long period!"

They ran, stumbling in the soft ashes, tripping over charred bones and rusted metal. Two men grabbed Jason under the arm and half carried him across the ground. It hadn't been planned that way, but it saved precious seconds. They dropped him against the wall and he fumbled out the bombs he had made. The charges from Krannon's gun, taken when he was killed, had been hooked together with a firing circuit. All the moves had been rehearsed carefully and they went smoothly now.

Jason had picked the metal wall as being the best spot to break in. It offered the most resistance to the native life, so the chances were it wouldn't be reinforced with sandbags or fill, the way other parts of the wall were. If he was wrong, they were all dead.

The first men had slapped their wads of sticky congealed sap against the wall. Jason pressed the charges into them and they stuck, a roughly rectangular pattern as high as a man. While he did this, the detonating wire was run out to its length and the raiders pressed back against the base of the wall. Jason stumbled through the ashes to the detonator, fell on it and pressed the switch at the same time.

Behind him a thundering bang shook the wall and red flame burst out. Rhes was the first one there, pulling at the twisted and smoking metal with his gloved hands. Others grabbed on and bent the jagged pieces aside. The hole was filled with smoke and nothing was visible through it. Jason dived into the opening, rolled on a heap of rubble and smacked into something solid. When he blinked the smoke from his eyes, he looked around him.

He was inside the city.

The others poured through now, picking him up as they charged in so he wouldn't be trampled underfoot. Someone spotted the spaceship and they ran that way.

A man ran around the corner of a building toward them. His Pyrran reflexes sent him springing into the safety of a doorway the same moment he saw the invaders. But they were Pyrrans too. The man slumped slowly back onto the street, three metal bolts sticking out of his body. They ran on without stopping, running between the low storehouses. The ship stood ahead.

Someone had reached it before them; they could see the outer hatch slowly grinding shut. A hail of bolts from the bows crashed into it with no effect.

"Keep going!" Jason shouted. "Get next to the hull before he reaches the guns."

This time three men didn't make it. The rest of them were under the belly of the ship when every gun let go at once. Most of them were aimed away from the ship, still the scream of shells and electric discharges were earshattering. The three men still in the open dissolved under the fire. Whoever was inside the ship had hit all the gun trips at once, both to knock out the attackers and summon aid. He would be on the screen now, calling for help. Their time was running out.

Jason reached up and tried to open the hatch, while the others watched. It was locked from the inside. One of the men brushed him aside and pulled at the inset handle. It broke off in his hand but the hatch remained closed.

The big guns had stopped now and they could hear again.

"Did anyone get the gun from the dead man?" he asked. "It would blow this thing open."

"No," Rhes said, "we didn't stop."

Before the words were out of his mouth, two men were running back toward the buildings, angling away from each other. The ship's guns roared again, a string of explosions cut across one man. Before they could change directions and find the other man he had reached the buildings.

He returned quickly, darting into the open to throw the gun to them. Before he could dive back to safety, the shells caught him.

Jason grabbed up the gun as it skidded almost to his feet. They heard the sound of wide open truck turbines screaming toward them as he blasted the lock. The mechanism sighed and the hatch sagged open. They were all through the airlock before the first truck appeared. Naxa stayed behind with the gun, to hold the lock until they could take the control room.

Everyone climbed faster than Jason, once he had pointed them the way, so the battle was over when he got there. The single city Pyrran looked like a pincushion. One of the techs had found the gun controls and was shooting wildly, the sheer quantity of his fire driving the trucks back.

"Someone get on the radio and tell the talkers to call the attack off," Jason said. He found the communications screen and snapped it on. Kerk's wide-eyed face stared at him from the screen.

"*You!*" Kerk said, breathing the word like a curse.

"Yes, it's me," Jason answered. He talked without looking up, while his hands were busy at the control board. "Listen to me, Kerk—and don't doubt anything I say. I may not know how to fly one of these ships, but I do know how to blow them up. Do you hear that sound?" He flipped over a switch and the faraway whine of a pump droned faintly. "That's the main fuel pump. If I let it run—which I won't right now—it could quickly fill the drive chamber with raw fuel. Pour in so much that it would run out of the stern tubes. Then what do you think would happen to your one-and-only spacer if I pressed the firing button? I'm not asking you what would happen to me—since you don't care—but you need this ship the way you need life itself.''

There was only silence in the cabin now. The men who had won the ship turned to face him. Kerk's voice grated loudly through the room.

"What do you want, Jason? What are you trying to do? Why did you lead those animals in here?" His voice cracked and broke as anger choked him and spilled over.

"Watch your tongue, Kerk," Jason said with soft menace. "These *men* you are talking about are the only ones on Pyrrus who have a spaceship. If you want them to share it with you, you had better learn to talk nicely. Now come over here at once—and bring Brucco and Meta." Jason looked at the older man's florid and swollen face and felt a measure of sympathy. "Don't look so unhappy, it's not the end of the world. In fact, it might be the beginning of one. And another thing, leave this channel open when you go. Have it hooked into every screen in the city so everyone can see what happens here. Make sure it's taped too, for replay."

Kerk started to say something, but changed his mind before he did. He left the screen, but the set stayed alive. Carrying the scene in the control room to the entire city.

27

The fight was over. It had ended so quickly the fact hadn't really sunk in yet. Rhes rubbed his hand against the gleaming metal of the control console, letting the reality of touch convince him. The other men milled about, looking out through the viewscreens or soaking in the mechanical strangeness of the room.

Jason was physically exhausted, but he couldn't let it show. He opened the pilot's medbox and dug through it until he found the stimulants. Three of the little gold pills washed the fatigue from his body, and he could think clearly again.

"Listen to me," he shouted. "The fight's not over yet. They'll try anything to take this ship back and we have to be ready. I want one of the techs to go over these boards until he finds the lock controls. Make sure all the airlocks and ports are sealed. Send men to check them, if necessary. Turn on all the screens to scan in every direction, so no one can get near the ship. We'll need a guard in the engine room; my control could be cut if they broke in there. And there had better be a room-by-room search of the ship, in case someone else is locked in with us."

The men had something to do now and felt relieved. Rhes split them up into groups and set them to work. Jason stayed at the controls, his hand next to the pump switch. The battle wasn't over yet.

"There's a truck coming," Rhes called, "going slow."

"Should I blast it?" the man at the gun controls asked.

"Hold your fire," Jason said, "until we can see who it is. If it's the people I sent for, let them through."

As the truck came on slowly, the gunner tracked it with his sights. There was a driver and three passengers. Jason waited until he was positive who they were.

"Those are the ones," he said. "Stop them at the lock, Rhes, make them come in one at a time. Take their guns as they enter, then strip them of *all* their equipment. There is no way of telling what could be a concealed weapon. Be specially careful of Brucco—he's the thin one with a face like an axe edge—make sure you strip him clean. He's a specialist in weapons and survival. And bring the driver, too; we don't want him reporting back about the broken airlock or the state of our guns."

Waiting was hard. His hand stayed next to the pump switch, even though he knew he could never use it. Just as long as the others thought he would.

There were stampings and muttered curses in the corridor; the prisoners were pushed in. Jason had one look at their deadly expressions and clenched fists before he called to Rhes.

"Keep them against the wall and watch them. Bowmen keep your weapons up." He looked at the people who had once been his friends and who now swam in hatred for him. Meta, Kerk, Brucco. The driver was Skop, the man Kerk had once appointed to guard him. He looked ready to explode now that the roles had been reversed.

"Pay close attention," Jason said, "because your lives depend upon it. Keep your backs to the wall and don't attempt to come any closer to me than you are now. If you do, you will be shot instantly. If we were alone, any one of you could undoubtedly reach me before I threw this switch. But we're not. You have Pyrran reflexes and muscles—but so do the bowmen. Don't gamble. Because it won't be a gamble. It will be suicide. I'm telling you this for your own protection. So we can talk peacefully without one of you losing his temper and suddenly getting shot. *There is no way out of this.* You are going to be forced to listen to everything I say. You can't escape or kill me. The war is over."

"And we lost—and all because of you, you *traitor!*" Meta snarled.

"Wrong on both counts," Jason said blandly. "I'm not a traitor because I owe my allegiance to all men on this planet, both inside the perimeter and out. I never pretended differently. As to losing, why you haven't lost anything. In fact you've won. Won your war against this planet, if you will only hear me out." He turned to Rhes, who was frowning in angry puzzlement. "Of course your people have won also, Rhes. No more war with the city, you'll get medicine, off-planet contact, everything you want."

"Pardon me for being cynical," Rhes said. "But you're promising the best of all possible worlds for everyone. That will be a little hard to deliver when our interests are opposed so."

"You strike through to the heart of the matter," Jason said. "Thank you. This mess will be settled by seeing that everyone's interests are not opposed. Peace between the city and farms, with an end to the useless war you have been fighting. Peace between mankind and the Pyrran life forms—because that particular war is at the bottom of all your troubles."

"The man's mad," Kerk said.

"Perhaps. You'll judge that after you hear me out. I'm going to tell you the history of this planet, because that is where both the trouble and the solution lie.

"When the settlers landed on Pyrrus three hundred years ago, they missed the one important thing about this planet, the factor that makes it different from any other planet in the galaxy. They can't be blamed for the oversight, they had enough other things to worry about. The gravity was about the only thing familiar to them, the rest of the environment was a shocking change from the climate-controlled industrial world they had left. Storms, vulcanism, floods, earthquakes—it was enough to drive them insane, and I'm sure many of them did go mad. The animal and insect life was a constant annoyance, nothing at all like the few harmless and protected species they had known. I'm sure they never realized that the Pyrran life was telepathic as well—"

"That again!" Brucco snapped. "True or not, it is of no importance. I was tempted to agree with your theory of *psionic* controlled attack on us, but the deadly fiasco you staged proved that theory wrong.''

"I agree," Jason answered. "I was completely mistaken when I thought some outside agency directed the attack on the city with *psi*onic control. It seemed a logical theory at the time and the evidence pointed that way. The expedition to the island *was* a deadly fiasco—only don't forget that attack was the direct opposite of what I wanted to have done. If I had gone into the cave myself, none of the deaths would have been necessary. I think it would have been discovered that the plant creatures were nothing more than an advanced life form with unusual *psi* ability. They simply resonated strongly to the *psi*onic attack on the city. I had the idea backward thinking they instigated the battle. We'll never know the truth, though, because they are destroyed. But their deaths did do one thing. Showed us where to find the real culprits, the creatures who are leading, directing and inspiring the war against the city.''

"*Who?*" Kerk breathed the question, rather than spoke it.

"Why, *you* of course," Jason told him. "Not you alone, but all of your people in the city. Perhaps you don't like this war. However, you are responsible for it and keep it going.''

Jason had to force back a smile as he looked at their dumbfounded expressions. He also had to prove his point quickly, before even his allies began to think him insane.

"Here is how it works. I said Pyrran life was telepathic—and I meant all life. Every single insect, plant and animal. At one time in this planet's violent history, these *psi*onic mutations proved to be survival types. They existed when other species died, and in the end I'm sure they cooperated in wiping out the last survivors of the non-*psi* strains. Cooperation is the key word here. Because while they still competed against each other under normal conditions, they worked together against anything that threatened them as a whole. When a natural upheaval or a tidal wave threatened them, they fled from it in harmony. You can see a milder form of this same behavior on any planet that is subject to forest fires. But here, mutual survival was carried to an extreme because of the violent conditions. Perhaps some of the life forms even developed precognition like the human quakemen. With this advance warning, the larger beasts fled. The smaller ones developed seeds, or burrs or eggs, that could be carried to safety by the wind or in the animals' fur, thus insuring racial survival. I know this is true because I watched it myself when we were escaping a quake.''

"Admitted—all your points admitted," Brucco shouted. "But what does it have to do with *us?* So all the animals run away together, what does that have to do with the war?"

"They do more than run away together," Jason told him. "They work together against any natural disaster that threatens them all. Some day, I'm sure, ecologists will go into raptures over the complex adjustments that occur here in the advent of blizzards, floods, fires and other disasters. There is only one reaction we really care about now, though. That's the one directed toward the city people. Don't you realize yet—they treat you all as another natural disaster!

"We'll never know exactly how it came about, though there is a clue in that diary I found, dating from the first days on this planet. It said that a forest fire seemed to have driven new species toward the settlers. Those weren't new beasts at all—just old ones with new attitudes. Can't you just imagine how those protected, overcivilized settlers acted when faced with a forest fire? They panicked, of course. If the settlers were in the path of the fire, the animals must have rushed right through their camp. Their reaction would undoubtedly have been to shoot the fleeing creatures down.

"When they did that, they classified themselves as a natural disaster. Disasters take any form. Bipeds with guns could easily be included in the category. The Pyrran animals attacked, were shot, and the war began. The survivors kept attacking and informed all the life forms what the fight was about. The radioactivity of this planet must cause plenty of mutations—and the favorable, survival mutation was now one that was deadly to man. I'll hazard a guess that the *psi* function even instigates mutations, some of the deadlier types are just too onesided to have come about naturally in a brief three hundred years.

"The settlers of course fought back, and kept their status as a natural disaster intact. Through the centuries, they improved their killing methods, not that it did the slightest good, as you know. You city people, their descendants, are heirs to this heritage of hatred. You fight and are slowly being defeated. How can you possibly win against the biologic reserves of a planet that can recreate itself each time to meet any new attack?"

Silence followed Jason's words. Kerk and Meta stood whitefaced as the impact of the disclosure sunk in. Brucco mumbled and checked points off on his fingers, searching for weak spots in the chain of reason. The fourth city Pyrran, Skop, ignored all these foolish words that he couldn't understand—or want to understand—and would have killed Jason in an instant if there had been the slightest chance of success.

It was Rhes who broke the silence. His quick mind had taken in the factors and sorted them out. "There's one thing wrong," he said. "What about us? We live on the surface of Pyrrus without perimeters or guns. Why aren't we attacked as well? We're human, descended from the same people as the junkmen."

"You're not attacked," Jason told him, "because you don't identify yourself as a natural disaster. Animals can live on the slopes of a dormant volcano, fighting and dying in natural competition. But they'll flee together when the volcano erupts. That eruption is what makes the mountain a natural disaster. In the case of human beings, it is their thoughts that identify them as life form or disaster. Mountain or volcano. In the city everyone radiates suspicion and death. They enjoy killing, thinking about killing, and planning for killing. This is natural selection too, you realize. These are the survival traits that work best in the city. Outside the city, men think differently. If they are threatened individually, they fight, as will any other creature. Under more general survival threats, they cooperate completely with the rules for universal survival that the city people break."

"How did it begin—this separation, I mean, between the two groups?" Rhes asked.

"We'll probably never know," Jason said. "I think your people must have originally been farmers, or *psi*onic sensitives who were not with the others during some natural disaster. They would of course act correctly by Pyrran standards, and survive. This could cause a difference of opinion with the city people who saw killing as the answer. It's obvious, whatever the reason, that two separate communities were established early, and soon separated except for the limited amount of barter that benefited both."

"I still can't believe it," Kerk mumbled. "It makes a terrible kind of truth, every step of the way, but I still find it hard to accept. There *must* be another explanation."

Jason shook his head slowly. "None. This is the only one that works. We've eliminated the other ones, remember? I can't blame you for finding it hard to believe, since it is in direct opposition to everything you've understood to be true in the past. It's like altering a natural law. As if I gave you proof that gravity didn't really exist, that it was a force altogether different from the immutable one we know, one you could get around when you understood how. You'd want more proof than words. Probably want to see someone walking on air."

"Which isn't such a bad idea at that," he added, turning to Naxa. "Do you hear any animals around the ship now? Not the ones you're used to, but the mutated, violent kind that live only to attack the city."

"Place's crawling with 'em," Naxa said. "Just lookin' for somethin' t' kill."

"Could you capture one?" Jason asked. "Without getting yourself killed, I mean."

Naxa snorted contempt as he turned to leave. "Beast's not born yet, that'll hurt me."

They stood quietly, each one wrapped tightly around by his own thoughts, while they waited for Naxa to return. Jason had nothing more to say. He would do one more thing to try to convince them of the facts; after that it would be up to each of them to reach a conclusion.

The talker returned quickly with a stingwing, tied by one leg to a length of leather. It flapped and shrieked and he carried it in.

"In the middle of the room, away from everybody," Jason told him. "Can you get that beast to sit on something and not flap around?"

"My hand good enough," he said, flipping the creature up so it clung to the back of his gauntlet. "That's how I caught it."

"Does anyone doubt that this is a real stingwing?" Jason asked. "I want to make sure you all believe there is no trickery here."

"The thing is real," Brucco said. "I can smell the poison in the wing claws from here." He pointed to the dark marks on the leather where the liquid had dripped. "If that eats through the gloves, he's a dead man."

"Then we agree it's real," Jason said. "Real and deadly, and the only test of the theory will be if you people from the city can approach it like Naxa here."

They drew back automatically when he said it. Because they knew that stingwing was synonymous with death. Past, present and future. You don't change a natural law. Meta spoke for all of them.

"We—can't. This man lives in the jungle, like an animal himself. Somehow he's learned to get near them. But you can't expect us to."

Jason spoke quickly, before the talker could react to the insult. "Of course I expect you to. That's the whole idea. If you don't hate the beast and expect it to attack you—why it won't. Think of it as a creature from a different planet, something harmless."

"I can't," she said. "It's a *stingwing!*"

As they talked, Brucco stepped forward, his eyes fixed steadily on the creature perched on the glove. Jason signaled the bowmen to

hold their fire. Brucco stopped at a safe distance and kept looking
steadily at the stingwing. It rustled its leathery wings uneasily and
hissed. A drop of poison formed at the tip of each great poison claw
on its wings. The control room was filled with a deadly silence.

Slowly he raised his hand. Carefully putting it out, over the
animal. The hand dropped a little, rubbed the stingwing's head
once, then fell back to his side. The animal did nothing except stir
slightly under the touch.

There was a concerted sigh, as those who had been unknowingly
holding their breath, breathed again.

"How did you do it?" Meta asked in a hushed voice.

"Hmm, what?" Brucco said, apparently snapping out of a daze.
"Oh, touching the thing. Simple, really. I just pretended it was one
of the training aids I use, a realistic and harmless duplicate. I kept
my mind on that single thought and it worked." He looked down at
his hand, then back to the stingwing. His voice was quieter now, as
if he spoke from a distance. "It's not a training aid, you know. It's
real. Deadly. The off-worlder is right. He's right about everything
he said."

With Brucco's success as an example, Kerk came close to the
animal. He walked stiffly, as if on the way to his execution, and
runnels of sweat poured down his rigid face. But he believed and
kept his thoughts directed away from the stingwing and he could
touch it unharmed.

Meta tried but couldn't fight down the horror it raised when she
came close. "I am trying," she said, "and I do believe you
now—but I just can't do it."

Skop screamed when they all looked at him, shouted it was all a
trick, and had to be clubbed unconscious when he attacked the
bowmen.

Understanding had come to Pyrrus.

28

"What do we do now?" Meta asked. Her voice was troubled,
questioning. She voiced the thoughts of all the Pyrrans in the room,
and the thousands who watched in their screens.

"What will we do?" They turned to Jason, waiting for an answer. For the moment their differences were forgotten. The people from the city were staring expectantly at him, as were the crossbowmen with half-lowered weapons. This stranger had confused and changed the old world they had known, and presented them with a newer and stranger one, with alien problems.

"Hold on," he said, raising his hand. "I'm no doctor of social ills. I'm not going to try and cure this planet full of musclebound sharpshooters. I've just squeezed through up to now, and by the law of averages I should be ten times dead."

"Even if all you say is true, Jason," Meta said, "you are still the only person who can help us. What will the future be like?"

Suddenly weary, Jason slumped into the pilot's chair. He glanced around at the circle of people. They seemed sincere. None of them even appeared to have noticed that he no longer had his hand on the pump switch. For the moment, at least, the war between city and country was forgotten.

"I'll give you my conclusions," Jason said, twisting in the chair, trying to find a comfortable position for his aching bones. "I've been doing a lot of thinking the last day or two, searching for the answer. The very first thing I realized, was that the perfect and logical solution wouldn't do at all. I'm afraid the old ideal of the lion lying down with the lamb doesn't work out in practice. About all it does is make a fast lunch for the lion. Ideally, now that you all know the real causes of your trouble, you should tear down the perimeter and have the city and forest people mingled in brotherly love. Makes just a pretty a picture as the one of lion and lamb. And would undoubtedly have the same result. Someone would remember how really filthy the grubbers are, or how stupid junkmen can be, and there would be a fresh corpse cooling. The fight would spread and the victors would be eaten by the wildlife that swarmed over the undefended perimeter. No, the answer isn't that easy."

As the Pyrrans listened to him, they realized where they were and glanced around uneasily. The guards raised their crossbows again and the prisoners stepped back to the wall and looked surly.

"See what I mean?" Jason asked. "Didn't take long, did it?" They all looked a little sheepish at their unthinking reactions.

"If we're going to find a decent plan for the future, we'll have to take inertia into consideration. Mental inertia, for one. Just because you know a thing is true in theory, doesn't make it true in fact. The barbaric religions of primitive worlds hold not a germ of scientific fact, though they claim to explain all. Yet if one of these savages has all the logical ground for his beliefs taken away, he doesn't stop believing. He then calls his mistaken beliefs 'faith' because he knows they are right. And he knows they are right because he has faith. This is an unbreakable circle of false logic that can't be touched. In reality, it is plain mental inertia. A case of thinking 'what always was' will also 'always be.' And not wanting to blast the thinking patterns out of the old rut.

"Mental inertia alone is not going to cause trouble—there is cultural inertia too. Some of you in this room believe my conclusions and would like to change. But will all your people change? The unthinking ones, the habit-ridden, reflex-formed people who *know* what is now, will always be. They'll act like a drag on whatever plans you make, whatever attempts you undertake to progress with the new knowledge you have."

"Then it's useless, there's no hope for our world?" Rhes asked.

"I didn't say that," Jason answered. "I merely mean that your troubles won't end by throwing some kind of mental switch. I see three courses open for the future, and the chances are that all three will be going on at the same time.

"First—and best—will be the rejoining of city and country Pyrrans into the single human group they came from. Each is incomplete now, and has something the other one needs. In the city here you have science and contact with the rest of the galaxy. You also have a deadly war. Out there in the jungle, your first cousins live at peace with the world, but lack medicine and the other benefits of scientific knowledge, as well as any kind of cultural contact with the rest of mankind. You'll both have to join together and benefit from the exchange. At the same time you'll have to forget the superstitious hatred you have of each other. This will only be done outside of the city, away from the war. Every one of you who is capable should go out voluntarily, bringing some fraction of the knowledge that needs sharing. You won't be harmed if you go in good faith. And you will learn how to live *with* this planet, rather than against it. Eventually you'll have civilized communities that won't be either 'grubber' or 'junkman.' They'll be Pyrran."

"But what about our city here?" Kerk asked.

"It'll stay right here—and probably won't change in the slightest. In the beginning you'll need your perimeter and defenses to stay alive, while the people are leaving. And after that it will keep going because there are going to be any number of people here who you won't convince. They'll stay and fight and eventually die. Perhaps you will be able to do a better job in educating their children. What the eventual end of the city will be, I have no idea."

They were silent as they thought about the future. On the floor, Skop groaned but did not move. "Those are two ways," Meta said. "What is the third?"

"The third possibility is my own pet scheme," Jason smiled. "And I hope I can find enough people to go along with me. I'm going to take my money and spend it all on outfitting the best and most modern spacer, with every weapon and piece of scientific equipment I can get my hands on. Then I'm going to ask for Pyrran volunteers to go with me."

"What in the world for?" Meta frowned.

"Not for charity. I expect to make my investment back, and more. You see, after these past few months, I can't possibly return to my old occupation. Not only do I have enough money now to make it a waste of time, but I think it would be an unending bore. One thing about Pyrrus—if you live—is that is spoils you for the quieter places. So I'd like to take this ship that I mentioned and go into the business of opening up new worlds. There are thousands of planets where men would like to settle, only getting a foothold on them is too rough or rugged for the usual settlers. Now can you imagine a planet a Pyrran couldn't lick after the training you've had here? And wouldn't you enjoy doing it?

"There would be more than pleasure involved, though. In the city, your lives have been geared for continual deadly warfare. Now you're faced with the choice of a fairly peaceful future, or staying in the city to fight an unnecessary and foolish war. I offer the third alternative of the occupation you know best, that would let you accomplish something constructive at the same time.

"Those are the choices. Whatever you decide is up to each of you personally."

Before anyone could answer, livid pain circled Jason's throat. Skop had regained consciousness and surged up from the floor. He pulled Jason from the chair with a single motion, holding him by the neck, throttling him. The bowmen tried to shoot, but held their fire because Jason was in the way.

"Kerk! Meta!" Skop shouted hoarsely. "Grab guns! Open the locks—our people'll be here, kill the damn grubbers and their lies!"

Jason tore at the fingers that were choking the life out of him, but it was like pulling at bent steel bars. He couldn't talk and the blood hammered in his ears and drowned his thoughts. It was over now and he had lost. They'd butcher each other in the spaceship and Pyrrus would keep on being a deathworld until every one of them was dead.

Meta hurtled forward like an uncoiled spring and the crossbows twanged. One bolt caught her in the leg, the other transfixed her upper arm. But she had been shot as she jumped and her inertia carried her across the room, to her fellow Pyrran and the dying off-worlder.

She raised her good arm and chopped down with the edge of her hand.

It caught Skop a hard blow on the biceps and his arm jumped spasmodically, his hand leaping from Jason's throat.

"What are you doing!" he shouted in strange terror to the wounded girl who fell against him. He pushed her away, still clutching Jason with his other hand. She didn't answer. Instead she chopped again, hard and true, the edge of her hand catching Skop across the windpipe, crushing it. He dropped Jason and fell to the floor, retching and gasping.

Jason watched the end through a haze, barely conscious.

Skop struggled to his feet, turned pain-filled eyes to his friends. "You're wrong," Kerk said. "Don't do it!"

The sound the wounded man made was more animal than human. When he dived toward the guns on the far side of the room, the crossbows twanged like harps of death. He skidded into the guns, his hand knocking them aside, but he was already dead.

When Brucco went over to help Meta, no one interfered. Jason gasped air back into his lungs, breathing in life. The watching glass eye of the viewer carried the scene to everyone in the city.

"Thanks, Meta . . . for understanding . . . as well as helping." Jason had to force the words out.

"Skop was wrong and you were right, Jason," she said. Her voice broke for a second as Brucco snapped off the feathered end of the steel bolt with his fingers, and pulled the shaft out of her arm. "I can't stay in the city; only people who feel as Skop did will be able to do that. And I'm afraid I can't go into the forest—you saw what luck I had with the stingwing. If it's all right, I'd like to come with you. I'd like to very much."

It hurt when he talked so Jason could only smile, but she knew what he meant.

Kerk looked down in unhappiness at the body of the dead man. "He was wrong—but I know how he felt. I can't leave the city, not yet. Someone will have to keep things in hand while the changes are taking place. Your ship is a good idea, Jason, you'll have no shortage of volunteers. Though I doubt if you'll get Brucco to go with you."

"Of course not," Brucco snapped, not looking up from the

compression bandage he was tying. "There's enough to do right here on Pyrrus. The animal life, quite a study to be made, probably have every ecologist in the galaxy visiting here before long. But I'll be first."

Kerk walked slowly to the screen overlooking the city. No one attempted to stop him. He looked out at the buildings, the smoke still curling up from the perimeter, and the limitless sweep of green jungle beyond.

"You've changed it all, Jason," he said. "We can't see it now, but Pyrrus will never be the way it was before you came. For better or worse."

"Better, damn it, better," Jason croaked, and rubbed his aching throat. "Now get together and end this war so people will really believe it."

Rhes turned and, after an instant's hesitation, extended his hand to Kerk. The grey-haired Pyrran felt the same repugnance himself about touching a grubber, the memory of a lifetime of disgust.

But they shook hands then because they were both strong men.

DEATHWORLD 2

For JOHN W. CAMPBELL
without whose aid this book—
and a good percentage of modern science fiction—
would never have been written.

All Nature is but Art, unknown to thee;
All Chance, Direction, which thou canst not see;
All Discord, Harmony not understood;
All partial Evil, universal Good:
And, spite of Pride, in erring Reason's spite,
One truth is clear, WHATEVER IS, IS RIGHT.
                    —ALEXANDER POPE, "An Essay on Man"

1

"Just a moment," Jason said into the phone, then turned away for a moment and shot an attacking horndevil. "No, I'm not doing anything important. I'll come over now and maybe I can help."

He switched off the phone and the radio operator's image faded from the screen. When he passed the gutted horndevil it stirred with a last spark of vicious life, and its horn clattered on his flexible metal boot; he kicked the body off the wall into the jungle below.

It was dark in the perimeter guard turret; the only illumination came from the flickering lights of the defense screen controls. Meta looked up swiftly at him and smiled, then turned her full attention back to the alarm board.

"I'm going over to the spaceport radio tower," Jason told her. "There is a spacer in orbit, trying to make contact in an unknown language. Maybe I can help."

"Hurry back," Meta said and, after a rapid check that all her alarms were in the green, she turned in the chair and reached up to him. Her arms held him, slim-muscled and as strong as a man's, but her lips were warm, feminine. He returned the kiss, though she broke away as suddenly as she had begun, turning her attention back to the alarm and defense system.

"That's the trouble with Pyrrus," Jason said. "Too much efficiency." He bent over and gave her a small bite on the nape of the neck and she laughed and slapped at him playfully without taking her eyes from the alarms. He moved—but not fast enough—and went out rubbing his bruised ear. "Lady weight-lifter!" he muttered under his breath.

The radio operator was alone in the spaceport tower, a teen-age boy who had never been offplanet, and therefore knew only Pyrran, while Jason, after his career as a professional gambler, spoke or had nodding acquaintance with most of the galactic languages.

"It's orbiting out of range now," the operator said. "Be back in a moment. Talks something different." He turned the gain up, and above the crackle of atmospherics a voice slowly grew.

"*. . . jeg kan ikke forsta . . . Pyrrus, kan dig hor mig . . . ?*"

"No trouble with that," Jason said, reaching for the microphone. "It's Nytdansk—they speak it on most of the planets in the Polaris area." He thumbed the switch on.

"*Pyrrus til rumfartskib*, over," he said, and opened the switch. The answer came back in the same language.

"Request landing permission. What are your coordinates?"

"Permission denied, and the suggestion strongly presented that you find a healthier planet."

"That is impossible, since I have a message for Jason dinAlt and I have information that he is here."

Jason looked at the crackling loudspeaker with new interest. "Your information is correct: dinAlt speaking. What is the message?"

"It cannot be delivered over a public circuit. I am now following your radio beam down. Will you give me instructions?"

"You do realize that you are probably committing suicide? This is the deadliest planet in the galaxy, and all the life forms, from the bacteria up to the clawhawks—which are as big as the ship you're flying—are inimical to man. There is a truce of sorts going now, but it is still certain death for an outworlder like you. Can you hear me?"

There was no answer. Jason shrugged and looked at the approach radar.

"Well, it's your life. But don't say with your dying breath that you weren't warned. I'll bring you in—but only if you agree to stay in your ship. I'll come out to you; that way you have a fifty-fifty chance that the decontamination cycling in your spacelock will kill the local microscopic life."

"That is agreeable," came the answer, "since I have no wish to die—only to deliver my message."

Jason guided the ship in, watched it emerge from the low-lying clouds, hover, then drop stern first with a grating crash. The shock absorbers took up most of the blow, but the ship had bent a support and stood at a decided angle.

"Terrible landing," the radio operator grunted, and turned back to his controls, uninterested in the stranger. Pyrrans have no casual curiosity.

Jason was the direct opposite. Curiosity had brought him to Pyrrus, involved him in the planet-wide war, and almost killed him. Now curiosity drove him towards the ship. He hesitated a moment as he realized that the radio operator had not understood his conversation with the strange pilot, and could not know that he planned to

nter the ship. If he was walking into trouble he could expect no
elp.

"I can take care of myself," he said to himself with a laugh, and
when he raised his hand his gun leaped out of the power holster
trapped to the inside of his wrist and slammed into his hand. His
ndex finger was already contracted, and when the guardless tripper
it it a single shot banged out, blasting the distant dartweed he had
imed at.

He was good, and he knew it. He would never be as good as the
ative Pyrrans, born and raised on this deadly planet, with its
oubled gravity, but he was faster and more deadly than any
ffworlder could possibly be. He could handle any trouble that
night develop—and he expected trouble. In the past he had had
nany differences of opinion with the police and various other
lanetary authorities, though he could think of none of them who
vould bother to send police across interstellar space to arrest him.

Why had this ship come?

There was an identification number painted on the spacer's stern,
nd a rather familiar heraldic device. Where had he seen that
efore?

His attention was distracted by the opening of the outer door of
he airlock and he stepped inside. Once it had sealed behind him, he
losed his eyes while the supersonics and ultraviolet of the decon
ycle did their best to eliminate the various minor life forms that had
ome in on his clothes. They finally finished, and when the inner
loor began to open he pressed tight against it, ready to jump through
s soon as it had opened wide enough. If there were any surprises he
vanted them to be his.

When he went through the door he realized he was falling. His
;un sprang into his hand and he had it half raised towards the man in
he spacesuit who sat in the control chair.

"Gas . . ." was all he managed to say, and he was out before he
it the metal deck.

Consciousness returned, accompanied by a thudding headache
hat made Jason wince when he moved, and when he opened his
:yes the pain of the light made him screw them shut again.
Vhatever the drug was that had knocked him out, it was fast-
vorking, and seemed to be oxidized just as quickly. The headache
aded to a dull throb, and he could open his eyes without feeling that
needles were being driven into them.

He was seated in a standard space-chair that had been equipped
vith wrist and ankle locks, which were now well secured. A man sat

in the chair next to him, intent on the spaceship's controls; the ship was in flight and well into space. The stranger was working the computer, cutting a tape to control their flight in jump space.

Jason took the opportunity to study the man. He seemed to be a little old for a policeman, though on second thought it was really hard to be sure of his age. His hair was grey and cropped so short it was like a skullcap, but the wrinkles in his leathery skin seemed to have been caused more by exposure than by advanced years. Tall and firmly erect, he appeared underweight at first glance, until Jason realized this effect was caused by the total absence of any excess flesh. It was as though he had been cooked by the sun and leached by the rain until only bone, tendon, and muscle were left. When he moved his head the muscles stood out like cables under the skin of his neck and his hands at the controls were like the browned talons of some bird. A hard finger pressed the switch that activated the jump control, and he turned away from the board to face Jason.

"I see you are awake. It was a mild gas. I did not enjoy using it, but it was the safest way."

When he talked his jaw opened and shut with the no-nonsense seriousness of a bank vault. His deepset, cold blue eyes stared fixedly from under thick dark brows. There was not the slightest element of humor in his expression or in his words.

"Not a very friendly thing to do," Jason said, while he quietly tested the restraining bands. They were locked and tight. "If I had any idea that your important personal message was going to be a dose of knockout gas I might have thought twice about guiding you in for a landing."

"Deceit for the deceitful," the snapping-turtle mouth bit out. "Had there been any other way to capture you, I would have used it. But considering your reputation as a ruthless killer, and the undoubted fact that you have friends on Pyrrus, I took you in the only manner possible."

"Very noble of you, I'm sure." Jason was getting angry at the other's uncompromising self-righteousness. "The end justifies the means and all that—not exactly an original argument. But I walked in with my eyes open and I'm not complaining." Not much, he thought bitterly. The next best thing to kicking this crumb around the block would be kicking himself for being so stupid. "But if it's not asking too much, would you mind telling me who you are and just why you have gone to all this trouble to obtain my undernourished body."

"I am Mikah Samon. I am returning you to Cassylia for trial and sentencing."

"Cassylia—I thought I recognized the identification on this ship. I suppose I shouldn't be surprised to hear that they are still interested in finding me. But you ought to know that there is very little remaining of the three billion, seventeen million credits that I won from your casino."

"Cassylia does not want the money back," Mikah said as he locked the controls and swung about in his chair. "They do not want you back either, since you are their planetary hero now. When you escaped with your ill-gotten gains they realized that they would never see the money again. So they put their propaganda mills to work and you are now known throughout all the adjoining star systems as 'Jason Three-Billion,' the living proof of the honesty of their dishonest games, and a lure for all the weak in spirit. You tempt them into gambling for money instead of working honestly for it."

"Pardon me for being slow-witted today," Jason said, shaking his head rapidly to loosen up the stuck synapses. "I'm having a little difficulty in following you. What kind of a policeman are you, to arrest me for trial after the charges have been dropped?"

"I am not a policeman," Mikah said sternly, his long fingers woven tightly together before him, his eyes wide and penetrating. "I am a believer in Truth—nothing more. The corrupt politicians who control Cassylia have placed you on a pedestal of honor. Honoring you, another and—if possible—a more corrupt man, and behind your image they have waxed fat. But I am going to use the Truth to destroy that image, and when I destroy the image I shall destroy the evil that produced it."

"That's a tall order for one man," Jason said calmly—more calmly than he really felt. "Do you have a cigarette?"

"There is of course no tobacco or spirits on this ship. And I am more than one man—I have followers. The Truth Party is already a power to be reckoned with. We have spent much time and energy in tracking you down, but it was worth it. We have followed your dishonest trail into the past, to Mahaut's Planet, to the Nebula Casino on Galipto, through a series of sordid crimes that turn an honest man's stomach. We have warrants for your arrest from each of these places, in some cases even the results of trials and your death sentence."

"I suppose it doesn't bother your sense of legality that those trials were all held in my absence?" Jason asked. "Or that I have only fleeced casinos and gamblers—who make their living by fleecing suckers?"

Mikah Samon wiped away this consideration with a wave of his hand. "You have been proved guilty of a number of crimes. No amount of wriggling on the hook can change that. You should be thankful that your revolting record will have a good use in the end. It will be the lever with which we shall topple the grafting government of Cassylia."

"I'm going to have to do something about that curiosity of mine," Jason said. "Look at me now"— He rattled his wrists in their restraining bands and the servo motors whined a bit as the detector unit came to life and tightened the grasp of the cuffs, limiting his movement. "A little while ago I was enjoying my health and freedom when they called me to talk to you on the radio. Then, instead of letting you plow into the side of a hill, I guide you in for a landing, and can't resist the impulse to poke my stupid head into your baited trap. I'm going to have to learn to fight those impulses."

"If that is supposed to be a plea for mercy, it is sickening," Mikah said. "I have never taken favors, nor do I owe anything to men of your type. Nor will I ever."

"Ever, like *never,* is a long time," Jason said very quietly. "I wish I had your peace of mind about the sure order of things."

"Your remark shows that there might be hope for you yet. You might be able to recognize the Truth before you die. I will help you, talk to you, and explain."

"Better the execution," Jason said chokingly.

2

"Are you going to feed me by hand—or unlock my wrists while I eat?" Jason asked. Mikah stood over him with the tray, undecided. Jason gave a verbal prod, very gently, because whatever else he was, Mikah was not stupid. "I would prefer you to feed me, of course—you'd make an excellent body servant."

"You are capable of eating by yourself," Mikah responded instantly, sliding the tray into the slots of Jason's chair. "But you will have to do it with only one hand, since if you were freed you would only cause trouble." He touched the control on the back of the chair and the right wrist lock snapped open. Jason stretched his cramped fingers and picked up the fork.

While he ate, Jason's eyes were busy. Not obviously, for a gambler's attention is never obvious, but many things can be seen if you keep your eyes open and your attention apparently elsewhere: a sudden glimpse of someone's cards, the slight change of expression that reveals a player's strength. Item by item, his seemingly random glance touched the contents of the cabin. Control console, screens, computer, chart screen, jump control, chart case, bookshelf. Everything was observed, considered, and remembered. Some combination of them would fit into the plan.

So far, all he had was the beginning and the end of an idea. Beginning: He was a prisoner in this ship, on his way back to Cassylia. End: He was not going to remain a prisoner—nor return to Cassylia. Now all that was missing was the vital middle. The end seemed impossible at the moment, but Jason never considered that it couldn't be done. He operated on the principle that you make your own luck. You kept your eyes open as things evolved, and at the right moment you acted. If you acted fast enough, that was good luck. If you worried over the possibilities until the moment had passed, that was bad luck.

He pushed the empty plate away and stirred sugar into his cup. Mikah had eaten sparingly and was now starting on his second cup of tea. His eyes were fixed, unfocused in thought as he drank. He started slightly when Jason spoke to him.

"Since you don't stock cigarettes on this ship, how about letting me smoke my own? You'll have to dig them out for me, since I can't reach the pocket while I'm chained to this chair."

"I cannot help you," Mikah said moving. "Tobacco is an irritant, a drug, and a carcinogen. If I gave you a cigarette I would be giving you cancer."

"Don't be a hypocrite!" Jason snapped, inwardly pleased at the rewarding flush in the other's neck. "They've taken the cancer-producing agents out of tobacco for centuries now. And if they hadn't—how does that affect this situation? You're taking me to Cassylia to certain death. So why should you concern yourself with the state of my lungs in the future?"

"I had not considered it that way. It is just that there are certain rules of life—"

"Are there?" Jason broke in, keeping the initiative and the advantage. "Not as many as you like to think. And you people who are always dreaming up the rules never carry your thinking far enough. You are against drugs. Which drugs? What about the tannic acid in that tea you're drinking? Or the caffeine in it? It's loaded with caffeine—a drug that is both a strong stimulant and a diuretic. That's why you won't find tea in spacesuit canteens. That's a case of a drug forbidden for a good reason. Can you justify your cigarette ban the same way?''

Mikah was about to speak, then thought for a moment. "Perhaps you are right. I am tired, and it is not important." He warily took the cigarette case from Jason's pocket and dropped it onto the tray. Jason didn't attempt to interfere. Mikah poured himself a third cup of tea with a slightly apologetic air.

"You must excuse me, Jason, for attempting to make you conform to my own standards. When you are in pursuit of the big Truths, you sometimes let the little Truths slip. I am not intolerant, but I do tend to expect everyone else to live up to certain criteria I have set for myself. Humility is something we should never forget, and I thank you for reminding me of it. The search for Truth is hard.''

"There is no Truth," Jason told him, the anger and insult gone now from his voice, since he wanted to keep his captor involved in the conversation. Involved enough to forget about the free wrist for a while. He raised the cup to his lips and let the tea touch his lips without drinking any. The half-full cup supplied an unconsidered reason for his free hand.

"No Truth?" Mikah weighed the thought. "You can't possibly mean that. The galaxy is filled with Truth; it's the touchstone of Life itself. It's the thing that separates Mankind from the animals.''

"There is no Truth, no Life, no Mankind. At least not the way you spell them—with capital letters. They don't exist.''

Mikah's taut skin contracted into a furrow of concentration. "You will have to explain yourself," he said. "For you are not being clear.''

"I'm afraid it's you who aren't being clear. You're making a reality where none exists. Truth—with a small *t*—is a description, a relationship. A way to describe a statement. A semantic tool. But Truth with a capital *T* is an imaginary word, a noise with no meaning. It pretends to be a noun, but it has no referent. It stands for nothing. It means nothing. When you say, 'I believe in Truth,' you are really saying, 'I believe in nothing.' ''

"You are incredibly wrong!" Mikah said, leaning forward, stabbing with his finger. "Truth is a philosophical abstraction, one of the tools that our minds have used to raise us above the beasts—

the proof that we are not beasts ourselves, but a higher order of creation. Beasts can be true—but they cannot know Truth. Beasts can see, but they cannot see Beauty."

"Arrgh!" Jason growled. "It's impossible to talk to you, much less enjoy any comprehensible exchange of ideas. We aren't even speaking the same language. Forgetting for the moment who is right and who is wrong, we should go back to basics and at least agree on the meaning of the terms that we are using. To begin with—can you define the difference between *ethics* and *ethos?*"

"Of course," Mikah snapped, a glint of pleasure in his eyes at the thought of a good rousing round of hairsplitting. "Ethics is the discipline dealing with what is good or bad, or right and wrong—or with moral duty and obligation. Ethos means the guiding beliefs, standards, or ideals that characterize a group or community."

"Very good. I can see that you have been spending the long spaceship nights with your nose buried in the books. Now make sure the difference between those two terms is very clear, because it is the heart of the little communication problem we have here. Ethos is inextricably linked with a single society and cannot be separated from it, or it loses all meaning. Do you agree?"

"Well . . ."

"Come, come—you *have* to agree on the terms of your own definition. The ethos of a group is just a catch-all term for the ways in which the members of a group rub against each other. Right?"

Mikah reluctantly gave a nod of acquiescence.

"Now that we agree about that, we can push on one step further. Ethics, again by your definition, must deal with any number of societies or groups. If there are any absolute laws of ethics, they must be so inclusive that they can be applied to *any* society. A law of ethics must be as universal of application, as is the law of gravity."

"I don't follow you. . . ."

"I didn't think you would when I got to this point. You people who prattle about your Universal Laws never really consider the exact meaning of the term. My knowledge of the history of science is a little vague, but I'm willing to bet that the first Law of Gravity ever dreamed up stated that things fell at such and such a speed, and accelerated at such and such a rate. That's not a law, but an observation that isn't even complete until you add 'on this planet.' On a planet with a different mass there will be a different observation. The *law* of gravity is the formula:

$$F = \frac{mM}{d^2}$$

and this can be used to compute the force of gravity between any two bodies anywhere. This is a way of expressing fundamental and unalterable principles that apply in all circumstances. If you are going to have any real ethical laws they will have to have this same universality. They will have to work on Cassylia or Pyrrus, or on any planet or in any society you can find. Which brings us back to you. What you so grandly call—with capital letters and a flourish of trumpets—'Law of Ethics' aren't laws at all, but are simply little chunks of tribal ethos, aboriginal observations made by a gang of desert sheepherders to keep order in the house—or tent. These rules aren't capable of any universal application; even you must see that. Just think of the different planets that you have been on, and the number of weird and wonderful ways people have of reacting to each other—then try and visualize ten rules of conduct that would be applicable in all these societies. An impossible task. Yet I'll bet that you have ten rules you want me to obey, and if one of them is wasted on an injunction against saying prayers to carved idols, I can imagine just how universal the other nine are. You aren't being ethical if you try to apply them wherever you go—you're just finding a particularly fancy way to commit suicide!''

''You are being insulting!''

''I hope so. If I can't reach you in any other way, perhaps insult will jar you out of your state of moral smugness. How dare you even consider having me tried for stealing money from the Cassylia casino, when all I was doing was conforming to their own code of ethics! They run crooked gambling games, so the law under their local ethos must be that crooked gambling is the norm. So I cheated them, conforming to their norm. If they have also passed a law that says cheating at gambling is illegal, the *law* is unethical, not the cheating. If you are bringing me back to be tried by that law you are unethical, and I am the helpless victim of an evil man.''

''Limb of Satan!'' Mikah shouted, leaping to his feet and pacing back and forth before Jason, clasping and unclasping his hands with agitation. ''You seek to confuse me with your semantics and so-called ethics, which are simply opportunism and greed. There is a Higher Law that cannot be argued—''

''That is an impossible statement—and I can prove it.'' Jason pointed at the books on the wall. ''I can prove it with your own books, some of that light reading on the shelf there. Not the Aquinas—too thick. But the little volume with 'Lull' on the spine. Is that Ramon Lull's *The Booke of the Ordre of Chyvalry?*''

Mikah's eyes widened. ''You know the book? You're acquainted with Lull's writing?''

"Of course," Jason said, with an offhandedness he did not feel, since this was the only book in the collection he could remember reading; the odd title had stuck in his head. "Now let me see it, and I shall prove to you what I mean." There was no way to tell from the unchanged naturalness of his words that this was the moment he had been working carefully towards. He sipped the tea, none of his tenseness showing.

Mikah Samon took the book down and handed it to him.

Jason flipped through the pages while he talked. "Yes . . . yes, this is perfect. An almost ideal example of your kind of thinking. Do you like to read Lull?"

"Inspirational!" Mikah answered, his eyes shining. "There is beauty in every line, and Truths that we have forgotten in the rush of modern life. A reconciliation and proof of the interrelationship between the Mystical and the Concrete. By manipulation of symbols, he explains everything by absolute logic."

"He proves nothing about nothing," Jason said emphatically. "He plays word games. He takes a word, gives it an abstract and unreal value, then proves this value by relating it to other words with the same sort of nebulous antecedents. His facts aren't facts—they're just meaningless sounds. This is the key point, where your universe and mine differ. You live in this world of meaningless facts that have no existence. My word contains facts that can be weighed, tested, proven related to other facts in a logical manner. My facts are unshakeable and unarguable. They exist."

"Show me one of your unshakeable facts," Mikah said, voice calmer now than Jason's.

"Over there," Jason said. "The large green book over the console. It contains facts that even you will agree are true—I'll eat every page if you don't. Hand it to me." He sounded angry, making overly bold statements, and Mikah fell right into the trap. He handed the volume to Jason, using both hands, for it was very thick, metal-bound, and heavy.

"Now listen closely and try and understand, even if it is difficult for you," Jason said, opening the book. Mikah smiled wryly at this assumption of his ignorance. "This is a stellar ephemeris, just as packed with facts as an egg is with meat. In some ways it is a history of mankind. Now look at the jump screen there on the control console and you will see what I mean. Do you see the horizontal green line? Well, that's our course."

"Since this is my ship and I am piloting it, I am aware of that," Mikah said. "Proceed with your proof."

"Bear with me," Jason told him. "I'll try to keep it simple.

Now, the red dot on the green line is our ship's position. The number above the screen is our next navigational point, the spot where a star's gravitational field is strong enough to be detected in jump space. The number is the star's code listing. BD89-046-229. I look it up in the book"—he quickly flipped the pages— "and find its listing. No name. A row of code symbols, though, that tells a lot about it. This little symbol means that there is a planet or planets suitable for man to live on. It doesn't say, though, if any people are there."

"Where does this all lead to?" Mikah asked.

"Patience—you'll see in a moment. Now look at the screen. The green dot approaching on the course line is the PMP—Point of Maximum Proximity. When the red dot and green dot coincide . . ."

"Give me that book," Mikah ordered, stepping forward, aware suddenly that something was wrong. He was just an instant too late.

"Here's your proof," Jason said, and hurled the heavy book through the jump screen into the delicate circuits behind. Before it hit, he had thrown the second book. There was a tinkling crash, a flare of light, and the crackle of shorted circuits.

The floor gave a tremendous heave as the relays snapped open, dropping the ship through into normal space.

Mikah grunted in pain, clubbed to the floor by the suddenness of the transition. Locked in the chair, Jason fought the heaving of his stomach and the blackness before his eyes. As Mikah dragged himself to his feet, Jason took careful aim and sent the tray and dishes hurtling into the smoking ruin of the jump computer.

"There's your fact," he said in cheerful triumph. "Your incontrovertible, gold-plated, uranium-cored fact.

"We're not going to Cassylia any more!"

3

"You have killed us both," Mikah said, his face strained and white, but his voice under control.

"Not quite," Jason told him cheerily. "But I have killed the jump control so we can't get to another star. However, there's nothing wrong with our space drive, so we can make a landing on one of the planets—you saw for yourself that there is at least one suitable for habitation."

"Where I will fix the jump drive and continue the voyage to Cassylia. You will have gained nothing."

"Perhaps," Jason answered in his most noncommittal voice, for he did not have the slightest intention of continuing the trip, no matter what Mikah Samon thought.

His captor had reached the same conclusion. "Put your hand back on the chair arm," he ordered, and locked the cuff into place again. He stumbled as the drive started and the ship changed direction. "What was that?" he asked.

"Emergency control. The ship's computer knows that something drastic is wrong, so it has taken over. You can override it with the manuals, but don't bother yet. The ship can do a better job than either of us, with its senses and stored data. It will find the planet we're looking for, plot a course, and get us there with the most economy of time and fuel. When we get into the atmosphere you can take over and look for a spot to set down."

"I do not believe a word you say now," Mikah said grimly. "I am going to take control and get a call out on the emergency band. Someone will hear it."

As he started forward the ship lurched again and all the lights went out. In the darkness, flames could be seen flashing inside the controls. There was a hiss of foam and they vanished. With a weak flicker the emergency lighting circuit came on.

"I shouldn't have thrown the Ramon Lull book," Jason said. "The ship can't stomach it any more than I could."

"You are irreverent and profane," Mikah said through his clenched teeth, as he went to the controls. "You attempt to kill us both. You have no respect for your own life or mine. You are a man who deserves the worst punishment the law allows."

"I'm a gambler," Jason laughed, "not at all as bad as you say. I take chances—but I only take them when the odds are right. You were carrying me back to certain death. The worst my wrecking the controls can do is to administer the same fate. So I took a chance. There is a bigger risk factor for you, of course, but I'm afraid I didn't take that into consideration. After all, this entire affair is your idea. You'll just have to take the consequences of your own actions, and not scold me for them."

"You are perfectly right," Mikah said quietly. "I should have been more alert. Now will you tell me what to do to save *both* our lives. None of the controls work.''

"None! Did you try the emergency override? The big red switch under the safety housing.''

"I did. It is dead too.''

Jason slumped back into the seat. It was a moment before he could speak. "Read one of your books, Mikah,'' he said at last. "Seek consolation in your philosophy. There's nothing we can do. It's all up to the computer now, and whatever is left of the circuits.''

"Can we help—can we repair anything?''

"Are you a ship technician? I'm not. We would probably do more harm than good.''

It took two ship-days of very erratic flight to reach the planet. A haze of clouds obscured the atmosphere. They approached from the night side, and no details were visible. Or lights.

"If there were cities we would see their lights—wouldn't we?'' Mikah asked.

"Not necessarily. Could be storms. Could be enclosed cities. Could be only ocean in this hemisphere.''

"Or it could be that there are no people down there,'' Mikah said. "Even if the ship should get us down safely, what will it matter? We will be trapped for the rest of our lives on this lost planet, at the end of the universe.''

"Don't be so cheerful,'' Jason said. "How about taking off these cuffs while we go down? It will probably be a rough landing and I'd like to have some kind of a chance.''

Mikah frowned at him. "Will you give me your word of honor that you will not try to escape during the landing?''

"No. And if I gave it—would you believe it? If you let me loose, you take your chances. Let's neither of us think it will be any different.''

"I have my duty to do,'' Mikah said. Jason remained locked in the chair.

They were in the atmosphere, and the gentle sighing against the hull quickly climbed the scale to a shrill scream. The drive cut out and they were in free fall. Air friction heated the outer hull white-hot, and the interior temperature quickly rose in spite of the cooling unit.

"What is happening?'' Mikah asked. "You are more acquainted with these matters. Are we through—are we going to crash?''

"Maybe. It can only be one of two things. Either the whole works have folded up—in which case we are going to be scattered in very small pieces all over the landscape; or the computer is saving itself for one last effort. I hope that's it. They build computers smart these days, all sorts of problem-solving circuits. The hull and engines are in good shape—but the controls are spotty and unreliable. In a case like this, a good human pilot would let the ship drop as far and fast as it could before switching on the drive. Then he'd turn it on full—thirteen G's or more, whatever he figured the passengers could take on the couches. The hull would take a beating, but who cares? The control circuits would be used the shortest amount of time in the simplest manner.''

"Do you think that is happening now?" Mikah asked, getting into his acceleration chair.

"That's what I *hope* is happening. Are you going to unlock the cuffs before you go to bed? It could be a bad landing, and we might want to go places in a hurry."

Mikah considered, then took out his gun. "I will unlock you, but I intend to shoot if you try anything. Once we are down, you will be locked again."

"Thanks for small blessings," Jason said when he was free, rubbing his wrists.

Deceleration jumped on them, kicked the air from their lungs in uncontrollable gasps, sank them deep into the yielding couches. Mikah's gun was pressed into his chest, too heavy to lift. It made no difference—Jason could not stand nor move. He hovered on the border of consciousness, his vision flickering behind a black and red haze.

Just as suddenly the pressure was gone.

They were still falling.

The drive groaned in the stern of the ship, and relays chattered. But it didn't start again. The two men stared at each other, unmoving, for the unmeasurable unit of time that the ship fell.

As the ship dropped it turned, and it hit at an angle. The end came for Jason in an engulfing wave of thunder, shock, and pain. The sudden impact pushed him against the restraining straps, burst them with the inertia of his body, hurled him across the control room. His last conscious thought was to protect his head. He was lifting his arms when he struck the wall.

There is a cold that is so chilling it is a pain, not a temperature. A cold that slices into the flesh before it numbs and kills.

Jason came to with the sound of his own voice crying hoarsely. The cold was so great it filled the universe. It was cold water, he realized as he coughed it from his mouth and nose. Something was around him, and it took an effort to recognize it as Mikah's arm; he was holding Jason's face above the surface while he swam. A receding blackness in the water could only have been the ship, giving off bubbles and groans as it died. The cold water didn't hurt now, and Jason was just relaxing when he felt something solid under his feet.

"Stand up and walk, curse you," Mikah gasped hoarsely. "I can't . . . carry you . . . can't carry myself. . . ."

They floundered out of the water side by side, four-legged crawling beasts that could not stand erect. Everything had an unreality about it, and Jason found it hard to think. He should not stop, that he was sure of, but what else could he do?

There was a flickering in the darkness, a wavering light coming towards them. Jason could not speak, but he heard Mikah cry out for help. The light came nearer; it was some kind of flare or torch, held high. Mikah pulled to his feet as the flame approached.

It was like a nightmare. It wasn't a man but a thing that held the flare. A thing of sharp angles, fang-faced and horrible. It had a clubbed extremity with which it struck down Mikah, who fell wordlessly, and the creature turned towards Jason. He had no strength to fight with, though he struggled to get to his feet. His fingers scratched at the frosted sand, but he could not rise; and exhausted with this last effort, he fell face down.

Unconsciousness pulled at his brain, but he would not submit. The flickering torchlight came closer, and the scuffle of heavy feet in the sand. He could not have this horror behind him, and with the last of his strength he levered himself over and lay on his back, staring up at the thing that stood over him, with the darkness of exhaustion filming his eyes.

4

It did not kill him at once, but stood staring down at him; and as the slow seconds ticked by and Jason was still alive, he forced himself to consider this menace that had appeared from the blackness.

"*K'e vi stas el* . . . ?" the creature said, and for the first time

Jason realized it was human. The meaning of the question picked at the edge of his exhausted brain; he felt he could almost understand it, though he had never heard the language before. He tried to answer, but there was only a hoarse gurgle from his throat.

"*Ven k'n torcoy—r'pidu!*"

More lights sprang from the darkness inland, and with them the sound of running feet. As they came closer, Jason had a clearer look at the man above him and could understand why he had mistaken him for some non-human creature. His limbs were completely wrapped in lengths of stained leather, his chest and body protected by thick overlapping leather plates covered with blood-red designs. Over his head was fitted the cochleate-shell of some animal, spiraling to a point in front; two small openings had been drilled in it for eye holes. Great, finger-long teeth had been set in the lower edge of the shell to heighten the already fearsome appearance. The only thing at all human about the creature was the matted and filthy beard that trickled out of the shell before the teeth. There were too many other details for Jason to absorb quickly; something bulky was slung behind one shoulder, dark objects at the waist; a heavy club reached and prodded Jason in the ribs, and he was too close to unconsciousness to resist.

A guttural command halted the torchbearers a full five meters from the spot where Jason lay. He wondered vaguely why the armored man had not let them approach closer, since the light from their torches barely reached this far; everything on this planet seemed inexplicable.

For a few moments Jason must have lost consciousness, for when he looked again the torch was stuck in the sand at his side and the armored man had one of Jason's boots off and was pulling at the other. Jason could only writhe feebly but could not prevent the theft; for some reason he could not force his body to follow his will. His sense of time seemed to have altered as well, and though every second dragged heavily by, events occurred with startling rapidity. The boots were gone now and the man fumbled at Jason's clothes, stopping every few seconds to glance up at the row of torchbearers.

The magnetic seals were alien to the strange creature, the sharp teeth sewn onto the leather over his knuckles dug into Jason's flesh as he struggled to open the seals or to tear the resistant metalcloth. He was growling with impatience when he accidentally touched the release button on the medikit and it dropped into his hand. This shining gadget seemed to please him; but when one of the sharp needles slipped through his thick handcoverings and stabbed him he howled with rage, throwing the machine down, and grinding it into a splintered ruin in the sand. The loss of his irreplaceable device goaded Jason into motion: he sat up and was trying to reach the medikit when unconsciousness surged over him.

Sometime before dawn the pain in his head drove him reluctantly back to awareness. There were some foul-smelling hides draped over him that retained a little of his body heat. He pulled away the stifling fold that covered his face and stared up at the stars, cold points of light that glittered in the frigid night. The air was a stimulant, and he sucked in deep gasps of it that burned his throat but seemed to clear his thoughts. For the first time he realized that his disorientation had been caused by that crack on the head he had received while the ship crashed; his exploring fingers found a swollen rawness on his skull. He must have a brain concussion: that would explain his earlier inability to move or think straight. The cold air was numbing his face, and he willingly pulled the hairy skin back over his head.

He wondered what had happened to Mikah Samon after the local thug in the horror outfit had bashed him with the club. This was a messy and unexpected end for the man after he had managed to survive the crash of the ship. Jason had no special affection for the undernourished zealot, but he did owe him a life. Mikah had saved him after the crash, only to be murdered himself by this assassin.

Jason made a mental note to kill the man just as soon as he was physically up to it; at the same time he was a little astonished at his reflexive acceptance of the need for this bloodthirsty atonement of a life for a life. Apparently his long stay on Pyrrus had trodden down his normal dislike for killing except in self-defense, and from what he had seen so far of this world the Pyrran training would certainly be most useful. The sky showed grey through a tear in the hide and he pushed the covering back to look at the dawn.

Mikah Samon lay next to him, his head projecting from a covering fur. His hair was matted and caked with dark blood, but he was still breathing.

"Harder to kill than I thought," Jason muttered as he levered himself painfully up onto one elbow and took a good look at this world where his spaceship sabotage had landed him.

It was a grim desert, lumped with huddled bodies, like the aftermath of a battle at world's end. A few of them were stumbling to their feet, holding their skins around them, the only signs of life in that immense waste of gritty sand. On one side a ridge of dunes cut off sight of the sea, but he could hear the dull boom of waves on the shore. White frost rimed the ground and the chill wind made his eyes blink and water. On the top of the dunes a remembered figure suddenly appeared, the armored man, doing something with what appeared to be lengths of rope; there was a metallic tinkling, suddenly cut off. Mikah Samon groaned and stirred.

"How do you feel?" Jason asked. "Those are two of the finest bloodshot eyes I have ever seen."

"Where am I . . . ?"

"Now, that is a bright and original question—I didn't pick you for the type who watched historical space opera on the TV. I have no idea where we are—but I can give you a brief synopsis of how we arrived here, if you are up to it."

"I remember we swam ashore, then something evil came from the darkness, like a demon from hell. We fought . . ."

"And he bashed in your head—one quick blow, and that was about all the fight there was. I had a better look at your demon, though I was in no better condition to fight him than you were. He's a man dressed in a weird outfit out of an addict's nightmare, and he appears to be the boss of this crew of rugged campers. Other than that, I have little idea of what is going on—except that he stole my boots, and I'm going to get them back if I have to kill him for them."

"Do not lust after material things," Mikah intoned seriously. "And do not talk of killing a man for material gain. You are evil, Jason, and . . . My boots are gone—and my clothes too!"

Mikah had thrown back his covering skins and made this startling discovery. "Belial!" he roared. "Asmodeus, Abaddon, Apollyon, and Baal-zebub!"

"Very nice," Jason said admiringly. "You really have been studying up on your demonology. Were you just listing them—or calling on them for aid?"

"Silence, blasphemer! I have been robbed!" He rose to his feet, and the wind whistling around his almost bare body quickly gave his skin a faint touch of blue. "I am going to find the evil creature that did this and force him to return what is mine."

Mikah turned to leave, but Jason reached out and grabbed his ankle with a wrestling grip, twisted it, and brought the man thudding to the ground. The fall dazed him, and Jason pulled the skins back over the rawboned form.

"We're even," Jason said. "You saved my life last night; just now I saved yours. You're bare-handed and wounded—while the old man of the mountain up there is a walking armory, and anyone with the personality to wear that kind of an outfit will kill you as easily as he picks his teeth. So take it easy and try to avoid trouble.

There's a way out of this mess—there's a way out of *every* mess if you look for it—and I'm going to find it. In fact, I'm going to take a walk right now and start my research. Agreed?''

A groan was the only answer, for Mikah was unconscious again, fresh blood seeping from his injured scalp. Jason stood up and wrapped the hides about his body as some protection from the wind, tying the loose ends together. Then he kicked through the sand until he found a smooth rock that would fit inside his fist with just the end protruding, and thus armed he made his way through the stirring forms of the sleepers.

When he returned, Mikah was conscious again, and the sun was well above the horizon. The people were all awake now, a shuffling, scratching herd of about thirty men, women, and children. They were identical in their filth and crude skin wrappings, milling about with random movements, or sitting blankly on the ground. They showed no interest at all in the two strangers. Jason handed a tarred leather cup to Mikah and squatted next to him.

''Drink that. It's water, the only thing there seems to be here to drink. I didn't find any food.'' He still had the stone in his hand, and while he talked he rubbed it on the sand: the end was moist and red and some long hairs were stuck in it.

''I took a good look around this camp, and there's very little more than you can see from here. Just this crowd of broken-down types, with few bundles rolled in hide, and some of them are carrying skin water bottles. They have a simple me-stronger pecking order, so I pecked a bit and we can drink. Food comes next.''

''Who are they? What are they doing?'' Mikah asked, mumbling a little, obviously still suffering the aftereffects of the blow. Jason looked at the contused skull, and decided not to touch it. The wound had bled freely and the blood had now clotted. Washing it off with the highly dubious water would accomplish little, and might add infection to their other troubles.

''I'm only sure of one thing,'' Jason said. ''They're slaves. I don't know why they are here, what they are doing, or where they are going, but their status is painfully clear—ours too. Old Nasty up there on the hill is the boss. The rest of us are slaves.''

''Slaves!'' Mikah exclaimed, horrified, the word penetrating through the pain in his head. ''It is abominable. The slaves must be freed.''

''No lectures, please, and try to be realistic—even if it hurts. There are only two slaves that need freeing here, you and I. These people seem nicely adjusted to the *status quo*, and I see no reason to change it. I'm not starting any abolitionist campaigns until I can see my way clearly out of this mess, and I probably won't start any then either. This planet has been going on a long time without me, and will probably keep rolling along once I'm gone."

"Coward! You must fight for the Truth, and the Truth will make you free."

"I can hear those capital letters again," Jason groaned. "The only thing right now that is going to make me free is me. Which may be bad poetry, but it is still the truth. The situation here is rough but not unbeatable, so listen and learn. The boss—his name is Ch'aka—seems to have gone off on a hunt of some kind. He's not far away and will be back soon, so I'll try to give you the entire setup quickly. I thought I recognized the language, and I was right. It's a corrupt form of Esperanto, the language all the Terido worlds speak. This altered language, plus the fact that these people live about one step above the Stone Age culture, is pretty sure evidence that they are cut off from any contact with the rest of the galaxy, though I hope not. There may be a trading base somewhere on the planet, and if there is we'll find it later. We have enough other things to worry about right now, but at least we can speak the language. These people have contracted a lot of sounds and lost some, and they've even introduced a glottal stop—something that *no* language needs; but with a little effort the meaning can be made out."

"I do not speak Esperanto."

"Then learn it. It's easy enough, even in this jumbled form. Now keep still and listen. These creatures are born and bred slaves, and it is all they know. There is a little squabbling in the ranks, with the bigger ones pushing the work on the weak ones when Ch'aka isn't looking, but I have the situation well in hand. Ch'aka is our big problem, and we have to find out a lot more things before we can tackle him. He is boss, fighter, father, provider, and destiny for this mob, and he seems to know his job. So try to be a good slave for a while."

"Slave! I?" Mikah arched his back and tried to rise. Jason pushed him back to the ground—harder than was necessary.

"Yes, you—and me too. That is the only way we are going to survive in this arrangement. Do what everyone else does; obey orders, and you stand a good chance of staying alive until we can find a way out of this tangle."

Mikah's answer was drowned out in a roar from the dunes as Ch'aka returned. The slaves climbed quickly to their feet, grabbing up their bundles, and began to form a single wide-spaced line. Jason helped Mikah to stand and wrap strips of skin around his feet, then

supported most of his weight as they stumbled to a place in the open
formation. Once they were all in position, Ch'aka kicked the
nearest one and they began walking slowly forward, looking carefully at the ground as they went. Jason had no idea of the significance of this action, but as long as he and Mikah weren't bothered it
didn't matter: he had enough work cut out for him just to keep the
wounded man on his feet. Somehow Mikah managed to dredge up
enough strength to keep going.

One of the slaves pointed down and shouted, and the line
stopped. He was too far away for Jason to make out the cause of the
excitement, but the man bent over and scratched a hole with a short
length of pointed wood. In a few seconds he dug up something
round and not quite as big as his hand. He raised it over his head and
brought the thing to Ch'aka at a shambling run. The slave-master
took it and bit off a chunk, and when the man who had found it
turned away he gave him a lusty kick. The line moved forward
again.

Two more of the mysterious objects were found, both of which
Ch'aka ate. Only when his immediate hunger was satisfied did he
make any attempt to be the good provider. When the next one was
found he called over a slave and threw the object into a crudely
woven basket the slave was carrying on his back. After this the
basket-toting slave walked directly in front of Ch'aka, who was
carefully watchful that every one of the things that was dug up went
into the basket. Jason wondered what they were—and they were
edible, an angry rumbling in his stomach reminded him.

The slave next in line to Jason shouted and pointed to the sand.
Jason let Mikah sink to a sitting position when they stopped, and
watched with interest as the slave attacked the ground with his piece
of wood, scratching around a tiny sprig of green that projected from
the desert sand. His burrowings uncovered a wrinkled grey object, a
root or tuber of some kind, from which the green leaves were
growing. It appeared to Jason as edible as a piece of stone, but
obviously not to the slave, who drooled heavily and actually had the
temerity to sniff the root. Ch'aka howled with anger at this, and
when the slave had dropped the root into the basket with the others
he received a kick so strong that he had to limp back painfully to his
position in the line.

Soon after this Ch'aka called a halt, and the tattered slaves
huddled around while he poked through the basket. He called them
over one at a time and gave them one or more of the roots, according
to some merit system of his own. The basket was almost empty
when he poked his club at Jason.

"K'e nam h'vas vi?" he asked.

"Mia namo estas Jason, mia amiko estas Mikah."

Jason had answered in correct Esperanto, which Ch'aka seemed to understand well enough, for he grunted and dug through the contents of the basket. His masked face stared at them, and Jason could feel the impact of the unseen watching eyes. The club pointed again.

"Where you come from? That your ship that burn, sink?"

"That was our ship. We come from far away."

"From other side of ocean?" This was apparently the largest distance the slaver could imagine.

"From the other side of the ocean, correct." Jason was in no mood to deliver a lecture on astronomy. "When do we eat?"

"You a rich man in your country, got a ship, got shoes. Now I got your shoes. You a slave here. My slave. You both my slaves."

'I'm your slave, I'm your slave," Jason said resignedly. "But even slaves have to eat. Where's the food?"

Ch'aka grubbed around in the basket until he found a tiny withered root that he broke in half and threw onto the sand in front of Jason.

"Work hard, you get more."

Jason picked up the pieces and brushed away as much of the dirt as he could. He handed one piece to Mikah and took a tentative bite out of the other one: it was gritty with sand and tasted like slightly rancid wax. It took a distinct effort to eat the repulsive thing, but he did. Without a doubt it was food, no matter how unwholesome, and would do until something better came along.

"What did you talk about?" Mikah asked, grinding his own portion between his teeth.

"Just swapping lies. He thinks we're his slaves, and I agreed. But it's just temporary," Jason added as anger colored Mikah's face and he started to climb to his feet. Jason pulled him back down. "This is a strange planet; you're injured, we have no food or water, and no idea at all how to survive in this place. The only thing we can do to stay alive is to go along with what Old Ugly there says. If he wants to call us slaves, fine—we're slaves."

"Better to die free than to live in chains!"

"Will you stop the nonsense! Better to live in chains and learn how to get rid of them. That way you end up alive-free rather than dead-free, a much more attractive state. Now shut up and eat. We can't do anything until you are out of the walking-wounded class."

For the rest of the day the line of walkers plodded across the sand, and in addition to helping Mikah, Jason found two of the *krenoj*, the edible roots. They stopped before dusk and dropped gratefully to the sand. When the food was divided they received a slightly larger portion, as evidence perhaps of Jason's attention to the work. Both men were exhausted and fell asleep as soon as it was dark.

During the following morning they had their first break from the walking routine. Their food searching always paralleled the unseen sea, and one slave walked the crest of the dunes that hid the water from sight. He must have seen something of interest, for he leaped down from the mound and waved both arms wildly. Ch'aka ran heavily to the dunes and talked with the scout, then booted the man from his presence.

Jason watched with growing interest as he unwrapped the bulky package slung from his back and disclosed an efficient-looking crossbow, cocking it by winding on a built-in crank. This complicated and deadly piece of machinery seemed very much out of place with the primitive slave-holding society, and Jason wished that he could get a better look at the device. Ch'aka fumbled a quarrel from another pouch and fitted it to the bow.

The slaves sat silently on the sand while their master stalked along the base of the dunes, then wormed his way over them and out of sight, creeping silently on his stomach. A few minutes later there was a scream of pain from behind the dunes and all the slaves jumped to their feet and raced to see. Jason left Mikah where he lay and was in the first rank of observers that broke over the hillocks and onto the shore.

They stopped at the usual distance and shouted compliments about the quality of the shot and what a mighty hunter Ch'aka was. Jason had to admit there was a certain truth in the claims. A large, furred amphibian lay at the water's edge, the fletched end of the crossbow bolt projecting from its thick neck and a thin stream of blood running down to mix with the surging waves.

"Meat! Meat today!"

"Ch'aka kills the *rosmaro!* Ch'aka is wonderful!"

"Hail, Ch'aka, great provider!" Jason shouted to get into the swing of things. "When do we eat?"

The master ignored his slaves, sitting heavily on the dune until he regained his breath after the stalk. Then, after cocking the crossbow again, he went over to the beast and with his knife cut out the quarrel, notching it against the bowstring still dripping with blood.

"Get wood for fire," he commanded. "You, Opisweni, you use the knife."

Shuffling backwards, Ch'aka sat down on a hillock and pointed the crossbow at the slave who approached the kill. Ch'aka had left his knife in the animal and Opisweni pulled it free and began methodically to flay and butcher the beast. All the time he worked he carefully kept his back turned to Ch'aka and the aimed bow.

"A trusting soul, our slave driver," Jason said to himself as he joined the others in searching the shore for driftwood. Ch'aka had the weapons, but he had a constant fear of assassination as well. If Opisweni tried to use the knife for anything other than the intended piece of work, he would get the crossbow quarrel in the back of his head. Very efficient.

Enough driftwood was found to make a sizable fire, and when Jason returned with his contribution the *rosmaro* had been hacked into large chunks. Ch'aka kicked his slaves away from the heap of wood and produced a small device from another of his sacks. Interested, Jason pushed as close as he dared, into the front rank of the watching circle. Though he had never seen a firemaker before, the operation of it was obvious to him. A spring-loaded arm drove a fragment of stone against a piece of steel, sparks flew out and were caught in a cup of tinder, where Ch'aka blew on them until they burst into flame.

Where had the firemaker and the crossbow come from? They were evidence of a higher level of culture than that possessed by those slave-holding nomads. This was the first bit of evidence Jason had seen that there might be more to the cultural life of this planet than they had seen since their landing. Later, while the others were gorging themselves on the seared meat, he drew Mikah aside and pointed this out.

"There's hope yet. These illiterate thugs never manufactured that crossbow or firemaker. We must find out where they came from, and see about getting there ourselves. I had a look at the quarrel when Ch'aka pulled it out, and I'll swear that it was turned from a piece of steel."

"This has significance?" Mikah asked, puzzled.

"It means an industrial society, and possible interstellar contact."

"Then we must ask Ch'aka where he obtained them and leave at once. There will be authorities, we will contact them, explain the situation, obtain transportation to Cassylia. I will not place you under arrest again until that time."

"How considerate of you!" Jason said, lifting one eyebrow. Mikah was absolutely impossible, and Jason probed at his moral armor to see if there were any weak spots. "Won't you feel guilty about bringing me back to get killed? After all, we are companions in trouble—and I did save your life."

"I will grieve, Jason. I can see that though you are evil you are not completely evil, and given the right training could be fitted for a useful place in society. But my personal grief must not be allowed to alter events: you forget that you committed a crime and must pay the penalty."

Ch'aka belched cavernously inside his shell helmet and howled at his slaves.

"Enough eating, you pigs! You get fat! Wrap the meat and carry it—we have light yet to look for *krenoj*. Move!"

Once more the line was formed and began its slow pace across the desert. More of the edible roots were found, and once they stopped briefly to fill the waterbags at a spring that bubbled up out of the sand. The sun dropped towards the horizon, and what little warmth it possessed was absorbed by a bank of clouds. Jason looked around and shivered; then he noticed the line of dots moving on the horizon. He nudged Mikah, who still leaned heavily on him.

"Looks like company coming. I wonder where they fit into the program."

Pain had blurred Mikah's attention and he took no notice and, surprisingly enough, neither did any of the other slaves, nor Ch'aka. The dots expanded and became another row of marchers, apparently absorbed in the same task as Ch'aka's group. They plodded forward, making a slow examination of the sand, and were followed behind by the solitary figure of their master. The two lines slowly approached each other, paralleling the shore.

Near the dunes was a crude mound of stones and Ch'aka's line of slaves stopped as soon as they reached it, dropping with satisfied grunts onto the sand. The cairn was obviously a border marker, and Ch'aka went to it and rested his foot on one of the stones, watching while the other line of slaves approached. They too stopped at the cairn and settled to the ground: both groups stared with dull-eyed lack of interest, and only the slave-masters showed any animation. The other master stopped a good ten paces before he reached Ch'aka and waved an evil-looking stone hammer over his head.

"Hate you, Ch'aka!" he roared.

"Hate you, Fasimba!" boomed back the answer.

The exchange was as formal as a *pas de deux*, and just about as war-like. Both men shook their weapons and shouted a few insults, then settled down to a quiet conversation. Fasimba was garbed in the same type of hideous and fear-inspiring outfit as Ch'aka, differing only in details. Instead of a conch, Fasimba's head was encased in the skull of one of the amphibious *rosmaroj*, brightened up with some extra tusks and horns. The differences between the two men were minor, and mostly a matter of decoration or variation of weapon design. They were obviously slave-masters and equals.

"Killed a *rosmaro* today, second time in ten days," Ch'aka said.

"You got a good piece coast. Plenty *rosmaroj*. Where the two slaves you owe me?"

"I owe you two slaves?"

"You owe me two slaves. Don't play like stupid. I got the iron arrows for you from the *d'zertanoj*. One slave you paid with died. You still owe other one."

"I got two slaves for you. I got two slaves I pulled out of the ocean."

"You got a good piece coast."

Ch'aka walked down his line of slaves until he came to the overbold one he had half crippled with a kick the day before. Pulling him to his feet, he booted him towards the other group.

"Here a good one," he said, delivering the goods with a parting kick.

"Looks skinny. Not too good."

"No, all muscles. Works hard. Doesn't eat much."

"You're a liar!"

"Hate you, Fasimba!"

"Hate you, Ch'aka! Where's the other one?"

"Got a good one. Stranger from the ocean. He can tell you funny stories, work hard."

Jason turned in time to avoid the full force of the kick, but it was still strong enough to knock him sprawling. Before he could get up, Ch'aka had clutched Mikah Samon by the arm and dragged him across the invisible line to the other group of slaves. Fasimba stalked over to examine him, prodding him with a spiked toe.

"Don't look good. Big hole on the head."

"He works hard," Ch'aka said. "Hole almost healed. He very strong."

"You give me new one if he dies?" Fasimba asked doubtfully.

"I'll give you. Hate you, Fasimba!"

"Hate *you*, Ch'aka!"

The slave herds were prodded to their feet and moved back the way they had come.

Jason shouted to Ch'aka. "Wait! Don't sell my friend. We work better together. You can get rid of someone else . . ."

The slaves gaped at this sudden outburst and Ch'aka wheeled, raising his club.

"You shut up. You're a slave. You tell me once more to do what and I kill you."

Jason kept still, since it was obvious that this was the only thing he could do. He had a few qualms about Mikah's possible fate: if he survived the wound, he was certainly not the type to bow to the inevitabilities of slave-holding life. But Jason had done his best to save him, and that was that. Now Jason would think about Jason for a while.

They made a brief march before dark, just until the other slaves were out of sight; then they stopped for the night. Jason settled himself into the lee of a mound that broke the force of the wind a bit and unwrapped a piece of scorched meat he had salvaged from the earlier feast. It was tough and oily, but far superior to the barely edible *krenoj* that made up the greater part of the native diet. He chewed noisily on the bone and watched while one of the other slaves sidled over towards him.

"Give me some your meat?" the slave asked in a whining voice, and only when she had spoken did Jason realize that this was a girl; all the slaves looked alike in their matted hair and skin wrappings. He ripped off a chunk of meat.

"Here. Sit down and eat it. What's your name?" In exchange for his generosity, he intended to get some information from the girl.

"Ijale." Still standing, she tore at the meat, held tightly in one fist while the index finger of her free hand scratched in her tangled hair.

"Where do you come from? Did you always live here—like this?" How do you ask a slave if she has always been a slave?

"Not here. I come from Bul'wajo first, then Fasimba, now I belong to Ch'aka."

"What or who is Bul'wajo? Someone like our boss Ch'aka?"

She nodded, gnawing at the meat.

"And the *d'zertanoj* that Fasimba gets his arrows from—who are they?"

"You don't know much," she said, finishing the meat and licking the grease from her fingers.

"I know enough to have meat when you don't have any—so don't abuse my hospitality. Who are the *d'zertanoj*?"

"Everyone knows who they are." She shrugged with incomprehension and looked for a soft spot in the sand to sit down. "They live in the desert. They go around in *caroj*. They stink. They have many nice things. One of them gave me my best thing. If I show it to you, you won't take it?"

"No, I won't touch it. But I would like to see anything they have made. Here, here's some more meat. Now let me see your best thing."

Ijale rooted in her skins for a hidden pocket and dragged out something concealed in her clenched fist. She held out her hand proudly and opened it, and there was enough light left for Jason to make out the rough form of a red glass bead.

"Isn't this very nice?" she asked.

"Very nice," Jason agreed, and for an instant felt a touch of real compassion when he looked at the pathetic bauble. The girl's ancestors had come to this planet in spaceships, with a knowledge of the most advanced sciences. Cut off, their children had degenerated into this: barely conscious slaves, who could prize a worthless piece of glass above all things.

"All right now," Ijale said, settling into the sand on her back. She unwrapped some skins and began to pull the others up around her waist.

"Relax," Jason told her. "The meat was a present—you don't have to pay for it."

"You don't want me?" she asked, surprised, pulling the skins back over her bare legs. "You do not like me? You think I am too ugly?"

"You're lovely," Jason lied. "Let's just say that I'm too tired."

Was the girl ugly or lovely? He couldn't tell. Her unwashed and tangled hair covered half of her face, while dirt threw an obscuring film over the rest. Her lips were chapped raw, and a red bruise covered one cheek.

"Let me stay with you tonight, even if you are too old to want me. Mzil'kazi wants me all the time, and he hurts me. See, there he is now."

The man she pointed to was watching from a healthy distance and skittered back even further when Jason looked up.

"Don't worry about Mzil'," Jason said. "We settled our relationship the first day I was here. You may have noticed the bump on his head." He reached for a rock and the watcher ran swiftly away.

"I like you. I'll show you my best thing again."

"I like you too. No, not now. Too many good things too fast will only spoil me. Good night."

5

Ijale stayed near Jason the next day, and took the next station in line when the endless *krenoj* hunt began. Whenever it was possible he questioned her, and before noon had extracted all of her meager knowledge of affairs beyond the barren coastal plain where they lived. The ocean was a mystery that produced edible animals, fish, and an occasional human corpse. Ships could be seen from time to time offshore, but nothing was known about them. On the other side the territory was bounded by desert even more inhospitable than the one in which they scratched out their existence—a waste of lifeless sand, habitable only by the *d'zertanoj* and their mysterious *caroj*. These last might be animals—or perhaps mechanical transportation of some kind; either was possible from Ijale's vague description. Ocean, coast, and desert—these made up all of her world, and she could conceive of nothing that might exist beyond.

Jason knew there was more; the crossbow was proof enough of that, and he had every intention of finding out where it came from. In order to do that he was going to have to change his slave status when the proper time came. He was developing a certain facility in dodging Ch'aka's heavy boot; the work was never hard, and there was ample food. Being a slave left him with no responsibilities other than obeying orders, and he had ample opportunity to discover what he could about this planet, so that when he finally did leave it he would be as well prepared as was possible.

Later in the day another column of marching slaves was sighted in the distance, on a course parelleling their own, and Jason expected a repeat performance of the previous day's meeting. He was agreeably surprised that it was not. The sight of the others threw Ch'aka into an immediate rage that sent his slaves rushing for safety in all directions. By leaping into the air, howling with anger, and beating his club against his thick leather armor, he managed to work himself into quite a state before starting off on a slogging run. Jason followed close behind him, greatly interested by this new turn of affairs.

Ahead of them the other group of slaves scattered, and from their midst burst another armed and armored figure. The two leaders churned towards each other at top speed, and Jason hoped for a shattering crash when they met. However, they slowed before they hit and began circling each other, spitting curses.

"Hate you, M'shika!"

"Hate you, Ch'aka!"

The words were the same, but they were shouted with fierce meaning, with no touch of formality this time.

"Kill you, M'shika! You coming again on my part of the ground with your carrion-meat slaves!"

"You lie, Ch'aka—this ground mine from way back."

"I kill you way back!"

Ch'aka leaped in as he screamed the words and swung a blow with his club that would have broken the other man in two if it had connected. But M'shika was expecting this and fell back, swinging a counterblow with his own club, which Ch'aka easily avoided. There followed a quick exchange of clubwork that did little more than fan the air, until suddenly both men were locked together and the fight began in earnest.

They rolled together on the ground, grunting savagely, tearing at each other. The heavy clubs were of no use this close and were dropped in favor of knives and knees: Jason could understand now why Ch'aka had the long tusks strapped to his kneecaps. It was a no-holds-barred fight, and each man was trying as hard as possible to kill his opponent. The leather armor made this difficult and the struggle continued, littering the sand with broken-off animal teeth, discarded weapons, and other debris. It looked as if it would be a draw, when both men separated for a breather; but they dived right back in again.

It was Ch'aka who broke the stalemate when he plunged his dagger into the ground and on the next roll caught the handle in his mouth. Holding his opponent's arms in both his hands he plunged his head down and managed to find a weak spot in the other's armor. M'shika howled and pulled free, and when he climbed to his feet blood was running down his arm and dripping from his fingertips. Ch'aka jumped after him but the wounded man grabbed up his club in time to ward off the charge.

Stumbling backward, he managed to pick up most of his discarded weapons with his wounded arm and beat a hasty retreat.

Ch'aka ran after him a short way, shouting praise of his own strength and abilities and of his opponent's cowardice. Jason saw a short, sharp horn from some sea animal lying in the churned-up sand and quickly picked it up before Ch'aka turned back.

Once his enemy had been chased out of sight, Ch'aka carefully searched the battle ground and salvaged anything of military value. Though there were still some hours of daylight left, he signaled that this was a halt and distributed the evening ration of *krenoj*.

Jason sat and chewed his portion reflectively, while Ijale leaned against his side, her shoulder moving rhythmically as she scratched some hidden mite. Lice were inescapable; they hid in the crevices of the badly cured hides and emerged to the warmth of human flesh. Jason had his quota of the pests, and found his scratching keeping time with hers. This syncopation of scratching triggered the anger that had been building within him, slow and unnoticed.

"I'm serving notice," he said, jumping to his feet. "I'm through with this slave business. Which way is the nearest spot in the desert where I can find the *d'zertanoj?*"

"Over there, a two-day walk. How are you going to kill Ch'aka?"

"I'm not going to kill Ch'aka, I'm just leaving. I've enjoyed his hospitality and his boot long enough."

"You can't do that," she gasped. "You will be killed."

"Ch'aka can't very well kill me if I'm not here."

"Everybody will kill you. That is the law. Runaway slaves are always killed."

Jason sat down again and cracked another chunk from his *kreno* and ruminated over it. "You've talked me into staying a while. But I have no particular desire now to kill Ch'aka, even though he did steal my boots. And I don't see how killing him will help me any."

"You are stupid. After you kill Ch'aka you'll be the new Ch'aka. Then you can do what you want."

Of course. Now that he had been told, the social setup appeared obvious. Because he had seen slaves and slaveholders, Jason had held the mistaken notion that they were different classes of society, when in reality there was only one class, what might be called the dog-eat-dog class. He should have been aware of this when he had seen how careful Ch'aka was never to allow anyone within striking distance of him, and how he vanished each night to some hidden spot. This was free enterprise with a vengeance, carried to its absolute extreme, with every man out for himself, every other man's hand turned against him, and your station in life determined by the strength of your arm and the speed of your reflexes. Anyone who stayed alone placed himself outside this society and was therefore an enemy of it and sure to be killed on sight. All of which added up to the fact that he had to kill Ch'aka if he wanted to get ahead. He still had no desire to do it; nevertheless he had to.

That night Jason watched Ch'aka when he slipped away from the others, and made a careful note of the direction that he took. Of course the slave-master would circle about before he concealed himself, but with a little luck Jason would find him. And kill him. He had no special love of midnight assassination, and until landing on this planet he had always believed that killing a sleeping man was a cowardly way to terminate another's existence. But special conditions demand special solutions, and he was no match for the heavily armored man in open combat; therefore the assassin's knife—or rather, the sharpened horn.

He managed to doze fitfully until some time after midnight; then he slipped silently from under his skin coverings. Ijale knew he was leaving; he could see her open eyes in the starlight, but she did not move nor say a word. Silently he skirted the sleepers and crept into the darkness between the dunes.

Finding Ch'aka in the wilderness of the desert night was not easy, but Jason persisted. He made careful sweeps in wider and wider arcs, working his way out from the sleeping slaves. There were gullies and shadowed ravines, and all of them had to be searched with utmost care. The slavemaster must be sleeping in one of them and would be alert for any sound.

The fact that Ch'aka had taken special precautions to guard against assassination was apparent to Jason only after he heard the bell ring. It was a tiny sound, barely detectable, but he froze instantly. There was a thin strand pressing against his arm, and when he drew back carefully the bell sounded again. He cursed silently for his stupidity, remembering only now about the bells he had heard before from Ch'aka's sleeping site. The slaver must surround himself every night with a network of string that would sound alarm bells if anyone attempted to approach in the dark. Slowly and soundlessly Jason drew back into the gulley.

With a thud of rushing feet Ch'aka appeared, swinging his club round his head and coming directly towards Jason. Jason rolled desperately sideways and the club crashed into the ground, then he was up and running at top speed down the gulley. Rocks twisted under his feet and he knew that if he tripped he was dead, but he had no choice other than flight. The heavily armored Ch'aka could not keep up with him, and Jason managed to stay on his feet until the other was left behind. Ch'aka shouted with rage and hurled curses after him, but he could not catch him. Jason, panting for breath, vanished into the darkness.

He made a slow circle back towards the sleeping camp. He knew the noise would have roused them and he stayed away for an estimated hour, shivering in the icy predawn, before he slipped back to his waiting skins. The sky was beginning to grey and he lay awake wondering if he had been recognized: he didn't think he had.

As the red sun climbed above the horizon, Ch'aka appeared on top of the dunes, shaking with rage.

"Who did it?" he screamed. "Who came in night?" He stalked among them, glaring right and left, and no one stirred except to draw away from his stamping feet. "Who did it?" he shouted again as he came near the spot where Jason lay.

Five slaves pointed silently at Jason, and Ijale shuddered and drew away from him.

Cursing their betrayal, Jason sprang up and ran from the whistling club. He had the sharpened horn in his hand but knew better than to try and stand up to Ch'aka in open combat; there had to be another way. He looked back quickly and saw his enemy still following, and in doing so he narrowly missed tripping over the outstretched leg of a slave.

They were all against him! They were all against each other, and no man was safe from any other man's hand. He ran free of the slaves and scrambled to the top of a shifting dune, pulling himself up the steep slope by clutching at the coarse grass. He turned at the top and kicked sand into Ch'aka's face, trying to blind him, but the slave-master swung down his crossbow and notched a steel quarrel, and Jason had to run. Ch'aka chased him again, panting heavily.

Jason was tired now, and he knew this was the best time to launch a counterattack. The slaves were out of sight, and it would be a battle between only the two of them. Scrambling up a slope of broken rock, he reversed himself suddenly and leaped back down. Ch'aka was taken by surprise and had his club only half raised when Jason was upon him, and he swung wildly. Jason ducked under the blow and used Ch'aka's momentum to help throw him as he grabbed the club arm and pulled.

Face down, the armored man crashed against the stones, and Jason was straddling his back even as he fell, clutching for his chin. He lacerated his fingers on a jagged tooth necklace, then grasped the man's thick beard and pulled back. For a single long instant, before he could writhe free and roll over, Ch'aka's head was stretched back, and in that instant Jason plunged the sharp horn deep into the soft flesh of the throat. Hot blood burst over his hand and Ch'aka shuddered horribly under him, and died.

Jason climbed to his feet, suddenly exhausted. He was alone with his victim. The cold wind swept about them, carrying the rustling grains of sand, chilling the sweat on his body. Sighing once, he wiped his bloody hands on the sand and began to strip the corpse. Thick straps held the shell helmet over the dead man's head, and when he unknotted them and pulled the helmet away he saw that Ch'aka was well past middle age. There was some grey in his beard, and his scraggly hair was completely grey; his face and balding head were pallid white from being concealed under the helmet.

It took a long time to get the wrappings and armor off and tie them on himself, but it was finally done. Under the skin and claw wrappings on Ch'aka's feet were Jason's boots, filthy but undamaged, and Jason drew them on happily. When at last, after scouring the helmet out with sand, he had strapped it on, Ch'aka was reborn. The corpse on the sand was just another dead slave. Jason scraped a shallow grave, interred the body, and covered it.

Then, slung about with weapons, bags, and crossbow, the club in his hand, he stalked back to the waiting slaves. As soon as he appeared they scrambled to their feet and formed a line. Jason saw Ijale looking at him worriedly, trying to discover who had won the battle.

"Score one for the visiting team," he called out, and she gave him a small, frightened smile and turned away. "About face all, and head back the way we came. There is a new day dawning for you slaves. I know you don't believe this yet, but there are some big changes in store."

He whistled while he strolled after the line and chewed happily on the first *kreno* that was found.

6

That evening they built a fire on the bench and Jason sat with his back to the safety of the sea. He took his helmet off—the thing was giving him a headache—and called Ijale over to him.

"I hear Ch'aka. I obey."

She ran hurriedly to him and flopped onto the sand, pulling open
her rawhide wrappings.

"What an opinion of men you have!" Jason exploded. "Si
up—all I want to do is talk to you. And my name is Jason, no
Ch'aka."

"Yes, Ch'aka," she said, darting a quick glance at his expose
face, then turning away. He grumbled, and pushed the basket o
krenoj over to her.

"I can see where it is not going to be an easy thing changing thi
social setup. Tell me, do you or any of the others ever have an
desire to be free?"

"What is free?"

"Well—I suppose that answers my question. Free is what yo
are when you are not a slave, or a slave owner, free to go where yo
want and do what you want."

"I wouldn't like that." She shivered. "Who would take care o
me? How could I find any *krenoj?* It takes many people together t
find *krenoj*—one alone would starve."

"If you are free you can combine with other free people and loo
for *krenoj* together."

"That is stupid. Whoever found would eat and not share unless
master made him. I like to eat."

Jason rasped his sprouting beard. "We all like to eat, but tha
doesn't mean we have to be slaves. But I can see that unless ther
are some radical changes in this environment I am not going to hav
much luck in freeing anyone, and I had better take all the precau
tions of a Ch'aka to see that I can stay alive."

He picked up his club and stalked off into the darkness, silentl
circling the camp until he found a good-sized knoll with smoot
sides. Working by touch he pulled the little pegs from their bag an
planted them in rows, carefully laying the leather strings in thei
forked tops. The ends of the strings were fastened to delicatel
balanced steel bells that tinkled at the slightest touch. Thus pro
tected, he lay down in the center of his warning spiderweb and sper
a restless night, half awake, waiting tensely for the bells to ring.

In the morning the march continued. They came to the barrie
cairn, and when the slaves stopped Jason urged them past it. The
did this happily, looking forward to witnessing a good fight fo
possession of the violated territory. Their hopes were justified whe
later in the day the other row of slaves was seen far off to the righ
and a figure detached itself and ran towards them.

"Hate you, Ch'aka!" Fasimba shouted as he ran up, only this time he meant what he said. "Coming on my ground, I kill you!"

"Not yet," Jason called out. "And hate you, Fasimba, sorry I forgot the formalities. I don't want any of your land, and the old treaty or whatever it is still holds. I just want to talk to you."

Fasimba stopped, but kept his stone hammer ready, very suspicious. "You got new voice, Ch'aka."

"I got new Ch'aka; old Ch'aka now pushing up daisies. I want to trade back a slave from you and then we'll go."

"Ch'aka fight hard. You must be good fighter, Ch'aka." He shook his hammer angrily. "Not as good as me, Ch'aka!"

"You're the tops, Fasimba; nine slaves out of ten want you for a master. Look, can't we get to the point, then I'll get my mob out of here." He looked at the row of approaching slaves, trying to pick out Mikah. "I want back the slave who had the hole in his head. I'll give you two slaves in trade, your choice. What do you say to that?"

"Good trade, Ch'aka. You pick one of mine, take the best, I'll take two of yours. But hole-in-head gone. Too much trouble. Talk all the time. I got sore foot from kicking him. Got rid of him."

"Did you kill him?"

"Don't waste slave. Traded him to the *d'zertanoj*. Got arrows. You want arrows?"

"Not this time, Fasimba, but thanks for the information." He rooted around in a pouch and pulled out a *kreno*. "Here, have something to eat."

"Where you get poisoned *kreno?*" Fasimba asked with unconcealed interest. "I could use a poisoned *kreno*."

"This isn't poisoned, it's perfectly edible, or at least as edible as these things ever are."

Fasimba laughed. "You pretty funny, Ch'aka. I give you one arrow for poisoned *kreno*."

"You're on," Jason said, throwing the *kreno* to the ground between them. "But I tell you it is perfectly good."

"That's what I tell man I give it to. I got good use for a poisoned *kreno*." He threw an arrow into the sand away from them and grabbed up the vegetable as he left.

When Jason picked up the arrow it bent, and he saw that it was rusted almost completely in two and that the break had been craftily covered by clay. "That's all right," he called after the retreating slaver. "Just wait until your friend eats the *kreno*."

They continued their march, first back to the boundary cairn with the suspicious Fasimba dogging their steps. Only after Jason and his band had passed the border did the others return to their normal foraging.

Then began the long walk to the borders of the inland desert. Since they had to search for *krenoj* as they went, it took them the better part of three days to reach their destination. Jason merely started the line in the right direction, but as soon as he was out of sight of the sea he had only a rough idea of the correct course. However, he did not confide his ignorance to the slaves and they marched steadily on, along what was obviously a well-known route to them. Along the way they collected and consumed a good number of *krenoj*, found two wells from which they refilled the skin bags, and pointed out a huddled animal sitting by a hole that Jason, to their unvoiced disgust, managed to miss completely with a bolt from the crossbow. On the morning of the third day Jason saw a line of demarcation on the flattened horizon, and before the midday meal they came to a sea of billowing, bluish-grey sand.

The ending of what he had been accustomed to thinking of as the desert was startling. Beneath their feet were sand and gravel, while occasional shrubs managed a sickly existence, as did some grass and the life-giving *krenoj*. Animals as well as men lived here and, ruthless though survival was, they were at least alive. In the waste ahead no life was visible or possible, though there seemed to be no doubt that the *d'zertanoj* lived there. This must mean that though it looked unlimited—as Ijale believed it to be—there were probably arable lands on the other side. Mountains as well, if they weren't just clouds, since a line of grey peaks could just be made out on the distant horizon.

"Where do we find the *d'zertanoj?*" Jason asked the nearest slave, who merely scowled and looked away. Jason was having a problem with discipline. The slaves would not do a thing he asked unless he kicked them. Their conditioning had been so thorough that an order unaccompanied by a kick just wasn't an order, and his continued reluctance to impose the physical coercion with the spoken command was being taken as a sign of weakness. Already some of the burlier slaves were licking their lips and sizing him up. His efforts to improve the life of the slaves were being blocked completely by the slaves themselves. With a muttered curse at the continued obduracy of these creatures, Jason kicked the man with the toe of his boot.

"Find them there by big rock," was the immediate response.

There was a dark spot at the desert's edge in the indicated direction, and when they approached this Jason saw that it was an outcropping of rock that had been built up with a wall of bricks and boulders to a uniform height. A good number of men could be concealed behind that wall, and he was not going to risk his precious slaves or even more precious skin anywhere near it. At his shout the line halted and sank down on the sand while he stalked a few meters in front, settling his club in his hand and suspiciously examining the structure.

That there were unseen watchers was proved when a man appeared from around the corner and walked slowly towards Jason. He was dressed in loose-fitting robes and carried a basket on one arm, and when he had reached a point roughly halfway between Jason and the rock he had just quitted, he halted and sat crosslegged in the sand, the basket at his side. Jason looked carefully in all directions, and decided the situation was safe enough. There were no places of concealment where armed men might have hidden, and he had no fear of the one man alone. Club ready, he walked out and stopped a full three paces from the other.

"Welcome, Ch'aka," the man said. "I was afraid we wouldn't be seeing you again after that little . . . difficulty we had."

He remained seated while he talked, stroking the few strands of his scraggly beard. His head was shaved smooth and was as sunburned and leathery as the rest of his face, the most prominent feature of which was a magnificent prow of a nose that terminated in flaring nostrils and was used as sturdy support for a pair of handmade sunglasses. They appeared to be carved completely of bone and fitted tightly to the face; their flat, solid fronts were cut with thin transverse slashes. This sort of eye protection could only have been for weak eyes, and the network of wrinkles suggested that the man was quite old and would present no danger to Jason.

"I want something," Jason said in straightforward, Ch'akaish manner.

"A new voice and a new Ch'aka—I bid you welcome. The old one was a dog, and I hope he died in great pain when you killed him. Now sit, friend Ch'aka, and drink with me." He carefully uncovered the basket and removed a stone crock and two crockery mugs.

"Where you get poison drink?" Jason asked, remembering his local manners. This *d'zertano* was a smart one; he had been able to tell instantly from Jason's voice that there had been a change in identity. "And what your name?"

"Edipon," the ancient said as, not insulted, he put the drinking apparatus back into the basket. "What is it that you want? Within reason, that is. We always need slaves and we are always willing to trade."

"I want slave you got. I trade you two for one."

The seated man smiled coldly from behind the shelter of his nose. "It is not necessary to talk as ungrammatically as the coastal barbarians, since I can tell by your accent that you are a man of education. What slave is it that you want?"

"The one you just received from Fasimba. He belongs to me." Jason abandoned his linguistic ruse and put himself even more on guard, taking a quick look around at the empty sands. This dried-up old bird was a lot brighter than he looked, and Jason would have to stay on guard.

"Is that all you want?" Edipon asked.

"All I can think of at this moment. You produce this slave and maybe we can talk some more business."

Edipon's laugh had very dirty overtones, and Jason sprang back when the oldster put two fingers into his mouth and whistled shrilly between them. There was the rustle of shifting sand, and Jason wheeled to see men apparently climbing out of the empty desert, pushing back wooden covers over which the sand had been smoothed. There were six of them with shields and clubs, and Jason cursed his stupidity at meeting Edipon on a spot of the other's choosing. He swung his club behind him, but the old man was already scampering for the safety of the rock. Jason howled in anger and ran at the nearest man, who was still only halfway out of his hiding place. The man took Jason's blow on his upraised shield and was toppled back into the pit by the force of it. Jason ran on, but another was ahead of him, swinging his own war club in readiness. There was no way around, so Jason ran into him at full speed with all of his pendant teeth and horns gnashing and clattering. The man fell back under the attack and Jason split his shield with his club, and would have done further damage had the other men not arrived at that moment and he had to face them.

It was a brief and wicked battle, with Jason giving just a little more than he received. Two of the attackers were down and a third was holding his cracked head when the weight of numbers carried Jason to the ground. He called to his slaves for aid, then cursed them when they only remained seated, while his arms were pinioned with rope and his weapons stripped from his body. One of the victors waved to the slaves who now docilely marched into the desert. Jason was dragged, snarling with rage, in the same direction.

There was a wide opening in the desert-facing side of the wall, and once through it Jason's anger instantly vanished. Here was one of the *caroj* that Ijale had told him about: there could be no doubt of it. He could now understand how, to her uneducated eye, there could exist an uncertainty as to whether the thing was an animal or not. The vehicle was a good ten meters long, and was shaped roughly like a boat; it bore on the front a large and obviously false animal head covered with fur, and resplendent with rows of carved teeth and glistening crystal eyes. Hide coverings and not very realistic legs were hung on the thing, surely not enough camouflage to fool a civilized six-year-old. This sort of disguise might be good enough to take in the ignorant savages, but the same civilized child would recognize this as a vehicle as soon as he saw the six large wheels underneath. They were cut with deep treads and made from some resilient-looking substance. No motive power was visible, but Jason almost hooted with joy at the noticeable smell of burnt fuel. This crude-looking contrivance had some artificial source of power, which might be the product of a local industrial revolution, or might have been purchased from off-world traders. Either possibility offered the chance of eventual escape from this nameless planet.

The slaves, some of them cringing with terror of the unknown, were kicked up the gangplank and into the *caro*. Four of the huskies who had subdued and bound Jason carried him up and dumped him onto the deck, where he lay quietly and examined what could be seen of the desert vehicle's mechanism. A post projected from the front of the deck, and one of the men fitted what could only be a tiller handle over the squared top of it. If this monolithic apparatus steered with the front pair of wheels it must be driven with the rear ones, so Jason flopped around on the deck until he could look towards the stern. A cabin, the width of the deck, was situated here, windowless and with a single inset door fitted with a grand selection of locks and bolts. Any doubt that this was the engine room was dispelled by the black metal smokestack that rose up through the cabin roof.

"We are leaving," Edipon screeched, and waved his thin arms in the air. "Bring in the entranceway. Narsisi, stand forward to indicate the way to the *caro*. Now—all pray as I go into the shrine to induce the sacred powers to move us towards Putl'ko." He started towards the cabin, then stopped to point to one of the club bearers. "Erebo, you lazy sod, did you remember to fill the watercup of the gods this time, for they grow thirsty?"

"I filled it, I filled it," Erebo muttered, chewing on a looted *kreno*.

Preparations made, Edipon went into the recessed doorway and pulled a concealing curtain over it. There was much clanking and rattling as the locks and bolts were opened and he let himself inside. Within a few minutes a black cloud of greasy smoke rolled out of the smokestack and was whipped away by the wind. Almost an hour passed before the sacred powers were ready to move, and they announced their willingness to proceed by screaming and blowing their white breath up in the air. Four of the slaves screamed counterpoint and fainted, while the rest looked as if they would be happier dead.

Jason had had some experience with primitive machines before, so the safety valve on the boiler came as no great surprise. He was also prepared when the vehicle shuddered and began to move slowly out into the desert. From the amount of smoke and the quantity of steam escaping from under the stern he didn't think the engine was very efficient, but primitive as it was it moved the *caro* and its load of passengers across the sand at a creeping yet steady pace.

More screams came from the slaves, and a few tried to leap over the side, but they were clubbed down. The robe-wrapped *d'zertanoj* were firmly working their way through the ranks of the captives, pouring ladlefuls of dark liquid down their throats. Some of the captives were slumped unconscious, or were dead, though the chances were better that they were merely unconscious, since there was no reason for their captors to kill them after going to such lengths to get them in the first place. Jason believed this, but the terrified slaves did not have the solace of his philosophy, so struggled on, thinking that they were fighting for their lives.

When Jason's turn came he did not submit meekly, in spite of his beliefs, and managed to bite some fingers and kick one man in the stomach before they sat on him, held his nose, and poured a measure of the burning liquid down his throat. It hurt and he felt dizzy, and he tried to will himself to throw up, but this was the last thing that he remembered.

7

"Drink some more of this," the voice said, and cold water splashed on Jason's face and some of it trickled down his throat, making him cough. Something hard was pressing into his back and his wrists hurt. Memory seeped back slowly—the fight, the capture, and the potion that had been forced upon him. When he opened his eyes he saw a flickering yellow lamp overhead, hung from a chain. He blinked at it and tried to gather enough energy to sit up. A familiar face swam in front of the light and Jason squinted his eyes at it and groaned.

"Is that you, Mikah—or are you just part of a nightmare?"

"There is no escape from justice, Jason. It is I, and I have some grave questions to put to you."

Jason groaned again. "You're real, all right. Even in a nightmare I wouldn't dare dream up any lines like that. But before the questions, how about telling me a thing or two about the local setup? You should know something, since you have been a slave of the *d'zertanoj* longer than I have." Jason realized that the pain in his wrists came from heavy iron shackles. A chain passed through them and was stapled to a thick wooden bar on which his head had been resting. "Why the chains—and what is the local hospitality like?"

Mikah resisted the invitation to impart any vital information and returned irresistibly to his own topic.

"When I saw you last you were a slave of Ch'aka, and tonight you were brought in with the other slaves of Ch'aka and chained to the bar while you were unconscious. There was an empty place next to mine and I told them I would tend you if they placed you there, and they did so. Now there is something I must know. Before they stripped you, I saw that you were wearing the armor and helmet of Ch'aka. Where is he—what happened to him?"

"Me Ch'aka," Jason rasped, and burst out coughing from the dryness in his throat. He took a long drink of water from the bowl. "You sound very vindictive, Mikah, you old fraud. Where is all the turn-the-other-cheek stuff now? Don't tell me you could possibly hate the man just because he hit you on the head, fractured your skull, and sold you down the river as a slave reject? In case you have been brooding over this injustice you can now be cheered, because the evil Ch'aka is no more. He is buried in the trackless wastes, and after all the applicants were sifted out I got the job."

"You killed him?"

"In a word—yes. And don't think that it was easy, for he had all the advantages and I possessed only my native ingenuity, which luckily proved to be enough. It was touch and go for a while, because when I tried to assassinate him in his sleep—"

"You *what?*" Mikah interrupted.

"Got to him at night. You don't think anyone in his right mind would tackle a monster like that face to face, do you? Though it ended up that way, since he had some neat gadgets for keeping track of people in the dark. Briefly, we fought, I won, I became Ch'aka, though my reign was neither long nor noble. I followed you as far as the desert, where I was neatly trapped by a shrewd old bird by the name of Edipon, who demoted me back to the ranks and took away all my slaves as well. Now that's my story. So tell me yours—where we are, what goes on here—''

''Assassin! Slaveholder!'' Mikah reared back as far as he could under the restraint of the chain, and pointed the finger of judgment at Jason. ''Two more charges must be added to your role of infamy. I sicken myself, Jason, that I could ever have felt sympathy for you and tried to help you. I will still help you, but only to stay alive so that you can be taken back to Cassylia for trial and execution.''

''I like that example of fair and impartial justice—trial *and* execution.'' Jason coughed again and drained the bowl of water. ''Didn't you ever hear of presumed innocence until proven guilt? It happens to be the mainstay of all jurisprudence. And how could you possibly justify trying me on Cassylia for actions that occurred on this planet—actions that aren't crimes here? That's like taking a cannibal away from his tribe and executing him for anthropophagy.''

''What would be wrong with that? The eating of human flesh is a crime so loathsome I shudder to think of it. Of course a man who does that must be executed.''

''If he slips in the back door and eats one of your relatives you certainly have grounds for action. But not if he joins the rest of his jolly tribe for a good roast of enemy. Don't you see the obvious point here—that human conduct can be judged only in relation to its environment? Conduct is relative. The cannibal in his society is just as moral as the churchgoer in yours.''

''Blasphemer! A crime is a crime! There are moral laws that stand above all human society.''

''Oh, no, there aren't. That's just the point where your medieval morality breaks down. All laws and ideas are historical and relative, *not* absolute. They are relevant to their particular time and place; taken out of context they lose their importance. Within the context of this grubby society, I acted in a most straightforward and honest manner. I attempted to assassinate my master—which is the only way an ambitious boy can get ahead in this hard world, and which was undoubtedly the way Ch'aka himself got the job in the first place. Assassination didn't work, but combat did, and the results were the same. Once in power, I took good care of my slaves, though of course they didn't appreciate it, since they didn' want good care: they only wanted my job, that being the law of the land. The only thing I really did wrong was not to live up to my obligations as a slaveholder and keep them marching up and down the beaches forever. Instead, I came looking for you and was trapped and broken back to slavery, where I belong for pulling such a stupid trick."

The door crashed open and harsh sunlight streamed into the windowless building. "On your feet, slaves!" a *d'zertano* shouted in through the opening.

A chorus of groans and shufflings broke out as the men stirred to life. Jason could see now that he was one of twenty slaves shackled to the long bar, apparently the entire trunk of a good-sized tree. The man chained at the far end seemed to be a leader of sorts, for he cursed and goaded the others to life. When they were all standing he snapped his commands in a hectoring tone.

"Come on, come on! First come, best food. And don't forget your bowls. Put them away so they can't drop out, remember nothing to eat or drink all day unless you have a bowl. And let's work together today, everyone pull his weight, that's the only way to do it. That goes for all you men, especially you new men. Give them a day's work here and they give you a day's food . . ."

"Oh, shut up!" someone shouted.

". . . and you can't complain about that," the man went on, unperturbed. "Now altogether . . . *one* . . . bend down and get your hands around the bar, get a good grip and . . . *two* . . . lift it clear of the ground, that's the way. And . . . *three* . . . stand up, and out the door we go."

They shuffled out into the sunlight and the cold wind of dawn bit through the Pyrran coverall and the remnants of Ch'aka's leather trappings that Jason had been allowed to keep. His captors had torn off the claw-studded feet but had not bothered the wrappings underneath, so they hadn't found his boots. This was the only bright spot on an otherwise unlimited vista of blackest gloom. Jason tried to be thankful for small blessings, but he could only shiver. As soon as possible this situation had to be changed, for he had already served his term as slave on this backward planet and was cut out for better things.

On order, the slaves dropped their bar against the wall of the yard and sat upon it. Presenting their bowls like scruffy penitents, they accepted dippers of lukewarm soup from another slave who pushed along a wheeled tub of the stuff: he was chained to the tub. Jason's appetite vanished when he tasted the sludge. It was *kreno* soup, and the desert tubers tasted even worse—he hadn't thought it was possible—when served up in a broth. But survival was more important than fastidiousness, so he gulped the evil stuff down.

Breakfast over, they marched out the gate into another compound, and fascinated interest displaced all of Jason's concerns. In the center of the yard was a large capstan into which the first group of slaves were already fitting the end of their bar. Jason's group, and the two others, shuffled into position and placed their bars, making a four-spoked wheel out of the capstan. An overseer shouted and the slaves groaned and threw their weight against the bars until they shuddered and began to turn; then trudging slowly, they kept the wheel moving.

Once this slogging labor was under way, Jason turned his attention to the crude mechanism they were powering. A vertical shaft from the capstan turned a creaking wooden wheel that set a series of leather belts in motion. Some of them vanished through openings into a large stone building, while the strongest strap of all turned the rocker arm of what could only be a counterbalanced pump. This all seemed like a highly inefficient way to go about pumping water, since there must be natural springs and lakes somewhere around. The pungent smell that filled the yard was hauntingly familiar, and Jason had just reached the conclusion that water couldn't be the object of their labors when a throaty gurgling came from the standpipe of the pump and a thick black stream bubbled out.

"Petroleum—of course!" Jason said out loud. Then when the overseer gave him an ugly look and cracked his whip menacingly, he bent his attention to pushing.

This was the secret of the *d'zertanoj*, and the source of their power. Hills towered above the surrounding walls and mountains were visible nearby. But the captured slaves had been drugged so they would not even know in which direction they had been brought to this hidden site, or how long the trip was. Here in this guarded valley they labored to pump the crude oil that their masters used to power their big desert wagons. Or did they use crude oil for this? The petroleum was gurgling out in a heavy stream now, and was running down an open trough that disappeared through the wall into the same building as the turning belts. What barbaric devilishness went on in there? A thick chimney crowned the building and produced clouds of black smoke, while from the various openings in the wall came a tremendous stench that threatened to lift the top off his head.

At the same moment that he realized what was going on in the building, a guarded door was opened and Edipon came out, blowing his sizable nose in a scrap of rag. The creaking wheel turned, and when its rotation brought Jason around again he called out to him.

"Hey, Edipon, come over here. I want to talk to you. I'm the former Ch'aka, in case you don't recognize me out of uniform."

Edipon gave him one look, then turned away, dabbing at his nose. It was obvious that slaves held no interest for him, no matter what their position had been before their fall. The slave driver ran over with a roar, raising his whip, while the slow rotation of the wheel carried Jason away. He shouted back over his shoulder.

"Listen to me—I know a lot, and can help you." Only a turned back was an answer, and the whip was already whistling down.

It was time for the hard sell. "You had better hear me—because I know that *what comes out first is best*. Yeow!" This last was involuntary as the whip landed.

Jason's words were without meaning to the slaves as well as to the overseer, who was raising his whip for another blow, but their impact on Edipon was as dramatic as if he had stepped on a hot coal. He shuddered to a halt and wheeled about, and even at this distance Jason could see that a sickly grey tone had replaced the normal brown color of his skin.

"Stop the wheel!" Edipon shouted.

This unexpected command drew the startled attention of everyone. The gape-mouthed overseer lowered his whip while the slaves stumbled and halted and the wheel groaned to a stop. In the sudden silence Edipon's steps echoed loudly as he ran to Jason, halting a hand's breadth away, his lips drawn back from his teeth with tension as if he were prepared to bite.

"What was that you said?" He hurled the words at Jason while his fingers half-plucked a knife from his belt.

Jason smiled, looking and acting calmer than he felt. His barb had gone home, but unless he proceeded carefully so would Edipon's knife—into Jason's stomach. This was obviously a very sensitive topic.

"You heard what I said—and I don't think you want me to repeat it in front of all these strangers. I know what happens here because I come from a place far away where we do this kind of thing all the time. I can help you. I can show you how to get more of the best, and how to make your *caroj* work better. Just try me. Only unchain me from this bar first and let's get to some place private where we can have a nice chat."

Edipon's thoughts were obvious. He chewed his lip and looked hotly at Jason, fingering the edge of his knife. Jason returned a smile of pure innocence and tapped his fingers happily on the bar, just marking time while he waited to be released. But in spite of the cold there was a rivulet of sweat trickling down his spine. He was gambling everything on Edipon's intelligence, believing that the man's curiosity would overcome the immediate desire to silence the slave who knew so much about things so secret, hoping that he would remember that slaves could always be killed, and that it wouldn't hurt to ask a few questions first. Curiosity won, and the knife dropped back into the sheath while Jason let his breath out in a relieved sigh. It had been entirely too close, even for a professional gambler; his own life on the board was a little higher stakes than he enjoyed playing for.

"Release him from the bar and bring him to me," Edipon ordered, then strode away in agitation. The other slaves watched wide-eyed as the blacksmith was rushed out, and with much confusion and shouted orders Jason's chain was cut from the bar where it joined the heavy staple.

"What are you doing?" Mikah asked, and one of the guards backhanded him to the ground. Jason merely smiled and touched his finger to his lips as the chain was released and they led him away. He was free from bondage, and he would stay that way if he could convince Edipon that he would be of better use in some capacity other than dumb labor.

The room they led him to contained the first touches of decoration or self-indulgence that he had seen on this planet. The furniture was carefully constructed, with an occasional bit of carving to brighten it, and there was a woven cover on the bed. Edipon stood by a table, tapping his fingers nervously on the dark polished surface.

"Lock him up," he ordered the guards, and Jason was secured to a sturdy ringbolt that projected from the wall. As soon as the guards were gone Edipon stood in front of Jason and drew his knife. "Tell me what you know, or I will kill you at once."

"My past is an open book to you, Edipon. I come from a land where we know all the secrets of nature."

"What is the name of this land? Are you a spy from Appsala?"

"I couldn't very well be, since I have never heard of the place." Jason pulled at his lower lip, wondering just how intelligent Edipon was, and just how frank he could be with him. This was no time to get tangled up in lies about the planetary geography: it might be best to try him on a small dose of the truth.

"If I told you I came from another planet, another world in the sky up among the stars, would you believe me?"

"Perhaps. There are many old legends that our forefathers came from a world beyond the sky, but I always dismissed them as religious drivel, fit only for women."

"In this case the girls happen to be right. Your planet was settled by men whose ships crossed the emptiness of space as your *caroj* pass over the desert. Your people have forgotten that, and have lost the science and knowledge you once had, but on other worlds the knowledge is still held."

"Madness!"

"Not at all. It is science, though many times confused as being the same thing. I'll prove my point. You know that I could never have been inside of your mysterious building out there, and I imagine you can be sure no one has told me its secrets. Yet I'll bet that I can describe fairly accurately what is in there—not from seeing the machinery, but from knowing what must be done to oil in order to get the products you need. You want to hear?"

"Proceed," Edipon said, sitting on a corner of the table and balancing the knife loosely in his palm.

"I don't know what you call it, the device, but in the trade it is a pot still used for fractional distillation. Your crude oil runs into a tank of some kind, and you pipe it from there to a retort, some big vessel that you can seal airtight. Once it is closed, you light a fire under the thing and try to get all the oil to an even temperature. A gas rises from the oil and you take it off through a pipe and run it through a condenser, probably more pipe with water running over it. Then you put a bucket under the open end of the pipe and out of it drips the juice that you burn in your *caroj* to make them move."

Edipon's eyes opened wider and wider while Jason talked, until they seemed almost bulging from his head. "Demon!" he screeched, and tottered towards Jason with the knife extended. "You couldn't have seen, not through stone walls. Only my family have seen, no others—I'll swear to that!"

"Keep cool, Edipon. I told you that we have been doing this stuff for years in my country." He balanced on one foot, ready for a kick at the knife in case the old man's nerves did not settle down. "I'm not out to steal your secrets. In fact, they are pretty small potatoes where I come from, where every farmer has a still for cooking up his own mash and saving on taxes. I'll bet I can even put in some improvements for you, sight unseen. How do you monitor the temperature on your cooking brew? Do you have thermometers?"

"What are thermometers?" Edipon asked, forgetting the knife for the moment, drawn on by the joy of a technical discussion.

"That's what I thought. I can see where your bootleg joy-juice is going to take a big jump in quality, if you have anyone here who can do some simple glass-blowing. Though it might be easier to rig up a coiled bi-metallic strip. You're trying to boil off your various fractions, and unless you keep an even and controlled temperature you are going to have a mixed brew. The thing you want for your engines are the most volatile fractions, the liquids that boil off first, like gasoline and benzene. After that you raise the temperature and collect kerosene for your lamps, and so forth right on down the line until you have a nice mass of tar left to pave your roads with. How does that sound to you?''

Edipon had forced himself into calmness, though a jumping muscle in his cheek betrayed his inner tensions. ''What you have described is the truth, though you were wrong on some small things. But I am not interested in your thermometer nor in improving our water-of-power. It has been good enough for my family for generations and it is good enough for me.''

''I suppose you think that line is original?''

''But there is something that you might be able to do that would bring you rich rewards,'' Edipon went on. ''We can be generous when needs be. You have seen our *caroj* and ridden on one, and seen me go into the shrine to intercede with the sacred powers to make us move. Can you tell me what power moves the *caroj?*''

''I hope this is the final exam, Edipon, because you are stretching my powers of extrapolation. Stripping away the 'shrines' and 'sacred powers,' I would say that you go into the engine room to do a piece of work with very little praying involved. There could be a number of ways of moving those vehicles, but let's think of the simplest. This is top of the head now, so no penalties if I miss any of the fine points. Internal combustion is out. I doubt if you have the technology to handle it, plus the fact there was a lot of do about the water tank and it took you almost an hour to get under way. That sounds as if you were getting up a head of steam— The safety valve! I forgot about that.

''So it is steam. You go in, lock the door, of course, then open a couple of valves until the fuel drips into the firebox, then you light it. Maybe you have a pressure gauge, or maybe you just wait until the safety valve pops to tell you if you have a head of steam. Which can be dangerous, since a sticking valve could blow the whole works right over the mountain. Once you have the steam, you crack a valve to let it into the cylinders and get the thing moving. After that you just enjoy the trip, of course making sure that the water is feeding to your boiler all right, that your pressure stays up, your fire is hot enough, all your bearings are lubricated, and the rest . . .''

Jason looked on astounded as Edipon did a little jig around the room, holding his robe up above his bony knees. Bouncing with excitement, he jabbed his knife into the table top and rushed over to

Jason and grabbed him by the shoulders, shaking him so that his chain rattled.

"Do you know what you have done?" he asked excitedly. "Do you know what you have said?"

"I know well enough. Does this mean that I have passed the exam and that you will listen to me now? Was I right?"

"I don't know if you are right or not; I have never seen the inside of one of the Appsalan devil-boxes." He danced around the room again. "You know more about their—what do you call it?— *engine*, than I do. I have only spent my life tending them and cursing the people of Appsala who keep the secret from us. But you will reveal it to us! We will build our own engines, and if they want water-of-power they will have to pay dearly for it."

"Would you mind being a little bit clearer," Jason asked. "I have never heard anything so confused in all my life."

"I will show you, man from a far world, and you will reveal the Appsalan secrets to us. I see the dawn of a new day for Putl'ko arriving."

He opened the door and shouted for the guards, and for his son, Narsisi. The latter arrived as they were unlocking Jason, who recognized him as the same droopy-eyed, sleepy-looking *d'zertano* who had been helping Edipon to drive their ungainly vehicle.

"Seize this chain, my son, and keep your club ready to kill this slave if he makes any attempt to escape. Otherwise, do not harm him, for he is very valuable. Come."

Narsisi tugged on the chain, but Jason only dug his heels in and did not move. They looked at him, astonished.

"Just a few things before we go. The man who is to bring the new day to Putl'ko is not a slave. Let us get that straight before this operation goes any further. We'll work out something with chains or guards so I can't escape, but the slavery thing is out."

"But—you are not one of us, therefore you must be a slave."

"I've just added a third category to your social order: employee. Though reluctant, I am still an employee, skilled labor, and I intend to be treated that way. Figure it out for yourself. Kill a slave, and what do you lose? Very little, if there is another slave in the pens that can push in the same place. But kill me, and what do you get? Brains on your club—and they do you no good at all there."

"Does he mean I can't kill him?" Narsisi asked his father, looking puzzled as well as sleepy.

"No, he doesn't mean that," Edipon said. "He means if we kill him there is no one else who can do the work he is to do for us. But I do not like it. There are only slaves and slavers; anything else is against the natural order. But he has us trapped between *satano* and the sandstorm, so we must allow him some freedom. Bring the slave now—I mean the employee—and we will see if he can do the things he has promised. If he does not, *I* will have the pleasure of killing him, because I do not like his revolutionary ideas.''

They marched single file to a locked and guarded building with immense doors, which were pulled open to reveal the massive forms of seven *caroj.*

"Look at them!'' Edipon exclaimed, and pulled at his nose. "The finest and most beautiful of constructions, striking fear into our enemies' hearts, carrying us fleetly across the sands, bearing on their backs immense loads, and only three of the damned things are able to move.''

"Engine trouble?'' Jason asked lightly.

Edipon cursed and fumed under his breath, and led the way to an inner courtyard where stood four immense black boxes painted with death heads, splintered bones, fountains of blood, and cabalistic symbols, all of a sinister appearance.

"Those swine in Appsala take our water-of-power and give nothing in return. Oh yes, they let us use their engines, but after running for a few months the cursed things stop and will not go again, then we must bring them back to the city to exchange for a new one, and pay again and again.''

"A nice racket,'' Jason said, looking at the sealed covering on the engines. "Why don't you just crack into them and fix them yourself? They can't be very complex.''

"That is death!'' Edipon gasped, and both *d'zertanoj* recoiled from the boxes at the thought. "We have tried that, in my father's father's day, for we are not superstitious like the slaves, and we know that these are man-made not god-made. However, the tricky serpents of Appsala hide their secrets with immense cunning. If any attempt is made to break the covering, horrible death leaks out and fills the air. Men who breathe the air die, and even those who are only touched by it develop immense blisters and die in pain. The man of Appsala laughed when this happened to our people, and after that they raised the price even higher.''

Jason circled one of the boxes, examining it with interest, trailing Narsisi behind him at the end of the chain. The thing was higher than his head and almost twice as long. A heavy shaft emerged through openings on opposite sides, probably the power takeoff for the wheels. Through an opening in the side he could see inset handles and two small colored disks, and above these were three funnel-shaped openings painted like mouths. By standing on tiptoe, Jason could look on top, but there was only a flanged, sooty opening there that must be for attaching a smokestack. There was only one more opening, a smallish one in the rear, and no other controls on the garish container.

"I'm beginning to get the picture, but you will have to tell me how you work the controls."

"Death before that!" Narsisi shouted. "Only my family—"

"Will you shut up!" Jason shouted back. "Remember? You're not allowed to browbeat the help any more. There are no secrets here. Not only that, but I probably know more about this thing than you do, just by looking at it. Oil, water, and fuel go in these three openings, you poke a light in somewhere, probably in that smoky hole under the controls, and open one of those valves for fuel supply; another one is to make the engine go slower and faster, and the third is for your water feed. The disks are indicators of some kind." Narsisi paled and stepped back. "So now keep still while I talk to your dad."

"It is as you say," Edipon said. "The mouths must always be filled, and woe betide if they go empty; for the powers will halt, or worse. Fire goes in here, as you guessed, and when the green finger comes forward this lever may be turned for motion. The next is for great speed, or for going slow. The very last is under the sign of the red finger, which when it points indicates need, and the handle must be turned and held turned until the finger retires. White breath comes from the opening in back. That is all there is."

"About what I expected," Jason muttered, and examined the container wall, rapping it with his knuckles until it boomed. "They give you the minimum of controls to run the thing, so you won't learn anything about the basic principles involved. Without the theory, you would never know what the handles control, or that the green indicator comes out when you have operating pressure, and the red one when the water level is low in the boiler. Very neat. And the whole thing sealed up in a can and booby-trapped in case you have any ideas of going into business for yourself. The cover sounds as if it is double-walled, and from your description I would say that it has one of the vesicant war gases, like mustard gas, sealed inside there in liquid form. Anyone who tried to cut their way in will quickly forget their ambitions after a dose of that. Yet there must be a way to get inside the case and service the engine; they aren't just going to throw them away after a few months' use. And considering the level of technology displayed by this monstrosity, I should be able to find the tricks and get around any other built-in traps. I think I'll take the job."

"Very well, begin."

"Wait a minute, boss. You still have a few things to learn about hired labor. There are always certain working conditions and agreements involved, all of which I'll be happy to list for you."

8

"What I do not understand is why you must have the other slave?" Narsisi whined. "To have the woman of course is natural, as well as to have quarters of your own. My father has given his permission. But he also said that I and my brothers are to help you, that the secrets of the engine are to be revealed to no one else."

"Then trot right over to him and get permission for the slave Mikah to join me in the work. You can explain that he comes from the same land that I do, and that your secrets are mere children's toys to him. And if your dad wants any other reasons, tell him that I need skilled aid, someone who knows how to handle tools and who can be trusted to follow directions exactly as given. You and your brothers have entirely too many ideas of your own about how things should be done, and a tendency to leave details up to the gods, and have a good bash with the hammer if things don't work the way they should."

Narsisi retired, seething and muttering to himself, while Jason huddled over the oil stove planning the next step. It had taken most of the day to lay down logs for rollers and to push the sealed engine out into the sandy valley, far from the well site; open space was needed for any experiments in which a mistake could release a cloud of war gas. Even Edipon had finally seen the sense of this, though all of his tendencies were to conduct the experiments with great secretiveness, behind locked doors. He had granted permission only after skin walls had been erected to form an enclosure that could be guarded; it was only incidental that they acted as a much appreciated windbreak.

After a good deal of argument the dangling chains and shackles had been removed from Jason's arms and lightweight leg-irons substituted. He had to shuffle when he walked, but his arms were completely free; this was a great improvement over the chains, even though one of the brothers kept watch with a cocked crossbow as long as Jason wasn't fastened down. Now he had to get some tools and some idea of the technical knowledge of these people before he could proceed, which would necessarily entail one more battle over their precious secrets.

"Come on," he called to his guard, "let's find Edipon and give his ulcers another twinge."

After his first enthusiasm, the leader of the *d'zertanoj* was getting little pleasure out of his new project.

"You have quarters of your own," he grumbled to Jason, "and the slave woman to cook for you, and I have just given permission for the other slave to help you. Now more requests—do you want to drain all the blood from my body?"

"Let's not dramatize too much. I simply want some tools to get on with my work, and a look at your machine shop or wherever it is you do your mechanical work. I have to have some idea of the way you people solve mechanical problems before I can go to work on that box of tricks out there in the desert."

"Entrance is forbidden."

"Regulations are snapping like straws today, so we might as well go on and finish off a few more. Will you lead the way?"

The guards were reluctant to open the refinery building gates to Jason, and there were worried looks and much rattling of keys. A brace of elderly *d'zertanoj*, stinking of oil fumes, emerged from the interior and joined in a shouted argument with Edipon, whose will finally prevailed. Chained again, and guarded like a criminal, Jason was begrudgingly led into the dark interior, the contents of which were depressingly anticlimactic.

"Really primitive," Jason sneered, and he kicked at the boxful of clumsy hand-forged tools. The work was of the crudest, the product of a sort of neolithic machine age. The distilling retort had been laboriously formed from sheet copper and clumsily riveted together. It leaked mightily, as did the soldered seams on the hand-formed pipe. Most of the tools were blacksmith's tongs and hammers for heating and beating out shapes on the anvil. The only things that gladdened Jason's heart were the massive drill press and lathe that worked off the slave-power drive belts. In the tool holder of the lathe was clamped a chip of some hard mineral that did a good enough job of cutting the forged iron and low-carbon steel. Even more cheering was the screw-thread advance on the cutting head, which was used to produce the massive nuts and bolts that secured the *caro* wheels to their shafts.

It might have been worse. Jason sorted out the smallest and handiest tools and put them aside for his own use in the morning. The light was almost gone now and there would be no more work this day.

They left in armed procession, as they had come, and two guards showed him to the kennel-like room that was to be his private quarters. The heavy bolt thudded shut in the door behind him and he winced at the thick fumes of kerosene through which the light of the single-wick lamp barely penetrated.

Ijale crouched over the small oil stove cooking something in a pottery vessel. She looked up and smiled hesitatingly at Jason, then turned quickly back to the stove. Jason walked over, sniffed, and shuddered.

"What a feast! *Kreno* soup, and I suppose followed by fresh *kreno* and *kreno* salad. Tomorrow I'll see about getting a little variety into the diet."

"Ch'aka is great," she whispered without looking up. "Ch'aka is powerful . . ."

"Jason is the name, I lost Ch'aka job when they took the uniform away."

". . . Jason is powerful to work charms on the *d'zertanoj* and make them do what he will. His slave thanks you."

He lifted her chin, and the dumb obedience in her eyes made him wince. "Can't we forget about the slavery bit? We are in this thing together and we'll get out of it together."

"We will escape, I know it. You will kill all the *d'zertanoj* and release your slaves and lead us home again where we can march and find *krenoj*, far from this terrible place."

"Some girls are sure easy to please. That is roughly what I had in mind, except when we get out of here we are going in the other direction, as far away from your *krenoj* crowd as I can get."

Ijale listened attentively, stirring the soup with one hand and scratching inside her leather wrappings with the other. Jason found himself scratching as well, and realized from the sore spots on his skin that he had been doing an awful lot of this since he had been dragged out of the ocean of this inhospitable planet.

"Enough is enough!" he exploded, and went over and hammered on the door. "This place is a far cry from civilization as I know it, but that is no reason why we can't be as comfortable as possible." Chains and bolts rattled outside the door and Narsisi pushed his gloom-ridden face in.

"Why do you cry out? What is wrong?"

"I need some water, lots of it."

"But you have water," Narsisi said, puzzled, and pointed to a stone crock in the corner. "There is water there enough for days."

"By your standards, Nars old boy, not mine. I want at least ten times as much as that, and I want it now. And some soap, if there is such stuff in this barbaric place."

There was a good deal of argument involved, but Jason finally got his way by explaining that the water was needed for religious rites, to make sure that he would not fail in the work tomorrow. It came in a varied collection of containers, along with a shallow bowl full of powerful soft soap.

"We're in business," Jason chortled. "Take your clothes off—I have a surprise for you."

"Yes, Jason," Ijale said, smiling happily and lying down on her back.

"No! You're going to get a bath. Don't you know what a bath is?"

"No," she said, and shuddered. "It sounds evil."

"Over here, and off with the clothes," he ordered, poking at a hole in the floor. "This should serve as a drain—at least the water went away when I poured some into it."

The water was warmed on the stove, but Ijale still crouched against the wall and shuddered when he poured it over her. She screamed when he rubbed the slippery soap into her hair; however, he continued, with his hand over her mouth so that she wouldn't bring in the guards. He rubbed the soap into his own hair too, and his scalp tingled delightfully with the refreshing treatment. Some of the soap went in his ears, muffling them, so that the first intimation he had that the door was opened was the sound of Mikah's hoarse shout. He was standing in the doorway, finger pointed, and shaking with wrath, and Narsisi was standing behind him, peering over Mikah's shoulder with fascination at this weird religious rite.

"Degradation!" Mikah thundered. "You force this poor creature to bend to your will, humiliate her, strip her clothes from her, and gaze upon her, though you are not united in lawful wedlock." He shielded his eyes from the sight with a raised arm. "You are evil, Jason, a demon of evil, and must be brought to justice—"

"Out!" Jason roared, and spun Mikah about and started him through the door with one of his practiced Ch'aka kicks. "The only evil here is in your mind, you snooping scut. I'm giving the girl the first scrubbing of her life, and you should be giving me a medal for bringing sanitation to the natives, instead of howling like that."

He pushed them both out the door and shouted at Narsisi: "I wanted this slave, but not now! Lock him up until morning, then bring him back." He slammed the door and made a mental note to get hold of a bolt to be placed on this side as well.

Ijale was shivering, and Jason rinsed off the suds with warm water and gave her a clean piece of fur to dry herself with. Her body, now that the dirt had been removed, looked young and strong, it was firm-breasted and wide-hipped— Then he recalled Mikah's accusations and, muttering angrily to himself, he turned away and stripped and scrubbed himself thoroughly, then used the last of the water to rinse out his clothes. The unaccustomed feeling of cleanliness raised his morale again, and he was humming as he blew out the lamp and finished drying himself in the darkness. He lay down and pulled up the sleeping furs, and was making plans for tackling the engine in the morning when Ijale's warm body pressed up against his, instantly driving away all thoughts of mechanical engineering.

"Here I am," she said, quite unnecessarily.

"Yes," he said, and coughed, for he was having some difficulty talking. "That's not really what I had in mind with the bath—"

"You are not too old. So what is wrong?" She sounded shocked.

"It's just that I don't want to take advantage, you must understand . . ." He was a little confused.

"What do you mean? You are one of *those* that doesn't like girls!" She started to cry and he could feel her body shaking.

"When in Rome—" he sighed, and patted her back.

There were more *krenoj* for breakfast, but Jason was feeling too good physically to mind. He was scrubbed pink and clean, and the itching was gone even from his sprouting beard. The metalcloth of his Pyrran coverall had dried almost as soon as it had been washed, so he was wearing clean clothes as well. Ijale was still recovering from the traumatic effects of her bath, but she looked positively attractive with her skin cleaned and her hair washed and combed a bit. He would have to find some of the local cloth for her, for it would be a shame to ruin the good work by letting her get back into the badly cured skins she was used to wearing.

It was with a sensation of positive good feeling that he bellowed for the door to be opened and stamped through the cool morning to his place of labor. Mikah was already there, looking scruffy and angry as he rattled his chains. Jason gave him the friendliest of smiles, which only rubbed salt into the other's moral wounds.

"Leg-irons for him, too," Jason ordered. "And do it fast. We have a big job to do today." He turned back to the sealed engine, rubbing his hands together with anticipation.

The concealing hood was made of thin metal that could not hide many secrets. He carefully scratched away some of the paint and discovered a crimped and soldered joint where the sides met, but no other revealing marks. After some time spent tapping all over with his ear pressed to the metal, he was sure that the hood was just what he had thought it was when he first examined the thing: a double-walled metal container filled with liquid. Puncture it and you were dead. It was there merely to hide the secrets of the engine, and served no other function. Yet it had to be passed to service the steam engine—or did it? The construction was roughly cubical, and the hood covered only five sides. What about the sixth, the base?

"Now you're thinking, Jason," he said to himself, and knelt down to examine it. A wide flange, apparently of cast iron, projected all around, and was penetrated by four large bolt holes. The protective casing seemed to be soldered to the base, but there must be stronger concealed attachments, for it would not move even after he carefully scratched away some of the solder at the base. Therefore the answer had to be on the sixth side.

"Over here, Mikah," he called, and the man detached himself reluctantly from the warmth of the stove and shuffled up. "Come close and look at this medieval motive power while we talk, as if we are discussing business. Are you going to co-operate with me?"

"I do not want to, Jason. I am afraid that you will soil me with your touch, as you have others."

"Well, you're not so clean now—"

"I do not mean physically."

"Well, I do. You could certainly do with a bath and a good shampoo. I'm not worried about the state of your soul; you can battle that out on your own time. But if you will work with me I'll find a way to get us out of this place and to the city that made this engine, because if there is a way off this planet we'll find it only in the city."

"I know that, yet still I hesitate."

"Small sacrifices now for the greater good later. Isn't the entire purpose of this trip to get me back to justice? You're not going to accomplish that by rotting out the rest of your life as a slave."

"You are the devil's advocate the way you twist my conscience —but what you say is true. I will help you here so that we can escape."

"Fine. Now get to work. Take Narsisi and have him round up at least three good-sized poles, the kind we were chained to in the pumping gang. Bring them back here, along with a couple of shovels."

Slaves carried the poles only as far as the outside of the skin

walls, for Edipon would not admit them inside, and it was up to
Jason and Mikah to drag them laboriously to the site. The *d'zertanoj*, who never did physical labor, thought it very funny when
Jason suggested that they help. Once the poles were in position by
the engine, Jason dug channels beneath it and forced them under.
When this was done he took turns with Mikah in digging out the
sand beneath, until the engine stood over a pit, supported only by
the poles. Jason let himself down and examined the bottom of the
machine. It was smooth and featureless.

Once more he scratched away the paint with careful precision,
until it was cleared around the edges. Here the solid metal gave way
to solder and he picked at this until he discovered that a piece of
sheet metal had been soldered at the edges and fastened to the
bedplate. "Very tricky, these Appsalanoj," he said to himself, and
attacked the solder with a knife blade. When one end was loose he
slowly pulled the sheet of metal away, making sure that there was
nothing attached to it, and that it had not been booby-trapped in any
way. It came off easily enough and clanged down into the pit. The
revealed surface was smooth hard metal.

"Enough for one day," Jason said, climbing out of the pit and
brushing off his hands. It was now almost dark. "We've accomplished enough for now, and I want to think a bit before I go ahead.
So far, luck has been on our side, but I don't think it should be this
easy. I hope you brought your suitcase with you, Mikah, because
you're moving in with me."

"Never! A sink of sin, depravity . . ."

Jason looked him coldly in the eye, and with each word he spoke
he stabbed him in the chest with his finger to drive home the point:
"You are moving in with me because that is essential to our plans.
And if you'll stop referring to my moral weaknesses I'll stop talking
about yours. Now come on."

Living with Mikah Samon was trying, but it was just barely
possible. Mikah made Ijale and Jason go to the far wall and turn
their backs and promise not to look while he bathed behind a screen
of skins. They did so, but Jason exacted a small revenge by telling
Ijale jokes so that they tittered together and Mikah would be sure
they were laughing at him. The screen of skins remained after the
bath, and was reinforced, and Mikah retired behind it to sleep.

The following morning, under the frightened gaze of his guards,
Jason tackled the underside of the baseplate. He had been thinking
about it a good part of the night, and he put his theories to the test at
once. By pressing hard on a knife he could make a good groove in
the metal. It was not as soft as the solder, but seemed to be some

simple alloy containing a good percentage of lead. What could it be concealing? Probing carefully with the point of the knife, he covered the bottom in a regular pattern. The depth of the metal was uniform except in two spots where he found irregularities; they were on the midline of the rectangular base, and equidistant from the ends and sides. Picking and scraping, he uncovered two familiar-looking shapes, each as big as his head.

"Mikah, get down in this hole and look at these things. Tell me what you think they are."

Mikah scratched his beard and prodded with his finger. "They're still covered with this metal. I can't be sure . . ."

"I'm not asking you to be sure of anything—just tell me what they make you think of."

"Why—big nuts, of course. Threaded on the ends of bolts. But they are so big. . . ."

"They would have to be if they hold the entire metal case on. I think we are getting very close now to the mystery of how to open the engine—and this is the time to be careful. I still can't believe it is as easy as this to crack the secret. I'm going to whittle a wooden template of the nut, then have a wrench made. While I'm gone you stay down here and pick all the metal off the bolt and out of the screw threads. We can think this thing through for a while, but sooner or later I'm going to have to take a stab at turning one of those nuts. And I find it very hard to forget about that mustard gas."

Making the wrench put a small strain on the local technology, and all of the old men who enjoyed the title of Masters of the Still went into consultation over it. One of them was a fair blacksmith, and after a ritual sacrifice and a round of prayers he shoved a bar of iron into the charcoal and Jason pumped the bellows until it glowed white hot. With much hammering and cursing, it was laboriously formed into a sturdy open-end wrench with an offset head to get at the countersunk nuts. Jason made sure that the opening was slightly undersized, then took the untempered wrench to the work site and filed the jaws to an exact fit. After being reheated and quenched in oil he had the tool that he hoped would do the job.

Edipon must have been keeping track of the work progress, for he was waiting near the engine when Jason returned with the completed wrench.

"I have been under," he announced, "and have seen the nuts that the devilish Appsalanoj have concealed within solid metal. Who would have suspected! It still seems to me impossible that one metal could be hidden within another. How could that be done?"

"Easy enough. The base of the assembled engine was put into a form and the molten covering metal poured into it. It must have a much lower melting point than the steel of the engine, so there would be no damage. They just have a better knowledge of metal technology in the city, and counted upon your ignorance.''

"Ignorance! You insult—"

"I take it back. I just meant they thought they could get away with the trick; and since they didn't, they are the stupid ones. Does that satisfy you?''

"What do you do next?''

"I take off the nuts and when I do there is a good chance that the poison-hood will be released and can simply be lifted off.''

"It is too dangerous for you to do. The fiends may have other traps ready when the nut is turned. I will send a strong slave to turn them while we watch from a distance. His death will not matter.''

"I'm touched by your concern for my health, but as much as I would like to take advantage of the offer, I cannot. I've been over the same ground and reached the reluctant conclusion that this is one job of work that I have to do myself. Taking off those nuts looks entirely too easy, and that's what makes me suspicious. I'm going to do it and look out for any more trickery at the same time—and that is something that only I can do. Now I suggest you withdraw with the troops to a safer spot.''

There was no hesitation about leaving; footsteps rustled quickly on the sand and Jason was alone. The leather walls flapped slackly in the wind, and there was no other sound. Jason spat on his palms, controlled a slight shiver, and slid into the pit. The wrench fitted neatly over the nut, he wrapped both hands around it, and, bracing his leg against the pit wall, began to pull.

And stopped. Three turns of the thread on the bolt projected below the nut, scraped clean of metal by the industrious Mikah. Something about them looked very wrong, though he didn't know quite what. But suspicion was enough.

"Mikah," he shouted, but had to call loudly two more times before his assistant poked his head tentatively around the screen. "Nip over to the petroleum works and get me one of their bolts threaded with a nut—any size, it doesn't matter.''

Jason warmed his hands by the stove until Mikah returned with the oily bolt, then waved him out to rejoin the others. Back in the pit, he held it up next to the protruding section of Appsalan bolt and almost shouted with joy. The threads on the engine bolt were canted at a slightly different angle: where one ran up, the other ran down. The Appsalan threads had been cut in reverse, with a lefthand thread.

Throughout the galaxy there existed as many technical and cultural differences as there were planets, but one of the few things they all had in common, inherited from their terrestrial ancestors, was a uniformity of thread. Jason had never thought about it before, but when he mentally ran through his experiences on different planets he realized that they were all the same. Screws went into wood, bolts went into threaded holes, and nuts all went onto bolts when you turned them with a clockwise motion. Counterclockwise removed them. In his hand was the crude *d'zertano* nut and bolt, and when he tried it it moved in the same manner. But the engine bolt did not: it had to be turned clockwise to *remove* it.

Dropping the nut and bolt, he placed the wrench on the massive engine bolt and slowly applied pressure in what felt like the completely wrong direction—as if he were tightening, not loosening. It gave slowly, first a quarter-turn, then a half-turn. Bit by bit the projecting threads vanished, until they were level with the surface of the nut. It turned easily now, and within a minute it fell into the pit. He threw the wrench after it and scrambled out. Standing at the edge, he carefully sniffed the air, ready to run at the slightest smell of gas. There was nothing.

The second nut came off as easily as the first, and with no ill effects. Jason pushed a sharp chisel between the upper case and the baseplate where he had removed the solder, and when he leaned on it the case shifted slightly, held down only by its own weight.

From the entrance to the enclosure he shouted to the group huddled in the distance. "Come on back—this job is almost finished."

They all took turns at sliding into the pit and looking at the projecting bolts, and made appreciative sounds when Jason leaned on the chisel and showed that the case was free.

"There is still the little matter of taking it off," he told them, "and I'm sure that grabbing and heaving is the wrong way. That was my first idea, but the people who assembled that thing had some bad trouble in store for anyone who tightened those nuts instead of loosening them. Until we find out what that is, we are going to tread very lightly. Do you have any big blocks of ice around here, Edipon? It is winter now, isn't it?"

"Ice? Winter?" Edipon mumbled, caught off guard by the change of subject. He rubbed at the reddened tip of his prominent nose. "Of course it is winter. Ice—there must be ice on the higher lakes in the mountain; they are always frozen at this time of the year. But what do you want ice for?"

"You get it and I'll show you. Have it cut in nice flat blocks that I can stack. I'm not going to lift off the hood—I'm going to drop the engine out from underneath it!''

By the time the slaves had brought the ice down from the distant lakes Jason had rigged a strong wooden frame flat on the ground around the engine and pushed sharpened metal wedges under the hood; then he had secured the wedges to the frame. Now, if the engine was lowered into the pit, the hood would stay above, supported by the wedges. The ice would take care of this. Jason built a foundation of ice under the engine and then slipped out the supporting bars. As the ice slowly melted, the engine would be gently lowered into the pit.

The weather remained cold, and the ice refused to melt until Jason had the pit rigged with smoking oil stoves. Water began to run down into the pit and Mikah went to work bailing it out, while the gap between the hood and the baseplate widened. The melting continued for the rest of the day and almost all of the night. Red-eyed and exhausted, Jason and Mikah supervised the soggy sinking, and when the *d'zertanoj* returned at dawn the engine rested safely in a pool of mud on the bottom of the pit: the hood was off.

"They're tricky devils over there in Appsala, but Jason dinAlt wasn't born yesterday,'' he exulted. "Do you see that crock sitting there on top of the engine?'' He pointed to a sealed container of thick glass, the size of a small barrel, filled with an oily greenish liquid; it was clamped down tightly with padded supports. "That's the booby-trap. The nuts I took off were on the threaded ends of two bars that held the hood on, but instead of being fastened directly to the hood they were connected by a crossbar that rested on top of that jug. If either nut was tightened instead of being loosened the bar would have bent and broken the glass. I'll give you exactly one guess as to what would have happened then.''

"The poison liquid!''

"None other. And the double-walled hood is filled with it too. I suggest that as soon as we have dug a deep hole in the desert the hood and container be buried and forgotten about. I doubt if the engine has many other surprises in store, but I'll be careful as I work on it.''

"You can fix it? You know what is wrong with it?'' Edipon was trembling with joy.

"Not yet. I have barely looked at the thing. In fact, one look was enough to convince that the job will be as easy as stealing *krenoj* from a blind man. The engine is as inefficient and clumsy in construction as your petroleum still. If you people put one tenth of the energy into research and improving your product as you do into hiding it from the competition, you would all be flying jets.''

"I forgive your insult because you have done us a service. You will now fix this engine and the other engines. A new day is breaking for us!''

Jason yawned. "Right now it is a new night that is breaking for me. I have sleep to make up. See if you can talk your sons into wiping the water off that engine before it rusts away, and when I get back I'll see what I can do about getting it into running condition.''

9

Edipon's good mood continued and Jason took advantage of it by extracting as many concessions as possible. By hinting that there might be more traps in the engine, he easily gained permission to do all the work on the original site instead of inside the sealed and guarded buildings. A covered shed gave them protection from the weather, and a test stand was constructed to hold the engines when Jason worked on them. This was of a unique design and was built to Jason's exacting specifications; and since no one, including Mikah, had ever heard of or seen a test stand before, Jason had his way.

The first engine proved to have a burnt-out bearing and Jason rebuilt it by melting down the original bearing metal and casting it in position. When he unbolted the head of the massive single cylinder he shuddered at the clearance around the piston; he could fit his fingers into the opening between the piston and the cylinder wall. By introducing cylinder rings, he doubled the compression and power output. When Edipon saw the turn of speed the rebuilt engine gave his *caro*, he hugged Jason to his bosom and promised him the highest reward. This turned out to be a small piece of meat every day to relieve the monotony of the *kreno* meals, and a doubled guard to make sure that his valuable property did not escape. Their food up to now had consisted only of *krenoj*, and Jason shuddered while he admitted that he was actually growing used to them.

Jason had his own plans and kept busy manufacturing a number of pieces of equipment that had nothing at all to do with his engine overhauling business. While these were being assembled he went about lining up a little aid.

"What would you do if I gave you a club?" he asked a burly slave whom he was helping to haul a log towards his workshop. Narsisi and one of his brothers lazed out of earshot, bored by the routine of the guard duty.

"What I do with club?" the slave grunted, forehead furrowing and mouth gaping with the effort of thought.

"That's what I asked. And keep pulling while you think. I don't want the guards to notice anything."

"If I have club, I kill!" the slave announced excitedly, fingers grasping early for coveted weapon.

"Would you kill me?"

"I have club, I kill you, you not so big."

"But if I gave you the club, wouldn't I be your friend? Then wouldn't you want to kill someone else?"

The novelty of this alien thought stopped the slave dead, and he scratched his head perplexedly until Narsisi lashed him back to work. Jason sighed and found another slave to try his sales program on.

It took a while, but the idea was eventually percolating through the ranks of the slaves. All they had to look forward to from the *d'zertanoj* was back-breaking labor and an early death. Jason offered them something else—weapons, a chance to kill their masters, and even more killing later when they marched on Appsala. It was difficult for them to grasp the idea that they must work together to accomplish this, and not kill Jason and each other as soon as they received weapons. It was a chancy plan at best, and would probably break down long before any visit could be made to the city. But the revolt should be enough to free them from bondage, even if the slaves fled afterwards. There were less than fifty *d'zertanoj* at this well station, all men, with their women and children at some other settlement further back in the hills. It would not be too hard to kill them or chase them off, and long before they could bring reinforcements Jason and his runaway slaves would be gone. There was just one factor missing from his plans, and a new draft of slaves solved even that problem for him.

"Happy days," he laughed, pushing open the door to his quarters and rubbing his hands together with glee. The guard shoved Mikah in after him and locked the door. Jason secured it with his own interior bolt, then waved the two others over to the corner furthest from the door and the tiny window opening.

"New slaves today," he told them, "and one of them is from

ppsala, a mercenary or a soldier that they captured on a skirmish.
e knows that they will never let him live long enough to leave here,
he was grateful for any suggestions I had."

"This is man's talk I do not understand," Ijale said, turning away
d starting towards the cooking fire.

"You'll understand this," Jason said, taking her by the shoulder.
The soldier knows where Appsala is and can lead us there. The
ne has come to think about leaving this place."

He had all of Ijale's attention now, and Mikah's as well. "How is
is?" she gasped.

"I have been making my plans. I have enough files and lockpicks
w to crack into every room in this place, a few weapons, the key
the armory, and every able-bodied slave on my side."

"What do you plan to do?" Mikah asked.

"Stage a slave revolt in the best style. The slaves fight the
'zertanoj and we get away, perhaps with an army helping us, but at
ast we get away."

"You are talking *revolution!*" Mikah bellowed, and Jason
mped him and knocked him to the floor. Ijale held his legs down
hile Jason squatted on his chest and covered his mouth.

"What is the matter with you? Do you want to spend the rest of
ur life rebuilding engines? They are guarding us too well for there
be much chance of our breaking out on our own, so we need
lies. We have them ready made—all the slaves."

"Brevilushun," Mikah mumbled through the restraining
ngers.

"Of course it's a revolution. It is also the only possible chance of
rvival that these poor devils will ever have. Now they are human
attle, beaten and killed on whim. You can't be feeling sorry for the
'zertanoj—every one of them is a murderer ten times over. You've
en them beat people to death. Do you feel they are too nice to
ffer a revolution?"

Mikah relaxed and Jason moved his hand slightly, ready to clamp
own if the other's voice rose above a whisper.

"Of course they are not nice," Mikah said. "They are beasts in
uman garb. I feel no mercy for them, and they should be wiped out
nd blotted from the face of the earth, as were Sodom and Gomor-
ah. But it cannot be done by revolution: revolution is evil, inher-
ntly evil."

Jason stifled a groan. "Try telling that to two-thirds of the
overnments that now exist, since that's how many were founded—
y revolution. Nice, liberal, democratic governments—that were
tarted by a bunch of lads with guns and the immense desire to run

things in a manner more beneficial to themselves. How else do yo get rid of the powers on your neck if there is no way to vote the away legally? If you can't vote them—shoot them."

"Bloody revolution, it cannot be!"

"All right, no revolution," Jason said, getting up and wiping h hands in disgust. "We'll change the name. How about calling it prison break? No, you wouldn't like that either. I have it— liberation! We are going to strike the chains off these poor peopl and restore them to the lands from which they were stolen. The litt fact that the slaveholders regard them as property and won't thin much of the idea, and therefore might get hurt in the proces shouldn't bother you. So—will you join me in this liberation mov ment?"

"It is still revolution."

"It is whatever I decide to call it!" Jason raged. "You com along with me on the plans, or you will be left behind when we g You have my word on that." He went over and helped himself some soup and waited for his anger to simmer down.

"I cannot do it . . . I cannot do it," Mikah brooded, staring in his rapidly cooling soup as into an oracular crystal ball, seekin guidance there. Jason turned his back on him.

"Don't end up like him," he warned Ijale, pointing his spoo back over his shoulder. "Not that there is much chance that yo ever will, coming as you do from a society with its feet firm planted on the ground, or on the grave, to be more accurate. Yo people see only concrete facts, and only the most obvious ones, an as simple an abstraction as 'trust' seems beyond you. While th long-faced clown can only think in abstractions of abstractions, an the more unreal they are the better. I bet he even worries about ho many angels can dance on the head of a pin."

"I do not worry about it," Mikah broke in, overhearing th remark. "But I do think about it once in a while. It is a problem th cannot be lightly dismissed."

"You see?"

Ijale nodded. "If he is wrong, and I am wrong—then you must the only one who is right." She nodded in satisfaction at th thought.

"Very nice of you to say so." Jason smiled. "And true too. I la no claims to infallibility, but I am damn sure that I can see th difference between abstractions and facts a lot better than either you, and I am certainly more adroit at handling them." He reache his hand over his shoulder and patted himself on the back. "Th Jason dinAlt fan-club meeting is now adjourned."

"Monster of arrogance!" Mikah exclaimed.

"Oh, keep still."

"Pride goeth before a fall! You are a maledicent and idolatrous anti-pietist . . ."

"Very good."

". . . and I grieve that I could have considered, for even a second, aiding you or standing by while you sin, and I fear for the weakness of my own soul that I have not been able to resist temptation as I should. It grieves me, but I must do my duty." He banged loudly on the door and called, "Guard! Guard!"

Jason dropped his bowl and started to scramble to his feet, but slipped in the spilled soup and fell. As he stood up again the locks rattled on the door, and it opened. If he could reach Mikah before the idiot opened his mouth he would close it forever, or at least knock him out before it was too late.

But it was already too late. Narsisi poked his head in and blinked sleepily; Mikah struck his most dramatic pose and pointed to Jason. "Seize and arrest that man. I denounce him for attempted revolution, for planning red murder!"

Jason skidded to a halt and back-tracked, diving into a bag of his personal belongings that lay against the wall. He scrabbled in it, then kicked the contents about, and finally came up with a metal-forming hammer that had a weighty solid lead head.

"More traitor you," Jason shouted at Mikah, and he ran at Narsisi, who had been dumbly watching the performance and mulling over Mikah's words. Slow as he appeared to be, there was nothing wrong with his reflexes, and his shield snapped up and took Jason's blow, while his club spun over neatly and rapped Jason on the back of the hand: the numbed fingers opened and the hammer dropped to the floor.

"I think you two better come with me; my father will know what to do," Narsisi said, pushing Jason and Mikah ahead of him out of the door. He locked it and called for one of his brothers to stand guard, then prodded his captives down the hall. They shuffled along in their leg-irons, Mikah nobly as a martyr and Jason seething and grinding his teeth.

Edipon was not at all stupid when it came to slave rebellions, and he sized up the situation even faster than Narsisi could relate it.

"I have been expecting this, so it comes as no surprise." His eyes held a mean glitter when he leveled them at Jason. "I knew the time would come when you would try to overthrow me, which was why I permitted this other one to assist you and to learn your skills. As I expected, he has betrayed you to gain your position, which I award him now.''

"Betray? I did this for no personal gain," Mikah protested.

"Only the purest of motives." Jason laughed coldly. "Don't believe a word this pious crook tells you, Edipon. "I'm not planning any revolution—he said that just to get my job."

"You calumniate me, Jason! I never lie—you are planning revolt. You told me—"

"Silence, both of you! Or I'll have both of you beaten to death. This is my judgment. The slave Mikah has betrayed the slave Jason, and whether the slave Jason is planning rebellion or not is completely unimportant. His assistant would not have denounced him unless he was sure that he could do the work as well, which is the only fact that has any importance to me. Your ideas about a worker class have troubled me, Jason, and I will be glad to kill them and you at the same time. Chain him with the slaves. Mikah, I award you Jason's quarters and his woman, and as long as you do the work well I will not kill you. Do it a long time and you will live a long time.''

"Only the purest of motives—is what what you said, Mikah?" Jason shouted back as he was kicked from the room.

The descent from the pinnacle of power was swift. Within half an hour new shackles were on Jason's wrist and he was chained to the wall in a dark room filled with other slaves. His leg-irons had been left on as an additional reminder of his new status. As soon as the door was closed he rattled the chains and examined them in the dim light of a distant lamp.

"How comes the revolution?" the slave chained next to him leaned over and asked in a hoarse whisper.

"Very funny, ha-ha," was Jason's answer, and then he moved closer for a better look at the man, who had a fine case of strabismus, his eyes pointing in independent directions. "You look familiar—are you the new slave I talked to today?"

"That's me, Snarbi, fine soldier, pikeman, checked out on club and dagger, seven kills and two possibles on my record. You can check it yourself at the guildhall."

"I remember it all, Snarbi, including the fact that you know your way back to Appsala."

"I been around."

"Then the revolution is still on; in fact, it is starting right now, but I want to keep it small. Instead of freeing all these slaves, what do you say to the idea that we two escape by ourselves?"

"Best idea I've heard since torture was invented. We don't need all these stupid types, they just get in the way. Keep the operation small and fast, that's what I always say."

"I always say that too," Jason agreed, digging into his boot with his fingertip. He had managed to shove his best file and a lockpick into hiding there while Mikah was betraying him back in their room. The attack on Narsisi with the hammer had just been a cover-up.

Jason had made the file himself after many attempts at manufacturing and hardening steel, and the experiments had been successful. He picked out the clay that covered the cut he had made in his leg-cuffs and tackled the soft iron with vigor; within three minutes they were lying on the floor.

"You a magician?" Snarbi whispered.

"Mechanic. On this planet they're the same thing." He looked around, but the exhausted slaves were all asleep and had heard nothing. Wrapping a piece of leather around the file to muffle the sound, he began to file a link in the chain that secured the shackles on his wrists. "Snarbi," he said quietly, "are we on the same chain?"

"Yeah, the chain goes through these iron cuff things and holds the whole row of slaves together. The other end goes out through a hole in the wall."

"Couldn't be better. I'm filing one of these links, and when it goes we're both free. See if you can't slip the chain through the holes in your shackles and lay it down without letting the next slave know what is happening. We'll wear the iron cuffs for now. There is no time to play around with them, and they shouldn't bother us too much. Do the guards come through here at all during the night to check on the slaves?"

"Not since I been here. They just wake us up in the morning by pulling the chain."

"Then let's hope that's what happens tonight, because we are going to need plenty of time. *There!*" The file had cut through the link. "See if you can get enough of a grip on the other end of this link while I hold this end, and we'll try to bend it open a bit."

They strained silently until the opening gaped wide enough and the link fell through. They slipped the chain and laid it silently on the ground, then moved noiselessly to the door.

"Is there a guard outside?" Jason asked.

"Not that I know. I don't think they have enough men here to guard all the slaves."

The door would not budge when they pushed against it, and there was just light enough to make out the large keyhole of a massive inset lock. Jason probed lightly with the pick, and curled his lip in contempt.

"These idiots have left the key in the lock." He pulled off the stiffest of his leather wrappings, and after flattening it out pushed it under the badly fitting bottom edge of the door, leaving just a bit to hold on to. Then through the keyhole he poked lightly at the key and heard it thud to the ground outside. When he pulled the leather back, the key was lying in the center of it. The door unlocked silently and a moment later they were outside, staring tensely into the darkness.

"Let's go! Run, get away from here," Snarbi said, but Jason grabbed him by the throat and pulled him back.

"Isn't there one bit of intelligence on this planet? How are you going to get to Appsala without food or water—and if you find some, how can you carry enough? If you want to stay alive, follow instructions. I'm going to lock this door first so that no one stumbles onto our escape by accident. Then we are going to get some transport and leave here in style. Agreed?"

The answer was only a choked rattle until Jason opened his fingers a bit and let some air into the man's lungs. A labored groan must have meant assent, for Snarbi tottered after Jason when he made his way through the dark alleys between the buildings.

Getting clear of the walled refinery town presented no problem, since the few sentries were looking for trouble only from the outside. It was equally easy to approach Jason's leather-walled worksite from the rear and slip through at the spot where Jason had cut the leather and sewn up the opening with thin twine.

"Sit here and touch nothing, or you will be cursed for life," he commanded the shivering Snarbi; then he slipped toward the front entrance with a small sledge hammer clutched in his fist. He was pleased to see one of Edipon's other sons on guard duty, leaning against a pole, dozing. Jason gently lifted his leather helmet with his free hand and tapped once with the hammer: the guard slept even more soundly.

"Now we can get to work," Jason said when he went back inside. He clicked a firelighter to the wick of a lantern.

"What are you doing?" Snarbi asked, terrified. "They'll see us, kill us—escaped slaves. . . ."

"Stick with me, Snarbi, and you'll be wearing shoes. Lights here can't be seen by the sentries—I made sure of that when I chose the site. And we have a piece of work to do before we leave—we have to build a *caro*."

They did not have to build it from scratch, but there was enough truth in the statement to justify it. His most recently rebuilt and most powerful engine was still bolted to the test stand, a fact that justified all the night's risks. Three *caro* wheels lay among the other debris of the camp, and two of them had to be bolted to the engine while it was still on the stand. The ends of the driving axle cleared the edges of the stand, and Jason threaded the securing wheel bolts into place and utilized Snarbi to tighten them. At the other end of the stand was a strong, swiveling post that had been a support for his test instruments, and seemed strangely large for this purpose. It was. When the instruments were stripped away, a single bar remained, projecting backwards like a tiller handle. When a third wheel was fitted with a stub axle and slid into place in the forked lower end of the post, the test stand looked remarkably like a three-wheeled, steerable, steam-engine-powered platform that was mounted on legs. That is exactly what it was, what Jason had designed it to be from the first, and the supporting legs came away with the same ease with which the other parts had been attached. Eventual escape had always taken first priority in his plans.

Snarbi dragged over the crockery jars of oil, water, and fuel while Jason filled the tanks. He started the fire under the boiler and loaded aboard tools and the small supply of *krenoj* he had managed to set aside from their rations. All of this took time; it would soon be dawn and they would have to leave before then, and he could no longer avoid making up his mind.

He could not leave Ijale here, and if he went to get her he could not refuse to take Mikah as well. The man had saved his life, no matter what murderous idiocies he had managed to pull since then. Jason believed that you owed something to a man who prolonged your existence, but he also wondered just how much he still owed. In Mikah's case, he felt the balance of the debt to be mighty small, if not overdrawn. Perhaps this one last time . . .

"Keep an eye on the engine—I'll be back as soon as I can," he said, jumping to the ground and putting on his equipment.

"You want me to do *what?* Stay here with this devil machine? I cannot! It will burn and consume me."

"Act your age, Snarbi, your physical age if not your mental one. This rolling junk pile was made by men and repaired and improved by me—no demons involved. It burns oil to make heat that makes steam that goes to this tube to push that rod to make those wheels go around so we can move, and that is as much of theory of the steam engine as you are going to get from me. Maybe you can understand this better—I, only I, can get you safely away from here. Therefore you will stay and do as I say, or I will beat your brains in. Clear?"

Snarbi nodded dumbly.

"Fine. All you have to do is sit here and look at this little green disk—see it? If it should pop out before I come back, turn *this* handle in *this* direction. Is that clear? That way, the safety valve won't blow and wake the whole country, and we'll still have a head of steam."

Jason went out past the still silent sentry and headed back towards the refinery station. Instead of a club or a dagger, he was armed with a well-tempered broadsword that he had managed to manufacture under the noses of the guards. They had examined everything he brought from the worksite, since he had been working in the evenings in his room, but they ignored everything he manufactured as being beyond their comprehension. This primordial mental attitude had been of immense value, for in addition to the sword he carried a sack of molotails, a simple weapon of assault whose origin was lost in pre-history. Small crocks were filled with the most combustible of the refinery's fractions and were wrapped around with cloth that he had soaked in the same liquid. The stench made him dizzy, and he hoped that they would repay his efforts when the time came. He could only hope, for they were completely untried. In use, one lit the outer covering and threw them. The crockery burst on impact and the fuse ignited the contents. Theoretically.

Getting back in proved to be as easy as getting out, and Jason felt a twinge of regret. His subconscious had obviously been hoping that there would be a disturbance and he would have to retreat to save himself—his subconscious obviously being very short on interest in saving the slave girl and his nemesis, particularly at the risk of his own skin. But he was back in the building where his quarters were, and was trying to peer around the corner to see if a guard was at the door. There was, and he seemed to be dozing, but something jerked him awake. He had heard nothing, but he sniffed the air and wrinkled his nose; the powerful smell of water-of-power from Jason's molotails had roused him and he spotted Jason before the latter could pull back.

"Who is there?" the guard shouted, and he advanced at a lumbering run.

There was no quiet way out of this, and Jason leaped out with an echoing shout and lunged. The blade went right under the man's guard—it must have been that he had never seen a sword before—and the tip caught him full in the throat. He expired with a bubbling wail that stirred voices deeper in the building. Jason sprang over the corpse and tore at the multifold bolts and locks that sealed the door. Footsteps were running in the distance when he finally threw the door open and ran in.

"Get out, and quick, we're escaping!" he shouted at them and pushed the dazed Ijale towards the door. He took a great deal of pleasure in landing a tremendous kick that literally lifted Mikah through the opening, where he collided with Edipon, who had just run up waving a club. Jason leaped over the tumbled forms, rapped Edipon behind the ear with the hilt of his sword, and dragged Mikah to his feet.

"Get out to the engine works," he ordered his still uncomprehending companions. "I have a *caro* there that we can get away in." They finally broke into clumsy motion.

Shouts sounded behind him and an armed mob of *d'zertanoj* ran into view. Jason pulled down the hall light, burning his hand on the hot base as he did so, and applied its open flame to one of his molotails. The wick caught with a burst of flame and he threw it at approaching soldiers before it could burn his hand more seriously. It flew towards them, hit the wall, and broke; inflammable fuel spurted in every direction but the flame went out.

Jason cursed, and grappled for another molotail, for if they didn't work he was dead. The *d'zertanoj* had hesitated a moment rather than walk through the puddle of spilled water-of-power, and in that instant he hurled the second fire bomb. This one burst nicely too, and lived up to its maker's expectations when it ignited the first molotail as well, and the passageway filled with a curtain of fire. Holding his hand around the lamp flame so it wouldn't go out, Jason ran after the others.

As yet, the alarm had not spread outside of the building. Jason bolted the door from the outside; by the time this was broken open and the confusion sorted out they would be clear of the buildings. There was no need for the lamp now and it would only give him away, so he blew it out. From the desert came a continuous ear-piercing scream.

"He's done it," Jason groaned. "That's the safety valve on the steam engine!"

He bumped into Ijale and Mikah, who were milling about confusedly in the dark, kicked Mikah again out of sheer hatred of all mankind, and led them towards the worksite at a dead run.

They escaped unharmed, mainly because of the confusion on all sides of them. The *d'zertanoj* seemed to have never experienced a night attack before, which they apparently thought this was, and they did an incredible amount of rushing about and shouting. The burning building and the unconscious form of Edipon that was carried from the blaze made the general excitement and disorder even worse. All the *d'zertanoj* had been roused by the scream of the safety valve, which was still bleeding irreplaceable steam into the night air.

In the confusion, the fleeing slaves were not noticed, and Jason led them around the guard post on the walls and directly towards the worksite. They were spotted as they crossed the empty ground, and after some hesitation the guard ran in pursuit. Jason was leading the enemy directly to his precious steam wagon, but he had no choice. In any case, the thing was making its presence known, and unless he reached it at once the head of steam would be gone and they would be trapped. He leaped the recumbent guard at the entrance and ran towards his machine. Snarbi was cowering behind one wheel, but there was no time to give him any attention. As Jason jumped onto the platform the safety valve closed, and the sudden stillness was frightening.

Frantically he spun valves and shot a glance at the indicator: there wasn't enough steam left to roll ten meters. Water gurgled and the boiler hissed and clacked at him, while cries of anger came from the *d'zertanoj* as they ran into the enclosure and saw the bootleg *caro*. Jason thrust the end of a molotail into the firebox; it caught fire and he turned and hurled it at them. The angry cries turned into screams of fear as the tongues of flame licked up at the pursuers, and they retreated in disorder. Jason ran after them and hastened their departure with another molotail. They seemed to be retreating as far as the refinery walls, but he could not be sure in the darkness whether some of them weren't creeping around to the sides.

He hurried back to the *caro*, tapped on the unmoving pressure indicator, and opened the fuel feed wide. As an afterthought he wired down the safety valve, since his reinforced boiler should hold more pressure than the valve had been originally adjusted for. Once this was finished, he could only wait, for there was nothing else that could be done until the pressure built up again. The *d'zertanoj* would rally, someone would take charge, and they would attack the worksite. If enough pressure built up before this happened, they could escape. If not . . .

"Mikah—and you too, you cowering slob Snarbi, get behind this thing and push," Jason said.

"What has happened?" Mikah asked"Have you started the revolution? If so, I will give no aid . . ."

"We're escaping, if that's all right with you. Just I, Ijale, and a guide to show us the way. You don't have to come."

"I will join you. There is nothing criminal in escaping from these barbarians."

"It's very nice of you to say so. Now push. I want this steamobile in the center, far from all the walls, and pointing towards the desert. Down the valley, I guess—is that right, Snarbi?"

"Down the valley, sure, that's the way." His voice was still rasping from the earlier throttling, Jason was pleased to notice.

"Stop it here, and everyone aboard. Grab on to those bars I've bolted along the sides so you won't get bounced off—if we ever start moving, that is."

Jason took a quick look through his workshop to make sure everything they might need was already loaded, then reluctantly he climbed aboard. He blew out the lantern and they sat there in the darkness while the tension mounted, their faces lit from below by the flickering glow from the firebox. There was no way to measure time; each second seemed to take an eternity to drag by. The walls of the worksite cut off any view of the outside, and within a few moments imagination had peopled the night with silent creeping hordes, huddling about the thin barrier of leather, ready to swoop down and crush them in an instant.

"Let's run for it," Snarbi gurgled, and he tried to jump from the platform. "We're trapped here, we'll never get away."

Jason tripped him and knocked him flat, then pounded his head against the floor planks a few times until he quieted.

"I can sympathize with that poor man," Mikah said severely. "You are a brute, Jason, to punish him for his natural feelings. Cease your sadistic attack and join me in a prayer."

"If this poor man you are so sorry for had done his duty and watched the boiler, we would all be safely away from here by now. And if you have enough breath for a prayer, put it to better use by blowing into the firebox. It's not going to be wishes, prayers, or divine intervention that gets us out of here—it's a head of steam . . . ."

A howled battle cry was echoed by massed voices, and a squad of d'zertanoj burst through the entrance. At the same instant the rear of the leather wall went down and more armed men swarmed over it. The immobile *caro* was trapped between the two groups of attackers, who laughed in glee as they charged. Jason, cursing, lit our molotails at the same time and hurled them, two and two, in opposite directions. Before they hit, he had jumped to the steam valve and wound it open; with a hissing clank the *caro* shuddered and got under way. For the moment the attackers were held back by the walls of flame, and they screamed as the machine moved away at right angles from between their two groups. The air whistled with crossbow bolts, but most were badly aimed and only a few thudded into the baggage.

With each revolution of the wheels their speed picked up, and when they hit the walls the hides parted with a creaking snap. Strips of leather whipped at them, then they were through. The shouts grew fainter and the fires grew dimmer behind them as they streaked down the valley at a suicidal pace, hissing and rattling over the bumps. Jason clung to the tiller and shouted for Mikah to come relieve him. For if he let go of the thing they would turn and crash in an instant, and as long as he held it he couldn't cut down the steam. Some of this finally got through to Mikah and he crawled forward, grasping desperately at every handhold, until he crouched beside Jason.

"Grab this tiller and hold it straight, and steer around anything big enough to see."

As soon as the steering was taken over, Jason worked his way back to the engine and throttled down; they slowed to a clanking walk, then stopped completely. Ijale moaned, and Jason felt as if every inch of his body had been beaten with hammers. There was no sign of pursuit; it would be at least an hour before they could raise steam in the *caro,* and no one on foot could possibly have matched their own headlong pace. The lantern he had used earlier had vanished during the wild ride, so Jason dug out another one of his own construction.

"On your feet, Snarbi," he ordered. "I've cracked us all out of slavery, and now it is time for you to do some of the guiding that you were telling me about. I never did have a chance to build headlights for this machine, so you will have to walk ahead with this light and pick out a nice smooth track going in the right direction."

Snarbi climbed down unsteadily and walked out in front of them. Jason opened the valve a bit and they clattered forward on his trail as Mikah turned the tiller to follow. Ijale crawled over and settled herself against Jason's side, shivering with cold and fright. He patted her shoulder.

"Relax," he said. "From now on this is just a pleasure trip."

10

They were six days out of Putl'ko and their supplies were almost exhausted. The country, once they were away from the mountains, became more fertile, and undulating pampas of grass with enough streams and herds of beasts to assure that they did not starve. It was fuel that mattered, and that afternoon Jason had opened their last jar. They stopped a few hours before dark, for their fresh meat was gone, and Snarbi took the crossbow and went out to shoot something for the pot. Since he was the only one who could handle the clumsy weapon with any kind of skill, in spite of his ocular deficiencies, and who knew about the local game, this task had been assigned to him. With longer contact, his fear of the *caro* had lessened, and his self-esteen rose with his ability as a hunter recognized. He strolled arrogantly out into the knee-high grass, crossbow over his shoulder, whistling tunelessly through his teeth. Jason stared after him and once again felt a growing unease.

"I don't trust that wall-eyed mercenary. I don't trust him for one second," he muttered.

"Were you talking to me?" Mikah asked.

"I wasn't, but I might as well now. Have you noticed anything interesting about the country we have been passing through, anything different?"

"Nothing. It is a wilderness, untouched by the hand of man."

"Then you must be blind, because I have been seeing things the last two days, and I know just as little about woodcraft as you do. Ijale," he called, and she looked up from the boiler over which she was heating a thin stew of their last *krenoj*. "Leave that stuff—it tastes just as bad whatever is done to it, and if Snarbi has any luck we'll be having roast meat. Tell me, have you seen anything strange or different about the land we passed through today?"

"Nothing strange, just signs of people. Twice we passed places where grass was flat and branches broken, as if a *caro* passed two or three days ago, maybe more. And once there was a place where someone had built a cooking fire, but that was very old."

"Nothing to be seen, Mikah?" Jason said, with raised eyebrows. "See what a lifetime of *kreno* hunting can do for the sense of observation and terrain."

"I am no savage. You cannot expect me to look out for that sort of thing."

"I don't. I have learned to expect very little from you besides trouble. Only now I am going to need your help. This is Snarbi's last night of freedom, whether he knows it or not, and I don't want him standing guard tonight, so you and I will split the shift."

Mikah was astonished. "I do not understand. What do you mean when you say this is his last night of freedom?"

"It should be obvious by now, even to you, after seeing how the social ethic works on this planet. What did you think we were going to do when we came to Appsala—follow Snarbi like sheep to the slaughter? I have no idea what he is planning; I just know he must be planning something. When I ask him about the city he only answers

in generalities. Of course he is a hired mercenary who wouldn't
know too much of the details, but he must know a lot more than he is
telling us. He says we are still four days away from the city. My
guess is that we are no more than one or two. In the morning I intend
to grab him and tie him up, then swing over to those hills there and
find a place to hole up. I'll fix some chains for Snarbi so he can't get
away, and then I'll do a scout of the city."

"You are going to chain this poor man, make a slave of him for
no reason!"

"I'm not going to make a slave of him, I'm just going to chain
him to make sure he doesn't lead us into some trap that will benefit
him. This souped-up *caro* is valuable enough to tempt any of the
locals, and if he can sell me as an engine-mechanic slave his fortune
is made."

"I will not hear this!" Mikah stormed. "You condemn the man
on no evidence at all, just because of your mean-minded suspicions.
Judge not lest ye be judged yourself! And you play the hypocrite as
well, because I well remember your telling me that a man is
innocent until proven guilty."

"Well, this man is guilty, if you want to put it that way, guilty of
being a member of this broken-down society, which means that he
will always act in certain ways at certain times. Haven't you learned
anything about these people yet? . . . Ijale!" She looked up from
her contented munching on a *kreno,* obviously not listening to the
argument. "Tell me, what is your opinion? We are coming soon to
a place where Snarbi has friends, or people who will help him. What
do you think he will do?"

"Say hello to the people he knows? Maybe they will give him a
kreno." She smiled in satisfaction at her answer, and took another
bite.

"That's not quite what I had in mind," Jason said patiently.
"What if we three are with him when we come to the people, and
the people see us and the *caro* . . ."

She sat up, alarmed. "We can't go with him! If he has people
there they will fight us, make us slaves, take the *caro.* You must kill
Snarbi at once."

"Bloodthirsty heathen . . ." Mikah began in his best denuncia-
tory voice, but stopped when he saw Jason pick up a heavy
hammer.

"Don't you understand yet?" Jason asked. "By tying up Snarbi
I'm only conforming to a local code of ethics, like saluting in the
army, or not eating with your fingers in polite society. In fact, I'm
being a little slipshod, since by local custom I really should kill him

before he can make trouble for us."

"It cannot be. I cannot believe it. You cannot judge and condemn a man upon such flimsy evidence."

"I'm not condemning him," Jason said with growing irritation. "I'm just making sure that he can't cause us any trouble. You don't have to agree with me to help me; just don't get in my way. And split the guard with me tonight. Whatever I do in the morning will be on my shoulders and no concern of yours."

"He is returning," Ijale whispered, and a moment later Snarbi came through the high grass.

"Got a *cervo,*" he announced proudly, and dropped the animal down before them. "Cut him up, makes good chops and roast. We eat tonight."

He seemed completely innocent and without guile; the only thing that appeared guilty about him was his shifty gaze, which could be blamed on his crossed eyes. Jason wondered for a second if his assessment of the danger was correct; then thought of where he was and lost his doubts. Snarbi would be committing no crime if he tried to kill or enslave them; he would just be doing what any ordinary slave-holding barbarian would do in his place. Jason searched through his toolbox for some rivets that could be used to fasten the leg-irons on the man.

They had a filling dinner and the others turned in at dusk and were quickly asleep. Jason, tired from the labors of the trip and heavy with food, forced himself to remain awake, trying to keep alert for trouble, both from within the camp and from without. When he became too sleepy, he paced around the camp until the cold drove him back to the shelter of the still warm boiler. Above him, the stars wheeled slowly, and when one bright one reached the zenith he estimated it was midnight, or a bit after. He shook Mikah awake.

"You're on now. Keep your eyes and ears open for anything stirring, and don't forget a careful watch there." He jerked his thumb at Snarbi's silent form. "Wake me up at once if there is anything suspicious."

Sleep came instantly, and Jason barely stirred until the first light of dawn touched the sky. Only the brightest stars were visible, and he could see a ground fog rising from the grass around them. Near him were the huddled forms of the two sleepers; the further one shifted in his sleep and Jason realized it was Mikah.

He bounded out of his skin covers and grabbed the other man by the shoulders. "What are you doing asleep?" he raged. "You were supposed to be on guard!"

Mikah opened his eyes and blinked with majestic assurance. "I was on guard, but towards morning Snarbi awoke and offered to take his turn. I could not refuse him.''

"You couldn't *what?* After what I said—''

"That was why. I could not judge an innocent man guilty and be a party to your unfair action. Therefore I left him on guard.''

"You left him on guard!" The words almost choked Jason. "Then where is he? Do you see anyone on guard?''

Mikah looked around in a careful circle and saw that there were only the two of them and the wakening Ijale. "He seems to have gone. He has proved his untrustworthiness, and in the future we will not allow him to stand guard.''

Jason drew his foot back for a kick, then realized he had no time for such indulgences and dived for the steamobile. The firemaker worked at the first try for a change, and he lit the boiler. It roared merrily, but when he tapped the indicator he saw that the fuel was almost gone. There should be enough left in the last jug to take them to safety before whatever trouble Snarbi was planning arrived—but the jug was gone.

"That tears it,'' Jason said bitterly after a hectic search of the *caro* and the surrounding plain. The water-of-power had vanished with Snarbi, who, afraid as he was of the steam engine, apparently knew enough from observing Jason fueling the thing to realize that it could not move without the vital liquid.

An empty feeling of resignation had replaced Jason's first rage: he should have known better than to trust Mikah with anything, particularly when it involved an ethical point. He stared at the man, now calmly eating a bit of cold roast, and marveled at his unruffled calm.

"This doesn't bother you,'' he said, "the fact that you have condemned us all to slavery again?''

"I did what was right. I had no other choice. We must live as moral creatures, or sink to the level of the animals.''

"But when you live with people who behave like animals—how do you survive?''

"You live as they do—as you do, Jason,'' he said with majestic judgment, "twisting and turning with fear, but unable to avoid your fate no matter how you squirm. Or you live as I have done, as a man of conviction, knowing what is right and not letting your head be turned by the petty needs of the day. And if one lives this way, one can die happy.''

"Then die happy!'' Jason snarled, and he reached for his sword, but he settled back again glumly without picking it up. "To think that I ever thought I could teach you anything about the reality of existence here, when you have never experienced reality before, nor ever will until the day you die. You carry your own attitudes, which are your reality, around with you all the time, and they are more solid to you than this ground we are sitting on."

"For once we are in agreement, Jason. I have tried to open your eyes to the true light, but you turn away and will not see. You ignore the Eternal Law for the exigencies of the moment, and are therefore damned."

The pressure indicator on the boiler hissed and popped out, but the fuel level was at the absolute bottom.

"Grab some food for breakfast, Ijale," Jason said, "and get away from this machine. The fuel is gone and it's finished."

"I shall make a bundle to carry, and we will escape on foot."

"No, that's out of the question. Snarbi knows this country, and he knew we would find out at dawn that he was missing. Whatever kind of trouble he is bringing is already on the way, and we wouldn't be able to escape on foot. So we might as well save our energy. But they aren't getting my hand-made, super-charged steamobile!" he added with sudden vehemence, snatching up the crossbow. "Back, both of you, far back. They'll make a slave of me for my talents, but no free samples go with it. If they want one of these hot-rod steam wagons they are going to have to pay for it!"

Jason lay down flat at the maximum range of the crossbow and his third quarrel hit the boiler. It went up with a most satisfactory bang and small pieces of metal and wood rained down all around. In the distance he heard shouting and the barking of dogs.

When he stood up he could see a distant line of men advancing through the tall grass, and when they were closer large dogs were also visible, tugging at their leashes. Though they must have come far in a few hours, they approached at a steady trot—experienced runners in thin leather garments, each carrying a short laminated bow and a full quiver of arrows. They swooped up in a semicircle, their great hounds slavering to be loosed, and stopped when the three strangers were within bow range. They notched their arrows and waited, alert, staying well clear of the smoking ruins of the *caro* until Snarbi finally staggered up, half supported by two other runners.

"You now belong to . . . the Hertug Persson . . . and are his slaves. . . ." Snarbi said. He seemed too exhausted to notice his surroundings. "What happened to the *caro?*" He screamed this last when he spotted the smoking wreck, and would have collapsed except for the sustaining arms. Evidently the new slaves decreased in value with the loss of the machine.

Snarbi stumbled over to it and, when none of the soldiers would help him, gathered up what he could find of Jason's artifacts and tools. When he had bundled them up, and the foot cavalry saw that he suffered no harm from the contact, they reluctantly agreed to carry them. One of the soldiers, identical in dress with the others, seemed to be in charge, and when he signaled a return they closed in on the three prisoners and nudged them to their feet with drawn bows.

"I'm coming, I'm coming," Jason said, gnawing on a bone, "but I'm going to finish my breakfast first. I see an endless vista of *krenoj* stretching before me, and I intend to enjoy this last meal before entering servitude."

The lead soldiers looked confused and turned to their officer for orders. "Who is this?" he asked Snarbi, pointing at the still seated Jason. "Is there any reason why I should not kill him?"

"You can't!" Snarbi choked, and turned a dirty shade of white. "He is the one who built the devil-wagon and knows all of its secrets. Hertug Persson will torture him to build another."

Jason wiped his fingers on the grass and stood up. "All right, gentlemen, let's go. And on the way perhaps someone can tell me just who Hertug Persson is and what is going to happen next."

"I'll tell you," Snarbi bragged as they started the march. "He is Hertug of the Perssonoj. I have fought for the Perssonoj and they knew me, and I saw the Hertug himself and he believed me. The Perssonoj are very powerful in Appsala and have many powerful secrets, but they are not as powerful as the Trozelligoj, who have the secret of the *caroj* and the *jetilo*. I knew I could ask any price of the Perssonoj if I brought them the secret of the *caroj*. And I will." He thrust his face close to Jason's with a fierce grimace. "You will tell them the secret. I will help them torture you until you tell."

Jason put out his toe as they walked and Snarbi tripped over it, and when the traitor fell he walked the length of his body. None of the soldiers paid any attention to this incident. When they had passed Snarbi staggered to his feet and tottered after them, shouting curses. Jason hardly heard them, for he had troubles enough as it was.

11

Seen from the surrounding hills, Appsala looked like a burning city that was being slowly washed into the sea. Only when they had come closer was it clear that the smoke was from the multifold chimneys, both large and small, that studded the buildings, and that the city began at the shore and covered a number of islands in what must be a shallow lagoon. Large seagoing ships were tied up at the seaward side of the city, and closer to the mainland smaller craft were being poled through the canals. Jason searched anxiously for a spaceport or any signs of interstellar culture, but saw nothing. Then the hills intervened as the trail cut off to one side and approached the sea some distance from the city.

A fair-sized sailing vessel was tied up at the end of a stone wharf, obviously awaiting them, and the captives were tied hand and foot and tossed into the hold. Jason managed to wriggle around until he could get his eye to a crack between two badly fitting planks, and he gave a running travelog of the short cruise, apparently for the edification of his companions, but really for his own benefit, since the sound of his own voice always cheered him and gave him courage.

"Our voyage is nearing its close, and before us opens up the romantic and ancient city of Appsala, famed for its loathsome customs, murderous natives, and archaic sanitation facilities, of which the watery channel this ship is now entering seems to be the major cloaca. There are islands on both sides, the smaller ones covered with hovels so decrepit that in comparison the holes in the grounds of the humblest animals are as palaces, while the larger islands seem to be forts, each one walled and barbicaned, and presenting a warlike face to the world. There couldn't be that many forts in a town this size, so I am led to believe that each one is undoubtedly the guarded stronghold of one of the tribes, groups, or clans that our friend Judas told us about. Look on these monuments to ultimate selfishness and beware: this is the end product of the system that begins with slaveholders like the former Ch'aka with their tribes of *kreno* crackers, and builds up through familial hierarchies like the *d'zertanoj,* and reaches its zenith of depravity behind those strong walls. It is still absolute power that rules absolutely, each man out for all that he can get, the only way to climb being over the bodies of others, and all physical discoveries and inventions being treated as private and personal secrets to be hidden and used only for personal gain. Never have I seen human greed and selfishness carried to such extremes, and I admire Homo sapiens' capacity to follow through on an idea, no matter how it hurts.''

The ship lost way as it backed its sails, and Jason fell from his precarious perch into the stinking bilge. "The descent of man," he muttered, and inched his way out.

Piles grated along the sides, and with much shouting and cursed orders the ship came to a halt. The hatch above was slid back and the three captives were rushed to the deck. The ship was tied up to a dock in a pool of water surrounded by buildings and high walls. Behind them a large sea gate was just swinging shut, through which the ship had entered from the canal. They could see no more because they were pushed into a doorway and through halls and past guards until they ended up in a large central room. It was unfurnished except for the dais at the far end on which stood a large rusty iron throne. The man on the throne, undoubtedly the Hertug Persson, sported a magnificent white beard and shoulder-length hair, his nose was round and red, his eyes blue and watery. He nibbled at a *kreno* impaled delicately on a two-tined iron fork.

"Tell me," the Hertug shouted suddenly, "why you should not be killed at once?"

"We are your slaves, Hertug, we are your slaves," everyone in the room shouted in unison, at the same time waving their hands in the air. Jason missed the first chorus, but came in on the second. Only Mikah did not join in the chant-and-wave, speaking instead in a solitary voice after the pledge of allegiance was completed.

"I am no man's slave."

The commander of the soldiers swung his thick bow in a short arc that terminated on the top of Mikah's head: he dropped stunned to the floor.

"You have a new slave, oh Hertug," the commander said.

"Which is the one who knows the secrets of the *caroj?*" the Hertug asked, and Snarbi pointed at Jason.

"Him there, oh Mightiness. He can make *caroj* and he can make the monster that burns and moves them. I know because I watched him do it. He also made balls of fire that burned the *d'zertanoj,* and many other things. I brought him to be your slave so that he could make *caroj* for the Perssonoj. Here are the pieces of the *caro* we traveled in, that were left after it was consumed by its own fire." Snarbi shook the tools and burnt fragments out onto the floor, and the Hertug curled his lip at them.

"What proof is this?" he asked, and turned to Jason. "These things mean nothing. How can you prove to me, slave, that you can do the things he says?"

Jason entertained briefly the idea of denying all knowledge of the matter, which would be a neat revenge against Snarbi, who would certainly meet a sticky end for causing all this trouble for nothing, but he discarded the thought as quickly as it had come. Partly for humanitarian reasons, for Snarbi could not help being what he was, but mostly because Jason had no particular desire to be put to the torture. He knew nothing about the local torture methods, and he wanted to keep it that way.

"Proof is easy, Hertug of all the Perssonoj, because I know everything about everything. I can build machines that walk, that talk, that run, fly, swim, bark like a dog, and roll on their backs."

"You will build a *caro* for me?"

"It could be arranged, if you have the right kind of tools for me to use. But I must first know what is the specialty of your clan, if you know what I mean. For instance, the Trozelligoj make motors, and the *d'zertanoj* pump oil: what do your people do?"

"You cannot know as much as you say if you do not know of the glories of the Perssonoj!"

"I come from a distant land and, as you know, news travels slowly around these parts."

"Not around the Perssonoj," the Hertug said scornfully, and he thumped his chest. "We can talk across the widths of the country, and always know where our enemies are. We can send magic to make light in a glass ball, or magic that will pluck the sword from an enemy's hand and drive terror into his heart."

"It sounds as if your gang has the monopoly on electricity, which is good to hear. If you have some heavy forging equipment—"

"Stop!" the Hertug interrupted. "Leave! Out—everyone except the *sciuloj*. Not the new slave, he stays here," he shouted when the soldiers seized Jason.

When the others had left, only a handful of men remained who were all a little long in the tooth. Each wore a brazen, sunburst-type decoration on his chest. They were undoubtedly adept in the secret electrical arts, and they fingered their weapons and grumbled with unconcealed anger at Jason's forbidden knowledge.

The Hertug spoke to him again. "You used a sacred word. Who

told it to you? Speak quickly, or you will be killed."

"Didn't I tell you I knew everything? I can build a *caro*, and, given a little time, I can improve on your electrical works, if your technology is on the same level as the rest of this planet."

"Do you know what lies behind the forbidden portal?" the Hertug asked, pointing to a barred, locked, and guarded door at the other end of the room. "There is no way you can have seen what is there, but if you can tell me what lies beyond it I will know you are the wizard that you claim you are."

"I have a very strange feeling that I have been over this ground once before." Jason sighed. "All right, here goes. You people here make electricity, maybe chemically, though I doubt if you would get enough power that way, so you must have a generator of some sort. That will be a big magnet, a piece of special iron that can pick up other iron, and you spin wire around fast next to it, and out comes electricity. You pipe this through copper wire to whatever devices you have—and they can't be very many. You say you talk across the country. I'll bet you don't talk at all, but send little clicks—I'm right, am I not?" The foot shuffling and the rising buzz from the adepts were sure signs that he was hitting close.

"I have an idea for you: I think I'll invent the telephone. Instead of the old clickety-clack, how would you like to *really* talk across the country? Speak into a gadget here, and have your voice come out at the far end of the wire?"

The Hertug's piggy little eyes blinked greedily. "It is said that in the old days this could be done, but we have tried and have failed. Can you do this thing?"

"I can—if we can come to an agreement first. But before I make any promises I have to see your equipment."

This brought mutters of complaint about secrecy, but in the end avarice won over taboo and the door to the holy of holies was opened for Jason while two of the *sciuloj*, with bared daggers ready, stood at his sides. The Hertug led the way, followed by Jason and his septuagenarian bodyguard, with the rest of the *sciuloj* tottering after. Each of them bowed and mumbled a prayer as he crossed the sacred threshold, while it was all Jason could do to keep himself from breaking into contemptuous laughter.

A rotating shaft—undoubtedly slave-powered—entered the large chamber through the far wall and turned a ramshackle collection of belts and pulleys that eventually hooked up to a crude and ugly machine that rattled and squeaked and shook the floor under their feet. At first sight it baffled Jason, until he examined its components and realized what it was.

"What else should I have expected?" he said to himself. "If there are two ways of doing anything, leave it to these people to use the worst one."

The final, cartwheel-sized pulley was fixed to a wooden shaft that rotated at an impressive speed, except when one of the belts jumped out of place, which was something that occurred with monotonous regularity. This happened while Jason was watching, and the shaft instantly slowed so that he could see that iron rings studded with smaller, U-shaped pieces of iron, were fixed all along its length. These were half hidden inside a birdcage of looped wires that was suspended about the shaft. The whole thing looked like an illustration from a bronze age edition of *First Steps in Electricity*.

"Does not your soul cringe in awe before these wonders?" the Hertug asked, noticing Jason's dropped jaw and glassy eye.

"It cringes all right," Jason told him. "But only in pain from that ill-conceived collection of mechanical misconceptions."

"Blasphemer!" the Hertug shrieked. "Slay him!"

"Wait a minute!" Jason said, holding tight to the dagger arms of the two nearest *sciuloj* and interposing their bodies between his body and the others' blades. "Don't misunderstand. That's a great generator you have there, a seventh wonder of the world—though most of the wonder is how it manages to produce any electricity. A tremendous invention, years ahead of its time. However, I might be able to suggest a few minor modifications that would produce more electricity with less work. I suppose that you are aware that an electric current is generated in a wire when a magnetic field is moved across it?"

"I do not intend to discuss theology with a non-believer," the Hertug said coldly.

"Theology or science, call it what you will, the answers still come out the same." Jason twisted a bit with his Pyrran-hardened muscles and the two old men squealed and dropped their daggers to the floor. The rest of the *sciuloj* seemed reluctant to press the attack. "But did you ever stop to think that you could get an electrical current just as easily by moving the *wire* through the magnetic field, instead of the other way around? You can get the same current flow that way with about a tenth of the work."

"We have always done it this way, and what was good enough for our ancestors—"

"I know, I know, don't finish the quote. I seem to have heard it before on this planet." The armed *sciuloj* began to close in on him again, their daggers ready. "Look, Hertug—do you want me slain or not? Let your boys know."

"Slay him not," the Hertug said after a moment's thought. "What he says may be true. He may be able to assist us in the operation of our holy machines."

With the threat removed for the moment, Jason examined the large, ungainly apparatus that filled the far end of the room, this time making some attempt to control his horrified reactions. "I suppose that your sacred wonder is your holy telegraph?"

"None other," the Hertug said reverently. Jason shuddered.

Copper wires came down from the ceiling above and terminated in a clumsily wound electromagnet positioned close to the flat iron shaft of a pendulum. When a current surged through the electromagnet it would attract the shaft; and when the current was turned off, the weight on the end of the pendulum would drag it back to somewhere near the vertical. A sharp metal scriber was fixed to the bottom of the weight, and the point of the scriber was dug into the wax coating of a long strip of copper. This strip ran in grooves so that it moved at right angles to the pendulum's swing, dragged forward by a weight-powered system of meshed wooden gears.

While Jason watched, the rattling mechanism jerked into motion. The electromagnet buzzed, the pendulum jerked, the needle drew an incision across the wax, the gears squeaked, and the cord fastened to a hole in the end of the strip began to draw it forwards. Attentive *sciuloj* stood ready to put another wax-coated strip into position when the first one was finished.

Close by, completed message strips were being made legible by pouring red liquid over them. This ran off the waxen surface but was trapped by the needle-scratched grooves. A shaky red line appeared running the length of the strips, with V-shaped extensions wherever the scribing needle had been deflected. These were carried to a long table where the coded information was copied off onto slates. Everything considered, it was a slow, clumsy, inept method of transmitting information. Jason rubbed his hands together.

"Oh, Hertug of all the Perssonoj," he intoned, "I have looked on your holy wonders and stand in awe, indeed I do. Far be it for a mere mortal to improve on the works of the gods, at least not right now, but it is within my power to pass on to you certain other secrets of electricity that the gods have imparted to me."

"Such as what?" the Hertug asked, eyes slitted.

"Such as the—let's see, what is the Esperanto word for it—such as the *akumulatoro*. Do you know of this?"

"The word is mentioned in some of the older holy writings, but that is all we know of it." The Hertug was licking his lips now.

"Then get ready to add a new chapter, because I'm going to

provide you with a Leyden jar, free and gratis, along with complete instructions on how to make more. This is a way of putting electricity in a bottle, just as if it were water. Then later we can go on to more sophisticated batteries."

"If you can do this thing you shall be suitably rewarded. Fail, and you will be . . ."

"No threats, Hertug; we've gone far beyond that stage. And no rewards either. I told you this was a free sample with no strings attached—perhaps just a few physical comforts for me while I'm working: the fetters struck off, a supply of *krenoj* and water, and such like. Then, if you like what I've done and want more, we can make a deal. Agreed?"

"I will consider your requests," the Hertug said.

"A simple yes or no will do. What can you possibly lose in an arrangement like this?"

"Your companions will be held prisoners to be slain instantly if you transgress."

"A fine idea. And if you want to get some work out of the one called Mikah—like hard labor, for instance—that is perfectly agreeable. I'll need some special materials that I don't see here. A wide-mouthed glass jar and a good supply of tin."

"Tin? I know it not."

"Yes, you do. It's the white metal you mix with copper to make your bronze."

"*Stano*. We have a goodly supply."

"Have them bring it around and I'll get to work."

In theory, a Leyden jar is simple enough to manufacture—if all the materials are on hand. Getting the correct materials was Jason's biggest problem. The Perssonoj did no glass blowing themselves, but bought everything they needed from the Vitristoj clan, who labored at their secret furnaces. These glass blowers produced a few stock-size bottles, buttons, drinking glasses, knobby plate glass, and half a dozen other items. None of their bottles could be adapted to this use, and they were horrified at Jason's suggestion that they produce a new bottle to his specifications. The offer of hard cash drained away most of their dismay, and after studying Jason's clay model they reluctantly agreed to produce a similar bottle for a staggering sum. The Hertug grumbled mightily, but finally he paid over the required number of stamped and punctured gold coins strung on a wire.

"Your death will be horrible," he told Jason, "if your *akumulatoro* fails."

"Have faith, and all will be well," Jason reassured him, and he returned to browbeating the metal workers, who suffered as they tried to hammer sheet tin into thin foil.

Jason had seen neither Mikah nor Ijale since they had all been dragged into the Perssonoj stronghold, but he did not worry about them. Ijale was well adapted to the slave life, so she would get into no trouble while he was selling the Hertug on the wonders of his electrical knowledge. Mikah, however, was not used to being a slave, and Jason cherished the hope that this would lead to bad trouble, resulting in physical contusions. After the last fiasco, his reservoir of good will for the man had drained dry.

"It has arrived," the Hertug announced, and he and all the *sciuloj* stood around mumbling suspiciously while the wrappings were removed from the glass jar.

"Not too bad," Jason said, holding it up to the light to see how thick the sides were. "Except that this is the large twenty-liter economy size—about four times as big as the model I sent them."

"For a large price a large jar," the Hertug said. "That is only right. Why do you complain? Do you fear failure?"

"I fear nothing. It's just a lot more trouble to build a model this size. It can also be dangerous; these Leyden jars can take quite a charge."

Ignoring the onlookers, Jason coated the jar inside and out with his lumpy tinfoil, stopping about two-thirds of the way up from the bottom. He then whittled a plug from *gumi*, a rubber-like material that had good insulating qualities, and drilled a hole through it. The Perssonoj watched, mystified, as he pushed an iron rod through this hole, then attached a short iron chain to the longer end, and fixed a round iron ball to the shorter.

"Finished," he announced.

"But—what does it do?" the Hertug asked, puzzled.

"I demonstrate." Jason pushed the plug into the wide mouth of the jar so that the chain rested on the inner lining of tinfoil. He pointed to the ball that projected from the top. "This is attached to the negative pole of your generator; electricity flows down through the rod and chain and is collected on the tin lining. We run the generator until the jar is full, then disconnect the input. The jar will then hold an electrical charge that we can draw off by hooking up to the ball. Understand?"

"Madness!" one of the older *sciuloj* cackled, and averted the infection of insanity by rotating his forefinger next to his temple.

"Wait and see," Jason said, with a calmness he did not feel. He had built the Leyden jar from a dim memory of a textbook illustration studied in his youth, and there was no guarantee the thing would work. He grounded the positive pole of the generator, then did the same with the outer coating of the jar by running a wire from it to a spike driven down through a cracked floor tile into the damp soil below.

"Let her roll!" he shouted and stepped back, arms folded.

The generator groaned and rotated, but nothing visible happened. He let it go on for several minutes, since he had no idea of its output or of the jar's capacity, and a lot depended on the results of this first experiment. Finally the sneering asides of the *sciuloj* grew louder, so he stepped forward and disconnected the jar with a flip of a dry stick.

"Stop the generator; the work is done. The *akumulatoro* is filled brimful with the holy force of electricity." He pulled over the demonstration unit he had prepared, a row of the crude incandescent light bulbs wired in series. There ought to be enough of a charge in the Leyden jar to overcome the weak resistance of the carbon filaments and light them up. He hoped.

"Blasphemy!" screeched the same elderly *sciulo*, shuffling forward. "It is sacred writ that the holy force can only flow when the road is complete, and when the road of flow is broken no force shall move. Yet this outlander dares tell us that holiness now resides in this jar to which but one wire was connected. Lies and blasphemy!"

"I wouldn't do that if I were you . . ." Jason suggested to the oldster, who was now pointing to the ball on top of the Leyden jar.

"There is no force here—there can be no force here. . . ." His voice broke off suddenly as he waved his finger an inch from the ball. A fat blue spark snapped between his fingertip and the charged metal, and the *sciulo* screamed hoarsely and dropped to the floor. One of his fellows knelt to examine him, then turned his frightened gaze to the jar.

"He is dead," he breathed.

"You can't say I didn't warn him," Jason said, then decided to press hard while luck was on his side. "It was *he* who blasphemed!" Jason shouted, and the old men cringed away. "The holy force was stored in the jar, and he doubted and the force struck him dead. Doubt no more, or you will all meet the same fate! Our work as *sciuloj*," he added, giving himself a promotion from slavery, "is to harness the powers of electricity for the greater glory of the Hertug. Let this be a reminder, lest we ever forget." They eyed the body, shuffled backwards, and got the idea very clearly.

"The holy force can kill," the Hertug said, smiling down at the corpse and dry-washing his hands. "This is indeed wonderful news. I always knew it could give shocks and cause burns, but never knew it held this great power. Our enemies will shrink before us."

"Without a doubt," Jason said, striking while the iron was hot and whipping out the drawings he had carefully prepared. "Take a look at these other wonders. An electrical motor to lift and pull things, a light called the carbon arc that can pierce the night, a way of coating things with a thin layer of metal, and many more. You can have them all, Hertug."

"Begin construction at once!"

"Instantly—as soon as we agree on the terms of my contract."

"I don't like the sound of that."

"You'll like it even less when you hear the details, but it will be well worth it." He bent forward and whispered in the Hertug's ear. "How would you like a machine that could blow down the walls of your enemies' fortresses so that you could defeat them and capture their secrets?"

"Clear the room," the Hertug commanded, and when they were alone he turned his shrewd little red eyes on Jason. "What is this contract you mentioned?"

"Freedom for me, a position as your personal adviser, slaves, jewels, girls, good food—all the usual things that go with the job. In return I will build for you all of the devices I have mentioned, and a good many more. There is nothing I cannot do! And all of this will be yours . . ."

"I will destroy them all—I will rule Appsala!"

"That's sort of what I had in mind. And the better things are for you, the better they will be for me. I ask no more than a comfortable life and the chance to work on my inventions, being a man of small ambition. I'll be happy puttering about in the lab—while you will rule the world."

"You ask much . . ."

"I'll supply much. I'll tell you what—take a day or two to make up your mind, while I produce one more invention for your instruction and edification."

Jason remembered the spark that had struck down the old man and it gave him fresh hope. It might be the way off this planet.

When will this be completed?'' the Hertug asked, poking at the parts spread over Jason's workbench.

"Tomorrow morning, though I work all night, oh Hertug. But even before it is finished I have another gift for you, a way to improve your telegraph system."

"It needs no improvement! It is as it was in our forefathers' days, and—"

"I'm not going to change anything; forefathers always know best, I agree. I'll just give you a new operating technique. Look at this—" and he held out one of the metal strips with the scribed wax coating. "Can you read the message?"

"Of course, but it takes great powers of concentration, for it is a deep mystery."

"Not that deep; in one look I divined all its horrible simplicity."

"You blaspheme!"

"Not really. Look here: that's a B, isn't it—two jiggles from the magic pendulum?"

The Hertug counted on his fingers. "It is a B, you are correct. But how can you tell?"

Jason concealed his scorn. "It was hard to figure out, but all things are as an open book to me. B is the second letter in the alphabet, so it is coded by two strokes. C is three—still easy; but you end up with Z, needing twenty-six bashes at the sending key, which is just a nonsensical waste of time. When all you have to do is modify your equipment slightly in order to send two different signals—let's be original and call one a 'dot' and the other a 'dash.' Now, using these two signals, a short and a long impulse, we can transcribe every letter of the alphabet in a maximum of four incre- ments. Understand?"

"There is a buzzing in my head, and it is difficult to follow . . ."

"Sleep on it. In the morning my invention will be finished, and at that time I will demonstrate my code."

The Hertug left, muttering to himself, and Jason finished the last windings on the armature for his new generator.

"What do you call it?" the Hertug asked, walking around the tall, ornate wooden box.

"This is an All Hail the Hertug Maker, a new source of worship, respect, and finance for Your Excellency. It is to be placed in the temple, or your local equivalent, where the public will pay for the privilege of doing you homage. Observe: I am a loyal subject who enters the temple. I give a donation to the priest and grasp this handle that projects from the side, and turn." He began cranking lustily and the sound of turning gears and a growing whine came from the cabinet. "Now watch the top."

Projecting from the upper surface of the cabinet were two curved metal arms that ended in copper spheres separated by an air space. The Hertug gasped and recoiled as a blue spark snapped across the gap.

"That will impress the peasants, won't it?" Jason said. "Now— observe the sparks and notice their sequence. First three short sparks, then three long ones, then three short ones again."

He stopped cranking and handed the Hertug a clearly inscribed sheet of vellum, a doctored version of the standard interstellar code. "Notice. Three dots stands for H and three dashes signify A. Therefore as long as this handle is turned the machine sends out H.A.H. in code, signifying *Huraoj al Hertug,* All hail the Hertug! An impressive device that will keep the priests busy and out of mischief and your loyal followers entertained. While at the same time it will cry your praises with the voice of electricity, over and over, night and day."

The Hertug turned the handle and watched the sparks with glowing eyes. "It shall be unveiled in the temple tomorrow. But there are sacred designs that must be inscribed on it first. Perhaps some gold . . ."

"Jewels too, the richer-looking the better. People aren't going to pay to work a holy hand-organ unless it looks impressive."

Jason listened happily as the sparks crackled out. They might be saying H.A.H. in the local code, but it would be S.O.S. to an offworlder. And any spaceship with a decent receiver that entered the atmosphere of this planet should pick up the broad-spectrum radio waves from the spark gap. There might even be one hearing the message now, turning the loop of the direction finder, zeroing in on the signal. If he only had a receiver he could hear their answering message, but it didn't matter, for shortly he would hear the roar of their rockets as they dropped on Appsala. . . .

Nothing happened. Jason had sent out the first S.O.S. over twelve hours earlier, but now he reluctantly abandoned any hope of immediate rescue. The best thing to do now was to get established soundly and comfortably while he waited for a ship to arrive. He did not let himself dwell on the possibility that a spacer might not approach this backwater planet during his lifetime.

"I have been considering your requests," the Hertug said, turning away from the spark-gap transmitter. "You might have a small apartment of your own, perhaps a slave or two, enough food to satisfy, and on holy days wine and beer. . . ."

"Nothing stronger?"

"You cannot obtain anything stronger; the Perssonoj wines from our fields on the slopes of Mount Malvigla are well known for their potency."

"They'll be even better known once I run them through a still. I can see a number of small improvements that will have to be made if I am to stay around here for any length of time. I may even have to invent the water closet before I get rheumatism from the drafts in your primitive jakes. There is a lot to be done. What we will have to do first is draw up a list of priorities, at the top of which will be money. Some of the things I plan to build for your greater glory will be a little expensive, so it would be best if we allowed for that by filling the treasury beforehand. I suppose you have no religious principles that forbid your getting richer?"

"None," the Hertug answered, very positively.

"Then we can let it rest there for now. With Your Excellency's permission, I shall repair to my new quarters and get some sleep, after which I shall prepare a list of projects for your edification and selection."

"That is satisfactory to me. And do not forget the things to make money."

"Top of the list."

Though Jason had the liberty of the sealed and holy workrooms, he had four bodyguard jailers who stayed very close to him the rest of the time, treading on his heels and breathing *kreno* fumes down the back of his neck.

"Do you know where my new quarters are?" Jason asked the captain of this guard, a surly brute named Benn't.

"Unnh," Benn't answered, and led the way into the drafty Perssonoj keep. They went up a tortuous stone staircase that led to the higher floors, then down a dark hall to a solid door where another guard was stationed. Benn't opened it with a heavy key that hung from his belt.

"This yours," he spat, with a jerk of his black-nailed thumb.

"Complete with slaves," Jason said, looking in and seeing Mikah and Ijale chained to the wall. "I'm not going to get much work out of those two if they are just being used as decorations. Do you have the key?"

With even less grace, Benn't dug a smaller key from his wallet and passed it to Jason; then he went out and locked the door behind him.

"I knew you would do something so they would not hurt you," Ijale said as Jason unlocked her iron collar. "I only feared a little bit."

Mikah maintained a stony silence until Jason began an inspection round of the rooms with Ijale, then he said coldly, "You have neglected to free me from these chains."

"I'm glad you noticed that," Jason said. "It saves my bringing it to your attention. Can you think of a better way to keep you out of trouble?"

"You are insulting!"

"I'm truthful. You lost me my steady job with the *d'zertanoj* and had me locked up as a slave. When I escaped I took you with me, and you repaid my generosity by allowing Snarbi to betray us to my present employer—and this position I obtained with no thanks to you."

"I did only what I thought was best."

"You thought wrong."

"You are a vindictive and petty man, Jason dinAlt!"

"You're damned right. You stay chained to that wall."

Jason put his arm through Ijale's and took her on a guided tour of the apartment. "In the most modern fashion the entrance opens directly into the main chamber, furnished with rustic split-log furniture and walls decorated with a fine variety of molds. A great place to make cheese, but unfit for human habitation. We'll let Mikah have it." He opened a connecting door. "This is more like it, a southern exposure, a view of the grand canal, and a bit of light. Windows of the best cracked horn, admitting both sunshine and fresh air. I'll have to put some glass in here. But right now a fire in that ox-roasting fireplace will have to do."

"*Krenoj!*" Ijale squealed, and ran to a basket set in an alcove. Jason shuddered. She smelled a few, pinching them between her fingers. "Not too old, ten days, maybe fifteen. Good for soup."

"Just what the old stomach yearns for," Jason said unenthusiastically.

Mikah bellowed from the other room. Jason started the fire

before he went to see what he wanted.

"This is criminal!" Mikah said, rattling his chains.

"I'm a criminal." Jason turned to leave.

"Wait! You cannot leave me like this. We are civilized men. Release me and I will give you my word that I bear you no ill will."

"That's very nice of you, Mikah, old son, but all the trust is gone from my previously trusting soul. I am a convert to the native ethos, and I now trust you just as far as I can see you. I'll give you that much. You can have the run of the place just to stop your bellowing."

Jason unlocked the chain that secured Mikah's iron collar to the wall, then turned away.

"You have forgotten the collar," Mikah said.

"Have I?" Jason answered, and his grin was more predatory than humorous. "I haven't forgotten how you betrayed me to Edipon, nor have I forgotten the collar. As long as you are a slave you cannot betray me again—so a slave you stay."

"I should have expected this of you." There was cold fury in Mikah's voice. "You are a dog, not a civilized man. I will *not* give you my word to assist you in any way; I am ashamed of myself for my weakness in even considering such a course. You are evil, and my life is dedicated to fighting evil—therefore I fight you."

Jason had his arm half-raised to strike, but instead he burst out laughing.

"You never cease to amaze me, Mikah. It seems impossible that one man could be so insensitive to facts, logic, reality, or what used to be called plain common sense. I'm glad you admitted that you are fighting me—it will make it easier to guard my back. And just so you won't forget and start acting chummy again, I'm keeping you a slave and treating you like a slave. So grab that stoneware crock over there and hammer for the guard and go fill it with water wherever slaves like you go to fetch water."

He turned on his heel and left the room, still seething with anger, but he tried to work up some enthusiasm for the meal Ijale had so carefully prepared.

With a full stomach and his feet toasting by the fire, Jason was almost comfortable. Ijale was crouched by the hearth doing a slow and clumsy job of repairing some skins with a large iron needle, while from the other room came the angry rattle of Mikah's chains. It was late and Jason was tired, but he had promised the Hertug a list of possible wonders and he wanted to finish it before he went to sleep. He looked up as the locks on the front entrance rattled open and the guard officer Benn't stamped in, followed by one of his soldiers, who carried a spluttering torch.

"Come," Benn't said, and pointed to the door.

"Where and why?" Jason asked, reluctant to face the damp discomfort of the keep.

"Come," Benn't repeated in the same unpleasant tone, and pulled his short stabbing sword from his belt.

"I'm learning to loathe you," Jason said, dragging himself reluctantly to his feet. He slipped his fur vest back on and went out past Mikah's brooding form. The guard at the door was gone and there was a dark shape on the floor just visible in the torchlight. Was it the guard? Jason started to turn when the door slammed behind them and the point of Benn't's sword jammed through his leather clothes and pinked the skin over his kidneys.

"Talk or move, you die," the soldier's voice grated in his ear.

Jason thought about it and decided not to move. Not that the threat disturbed him, for he was sure he could disarm Benn't and reach the other soldier before he could draw his sword, but he was interested in this new development. He had more than a strong suspicion that what was happening was unknown to the Hertug, and he wondered just where it would lead.

He regretted his decision instantly. A foul-tasting rag was stuffed into his mouth and tied in place with straps that cut into his neck and jaws. His arms were tied at the same moment and a second sword was pressed into his side. Resistance was impossible now, without serious risk, so he marched humbly up the stairs when prodded, and out onto the flat roof of the building.

The soldier put out his torch and they were in the black night, cold sleet blowing about them. They stumbled across the slippery tiles. The parapet was invisible in the darkness and when it hit Jason's legs just below the knees he tottered and would have gone over if the soldiers hadn't dragged him back. Working silently and swiftly, they knotted a rope under his arms and lowered him over the edge. Jason cursed inside the gag as he bumped painfully down the rough outer facing of the building, then recoiled as he went up to his knees in icy water. This side of the Perssonoj keep dropped sheer to the canal and Jason hung there, immersed to his waist, as the barely visible shape of a boat loomed out of the sleet-filled darkness. Rough hands pulled him in and dumped him down, and a few moments later the boat rocked as his kidnapers descended the rope and dropped in beside him. Oars squeaked and they moved off. No alarm had been raised.

The men in the boat ignored him; in fact, they used him for a footrest until he squirmed away. There was little enough to see, lying flat as he was, until more flares appeared and he saw that they were rowing through a large sea gate, much like the one at the entrance to the Perssonoj keep. It did not take much deliberation to realize that he had been picked up by one of the competing organizations. When the boat stopped he was thrown onto the dock, then hauled through damp stone halls to face a high, rusty iron portal. Benn't had vanished—probably after receiving his thirty pieces of silver—and the new guards were silent. They untied him, pulled the gag from his mouth, pushed him through the iron door, and slammed it shut behind him. He was left alone to face the spine-chilling terrors of the chamber.

There were seven figures seated on a high dais, robed, armored, and fearfully masked. Each leaned on a meter-long broadsword. Oddly shaped lamps burned and smoked about them and the air was thick with the reek of hydrogen sulphide.

Jason laughed coldly and looked around for a chair. None was visible, so he took a sputtering lamp, shaped like a snake with a flame in its mouth, from a nearby table and put it on the floor, and then sat on the table. He turned a contemptuous eye on the horrors before him.

"Stand, mortal!" the central figure said. "To sit before the Mastreguloj is death!"

"I sit," Jason said, making himself comfortable. "You didn't kidnap me just to kill me, and the sooner you realize that horror-comic outfits don't bother me, the quicker we will be able to get down to business."

"Silence! Death is at hand!"

"Ekskremento!" Jason sneered. "Your masks and threats are of about the same quality as those of the desert slavers. Let's get down to facts. You have been collecting rumors about me and they have got you interested. You have heard about the supercharged caro, and spies have told you about the electronic prayer wheel in the temple—maybe more. It all sounded so good that you wanted me for yourselves, and you tried the foolproof Appsalan dodge of a little money in the right places. And here I am."

"Do you know to whom you talk?" the masked figure on the far right asked in a high-pitched, shaking voice. Jason examined the speaker carefully.

"The Mastreguloj? I've heard about you. You are supposed to be the witches and warlocks of this town, with fire that burns in water, smoke that will burn the lungs, water that will burn the flesh, and so forth. My guess is that you are the local equivalents of chemists; and though there aren't supposed to be very many of you, you are nasty enough to keep the other tribes frightened."

"Do you know what this contains?" the man asked, holding up a glass sphere with some yellowish liquid in it.

"I don't know, and I couldn't care less."

"It contains the magic burning water that will sear you and char you in an instant if it touches—"

"Oh, come off it! There's nothing in there but some common acid, probably sulphuric, because the other acids are made from it, and there is also the strong clue of rotten egg reek that fills this room."

His guess seemed to have struck home; the seven figures stirred and muttered to each other. While they were distracted, Jason stood up and walked slowly towards them. He had had enough of the scientific quiz games and felt bitter about being kidnaped, tied, dunked, and walked on. These Mastreguloj were feared and avoided by the others in Appsala, but they weren't a large enough clan for what he had in mind. For a number of good reasons he had backed the Perssonoj to win and he wasn't changing sides now.

Among the trivia cluttering the back of his mind was a statement he had read once in a book about famous escapes. He had noted it because he had a professional interest in escaping, since, on many occasions his aims and the police's had differed. The conclusion he had reached by a study of escapees was that the best time to escape was as soon as possible after you have been captured. Which was now.

The Mastreguloj had made a mistake by seeing him alone; they were so used to cowing and frightening people that they were getting careless—and old. From their voices and from the way they acted, he was sure that there were no young men on the dais, he was equally certain that the man on the right end was well into senility. His voice had revealed it, and now that Jason was closer he could see the palsied vibration that shook the large sword the man held before him.

"Who revealed the secret and sacred name of *sulfurika acido?*" the central figure boomed. "Speak, spy, or we will have your tongue torn from your head, fire poured into your bowels—"

"Don't do that," Jason pleaded, kneeling and clasping his hands prayerfully before him. "Anything but that! I'll talk!" He shuffled forward on his knees closer to the dais, bearing to the right as he did so. "The truth will out, I can no longer conceal it—here is the man who told me all the sacred secrets." He pointed to the oldster on the right, and when he did so his hand came close to the long sword the man held.

As Jason stood up, he reached out and plucked the sword from the old man's loose grip and pushed him sideways into the next chair— both men went over with a satisfactory crash.

"Death to unbelievers!" he shouted, and pulled down the black hanging with skull-and-demon pattern that covered the back wall. He threw it over the two men near him, who were just struggling to their feet, and he saw a small door that had been concealed behind the drapery. Pushing it open, he jumped through into the lamplit corridor beyond and almost into the arms of the two guards stationed there. The benefit of surprise was on his side. The first one collapsed when Jason rapped him on the head with the flat of his blade, and the second dropped his own sword when Jason's point took him in the upper arm. His Pyrran training was serving him now. He could move faster and kill quicker than any of the Appsalans. He proved this when he ran around a corner, going in the direction of the entrance, and almost ran into Benn't, his former guard.

"Thanks for bringing me here—I didn't have enough troubles," Jason said, beating the other's sword aside. "And while being a paid traitor is normal in Appsala, it wasn't nice to kill one of your own men." His sword swung and tore Benn't's throat open, almost taking his head off at the same time. The broadsword was heavy and hard to swing, but once it started moving it sliced through anything in its way. Jason ran on and enthusiastically attacked the guards in the front hall.

The only advantage he had was again the element of surprise, so he moved as fast as he could. Once they united, they could capture and kill him, but it was late at night and the last thing the bored guards expected was this demoniacal attack from their rear. One went down, another staggered away with blood spouting from a butchered arm, and Jason was throwing his weight on the pivoted bar that sealed the entrance. From the corner of his eye he saw one of the masked Mastreguloj appear from the council room by way of the main entrance.

"Die!" the man shrieked, and hurled a glass sphere at Jason's head.

"Thanks," Jason said, catching the thing neatly in midair with his free hand. He slipped it inside his clothes as he pulled the door open.

Pursuit was just being organized when he ran down the slippery stairs and jumped into the nearest boat. It was too large for him to row easily, but he cut the painter and pushed off with a leaf-shaped oar. There was a sluggish tide moving in the channel, and he let it carry him away as he dropped the oars on the tholepins and pulled lustily. Figures appeared on the stairs, there were shouts and the flicker of torches, then a cloud of sleet blew in between and they were lost from view. Jason rowed on into the darkness, smiling grimly to himself.

13

He rowed until the exercise warmed him, then let the boat drift with the tide. It bumped against unseen obstacles in the dark, and whirled about when it came to another canal. Jason pulled lustily into this, and made his way through a maze of dimly seen waterways between low islands and cliff-like walls. When he was sure his trail was sufficiently confused he pulled to the nearest shore where he could beach the boat. It came to a stop and he jumped out, ankle deep in the wet sand, and he pulled it as far up as he could.

When he could no longer move it he climbed back in, put the glass capsule out of reach in the bilge where it could not be broken accidentally, and settled down to wait for dawn. He was chilled and shivering, and before the first grey light penetrated the sleet he was in a foul humor.

Dim shapes slowly resolved themselves from the darkness—some small boats nearby, drawn up on shore and securely chained to piles, and further back small, squat buildings. A man crawled from one of the hovels, but as soon as he saw Jason and his boat he squealed and vanished from sight. There were stirrings and mumblings inside, and Jason climbed out onto the shore and swung the broadsword a few times to loosen up his muscles.

About a dozen men came hesitantly down to the shore to face him, clutching clubs and oars, almost shivering with fright.

"Go, leave us in peace," the leader said, extending his index finger and little finger to avert the evil eye. "Take your foul bark, Mastregulo, and depart our shores. We are but poor fisherfolk . . ."

"I have nothing but sympathy for you," Jason said, leaning on the sword. "And I have no more love for the Mastreguloj than you have."

"But your boat—there is the sign," and the leader pointed to a hideous bit of carving on the bow.

"I stole it from them."

The fishermen moaned and milled about, some running away, while a few dropped to their knees to pray. One threw his club at Jason, a half-hearted attempt that Jason parried easily with his sword.

"We are lost," the leader wailed. "The Mastreguloj will follow, sight this craft of ill omen, and fall upon us and kill us all. Take it, leave at once!"

"There's something in what you say," Jason agreed. The boat was a handicap. He could barely manage it alone and it was too easily identified to enable him to move about unnoticed. Keeping a wary eye on the fishermen, he retrieved the glass ball and then put his shoulder to the bow, sliding the boat back into the water, where the current caught it and soon carried it out of sight.

"That problem is taken care of," Jason said. "Now I have to get back to the Perssonoj stronghold. Which of you wants the ferry job?"

The fishermen began to drift away, and Jason planted himself in front of the leader before he could vanish too. "Well, how about it?"

"I don't think I could find it," the man said, going white under his wind-burned skin. "Fog, plenty of sleet, I never go that way . . ."

"Come on, now, you'll be well paid, just as soon as we land. Name your price."

The man gave a mean laugh and tried to edge away.

"I see what you mean," Jason said, putting his sword in the other's way. "Credit is one custom that doesn't mean much here."

Jason looked thoughtfully at the sword and realized for the first time that the bumps on the hilt were faceted stones in ornate settings. He pointed to them. "Here we go, payment in advance if you can find me a knife to pry these out with. As a down payment, that red one that looks like a ruby; then the green one when we get there."

With a bit of arguing, and the addition of another red stone, avarice won over fear, as usual, and the fisherman pushed a small and badly joined boat into the canal. He rowed while Jason bailed and they began a surreptitious tour of the back canals. Aided by sleet, fog, and the fisherman's suddenly regained and intimate knowledge of the waterways, they arrived unobserved at some crumbled stone steps leading to a barred gate. The man swore that this was an entrance to the Perssonoj stronghold. Jason, well versed in local custom by now, was aware that it might be something quite different, even a way to the Mastreguloj he had just left, and he kept one foot in the boat until a guard appeared with the characteristic Perssonoj sunburst on his cloak. The fisherman received the final payment with astonishment and rowed quickly away, muttering to himself. Another guard was called, Jason's sword was taken from him, and he was quickly brought to the Hertug's audience chamber.

"Traitor!" the Hertug shouted, dispensing with all formalities. "You conspire to kill my men and flee, but I have you now—"

"Oh, stop it!" Jason said irritably, and shrugged away the guards who were holding his arms. "I returned voluntarily, and that should mean something, even in Appsala. I was kidnaped by the Mastreguloj, with the aid of a traitor in your guard—"

"His name!"

"Benn't, deceased—I saw to that myself. Your trusted captain sold you out to the competition, who wanted me to work for them, but I didn't accept. I didn't think too much of their outfit and I left before they got around to making an offer. But I brought a sample back with me." Jason pulled out the glass sphere of acid and the guards dropped back, screaming, and even the Hertug went white.

"The burning water!" he gasped.

"Exactly. And as soon as I get some lead it is going to become part of the wet cell battery I was busy inventing. I'm annoyed, Hertug—I don't like being kidnaped and pushed around. Everything about Appsala annoys me, and I have some plans for the future. Clear these men out so I can tell my plans to you."

The Hertug chewed his lip nervously and looked at the guards. "You came back," he said to Jason—"why?"

"Because I need you just as much as you need me. You have plenty of men, power, and money. I have big plans. Now clear the serfs out."

There was a bowl of *krenoj* on the table and Jason rooted around for a fresh one and bit off a piece. The Hertug was thinking hard.

"You came back," he said again. He seemed to find this fact astonishing. "Let us talk."

"Alone."

"Clear the chamber," he ordered, but he took the precaution of having a cocked crossbow placed before him. Jason ignored it; he had expected no less. He crossed to the badly glazed window and looked out at the island city. The storm had stopped finally, and weak sunshine was lighting up the rain-darkened roofs.

"How would you like to own all that?" Jason asked.

"Speak on." The Hertug's little eyes glittered.

"I mentioned this before, but now I mean it—seriously. I am going to reveal to you every secret of every other clan on this damned planet. I'm going to show you how the *d'zertanoj* distill oil, how the Mastreguloj make sulphuric acid, how the Trozelligoj build engines. Then I'm going to improve your weapons of war, and introduce as many new ones as I can. I will make war so terrible that it will no longer be possible. Of course it will still go on, but your troops will always win. You'll wipe out the competition, one by one, starting with the weakest ones, until you will be the master of this city, then of the whole planet. The riches of a world will be yours, and your evenings will be enlivened by the horrible deaths you will mete out to your enemies. What do you say?"

"*Supren la Perssonoj!*" the Hertug shouted, leaping to his feet.

"That's what I thought you would say. If I'm going to be stuck here for any length of time I want to get in a few body blows to the system. I have been entirely too uncomfortable, and it is time for a change."

14

The days grew longer, the sleet turned to rain, but even that finally stopped. The last clouds eventually blew out to sea and the sun shone down on the city of Appsala. Buds opened, flowers blossomed and filled the air with perfume, while from the warming waters of the canals there rose another odor, less pleasant, that Jason could just as well have done without. But he had very little time to notice it, for he was working long hours at both research and production, a constantly exhausting task. Pure research and production development were expensive, and when the bills mounted too high the Hertug scratched in his beard and mumbled about the good old days. Then Jason had to drop everything and produce a fresh miracle or two. The arc light was one; then the arc furnace, which helped with the metallurgical work and made the Hertug very happy, particularly when he found out how good it was for torture and fed a captured Trozelligo into it until he told them what they wanted to know. When this novelty palled, Jason introduced electroplating, which helped fill the treasury both through jewelry sales and counterfeiting.

After opening the Mastreguloj glass sphere with elaborate precautions, Jason satisfied himself that it did contain sulphuric acid, and he constructed a heavy, but effective, storage battery. Still angry over the kidnaping, he led an attack on a Mastreguloj barge and captured a large supply of acid, as well as assorted other chemicals. These he was testing whenever he had the time. He had followed a number of deadend trails, but had been forced to abandon them. The formula for gunpowder escaped him, and this depressed him, though it cheered his assistants who had been raking through old manure piles for supplies of saltpeter.

He had more success with *caroj* and steam engines, because of previous experience, and developed a lightweight, sturdy marine engine. In his spare moments he invented movable type, the telephone, and the loudspeaker—which, with the addition of the phonograph record, did wonders for the religious revenue in production of spirit voices. He also made a naval propeller to go with his engine, and was busily perfecting a steam catapult. For his own pleasure he had set up a still in his rooms, with which he manufactured a coarse but effective brandy.

"All in all, things aren't going too badly," he said, lolling back in his upholstered easy chair and sipping a glass of his latest and best. It had been a warm day, and more than a bit choking with the effluvia that rose from the canals, but now the evening sea breeze was cool and sweet as it blew in through the open windows. Under his belt was a fine steak, cooked on a charcoal grill of his own invention, served with mashed *krenoj* and bread baked from flour ground in his recently invented mill. Ijale was singing in the kitchen as she cleaned up, and Mikah was industriously running a brush through the pipes of the still, clearing away the dregs of the last batch.

"Sure you won't join me in a quick one?" Jason asked, brimming with the milk of human kindness.

"Wine is a mocker, strong drink is raging. . . . Proverbs," Mikah declaimed in his best style.

"Wine that maketh glad the heart of man. Psalms. I've read the Book too. But if you won't have a friendly cup, why don't you have a refreshing glass of water and take a rest? That job can wait until morning.''

''I am your slave,'' Mikah said darkly, touching the iron collar about his neck for an instant, then turning back to his work.

''Well, you have only yourself to blame. If you were more trustworthy I would give you your freedom. In fact, why don't I do that? Just give me your word that you'll not cook up any more trouble, and I'll have you out of that collar before you can say antidisestablishmentarianism. I think I'm in well enough with the Hertug to ride any minor troubles you might cause. What do you say? As narrow-minded as your conversation is, it's at least twice as good as anything else I can find on this planet.''

Mikah touched the collar again and looked doubtful for just a moment. Then he shouted ''No!'' and jerked his fingers away as if they were burnt. ''Behind me, Satan! Down! I will give you no pledges, nor will I put my honor in fief to such as you. Better to serve in bondage until the day of liberation when I will see you standing trial for such crimes as this, standing before a bar of justice, being sentenced and doomed.''

''Well, you leave little doubt as to your ambitions.'' Jason drained the glass appreciatively and refilled it. ''I hope they work out, at least the day of liberation part; after that I find our opinions of the correct course differ a little. But have you ever stopped to think how far away that day of liberation may be? And just what are you doing to bring it about?''

''I can do nothing—I am a slave!''

''Yes, and we both know why. But aside from that, do you think you could do any better if you were free? I'll answer for you. No. But I can do better, and I have come up with a few answers. For one thing, there are no offworlders besides us on this forsaken planet. I found some crystals that resonate nicely and I built a crystal radio. I didn't hear a thing except atmospherics and my own holy S.O.S.''

''What blasphemy do you speak?''

''Didn't I ever tell you? I built a simple radio disguised as an electronic prayer wheel and the faithful have been broadcasting religiously since the first day.''

''Is nothing sacred to you, blasphemer?''

''We'll go into that some other time—though I can't see what you are complaining about now. Do you mean you *respect* this phoney religion with great god Elektro and all the rest? You should be thankful that I am getting some productive mileage out of the worshipers. If any spacer ever gets near the atmosphere of this planet, it will pick up the call for help and head this way."

"How soon?" Mikah asked, interested in spite of himself.

"It could be in five minutes—or in five hundred years. Even if someone is looking for you, there are a lot of planets in this galaxy. I doubt if the Pyrrans will come after me—they have only one spaceship and have plenty of uses for it. What about your people?"

"They will pray for me, but they cannot search. Most of our money was used to obtain the ship you so willfully destroyed. But what of other ships? Surely traders, explorers . . ."

"Chance—it depends completely on the hazards of chance. As I said, five minutes from now, five centuries—or never. The blind workings of chance."

Mikah sat down heavily, wrapped in gloom, and Jason—despite the fact that he realized he should know better—felt a momentary pang of pity. "But cheer up, things aren't that bad here," he said. "Just compare our present position with our first job *kreno* hunting in Ch'aka's merry band. Now we have a place with comfortable furnishings, heating, good food, and as fast as I can invent them, all the modern conveniences. For my own comfort, plus the fact that I hate so many of the people involved, I am going to drag this world out of its dark age and get it headed into the glories of the technological future. Did you think I was going to all this trouble just to help the Hertug?"

"I do not understand."

"That's fairly typical. Look, we have here a static culture that is never going to change without a large charge of explosive put in the proper place. That's me. As long as knowledge is classified as an official secret, there will be no advance. There will probably be slight modifications and improvements within these clans as they work on their specialties, but nothing of any vital importance. I'm ruining all that. I'm letting our Hertug have the information possessed by every other tribe, plus a lot of gadgets they don't know about yet. This destroys the normal check and balance that keep these warring mobs roughly equal, and if he runs his war right— meaning my way—he can pick them off one by one . . ."

"War?" Mikah asked, his nostrils flaring, the old light back in his eyes. "Did you say *war?*"

"That's the word," Jason answered, complacently sipping at his glass, drunk with his own vision and half-stoned on the home brew so that he did not notice the warning signs. "As someone once said, you can't make an omelet without breaking eggs. Left alone, this world will stumble on in its orbit forever with ninety-nine per cent of the population doomed to disease, poverty, filth, misery, slavery, and all the rest. I'm going to start a war, a nice, clean scientific one that will wipe out the competition. When it is all over this will be a far, far better place for everyone. The Hertug will have cleaned up the other mobs and will be dictator. The work I am doing is already too much for the ancient *sciuloj*, and I have been subcontracting to slaves and training younger technicians from the family. When I am through there will be crossfertilization of all the sciences, and industrial revolution will be in full swing here. There will be no turning back, because the old ways will be dead. Machines, capital, entrepreneurs, leisure, the arts . . ."

"You are a monster!" Mikah rasped through his teeth. "To satisfy your own ego you would even start war and condemn thousands of innocents to death. I will stop you, if it costs me my life!"

"Whazzat . . . ?" Jason said, lifting his head. He had drifted off to sleep, worn out from work and lulled by his own golden vision.

But Mikah did not answer. He had his back turned and was bent over the still, cleaning it. His face was flushed and his teeth were clamped so hard into his lip that a thin trickle of blood ran down his chin. He had finally learned the benefits of silence at certain times, though the effort of maintaining it was almost killing him.

In the courtyard of the Perssonoj keep was a great stone tank kept filled with fresh water pumped from barges. Here the slaves met as they drew their supplies, and here was the center of gossip—and intrigue. Mikah waited his turn at the tap to fill his bucket, but at the same time he examined the faces of the other slaves, looking for the one who had talked to him a few weeks earlier, whom he had ignored at the time. He finally saw him, dragging in faggots of firewood from the unloading dock, and went over to him.

"I will help," Mikah whispered as he passed. The man smiled crookedly.

"At last you are being wise. All will be arranged."

It was full summer. The days were hot and humid, the air cooling off only after dark. Jason had reached the proving stages of his steam catapult when he was forced to violate his rule of doing only day work. At the last minute he decided on an evening test, since with the oil-fired boiler working full blast the heat was unbearable during the daytime. Mikah had gone out for water to refill their kitchen tank—he had forgotten it during the day—so Jason did not see him when he went down to the workshop after dinner. Jason's assistants had the boiler hot and a head of steam up: the tests began.

Because of the hiss of leaking steam and the general uproar of the mechanism, the first sign he had that anything was wrong was when a soldier burst in with blood soaking his leather from a crossbolt quarrel stuck in his shoulder.

"Attacking—Trozelligoj!" he gasped.

Jason shouted orders, but was ignored in the concerted rush to the door. Cursing, he stayed long enough to damp the fire and open a bleed valve so the boiler wouldn't blow up while he was away. Then he followed the others out of the door, going by way of the rack that held his experimental weapons, and without stopping he pulled from it a newly constructed morning star, an ugly-looking weapon consisting of a thick handle surmounted by a bronze ball into which were set machined steel spikes. It balanced nicely in the hand and whistled in the air when he swung it.

He ran through the dark halls toward the sounds of distant shouting, which seemed to be coming from the courtyard. As he went by the stairs that led to the upper floors, he was vaguely aware of a clatter from somewhere above, and a muffled shout. Going out the wide main entrance that opened onto the courtyard, he saw that the battle was in its final stages and would be won without any help from him.

Carbon arcs lit the scene with a harsh light. The sea gate leading into the pool had been crashed partly open by a barge with a pointed prow, which still remained there, caught fast in the splintered gates. Unable to force their way into the courtyard, the Trozelligoj had attacked along the wall and wiped out most of the guard there. But before they could reach the courtyard and bring reinforcements over the wall, the counterattack of the aroused defenders had halted them. Success was now impossible and they were retreating slowly, fighting a rear-guard action. Men were still dying, but the battle was over. Corpses, most of them studded with bolts from the crossbows, floated in the water, and the wounded were already being dragged away. There was nothing much here that Jason could do, and he wondered what reason lay behind the midnight attack.

At the same moment he felt a presentiment of further trouble clutch at his insides. What was wrong? The attack was beaten off, yet he felt that something was not right, something important. Then he remembered the sounds he had heard coming down the stairwell —heavy feet and the clattering of weapons. And the shout, cut off as if someone had been silenced. The sounds had meant little when he heard them; if he had thought about them at all he had assumed that more soldiers were coming to join in the battle.

"But I was the last one to come through this door! No one came down the stairs!'' Even as he was saying the words, he was running towards the stairs, and he bounded up them three at a time.

There was a crash from somewhere above, and the clank of metal on stone. Jason burst out into the hallway, stumbling and half falling over a body huddled there, and he realized that the sounds of fighting were coming from his own rooms.

Inside them it was a madhouse, a slaughterhouse; only one lamp lay unbroken, and in its uncertain light soldiers stumbled over the crushed remains of his furnishings, struggled, and died. The rooms seemed smaller, filled now with fighting men, and Jason leaped over a pair of tangled corpses to join the thin ranks of the Perssonoj.

"Ijale," he shouted, "where are you?" and swung the morning star against the helmet of a charging soldier. The man went down, taking another with him, and Jason jumped into the opening.

"There is the one!" a voice shouted from the rear ranks of the Trozelligoj, and Jason was almost swamped as the attackers turned their attention to him. There were so many of them that they got in each other's way as they pressed the attack home with desperate fury. They were trying to disable him, attempting to cut his legs from under him or put a crossbow bolt through his arm. A sword sliced into his calf before he could deflect it, and his arm ached with the effort needed to keep the morning star a twirling web of death in front of him. He was aware only of the desperate men who were attacking him, and did not know that word of this raid had spread and that more defenders had arrived until the soldiers in front of him were swept back by a rush of Perssonoj.

Jason wiped the sweat from his eyes with his sleeve and stumbled after them. There were more torches now, and he could see that the outnumbered raiders were in retreat, fighting a rear-guard defense shoulder to shoulder while others struggled to get through the wide windows that faced the canal. His carefully installed glass panes were now broken shards underfoot, while hooks and grappling irons were sunk into the frame and wall, and thick ropes passed out through the opening.

A crossbow squad rushed in and brought down the last of the rear-guard and Jason led the rush to the window. Dark forms were vanishing out of sight down the wall, clambering in desperate haste down the hanging rope ladders. The shouting victors began to saw through the ropes until Jason knocked them aside with a sweep of his arm.

"No—follow them!" he shouted, and swung his leg over the windowsill. With the haft of the morning star clutched in his teeth, he climbed down the swaying rope ladder, cursing indistinctly its swaying rungs.

When he reached the bottom he saw that the ends of the ropes trailed in the water, and he could hear the sound of hurried oars vanishing in the darkness.

Jason was suddenly and painfully aware of his wounded leg, as well as of his state of exhaustion: he was not going to attempt to climb back up.

"Have them bring a boat around," he told the soldier who had followed him down. Then he hung there, his arm hooked over a rung, until the boat appeared. The Hertug himself was in the bow, a naked sword in his hand.

"What is this attack? What is the meaning of it?" the Hertug demanded. Jason hauled himself wearily into the boat and sank onto a bench.

"It's obvious enough now—the whole attack was just meant to get me."

"What? It cannot be . . ."

"It certainly is, if you just look at it closely for a moment. The attack on the sea gate was never meant to succeed; it was just a distraction while the real plan to kidnap me was pushed through. It was only chance that I was working in the shop tonight—I'm usually asleep by this time."

"Who would want you? Why?"

"Haven't you waked up to the fact yet that I'm the most valuable piece of property in Appsala? The Mastreguloj were the first to realize that; they even successfully kidnaped me, as you may remember. We should have been alert for a Trozelligoj attack; after all, they must know by now that I'm making steam engines, their old monopoly."

The boat swung in through the splintered sea gate and ground against the dock, and Jason swung painfully ashore.

"But how did they get in and find your quarters?" the Hertug asked.

"It was an inside job, a traitor, as always on this pest-ridden planet. Someone who knew the routine, who could set the hook and drop the first ladder down to the waiting boats just before the attack. It wasn't Ijale—they must have captured her."

"I will discover who the traitor is!" the Hertug raged. "I'll feed him into the arc furnace an inch at a time."

"I know who it is," Jason told him, and there was an ugly glitter in his eye. "I heard his voice when I came in, telling them who I was. I recognized the voice—it was my slave, Mikah."

15

"They'll pay—oh, how they'll pay for this!" the Hertug growled, grating his teeth together with a horrible sound. He was sipping at a glass of Jason's brandy, and his eyes and nose were even redder than usual.

"I'm glad to hear you say that, because it's just what I had in mind," Jason said, leaning back on a couch with an even bigger glass balanced on his chest. He had washed out the cut on his leg with boiled water and bound it with sterile bandages. It was throbbing a bit now, but he doubted if it would give him much trouble. He ignored it and made his plans. "Let's start the war now," he said.

The Hertug blinked. "Isn't that sudden? I mean, are we ready yet?"

"They invaded your castle, killed your soldiers, wrecked your—"

"Death to the Trozelligoj!" the Hertug screamed and crashed his glass against the wall.

"That's more like it. Don't forget what stab-in-the-back bastards they are, pulling a stunt like this. You can't let them get away with it. Plus the fact that we had better start the war soon, or we will never have a chance. If the Trozelligoj will go to this much trouble to grab me, they must be very worried. Since this plan didn't succeed, they will be thinking next of a stronger attack—and will probably get some of the other clans to help with it. They are all beginning to fear you, Hertug, so we had better get the war rolling before they decide to get together and wipe us out. We can still take the clans on, one at a time, and be sure of victory."

"It would help if we had more men, and a little time . . ."

"We have about two days—that's as long as it will take me to equip my invasion fleet. That will give you enough time to call in the reserves from the country. Strip the estates, because we want to attack and take the Trozelligoj fortress, and this is the only chance we will have. And the new steam catapult will do the job."

"It has been tested?"

"Just enough to show it will do what it was designed to do. We can do the ranging and sighting with the Trozelligoj for a target. I'll start work at first light, but I suggest that you get the messengers out now so that the men can get here in plenty of time. Death to the Trozelligoj!"

"Death!" the Hertug echoed, and he grimaced horribly as he rang for the servant.

There was much to be done, and Jason accomplished it by going without sleep. When he became tired he would think about the treacherous Mikah, and wonder what had happened to Ijale, and anger would drive him back to work. He had no assurance that Ijale was even alive; he just assumed that she had been kidnaped as part of his household. As for Mikah, he was going to have a lot to answer for.

Because the steam engine and propeller had already been installed in a ship and tested inside the sea gate, finishing the warship did not take very long. It was mostly a matter of bolting on the iron plates he had designed to shield it down to the waterline. The plating was thicker at the bow, and he saw to it that heavier internal bracing was installed. At first he had thought to install the steam catapult on the warship, but then had decided against it. A simpler way was better. The catapult was fitted into a large, flat-bottomed barge, along with the boiler, tanks of fuel, and a selection of carefully designed missiles.

The Perssonoj were pouring in, all of them fuming with anger over the back-stabbing attack and thirsting for vengeance. In spite of their shouting Jason snatched a few hours' sleep on the second night and had himself waked at dawn. The fleet was assembled, and with much drum-beating and off-key bugling they set sail.

First came the warship, the "Dreadnaught," with Jason and the Hertug on its armored bridge; this towed the barge. In line astern were a great variety of vessels of all sizes, loaded with the troops. The entire city knew what was happening and the canals were deserted, while the Trozelligoj fortress was sealed, barred, and waiting. Jason let go a blast of the steam whistle, well out of arrow range of the enemy walls, and the fleet reluctantly halted.

"Why don't we attack?" the Hertug asked.

"Because we have them in range, while they can't reach us. See." Immense, iron-headed spears plunged into the water a good thirty meters from the bow of the ship.

"*Jetilo* arrows." The Hertug shuddered. "I've seen them pass through the bodies of seven men without being slowed."

"Not this time. I'm about to show you the glories of scientific warfare."

The fire from the *jetiloj* was no more effective than the shouting soldiers on the walls who were clashing swords on shields and hurling curses, and it soon stopped. Jason transferred to the barge and saw that it was anchored firmly, pointing its bow directly at the fortress. While the steam pressure was building up, he aimed the centerline of the catapult and took a guess at the elevation.

The device was simple, but powerful, and he had high hopes for it. On the platform, which could be rotated and elevated, was mounted a single large steam cylinder with its piston connected directly to the short arm of a long lever. When steam was admitted to the cylinder, the short but immensely powerful stroke of the piston was turned by mechanical advantage into flailing speed at the far end of the arm. This whipped up and crashed into a padded crossarm and was stopped, but whatever load was placed in the cup on the end of the arm went speeding off through the air. The mechanism had been tested and worked perfectly, though no shots had yet been fired.

"Full pressure," Jason called out to his technicians. "Load one of the stones into the cup." He had prepared a variety of missiles, all of them weighing the same in order to simplify ranging problems. While the weapon was being loaded he checked the flexible steam lines once more: they had been the hardest thing to manufacture, and they still had a tendency to leak under pressure and continued use.

"Here goes!" he shouted, and pulled down on the valve.

The piston drove out with a satisfactory speed, the arm whipped up and crashed resoundingly into the stop—while the stone went whistling away, a dwindling dot. All the Perssonoj cheered. But the cheering stopped when the stone kept on going, clearing the topmost turret of the keep by a good fifty meters, and vanished on the other side. The Trozelligoj burst into raucous cheering of their own when it splashed harmlessly into the canal on the far side.

"Just a ranging shot," Jason said offhandedly. "A little less elevation and I'll drop one like a bomb into their courtyard."

He cracked the exhaust valves and gravity drew the long arm back to the horizontal, at the same time returning the piston for the next shot. Jason carefully shut the valve and cranked on the elevation wheel. A stone was loaded and he fired again.

This time only the Trozelligoj in the fortress cheered as the stone mounted almost straight up, then dropped to sink one of the attacking boats less than fifty meters from the barge.

"I do not think much of your devilish machine," the Hertug said. He had come back to watch the firing.

"There are always field problems," Jason answered through tight lips. "Just watch the next shot." He decided to abandon any more attempts at fancy high trajectories, and to let fly head-on, for the machine was far more powerful than he had estimated. Cranking furiously on the elevation wheel, he raised the rear of the catapult until the stone would leave the cup almost parallel with the water.

"This is the shot that tells," he announced with much more conviction than he felt, and crossed the fingers of his free hand as he fired. The stone hummed away and hit just below the top of the crenellated wall. It blasted out a great chunk of masonry and utterly demolished the soldiers who had been standing there. There were no more cheers heard from the beseiged Trozelligoj.

"They cower in fear!" the Hertug screamed exultantly. "Attack!"

"Not quite yet." Jason explained patiently. "You're missing the whole point of siege weapons. We do as much damage to them as we can before attacking—it helps the odds." He gave the aiming wheel a turn and the next missile bit a piece out of the wall further along. "And we change ammunition too, just to keep them on the jump."

When the stones had worked along the wall and were beginning to tear holes in the main building, Jason raised the sights a bit. "Load on a special," he ordered. These were oil-soaked bundles of rags weighted with stones and bound about with ropes.

When the special was seated in the cup he ignited it himself and did not shoot until it was burning well. The rapid journey through the air fanned it into a roaring blaze that burst expansively on the thatched roof of the enemy keep, which began immediately to crackle and smoke. "We'll try a few more of those," Jason said, happily rubbing his hands together.

The outer wall was pierced in a number of places, two towers were down, and most of the roof was on fire before the desperate Trozelligoj made an attempt to strike back. Jason had been waiting for this, and noticed at once when the sea gates began to swing open.

"Cease fire," he ordered, "and keep your eyes on the pressure. I'll personally murder every one of you that survives if you let that boiler blow up." He jumped for the manned boat he had waiting alongside. "Pull for the battleship!" he said and the boat bobbed as the Hertug hurtled after him.

"The Hertug always leads!" he shouted, and almost beheaded

one of the oarsmen with his wildly waving sword.

"That's all right by me," said Jason, "but just watch where you are putting that sword, and keep your head down when the shooting starts."

When Jason reached the bridge of the "Dreadnaught" he saw that the clumsy-looking Trozelligoj side-wheeler had thrashed through the sea gate and was heading directly towards them. Jason had heard bloodchilling descriptions of this powerful weapon of destruction, and he was pleased to see that it was just a ramshackle and unarmored vessel, as he had expected. "Full speed ahead," he bellowed into the speaking tube, and took the wheel himself.

The ships, head-on to each other, closed rapidly, and spears from the *jetiloj,* the oversize crossbows, rattled off the "Dreadnaught's" armor plate and splashed into the water. They did no harm and the two vessels still rushed towards each other on a collision course. The sight of the low, beetle-like and smoke-belching form of the "Dreadnaught" must have shaken the enemy captain, and he must have realized that collision at this speed could not do his ship much good, for he suddenly turned the ship away. Jason spun the wheel to follow the other, and kept his bow aimed at the ship's flank.

"Brace yourselves—we're going to hit!" he shouted as the high dragon prow of the other ship flashed past, frightened faces at the rail. Then the metal ram of the "Dreadnaught's" bow hit squarely in the middle of the dripping boards of the port paddle wheel and crashed on deep into the ship's hull. The shuddering impact hurled them from their feet as the "Dreadnaught" slammed to a stop.

"Reverse engines so we can pull free!" Jason ordered, and spun the wheel hard over.

A soldier who had jumped or been knocked from the other ship fell to the armored deck of the "Dreadnaught." Howling battle cries, the Hertug climbed out of the bridge window and attacked the dazed man, slashing him across the neck and then kicking his body into the water. Screams, thuds, and the shrill hiss of leaking steam came from the side-wheeler. The Hertug dived back to the safety of the bridge just as the first crossbow bolts slammed down from above.

The propeller whirled, full speed astern, but the "Dreadnaught" only vibrated, and did not move. Jason muttered, and threw the steering wheel hard in the opposite direction. The ship rocked and levered free, then began to move smoothly astern. Water gurgled and rushed into the holed side-wheeler, which began immediately to list and settle.

"Did you see the way I vanquished the knave who dared attack us?" the Hertug asked with immense satisfaction.

"You still swing a wicked sword," Jason told him. "Did *you* see the way I knocked a hole into that barge? Ahh! There goes the boiler," he added as a tremendous jarring thud came from the stricken enemy, followed by a cloud of steam and smoke as she broke in two and swiftly sank.

By the time Jason had swung the battleship back towards their position, the side-wheeler was gone and the sea gates closed again. "Run the survivors down," the Hertug ordered, but Jason ignored him.

"There is water below," a man said, poking his head up through a hatch. "It is sloshing over our feet."

"Some of the seams opened after the crash," Jason told him. "What did you expect? This is why I installed the pumps, and we have ten extra slaves aboard. Put them to work."

"It is a day of victory," the Hertug said, looking happily at the blood on his sword. "How the swine must regret their attack on our keep!"

"They'll regret it even more before the day is over," Jason said. "We're moving into the last phase now. Are you sure that your men know what to do?"

"I have told them myself many times, and have given them the printed sheets of orders that you prepared. All is ready for the signal. When shall I give it?"

"Very soon. You stay here on the bridge, with your hand on the whistle, while I have a few more shots."

Jason transferred to the barge and planted some of the fire-bomb specials on the roof to keep the fire roaring. He followed these with half a dozen rounds of canister shot—leather bags of fist-size stones that burst when fired—and cleared away all the firefighters and soldiers who were foolish enough to expose themselves. Then he worked the heavy stones back along the wall, crumbling it ever more, until his hurtling missiles reached the sea gate. It took just four shots to batter the heavy timber into splinters and leave the gates a sagging wreck. The way was open. Jason waved his arm and jumped for the boat. The whistle screamed three times and the waiting Perssonoj vessels began to move to the attack.

Because there was no one he could trust to do an adequate job, Jason was not only commander-in-chief of the attackers, but also gun layer, artilleryman, ship's captain, and all the rest, and his legs were getting tired from running back and forth. Climbing to the bridge of the "Dreadnaught" was an effort. Once the attackers were inside the stronghold he could relax and let them finish the job in their efficiently bloodthirsty manner. He had done his part: he had weakened the defenders and caused a good number of casualties; now the forces would join in hand-to-hand combat, opening the way to complete victory.

The smaller vessels, propelled by sail and oar, were halfway to the battered walls before the "Dreadnaught" got moving, but the steam-powered battleship soon caught up with them. The attackers opened ranks and the hurtling ship plunged through, aimed directly at the drooping ruins of the sea gate. The armored bow hit, tore them screaming from their hinges, and plowed on into the pool inside. Even with full speed astern, they were making headway when they hit the dock and shuddered to a stop, with the sharp prow jammed deep into the pilings. Behind them came the roaring Perssonoj and from ahead the defending Trozelligoj, and in an instant deadly battle was joined. The Hertug's noble bodyguard were in the first wave and were waiting to protect their leader as he rushed off to the attack.

Jason slipped an emergency flask of home distillate from its padded rack and downed a stimulating dose. He poured a second one into a beaker to enjoy more slowly, and watched the battle from his vantage point on the bridge.

From the first instant that the forces met, the outcome had never been in doubt. The defenders were battered, burned, and outnumbered, and they were suffering from crushed morale. They could only fall back as the Perssonoj charged over the crumbled walls and in through the open sea gate. The courtyard was swept clear and the battle moved off into the depths of the keep: it was time for Jason to do his next part.

He drained his beaker, slipped a small shield on his left arm, and grabbed up the morning star, which had proved so useful already. Ijale was somewhere in there, he was sure, and he had to find her before there were any unfortunate accidents. He felt a responsibility for the girl—she would still be walking the coastal deserts in a slave band if he hadn't come along. For better or worse, she was in this trouble because of him, and he had to get her out of it safely. He hurried ashore.

The fire in the damp thatch of the roof seemed to have gone out without causing any further damage to the stone building, but it still smoked and the halls were thick with the reek of it. In the entrance hall there was just death—bodies and blood and a few wounded. Jason kicked open a door and went deeper into the keep. A last battle was being fought by the outnumbered defenders in the main dining hall, but he skirted it and pushed through into the kitchens. Here there were only slaves cowering under the tables, and the chief cook, who attacked him with a cleaver. Jason disarmed him with a twitch of the morning star, and threatened painful death if the man didn't tell him where Ijale was. The cook talked, willingly, clutching his bloody arm, but he knew nothing. The slaves only gabbled in fear, and were hopeless. Jason pushed on.

A fearful roar of voices and a constant crashing drew him to the major remaining conflict in what was obviously the main hall, lit by tall windows and hung with flags and pennants. It was a shambles now as the warring groups surged back and forth, slipping in the blood and on the bodies of the wounded and dead. A flurry of bolts from crossbowmen at the far end of the hall drove the fighting men apart, forcing the attackers to raise their shields to defend themselves.

A line of armored and shielded men stretched across the room, and at their rear was a smaller knot of men, more gayly decorated and jeweled, undoubtedly the noble family of the Trozelligoj themselves. They were on the dining dais, now swept clear of furniture, and could look over the heads of the men battling below them. One of them caught sight of Jason when he entered and pointed towards him with his sword, while talking rapidly with the others. Then they all turned their attention to him and the group opened up.

Jason saw that they held Ijale, cruelly chained and bound, and that one of them had his sword pressed to her bosom. They waved his attention to this and their meaning was obvious enough: do not attack, or she dies. They had no idea what she meant to him, or if she meant anything at all, but they must have suspected him of some affection. They were about to be slaughtered, so any desperate move was worth trying.

Jason's reaction was a roaring rage that sent him hurtling forward. Logically, he knew that there could be no compromise now; victory was at hand, and any attempt to reason with the Hertug or the desperate Perssonoj would be sure to result in Ijale's death. He must reach her!

The Trozelligoj soldiers were knocked aside as he plunged into them from the rear and flung himself on the guarding line of armored men. An arrow hurtled by, barely missing him, but unnoticed, and he was upon them. The suddenness of his attack and his charging weight drove the line back for an instant and his morning star whistled through a gap between two shields, hitting square on a helmeted face. He caught a descending sword on his shield and slammed into the man he had hit, who went down. Once past the soldiers, he did not stay to battle but pushed on, while the line tried to close to face the enemy who had rushed to take advantage of Jason's suicidal attack.

There was another member of the group on the dais whom Jason had not noticed before; he glimpsed him now as he attacked. It was Mikah, the traitor, here! He stood next to Ijale, who was going to be murdered because Jason could not possibly reach her in time. The sword was already plunging down to slay her.

Jason had just an instant's sight of Mikah as the latter stepped forward and clutched the swordsman's shoulders and hurled him backwards to the floor. Then Jason was attacked from all sides at once and was fighting desperately for his life.

The odds were too great—five, six to one—all of the attackers armored and desperate. But he did not have to win, only to hold them off a few seconds longer until his own men arrived. They were just behind him; he could hear their victorious roar as the line of defenders went down. Jason caught one sword on his shield, kicked another attacker aside, and beat off a third with his morning star.

But there were too many. They were all about him. He thrust two aside, then turned to face the others behind him. There—the old man, the leader of these people, anger in his eyes . . . a long sword in his hands . . . thrusting.

"Die, demon! Die, destroyer!" the Trozelligoj screeched and lunged.

The long, cool blade caught Jason just above the belt, thrust into his body with a searing pain, transfixed him, emerging from his back.

16

It was pain, but it was not unbearable. What was unendurable was the sure knowledge of death. The old man had killed him. It was all over. Almost without malice, Jason raised his shield and pushed it against the man, sending him stumbling backwards. The sword remained, slim shining death through his body.

"Leave it," Jason said hoarsely to Ijale, who raised her chained hands to pull it out, her eyes numb with terror.

The battle was over, and through the blurring of pain Jason could see the Hertug before him, the awareness of death written also on his face. "Cloths," Jason said, as clearly as he could. "Have them ready to press to the wounds when the sword is removed."

Strong hands of the soldiers held him up and the cloths were ready. The Hertug stood before Jason, who merely nodded and closed his eyes. Once more the pain struck at him and he fell. He was lowered to the carpet, his clothes were torn open, the flow of blood compressed beneath the waiting bandages.

As he lost consciousness, grateful for this relief from agony, he wondered why he bothered. Why prolong the pain? He could only die here, light years from antiseptics and antibiotics, with destruction pushed through his guts. He could only die . . .

Jason struggled back to awareness just once to see Ijale kneeling over him with a needle and thread, sewing together the raw lips of the wound in his abdomen. The light went away again, and the next time he opened his eyes he was in his own bedroom looking at the sunlight flooding in through the broken windows. Something obscured the light, and first his forehead and his cheeks, then his lips, were moistened and cooled. It made him realize how dry his throat was and how strong the pain was.

"Water . . ." he rasped, and was surprised at the weakness of his voice.

"It was told me that you should not drink—with a cut there," Ijale said, pointing to his body, her lips taut.

"I don't think it will matter . . . one way or the other," he told her, the knowledge of impending death more painful by far than the wound. The Hertug appeared beside Ijale, his drawn expression a mirror image of hers, and held a small box out to Jason.

"The *sciuloj* have obtained these, the roots of the *bede* that deaden pain and make it feel distant. You must chew on it, though not too much; there is great danger if too much of the *bede* is taken."

Not for me, Jason thought, forcing his jaws to chew the dry, dusty root. *A pain killer, a narcotic, a habit-forming drug . . . I'm going to have very little time to get the habit.*

Whatever the drug was, it worked fine and Jason was grateful. The pain slipped away, as did his thirst, and though he felt a little lightheaded he was no longer exhausted. "How did the battle go?" he asked the Hertug, who was standing, arms folded, scowling at fate.

"Victory is ours. The only surviving Trozelligoj are our slaves;

their clan has ceased to exist. Some soldiers fled, but they do not count. Their keep is ours, and the most secret chambers where they build their engines. If you could but see their machines . . ." At the realization that Jason could not see them, and would see but little else, the Hertug fell to scowling again.

"Cheer up," Jason told him. "Win one, win them all. There are no other mobs strong enough to stand up to you now. Keep moving before they can combine. Pick off the most unfriendly ones first. If possible, try not to kill all their technicians; you'll want someone to explain their secrets after you have beaten them. Move fast, and by winter you'll own Appsala."

"We'll give you the finest funeral Appsala has ever seen," the Hertug burst out.

"I'm sure of it. Spare no expense."

"There will be feasts and prayers, and your remains will be turned to ash in the electric furnace in the honor cf the god Elektro."

"Nothing could make me happier . . ."

"And afterwards they will be taken to sea at the head of a magnificent funeral procession, ship after ship, all of them heavily armed so that on the return voyage we can fall on the Mastreguloj and take them unawares."

"That's more like it, Hertug. I thought for a while there that you were getting too sentimental."

A crashing at the door drew Jason's attention and he turned his head, slowly, to see a group of slaves dragging heavily insulated cables into the room. Others carried boxes of equipment, and behind them came the slave overseer cracking his whip, driving Mikah's tottering, chained figure before him. Mikah was booted into a corner, where he collapsed.

"I was going to kill the traitor," the Hertug said, "until I thought how nice it would be for you to torture him to death yourself. You'll enjoy that. The arc furnace will be hot soon and you can cook him bit by bit, send him ahead as a sacrifice to Elektro to smooth the way for your coming."

"That's very considerate of you," Jason said, eying Mikah's battered form. "Chain him to the wall, then leave us, so that I may think of the most ingenious and terrible tortures for him."

"I shall do as you ask. But you must let me watch the ceremony. I am always interested in something new in torture."

"I'm sure you are, Hertug."

They left, and Jason saw Ijale stalking Mikah with the kitchen knife.

"Don't do it," Jason told her. "It's no good, no good at all."

She obediently put the knife down, and took up the sponge to wipe Jason's face. Mikah lifted his head and looked at Jason. His face was bruised, and one eye was puffed shut.

"Would you tell me," Jason asked, "just what in hell you thought you were doing by betraying us and trying to get me captured by the Trozelligoj?"

"Though you torture me, my lips are eternally shut."

"Don't be a bigger idiot than usual. No one's going to torture you. I just wonder what you had in mind this time—what ever led you to pull this kind of stunt?"

"I did what I thought best," Mikah answered, drawing himself up.

"You *always* do what you think best—only you usually think wrong. Didn't you like the way I treated you?"

"There was nothing personal in what I did. It was for the good of suffering mankind."

"I think you did it for the reward and a new job, and because you were angry at me," Jason needled, knowing Mikah's weaknesses.

"Never! If you must know . . . I did it to prevent war. . . ."

"Just what do you mean by that?"

Mikah scowled, looking ominous and judicial in spite of his baatered eye. His chains rattled as he pointed an accusing finger at Jason.

"Deep in drink one day you did confess your crime to me, and did speak of your plans to wage deadly war among these innocent people, to embroil them in slaughter and to set cruel despotism about their necks. I knew then what I had to do. You had to be stopped. I forced my lips shut, not daring to say a word lest I reveal my thoughts, because I knew a way.

"I had been approached by a man in the hire of the Trozelligoj, a clan of honest laborers and mechanics, he assured me, who wished to hire you away from the Perssonoj at a good wage. I did not answer him at the time, because any plan to free us would involve violence and loss of life, and I could not consider this even though refusing meant my remaining in chains. Then, when I learned of your bloodthirsty intentions, I examined my conscience and saw what had to be done. We would all be removed from here, taken to the Trozelligoj, who promised that no harm would come to you, though you would be kept a prisoner. The war would be averted."

"You are a simple fool," Jason said, without passion. Mikah flushed.

"I do not care what your opinion is of me. I would act the same again if there was the opportunity."

"Even though you now know that the mob you were selling out to are no better than the ones here? Didn't you stop one of them from killing Ijale during the fighting? I suppose I should thank you for that—even though you are the one who got her into the spot."

"I do not want your thanks. It was the passion of the moment that made them threaten her. I cannot blame them. . . ."

"It doesn't matter one way or the other. The war is over; they lost, and my plans for an industrial revolution will go through without a hitch, even without my personal attention. About the only thing you have accomplished is to bring about my death—which I find very hard to forgive."

"What madness . . . ?"

"*Madness,* you narrow-minded fool!" Jason pushed himself up on one arm, but had to drop back as an arrow of pain shot through the muffling layers of the drug. "Do you think I'm lying here because I'm tired? Your kidnaping and intriguing led me a lot further into battle than I ever intended, and right onto a long, sharp, unsanitary sword. It stuck me like a pig."

"I don't understand what you are saying."

"Then you are being very dim. I was run through, front to back. My knowledge of anatomy is not as good as it might be, but at a guess I would say no organ of vital importance was penetrated. If my liver or any major blood vessels had been punctured, I wouldn't be talking to you now. But I don't know of any way to make a hole through the abdomen without cutting a loop or two of intestine, slicing up the peritoneum and bringing in a lot of nice hungry bacteria. In case you haven't read the first-aid book lately, what happens next is an infection called peritonitis, which, considering the medical knowledge on this planet, is one hundred per cent fatal."

This shut Mikah up nicely, but it didn't cheer Jason very much, so he closed his eyes for a little rest. When he opened them again it was dark and he dozed on and off until dawn, when he had to wake Ijale to tell her to bring him the bowl of *bede* roots. She wiped his forehead and he noticed the expression on her face.

"Then it's not getting hotter in here," he said. "It's me."

"You were hurt because of me," Ijale wailed, and she began to cry.

"Nonsense!" Jason told her. "No matter what way I die, it will be suicide. I settled that a long time ago. On the planet where I was born there was nothing but sunny days and endless peace and a long, long life. I decided to leave, preferring a short, full one to a long and empty one. Now let's have a bit more of that root to chew on, because I would like to forget my troubles.''

The drug was powerful, and the infection was deep. Jason drifted along sinking into the reddish fog of the *bede,* then coming back up out of it to find nothing changed. Ijale was still there, tending him, Mikah in the far corner brooding in his chains. He wondered what would happen to them when he died, and the thought troubled him.

It was during one of these black, conscious moods that he heard the sound, a growing rumble that suddenly cracked the air outside, then died away. He levered himself up onto his elbows, heedless of the pain, and shouted.

''Ijale, where are you? Come here at once!''

She ran in from the other room, and he was conscious of shouts outside, voices on the canal, in the courtyard. Had he really heard it? Or was it a feverish hallucination? Ijale was trying to force him down, but he shrugged her away and called to Mikah. ''Did you hear anything just then? Did you hear it?''

''I was asleep—I think I heard . . .''

''What?''

''A roar—it woke me up. It sounded like . . . but it is impossible . . .''

''Impossible? Why impossible? It was a rocket engine, wasn't it? Here on this primitive planet.''

''But there are no rockets here.''

''There are now, you idiot. Why do you think I built my radio-broadcasting prayer wheel?'' He frowned in sudden thought, trying to cudgel his fogged and fevered brain into action.

''Ijale,'' he called, rooting under his pillow for the purse concealed there. ''Take this money—all of it—and get down to the Temple of Elektro and give it to the priests. Don't let anyone stop you, because this is the most important thing you have ever done. They have probably stopped grinding the wheel and have all gone outside for a look at the excitement. That rocket will never find the right spot without a guide beam—and if it lands any place else in Appsala there could be trouble. Tell them to crank, and not to stop cranking, because a ship of the gods is on the way here and it needs all the prayers it can get.''

She ran out and Jason sank back, breathing rapidly. Was it a spaceship out there that had picked up his S.O.S.? Would it have a doctor or a medical machine that could cure him at this advanced stage of infection? It must have, every ship carried some medical provision. For the first time since he had been wounded he allowed himself to believe that there might be a chance he could survive, and a black weight lifted from him. He even managed a smile at Mikah.

"I have a feeling, Mikah old son, that we have eaten our last *kreno*. Do you think you can bear up under that burden?"

"I will be forced to turn you in," Mikah said gravely. "Your crimes are to serious to conceal; I cannot do otherwise. I must tell the captain to notify the police . . ."

"How did a man with your kind of mind live this long?" Jason asked coldly. "What's to stop me from having you killed and buried right now so that you could make no charges?"

"I do not think you would do that. You are not without a certain kind of honor."

" 'Certain kind of honor'! A word of praise from you! Can it be possible that there is the tiniest of chinks in the rock-ribbed fastness of your mind?"

Before Mikah could answer the roar of the rocket returned, coming lower and not dying away as before, but growing louder instead, becoming deafening, and a shadow moved across the sun.

"Chemical rockets!" Jason shouted over the noise. "A pinnace or landing boat from a spacer . . . it must be zeroing in on my spark radio—there's no possibility of coincidence here." At that moment Ijale ran into the room and hurled herself down by Jason's bed.

"The priests have fled," she wailed; "everyone is in hiding. A great fire-breathing beast has come down to destroy us all!" Her voice was suddenly a shout as the roar in the courtyard outside stopped.

"It's down safely," Jason breathed, then pointed to his drawing materials on the table. "The paper and a pencil, Ijale. Let me have them. I'm going to write a note that I want you to take down to the ship that landed." She recoiled, shivering.

"You mustn't be afraid, Ijale, it's just a ship like the ones that you have been in, only one made to sail in the air rather than on the water. It will have people in it who won't harm you. Go out and show them this note, then bring them here."

"I am afraid . . ."

"Don't be; no harm will come of this. The people in the ship will help me, and I think they can make me well again."

"Then I go," she said simply, rising and forcing herself, still shaking, out of the door.

Jason watched her leave. "There are times, Mikah," he said, "when I'm not looking at you, that I can be proud of the human race."

The minutes stretched out and Jason found himself pulling at the blankets, twisting them with his fingers, wondering what was happening outside in the courtyard. He started as there was a sudden clanging on metal, followed immediately by a rapid series of explosions. Were the fools attacking the ship? He writhed and cursed at his own weakness when he tried to get up. All he could do was lie there and wait—while his existence lay in others' hands.

More explosions sounded—inside the building this time—as well as shouts and a loud scream. Running footsteps came down the hall and Ijale hurried in and Meta, gun still smoking in her hand, entered behind her.

"It's a long way from Pyrrus," Jason said, resting his eyes on the troubled beauty of her face, on the familiar woman's body in the harsh metalcloth suit. "But I can't think of anyone I would rather see come through that door. . . ."

"You're hurt!" She ran swiftly to him, kneeling on the far side of the bed so that she still faced the open door. When she took up his hand her eyes widened at the dry heat of his skin. She said nothing, but unclipped the medikit from her belt and pressed it against the skin of his forearm. The analyzing probe pushed down and it clicked busily, injecting him with one hypodermic needle, then with three more in rapid succession. It buzzed a bit more, then gave him a swift vaccination and switched on the "treatment completed" light.

Meta's face was close above his; she bent a little nearer and kissed him on his cracked lips and a curl of golden hair fell forward onto his cheek. She was a woman, but a Pyrran woman, and she kissed him with her eyes open, and without even pulling away fired a shot that blew out a corner of the door frame and drove back the soldiers in the hall.

"Don't shoot them," Jason said, when she had reluctantly drawn away. "They're supposed to be friends."

"Not my friends. As soon as I left the lifeboat they fired on me with some sort of primitive projectile weapon, but I took care of that. They even fired at the girl who brought your message, until I blew one of the walls down. Are you feeling better?"

"Neither good nor bad, just dizzy from the shots you gave me. But we had better get to the ship. I'll see if I can walk." He threw his legs over the edge of the bed and collapsed, face down on the floor. Meta dragged him back onto the bed and arranged the blankets over him again.

"You must stay here until you are better. You are too sick to move now."

"I'll be a lot sicker if I stay. As soon as the Hertug—he's the one in charge here—realizes that I may be leaving, he will do anything to keep me here, no matter how many men he loses doing it. We are going to have to move before his evil little mind reaches that conclusion."

Meta was looking around the room, and her glance slid over Ijale—who was crouched down staring at her—as if she were part of the furnishings, then stopped at Mikah. "Is that creature chained to the wall dangerous?" she asked.

"At times he can be; you have to keep a close eye on him. He's the one who seized me on Pyrrus."

Meta's hand flew to a pouch at her waist and she slipped an extra gun into Jason's hand. "Here is a gun—you will want to kill him yourself."

"See, Mikah," Jason said, feeling the familiar weight of the weapon in his palm. "Everyone wants me to kill you. What is there about you that makes everyone loathe you so?"

"I am not afraid to die," Mikah said, raising his head and squaring his shoulders, but not looking very impressive with his scraggly grey beard and the chains he wore.

"Well, you should be." Jason lowered the gun. "It's surprising that someone with your passion for doing the wrong thing has lasted this long."

He turned to Meta. "I've had enough of killing for a while," he told her; "this planet is steeped in it. And we'll need him to help carry me downstairs, I don't think I can make it on my own, and he's probably the best stretcher bearer we can find."

Meta turned towards Mikah and her gun shot from its power holster into her hand and fired. He recoiled, raising his arm before his eyes, then seemed shocked to find himself still alive. Meta had freed him by shooting his chains away. She slid over to him with the effortless grace of a stalking tiger and pushed the still smoking muzzle of her gun deep into his midsection.

"Jason doesn't want me to kill you," she purred, and twisted the gun a bit deeper, "but I don't always do what he tells me. If you want to live a while you will do what *I* say. You will take the top off that table to make a stretcher. You will help carry Jason on it down to the rocket. Cause any kind of trouble, and you will be dead. Do you understand?"

Mikah opened his mouth for a protest, or perhaps for one of his speeches, but something in the icy bitterness of the girl stayed him. He merely nodded and turned to the table.

Ijale was crouched next to Jason's bed now, holding tight to his hand. She had not understood a word of any of the off-world languages they had spoken.

"What is happening, Jason?" she pleaded. "What was the shiny thing that bit your arm? This new one kissed you, so she must be your woman, but you are strong and can have two women. Do not leave me."

"Who is the girl?" Meta asked coldly. Her power holster buzzed and the muzzle of her gun slipped in and out.

"One of the locals, a slave who helped me," Jason said with an offhandedness he did not feel. "If we leave her here they will probably kill her. She'll come with us. . . ."

"I don't think that is wise." Meta's eyes were slitted, and her gun seemed about to leap into her hand. A Pyrran woman in love was still a woman—and still a Pyrran, a terribly dangerous combination. Luckily a stir at the door distracted her and she blasted two shots in that direction before Jason could stop her.

"Hold it—that's the Hertug. I recognized his heels as he dived for safety."

A frightened voice quavered from the hall. "We did not know this one was your friend, Jason. Some soldiers, too enthusiastic, shot too soon. I have had them punished. We are friends, Jason. Tell the one from the ship not to make more of the blowing up, so that I can enter and talk to you."

"I do not understand his words," Meta said, "but I don't like the sound of his voice."

"Your instincts are perfectly right, darling," Jason told her. "He couldn't be more two-faced if he had eyes, nose, and mouth on the back of his head."

Jason chuckled, and realized he was getting light-headed with all the battling drugs and toxins in his system. Clear thinking was an effort, but it was an effort that had to be made. They still weren't out of trouble and, as good a fighter as Meta was, she couldn't be expected to beat an entire army. And that's what would be called out to stop them if he didn't watch his step.

"Come on in, Hertug," he called out. "No one will hurt you— these mistakes happen." And then to Meta: "Don't shoot—but don't relax either. I'll try to talk him out of causing trouble, but I can't guarantee it, so stand ready for anything."

The Hertug took a quick look in the door and bobbed out of sight again. He finally rallied the remains of his nerve and shuffled in hesitantly.

"That's a nice little weapon your friend has, Jason. Tell him"— he blinked nearsighted eyes at Meta's uniform—"I mean her, that we'll trade some slaves for one. Five slaves, that's a good bargain."

"Say seven."

"Agreed. Hand it over."

"Not this one; it has been in her family for years and she couldn't bear to part with it. But there is another one in the ship she arrived in—we'll go down and get it."

Mikah had finished dismembering the table and he laid the top of it next to Jason's bed; then he and Meta slid Jason carefully onto it. The Hertug wiped his nose with the back of his hand, and his blinking red eyes took everything in.

"In the ship there are things that will make you well," he said, showing more intelligence than Jason had given him credit for. "You will not die, and you will leave in the sky ship?"

Jason groaned and writhed on the stretcher, clutching at his side in agony. "I'm dying, Hertug! They take my ashes to the ship, a space-going funeral barge, to scatter them among the stars—"

The Hertug dived for the doorway, but Meta was on him in the same instant, swinging his arm up behind his back until he screamed, and digging her gun into his kidneys.

"What are your plans, Jason?" she asked calmly.

"Let Mikah carry the front of the stretcher, and the Hertug and Ijale can hold up the back. Keep the old boy under your gun, and with a little luck we'll get out of here with whole skins."

They went out that way, slowly and carefully. The leaderless Perssonoj could not make up their minds what to do; the pained shouts from the Hertug only rattled them, as did Jason's shots, which blasted chunks of masonry and blew out windows. He enjoyed the trip down the stairs and across the courtyard, and cheered himself by putting a shot near any head that appeared. They reached the rocket without difficulty.

"Now comes the hard part," Jason said, wrapping an arm about Ijale's shoulders and throwing most of his weight on the other arm, clutched tight on Mikah's neck. He couldn't walk, but they could hold him up and drag him aboard. "Stay in the door, Meta, with a firm grip on the old buzzard. Expect anything to happen, because there is no such thing as loyalty here, and if they have to kill the Hertug to get you they won't hesitate for an instant."

"That is logical," Meta agreed. "After all, it is war."

"Yes, I suppose a Pyrran would look at it that way. Stand ready. I'll warm the engines, and when we're ready to take off I'll blow the siren. Drop the Hertug, close the lock, and get to the controls as fast as you can—I don't think I could manage a takeoff. Understand?"

"Perfectly. Go—you are wasting time."

Jason slumped in the co-pilot's seat and ran through the starting cycle as fast as he could. He was just reaching for the siren button when there was a jarring thump and the whole ship shook, and—for one heartstopping second—it rocked and almost fell over. It slowly righted itself and he hit the alarm. Before it stopped echoing, Meta was in the pilot's seat and the little rocket blasted skywards.

"They are more advanced than I thought they would be on this primitive world," she said, as soon as the first thrust of acceleration eased. "There was a great, ugly machine in one of the buildings that suddenly smoked and threw a rock that took most of our port fin away. I blew it up, but the one you call the Hertug escaped."

"In some ways they are very advanced," Jason said, feeling too weak to admit that they had been almost finished off by his own invention.

17

With Meta's skillful piloting, they slid easily into the open hold of the Pyrran spacer that was orbiting just outside the atmosphere. Being in free fall eased Jason's pain enough for him to make sure that the wide-eyed and terrorized Ijale was strapped into an acceleration couch before he collapsed. After that he floated towards a bunk himself, and before he reached it passed out with a happy smile: the slaveholding monomaniacs already seemed far behind.

When he awoke much of the pain and discomfort was gone, as well as the fever; and though he was dreadfully weak he was able to pull himself through the passageways to the control room. Meta was plotting a course on the computer.

"Food!" Jason croaked, clutching at his throat. "My tissues exhaust themselves making repairs and I starve."

Meta wordlessly passed him a squeeze-flask dinner, managing to do it in such a way that he knew she was angry about something. As he put the tube in his mouth he saw Ijale crouched on the far side of the compartment—at least, crouching as much as she was capable of in free fall.

"My, that was good!" Jason exclaimed with false joviality. "Are you flying this ship alone, Meta?"

"Of course I'm alone." She said it in such a way that it sounded more like: *Aren't you a fool?* "I was allowed to take the ship, but no one could be spared to go with me."

"How did you find me?" he asked, trying to discover a subject that she might warm to.

"That should be obvious. The operator at the spaceport noted the insignia when the spacer left with you in it, and when he described it Kerk recognized it as Cassylian. I went to Cassylia and investigated; they identified the ship, but there was no record of it having returned. Then I followed a reverse course to Pyrrus and found three possible planets near enough to the course to have registered in the ship during jump-space flight. Two of them are centrally organized, with modern spaceports and flight controls, and would have known if the ship I was seeking had landed, or even crashed. It hadn't. Therefore the ship must have landed on the third one, the planet we have just left. As soon as I entered the atmosphere I heard the distress signal and came as fast as I could. . . . What are you going to do with that woman?"

These last words were spoken in an icy tone. Ijale crouched lower, not understanding a word of the conversation, but obviously petrified with fear.

"I haven't really thought about it yet . . ."

"There is only room for one woman in your life, Jason. Me. I'll kill anyone who thinks differently."

Without a doubt she meant it; and if Ijale was going to live much longer she had to be separated as quickly as possible from the deadly threat of female Pyrran jealousy. Jason thought fast.

"We'll stop at the next civilized planet and let her off. I have enough money to leave a deposit in a bank that will last her for years. And I'll make arrangements for it to be paid out only a bit at a time, so no matter how she is cheated she will always have enough. I'm not going to worry about her—if she was able to live in the *kreno* legion she can get along anywhere on a settled world."

He could already hear the complaints that would come when he broke the news to Ijale, but it was for her own survival.

"I shall care for her and lead her in the paths of righteousness," a remembered voice spoke from the doorway. Mikah stood there, cluthing at the jamb, bushy-bearded and bright-eyed.

"That's a wonderful idea!" Jason agreed enthusiastically. He turned to Ijale and spoke to her in her own language. "Did you hear that? Mikah is going to take you home with him and look after you. I'll arrange for some money to be paid to you for all your needs— he'll explain to you all about money. I want you to listen to him carefully, note exactly what he says, then do the exact opposite.

You must promise me you will do that, and never break your word. In that way, though you may make some mistakes, and will sometimes be wrong, the rest of the time things will go very smoothly."

"I cannot leave you! Take me with you—I'll be your slave always!" she wailed.

"What did she say?" Meta snapped, catching some of the meaning.

"You are evil, Jason," Mikah declaimed, getting the needle back into the familiar groove. "She will obey you, I know that, so no matter how I labor she will always do as you say."

"I sincerely hope so," Jason said fervently. "One has to be born into your particular brand of illogic to get any pleasure from it. The rest of us are happier bending a bit under the impact of existence, and exacting a mite more pleasure from the physical life around us."

"Evil I say, and you shall not go unpunishcd." Mikah's hand appeared from behind the door jamb, and it held a pistol that he had found below. "I am taking command of this ship. You will secure the two women so that they can cause no trouble; then we will proceed to Cassylia for your trial."

Meta had her back turned to Mikah and was sitting in the control chair a good five meters from him, her hands filled with navigational notes. She slowly raised her head and looked at Jason and a smile broke across her face.

"You said you didn't want him killed."

"I still don't want him killed, but I also have no intention of going to Cassylia." He echoed her smile, and turned away.

He sighed happily, and there was a sudden rush of feet behind his back. No shots were fired, but a hoarse scream, a thud, and a sharp cracking noise told him that Mikah had lost his last argument.

DEATHWORLD 3

for
Kingsley and *Jane*
—gratefully

1

Guard Lieutenant Talenc lowered the electronic binoculars and twisted a knob on their controls, turning up the intensity to compensate for the failing light. The glaring white sun dropped behind a thick stratum of clouds, and evening was close, yet the image intensifier in the binoculars presented a harshly clear black-and-white image of the undulating plain. Talenc cursed under his breath and swept the heavy instrument back and forth. Grass, a sea of wind-stirred, frost-coated grass. Nothing.

"I'm sorry, but I didn't see it, sir," the sentry said reluctantly. "It's always just the same out there."

"Well I saw it—and that's good enough. Something moved and I'm going to find out what it is." He lowered the binoculars and glanced at his watch. "An hour and a half until it gets dark, plenty of time. Tell the officer of the day where I've gone."

The sentry opened his mouth to say something, then thought better of it. One did not give advice to Guard Lieutenant Talenc. When the gate in the charged wire fence opened, Talenc swung up his laser rifle, settled the grenade case firmly on his belt, and strode forth—a man secure in his own strength, a one time unarmed-combat champion and veteran of uncounted brawls. Positive that there was nothing in this vacant expanse of plain that he could not take care of.

He had seen a movement, he was sure of that, a flicker of motion that had drawn his eye. It could have been an animal; it could have been anything. His decision to investigate was prompted as much by the boredom of the guard routine as by curiosity. Or duty. He stamped solidly through the crackling grass and turned only once to look back at the wire-girt camp. A handful of low buildings and tents, with the skeleton of the drill tower rising above them, while the clifflike bulk of the spaceship shadowed it all. Talenc was not a sensitive man, yet even he was aware of the minuteness of this lonely encampment, set into the horizon-reaching plains of emptiness. He snorted and turned away. If there was something out here, he was going to kill it.

A hundred meters from the fence there was a slight dip, followed by a rising billow, an irregularity in the ground that could not be seen from the camp. Talenc trudged to the top of the hillock and gaped down at the group of mounted men who were concealed behind it.

He sprang back instantly, but not fast enough. The nearest rider thrust his long lance through Talenc's calf, twisted the barbed point in the wound and dragged him over the edge of the embankment. Talenc pulled up his gun as he fell, but another lance drove it from his hand and pierced his palm, pinning it to the ground. It was all over very quickly, one second, two seconds, and the shock of pain was just striking him when he tried to reach for his radio. A third lance through his wrist pinioned that arm.

Spread-eagled, wounded, and dazed by shock, Guard Lieutenant Talenc opened his mouth to cry aloud, but even this was denied him. The nearest rider leaned over casually and thrust a short saber between Talenc's teeth, deep into the roof of his mouth, and his voice was stilled forever. His leg jerked as he died, rustling a clump of grass, and that was the only sound that marked his passing. The riders gazed down upon him silently, then turned away with complete lack of interest. Their mounts, though they stirred uneasily, were just as silent.

"What is all this about?" the officer of the guard asked, buttoning on his weapon belt.

"It's Lieutenant Talenc, sir. He went out there. Said he saw something, and then went over a rise. I haven't seen him since, maybe ten, fifteen minutes now, and I can't raise him on the radio."

"I don't see how he can get into any trouble out there," the officer said, looking out at the darkening plain. "Still—we had better bring him in. Sergeant." The man stepped forward and saluted. "Take a squad out and find Lieutenant Talenc."

They were professionals, signed on for thirty years with John Company, and they expected only trouble from a newly opened planet. They spread out as skirmishers and moved warily away across the plain.

"Anything wrong?" the metallurgist asked, coming out of the drill hut with an ore sample on a tray.

"I don't know . . ." the officer said, just as the riders swept out of the concealed gully and around both sides of the knoll.

It was shocking. The guardsmen, trained, deadly and well-

armed, were overrun and destroyed. Some shots were fired, but the
riders swung low on their long-necked mounts, keeping the animals' thick bodies between themselves and the guns. There was the
twang of suddenly released bowstrings and the lances dipped and
killed. The riders rolled over the guardsmen and rode on, leaving
nine twisted bodies behind them.

"They're coming this way!" the metallurgist shouted, dropping
the tray and turning to run. The alarm siren began to shriek and the
guards poured out of their tents.

The attackers hit the encampment with the sudden shock of an
earthquake. There was no time to prepare for it, and the men near
the fence died without lifting their weapons. The attackers' mounts
clawed at the ground with pillar-like legs and hurled themselves
forward; one moment a distant threat, the next an overwhelming
presence. The leader hit the fence, its weight tearing it down even as
electricity arced brightly and killed it, its long thick neck crashing to
the ground just before the guard officer. He stared at it, horrified,
for just an instant before the creature's rider planted an arrow in his
eye socket and he died.

Murder, whistling death. They hit once and were gone, sweeping
close to the fence, leaping the body of the dead beast, arrows
pouring in a dark stream from their short, laminated bows. Even in
the half darkness, from the backs of their thundering, heaving
mounts, their aim was excellent. Men died, or dropped, wounded.
One arrow even tore into the gaping mouth of the siren so that it
rattled and moaned down into silence.

As quickly as they had struck they vanished, out of sight in the
ravine behind the shadowed rise, and, in the stunned silence that
followed, the moans of the wounded were shockingly loud.

The light was almost gone from the sky now and the darkness
added to the confusion. When the glow tubes sprang on, the camp
became a pool of bloody murder set in the surrounding night. Order
was restored only slightly when Bardovy, the expedition's commander, began bellowing instructions over the bullhorn. While the
medics separated the dying from the dead, mortars were rushed out
and set up. One of the sentries shouted a warning and the big
battlelamp was turned on—and revealed the dark mass of riders
gathering again on the ridge.

"Mortars, fire!" the commander shouted with wild anger. "Hit
them hard!"

His voice was drowned out as the first shells hit, round after
round poured in until the dust and smoke boiled high and the
explosions rolled like thunder.

They did not realize that the first charge had been only a feint and that the main attack was hitting them from the opposite side of the camp. Only when the beasts were in among them and they began to die did they know what had happened. Then it was too late.

"Close the ports!" the duty pilot shouted from the safety of the spacer's control room high above, banging the airlock switches as he spoke. He could see the waves of attackers sweeping by, and he knew how lethargic was the low-geared motion of the ponderous outer doors. He kept pushing at the already closed switches.

In a wave of shrieking brute flesh, the attackers rolled over the charged fence. The leading ones died and were trampled down by the beasts behind, who climbed their bodies, thick claws biting deep to take hold. Some of the riders died as well, and they appeared to be as dispensable as their mounts, for the others kept on coming in endless waves. They overwhelmed the encampment, filled it, destroyed it.

"This is Second Officer Weiks," the pilot said, activating all the speakers in the ship. "Is there any officer aboard who ranks me?" He listened to the growing silence and, when he spoke again, his voice was choked and unclear.

"Sound off in rotation, officers and men, from the Engine Room north. Sparks, take it down."

Hesitantly, one by one, the voices checked in, while Weiks activated the hull scanners and looked at the milling fury below.

"Seventeen—that's all," the radio operator said with shocked unbelief, his hand over the microphone. He passed the list to the Second Officer, who looked at it bleakly, then slowly reached for the microphone.

"This is the bridge," he said. "I am taking command. Run the engines up to ready."

"Aren't we going to help them?" a voice broke in. "We can't just leave them out there."

"There is no one out there to leave," Weiks said slowly. "I've checked on all the screens and there is nothing visible down there except these—attackers and their beasts. Even if there were, I doubt if there is anything we could do to help. It would be suicide to leave the ship. And we have only a bare skeleton flight crew aboard as it is."

The frame of the ship shivered as if to add punctuation to his words.

"One of the screens is out—there goes another—they hit it with something. And they're fixing lines to the landing legs. I don' know if they can pull us over—and I don't want to find out. Secure to blast in sixty-five seconds.''

"They'll burn in our jets, everything, everyone down there," the radio operator said, snapping his harness tight.

"Our people won't feel it," the pilot said grimly, "and—let's see how many of the others we can get."

When the spacer rose, spouting fire, it left a smoking, humped circle of death below it. But, as soon as the ground was cool enough, the waiting riders pressed in and trampled through the ash. More and more of them, appearing out of the darkness. There seemed no end to their teeming numbers.

2

"Pretty stupid to get hit by a sawbird," Brucco said, helping Jason dinAlt to pull the ripped metalcloth jacket off over his head.

"Pretty stupid to try and eat a peaceful meal on this planet!" Jason snapped back, his words muffled by the heavy cloth. He pulled the jacket free and winced as sharp pain cut into his side. "I was just trying to enjoy some soup, and the bowl got in the way when I had to fire."

"Only a superficial wound," Brucco said, looking at the red gash on Jason's side. "The saw bounced off the ribs without breaking them. Very lucky."

"You mean lucky I didn't get killed. Whoever heard of a sawbird in the mess hall?''

"Always expect the unexpected on Pyrrus. Even the children know that." Brucco sloshed on antiseptic and Jason ground his teeth together tightly. The phone pinged and Meta's worried face appeared on the screen.

"Jason—I heard you were hurt," she said.

"Dying," he told her.

Brucco sniffed loudly. "Nonsense. Superficial wound, fourteen centimeters in length, no toxins."

"Is that all?" Meta said, and the screen went dark.

"Yes, that's all," Jason said bitterly. "A liter of blood and a kilo of flesh, nothing more bothersome than a hangnail. What do I have to do to get some sympathy around here—lose a leg?"

"If you lost a leg in combat, there might be sympathy," Brucco said coldly, pressing an adhesive bandage into place. "But if you lost a limb to a sawbird in the mess hall, you would expect only contempt."

"Enough!" Jason said sharply, pulling his jacket back on. "Don't take me so literally and, yes, I know all about the sweet consideration I can expect from you friendly Pyrrans. I don't think I'll ever miss this planet, not for five minutes."

"You're leaving?" Brucco asked, brightening up. "Is that what the meeting is about?"

"Don't sound so wildly depressed at the thought. Try to control your impatience until 1500 hours, when the others will be here. I play no favorites. Except myself, that is," he added, walking out stiffly, trying to move his side as little as possible.

It was time for a change, he thought, looking out of a high window across the perimeter wall to the deadly jungle beyond. Some light-sensitive cells must have caught the motion because a tree branch whipped forward and a sudden flurry of thorndarts rattled against the transparent metal of the window. His reflexes were so well trained by now that he did not move a muscle.

Past time for a change. Every day on Pyrrus was another spin of the wheel. Winning was just staying even, and when your number came up, it was certain death. How many people had died since he first came here? He was beginning to lose track, to become as indifferent to death as any Pyrran.

If there were going to be any changes made, he was the one who would have to make them. He had thought once that he had solved this planet's deadly problems, when he had proved to them that the relentless, endless war was their own doing. Yet it still went on. Knowledge of the truth does not always mean acceptance of it. The Pyrrans who were capable of accepting the reality of existence here had left the city and had gone far enough away to escape the pressure of physical and mental hatred that still engulfed it. Although the remaining Pyrrans might give lip-service to the concept that their own emotions were keeping the war going, they did not really believe that this was true. And each time they looked out at the world that they hated, the enemy gained fresh strength and pressed the attack anew. When Jason thought of the only possible end for the city, he grew depressed. There were so many of the people left who would not accept the change—or help of any kind. They were as much a part of this war and as adapted to the war as the hyperspecialized life forms outside, molded in the same way by the same generations of mixed hatred and fear.

There was one more change coming. He wondered how many of them would accept it.

It was 1520 hours before Jason made his appearance in Kerk's office. He had been delayed by a last-minute exchange of messages on the jump-space communicator. Everyone in the room shared the same expression, cold anger. Pyrrans had very little patience and even less tolerance for a puzzle or a mystery. They were so alike—yet so different.

Kerk, gray-haired and stolid, able to control his expression better than the others. Practice, undoubtedly, from dealing so much with off-worlders. This was the man whom it was most important to convince because, if the slapdash, militaristic Pyrran society had any leader at all, he was the one.

Brucco, hawk-faced and lean, his features set in a perpetual expression of suspicion. The expression was justified. As physician, researcher and ecologist, he was the single authority on Pyrran life forms. He had to be suspicious. Though at least there was one thing in his favor: he was scientist enough to be convinced by reasoned fact.

And Rhes, leader of the outsiders, the people who had adapted successfully to this deadly planet. He was not possessed by the reflex hatred that filled the others, and Jason counted upon him for help.

Meta, sweet and lovely, stronger than most men, whose graceful arms could clasp with passion—or break bones. Does your coldly practical mind—hidden in that beautiful female body—know what love is? Or is it just pride of possession you feel toward the off-worlder Jason dinAlt? Tell him sometime; he would like to know. But not right now. You look just as impatient and dangerous as the others.

Jason closed the door behind him and smiled insincerely.

"Hello there, everybody," he said. "I hope you didn't mind my keeping you waiting?" He went on quickly, ignoring the angry growls from all sides.

"I'm sure that you will all be pleased to hear that I am broke, financially wiped out, and sunk."

Their expressions cleared as they considered the statement. One thought at a time—that was the Pyrran way.

"You have millions in the bank," Kerk said, "and no way of gambling and losing them."

"When I gamble, I win," Jason informed him with calm dignity. "I am broke because I have spent every last credit. I have purchased a spaceship, and it is on its way here now."

"Why?" Meta asked, speaking the question that was foremost in all their minds.

"Because I am leaving this planet and I'm taking you—and as many others as possible—with me."

Jason could read their mixed feelings easily. For better or for worse—and it was certainly worse than any other planet in the known galaxy—this was their home. Deadly and dangerous, but still theirs. He had to make his idea attractive, to gain their enthusiasm and make them forget any second thoughts that they might have. The appeal to their intelligence would come later; first he must appeal to their emotions. He knew well this single chink in their armor.

"I've discovered a planet that is far more deadly than Pyrrus."

Brucco laughed with cold disbelief, and they all nodded in agreement with him.

"Is that supposed to be attractive?" Rhes asked, the only Pyrran present who had been born outside the city and was therefore immune to their love of violence. Jason gave him a long, slow wink to ponder over while he went on to convince the others.

"I mean deadly because it contains the most dangerous life form ever discovered. Faster than a stingwing, more vicious than a horndevil, more tenacious than a clawhawk—there's no end to the list. I have found the planet where these creatures abide."

"You are talking about men, aren't you?" Kerk said, quicker to understand than the others, as usual.

"I am. Men who are more deadly than the ones here, because Pyrrans have been bred by natural selection to defend themselves against any dangers. *Defend*. What would you think of a world where men have been bred for some thousands of years to attack, to kill and destroy, without any thought of the consequences? What do you think the survivors of this genocidal conflict would be like?"

They considered it and, from their expression, they did not think very much of the idea. They had taken sides, united against a common enemy in their thoughts, and Jason hurried on while he had them in agreement.

"I'm talking about a planet named 'Felicity,' apparently called this to sucker in the settlers, or for the same reason that big men are called 'Tiny.' I read about it some months back in a newsfax, just a small item about an entire mining settlement being wiped out. This is a hard thing to do. Mining-operation teams are tough and ready for trouble—and the John & John Minerals Company's are the toughest. Also—and equally important—John Company does not play for small stakes. So I got in touch with some friends and sent them some money to spread around, and they managed to contact one of the survivors. It cost me a good deal more to get accurate information from him, but it was well worth it. Here it is." He paused for dramatic effect and held up a sheet of paper.

"Well, read it. Don't just wave it at us," Brucco said, tapping the table irritably.

"Have patience," Jason told him. "This is an engineer's report, and it is very enthusiastic in a restrained engineering way. Apparently Felicity has a wealth of heavy elements, near the surface and confined to a relatively restricted area. Opencut mining should be possible and, from the way this engineer talks, the uranium ore sounds like it is rich enough to run a reactor without any refining."

"That's impossible," Meta broke in. "Uranium ore in a free state could not be so radioactive that—"

"Please," Jason said, holding both hands in the air. "I was just making a small exaggeration to emphasize a point. The ore is rich, let it go at that. The important thing now is that, in spite of the quality of the ore, John Company is not returning to Felicity. They had their fingers burned once, badly, and there are plenty of other planets they can mine with a lot less effort. Without having to face dragon-riding barbarians who appear suddenly out of the ground and attack in endless waves, destroying everything they come near."

"What is all that last bit supposed to mean?" Kerk asked.

"Your guess is as good as mine. This is the way the survivors described the massacre. The only thing we can be sure about it is that they were attacked by mounted men, and that they were licked."

"And this is the planet you wish us to go to," Kerk said. "It does not sound attractive. We can stay here and work our own mines."

"You've been working your mines for centuries, until some of the shafts are five kilometers deep and producing only second-rate ore—but that's not the point. I'm thinking about the people here and what is going to happen to them. Life on this planet has been irreversibly changed. The Pyrrans who were capable of making an adjustment to the new conditions have done so. Now—what about the others?"

Their only answer was a protracted silence.

"It's a good question, isn't it? And a pertinent one. I'll tell you what's going to happen to the people left in this city. And when I tell you, try not to shoot me. I think you have all outgrown that kind of instant reflex to a difference of opinion. At least I hope that everyone in this room has. I wouldn't tell this to the people out there in the city. They would probably kill me rather than hear the truth. They don't want to find out that they are all condemned to certain death by this planet."

There was the thin whine of an electric motor as Meta's gun sprang halfway out of its power holster, then slipped back. Jason smiled at her and waggled his finger; she turned away coldly. The others controlled their trigger reflexes better.

"That is not true," Kerk said. "People are still leaving the city—"

"And returning in about the same numbers. Argument invalid. The ones who were able to leave have done so; only the hard core is left."

"There are other possible solutions," Brucco said. "Another city could be constructed—"

The rumble of an earthquake interrupted him. They had been feeling tremors for some time, so commonplace on Pyrrus that they were scarcely aware of them, but this one was much stronger. The building moved under them and a jagged crack appeared in the wall, showering cement dust. The crack intersected the window frame and, although the single pane was made of armorglass, it fractured under the strain and crashed out in jagged fragments. As though on cue, a stingwing dived at the opening, ripping through the protective netting inside. It dissolved in a burst of flame as their guns surged from their power holsters and four shots fired as one.

"I'll watch the window," Kerk said, shifting his chair so he could face the opening. "Go on."

The interruption, the reminder of what life in this city was really like, had thrown Brucco off his pace. He hesitated a moment, then continued.

"Yes . . . well, what I was saying—other solutions are possible. A second city, quite distant from here, could be constructed, perhaps at one of the mine sites. Only around this city are the life forms so deadly. This city could be abandoned and—"

"And the new city would recapitulate all the sins of the old. The hatred of the remaining Pyrrans would recreate the same situation. You know them better than I do, Brucco, isn't that what would happen?"

Jason waited until Brucco had nodded a reluctant yes.

"We've been over this ground before and there is only one possible solution. Get those people off Pyrrus and to a world where they can survive without a constant, decimating war. *Any* place would be an improvement over Pyrrus. You people are so close to it that you seem to have forgotten what a hell this planet really is. I know that it's all that you have and that you're adjusted to it, but it is really not very much. I've proved to you that all of the life forms here are telepathic to a degree and that your hatred of them keeps them warring upon you. Mutating and changing and constantly getting more vicious and deadly. You have admitted that. But it doesn't change the situation. There are still enough of you Pyrrans hating away to keep the war going. Sanity save me but you are a pigheaded people! If I had any brains, I would be well away from here and leave you to your deadly destiny. But I'm involved, like it or not. I've kept you alive and you've kept me alive and our futures run on the same track. Besides that, I like your girls."

Meta's sniff was loud in the listening silence.

"So—jokes and arguments aside, we have a problem. If your people stay here, they eventually die. All of them. To save them, you are going to have to get them away from here, to a more friendly world. Habitable planets with good natural resources are not always easy to find, but I've found one. There may be some differences of opinion with the natives, the original settlers, but I think that should make the idea more interesting to Pyrrans rather than the other way around. Transportation and equipment are on the way. Now who is in with me? Kerk? They look to you for leadership. Now —lead!"

Kerk squinted his eyes dangerously at Jason and tightened his lips with distaste. "You always seem to be talking me into doing things I do not really want to do."

"A measure of maturity," Jason said blandly. "The ego rising triumphant over the id. Does that mean that you will help?"

"It does. I do not want to go to another planet and I do not enjoy the thought. Yet I can see no other way to save the people in the city from certain extinction."

"Good. And you, Brucco? We'll need a surgeon."

"Find another one. My assistant, Teca, will do. My studies of the Pyrran life forms are far from complete. I am staying in the city as long as it is here."

"It could mean your life."

"It probably will. However, my records and observations are indestructible."

No one doubted that he meant it—or attempted to argue with him. Jason turned to Meta.

"We'll need you to pilot the ship after the ferry crew has been returned."

"I'm needed here to operate our Pyrran ship."

"There are other pilots. You've trained them yourself. And if you stay here, I'll have to get myself another woman."

"I'll kill her if you do. I'll pilot the ship."

Jason smiled and blew her a kiss that she pretended to ignore. "That does it then," he said. "Brucco will stay here, and I guess Rhes will also stay to supervise the settling of the city Pyrrans with his people."

"You have guessed wrong," Rhes told him. "The settlements are now handled by a committee and going as smoothly as can be expected. I have no desire to remain—what is the word?—a backwoods rube for the rest of my life. This new planet sounds very interesting and I am looking forward to the experience."

"That is the best news I have heard today. Now let's get down to facts. The ship will be here in about two weeks, so if we organize things now, we should be able to get the supplies and people aboard and lift soon after she arrives. I'll write up an announcement that loads the dice as much as possible in favor of this operation, and we can spring it on the populace. Get volunteers. There are about 20,000 people left in the city, but we can't get more than about 2,000 into the ship—it's a demothballed armored troop carrier called the *Pugnacious,* left over from one of the Rim Wars—so we can pick and choose the best. Establish the settlement and come back for the others. We're on our way."

Jason was stunned, but no one else seemed surprised.

"One hundred and sixty-eight volunteers—including Grif, a nine-year-old boy—out of how many thousand? It just isn't possible."

"It is possible on Pyrrus," Kerk said.

"Yes, it's possible on Pyrrus, but only on Pyrrus." Jason paced the room, with a frustrating, dragging step in the doubled gravity, smacking his fist into his open palm. "When it comes to unthinking reflex and sheer bullheadedness, this planet really wins the plutonium-plated prize. 'Me born here. Me stay here. Me die here. Ugh.' Ugh is right!" He spun about to stab his finger at Kerk—then grabbed at his calf to rub away the cramp brought on by overexertion in the heightened gravity.

"Well, we're not going to worry about them," he said. "We'l

save them in spite of themselves. We'll take the one hundred and sixty-eight volunteers and we'll go to Felicity, and we'll lick the planet and open the mine—and come back for the others. That's what we're going to do!"

He slumped in the chair, massaging his leg, as Kerk went out. "I hope . . ." he mumbled under his breath.

3

Muffled clanking sounded in the airlock as the transfer-station mechanics fastened the flexible tubeway to the spacer's hull. The intercom buzzed as someone plugged into the hull jack outside.

"Transfer Station 70 Ophiuchi to *Pugnacious*. You are sealed to tubeway, which is now pressurized to ship standard. You may open your outer port."

"Stand by for opening," Jason said, and turned the key in the override switch that permitted the outer port to be open at the same time as the inner one.

"Good to be back on dry land," one of the ferry crewmen said as they came into the lock, and the others laughed uproariously, as though he had said something exceedingly funny. All of them, that is, except the pilot, who scowled at the opening port, his broken arm sticking out stiffly before him in its cast. None of them mentioned the arm or looked in his direction, but he knew why they were laughing.

Jason did not feel sorry for the pilot. Meta always gave fair warning to the men who made passes at her. Perhaps, in the romantically dim light of the bridge, he had not believed her. So she had broken his arm. Tough. Jason kept his face impassive as the man passed by him and out into the tubeway. This was constructed of transparent plastic, an undulating umbilical cord that connected the spacer to the transfer station, the massive, light-sprinkled bulk that loomed above them. Two other tubeways were visible, like theirs, connecting ships to this way station in space, balanced in a null-g orbit between the suns that made up the two star system. The smaller companion, 70 Ophiuchi B, was just rising behind the station, a tiny disk over a billion miles distant.

"We've got a parcel here for the *Pugnacious*," a clerk said, floating out of the mouth of the tubeway. "A transhipment waiting your arrival." He extended a receipt book. "Want to sign for it?"

Jason scrawled his name, then moved aside as two freight handlers maneuvered the bulky case down the tube and through the lock. He was trying to work a pinch bar under the metal sealing straps when Meta came up.

"What is that?" she asked, twisting the bar from his hands with an easy motion and jamming it deep under the strap. She heaved once and there was the sharp twang of fractured metal.

"You'll make some man a fine husband," Jason told her, dusting off his fingers. "I bet you can't do the other two that easily." She bent to the task. "This is a tool, something that we are going to need very much if we are going into the planet-busting business. I wish I had had one when I first came to Pyrrus, it might have saved a good number of lives."

Meta threw back the cover and looked at the wheeled ovoid form. "What is it—a bomb?" she asked.

"Not on your life. This is something much more important." He tilted up the crate so that the object rolled out onto the floor.

It was an almost featureless, shiny metal egg that stood a good meter high with its small end up. Six rubber-tired wheels, three to a side, held it clear of the floor, and the top was crowned by a transparent-lidded control panel. Jason reached down and flipped up the lid, then punched a button marked *on* and the panel lights glowed.

"What are you?" he said.

"This is a library," a hollow, metallic voice answered.

"Of what possible use is that?" Meta said, turning to leave.

"I'll tell you," Jason said, putting out his hand to stop her, ready to move back quickly if she tried any arm-busting tricks. "This device is our intelligence, in the military sense, not the IQ. Have you forgotten what we had to go through to find out anything at all about your planet's history? We needed facts to work from and we had none at all. Well, we have some now." He patted the library's sleek side.

"What could this little toy possibly know that could help us?"

"This little toy, as you so quaintly put it, costs over 982 thousand credits, plus shipping charges."

She was shocked. "Why—you could outfit an army for that much. Weapons, ammunition . . ."

"I thought that would impress you. And will you please get it through your exceedingly lovely blond head that armies aren't the solution to every problem. We are going to bang up against a new culture soon, on a new planet, and we want to open a mine in the right place. Your army will tell us nothing about mineralogy or anthropology or ecology or exobiology—"

"You are making those words up."

"Don't you just wish I were! I don't think you quite realize how much of a library is stuffed into this creature's metal carcass. Library," he said, pointing to it dramatically, "tell us about yourself."

"This is a model 427-1587, Mark IX, improved, with photodigital laser-based recorder memory and integrated circuit technology—"

"Stop!" Jason ordered. "Library, you will have to do better than that. Can't you describe yourself in simple newsfax language?"

"Well, hello there," the library chortled. 'I'll bet you never saw Mark IX before, the ultimate in library luxury—"

"We've hit the *sales talk* button, but at least we can understand it."

"—and the very newest example of what the guys who built this machine like to call 'integrated circuit technology.' Well, friends, you don't need a galactic degree to understand that the Mark IX is something new in the universe. That 'integrated so-and-so' double-talk just means that this is a thinking machine that can't be beat. But everyone needs something to think about as well as to think with, and just like the memory in your head, the Mark IX has a memory all its own. A memory that contains the *entire library* at the University of Haribay, holding more books than you could count in a lifetime. These books have been broken down into words and the words have been broken down into bits, and the bits have been recorded on little chips of silicon inside the Mark IX's brain. That memory part of the brain is no bigger than a man's clenched fist—a *small* man's fist—because there are over 545 million bits to every ten square millimeters. You don't even have to know what a bit is to know that that is impressive. All of history, science and philosophy are in this brain. Linguistics, too. If you want to know the word for 'cheese' in the basic galactic languages, in the order of the number of speakers, it is this—"

As the high-speed roar of syllables poured out Jason turned to Meta—and found she was gone.

"It can do other things besides translate 'cheese,' " he said, pressing the *off* button. "Just wait and see."

The Pyrrans were happy enough to vegetate, to doze and yawn, like tigers with full stomachs, during the trip to Felicity. Only Jason felt the urge to use the time efficiently. He searched all the cross-references in the library for information about the planet and the solar system it belonged to, and was drawn from his studies only by Meta's passionate, yet implacable, grasp. She felt that there were far more interesting ways to pass the long hours, and Jason, once he had been severed from his labors, enthusiastically agreed with her.

One ship-day before they were scheduled to drop from jump-space into the Felicity system, Jason called a general meeting in the dining room.

"This is where we are going," he said, tapping a large diagram hung on the wall. There was absolute silence and 100 percent attention, for a military-style briefing was meat and drink to the Pyrrans.

"The planet is called 'Felicity,' the fifth planet of a nameless class-F1 star. This is a white star with about twice the luminosity of Pyrrus's own G2 sun and it puts out a lot more ultraviolet. You can look forward to getting nice suntans. The planet has nine-tenths of its surface covered by water, with a few chains of volcanic islands and only one land mass big enough to be called a continent. This one. As you can see, it looks like a flattened-out dagger, point downward, divided roughly in the middle by the guard. The line here, represented by the guard, is an immense geological fault that cuts across the continent from one side to the other, an unbroken cliff that is three to ten kilometers high across the entire land mass. This cliff and the range of mountains behind it have had a drastic effect on the continental weather. The planet is far hotter than most other habitable ones—the temperature at the equator is close to the boiling point of water—and only this continent's location right up near the northern pole makes life bearable. Moist, warm air sweeps north and hits the escarpment and the mountains, where it condenses as rain on the southern slopes. A number of large rivers run south from the mountains and signs of agriculture and settlements were seen here—but were of no interest to the John Company men. The magnetometers and gravitometers didn't twitch a needle. But up here"—he tapped the northern half of the continent, the "handle" of the dagger—"up here the detectors went wild. The mountain building that pushed the northern half up so high, causing this continent-splitting range in the middle, stirred up the heavy metal deposits. Here is where the mines will have to be, in the middle of the most desolate piece of landscape I have ever heard about. There is little or no water, the mountain range stops most of it, and what does get past the mountains usually falls as snow on this giant plateau. It is frigid, high, dry, and deadly—and it never changes. Felicity has almost no axial tilt to speak of, so the seasonal changes are so slight they can scarcely be noticed. The weather in any spot remains the same all of the time. To finish off this highly attractive picture of the ideal settlement site, there are men who live up here who are as deadly—or deadlier—than any life forms you ever faced on Pyrrus. Our job will be to sit right down in the middle of them, build a settlement and open a mine. Do I hear any suggestions as to how this can be done?"

"I know," Clon said, standing slowly. He was a hulking, burly man with a thick and protruding brow ridge. The weight of this bony ledge must have been balanced by even thicker bone in the skull behind, leaving room for only the most miniscule of brain cavities. His reflexes were excellent, undoubtedly short-circuited in his spinal column like some contemporary dinosaur, but any thoughts that had to penetrate his ossified cranium emerged only with the most immense difficulty. He was the last person Jason expected to answer.

"I know," Clon repeated. "We kill them all. Then they don't bother us."

"Thanks for the suggestion," Jason said calmly. "Your chair's right behind you, that's it. Your suggestion is a sound Pyrran one, Pyrran also in the fact that you want to apply it to a second planet even though it failed on the first one. Attractive as it may look, we shall not indulge in genocide. We shall use our intelligence to solve this problem, not our teeth. We are trying to open this world up, not close it forever. What I propose is an open camp, the opposite of the armed *laager* the John Company men built. If we are careful, and watch the surrounding countryside carefully, we should not be taken by surprise. My hope is that we will be able to contact the locals and find out what they have against miners or off-worlders, and then try to change their minds. If anyone has a better suggestion for a plan of action, let me know now. Otherwise, we land as close to the original site as we can and wait for contact. Our eyes are open, we know what happened to the first expedition, so we will be very careful that it doesn't happen to us."

Finding the original mine site was very easy. A year's slow growth of the sparse vegetation had not been enough to obscure the burned scar on the landscape. The abandoned heavy equipment showed clearly on the magnetometer, and the *Pugnacious* sank to the ground close by. From above, the rolling steppe had appeared to be empty of life, and it looked even more so once they were down. Jason stood in the open airlock and shivered as the first blast of dry, frigid air hit him, the grass rustling to its passing, while grains of sand hissed against the metal of the hull. He had planned to be first out, but Rhes happened to knock against him as Kerk came up so that the gray-haired Pyrran slipped by and leaped to the ground.

"A lightweight planet," he said as he turned slowly, his eyes never still. "Can't be over 1G. Like floating, after Pyrrus."

"It's closer to 1.5G," Jason said, following him out just as warily. "But anything is better than 2G."

The first landing party, ten men in all, emerged from the ship and carefully surveyed the area. They stayed close enough to be able to call to one another, yet not so close that they blocked each other's vision or field of fire. Their guns stayed in their power holsters and they walked slowly, apparently indifferent to the frigid wind and blown sand that reddened Jason's skin and made his eyes water. In their own, strictly Pyrran way, they were enjoying themselves after the forced relaxation of the voyage.

"Something moving 200 meters to the southeast," Meta's voice spoke in their earphones. She was one of the observers at the viewports in the ship above.

They spun and crouched, ready for anything. The undulating plain still appeared to be empty, but there was a sudden hissing as an arrow arced toward Kerk's chest. His gun sprang into his hand and he shot it from the air as calmly and efficiently as he would have dispatched an attacking stingwing. Another arrow flashed toward them and Rhes stepped aside so that it missed him. They all waited, alert, to see what would happen next.

An attack, Jason thought, or is it just a diversion? It can't be possible—so soon after our arrival—that any kind of concerted attack could be launched. Yet, why not?

His gun jumped into his hand and he started to wheel about—just as hard pain slammed into his head. He had no awareness of falling, just a sudden and complete blackness.

4

Jason did not enjoy being unconscious. A red, cloying pain engulfed him and, barely rational, he had the feeling that, if he could only wake up all the way, he could take care of everything. For some reason he could not understand, his head was rocking back and forth, adding immeasurably to the agony, and he kept wishing it would stop, but it did not.

After what must have been a very long time, he realized that, when he was feeling the pain, he must be conscious, or very close to it, and he should use these periods most advantageously. His arms were secured in some manner—he could feel that even if he could not see them—but they still had some degree of movement. The bulk of the power holster was there, pressed between his arm and his side, but the gun would not leap into his hand. His groping fingers eventually found out why when they contacted the ragged end of the cable that connected the gun with the holster.

His shattered thoughts groped for understanding with the same disconnected numbness as had his fingers. Something had happened to him; someone, not something, had hit him. Taken his gun away. What else? Why couldn't he see anything? Anything other than a diffuse redness when he tried to open his eyes. What else was gone? His equipment belt, surely. His fingers fumbled back and forth at his waist but could not find it.

They touched something. In its separate holder the medikit still remained on the back of his hip. Careful not to hit the *release* button—if it slipped out of his hand, it was gone—he pressed the heel of his hand up against the device until his flesh contacted the actuating probe. The analyzer buzzed distantly and he never felt the stab of the hypodermic needles through the all-pervading agony in his head. Then the drug took effect and the pain began to seep away.

Without the overriding presence of the pain, he could concentrate that small remaining part of his consciousness on the problem of his eyes. They could not be opened: something was sealing them shut. Something that might or might not be blood. Something that prob-

ably was blood considering the condition of his head, and he smiled
at his success in completing this complicated line of thought.

Concentrate on one eye. Concentrate on right eye. Squeeze tight
shut until it hurt, pull with lids to open. Squeeze shut again. It
worked, the pulling, squeezing, tears-dissolving, and he felt the lids
start to part stickily.

The white-burning sun shone directly into his eye and he had to
blink and look away. He was moving backward across the plains, a
jarring and uneven ride, and there was something like a grid not too
far from his face. The sun touched the horizon. That was important,
he kept telling himself, to remember that the sun touched the
horizon directly behind him, or perhaps a little bit to the right.

Right. Setting. A little to the right. The medikit's drugs and the
traumatic shock were pushing him under again. But not yet. Setting. Behind. To the right.

When the last white glimmer dropped behind the horizon, he
closed the tortured eye and this time welcomed unconsciousness.

"_____!" a voice roared, an incomprehens-
ible gout of sound. The sharp pain in his side made a far stronger
impression and Jason rolled away from it, trying to scramble to his
feet at the same time. Something hard and unyielding bruised his
back and he dropped onto all fours. It was time to open his eyes, he
decided, and he brushed at his sealed eyelids and managed to unglue
them. One look convinced him that he had been far happier with
them shut, but it was too late for that now.

The voice belonged to a big, burly man who clutched a two-
meter-long lance, with which he had been prodding Jason's ribs.
When he saw that Jason was sitting up with his eyes open, he pulled
back the lance and leaned on it, examining his captive. Jason
understood their relative positions when he realized that he was in a
bell-shaped cage of iron bars, the top of which just cleared his head
when he was sitting down. He leaned against the bars and studied
his captor.

He was a warrior, that was clear, arrogant and self-assured, from
the fanged animal skull that decorated the top of his padded helm to
the needle-sharp prickspurs on the heels of his knee-high boots. A
molded breastplate, apparently made of the same kind of material as
his helm, covered the upper half of his body and was painted in
garish designs around the central figure of an unidentifiable animal.
In addition to the lance, the man had an efficient-looking short
sword slung, without scabbard, through a thong on his belt. His skin
was tanned and wind-burned, glistening with some oily substance

and, standing upwind of Jason, he exuded a rich and unwashed animal odor.

"_____!" the warrior shouted, shaking the lance in Jason's direction.

"That's a pretty poor excuse for a language!" Jason shouted back.

"_____!" the man answered, in a shriller voice this time, accompanied with sharp clicking sounds.

"And that one is not much better."

The man cleared his throat and spat in Jason's general direction. *"Bowab* you," he said, "you can speak the in-between tongue?"

"Now that's more like it. A broken-down and corrupt form of standard English. Probably used as some sort of second language. I suppose that we'll never know who originally settled this planet, but one thing is certain—they spoke English. During the Breakdown, when communication was cut off between all the planets, this fine world slipped down into dog-eat-dog barbarism and must have generated a lot of local dialects. But at least they kept the memory of English, debased though it is, as a common language among the tribes. It's just a matter of speaking it badly enough to be understood."

"What you say?" the warrior growled, shaking his head over Jason's incomprehensible burble of words.

Jason tapped his chest and said, "Sure, me speak in-between tongue just as good as you speak in-between tongue."

This apparently satisfied the warrior because he turned and pushed his way through the throng. For the first time, Jason had a chance to examine the passing men who had just been a blur in the background before. All males, and all warriors, dressed in numerous variations on a single theme. High boots, swords, half armor and helms, spears and short bows decorated in weird and colorful patterns. Beyond them and on all sides were rounded structures colored the same yellowish gray as the sparse grass that covered the plains. Something moved through the crowd, and the men gave way to a swaying beast and rider. Jason recognized the creature from the description given by the survivors of the massacre, of the mounts that had been ridden during the attack.

It was horselike in many ways, yet twice as big as any horse, and covered with shaggy fur. The creature's head had an equine appearance, but it was disproportionately tiny and set at the end of a moderately long neck. It had long limbs, especially the forelegs, which were decidedly longer than the hind legs, so that its back sloped downward from the withers to the rump, terminating in a tiny, flicking tail. The strong, thick toes on each foot had sharp claws that dug into the ground as the beast paced by, guided by the rider who sat just behind the forelimbs at the highest point on the humped back.

A harsh blast on a metallic horn drew Jason's attention and he turned to see a compact group of men striding toward his cage. Three soldiers with lowered lances led the way, followed by another with a dangling standard of some kind on a pole. Warriors with drawn swords walked alertly, surrounding the two central figures. One of them was the lance-jabber who had prodded Jason to life. The other, a head taller than his companions, had a golden helm and breastplate inset with jewels, while curling horns sprouted from both sides of his helm.

He had more than that, Jason saw when he approached the cage. The look of the hawk, or a great jungle cat secure in his rule. This man was the leader and he knew it, accepted it automatically. He, a warrior, leader of warriors. His right hand rested on the pommel of his bejeweled but efficient-looking sword while he stroked the sweep of his great red mustachios with the scarred knuckles of his left hand. He stopped close to the bars and stared imperiously at Jason, who tried, but failed, to return the other's gaze with the same intensity. His cramped position inside the cage and his battered, scruffy appearance did not help his morale.

"Grovel before Temuchin," one of the soldiers ordered, and buried the butt end of his lance in the pit of Jason's stomach.

It might have been easier to grovel, but Jason, bent double with the pain, kept his head up and his eyes fixed on the other.

"Where are you from?" Temuchin asked, his voice so used to command that Jason found himself answering at once.

"From far away, a place you do not know."

"Another world?"

"Yes. Do you know about other worlds?"

"Only from the songs of the jongleurs. Until the first ship came down, I did not think they were true. They are."

He snapped his fingers and one of the men handed him a blackened and twisted recoilless rifle. "Can you make this spout fire again?" he asked.

"No." It must have been one of the weapons of the first expedition.

"What about this?" Temuchin held up Jason's own gun, its cable dangling where it had been torn from his power holster.

"I don't know." Jason was just as calm as the other. Let him just get his hands on the gun. "I will have to look at it closely."

"Burn this one, too," Temuchin said, throwing the gun aside. "Their weapons must be destroyed by fire. Now tell me at once, other-world man, why do you come here?"

He'd make a good poker player, Jason thought. I can't read his cards and he knows all of mine. Then what should I tell him? Why not the truth?

"My people want to take metal from the ground," he said aloud. "We harm no one, we will even pay—"

"No." There was a flat finality to the sound. Temuchin turned away.

"Wait, you haven't heard everything."

"It is enough," he said, halting for a moment and speaking over his shoulder. "You will dig and there will be buildings. Buildings make a city and there will be fences. The plains are always open." And then he added in the same flat voice.

'Kill him.''

As the band of men turned to follow Temuchin, the standard-bearer passed in front of the cage. His pole was topped with a human skull and Jason saw that the banner itself was made up of string after string of human thumbs, mummified and dry, knotted together on thongs.

"Wait!" Jason shouted at their retreating backs. "Let me explain. You can't just do this—"

But, of course, he could. A squad of soldiers surrounded the cage and one of them bent underneath it and there was the rattling of chains. Jason cowered back as the entire cage swung up on creaking hinges, and he clutched at the bars as the soldiers reached for him.

He sprang over them, kicking one in the face as he went by and crashed into the soldiers beyond. The results were a foregone conclusion, but he made the most of the occasion. One soldier lay sprawled on the ground and another sat up holding his head when the rest carried Jason away. He cursed them, in six different languages, even though his words had as much effect on the stolid, expressionless men as had his blows.

"How far did you travel to reach this planet?" someone asked.

"*Ekmortu!*" Jason mumbled, spitting out blood and the chipped corner of a tooth.

"What is your home world like? Much as this one? Hotter or colder?"

Jason, being carried face down, twisted his head around to look at his questioner, a gray-haired man in ragged leather garments that had once been dyed yellow and green. A tall, sleepy-eyed youth stumbled after him dressed in the same motley, though his were not so completely obscured by grime.

"You know so many things," the old man pleaded, "so you must tell me something."

The soldiers pushed the two men away before Jason could oblige by telling him some of the really pithy things that came to mind. With so many men holding him, he was completely helpless when they backed him against a thick iron pole set firmly in the ground and tore at his clothing. The metalcloth and fasteners resisted their fingers until one of them produced a dagger and sawed through the material, ignoring the fact that he was slicing Jason's skin at the same time. When his clothing had been pulled open to his waist, Jason was bleeding from a dozen cuts and was groggy from the mauling he had taken. He was pushed to the ground and a leather rope lashed around his wrists. Then the soldiers went away.

Although it was early afternoon, the temperature must have been just above the freezing point. With his insulated clothing stripped away, the shock of the cold air on his body brought him instantly to full, shivering consciousness.

What the next step would be was obvious. The strap that secured his wrists was a good three meters long and the other end was fastened to the top of the pole. He was alone in the center of a cleared area, and there was a bustle on all sides as the hump-backed riding beasts were saddled and mounted. The first man ready uttered a piercing, warbling cry and charged at Jason with his lance leveled. The beast ran with frightful speed, claws digging into the soil, hurtling forward like an unleashed thunderbolt.

Jason did the only thing possible, jumping to the other side of the pole and keeping it between himself and the attacking rider. The man jabbed with his lance but had to pull it back swiftly as he went by the pole.

Only fighting intuition saved Jason then, for the sound of the second beast's charge was lost in the thunder of the first. He grabbed the pole and spun around it. The lance clanged against the metal as the second attacker went by.

The first man was already turning his mount and Jason saw that a third had saddled up and was ready to attack. There could be only one possible outcome to this game of deadly target practice: he could dodge just so often.

"Time to change the odds," he said, bending and groping in the top of his right boot. His combat knife was still there.

As the third man started his charge, Jason flipped the knife into the air and caught the hilt between his teeth, then sawed his leather bindings against its razor edge. They fell away and he crouched behind the slim pole to avoid the stabbing lance. The charge went by and Jason attacked.

He sprang, the knife in his left hand, reaching out with his right to grab the rider's leg in an attempt to unseat him. But the creature was moving too fast and he slammed into its flank behind the saddle, his fingers clutching at the beast's matted fur.

After that everything happened very fast. As the rider twisted about, trying to stab down and back at his attacker, Jason sank his dagger right up to its hilt in the animal's rump.

The needlelike spikes of the prickspurs that the warriors used in place of rowels on their spurs indicated that the creatures they rode must not have very sensitive nervous systems. This was true of the thick hide and pelt over the ribs, but the spot that Jason's dagger hit, not too far below the animal's tail, appeared to be of a different nature altogether. A rippling shudder passed through the creature's flesh and it exploded forward as though a giant spring had been released in its guts.

Already off balance, the rider was tipped from his saddle and disappeared. Jason, clutching at the fur and worrying the knife deeper with his other hand, managed to hold on through one bound, then a second. There was the blurred vision of men and animals streaming by while Jason fought to keep his grip. This proved impossible and, on the third ground-shaking leap, he was tossed free.

Sailing headlong through the air, Jason saw he was aiming toward the space between two of the dome-shaped structures. This was certainly better than hitting one of them, so he relaxed and tucked his chin under as he struck the ground and did a shoulder roll, then another. Landing on his feet, he ran, his speed scarcely diminished.

The domed structures, dwellings of some kind, were scattered about with lanes between them. He was in a wide, straight lane and thoughts of spearheads between the shoulder blades sent him darting off at right angles at the next opening. Outraged cries from behind him indicated that his pursuers did not think highly of his escape. So far, he was ahead of the pack and he wondered how long he could keep it that way.

A leather flap was thrown back on one of the domes ahead and a gray-haired man looked out—the same one who had been trying to question Jason earlier. He appeared to take in the situation in a glance and, opening the flap wider, he motioned Jason toward it.

It was a time for quick decisions. Still running headlong, Jason glanced around and saw that, for the moment, no one else was in

sight. Any port in a storm. He dived through the opening dragging
the old man after him. For the first time he was aware that the
combat knife was still in his hand, so he pressed it up through the
other's beard until the point touched his throat.

"Give me away and you're dead," he hissed.

"Why should I betray you?" the man cackled. "I brought you
here. I risk all for knowledge. Now back, while I close the opening." Ignoring the knife, he began to lace the flap shut.

Looking quickly about the dark interior, Jason saw that the
sleepy-eyed youth was dozing by a small fire, over which hung an
iron pot. A withered crone was stirring something in the pot,
completely ignoring the commotion at the entrance.

"In back, down," the man said, pushing at Jason. "They'll be
here soon. They mustn't find you, oh no."

The shouting was coming closer outside and Jason could see no
reason to find fault with the plan. "But the knife is still ready," he
warned, as he sat against the back wall and allowed a collection of
musty skins to be draped over his shoulders.

Heavy feet thundered by, shaking the earth, and voices could be
heard from all sides now. Graybeard hung a leather shawl over
Jason's head so that it obscured his face, then scrabbled in a pouch at
his belt for a reeking clay pipe that he poked into Jason's mouth.
Neither the old woman nor the youth paid any attention to all of this.

They still did not look up when a helmeted warrior tore open the
entrance and poked his head inside.

Jason sat, motionless, looking out from under the leather hood,
the hidden knife in his hand, ready to dive across the floor and sink it
into the intruder's throat.

Looking quickly about the dark interior, the intruder shouted
what could only have been a question. Graybeard answered with a
negative grunt—and that was all there was to it. The man vanished
as quickly as he had come and the old woman tottered over to lace
the entrance tightly shut again.

In his years of wandering around the galaxy, Jason had encountered very little unselfish charity and was justifiably suspicious. The
knife was still ready. "Why did you take the risk of helping me?"
he asked.

"A jongleur will risk anything to learn new things," the man
answered, settling himself cross-legged by the fire. "I am above the
petty squabbles of the tribes. My name is Oraiel, and you will begin
by telling me your name."

"Riverboat Sam," Jason said, putting the knife down long
enough to pull up the top of his metalcloth suit and push his arms

into it. He lied by reflex, like playing his cards close to his chest. There were no threatening moves. The old woman mumbled over the fire while the youth squatted behind Oraiel, sinking into the same position.

"What world are you from?"

"Heaven."

"Are there many worlds where men live?"

"At least 30,000, though no one can be completely sure of the exact number."

"What is your world like?"

Jason looked around, and, for the first time since he had opened his eyes in the cage, he had a moment to stop and think. Luck had been with him so far, but he was still a long way from getting out of this mess alive.

"What is your world like?" Oraiel repeated.

"What's your world like, old man? I'll trade you fact for fact."

Oraiel was silent for a moment and a spark of malice glinted in his half-closed eyes. Then he nodded. "It is agreed. I will answer your questions if you will answer mine."

"Fine. You'll answer mine first as I have more to lose if we're interrupted. But before we do this twenty-questions business, I have to take an inventory. Things have been too busy for this up until now."

Though his gun was gone, the power holster was still strapped into place. It was worthless now, but the batteries might come in useful. His equipment belt was gone and his pockets had been rifled. Only the fact that the medikit was slung to the rear had saved it from detection. He must have been lying on it when they searched him. His extra ammunition was gone as well as the case of grenades.

The radio was still there! In the darkness they must not have noticed it in the flat pocket almost under his arm. It only had line-of-sight operation, but that might be enough to get a fix on the ship or even call for help.

He pulled it out and looked gloomily at the crushed case and the fractured components that were leaking from a crack in the side. Some time during the busy events of the last day, it had been struck by something heavy. He switched it on and got exactly the result he expected. Nothing.

The fact that the chronometer concealed behind his belt buckle was still keeping perfect time did little to cheer him. It was 10 in the morning. Wonderful. The watch had been adjusted for the 20-hour day when they had landed on Felicity, with noon set for the sun at the zenith at the spot where they had landed.

"That's enough of that," he said, making himself as comfortable as was possible on the hard ground and pulling the furs around him. "Let's talk, Oraiel. Who is the boss here, the one who ordered my execution?"

"He is Temuchin the Warrior, The Fearless One, He of the Arm of Steel, The Destroyer—"

"Fine. He's on top. I can tell that without the footnotes. What has he got against strangers—and buildings?"

" 'The Song of the Freemen,' " Oraiel said, digging his elbow into the ribs of his assistant. The youth grunted and rooted about in the tangled furs until he produced a lutelike instrument with a long neck and two strings. Plucking the strings for accompaniment he began to sing in a high-pitched voice.

> Free as the wind,
> Free as the plain on which we wander,
> Knowing no home,
> Other than our tents. Our friends
> The Moropes,
> Who take us to battle,
> Destroying the buildings,
> Of those who would trap us . . .

There was more like this and it went on for an unconscionably long time, until Jason found himself beginning to nod. He interrupted, broke off the song, and asked some pertinent questions.

A picture of the realities of life on the plains of Felicity began to emerge.

From the oceans on the east and west, and from the Great Cliff in the south, to the mountains in the north there stood not one permanent building or settlement of man. Free and wild, the tribes roved over the grass sea, warring on themselves and each other in endless feuds and conflicts.

There had been cities here, some of them were even mentioned by name in the Songs, but now, only their memory remained, and an uncompromising hatred. There must have been a long and bitter war between two different ways of life, if the memory, generations later, could still arouse such strong emotions. With the limited natural resources of these arid plains, the agrarians and the nomads could not possibly have lived side by side in peace. The farmers would have built settlements around the scant water sources and fenced out the nomads and their flocks. In self-defense, the nomads would have had to band together in an attempt to destroy the settlements. They had succeeded so well in this genocidal warfare that the only trace of their former enemies that remained was a hated memory.

Crude, unlettered, violent, the barbarian conquerors roamed the high steppe in tribes and clans, constantly on the move as their stunted cattle and goats consumed the scant grass that covered the plains. Writing was unknown; the jongleurs—the only men who could pass freely from tribe to tribe—were the historians, entertainers and bearers of news. No trees grew in this hostile climate so wooden utensils and artifacts were unknown. Iron ore and coal were apparently plentiful in the northern mountains, so iron and mild steel were the most common materials used. These, along with animal hides, horns and bones, were almost the only raw materials available. An outstanding exception were the helms and breastplates. While some were made of iron, the best ones came from a tribe in the distant hills who worked a mine of asbestos-like rock. They shredded this to fibers and mixed it with the gum of a broad-leaved plant to produce what amounted to an epoxy-fiberglass material. It was light as aluminum, strong as steel, and even more elastic than the best spring steel. This technique, undoubtedly inherited from the first, pre-Breakdown settlers on the planet, was the only thing that physically distinguished the nomads from any other race of iron-age barbarians. Animal droppings were used for cooking fuel; animal fat, for lamps. Life tended to be nasty, brutish and short.

Every clan or tribe had its traditional pasture ground over which it roamed, though the delimitations were vague and controversial, so that wars and feuds were a constant menace. The domed tents, *camachs*, were made of joined hides over iron poles. They were erected and struck in a few minutes, and when the tribe moved on, they were carried, with the household goods, on wheeled frames called *escungs*, like a travois with wheels, which were pulled by the *moropes*.

Unlike the cattle and goats, which were descendants of terrestrial animals, the *moropes* were natives of the high steppes of Felicity. These claw-toed herbivores had been domesticated and bred for centuries, while most of their wild herds had been exterminated. Their thick pelts protected them from the eternal cold, and they could go as long as 20 days without water. As beasts of burden—and chargers of war—they made existence possible in this barren land.

There was little more to tell. The tribes roved and fought, each speaking its own language or dialect and using the neutral in-between tongue when they had to talk to outsiders. They formed alliances and treacherously broke them. Their occupation and love was war and they practiced it most efficiently.

Jason digested this information while he attempted, less success-fully, to digest the unchewable lumps from the stew that he had forced himself to swallow. For drink there had been fermented *morope* milk, which tasted almost as bad as it smelled. The only course he had missed was the one reserved for warriors, a mixture of milk and still-warm blood, and for this he was grateful.

Once Jason's curiosity had been satisfied, Oraiel's turn had come and he had asked questions endlessly. Even while Jason ate, he had had to mumble answers, which the jongleur and his apprentice filed away in their capacious memories. They had not been disturbed, so he considered himself safe—for the time being. It was already late in the afternoon and he had to think of a way to escape and return to the ship. He waited until Oraiel ran out of breath then asked some pointed questions of his own.

"How many men are there in this camp?"

The jongleur had been sipping steadily at the *achadh*, the fer-mented milk, and was beginning to rock back and forth. He mum-bled and spread his arms wide. "They are the sons of the vulture," he intoned. "Their numbers blacken the plain and the fearful sight of them strikes terror—"

"I didn't ask for a tribal history, just a nice round figure."

"Only the gods know. There may be a hundred, there may be a million."

"How much is 20 and 20?" Jason interrupted.

"I do not bother my thoughts with such stupid figurations."

"I didn't think you could do higher mathematics—like counting to one hundred and other exotic computations."

Jason went over and peered out of the opening between the laces. A blast of frigid air made his eyes water. High, icy clouds drifted across the pale blueness of the sky, while the shadows were growing long.

"Drink," Oraiel said, waving the leathern bottle of *achadh*. "You are my guest and you must drink."

The silence was broken only by the rasp of sand as the old woman scrubbed out the cooking pot. The apprentice's chin was on his chest and he appeared to be asleep.

"I never refuse a drink," Jason said, and walked over and took the bottle.

As he raised it to his lips, he saw the old woman glance up

quickly, then bend low again over her work. There was a slight stirring behind him.

Jason hurled himself sideways, the drinking skin went flying and the club skinned his ear and crashed into his shoulder.

Still rolling, without looking, Jason kicked backward and his foot caught the apprentice in the pit of the stomach. He folded nicely and the spiked iron bar rolled free of his limp hands.

Oraiel, no longer drunk, pulled a long, two-handed sword from under the furs beside him and swung on Jason. Though the spikes had missed, the bar itself had numbed Jason's right shoulder and his arm, which hung limply at his side. There was nothing wrong with his left arm, however, so he flung himself inside the arc of the sword before it could descend and locked his hand around the jongleur's throat, thumb and index finger on the major blood vessels. The man kicked spasmodically, then slumped unconscious.

Always aware of his flanks, Jason had been trying to keep one eye on the old woman, who now produced a gleaming, saw-edged knife—the *camach* was an armory of concealed weapons—and hopped to the attack. Jason dropped the jongleur and chopped her wrist so the knife fell at his feet.

The entire action had taken about ten seconds. Oraiel and his apprentice were draped over each other in an unconscious huddle, while the crone sobbed by the fire, cradling her wrist.

"Thanks for the hospitality," Jason said, trying to rub some life back into his numbed arms. When he could move his fingers again, he tied and gagged the woman, then the others, arranging them in a neat row on the floor. Oraiel's eyes were open, radiating bloodshot waves of hatred.

"As ye sow, so shall ye reap," Jason said, picking over the furs. "That's another one you can memorize. I suppose you can't be blamed for trying to get your information, and the reward money as well. But you were being a little too greedy. I know that you're sorry now and want me to have enough of these moth-eaten furs to disguise myself with, as well as that greasy fur hat which has seen better days, and perhaps a weapon or two."

Oraiel growled and frothed a little around his gag.

"Such language," Jason said. He pulled the hat low over his eyes and picked up the spiked club, which he had wrapped in a length of leather. "Neither you nor the old girl have enough teeth for the job, but your assistant has a fine set of choppers. He can chew through the leather gag, then chew the thongs on your wrists. By which time I shall be far from here. Be thankful I'm not one of your own kind, or you would be dead right now." He picked up the skin of *achadh* and slung it from his shoulder. "I'll take this for the road."

There was no one in sight when he poked his head out of the *camach,* so he stopped long enough to lace the flap tightly behind him. He squinted up at the sky once, then turned away among the domed rows.

Head down, he shuffled away through the barbarian camp.

5

No one paid him the slightest attention.

Bundled as they were against the perpetual cold, most of the people looked as ragged and nondescript as he did, male and female, young and old. Only the warriors had any distinction of dress, and they could be easily avoided by scuttling off between the *camachs* whenever he saw one approaching. The rest of the citizenry avoided them as well, so no notice was taken of his actions.

There appeared to be no organized planning of the encampment that he could see. The *camachs* staggered in uneven rows, thrown up apparently wherever the owners had stopped. They thinned out after a while and Jason found himself skirting a herd of small, shaggy and evil-looking cows. Armed guards, holding tethered *moropes,* were scattered about, so he made his way by as quickly as was prudent. He heard—and smelled—a flock of goats nearby, and avoided them as well. Then, suddenly, he was at the last *camach,* and the featureless plain was ahead, stretching out to the horizon. The sun was almost down and he squinted at it happily.

"Setting right behind me, or just a little to the right. I remember that much about the ride here. Now if I reverse the direction and march into the sunset I should come to the ship."

Sure, he thought, if I can make as good time as the thugs did who brought me here. And if I am going in the right direction, and they made no turns. And if none of these bloodthirsty types find me. If—

Enough ifs. He shook his head and braced his shoulders, then took a swig of the foul *achadh.* As he raised the skin to his mouth, he looked about him and saw that he was unobserved. Wiping his mouth on his sleeve, he strolled out into the empty steppe.

He did not go far. As soon as he found a gully that would shelter him from view of the encarpment, he dropped down into it. It gave him some protection from the wind, and he pulled his knees up to his chest to conserve heat, then waited there until it was completely dark. It wasn't the most morale-building way to spend the time, chilled and getting colder as the wind rustled the grass above his head, but there was no other way. He put a rock on the far wall of the gully, ready to mark the exact spot where the sun set, then huddled back against the opposite wall. He brooded about the radio, and even opened it to see if anything could be done, but it was unarguably beyond repair. After that, he just sat and waited for the sun to reach the western horizon and for the stars to come out.

Jason wished that he had done some more stellar observation before the ship had landed, but it was a little late for that now. The constellations would be unfamiliar and he had no idea if there was a pole star or even a close circumpolar constellation that he could set his course by. One thing he did remember from constant examination of the maps and charts as they prepared for the landing, was that they had set down almost exactly on the seventieth parallel, at 70 degrees of north latitude right on the head.

Now what did this mean? If there were a north polar star, it would be exactly 70 degrees above the northern horizon. Given a few nights and a protractor, it would be easy enough to find. But his present situation did not allow much time for casual observation. Or the temperature either; he stamped his feet to see if they still had any sensation remaining in them.

The north polar axis would be 70 degrees above the northern horizon, which meant that the sun at noon would be exactly 20 degrees above the southern horizon. It had to be this way every day of the year, because the axis of rotation of the planet was directly vertical to the plane of the ecliptic. No nonsense here about long days and short days—or even seasons for that matter. At any single spot on the planet's surface the sun always rose from the same place on the horizon. Day after day, year after year, it cut an identical arc across the sky, then set at the same spot on the western horizon as it had the night before. Day and night, all over the planet, were always of equal length. The angle of incidence of the sun's rays would always remain the same as well, which meant that the amount of radiation reaching any given area would remain constant the year round.

With days and nights of equal length, and the energy input always equal, the weather always remained the same and you were stuck with what you had. The tropics were always hot; the poles, locked in a frigid and eternal embrace.

The sun was now a dim yellow disk balanced on the sharp line of the horizon. At this high latitude, instead of dropping straight down out of sight, it slithered slantways along the horizon. When half the disk was obscured, Jason marked the spot on the far rim, then went over and stood the pointed stone up at that spot. Then he returned to the spot where he had been sitting and squinted along his bearing marker.

"Very fine," he said out loud. "Now I know where the sun sets—but how do I follow that direction after dark? Think, Jason, think, because right now your life depends upon it." He shivered, surely because of the cold.

"It would help if I knew just where on the horizon the sun set, how many degrees west of north. With no axial tilt, the problem should be a simple one." He scratched arcs and angles in the sand and mumbled to himself. "If the axis is vertical, every day must be an equinox, which means that day and night are equal every day, which means—ho-ho!" He tried to snap his fingers, but they were too cold to respond.

"That's the answer! If the length of the night is to equal the length of the day, then there is only one place for the sun to set and rise, at every latitude from the equator north and south. The sun will have to cut a 180-degree arc through the sky, so it must rise due east and set due west. Eureka!"

Jason put his right arm straight out from his shoulder and shuffled around until his finger was pointing exactly at his marker.

"This is simplicity itself. I am pointing west and facing due south. Now I craftily pull up my left arm and I am pointing due east. All that remains now is to stand in this uncomfortable position until the stars come out."

In the high, thin air, the first stars were already appearing in the east, though twilight still lingered on the opposite horizon. Jason thought for a moment and decided that he could improve upon the accuracy of the finger-pointing technique. He put a stone on the eastern rim of the gully, just above the spot where he had been sitting. Then he climbed the opposite wall and sighted at it over the first marker stone. A bright blue star lay close to the horizon in the correct spot, and a clear Z-shaped constellation was beginning to be visible around it.

"My guiding star, I shall follow you from afar," Jason said, and snapped open his belt buckle to look down at the illuminated face of his watch. "Got you. With a 20-hour day, I can say ten hours of darkness and ten of light. So right now I walk directly away from my star. In five hours it will hit its zenith in the south, right on a line with my left shoulder as I walk. Then it swoops around and dives down to set directly in front of me about dawn. This is simplicity itself as long as I make adjustments for the new position every hour, or half hour, to allow for the changed position with the passage of time. Hah!''

Snorting this last, he made sure that the Z was directly behind his back, shouldered his club and tramped off in the correct direction. Everything seemed secure enough, but he wished, neither for the first nor the last time, that he had a gyrocompass.

The temperature dropped quickly as the night advanced, and in the clear, dry air the stars burned in distant, twinkling points. Overhead, the constellations wheeled silently high, while the little Z hurried in its low arc until it stood at its zenith at midnight. Jason checked his watch, then dropped onto a crackling hummock of grass. He had been walking for over five hours with only a single break. In spite of his training at 2G on Pyrrus, the going was hard. He swigged from the drinking skin and wondered what the temperature was. In spite of its mildly alcoholic content, the *achadh* was a half-frozen slush.

Felicity had no moons, but there was more than enough light to see by from the stars. The frigid grayness of the plain stretched away on all sides, silent and motionless except for the dark, moving mass coming up behind him.

Slowly, Jason sank to the ground and lay there, frozen, while the *moropes* and their riders came near, the ground shivering with the rumble of their feet. They passed, no more than 200 meters from where he lay, and he pressed flat and watched the dark, silent silhouettes until they vanished out of sight to the south.

"Looking for me?" he asked himself, standing and brushing at the furs. "Or are they heading for the ship?"

This latter seemed the most obvious answer. The compactness of the group and their hurried pace indicated some specific destination. And why not? He had been brought from the ship along this route, so it was perfectly understandable that others should follow it as well. He considered going over to attempt to follow their trail, but did not think too highly of the idea. There could be a good bit of traffic back and forth from the ship, and he did not feel like being caught on the barbarian highway by daylight.

When he stood up the wind had a chance to get at him, and a fit of shivering shook him with a giant hand. He was as rested as he was ever going to be, so he might as well press on before he froze to death. Slinging the drinking skin over his shoulder and picking up the club, he began walking again in the correct direction, paralleling the raiders' track.

Twice more during that seemingly endless night, groups of raiders hurried by in the same direction, while Jason concealed himself against chance observation. Each time it was harder to get up and go on, but the cold ground was a good persuader. By the time the sky began to lighten in the east, the 1.5 gravity had exacted its toll. It took Jason an effort of will to put one foot in front of the other. His guiding constellation was on the horizon, fading in the spreading grayness of dawn, and he went on until it was gone.

It was time to stop. Only by promising himself that he would not walk after sunrise had he managed to keep going at all. He could guide himself easily enough by the sun during the day, but it would be too dangerous. A moving figure could easily be seen at great distances on these plains. And, as the ship was not yet in sight, there was a good deal more walking to be done. He would have to get some rest if he were to go on, and this was possible only during the day.

He half fell, half crawled into the next gully. There was a small overhanging ledge, on the northern side where the sun would strike all day, just the burrow for him. The ledge would keep the wind off him and shield him from sight from above. Pulling his legs up to his chest, he tried to ignore the cold of the ground that struck through his furs and insulated clothing. While he was wondering if, chilled, uncomfortable, exhausted, stifling, he could possibly fall asleep, he fell asleep.

Some sound, some presence bothered him, and he opened one eye and peered out from under the edge of the hat. Two gray-furred animals, with skinny tails and long teeth, were surveying him with wide eyes from the other side of the gully. He said ''Boo'' and they vanished. The sun felt almost warm now and the ground had either warmed up or his side was too numb to feel anything. He went to sleep again.

The next time he awoke the sun had dropped behind the gully wall and he was in shadow. He knew just what a slab of meat in a frozen-food locker felt like. Moving took almost more effort than he cared to make, and he was afraid that, if he struck his hands or feet against anything, they would crack off. There was still some *achadh* left in the skin and he swilled it down, which brought on an extended coughing fit. When it was over he felt weaker, though a little bit more alive.

Once again he took his direction from the setting sun and, when the stars came out, started on his way. Walking was much worse than it had been the preceding night. Exertion, his wounds, the lack of food and the heightened gravity exacted their toll. Within an hour he was tottering like an octogenarian and knew that he could not go on like this. He dropped to the ground, panting with exhaustion, and pressed the release that dropped the medikit into his hand.

"I've been saving you for the last round. And, if I am not mistaken, I have just heard the final bell ringing."

Cackling feebly at this insipid witticism, he adjusted the control dial for *stimulants, normal strength*. He pressed the actuator to the inside of his wrist and felt the sharp bite of the needles striking home.

It worked. Within sixty seconds he became aware that his fatigue was beginning to slip away, masked behind a curtain of drugs. When he stood, he experienced a certain numbness in his limbs, but no tiredness at all.

"Onward!" he shouted, marking his guiding constellation as he slipped the medikit back into its holder.

The night was neither long nor short; it just passed in a pleasant haze. Under the stress of the drugs, his mind worked well and he tried not to think of the physical toll they were exacting. A number of war parties passed, all coming from the direction of the ship, and he hid each time even though most of them were far distant. He wondered if some battle had been fought and if they might have been beaten. Each time, he changed his course slightly to come closer to their line of march, so that there would be no chance of his getting lost.

Soon after three in the morning, Jason found himself stumbling and, at one point, actually trying to walk along on his knees. A full turn of the medikit control set it for *stimulants, emergency strength*. The injections worked and he went on again at the same regular pace.

It was almost dawn when he began to smell the first traces of some burned odor—which grew stronger with each pace forward. When the sky began to gray in the east, the smell was sharp in his nostrils, and he wondered what significance it might have. Unlike the previous morning, he did not stop but pressed on. This was the last day that he had and he must reach the ship before the stimulants wore off. It could not be too far ahead. He would just have to stay alert and chance walking during the day. He was much smaller than the *moropes* and their riders and, given any luck at all, he should be able to spot them first.

When he walked into the blackened area of grass, he would not believe it. A fire perhaps, accidentally ignited. It had burned in an exactly circular pattern.

Only when he recognized the rusted and destroyed forms of the mining machinery did he dare admit the truth.

"I'm here. Back at the same spot. This is where we landed."

He staggered crazily in a circle, looking at the massive emptiness stretching away on all sides.

"This is it!" he shouted. "This is where the ship was. We put the *Pugnacious* down right here next to the original landing site. Only the ship isn't here. They've left—gone without me. . . ."

Despair froze him and his arms dropped to his sides as he stood there, tottering, his strength gone. The ship, his friends, they were gone as well.

From close by came the rumble of heavy, running feet.

Over the hill rushed five *moropes,* their riders shouting with predatory glee as they lowered their lances for the kill.

6

With conditioned reflex Jason swung up his arm, his hand crooked and ready for the gun—before he remembered that he had been disarmed.

"Then we'll do this the old-fashioned way!" he shouted, swinging the iron club in a whistling circle. The odds were well against him, but before he went down they would know that they had been in a fight.

They came in a tight knot, each man trying to be first to the kill, jostling one another and leaning far forward with outstretched lances. Jason stood ready, legs wide, waiting for the last possible instant before he moved. The shrieking riders were at the edge of the burnt area.

A muffled explosion was followed instantly by a great, rolling cloud of vapor that hid the attackers from sight. Jason lowered his club and stepped back as a tendril of the cloud twisted toward him. Only one *morope* made it through the gray vapor, carried along by its momentum, skidding and collapsing with a ground-shaking thud. Its rider catapulted toward Jason and even managed to crawl a short distance further, his jaw working with silent hatred, before he, too, collapsed.

When a wisp of the thinned-out gas reached Jason he sniffed, then moved quickly away. Narcogas. It worked instantly and thoroughly on any oxygen-breathing animal, producing paralysis and unconsciousness for about five hours, after which the victim recovered completely, with nothing worse than the nasty side effect of a skull-splitting headache.

What had happened? The ship had certainly gone, and there was no one else in sight. Fatigue was winning out over the effects of the stimulants and his thinking was getting muzzy. He heard the growling rumble for some seconds before he recognized the source of the sound. It was the rocket launch from the *Pugnacious*. Blinking up into the clear brightness of the morning sky, he saw the high contrail stretching a white line across the sky toward him, growing larger with each passing second. The launch was first a black dot, then a growing shape, finally a flame-spouting cylinder that touched down less than a hundred meters away. The lock spun open and Meta dropped to the ground, even before the shock absorbers had damped the landing impact.

"Are you all right?" she called, running swiftly to him, the questing muzzle of her gun looking for enemies on all sides.

"Never felt better," he said, leaning on the club so he would not fall down. "What kept you? I thought you had all pulled out and forgotten about me."

"You know we wouldn't do that." She ran her hands over his arms, his back while she talked, as though looking for broken bones—or simply reassuring herself of his presence. "We could not stop them from taking you away, although we tried. Some of them died. An attack was launched on the ship at the same time."

Jason could well understand the shock of battle and dogged resistance behind her matter-of-fact words. It must have been brutal.

"Come to the launch," she said, putting his arm across her shoulders so she could bear part of his weight. He did not protest. "They must have been concealed on all sides and reinforcements kept arriving. They are very good fighters and do not ask for quarter, nor do they expect it. Kerk soon realized that there would be no end to the battle and that we could not help you by staying there. If you did succeed in escaping—which he was sure you would if you were still alive—it would have been impossible for you to reach the ship. Therefore, under cover of counterattacks, we placed a number of spyeyes and microphones, as well as planting a good store of land mines and remote-controlled gas bombs. After that we left, and the ship has set up a base somewhere in the northern mountains. I dropped off at the foothills with the launch and have been waiting ever since. I came as soon as I could. Here, into the cabin."

"You timed it very well, thank you. I can do that myself."

He couldn't, but he wouldn't admit it, and made believe that he had climbed the ladder instead of being boosted in by a powerful push from her feminine right arm.

Jason staggered over and dropped into the copilot's acceleration couch while Meta sealed the lock. Once it was closed, the tension drained from her body as her gun whined back into its power holster. She hurried to his side, kneeling so she could look into his face.

"Take this filthy thing off," she said, hurling the fur cap to the floor. She ran her fingers through his hair and touched her fingertips lightly to the bruises and frostbite marks on his face. "I thought you were dead, Jason, really I did. I never thought I would see you again."

"Did that bother you so much?"

He was exhausted, his strength stretched well beyond the breaking point so that waves of blackness threatened to obscure his vision. He fought them away. He felt that, at this moment, he was closer to Meta than he had ever been before.

"It did, it bothered me. I don't know why." She kissed him suddenly, hard, forgetting the condition of his cracked and battered lips. He did not complain.

"Perhaps you are just used to having me around," he said, far more casually than he felt.

"No, it is not that. I have had men around before."

Oh, thanks, he thought.

"I have had two children. I am twenty-three years old. While piloting our ship, I have been to many planets. I used to think that I knew all there was to know, but now I do not believe so. You have taught me many new things. When that man, Mikah Samon, kidnapped you, I found out something I did not know about myself. I had to find you. These are very un-Pyrran things to feel, for we are taught to always think of the city first, never of other people. Now I am very mixed up. Am I wrong?"

"No," he said, fighting back the threat of overwhelming darkness. "Quite the opposite." He pressed his cracked and dirt-grimed fingers to the resilient warmth of her arm. "I think you are more right than any of the trigger-happy butchers in your tribe."

"You must tell me. Why do I feel this way?"

He tried to smile, but it hurt his face.

"Do you know what marriage is, Meta?"

"I have heard of it. A social custom on some planets. I do not know what it is."

An alarm buzzed angrily on the control board and she turned at once to it.

"You still don't know, and maybe it's better that way. Maybe I'll never tell you." He smiled, his chin touched his chest and he fell instantly asleep.

"There are more of them coming," Meta said, switching off the alarm and glancing into the viewscreen. There was no answer. When she saw what had happened, she quickly tightened the straps to secure him in the couch, then began the takeoff procedure. She neither noticed nor cared if any attackers were under the jets when she blasted skyward.

The pressure of deceleration woke Jason as they dropped down for the landing. "Thirsty," he said, smacking his dry lips together. "And hungry enough to eat one of those *moropes* raw."

"Teca is on the way," she told him, flipping off the switches as the launch grounded.

"If he is the same kind of sawbones his mentor, Brucco, is, he'll put me under for recovery therapy and keep me unconscious for a week. No can do." He turned his head, slowly, to look as the inner port opened. Teca, a brisk and authoritative young man, whose enthusiasm for medicine far exceeded his knowledge, climbed in.

"No can do," Jason repeated. "No recovery therapy. Glucose drip, vitamin injections, artificial kidney, whatever you wish as long as I'm conscious."

"That's what I like about Pyrrans," Jason said, as they carried him from the launch on a stretcher, the glucose-drip bottle swinging next to his head. "They let you go to hell in your own way."

Meta saw to it that it took a good while for the leaders of the expedition to gather. Jason, whose eyes had closed in the middle of a grumbled complaint, spent the time in a deep, restorative sleep. He woke up when the hum of conversation began to fill the ward-room.

"Meeting will come to order," he said in what was intended to be a firm, commanding voice. It came out as a cracked whisper. He turned to Teca. "Before the meeting begins, I would like some syrup for my throat and a shot to wake me up. Can you take care of that?''

"Of course, I can," Teca said, opening his kit. "But I think it unwise due to the strain already imposed on your system." However, he did not let his thoughts interfere with the swift execution of his duties.

"That's better," Jason said as the drugs once more wiped away the barrier of fatigue. He would pay for this—but later. The work must be done now.

"I've found out the answers to some of our questions," he told them. "Not all, but enough for a beginning. I know now that, unless some profound changes are made, we are not going to be able to establish a mining settlement. And when I say 'profound,' I mean it. We are going to have to change the complete mores, taboos and cultural motivations of these people before we can get our mine into operation."

"Impossible," Kerk said.

"Perhaps. But it is better than the only other alternative—which is genocide. As things stand now, we would have to kill every one of those barbarians before we could be assured of establishing a settlement in peace."

A depressed silence followed this statement. The Pyrrans knew what this meant because they were themselves unwilling genocide victims of their home planet.

"We will not consider genocide," Kerk said, and the others unconsciously nodded their heads. "But your other alternative sounds too unreasonable."

"Does it? You might recall that we are all here now because the mores, taboos and cultural motivations of your people have recently been turned upside down. What's good enough for you is good enough for them. We bore from within, utilizing those two ancient techniques known as 'Divide and rule' and 'If you can't lick 'em, join 'em!' ''

"It would help us," Rhes said, "if you explained what the mores exactly are that we are supposed to be disrupting."

"Didn't I tell you yet?" Jason searched his memory and realized that he hadn't. In spite of the drugs, he was not thinking so clearly as he should. "Then let me explain. I have recently had an involuntary indoctrination into how the locals live. 'Nastily' is one word for it. They are broken up into tribes and clans, all of whom seem to be perpetually at war with the others. Occasionally two or more of the tribes will join together to wipe out one of the others whom they all agree needs wiping out. This is always done under the leadership of a warlord, someone smart enough to make an alliance and strong enough to keep it working. Temuchin is the name of the chief who organized the tribes to destroy the John Company expedition. He is so good at his job that, instead of breaking up the alliance when the threat was over, he kept it going and has even added to it. The anti-city taboo appears to be one of the strongest they have, so it was easy to get recruits. He has kept his army busy ever since, consolidating more and more area under his control. When we arrived, it gave his recruiting an even bigger boost. Temuchin is our main problem. We can get nowhere so long as he is leading the tribes. The first thing we must do is to take away his reason for this holy war, and we can do that easily enough by leaving.''

''Are you sure that you are not feverish?'' Meta asked.

''Thank you for the consideration, but I am fine. I mean we must convince the tribes that we have left. Another landing must be made on the same site and some sort of digging in got under way. Trouble will arrive quickly enough and we'll have to fight them off to prove that we mean business. At the same time we will try to talk to them through loudspeakers, apparently to convince them of our peaceful intent. We'll tell them all about the nice things we will give them if they let us alone. This will only make them fight harder. Then we will threaten to leave forever if they don't stop. They won't stop. So we blast off, straight up, and drop back to a hiding place in the mountains on a ballistic orbit so we won't be seen. That is stage one.''

''I assume there is a stage two,'' Kerk said with marked lack of enthusiasm, ''for up to now it looks very much like a retreat.''

''That's just the idea. In stage two we find an isolated spot in the mountains that simply cannot be reached on foot. We build a model village there to which we transplant, entirely against their will, one of the smaller tribes. They will have all the most modern sanitary conveniences, hot water, the only flush toilets on the entire planet, good food and medical aid. They will hate us for it and do everything possible to kill us and to escape. We will release them—when this affair is over. But in the meanwhile we will utilize their *moropes* and *camachs* and the rest of their barbaric devices.''

''What in the world for?'' Meta asked.

''To form our own tribe, that's what for. The fighting Pyrrans. Tougher, nastier and more faithful to the taboos than any other tribe. We'll bore from within. We'll be so good at the barbarian game that our chief, Kerk the Great, will be able to squeeze Temuchin out of the top job. I know you will be able to get the operation rolling before I return.''

"I did not know you were going," Kerk said, his baffled expression mirrored by the others. "What are you planning to do?"

Jason plucked an invisible string in midair. "I," he announced, "am going to become a jongleur. A wandering troubadour and spy, to sow dissent and prepare the way for your arrival."

7

"If you laugh—or even smile—I'll break your arm," Meta said through tightly clenched teeth.

Jason had to use every iota of his gambler's facial control to maintain his bland, slightly bored expression. He knew she meant it about the broken arm. "I never laugh at a lady's new clothes," he said. "If I did, I would have split my sides many, many planets ago. I think you look fine for the job."

"You would," she hissed. "I think I look like some furry animal that has been run over by a ground car."

"Look, Grif is here," he said, pointing. She automatically turned toward the door. It was a timely entrance because, now that she had mentioned it, she did look like . . .

"Well, Grif, come in, my boy!" Making believe that the wide grin and hearty laugh were for the grim-faced nine-year-old.

"I don't like this," Grif said, flushed and angry. "I don't like looking funny. No one wears clothes like this."

"All three of us do," Jason said, aiming his remarks at the boy but hoping they would register with Meta. "And where we are going, it is the usual dress. Meta here is in the height of fashion among the plains tribes." She was wrapped in stained leather and furs, her angry face scowling out from under a shapeless hood. He looked quickly away. "While you and I wear the indifferent motley of a jongleur and his apprentice. You'll soon see how well we fit in."

Time to change the subject from their ludicrous apparel. He looked closely at Grif's face and hands, then at Meta's.

"The ultraviolet and the tanning drugs have worked fine," he said as he took a small leather bag from the sack at his waist. "You skins are about the same color as the tribesmen's, but there is one thing missing. As protection against the cold and wind, they grease their faces heavily. Wait, stop!'' he said as both Pyrrans clenched their fists and death fluttered close. ''I'm not asking you to smear on the rancid *morope* fat they use. This is clean, neutral, odorless silicone jelly that will be good protection. Take my word for it—you'll need it.''

Jason quickly dug out a glob and rubbed it onto his cheeks. Reluctantly, the other two did the same. Before they were finished, the Pyrran scowls had deepened, which Jason had not thought possible. He wished they would relax—or this game would be over before it began. In the past week, once the others had approved, their plans had moved on teflon bearings. First the planned ''retreat'' from the planet, then the establishing of a base in this isolated valley. It was surrounded by vertical peaks on all sides and completely inaccessible except by air. Their resettlement camp was in the mountains nearby, a bit of plateau that was really only a large ledge set in a gigantic vertical cliff, a natural escape-proof prison. It was already occupied by a clean and embittered family of nomads, five males and six females, that had been caught away from their tribe and quieted by narcogas. Their artifacts and clothes, suitably cleaned and deloused, had been turned over to Jason—as had their *moropes*. Everything was ready now to penetrate Temuchin's army, if Jason could only get these single-minded Pyrrans to cooperate.

''Let's go,'' Jason said. ''It should be our turn by now.''

With its capacious holds and cabins, the *Pugnacious* was still being used as a base, though some of the prefabs were almost erected. As they went down the corridor toward the lock, they met Teca coming from the opposite direction.

''Kerk sent me,'' he said. ''They're almost ready for you.''

Jason merely nodded and they started by him. Relieved of his message, Teca noticed for the first time their exotic garb and grease-covered faces. And the fierce scowls on the Pyrrans' faces. It was all very much out of place in the metal and plastic corridor. Teca looked from one to the other, then pointed at Meta.

''Do you know what you look like?'' he said, and made the very great mistake of smiling.

Meta turned toward him, snarling, but Grif was closer, standing just next to the man. He sank his fist, with all of his weight, deep into Teca's midriff.

Grif was only nine—but he was a Pyrran nine-year-old. Teca had not expected the attack nor was he prepared for it. He said something like *whuf* as the air was driven from his chest, and sat down suddenly on the deck.

Jason waited for the mayhem to follow. Three Pyrrans fighting—and all of them angry! But Teca's mouth dropped open as he looked, wide-eyed, from one to another of the furry trio who surrounded him.

It was Meta who burst out laughing, and Grif followed an instant later. Jason joined in out of pure relief. Pyrrans rarely laugh, and when they do it is only at something broad and obvious, like a man's being knocked suddenly onto his backside. It broke the tension and they roared until their eyes streamed, laughing even harder when the redfaced Teca climbed to his feet and stalked angrily away.

"What was all that about?" Kerk asked when they emerged into the frigid night air.

"You would never believe me if I told you," Jason said. "Is that the last one?"

He pointed to the unconscious *morope* that was being rolled into heavy cable sling. The launch, with vertijets screaming, was hovering above them and lowering a line with a stout hook at the end.

"Yes, the other two have already been delivered, along with the goats. You go out in the next trip."

They looked on in silence while the hook was slipped through the rings in the net and the launch was waved away. It rose quickly, the legs of its unconscious burden dangling limply, and vanished into the darkness.

"What about the equipment?" Jason said.

"It has all been moved out. We set up the *camach* for you and put everything inside it. You three look impressive in those outfits. For the first time, I think you may get away with this masquerade."

There were no hidden meanings in Kerk's words. Out here in the cold night, with a knifelike wind biting deep, their costumes were not out of place. They certainly were as effective as Kerk's insulated and electrically heated suit. Better perhaps. While his face was exposed, theirs were protected by the grease. Jason looked closer at Kerk's cheeks.

"You should go inside," he said, "or rub some of this grease on. It looks like you're getting frostbitten."

"Feels like it, too. If you don't need me here any more, I'll and thaw out."

"Thanks for the help. We'll take it from here."

"Good luck then," Kerk said, shaking hands with them and

including the boy. "We'll keep a full-time radio watch so you can contact us."

They waited silently until the launch returned. They boarded quickly and the trip to the plains did not take very long, which was all for the best, as the interior of the cabin felt stuffy and tropical after the night air.

When the launch had set them down and gone, Jason pointed to the rounded form of the *camach.* "Get inside and make yourselves at home," he said. "I'm going to make sure that the *moropes* are staked down so they don't wander away when they come to. You'll find an atomic power pack there, as well as a light and a heater to plug in. We might as well enjoy the benefits of civilization one last evening."

By the time he had finished with the beasts, the *camach* had warmed up, and cheering light filtered through the lashings around the door flap. Jason laced it behind him and took off his heavy outer furs as the others had done. He rooted an iron pot from one of the hide boxes and filled it with water from a skin bag. This, and the other bags, had been lined with plastic which had not only leak-proofed them, but made a marked difference in the quality of the water. He put it on the heater to boil. Meta and the boy sat silently, watching every move he made.

"This is *char,"* he said, breaking a crumbly black lump off the larger brick. "It's made from one of the shrubs, the leaves are moistened and compressed into blocks. The taste is bearable and we had better get used to it." He dropped the fragments into the water, which instantly turned a repellent shade of purple.

"I don't like the way it looks," Grif said, eyeing it suspiciously. "I don't think I want any."

"You better try it in spite of that. We are going to have to live just like these nomads if we are to escape detection. Which brings up another very important point."

Jason pulled his sleeve up as he spoke and began to unstrap his power holster—while the other two looked on with shocked, widened eyes.

"What is wrong? What are you doing?" Meta asked when he took the gun off and stowed it in the metal trunk. A Pyrran wears his gun every hour of the day and night. Life is unimaginable without one.

"I'm taking off my gun," he patiently explained. "If I used it, or if a tribesman even saw it, our disguise would be penetrated. I'm going to ask you to put yours in here, too—"

Before the words were out of his mouth there was a sharp ripping sound as both of the other guns tore through the leather clothing and slapped into their owners' hands. Jason looked calmly at the unwavering muzzles.

"That is exactly what I mean. As soon as you people get excited, *zingo,* out come the guns. It's not that you can't be trusted; it's just that your reflexes are wrong. We're going to have to lock the guns away where we can get at them in an emergency, but where their presence can't betray us. We'll just have to handle the locals with their own weapons. Look here."

The guns zipped back into their power holsters as the Pyrrans' attention was captured by Jason's display. He unrolled a skin that clanked heavily. It was filled with a wicked assortment of knives, swords, clubs and maces.

"Nice, aren't they?" Jason asked, and they both nodded agreement. Babies and candy: Pyrrans and weapons. "With these we'll be just as well armed as anyone else—in fact better. For any one Pyrran is better than any three barbarians. I hope. But we're shading the odds with these. With the exception of one or two items, they are all copies of local artifacts, only made of much better steel, harder and with a more permanent edge. Now give me the guns."

Only Grif's gun appeared in his hand this time, and he had the intelligence to be a little chagrined as he let it slip back into the power holster. Fifteen solid minutes of wheedling and arguing reluctantly convinced Meta she should part with her weapon, and it took the two of them an hour more to disarm the boy. It was finally done and Jason poured out mugs of *char* for his unhappy partners— both of whom clutched swords to solace themselves.

"I know this stuff is terrible," he said, seeing the shocked expressions that appeared on their faces when they drank. "You don't have to learn to like it, but at least teach yourselves to drink it without looking as though you're being poisoned."

Except for occasional horrified looks at their bare right arms, the Pyrrans forgot the loss of guns while they readied the *camach* for the night. Jason unrolled the fur sleeping bags and turned off the heater while they packed the extra weapons away.

"Bedtime," he announced. "We have to get up at dawn to move to this spot on the chart. There is a small band of nomads going in the direction of what we think is Temuchin's main camp, and we want to meet them here. Join forces, practice our barbarian skills, and let them bring us into the camp without too much notice being taken of us."

Jason was up before dawn and had all the off-planet devices

sealed into the lockbox before he woke the others. He had left out three self-heating meal packs but he would not let them be opened until the *escung* had been loaded. It was a clumsy, time-consuming job this first time, and he was relieved that his angry Pyrrans had been disarmed. The skin cover was pulled off the *camach* and the iron supporting poles were collapsed. These were tied onto the frame of the wheeled travois to act as a support for the rest of the luggage. The sun was well above the horizon and they were sweating, despite the lung-hurting chill air, before they were through loading everything aboard the *escung*. The *moropes* were rumbling deep in their chests as they grazed, while the goats were spread out on all sides nibbling the scant grass. Meta looked pointedly at all this eating and Jason got the hint.

"Come and get it," he said. "We can harness up after we eat." He pulled the opening tab on his pack and steam rose at once from its contents. They broke off the attached plastic spoons and ate in hungry silence.

"Duty calls," Jason announced, scraping up the last morsel of meat. "Meta, use your knife and dig a nice deep hole to bury these meal packs. I'll saddle the *moropes* and harness the one that pulls the *escung*. Grif, take that basket, there on top, and pick up all the *morope* chips. We don't want to waste a natural resource."

"You want me to *what?*"

Jason smiled falsely and pointed to the ground near the big herbivores. "Dung. Those things there. We save them and dry them, and that is what we use from now on to heat and cook with." He swung the nearest saddle onto his back and made believe he did not hear the boy's answering remark.

They had observed how the nomads handled the big beasts and had had some practice themselves, but it was still difficult. The *moropes* were willing but incredibly stupid, and responded best only to the application of direct force. They were all almost exhausted by the time they moved out, Jason leading the way on one riding *morope* and Meta on the second. Grif, perched high on the loaded *escung*, trailed behind, riding backward to keep an eye on the goats. These animals trailed after, grabbing mouthfuls of grass as they went, conditioned to stay close to their owners who supplied the vital water and salt.

By early afternoon they were saddle-sore and weary, when they saw the cloud of dust moving diagonally across their front.

"Just sit quiet and keep your weapons handy," Jason said, "while I do the talking. Listen to the way they speak this simplified language so that later on you'll be able to do it yourself."

As they came closer, the dark blobs of *moropes* could be made out, with the scattered specks of the goat herds behind. Three *moropes* swung away from the larger group and headed their way at a dead run. Jason held up his hand for his party to halt, then cursed as he threw all of his weight on the reins to bring his hulking mount to a stop. Sensation penetrated its tiny brain and it shuddered to a halt and began instantly to graze. He loosened his knife in its sheath and noticed that Meta's right hand was unconsciously flexing, reaching for the gun that was not there. The riders thundered up, stopping just before them.

The leader had a dirty black beard and only one eye. The red, raw appearance of the empty socket suggested that the eyeball had been gouged out. He wore a dented metal helm that was crowned with the skull of some long-toothed rodent.

"Who are you, jongleur?" he asked, shifting a spiked mace from one hand to the other. "Where you go?"

"I am Jason, singer of songs, teller of tales, on my way to the camp of Temuchin. Who are you?"

The man grunted and picked at his teeth with one blackened nail.

"Shanin of the rat tribe. What do you say to rats?"

Jason had not the slightest idea what one said to rats, though he could think of a few possibly inappropriate remarks. He noticed now that the others had the same type of skull, rats' skulls undoubtedly, mounted on their helms. The symbol of their tribe, perhaps, different skulls for different tribes. But he remembered that Oraiel had no such decoration, and that the jongleurs were supposed to stay outside of tribal conflicts.

"I say hello to rats," he improvised. "Some of my best friends are rats."

"You fight feud with rats?"

"Never!" Jason answered, offended by the suggestion.

Shanin seemed satisfied and went back to picking his teeth. "We go to Temuchin, too," he said indistinctly around his finger. "I have heard Temuchin strikes against the mountain weasels so we join him. You ride with us. Sing for me tonight."

"I hate mountain weasels, too. I'll sing tonight."

At a grunted command the three men wheeled and galloped away. That was all there was to it. Jason's party followed and slowly caught up with the moving column of *moropes,* swinging in behind them so that their herd of goats did not mix with the others.

"That's what all the goat leads are for," Jason said, coughing in the cloud of dust that hung heavy in the air. "As soon as we stop, want you two to secure all our animals so they can't get lost in the other herd.''

"Aren't you planning to help?'' Meta asked coldly.

"Much as I would love to, this is a male-oriented, primitive society and that sort of thing just isn't done. I'll do my share of the work out of sight in the tent, but not in public.''

It was a short day, which the disguised off-worlders appreciated, because the nomads reached their goal, a desert well, early in the afternoon. Jason, saddle-sore and stiff, slid to the ground and hobbled in small circles to work the circulation back into his numb legs. Meta and Grif were rounding up and tethering the protesting goats, which induced Jason to take a walk around the camp to escape her daggerlike glances. The well interested him: he came to look and stayed to help. Only men and boys were gathered here since there seemed to be a sexual taboo connected with the water. This was understandable, as water was as essential to life as hunting ability in this semiarid desert.

A rock cairn marked the well, which the men removed to disclose a beaten iron cover. This was heavily greased to retard its rusting, though the covering rocks had cut through the grease and streaks of oxidation were beginning to form. When the cover had been lifted aside, one of the men thoroughly greased it again on both sides. The well itself was about a meter in diameter and impressively deep, lined with stones so perfectly cut and set that they locked into place without mortar. They were ancient and much worn about the mouth, grooved by centuries of use. Jason wondered who the original builders had been.

Getting the water out of the well was done in the most primitive way possible—by dropping an iron bucket down the shaft, then pulling it up again with a braided leather rope. Only one man at a time could work at this, straddling the well head and pulling the rope up hand over hand. It was tiring work and the men changed position often, standing about to talk or to bring the filled waterskins back to their *camachs*. Jason took his turn at the well, then wandered back to see how the work was coming.

All the goats had been tethered, and Meta and Grif had the iron *camach* frame erected while they struggled to drag the cover into place. Jason contributed his mite by hauling their lockbox from the pile of gear and sitting on it. Its tattered leather cover disguised the alloy container inside, secured with a lock that could only be opened by the fingerprint of one of the three of them. He plucked at the two-stringed lute that he had made in frank imitation of the one he had seen the jongleur use, and hummed a song to himself. A passing tribesman stopped and watched the *camach* being erected. Jason recognized the man as one of the riders who had intercepted them earlier and decided to take no notice of him. He plinked out a version of a spaceman's drinking song.

"Good strong woman but stupid. Can't put up a *camach* right," the tribesman said suddenly, pointing with his thumb.

Jason had no idea what he should say, so he settled for a grunt. The man persisted, scratching in his beard while he openly admired Meta.

"I need a strong woman. I'll give you six goats for this one."

Jason saw that it was more than her strength that the man admired. Meta, working hard, had taken off her heavy outer furs, and her slim figure was far more attractive than the squat and solid ones of the nomad women. Her hair was neat, her teeth unbroken, her face unmarked or scarred.

"You wouldn't want her," Jason said. "She sleeps late, eats too much. Costs too much. I paid twelve goats for her."

"I'll give you ten," the warrior said, walking over and grabbing Meta by the arm and pulling her about so he could look at her.

Jason shuddered. Perhaps the tribeswomen were used to being treated like chattels, but Meta certainly wasn't. Jason waited for the explosion, but she surprised him by pulling her arm away and turning back to her work.

"Come here," Jason told the man. He had to break this up before it went too far. "Come have a drink. I have good *achadh.*"

It was too late. The warrior shouted in anger at being resisted by a mere woman and, with his bunched fist, struck her over the ear, then reached to pull her about again.

Meta stumbled from the force of the unexpected blow and shook her head. When he pulled at her this time, she did not resist but spun about, bringing up her arm at the same time. The stiffened outer edge of her hand caught him across the larynx, almost fracturing it, rendering him voiceless. She stood, ready now, while the man doubled over, coughing hoarsely and spitting up blood.

Jason tried to spring forward, but it was over before he had taken a single pace.

The warrior's fighting reflexes were good—but Meta's were even better. He came out of the crouch, blood streaming down his chin, with a knife in his hand, swinging it up underhand in a wicked knifefighter's thrust.

Meta clutched his wrist with both her hands, twisting at the same instant so that the knife went by her. She continued to twist, levering the man's arm up behind his back, exerting bone-breaking pressure so that the knife dropped from his powerless fingers. She could have left it at this, but, because she was a Pyrran, she did not.

She caught the knife before it touched the ground, straightened and brought it slanting up into the man's back, below and inside his rib cage, sinking it to the hilt so the blade penetrated his lung and heart, killing him instantly. When she released him, he sank, unmoving, to the ground.

Jason sank back onto the lockbox and, as though by chance, his forefinger touched the keying plate and he felt the click as the bolt unlatched. A number of onlookers had watched the encounter and a hum of astonishment filled the air. One woman waddled over and picked up the man's arm, which dropped limply when she released it. "Dead!" she said in an astonished voice and looked wonderingly at Meta.

"You two—over here!" Jason called out, using their own "tribal" tongue that the crowd would not understand. "Keep your weapons handy and stand close. If this really gets rough, there are gas grenades and your guns in here. But once we use them, we'll have to wipe out or capture the entire tribe. So let's save that as a last resort."

Shanin, with a score of his warriors behind him, pushed through the crowd and looked unbelievingly at the dead man. "Your woman kill this man with his own knife?"

"She did—and it was his own fault. He pushed her around, started trouble, then attacked her. It was just self-defense. Ask anyone here." There was a mutter of agreement from the crowd.

The chief seemed more astonished than angry. He looked from the corpse to Meta, then swaggered over and took her by the chin, turning her head back and forth while he examined her. Jason could see her knuckles go white but she kept her control.

"What tribe she from?" Shanin asked.

"From far away, in the mountains, far north. Tribe called the . . . Pyrrans. Very tough fighters."

Shanin grunted. "I never heard of them." As though his encyclopedic knowledge ruled them out of existence. "What's their totem?"

What indeed, Jason thought? It couldn't be a rat or a weasel. What kind of animals had they seen in the mountains? "Eagle," he announced, with more firmness than he felt. He had seen something that looked like an eagle once, circling the high peaks.

"Very strong totem," Shanin said, obviously impressed. He looked down at the dead man and stirred him with his foot. "He has a *morope,* some furs. Woman can't have them.'' He looked up shrewdly at Jason, waiting for an answer.

The answer to that one was easy. Women, being property themselves, could not own property. And to the victor went the spoils. Don't let anyone ever say that dinAlt was not generous with secondhand *moropes* and used furs.

''The property is yours, of course, Shanin. That is only right. I would never think of taking them, oh no! And I shall beat the woman tonight for doing this.''

It was the right answer and Shanin accepted the booty as his due. He started away, then called back over his shoulder. ''He could not have been a good fighter if a woman killed him. But he has two brothers.''

That meant something all right, and Jason gave it some thought as the people in the crowd dispersed, taking the dead man with them. Meta and Grif finished erecting the cover on the *camach* and carried all of their goods inside. Jason dragged in the lockbox himself, then sent Grif to tether the goats closer in, near their *moropes.* The killing could lead to trouble.

It did, and faster than Jason had imagined. There were some thuds and a shrill scream outside and he raced for the entrance. Most of the action was over by the time he reached it.

A half dozen boys, relatives perhaps of the dead man, had decided to exact a little revenge by attacking Grif. Most of them were older or bigger than he, so they must have planned on a quick attack, a beating and a hasty retreat. It did not work out quite as planned.

Three boys had grabbed him, to hold him securely while the others administered the drubbing. Two of these now lay unconscious on the ground, for the Pyrran boy had cracked their skulls together, while the third rolled in agony after having been kneed in the groin. Grif was kneeling on the neck of the fourth boy while attempting to break the leg of the fifth by twisting it up behind his back. The sixth boy was trying to get away and Grif was reaching for his knife to stop him before he made his escape.

''Not the knife!'' Jason shouted, and helped the survivor on his way with a good boot in the coccyx. ''We're in enough trouble without another killing.''

Scowling, deprived of his pleasure, Grif elicited both a shrill scream, with an extra ankle twist, and a choked groan, from under his grinding knee. Then he stood and watched while the survivors limped and crawled from the area of combat. Except for a rapidly blackening eye and a torn sleeve, he himself was unhurt. Jason, speaking calmly, managed to get him inside the *camach,* where Meta put a cold compress on his eye.

Jason laced up the entrance and looked at his two Pyrrans, their tempers still aroused, stalking around as though still looking for trouble.

"Well," he said, shrugging his shoulders, "no one can say that you don't make a strong first impression."

8

> Though they had the swords of lightning,
> Die they did in countless numbers. Arrows' flight
> Did speak to strangers,
> Bidding them to leave our pastures . . .

"I speak with the voice of Temuchin, for I am Ahankk, his captain," the warrior said, throwing open the entrance to Shanin's *camach.*

Jason broke off his "Ballad of the Flying Strangers" and turned slowly to see who had caused the welcome interruption. His throat was getting sore and he was tired of singing the same song over and over. His account of the spaceship's defeat was the pop hit of the encampment.

The newcomer was a high-ranking officer, that was obvious. His breastplate and helm were shiny and undented, and even set with a few roughly cut jewels. He swaggered as he walked, planting his feet squarely as he stood before Shanin, his hand resting on his sword pommel.

"What does Temuchin want?" Shanin asked coldly, his hand on his own sword, not liking the newcomer's manner.

"He will hear the jongleur who is called Jason. He is to come at once."

Shanin's eyes narrowed to cold slits. "He sings for me now. When he is through, he will come to Temuchin. Finish the song," he said turning to Jason.

To a nomad chief all chiefs are equal and it is hard to convince them differently. Temuchin and his officers had plenty of experience and knew all the persuasive arguments. Ahankk whistled shrilly and a squad of heavily armed soldiers with drawn bows pushed into the *camach*. Shanin was convinced.

"I am bored with this croaking," he announced, yawning and turning away. "I will now drink *achadh* with one of my women. All leave."

, Jason went out with his honor guard and turned toward his *camach*. The officer stopped him with a broad hand against his chest. "Temuchin will hear you now. Turn that way."

"Take your hand from me," Jason said in a low voice that the nearby soldiers could not hear. "I go to put on my best jacket and to get a new string for this instrument because one of these is almost broken."

"Come now," Ahankk said loudly, leaving his hand where it was and giving Jason a shove.

"We will first visit my *camach*. It is just over there," Jason answered just as loudly. At the same time he reached up and took hold of the man's thumb. This is a good grip at any time, and his 2G-hardened muscles added the little extra something that made the thumb feel as if it were being torn from the hand. The officer writhed and resisted, pulling at his sword clumsily, crosswise, for it was his sword hand that Jason was slowly rending.

"I'll kill you with this knife that is pushed against your middle if you draw your sword," Jason said, holding the lute under his arm and pressing the bone pick into Ahankk's stomach. "Temuchin said to bring me, not kill me. He will be angry if we fight. Now—which do you choose?"

The man struggled for another moment, lips drawn back in anger, then released his sword. "We shall go to your *camach* first so you can dress in something more fitting than those rags," he ordered aloud.

Jason let go of the thumb and started off, turned slightly sideways so he could watch the officer. The man walked beside him calmly enough, rubbing his injured thumb, but the look he directed at Jason was pure hatred. Jason shrugged and went on. He had made an enemy, that was certain, yet it was imperative that he go to the tent first.

The trek with Shanin and his tribe had been exhausting but uneventful. There had been no more trouble from the relatives of the slain man. Jason had utilized the time well to practice his jongleur's art and to observe the customs and culture of the nomads. They had reached Temuchin's camp and settled in over a week ago.

"Camp" was not an apt designation, because the nomads were spread out for miles along the polluted, refuse-laden stream they called a river, but the biggest river apparently in the entire land. Because the animals had to compete for the scant forage, a good deal of territory was needed for each tribe. There was a purely military camp in the center of all these settlements but Jason had not yet been near it. Nor was he in a hurry to. There was enough for him to observe and record on the outskirts before he would be sure enough of himself to penetrate to the heart of the enemy. In addition, Temuchin had once seen him, face to face, and he appeared to be the kind of man who would have a good memory. Jason's skin was darker now, and he had used a pilating agent to hurry the growth of a thick and sinister mustache that hung almost to his chin on both sides of his mouth. Teca had inserted plugs that changed the shape of his nose. He hoped it would be enough. Yet he wondered how the war chief had heard—and what he had heard--about him.

"Rise, awake," he shouted, throwing open the flap of his *camach*. "I shall go before the great Temuchin and I must dress accordingly." Meta and Grif looked coldly at Jason and the officer who had followed him and made no attempt to move.

"Get cracking," Jason said in Pyrran. "Rush around and look like you're impressed, offer this elegant slob a drink and stuff like that. Keep his attention off me."

Ahankk took a drink, but he still kept a wary eye on Jason.

"Here," Jason said, holding the lute out to Grif. "Put a new string on this thing, or make believe you are changing it if you can't find one. And *don't* lose your temper when I shove you. It's just part of the act."

Grif scowled and growled, but otherwise reacted well enough when Jason bullied him off to work with the lute. Jason shed his jacket, rubbed fresh grease into his face and a little onto his hair for good measure, then opened the lockbox. He reached in and took out his better jacket, palming a small object at the same time.

"Now hear this," he called out in Pyrran. "I'm being rushed to see Temuchin and there is no way out of it. I've taken one of the dentiphones and I've left two more on top. Put them on as soon as I've gone. Stay in touch and stay alert. I don't know how the interview is going to turn out, but if there is any trouble, I want us to be in contact at all times. We may have to move fast. Stick with it, gang, and don't despair. We'll lick them yet."

As he slipped into the jacket he screamed at them in in-between. "Give me the lute—and hurry! If anything is disturbed or there is any trouble while I am gone, I will beat you both." He stalked out.

They rode in a loose formation, and perhaps it was only accidental that there were soldiers on all sides of Jason. Perhaps. What had Temuchin heard and why did he want to see him? Speculation was useless and he tried to drop the train of thought and observe his surroundings, but it kept creeping back.

The afternoon sun was low behind the *camachs* when they approached the military camp. The herds were gone and the tents were arranged in neat rows. There were troops on all sides. A wide avenue opened up with a very large, black *camach* at the far end, guarded outside by a row of spearmen. Jason did not need any diagrams to know whose tent this was. He slid from his *morope*, tucked the lute under his arm, and followed his guiding officer with what he intended to be a proud but not haughty gait. Ahankk went in front of Jason to announce him, and as soon as his back was turned, Jason slipped the dentiphone into his mouth and pushed it into place with his tongue. It fitted neatly over an upper back molar, and the power would be turned on automatically by contact with his saliva. "Testing, testing, can you hear me?" he whispered under his breath. The microminiaturized device had an automatic volume control and could broadcast anything from a whisper to a shout.

"Loud and clear," Meta's voice rustled in his ear, inaudible to anyone but him. The output was fed as mechanical vibration into his tooth, thence to his skull and ear by bone conduction.

"Step forward!" Ahankk shouted, rudely jerking Jason from his radiophonic communication by grabbing his arm. Jason ignored him, pulling away and walking alone toward the man in the high-backed chair. Temuchin had his head turned as he talked to two of his officers, which was for the best, for Jason could not control a look of astonishment as he realized what the throne was made of. It was a tractor seat, supported and backed by recoilless rifles bound together. These were slung with leathern strings of desiccated thumbs, some of them just bone with a few black particles of flesh adhering. Temuchin, slayer of the invaders—and here was the proof.

Temuchin turned as Jason came close, fixing him with a cold, expressionless gaze. Jason bowed, more to escape those eyes than from any obsequious desires. Would Temuchin recognize him? Suddenly the nose plugs and drooping mustache seemed to him the flimsiest excuse for a disguise. He should have done better. Temuchin had stood this close to him once before. Surely he would recognize him. Jason straightened up slowly and found the man's chill eyes still fixed on him. Temuchin said nothing.

Jason knew he should stay quiet and let the other talk first. Or was that right? That is what he would do as Jason—attempt to outface and outpoint the other man. Stare him down and get the upper hand. But surely that was not to be expected of an itinerant jongleur? He must certainly feel a little ill at ease, no matter how snow-driven his conscience.

"You sent for me, great Temuchin. I am honored." He bowed again. "You will want me to sing for you."

"No," Temuchin said coldly. Jason allowed his eyebrows to rise in mild astonishment.

"No songs? What, then, will the leader of men have from a poor wanderer?"

Temuchin swept him with his frigid glance. Jason wondered how much was real, how much shrewd role-playing to impress the locals.

"Information," Temuchin said just as the dentiphone hummed to life inside Jason's mouth and Meta's voice spoke. "Jason—trouble. Armed men outside telling us to come out or they will kill us."

"That is a jongleur's duty, to tell and teach. What would you know?" Under his breath he whispered, "No guns! Fight them—I'll get help."

"What was that?" Temuchin asked, leaning forward threateningly. "What did you whisper."

"It was nothing, it was—" Damn, you couldn't say "nervous habit" in in-between. "It is a jongleur's . . . way. Speaking the words of a song quietly, so they will not be forgotten."

Temuchin leaned back, a frown cutting deep lines in his forehead. He apparently did not think much of Jason's rehearsing during an audience. Neither did Jason. But how could he help Meta and Grif?

"Men—breaking in!" her shouting voice whispered silently.

"Tell me about this Pyrran tribe," Temuchin said.

Jason was beginning to sweat. Temuchin must have a spy in the tribe, or Shanin had volunteered information. And the dead man's family seemed to be out for vengeance now, knowing he was away from the camp. "Pyrrans? They're just another tribe. Why do you want to know?"

"What?" Temuchin lunged to his feet pulling at his sword. "You dare to question me?"

"Jason!"

"Wait, no." Jason felt the perspiration beginning to form droplets under the layer of grease on his face. "I spoke wrong. Damn this in-between tongue. I meant to say, *What* do you want to know?

I will tell you whatever I can.''

"There are many of them. Swords and shields. They attack Grif, all together.''

"I have never heard of this tribe. Where do they keep their flocks?''

"The mountains . . . in the north, valleys, remote, you know . . .''

"Grif is down, I cannot fight them all.''

"What does that mean? What are you hiding? Perhaps you do not understand Temuchin's law. Rewards to those who are with me. Death to those who oppose me. The slow death for those who attempt to betray me.''

"The slow death?'' Jason said, listening for the words that did not come.

Temuchin was silent a moment. "You do not appear to know much, jongleur, and there is something about you that is not right. I will show you something that will encourage you to talk more freely.'' He clapped his hands and one of the attentive officers stepped forward. "Bring in Daei.''

Was that a muffled breathing? Jason could not be sure. He brought his attention back to the *camach* and looked, astonished, at the man on the litter that was set down before them. The man was tied down by a tight noose about his neck. He did not try to loosen the rope and escape because there were just raw stumps where his fingers should have been. His bare, toeless feet had received the same treatment.

"The slow death,'' Temuchin said, staring fixedly at Jason. "Daei left me to fight with the weasel clans. Each day one joint is cut off each limb. He has been here many days. Now, today's justice.'' He raised his hand.

Soldiers held the man although he made no attempt to struggle. Thin strips of leather were sunk deep into the flesh of his wrists and ankles and knotted tight. His right arm was pressed against the ground and one soldier made a swift chop with an ax. The hand jumped off, spurting blood. The men methodically went to the other arm, then the legs.

"He has two more days to go, as you can see,'' Temuchin said. "If he is strong enough to live that long, I may be merciful on the third day. I may not be. I have heard of one man who lived a year before reaching his last day.''

"Very interesting,'' Jason said. "I have heard of the custom but it slipped my mind.'' He had to do something quickly. He could hear the hammer of *moropes'* feet outside, and men's shouts.

"Did you hear that? A whistle?"

"Have you gone mad?" Temuchin asked, annoyed. He waved angrily and the now unconscious man was carried out, the dismembered extremities kicked aside.

"It was a whistle," Jason said, starting toward the entrance. "I must step outside. I will return at once."

The officers in the tent, no less than Temuchin, were dumbfounded by this. Men did not leave his presence this way.

"Just a moment will do it."

"Stop!" Temuchin bellowed, but Jason was already at the entrance. The guard there barred his way, pulling out his sword. Jason gave him the shoulder, sending him spinning, and stepped outside.

The outer guards ignored him, unaware of what was happening inside. Walking casually but swiftly, Jason turned right and had reached the corner of the large *camach* before his pursuers burst out behind him. There was a roar and the chase was on. Jason turned the corner and raced full tilt along the side.

Unlike the smaller, circular *camachs,* this one was rectangular, and Jason reached and dived around the next corner before the angry horde could see where he had gone. Shouts and hoarse cries echoed behind as he raced full tilt around the structure. Only when he reached the front again did he slow to a walk as he turned the last corner.

The pursuit was all streaming off in the opposite direction, bellowing distantly like hounds. The two guards who had been at the entrance were gone and all the other nearby ones were looking in the opposite direction. Walking steadily Jason came to the entrance and went inside. Temuchin, who was pacing angrily, was aware that someone had come in.

"Well!" he shouted. "Did you catch—you!" He stepped back and drew his sword with a lightning slash.

"I am your loyal servant, Temuchin," Jason said flatly, folding his arms and not retreating. "I have come to report rebellion among your tribes."

Temuchin did not strike—nor did he lower his sword.

"Speak quickly. Your death is at hand."

"I know you have forbidden private feuds among those who serve you. There are some who would slay my servant because she killed a man who attacked her. I have been near her ever since this happened—until today. Therefore I asked a trusted man to watch and to report to me. I heard his whistle, because he dared not enter the *camach* of Temuchin. I have just talked to him. Armed men have attacked my *camach* in my absence and taken my servants. Yet

I have heard that there is one law for all who follow Temuchin. I ask you now to declare about this.''

There was the thud of feet behind Jason as his pursuers caught up and stormed through the entrance. They slid to a stop, piling up behind each other as they saw the two men facing each other—Temuchin with his sword still raised.

He glared at Jason, the sword quivering with the tension in his muscles. In the silence of the *camach* they could clearly hear his teeth grate together as he brought the sword down—point first into the dirt floor.

''Ahankk!'' he shouted, and the officer ran forward, slapping his chest. ''Take four hands of men and go to the tribe of Shanin of the rat clan—''

''I can show you—'' Jason interrupted.

Temuchin wheeled on him, thrust his face so close that Jason could feel his breath on his cheek, and said, ''Speak once again without my permission and you are dead.''

Jason nodded, nothing more. He knew he had almost overplayed his hand. After a moment, Temuchin turned back to his officer.

''Ride at once to this Shanin and command him to take you to those who have taken the Pyrran servants. Bring all you find there here, as many alive as possible.''

Ahankk saluted as he ran out: obedience counted before courtesy in Temuchin's horde.

Temuchin paced back and forth in a vile temper, and the officer and men withdrew silently, from the *camach* or back against its walls. Only Jason stood firm—even when the angry man stopped and shook his large fist just under Jason's nose.

''Why do I allow you to do this?'' he said with cold fury. ''Why?''

''May I answer?'' Jason asked quietly.

''Speak!'' Temuchin roared, hanging over him like a falling mountain.

''I left Temuchin's presence because it was the only way I could be sure that justice would be done. What enabled me to do this is a fact I have concealed from you.''

Temuchin did not speak, though his eyes blazed with anger.

''Jongleurs know no tribe and wear no totem. This is the way it should be, for they go from tribe to tribe and should bear no allegiance. But I must tell you that I was born in the Pyrran tribe. They made me leave and that is why I became a jongleur.''

Temuchin would not ask the obvious question and Jason did not allow the expectant silence to become too long.

"I had to leave because—this is very hard to say—compared to the other Pyrrans . . . I was so weak and cowardly."

Temuchin swayed slightly and his face suffused with blood. He bent and his mouth opened—and he roared with laughter. Still laughing, he went to his throne and dropped into it. None of the watchers knew what to make of this; therefore they were silent. Jason allowed himself the slightest smile but said nothing. Temuchin waved over the servant with a leathern blackjack of *achadh,* which he drained at a single swallow. The laughing died away to a chuckle, then to silence. He was his cold, controlled self once more.

"I enjoyed that," he said. "I find very little to laugh at. I think you are intelligent, perhaps too intelligent for your own good, and you may someday have to die for that. Now you will tell me about your Pyrrans."

"We live in the mountain valleys to the north and rarely go down to the plains." Jason had been working on this cover story since he had first joined the nomads; now was the time to put it to the test. "We believe in the rule of might, but also the rule of law. Therefore we seldom leave our valleys and we kill anyone who trespasses. We are the Pyrrans of the eagle totem, which is our strength, so that even one of our women can kill a plains warrior with her hands. We have heard that Temuchin is bringing law to the plains, so I was sent to find out if this were true. If it is true, the Pyrrans will join Temuchin—"

They both looked up at the sudden interruption—Temuchin because there were shouts and commands as a group of *moropes* reined up outside the *camach,* Jason because a weak voice had very clearly said "Jason" inside his head. He could not tell whether it was Meta or Grif.

Ahankk and his warriors came in through the entrance, half carrying, half pushing their prisoners. One wounded man, drenched with blood, and his unharmed companion, Jason recognized as two of the nomads from Shanin's tribe. Meta and Grif were brought in and dropped onto the ground, bloody, battered and unmoving. Grif opened his one uninjured eye and said "Jason . . . ," then slumped unconscious again. Jason started forward, then had enough self-control to halt, clenching his fists until his nails dug deep into his palms.

"Report," Temuchin ordered. Ahankk stepped forward.

"We did as you ordered, Temuchin. Rode fast to this tribe and the one Shanin took us to a *camach.* We entered and fought. None escaped, but we had to kill to subdue them. Two have been captured. The slaves breathe so I think they are alive.''

Temuchin rubbed his jaw in obvious thought. Jason took a long chance and spoke.

"Do I have Temuchin's permission to ask a question?''

Temuchin gave him a long, hard look, then nodded agreement.

"What is the penalty for rebellion and private vengeance in your horde?''

"Death. Is there any other punishment?''

"Then I would like to answer a question that you asked earlier. You wanted to know what Pyrrans are like. I am the weakest of all the Pyrrans. I would like to kill the unwounded prisoner, with one hand, with a dagger alone, with one stroke—no matter how he is armed. Even with a sword. He looks to be a good warrior.''

"He does,'' Temuchin said, looking at the big, burly man who was almost a head taller than Jason. "I think that will be a very good idea.''

"Tie my hand,'' Jason ordered the nearest guard, placing his left arm behind his back. The prisoner was going to die in any case, and if his death could be put to a good use, that would probably be more than the man had contributed to any decent cause in his entire lifetime. Being a hypocrite, Jason? a tiny inner voice asked, and he did not answer because there was a great deal of truth in the charge. At one time he had disliked death and violence and sought to evade it. Now he appeared to be actively seeking it.

Then he looked at Meta, unconscious and curled in pain upon the ground, and his knife whispered from its sheath. A demonstration of unusual fighting ability would interest Temuchin. And that ignorant barbarian with the hint of a smug smile badly needed killing.

Or he would be killed himself if he hadn't planted the suggestion strongly enough. If they gave that brute a spear or a club, he would easily butcher Jason in a few minutes.

Jason did not change expression when the soldiers released the man and Ahankk handed him his own long two-handed officer's sword. Good old Ahankk: it sometimes helped to make an enemy. The man still remembered the thumb-twisting and was getting his own back. Jason slapped his broad-bladed knife against his side and let it hang straight down. It was an unusual knife that he had forged and tempered himself, after an ancient design called the "bowie." It was as broad as his hand, with one edge sharpened the length of the blade, the other for less than half. It could cut up or down and could stab, and it weighed more than two kilos. And it was made of the best tool steel.

The man with the sword shouted once and swung the sword high, running forward. One blow would do it, a swing with all of his weight behind it that no knife could possibly stop. Jason stood as calmly as he could and waited.

Only when the sword was swinging down did he move, stepping forward with his right foot and bracing his legs. He swung the knife up, with his arm held straight and his elbow locked, then took the force of the blow full on the edge of his knife. The strength of the swing almost knocked the knife from his hand and drove him to his knees. But there was a brittle clang as the mild steel struck the toolsteel edge, all of the impact coming suddenly on this small area, and the sword snapped in two.

Jason had the barest glimpse of the shocked expression on his face as the man's arms swung down, his hands still locked tightly about the hilt that supported the merest stub of a blade. The force of the blow had knocked Jason's arm down and he moved with the motion, letting the knife swing down and around—and up.

The point tore through the leather clothing and struck the man low in the abdomen, penetrating to the hilt. Bracing himself, Jason jerked upward with all his strength, cutting a deep and hideous wound through the man's internal organs until the blade grated against the clavicle in his chest. He held the knife there as the man's eyeballs rolled back into his head and Jason knew that he was dead.

Jason pulled the knife out and stepped back. The corpse slid to the floor at his feet.

"I will see that knife," Temuchin said.

"We have very good iron in our valley," Jason told him, bending to wipe the knife on the dead man's clothing. "It makes good steel." He flipped the knife in the air, catching it by the tip, and extended the hilt to Temuchin, who examined it for a moment, then called to the soldiers.

"Hold the wounded one's neck out," he said.

The man struggled for a moment, then sank into the apathy of one already dead. Two soldiers held him while a third clutched his long hair with both hands and pulled him forward, face downward, with his dirt-lined neck bare and straight. Temuchin walked over, balancing the knife in his hand, then raised it straight over his head.

With a single galvanic thrust of his muscles, he swung the knife down against the neck and a meaty *chunnk* filled the silent *camach*.

The tension released, the soldier moved back a step, the severed head swinging from his fingers. The blood-spurting body was unceremoniously dropped to the ground.

"I like this knife," Temuchin said. "I will keep it."

"I was about to present it to you," Jason said, bowing to hide his scowl. He should have realized that this would happen. Well, it was just a knife.

"Do your people know much of the old science?" Temuchin asked, dropping the knife for a servant to pick up and clean. Jason was instantly on his guard.

"No more or less than other tribes," he said.

"None of them can make iron like this."

"It is an old secret, passed on from father to son."

"There could be other old secrets." His voice was as hard and cold as the steel itself.

"Perhaps."

"There is a lost secret then that you may have heard of. Some call it 'flamepowder' and others, 'gunpowder.' What do you know of this?"

Indeed, what do I know of this? Jason thought, trying to read something from the other's fixed expression. What could a barbarian jongleur know of such things?

And if this was a trap, what should Jason tell him?

9

Meta made no protest as Jason washed the dirt from her cuts and sprayed them with dermafoam. The medikit had sewn 14 stitches into the cut on her skull, but he had done this while she was still unconscious and had covered the shaved area with a bandage. She had come to right after this, but had not moved or complained when he had put two more stitches in her split upper lip.

Grif breathed a hoarse snore from the mound of furs where Jason had placed him. The boy's wounds were mostly superficial and the medikit had advised sedation, which suggestion Jason had complied with.

"It's all over now," Jason said. "You had better get some rest."

"There were too many of them," Meta said, "but we did the best we could. Let me have a mirror. They surprised me, going for the boy first, but it was a wise plan. He went down at once. Then they came at me and I could not talk to you any more." She took the polished steel mirror from Jason, had one brief glance and handed it back. "I look terrible. It must have been a quick fight. I don't remember too clearly. Some of them had clubs, the women, and they tried to hit my legs. I know I killed at least three or four, one of the women, before I went down. What happened then?"

Jason took the *achadh* skin and worked the hidden valve on the mouthpiece that sealed off the fermented milk and opened the reservoir of spiced alcohol that the Pyrrans favored.

"Drink?" he asked, but she shook her head. He joined himself and had a long one. "Skipping the finer details for the moment, I managed to send some of the troopers after you. They brought back both of you, and a few rat survivors—all of whom are now dead. I killed the unwounded one myself in true Pyrran-vengeance fashion, for which I do not feel too ashamed. But I had to give my knife to Temuchin, who instantly spotted the advanced level of technology. I'm very glad now that I hand-forged it and that the tool marks can still be seen. Right away he asked me if we Pyrrans knew anything about gunpowder, which rocked me. I played it slippery, told him I knew nothing—just the name—but perhaps others in the tribe knew more. He bought that for the time being—I think. You just can't tell with that guy. But he wants us to move in. At dawn we have to truck our *camach* into the camp next to his, and say good-bye to Shanin and his rats, whom we shall not miss. And in case we should change our minds, there is a squad of Temuchin's boys waiting outside. I still haven't decided whether we are prisoners or not."

"I know I look terrible this way," she said, her head nodding.

"You'll always look good to me," Jason told her cheeringly, then realized that he meant it. He twisted the medikit to *full sedation* and pressed it to her arm. She did not protest. With more than a small amount of guilt, and the feeling that he alone was responsible for their danger and pain, Jason laid her down on the furs next to the boy and covered them both. What bit of insane stupidity was it that had permitted him to involve a woman and a child in this murderous business? Then he remembered that conditions here were still far better than they were on Pyrrus, and he had probably saved their lives by getting them away. He looked at their bruises and shuddered, and wondered if they would thank him for it.

In the morning the two wounded Pyrrans had just enough strength to stumble out of the *camach* so that Jason could supervise its dismantling by the soldiers. They grumbled about woman's work, but Jason would allow none of Shanin's tribespeople near any of his belongings. After all the recent deaths, he was sure that his feud had widened its boundaries until it took in a good portion of the tribe. It was only after Jason had lubricated their spirits with a large skin of high-proof *achadh* that the soldiers buckled down to finish the job and to load the *escung*. Jason strapped Meta and Grif in under the furs, in much the same way that he had been carried after his capture, and the small caravan set out, hurried on its way by many dark looks.

In Temuchin's own camp, there were enough females who could be drafted for the degrading labor so that the men could stand and watch, which was their normal contribution. Jason could not stay to supervise. He left this to Meta, because a message arrived demanding his instant appearance before Temuchin.

The two guards at the entrance to the warlord's *camach* stood aside when Jason approached. At least he had some prestige among the enlisted men. Temuchin was alone, holding Jason's knife, which was drenched with blood. Jason stopped, then relaxed when Temuchin seized the point and, with a quick snap of his wrist, sent it whistling through the air to sink deep into the carcass of a goat that he was using for a target.

"This knife has good balance," Temuchin said. "Throws well."

Jason nodded silently for he knew that he had not been summoned to an audience just to hear that.

"Tell me all you know about gunpowder," Temuchin said, bending over to retrieve the knife.

"There is very little to tell."

Temuchin straightened and his eyes caught Jason's as he tapped the hilt of the knife against the calloused palm of his hand. "Tell me everything you know. Instantly. If you had gunpowder, could you make it blow up with the big noise instead of burning with smoke?"

This was the clinch. If Temuchin thought that he were lying, that big knife would sink into his gut as easily as it went into the goat's. The warlord had some very specific ideas about the physical nature of gunpowder, so he was not bluffing. Time to take a chance.

"Though I have never seen gunpowder, I know what is said about it. I have heard how to make it explode."

"I thought you might." The knife as it sank deep into the goat's flesh. "I think you know other things that you are not telling me."

"Men have secrets that they swear never to reveal. But Temuchin is my master and I will help him in every way that I can."

"Good. Don't forget that. Now tell me what you know about the people in the lowlands."

"Why—nothing," Jason said, astonished. The question had come as a complete surprise.

"You and everyone else. That is changing now. I know some things about the lowlanders and I am going to learn more. I am going to raid the lowlands and you are coming with me. I can use some of this gunpowder. Prepare yourself. We leave at midday. You are the only one who knows it is not a simple hunting expedition, so talk of the matter only at the risk of your life."

"I would rather die than speak a word of this to anyone."

Jason returned to his *camach,* deep in thought, and instantly told Meta everything he had just learned.

"This sounds very strange," she said, hobbling to the fire, her muscles stiff from the beating she had undergone. "I am hungry and cannot make this fire burn."

Jason fanned the fire, and coughed and averted his head when he caught a lungful of pungent smoke. "I don't think you are using first-rate *morope* chips here. They have to be well dried to burn evenly. It sounded strange to me, too. How can he get down a vertical cliff over ten kilometers high? Yet he knows about gunpowder, and he certainly never found out about that here on the plateau." He coughed again then kicked sand over the fire. "Enough of that. You and Grif need something more nutritious than goat stew in any case. I'll crack out a couple of meal packs."

Meta picked up a war ax and stood by the entrance to make sure that Jason was not disturbed when he opened the lockbox. He took out the meal packs and unsealed them, then pointed to the radio.

"Report to Kerk at midnight. Let him know everything that is happening. You should be safe enough here, but if it looks like there will be any difficulty, tell him to pull you out."

"No. We will stay here until you return." She plunged her spoon into the food and ate hungrily. Grif took the other pack and Jason stood guard at the entrance during the meal.

"Put the empty cans into the lockbox until we find a safer spot to bury them. I wish there was more I could do."

"Don't worry about us. We know how to take care of ourselves," Meta told him firmly.

"Yes," Grif agreed, unsmiling. "This planet is very soft after Pyrrus. Only the food is bad."

Jason looked at them both, battered yet undefeated. He opened his mouth, then closed it because there was really nothing that he could say. He packed a leathern bag with the supplies he might need for the trip, extra clothing, and a microminiaturized transceiver that slipped into the hollow handle of his war ax. This and a short sword were his only weapons. He had tried using the laminated horn bows, but he was so improficient that he was better off not having one of the things around. Slinging a shield from his left arm, he waved good-bye and left.

When Jason rode up on his *morope,* he saw that a small force of less than 50 men had assembled for the expedition. They carried no extra equipment or supplies and it was obvious that it would not be a prolonged trip. Only after Jason had intercepted a number of cold glances did he realize that he was the only outsider there. All the others were either high-ranking officers and close associates of Temuchin or members of his own tribe.

"I can keep secrets, too," Jason told Ahankk, who rode close, scowling, but he received only a fine selection of grating curses in return. As soon as the warlord appeared, they rode off in a double column, following his lead.

It was hard riding and Jason was thankful for the weeks he had spent in the saddle. At first they started toward the foothills to the east, but as soon as they were hidden from sight of the camp and sure that they were not observed by stragglers, they turned and moved south at a ground-eating pace. The mountains rose up on all sides of them as they rode from valley to valley, climbing steadily. Jason, breathing through his fur neckpiece, could not believe that throat-hurting air could be so cold, yet it did not seem to bother anyone else.

They grabbed a quick, unheated meal at sunset, then kept on going. Jason could see the sense in this; he had almost frozen to the ground during their brief halt. They were in single file now. The trail was so narrow that Jason, like many of the others, dismounted to lead his *morope,* in an attempt to warm himself above the congealing point by the exertion. The cold light of the star-filled sky lit their way.

Coming to a junction of two valleys, Jason looked to his right, at the gray sea spreading out in the distance beyond the nearly vertical cliffs. Sea?! He stopped so suddenly that his *morope* trod on his heels and he had to jump aside to avoid being trampled.

No, it couldn't be the sea. They were in the middle of the continent. And too high up. Realization came late—he was looking at a sea rightly enough, the top of a sea of clouds. Jason watched until a turn in the trail took them from sight. The trail was dipping downward now as he knew it must. He halted his *morope* so that he could climb back into the saddle. Somewhere up ahead was the edge of the world.

Here the domain of the nomads ended at the continent-spanning cliff, a solid wall of rock reaching up from the plains below. Here also, was where the weather ended. The warm southern winds blowing north struck the cliff, were forced upward and condensed as clouds, to then bring their burden of water back to the land below as rain. Jason wondered if they ever saw the sun at all this close to the escarpment. A glistening dusting of snow in the hollows showed that severe storms pushed even over the top of this natural barrier.

As the trail dropped it passed through a narrow pass and, once inside, Jason saw a stone hut under an overhang of rock, where guards stood and stoically watched them pass. Whatever their destination was, it must be close. A short while later they halted and word was passed back to Jason to wait on Temuchin. He shuffled to the head of the procession as fast as his numbed muscles would permit.

Temuchin was chewing steadily on a resistant piece of dried meat, and Jason had to wait until he had washed this morsel down with some of the half-frozen *achadh*. The sky was lightening in the east and, by the traditional nomad test, it was almost dawn, the moment when a black goat's hair could be told from a white.

"Bring my *morope*," Temuchin commanded as he strode away. Jason grabbed the reins of the tired, snapping beast and dragged it after the warlord. Three officers followed after him. The trail took two more sharp turnings and opened out onto a broad ledge, the farther side of which was the sheer edge of the cliff. Temuchin walked over and stared down at white-massed clouds not far below. But it was the rusty chunk of machinery that fascinated Jason.

The most impressive part was the massive A frame that was seated deep into the living rock at the cliff's edge, projecting outward and overhanging the abyss below. This had been hand-forged, all eight meters of its length, and what a prodigious labor that must have been. It was stabilized with cross-brace rods and rested against a ridge of rock at the lip of the drop that raised it to a 45-degree angle. The entire frame was pitted and scratched with rust, although some attempt had been made to keep it greased. A length of flexible black material led over a pulley wheel at the point of the A and back through a hole in a buttress of rock behind. Aroused now by curiosity, Jason went around the rock to admire the device behind it.

In its own way, this engine, though smaller, was more spectacular than the supporting frame on the cliff. The black ropelike material came through the hole and wound around a drum. This drum, on an arm-thick shaft, was held to the back of the vertical rock face by four sturdy legs. It could obviously take an immense strain as there was nothing to uproot: all of the pressure would be carried directly to the rock face, seating the legs even more firmly. A meter-wide gear wheel, fitted to the end of the drum, meshed with a smaller pinion gear that could be turned by a long crank handle. This was apparently made of wood, but Jason did not pay much attention to the fact. A number of pawls and ratchets made sure that nothing could slip.

It did not take a mechanical genius to understand what the device was for. Jason turned to Temuchin, forcefully controlling the tendency for one eyebrow to lift, and said: "Is this the mechanism by which we are supposed to descend to the lowlands?"

The warlord seemed about as impressed by the machine as Jason was himself.

"It is. It does not appear to be the sort of thing one would usually risk one's life with, but we have no choice. The tribe which built and operated it, a branch of the stoat clan, have sworn that they used it often to raid the lowlands. They told many tales, and had wood and gunpowder to prove it. The survivors are here and they will operate the thing. They will be killed if there is any trouble. We will go first."

"That won't help us very much if something goes wrong."

"Man is born to die. Life consists only of a daily putting off of the inevitable."

Jason had no answer to this one. He looked up as, with pained cries, a group of men and squat women were driven down the hill toward the winch.

"Stand back and let them do their work," Temuchin ordered, and the soldiers instantly withdrew. "Watch them closely and if there is treachery or mistakes, kill them at once."

Thus encouraged, the stoat clansmen turned to their jobs. They appeared to know what they were doing. Some turned the handle while others adjusted the clanking pawls. One man even pulled himself out on the frame, far over the cliff's edge, to grease the pulley wheel on its end.

"I will go first," Temuchin said, slinging a heavy leather harness around his body under his arms.

"I hope that rope thing is long enough," Jason said, and instantly regretted it when Temuchin turned to glare at him.

"You will come next, after you have sent down my *morope*. See that it is blindfolded so it does not panic. Then you, then another *morope*, in that order. The *moropes* will be brought to the cliff only one at a time so they do not see what is happening to the others." He turned to the officers. "You have heard my orders."

Chanting in unison, the stoats turned the handle to wind the rope onto the drum, the pawls slowly clanking over. The pressure came on the harness but the rope stretched and thinned before Temuchin was lifted from the ground. Then his toes swung clear and he grabbed the rope as he swung out over the abyss, oscillating slowly up and down. When the bobbing had damped the operators reversed the motion and he slowly dropped from sight. Jason went to the lip and saw the warlord's figure get smaller and finally vanish into the woolly clouds below. A piece of rock broke loose under the pressure of Jason's toe and he stepped backward quickly.

Every hundred meters, more or less, the men slowed and worked cautiously as a blob appeared where two sections of the elastic rope were joined together. They turned the handle carefully until the knot had cleared the pulley, then went back to their normal operating speed. Men changed positions on the cranks without stopping so that the rope moved out and down continuously.

"What is this rope?" Jason asked one of the stoats who seemed to be supervising the operation, a greasy-haired individual whose only tooth appeared to be a yellowed fang that projected above his upper lip.

"Plant things, growing things—long with leaves. What you call them *mentri*—"

"Vines?" Jason guessed.

"Yah, vines. Big, hard to find. Grow down the cliff. Stretch and very strong."

"They had better be," Jason said, then pointed and grabbed the man as the vine rope suddenly began to bounce up and down. He wriggled in Jason's numbing grip and hurried to explain.

"All right, good. That means the man is down, let the vine go; it bounces up and down. Bring up!" he added, shouting at the crank operators.

Jason loosened his grip on the man, who moved quickly away rubbing the injured spot. It made sense; when Temuchin had let go of the rope, the sudden decrease in weight on the cable would have caused it to oscillate, though not too much. His weight was surely only a small part of the overall weight of that massive length of cable.

"The *morope* next," Jason ordered when the hook and sling were finally hauled up to the clifftop once more. The beast was led forward, blinking its red little eyes suspiciously at the brink ahead. The stoats efficiently fitted a broad harness about its body, then covered its eyes with a leather sack pulled down tight and tied under its jaw. After the hook had been attached, the *morope* stood patiently until it began to feel its weight coming off the ground. Then, panic-stricken, it began to struggle, its claws raking grooves in the dirt and cracking chips from the stone. But the operators had experience with this as well. The man whom Jason had been talking to ran up with a long-handled sledgehammer and, with a practiced swing, hit a mark on the bag, which must have been right above the creature's eyes. It went instantly limp. With much shouting and heaving, the dead weight was swung clear of the ground and started over the edge.

"Hit just right," the man said. "Too hard, kill it. Not hard enough, it wake up soon and jump around, break rope."

"Well hit," Jason said, and hoped that Temuchin was not standing directly below.

Nothing appeared to be wrong and the rope vine clanked out endlessly. Jason found himself dozing off and stepped farther back from the edge. Suddenly there were shouts and he opened his eyes to see the rope jerking back and forth, heaving with great bounces. It even jumped from the pulley and one of the men had to climb up to reseat it.

"Did it break?" Jason asked the nearest operator.

"No, good, all fine. Just bounce big when the *morope* come off."

This was understandable. When the greater weight of the large beast was removed the elastic vine would do a great deal of heaving about. The motion had damped and they were bringing it up now. Jason realized that he was next and was aware of a definite dropping sensation in his stomach. He would have given a great deal not to suffer a descent on this iron-age elevator.

The beginning alone was bad enough. He realized that his feet were dragging free of the rock as the tension came on the vine and he automatically scratched with his toes, trying to stay on the solid mountaintop. He did not succeed. The wheel turned another clank and he was airborne, swinging out from the cliff and above the cloud-bottomed drop. He took one look down between his twirling feet, then riveted his attention straight ahead. The clifftop slowly rose above his head and the grim-faced nomads vanished from sight. He tried to think of something funny to say but, for once, was completely out of humorous ideas. Rotating slowly as he dropped, he could, for the first time, see the continent-spanning cliff sweeping away on both sides and could appreciate the incredible vastness of it. The air was clear and dry with the early-morning sun lighting up the rock face so that every detail could be plainly seen.

Below was the white sea of the clouds, washing and breaking against the base of the continentwide cliff. The jagged gray mountains that could be seen rising behind it were dwarfed by comparison. Against the immensity of this cliff, Jason felt like a spider on a thread, drifting down an endless wall, moving yet seemingly suspended forever at the same spot because the scale was so large. As he rotated, he looked first right, then left, and in each direction the grained escarpment ran straight to the horizon, still erect and skytouching where it dimmed and vanished.

Jason could see now that the point on the cliff above, where the winch had been placed, was much lower than the rest of the stone barrier. He assumed that there was a matching rise in the ground below, for at any other spot along the cliff the length of the vine rope would not have been strong enough to support its own weight, exclusive of any added burden. The clouds rose up steadily below him until he felt he could almost reach out and kick them. Then the first damp tendrils of the fog touched him, and a few moments later the clouds closed around and he was alone in the gray world of nothingness.

The last thing that he expected to do, dangling at the end of the kilometer-long bobbing strand, was to fall asleep. But he did. The rocking motion, the fatigue of the day and night ride, and the blankness of his surroundings all contributed their bit. He relaxed, his head dropped, and in a few moments he was snoring lustily.

He awoke when the rain began trickling inside his collar and down his back. Though the air was much warmer he shivered and pulled his collar tight. It was one of those drizzling, dripping all-day rains that seem never to end. Through it he could make out the streaked face of the cliff still moving by, and when he bent and looked between his toes, something indeterminate was visible below. What? People? Friend or foe? If the locals knew about the winch that was out of sight in the clouds above, they might possibly keep a massacre party waiting here. He swung the war ax out of his belt and slipped the thong about his wrist. Individual boulders were standing out below, set in a drab field of rain-soaked grass. The air was humid and sticky.

"Unbuckle that harness and be ready to let go of it," Temuchin ordered, coming into sight as he stalked across the field below. "What is the ax for?"

"Anyone other than you who might be waiting," Jason answered, securing the ax in his belt again and working at the leather harness. A sudden stretch on the flexible rope lowered him to within feet of the grass.

"Let go!" Temuchin ordered, and Jason did, unfortunately just as the rope started up again. He rose a few feet and, for one instant, was suspended in midair, unmoving and unsupported, before he fell heavily. He rolled when he hit and jammed the hilt of his sword painfully into his ribs, but was otherwise undamaged. There was a quick *whoosh* above them as the rope, relieved of its burden, contracted and snapped upward.

"This way," Temuchin said, turning and walking off while Jason struggled to his feet. The grass was slippery and wet, and mud squelched up around his boots when he walked. Temuchin went around a pillar of rock and pointed up at its ten-meter-high summit.

"You can watch from there to see when your *morope* arrives. Wake me then. My beast is grazing on this side. Be sure it does not stray." Without waiting for an answer, Temuchin lay down in a relatively dry spot in the lee of the rock and pulled a flap of leather over his face.

Sure, Jason said to himself, just the job I wanted in the rain. A nice wet rock and a tremendous view of absolutely nothing. He pulled himself up the steeply slanted stone and sat down on its rounded peak.

Thoughts of sleep were gone now; even sitting comfortably was impossible on the knobby hardness, so Jason writhed and suffered. The silence was disturbed only by the endless susurration of the falling rain, broken by an occasional trumpet of satiated joy from the *morope* as it enjoyed the unaccustomed banquet. From time to time the sheets of rain shifted, opening up a view down the hillside of grass pastures, with quick rivulets and dark-stained stones pushing up through the greenery. Ages of rain and damp discomfort passed before Jason heard hoarse breathing overhead and could make out a dim form dropping down slowly through the haze. He slid to the ground and Temuchin was awake and alert the instant Jason touched his shoulder.

There was something awe-inspiringly impressive about the great bulk of the limp *morope,* apparently unsupported, that swung down over their heads. Its legs were beginning to twitch and its breathing grew faster.

"Quickly," Temuchin ordered. "It is beginning to awake."

A sudden bounce dropped the *morope* lower and they grabbed for it, but the return contraction pulled it out of reach again. It was beginning to turn its head and was attempting to lift its neck. The next drop brought it almost to the ground and Temuchin leaped for its neck, grabbing it and hanging on, his added weight pulling the foreparts of the creature to the damp ground.

"Unbuckle it!" he shouted.

Jason dived for the straps. The buckles were easy-opening, being released by throwing back an iron handle. It would have been impossible to open normal buckles against the tension of the taut, stretched cable. The *morope* was beginning to thrash about when Jason threw open the last buckle—and leaped clear. The contraction of the elastic cable pulled the harness out from under the *morope*, raking its flesh so that it bellowed with pain, half flipping it over. The jangling harness, with a departing hiss, instantly vanished from sight in the rain.

The rest of the day settled into routine. Now that Jason knew what to do, Temuchin proved himself an experienced field soldier by taking advantage of the lull to catch up on his sleep. Jason wished he could join him, but he had been left in charge and he knew better than to try and avoid the responsibility. Soldiers and mounts dropped out of the rain-filled sky at regular intervals and Jason organized the operation. Some of the soldiers watched the field of grazing *moropes* while others stood by to land the new arrivals. The rest slept, except for Ahankk, who, in Jason's opinion, seemed to have fine vision and who therefore occupied the lookout position. Twenty-five *moropes* and 26 men were down before the end suddenly came.

The work party were half dozing, depressed by the endless rain, when Ahankk's hoarse call jabbed them to instant awareness. Jason looked up and had a brief vision of a dark form hurtling down, apparently right at them. This was just an illusion of the mist for the *morope* grew in size and struck the landing spot, plunging to the ground like a falling rock and hitting with a sickening, explosive sound. A great length of rope fell on and around it, the end landing not far from Jason and the soldiers.

There was no need to call Temuchin. He had been awakened by the shout and the sound of impact. He turned away after a single glance at the bloody, deformed corpse of the beast.

"Tie four *moropes* to the harness. I want it dragged away from here, along with that rope." While his lieutenants jumped to obey him, he turned to Jason. "This is why I sent a man first, then a *morope*. Two of the men will have to ride double. The stoats warned me that the rope broke after use, and that there was no possible way to tell when this would be. It usually breaks under a heavy load."

"But has been known to snap when letting a man down. I can see why you went first. You'd make a good gambler, warlord," Jason said.

"I am a good gambler," Temuchin told him calmly, running a

scrap of oiled leather over his rusting sword. "There is just one rope in reserve, so I left orders to halt the drop if this one should break. A new rope will be in place by the time we return and a guard will be lowered and waiting for us. Now—we ride."

10

"Is it permitted to ask where we are going?" Jason said as the war party moved slowly down the grassy hillside. They were spread out in a wide crescent with Temuchin and Jason at the center, with the *moropes* dragging the carcass of their fellow close by.

"No," Temuchin said, which pretty well took care of that.

It was a smooth descent, as though the plains below were rising up to meet the escarpment, now invisible in the rain behind them. Grass and small shrubs covered the hill, cut through by streams and freshets. As they went lower, these joined to form good-size brooks. The *moropes* splashed through them, snorting at the presence of such prodigious amounts of water. And the temperature rose. Jason and the others opened the ties that sealed their clothing and he was happy to tilt his helm back so the fine drizzle fell onto his overheated face. He wiped away the layer of grease that had covered his skin and began to think about the possibilities of bathing again.

The hill ended suddenly in a ragged cliff above a foam-flecked river. Temuchin ordered the corpse of the fallen animal and the festoons of rope dragged forward to the brink, where a squad of soldiers heaved and tipped it over the edge. It hit the water with a showering splash and, with a last, almost flippant wave of one claw-studded paw, it was whirled away and vanished from sight. Without hesitation Temuchin turned their course southwest along the river's bank. It was obvious that he had been forewarned of this obstacle, and the march continued at its kilometer-eating pace.

By late afternoon the rain had stopped and the character of the country had completely changed. Patches of brush and wood dotted the plain and, not far ahead, an extensive forest was visible under the lowering sky. As soon as Temuchin saw it, he halted the march

"Sleep," he ordered. "We move again at nightfall."

Jason did not have to be ordered twice. He was off his mount while the others were still stopping; he curled up on the grass and closed his eyes. The *morope's* reins were tied about his ankle. After the skullbanging, the grazing, drinking and galloping, the creature was happy to rest, too. It stretched full length on the ground, its chin extended in the rich grass, from which it pulled a clump to hold in its mouth while it slept.

The sky was dark, but to Jason it felt as though he had just closed his eyes when the steel fingers sank into his leg and shook him awake.

"We ride," Ahankk said. Jason sat up, his stiff muscles creaking with the effort, and rubbed the granules of sleep from his eyes. He had washed out the dregs of *achadh* from his drinking skin earlier in the day and filled it with fresh stream water. He drank his fill and then sprayed a goodly quantity over his face and head. There was no water shortage in this land.

They rode out in a single file, Temuchin leading and Jason one but last from the rear. Ahankk rode as rearguard, and it was obvious from his hot gaze and ready sword that Jason was what he was guarding. The exploring party was now a war party and the nomads needed no aid and expected only interference from a wandering jongleur. He was safe in the rear, where he could not cause any trouble. If he did, he would be killed instantly. Jason rode quietly, trying to generate an aura of innocent compliance with the set of his shoulders.

There was no sound, even when they entered the woods. The padded feet of each *morope* fell in easy rhythm in the tracks of the preceding beast. Leather did not creak and metal did not rattle. They were spectral forms moving through rain-sodden silence. The trees opened up and Jason was aware that they had entered a clearing. A dim light was visible in the near distance and, by glancing out of the corners of his eyes at it, Jason could make out the dark form of a building.

Still silent, the soldiers had made a smooth right turn and were moving on the building in a single line. They were no more than a few meters from the structure when a rectangle of light suddenly appeared as a door was opened. A man, silhouetted sharply against the light, stood in the opening.

"Save him—kill the rest!" Temuchin shouted, and the attackers leaped forward before the words were out of his mouth.

Chance put Jason near the man in the open doorway, yet everyone else seemed to get there first. The man leaped back with a hoarse cry, trying to close the door, but three men hit it at once, driving it open and sending him back. All three of them remained flat on the floor where they had fallen, and Jason, who had just slid from his *morope's* back, saw why. Five more of the men, two kneeling and three standing, had stopped at the open doorway with drawn bows. Two, three times they fired and the air hissed and thrummed from their bowstrings and the arrows' flight. Jason reached them as they stopped the firing and charged into the building. He was right behind them, but the fight was over.

The barnlike room, lit by a single spluttering candle, was filled to overflowing with death. Toppled tables and chairs made a ragged jumble into which were mixed the dead and dying. A gray-haired man with an arrow in his chest moaned and stirred; a soldier bent over and severed his throat with a chop of his ax. There were crashes as the building was broken into from the rear by the rest of the nomads, who had surrounded it. Escape was impossible.

One man was still alive, still fighting, the man who had stood in the doorway. He was tall and shock-headed, dressed in rough homespun, and he laid about him with an immense quarterstaff. It would have been simple enough to kill him—an arrow would have done it—but the nomads wanted to capture him and had never encountered this simple weapon before. One already sat on the floor, clutching his leg, and a second was disarmed even as Jason watched, his sword clanging into a corner. The lowlander had his back to the wall and was unapproachable from the front.

Jason could do something about this. He looked around swiftly and saw a rack of simple farm implements against the wall. One of these was a long-handled shovel that looked as if it would do. He grabbed it in both hands and banged the center down hard against his knee. It bent but did not break. Well-seasoned wood.

"I'll take him!" Jason shouted, running to the fight. He was an instant late because the quarterstaff landed square on the swordsman's arm, snapping the bones and sending the man's weapon flying. Jason took his place and swung the shovel at the lowlander's ankles.

The man quickly spun the end of his staff down to counter the blow, and when the weapons crashed together, Jason used the force of impact to reverse his direction of motion, bringing the handle end of the shovel around toward the lowlander's neck. The man parried this blow in time as well, but in doing so he had to step aside, away from the wall, and this was all that was needed.

Ahankk, who had come in with Jason, swung the flat of his ax against the man's skull and he dropped, unconscious, to the floor

Jason threw away the shovel and picked up the fallen quarterstaff. It was a good two meters long, made of tough and flexible wood bound about with iron rings.

"What is that?" Temuchin asked. He had watched the end of the brief battle.

"A quarterstaff. A simple but effective weapon."

"And you know how to use it? You told me you knew nothing about the lowlands." His face was expressionless as he talked, but there was a glow like an inner fire in his eyes. Jason realized that he had better make the explanation good or he would join the rest of the corpses.

"I still know nothing about the lowlands. But I learned to handle this weapon when I was a child. Everyone in my . . . tribe uses them." He did not bother to add that the tribe he was talking about was not the Pyrrans, but the agrarian community on Porgorstor-saand, far across the galaxy, where he had grown up. With rigid class and social distinctions, the only real weapons were borne by the soldiers and the aristocracy. But you can't deny a man a stick when he lives in a forest, so quarterstaffs were in common use, and at one time Jason had been proficient in the use of this uncompli-cated yet decisive weapon.

Temuchin turned away, satisfied for the moment, while Jason spun the staff experimentally. It was nicely weighted.

The nomads were efficiently looting the building, which appeared to be a farm of some kind. The livestock were kept under the same roof and all of the animals had been butchered when the soldiers had broken in. When Temuchin said kill, he meant kill. Jason looked at the carnage but would permit himself no change of expression, even when one of the men, looking for booty, turned over a wooden chest. There was a baby behind it, perhaps thrust there at the last minute by one of the women now dead upon the floor, and the soldier skewered it unemotionally with a quick stab of his sword.

"Bind that one and bring him," Temuchin ordered, brushing the dirt from a piece of cooked meat that had been knocked to the floor in the attack, then taking a bite from it.

Swift, tight turns of leather secured his wrists behind his back; then the prisoner was propped against the wall. When three buckets of water dashed into his face had failed to bring him around, Temuchin heated the tip of his dagger blade in a burning candle and pressed it into the soft flesh of the man's arm. He moaned and tried to pull away, then opened his eyes, which swam blearily with the aftereffects of the blow.

"Do you speak the in-between tongue?" Temuchin asked. When the man answered something incomprehensible, the warlord struck him, carefully, on the purple and enflamed wound made by the earlier blow. The farmer screamed and tried to get away, but still answered in the same unknown language.

"The fool cannot speak," Temuchin said.

"Let me," one of his officers said, stepping forward. "What he talks is not unlike the tongue of the hill-serpent clan in the far east near the sea."

Communication was established. With laborious rephrasings and repeatings, the message was communicated to the farmer that he would be killed if he did not help them. No promises were made for what would happen if he did, but the lowlander was not in the best of bargaining positions. He quickly agreed.

"Tell him we wish to go to the place of the soldiers," Temuchin said, and their prisoner bobbed his head in quick agreement. Understandable. A peasant in a primitive economy has little love for the tax-collecting, oppressing soldiers. He babbled in his hurry to convey information. The translator interpreted his words.

"He says that there are many soldiers there, two hands, perhaps five hands of them. They are armed and the place is strong. They have something else, some kind of weapons, but I cannot make out what the creature is talking about."

"Five hands of men," Temuchin said, smiling and looking out of the corners of his eyes. "I am frightened."

The nomads nearby hooted with laughter and struck each other on the back, then hurried to tell the others. Jason did not think it a great witticism, but he could find no fault with the men's morale.

A sudden silence passed over them as two of the soldiers slowly approached, supporting and half dragging one of their comrades. The man hopped on one leg, fighting to keep the other foot clear of the ground, and when he raised his pain-twisted face to Temuchin Jason recognized him as the one injured in the battle with the quarterstaff-wielding peasant.

"What has happened?" Temuchin asked, all traces of laughter gone from his voice.

"My leg . . ." the man, a minor chieftain, answered hoarsely

"Let me see," the warlord ordered, and the soldier's boot was quickly cut open.

The man's knee had been shattered brutally, the kneecap fractured so badly that pieces of white bone had penetrated the skin. Slow trickles of blood seeped from the wound. The soldier must be suffering incredible pain, yet he made no outcry. Jason knew that would take skilled surgery and bone replacement to enable the man to walk again, and wondered what his fate would be on this barbarian world. He found out quickly.

"You cannot walk, you cannot ride, you cannot be a soldier," Temuchin said.

"I know that," the man said, straightening and throwing off the hands of the men who helped him. "But if I am to die, I wish to die in combat and be buried with my thumbs. I cannot hold a sword to fight the demons in the underworld if I have no thumbs."

"That is the way it will be,." Temuchin said, drawing his sword. "You have been a good soldier and a good friend and I wish you success in your battles to come. I will fight you myself for it is an honor to be sent below by a warlord."

The battle was no ritual, and the wounded man did well despite his injured leg. But Temuchin fought so that the other had to turn toward his wounded side, but he could not, so a quick thrust caught him under the ribs and he died.

"There was another wounded man," Temuchin said, still holding his bloody sword. The soldier with the broken arm stepped forward, the arm in a sling.

"The arm will get better," he said. "The skin did not break. I can fight and ride, though I cannot shoot a bow."

Temuchin hesitated a moment before he answered. "We need every man that we have. Do those things and you will return with us to the camp. We will ride as soon as this man is buried." He turned to Jason.

"Ride in front with me," he ordered, "and do not make any stupid noise." He apparently did not think much of Jason's soldiering ability, and Jason did not feel like correcting him. "This place of the soldiers is what we are looking for. The stoat clan has raided this country in the past, but with no more than two or three men at a time as to send more *moropes* down is dangerous. They avoid the soldiers and attack these farms. But they have fought the soldiers and it is from them that I learned of the gunpowder. They killed one soldier and took his gunpowder, but when I put fire to it, it merely burned. Yet the stoats swear that it blew up, and others have said the same and I do not doubt them. We will capture the gunpowder and you will make it blow up."

"Take me to it," Jason said, "and I'll show you how it's done."

They blundered through the forest until well after midnight before their prisoner tearfully admitted that he had lost his way in the darkness. Temuchin beat him until he howled with pain then, reluctantly, ordered the men to rest until morning. The rain had begun again and they sought what comfort they could find under the dripping trees.

Jason had a bad taste in his mouth. It wasn't the dung-cooked food this time or the filthy *achadh,* but the massacre at the farm. Get close to the trees and you don't see the forest. He had been living with the nomads, living like a nomad, and had become part of their culture. They were interesting people and, since moving to Temuchin's camp, he had found them a warm, if not exactly the galaxy's most humorous, people, and at least it was possible to get along with them. They were honest in their own way and respected their own code of laws. They were also cold-blooded murderers and killers. It did not matter that they killed according to their own sets of values. This did not change the situation. Jason could still see the sword thrusting into the infant and he moved uncomfortably on the sodden leaves.

He had been among the trees and forgotten the forest. He had forgotten that these people had slaughtered the first mining expedition and would relish nothing better than doing the same to any other off-worlders that they met. He was a spy in their midst and he was working for their complete downfall.

That was more like it. He could live with himself as long as it was constantly clear that he was just playing a role, not enjoying himself, and that all this masquerading had some purpose. He had to wreck the social structure of these nomads and see to it that the Pyrrans opened their mines in safety.

Alone in the wet night, chilled and depressed, it looked like a very dim possibility. The hell with that. He twisted and attempted to get comfortable and go to sleep but the images of the massacre kept interfering.

In your own way, Temuchin, you are a great man, he thought. But I am going to have to destroy you. The rain fell remorselessly.

At first light they moved out again, a silent column through the fog-shrouded forest. The captive peasant chattered his teeth in fear until he recognized a clearing and a path. Smiling and happy now, he showed them the correct way. A wad of his clothing was stuffed into his mouth so that he could not give any alarm.

A crackling of broken twigs sounded ahead and there was the sound of voices.

The column stopped with instant silence and a sword was pressed against the prisoner's neck. Nothing moved. The voices ahead grew louder and two men came around a turning of the trail. They walked two, three paces before they were aware of the motionless, silent forms so close to them in the fog. Before they could act, a half dozen arrows had snuffed out their lives.

"What are those stick things they carry?" Temuchin said to Jason.

Jason slid to the ground and turned the nearest corpse over with his boot. The man wore a lightweight steel breastplate and a steel helm; other than that, he was unarmored, dressed in coarse cloth and leather. He had a short sword in his belt and still clutched in his hand what could only have been a primitive musket.

"It is what is called a 'gun,' " Jason said, picking it up. "It uses gunpowder to throw a piece of metal that can kill. The gunpowder and metal are put down this tube here. When this little lever on the bottom is pulled, this stone throws a spark down into the gunpowder, which blows up and shoots the metal out."

When Jason looked up, he saw that every man within hearing had his bow and arrow aimed at his throat. He put the weapon down carefully and pulled two leather bags from the dead soldier's belt and looked inside of them. "Just what I thought. Bullets and cloth patches here—and this is gunpowder." He handed the second bag up to Temuchin, who looked into and smelt it.

"There is not very much here," he said.

"It doesn't take very much, not for these guns. But there is sure to be a bigger supply in the place where these men came from."

"That is what I thought," Temuchin said, and he waved the raiding party on as soon as the arrows had been retrieved and the bodies relieved of their thumbs and rolled aside. He took both muskets himself.

Less than a ten-minute ride along the trail brought them to the edge of a clearing, a large meadow that flanked a smoothly flowing river. At the water's edge stood a squat and solid stone building with a high tower in its center. Two figures were visible at the top of the tower.

"The prisoner says that this is the place of the soldiers," said the officer who had been translating.

"Ask him if he knows how many entrances there are," Temuchin ordered.

"He says that he does not know."

"Kill him."

A swift sword thrust eliminated the prisoner and his corpse was dumped into the brush.

"There is only that one small door on this side and the narrow holes through which bows and the gun thing may be fired,"

Temuchin said. "I do not like it. I want two men to look at the other sides of this building and tell me what they see. What is that round thing above the wall?" he asked Jason.

"I don't know—but I can guess. It could be a gun, the same as these only much bigger, that would throw a large piece of metal."

"I thought so, too," Temuchin said, and narrowed his eyes in thought. He issued orders to two men, who turned and rode back along the trail.

The scouts dismounted and vanished silently into the underbrush. These men, who had learned to conceal themselves in the apparently barren plains, could disappear completely in the wooded cover. With a predator's patience, the warriors, still mounted, waited silently for the scouts to come back.

"It is as I thought," Temuchin said when they had returned and reported to him. "This place is well made and is built only for fignting. There is one more door, the same size on the other side by the water. If we wait until nightfall, we can take the place easily, but I do not wish to wait. Can you fire this gun?" he asked Jason.

Jason nodded reluctantly, because he already had a very good idea what Temuchin had in mind—even before he saw the two men returning with one of the dead soldiers. Everyone fought in Temuchin's horde, even lute-playing gunpowder experts. Jason tried to think of a way out of this fix, but he could not, so he volunteered before he was drafted. It made no difference at all to Temuchin. He wanted the gate open and Jason was the best man for the job.

By rearranging the soldier's uniform, he managed to conceal the arrow holes and most of the blood, then he rubbed mud over the rest of the bloodstains to disguise them. A fine rain was beginning to fall and this would be a help. While he was putting on the uniform, Jason called for the officer who had been translating and had him repeat over and over again the simple phrase "Open—quickly!" in the local tongue, until Jason felt he had it right. Nothing complicated. If they insisted on conversation before they let him in, he was as good as dead.

"You understand what you are to do?" Temuchin asked.

"Simple enough. I come up to that gate from downriver, while the rest of you wait at the edge of the forest upriver. I tell them to open up. They open up. I go in and do my best to see that the gate stays open until you and the rest arrive."

"We will be very quick."

"I know that, but I'm going to be very alone." Jason had one of the soldiers hold his helmet over the pan of the musket while Jason blew out the possibly damp gunpowder. He did not want a misfire with his single shot. He shook fresh powder into the pan, then wrapped a piece of leather around to keep it dry. He pointed to the gun.

"This thing will fire only once for I'll have no time to reload. And I don't think much of this government-issue short sword. So, if you don't mind too much, I would like to borrow back my Pyrran knife."

Temuchin merely nodded and passed it over. Jason threw away the sword and slipped the knife into his belt in its place. The helmet smelled of rank sweat, but it rode low on his head, which was fine. He wanted his face concealed as much as possible.

"Go now," Temuchin ordered, irritated at the delay the donning of the disguise had caused. Jason smiled coldly and turned and walked away into the woods.

Before he had gone 50 meters he was soaked to the waist by the dense, waterlogged underbrush. This was the least of his troubles. Pushing his way through the sodden forest, he wondered how he had become involved in this latest bit of madness. Gunpowder, that was the reason. He cursed loudly and fluently, then peered out at the fortified building, now barely visible through the falling rain. Another 20 meters should do it. He pushed on, then left the shelter of the trees and walked ahead until he reached the riverbank. The water swirled by, laden with mud, and the rain spattered onto its surface, making an endless series of conjoining rings. He wanted to check the powder in the pan, but knew it was wiser not to. Do it, that's all, do it. Lowering his head he trudged toward the building, just visible through the rain.

If the men in the watchtower were looking at him, they gave no sign. Jason plodded closer, looking up under the edge of the helmet, the gun clutched across his chest. Now he was close enough to see the crumbled mortar between the roughly cut stones and the heavy bolts that studded the wood of the door ahead. He was close to the wall when one of the soldiers leaned out of the tower and called down to him incomprehensible words. Jason waved and trudged on.

When the man called again, Jason waved and shouted "Open!" in what he hoped was the correct accent. He made his voice as harsh as possible to disguise any inaccuracies. Then he was against the wall and out of sight of the men in the tower, who were still calling out to him. The door, solid and unmoving was just before him. Nothing happened, and the tension tightened another notch. There was a scratching sound and he saw a gun barrel coming out of a narrow window to the right of the door.

"Open—quickly!" he shouted and hammered on the door. "Open!" He pressed flat against the door so the gun could not bear on him and hammered again with the butt of the musket.

There were sounds inside the fortified building, voices and moving about, but the pulse of Jason's blood sounded even louder in his ears, thudding like a hidden drum, with a measureless time between each beat. Could he get away? Both sides would shoot him if he tried. But he could not stay here, powerless and trapped. As he raised his musket to hammer on the door again, he heard the rattle of heavy chains inside and a grating sound remarkably like that made by the sliding of an iron bolt. He cocked the flintlock through the protecting cover and released one side so that the leather could be pulled quickly away. The instant the door started to open he crashed his shoulder against it with all of his weight and pushed through, slamming it wide as hard as he could.

He kept moving, through the short archway and into the open square that the building was built around. Out of the corner of his eye he was barely aware of the man who had opened the door, now crushed by it, slumping to the ground. That was all he had time to notice because he saw that he was about to be killed.

Strike hard and fast and do not stop—that was what the nomads did and they were right. One soldier with a sword in his hand stood to the side, while directly in front of Jason were a number of others with guns leveled and ready to fire. Before the surprised men could shoot, Jason shouted and dived into their midst. Just before he hit them he pulled the trigger and was pleasantly surprised when the musket went off with a hollow boom and one of the men clutched his chest and fell. That was the last fact that Jason remembered clearly. He left the ground in a blocking dive, swinging the gun barrel and butt as he did, and crashed into them.

It was very confusing. After the first impact, he threw the gun at a soldier, kicked another one as he pulled out the heavy knife and swung it wildly. One man fell on him, dead or wounded, and Jason clutched his body for protection and lunged out with the knife again and again.

There was a sharp pain in his leg, then in his side and arm, and a loud ringing sounded in his head. He swung the knife in an arc and realized that he was falling. The ground felt good and so did the weight of the man lying, unmoving, on top of him. Above him the officer appeared, wild-eyed and raging, stabbing down with his sword. Jason parried it almost contemptuously with the knife, then stabbed upward to sink his blade in just above the man's groin. Blood spurted and the officer screamed and fell, and Jason had to push the body aside to see. By the time he did this, the quick battle had been decided.

The first of Temuchin's soldiers arrived, plunging headlong through the gate. He must have ridden at full speed toward the opening and dived from his saddle as the beast turned away. It was Temuchin himself, Jason realized, as the red-maned barbarian roared and swung his sword to cut down two attacking soldiers. After that, it was all over but the mopping up.

Once the immediate dangers had been cleared from around him, Jason stumbled over and dropped with his back against the wall. The ringing in his head ebbed away to a dull buzzing, and when he took his helmet off, he found an immense dent in its side. But at least there seemed to be no matching dent in his head. He touched his fingers to the sore spot on his skull, then examined them carefully. No blood. But there was enough on his side and dripping down his leg to make up for it. A shallow cut in his hip, just under the half armor, had produced a sopping amount of blood, though the wound itself was superficial, as was the slice in his arm. The wound in his leg had bled only slightly, although it was the more serious of the two, a deep stab wound in his thigh muscles. It hurt, yet he could walk; he had no intention of being exterminated for being found wanting like the soldier at the farm. There were some strips of sterilized suede in his saddlebags, for bandaging, but the blood would just have to drip until he got to them.

From the moment when Temuchin dived through the doorway there had been no slightest doubt as to the outcome of the battle. The garrison soldiers had never before faced an enemy to match the barbarous fiends who now fell upon them. The muskets were more of a hindrance than a help, because the bows fired far faster and more accurately than the clumsy, sightless muzzle-loaders. Some soldiers fled and some stood and fought, but the outcome was the same in either case. They were slaughtered. The screams grew fainter and more distant as the survivors tried to escape into the building.

Blood mixed with rain in the sodden courtyard and there were bodies heaped on every side. A single nomad lay slumped in the doorway where a bullet had stopped him, and he appeared to be the only casualty suffered by the raiders. A motion caught Jason's eye and he saw a soldier raise his head above the top of the watchtower where he had been hiding. Something twanged sharply and an arrow sank into the man's eyesocket; he dropped back out of sight more permanently this time.

There were no more groans or appeals for mercy: the fort had been taken. The nomads moved silently among the corpses, bending to their grisly amputation ritual. Temuchin came from one of the doorways, his sword red and dripping, and waved one of his men to the huddled collection of bodies near the gate that they had forced.

"Three of these belong to the jongleur," he said. "The rest of the thumbs are mine." The soldier bowed and took out his dagger. Temuchin turned to Jason. "There are rooms in here with many things. Find the gunpowder."

Jason stood up, a lot faster than he really wanted to, and realized that he still held the bloody knife. He wiped it on the clothing of the nearest corpse and held it out to Temuchin, who took it without a word, then turned and went back into the building. Jason followed, trying vainly to walk without hobbling.

Ahankk and another officer were guarding the door of a low-ceilinged storeroom. The nomads were looting the bodies and the rest of the fortress, but were not permitted here. Jason pushed by and stopped just inside the doorway. There were baskets of lead bullets, fist-sized cannon balls, extra muskets and swords, and a number of squat barrels sealed with wooden plugs.

"Those have the right look," Jason said, pointing, then put up his arm to stop Temuchin when he started forward. "Don't walk in here. See those gray grains on the floor near the open keg? That looks very much like spilled gunpowder and it can catch fire when you walk on it. Let me sweep it up before anyone else comes in here."

Bending over sent a dagger of pain through his side and leg which Jason did his best to ignore. Using a bunched-up piece of cloth, he made a clean path across the room. The open barrel did contain gunpowder. He let the rough granules slide back through the hole, then pushed home the bung. Picking the barrel up as gently as he could, he carried it over and gave it to Ahankk. "Don't drop this, bang it, set fire to it or let it get wet. And send down"—he counted quickly—"nine men for the rest of the gunpowder. Tell them what I just told you."

Ahankk turned away and there was a crashing explosion outside followed by a distant boom. Jason jumped to the window and saw that a big bite had been taken out of the watchtower. Fragments of stone dropped into the mud and a cloud of dust was soaked up by the rain. The walls vibrated with the impact and the distant explosion sounded again. A nomad ran in through the gate, shouting loudly in his own tongue.

"What is he saying?" Jason asked.

Temuchin clenched his fists. "Many soldiers coming. They are firing a large gun that makes that noise. Many hands of soldiers, more than he can count."

11

There was no panic and scarcely any excitement. War was war, and the strange environment, the rain, the novel weapons—none of this could affect either the barbarians' calm or their fighting ability. Men who attack spaceships have only contempt for muzzle-loading cannon.

Ahankk took charge of the detail to carry the gunpowder, while Temuchin himself went to the battered watchtower to see what kind of force was attacking. Another cannon ball hit the wall and bullets hummed by like lethal bees while he stood there, unmoving, until he had seen enough. He leaned over and shouted orders down to his men.

Jason trailed after the men who were carrying the gunpowder, and when he emerged, he discovered that the warlord was the only other living person left inside the fort.

"Through that door," Temuchin ordered, pointing to the gate that opened onto the riverbank. "The ones who come cannot see that side yet, and all the *moropes* are there and behind this building. All of you with the gunpowder mount up and, when I signal the charge, you will go at once to the trees. The rest of us will delay the soldiers and then join you."

"How many men do you think are attacking?" Jason asked, as the gunpowder bearers hurried out.

"Many. Two hands times the count of a man, perhaps more. Go with the gunpowder, the attack is close." It was, too. Bullets splattered against the wall and spanged in through the firing slits. The roar of attacking voices sounded just outside.

The count of a man, Jason thought, hopping and hobbling to his *morope,* which was being held outside. All of a man's fingers and toes, twenty. And a hand times that would be a hundred, two hands two hundred. And their party numbered 23 at the most, if no more of the men had been killed during the last attack. Ten men, each to carry a barrel of gunpowder, with Jason along as technical adviser, left 13 lancers for the attack. Thirteen against a couple of hundred. Good barbarian odds.

Events moved fast after that. Jason barely had time to haul himself into the saddle before the gunpowder party wheeled away, and he made a tardy rearguard. They reached the back of the building just as the first attackers appeared. The remaining 13 riders charged out and the victorious roar of the foot soldiers turned instantly into mingled cries of shock and pain. Jason stole one glance over his shoulder and saw the cannon upended, men fleeing in all directions, while the *moropes* and their bloodthirsty riders cut a swathe of death through the ranks. Then the trees were before him and he had to avoid the whipping branches.

They waited just inside the screen of the woods. Within a minute there was the *thud-thud* of galloping *moropes* and seven of them plunged through the sodden brush. One of the beasts was carrying two riders. Their numbers were decreasing with every encounter.

"Go on," Temuchin ordered. "Follow the trail back the way we came. We will stay here and slow down any who try to follow."

As Jason and the powder team left, the survivors were dismounting and taking cover at the edge of the open field. It would take a determined attack to press home against the deadly arrows that would emerge from the obscuring forest.

Jason did not enjoy the ride. He had not dared to bring his medikit, though he wished now that he had taken this risk. Neither had he ever before tried to bandage two slippery wounds on himself, with cardboard-stiff chamois, while charging along a twisting trail on a hump-backed *morope*. It was his fond hope that he would never have to do it again. Before they reached the sacked farmhouse, the other riders caught up with them and the entire party galloped on in exhausted silence. Jason was hopelessly lost on the foggy, tree-shrouded paths, which all looked alike to him. But the nomads had far better eyes for the terrain and rode steadily toward their objective. The *moropes* were faltering and could be kept moving only by constant application of the prickspurs. Blood streamed down their sides and soaked into their damp fur.

When they reached the river, Temuchin signaled a stop.

"Dismount," he ordered, "and take only what you must have from your saddlebags. We leave the beasts here. One at a time now, over that rise to the river.'' He moved off first, leading his own mount.

Jason was too foggy from exhaustion and pain to realize what was happening. When he finally pulled his mount forward, he was surprised to see a knot of men on the riverbank with not a single *morope* in sight.

''Do you have everything you want?'' Temuchin asked, taking Jason's bridle and pulling the *morope* close to the bank. As Jason nodded, he whipped the bowie knife across in a wicked, backhand slash that cut the creature's throat and almost severed its head from its body. He moved quickly to avoid the pulsing gout of blood, then put his foot against the swaying animal and pushed it sideways into the river. The swift current carried it quickly from sight.

''The machine cannot lift a *morope* up the cliff,'' Temuchin said. ''And we do not want their bodies near the landing spot or the place will be known and soldiers will wait there. We walk.'' He looked at Jason's wounded leg. ''You can walk, can't you?''

''Great,'' Jason said. ''Never felt better. A little hike after a couple of nights without sleep and a thousand-kilometer ride is just what I need. Here we go.'' He walked off as swiftly as he could, trying not to limp. ''We'll get this gunpowder back and I'll show you just how to use it,'' he reminded, just in case the warlord had forgotten.

It was not a very nice walk. They did not stop, but instead, to relieve each other, passed the barrels from one to another without halting. At least Jason and the other three walking wounded missed this assignment. Trudging uphill on the slippery grass was not easy. Jason's leg was a pillar of pain that bled a steady trickle of blood down into his boot top. He kept falling behind, and the march was endless. All of the others had passed him and, at one point, they were out of sight over a ridge ahead. He wiped the rain and sweat from his eyes and limped on, trying to follow their vague path in the tall grass, which was already straightening up and blurring the signs. Temuchin appeared on the hilltop above and looked back at him, fingering his sword hilt, and Jason put on a lung-destroying burst of speed. If he faltered, he would join the *moropes*.

An indeterminate period of time later, it came as a complete shock when he stumbled into the small group of men sitting on the grass, their backs to a familiar tower of rock.

''Temuchin has gone,'' Ahankk said. ''You will go next. Each of the first ten men on the rope will carry up a barrel of this gunpowder.''

"That's a great idea," Jason said collapsing inertly onto the soggy grass. It was an unconscionably long time before he could even struggle to a sitting position to do what he could to fix his crude bandages. One of the men carried over a barrel of gunpowder that had been secured in a harness of leather straps, with a loop to go around Jason's neck. The rope came down soon after this and he allowed himself to be strapped into it. This time the possibility of falling did not trouble him in the slightest. He rested his head on the gunpowder and fell asleep as soon as the lift began, nor did he awake until they pulled him to the clifftop and his forehead banged against the rock. Fresh *moropes* were waiting and he was permitted to return alone to the camp, without the gunpowder. He allowed the animal to go at its slowest pace so that the ride was not unbearable, but when he reached his own *camach,* he found that he did not possess the strength to dismount.

"Meta," he croaked. "Help a wounded veteran of the wars." He swayed when she poked her head out of the flap, then let go. She caught him before he hit the ground and carried him in her arms into the tent. It was a pleasant experience.

"You should eat something," Meta said sternly. "You have had enough to drink."

"Nonsense," he said, sipping from the iron cup and smacking his lips. "I don't have tired blood—I have no blood. The medik said that I was partially exsanguinated and gave me a stiff iron injection to make up for it. Besides, I'm too tired to eat."

"The readings also said that you needed a transfusion."

"A little hard to do that here. I'll drink plenty of water and have goat's liver for dinner every night."

"Open!" someone shouted, pulling at the laced and knotted entrance flap of the *camach.* "I speak with the voice of Temuchin."

Meta put the medikit under a fur and went to the entrance. Grif who had been fanning the fire, picked up a lance and balanced it in his hand. A soldier poked his head in.

"You will come to Temuchin now."

"I come at once, tell him that."

The soldier started to argue, but Meta twisted his nose and pushed him back through the opening. She laced it shut again.

"You cannot go," she said.

"I have no choice. We've sutured the wounds by hand with gut that's acceptable, and the antibiotics are not detectable. The iron already seeping into my bone marrow."

"That is not what I meant," Meta said angrily.

"I know what you meant, but there is very little we can do about it." He pulled out the medikit and twisted the control dial. "Pain killer in the leg so I can walk on it, and a nice big shot of stimulant. I'm taking years off my life with this drug addiction, and I hope someone appreciates it."

When he stood up, Meta grabbed him by the arms. "No, you cannot," she said.

He used a gentler warfare, taking her face in his hands and kissing her. Grif snorted with contempt and turned back to his fire. Her hands relaxed.

"Jason," she said haltingly. "I don't like this. There is nothing I can do to help."

"There's plenty, but not at this moment. Just hold the fort for a while longer. I'm going to show Temuchin how to make his big bang, and then we're going to get out of here, back to the ship. I'll tell him I am going to bring the Pyrran tribe in, which is just what I intend to do. Along with some other things. The wheels are turning and plans are being made, and there is a new day coming soon to Felicity." The drugs were making him light-headed and elated, and he believed every word he said. Meta, who had spent too long a time bent over a dung fire in this frozen campsite, was not quite so enthusiastic. But she let him go. Duty comes first—that is a lesson every Pyrran learns in the nursery.

Temuchin was waiting, showing no sign of the strain of the past days, pointing to the barrels of gunpowder on the floor of his *camach*.

"Make it explode," he commanded.

"Not in here and not all at once, unless you are planning a mass suicide. What I need is some sort of container that I can seal, and not too big a one either."

"Speak your needs. What you must have will be brought in here."

The warlord obviously wanted his explosive experiments classified Top Secret, which was all right with Jason. The *camach* was warm and relatively comfortable, with food and drink close at hand. He sank into the furs and worried a baked goat's leg until his materials had been assembled; then, after wiping his hands on his jacket, he set to work.

A number of clay pots had been assembled and Jason chose the smallest one, little more than a cup in size. Then he worked out the plug from one of the barrels and carefully shook some of the gunpowder out onto a sheet of leather. The grains were not very uniform, but he doubted if this would affect the speed of burning very much. This stuff had certainly worked well enough in the muskets. Using a scoop formed of stiff leather, he carefully loaded the pot until it was half full. A trimmed piece of chamois fitted on top of the granules and he tamped it down gently with the rounded end of a worn thighbone. Temuchin stood behind him watching every step of the process closely. Jason explained.

"The granules should be close together for even burning, for smooth burning makes the best banging. Or so I have been told by the men in the tribe who know about this sort of thing. This is all as new to me as it is to you. Then the leather goes in to hold the gunpowder in place and to act as a waterproof shield." Jason had ready a mixture of water, dirt from the *camach* floor and crumbled dung. This made a damp, claylike substance that he now pushed into the pot to seal it. He patted it smooth and pointed.

"It is said that in order to explode, the gunpowder must be completely contained. If there are any openings, the fire rushes out through them and the substance simply burns."

"How does the fire reach it now?" Temuchin asked, frowning in concentration as he forced himself to follow the unaccustomed technical explanations. For an illiterate who couldn't count very well and did not have a shard of technical knowledge, he was doing all right. Jason took up one of the heavy iron needles that were used for sewing the *camach* covers.

"You've asked the right question. The plug is dry enough now, so I can poke a hole through it with this, through the mud and the leather, right down to the powder. Then, using the other end of the needle, I'll push this piece of cloth all the way down into the hole. I liberated the cloth from one of your men who liberated it from a lowlander's back. I have soaked the cloth in oil so that it will burn easily." He hefted the pot-grenade in his hand. "So I think that we are ready to go."

Temuchin stalked out and Jason, with the bomb in one hand and the flickering oil lamp in the other, followed at a suitable distance. A large area had been cleared before the warlord's *camach* and the soldiers held the curious at a suitable distance. The word had been quickly passed that something strange and dangerous was going to happen, so men had come flocking from all parts of the sprawling camp. They were packed solidly into the spaces between the surrounding *camachs*. Jason placed the bomb carefully in the ground and raised his voice.

"If this works there should be a loud noise, smoke and flame. Some of you here know what I mean. So—here goes."

He bent and applied the lamp to the fuse, holding it there until the cloth smoldered and burst into flame. It was burning slowly enough so that he could stand for a few seconds to make sure that it was going well. It was. Only then did he turn and stroll back to the *camach* next to Temuchin.

Even Jason's drug-induced confidence did not survive the anticlimax. The fuse burned, smoked, gave off some sparks and then apparently went out. Jason made himself wait a long time, in spite of the impatient murmurs and occasional angry shouts. He had no desire to bend over the bomb and have it blow up in his face. Only when Temuchin began to finger his knife in a suggestive manner did Jason walk out, hoping that he appeared to be more relaxed than he felt, to look down at the charred fuse opening. He nodded once sagely, then headed back to the *camach*.

"The fuse went out before it reached the gunpowder. We need a bigger hole or a better fuse—and I have just remembered another stanza of the 'Song of the Bomb' that speaks about that. I will do it now. Do not let anyone approach it until I return." Before he could get any arguments, he went back into the *camach*.

The best fuses contained gunpowder, so they could burn even without a supply of air. He needed a gunpowder fuse to get down through that layer of mud. There was plenty of powder here—but what could he roll it in? Paper was best, but in short supply at the present moment. Or was it? He made sure that the entrance was well secured and that he was alone in the tent. Then he rooted to the bottom of his waist wallet and dug out his medikit. He had brought it despite the risk, because he had no idea how long this session would take and had not wanted to run any risk of passing out before it was over.

It took just a second to press, twist and pull open the recharging chamber. Folded above the ampules was the inspection and recharge sheet, just big enough for his needs. He slipped the medikit out of sight again.

Making the fuse was simple enough, though he practically had to twist each grain of powder into the paper separately to make sure they didn't lump together and burn too fast. When the job was done, he rubbed oil and lampblack into the paper to disguise its pristine whiteness. "This should do it," he said, taking the fuse and the needle and going back to the demonstration.

It almost did a lot more than he had bargained for. The nomads were jeering openly now and making rude noises, and Temuchin was white with rage. The bomb was still sitting innocently where he had left it. Pretending not to hear the unflattering remarks, Jason bent over the bomb and made a new hole in the clay seal. He was taking no chances of poking a smoldering fragment of rag down into the gunpowder. It was a chancy business, and the sweat on his forehead had nothing to do with the chilling temperature of the morning air as he pushed home the new fuse.

"This is the one that works," he said as he applied the flame.

The paper smoked lustily and crackled as a shower of sparks flew into the air. Jason had one brief, horrified glimpse of the flame streaking down the oily gunpowder fuse, then he turned and dived for safety.

This time the results were very impressive. The bomb exploded with a highly satisfactory roar and pieces of jagged pottery whistled away in every direction, ripping holes in a score of *camachs* and inflicting minor wounds on some of the spectators. Jason was so close to the blast that it rolled him over and over on the ground.

Temuchin still stood unmoving at the opening of the *camach,* but he did look a slight bit more pleased now. The few shouts of pain from the audience were drowned out in the enthusiastic cries and happy back-slapping. Jason sat up shakily and felt himself all over, but could find nothing broken that had not been broken before.

"Can you make them bigger?" Temuchin asked, an anticipatory gleam of destruction in his eye.

"They come in all sizes. Though I could give you a more exact idea if you would let me know just what use you have in mind for them."

A stir on the other side of the field distracted Temuchin before he could answer. A number of men on *moropes* were trying to force their way through the crowd and the bystanders did not like the idea. There were angry shouts and at least one broken-off scream.

"Who approaches without permission?" Temuchin said, and when he reached for his sword, his personal guard drew their weapons and formed up close to him. The first row of onlookers jumped aside rather than be trampled and a *morope* and rider came through.

"What made that noise?" the rider asked, his voice just as used to automatic command as was Temuchin's.

It was a voice that was very familiar to Jason.

It was Kerk.

Temuchin went striding forward in cold anger, his men grouped around him, while Kerk dismounted and was joined by Rhes and the other Pyrrans. A really beautiful battle was in the making.

"Wait!" Jason shouted, and ran to get between the two groups who were on obvious collision course. "These are the Pyrrans!" h shouted. "My tribe. Warriors who have come to join the forces of Temuchin." Out of the corner of his mouth he hissed at Kerk. "Relax! Bend the knee a bit before we all get massacred."

Kerk did nothing of the sort. He stopped, looking just as irritated as Temuchin, and fingered his sword hilt in the same threatening manner. Temuchin came on like an avalanche and Jason had to step back or he would have been crushed between the two men. When Temuchin stopped his toes were touching Kerk's and they glared at each other with almost eyeball-to-eyeball contact.

They were very much alike. The warlord was taller, but the solid breadth of the Pyrran could never be mistaken for fat. Their apparel was just as impressive, as Kerk had followed Jason's radioed instructions. His breastplate sported a multicolored and severely two-dimensional design of an eagle, while the eagle's skull itself crowned his helm.

"I am Kerk, leader of the Pyrrans," he said, slipping his sword up and down with an irritating, grating sound.

"I am Temuchin, warlord of the tribes. You will bow to me."

"Pyranns bow to no man."

Temuchin rumbled deep in his throat like an infuriated carnivore and began to draw his sword. Jason resisted an impulse to cover his eyes and flee. This would be bloody murder.

Kerk knew what he was doing. He had not come here to depose Temuchin—at least not right now—so he did not reach for his own sword. Instead, his hand moved with the cracking speed that only Pyrrans have developed, and he seized the wrist of Temuchin's sword arm.

"I do not come to fight you," he said calmly. "I come as an equal to side with you in your cause. We will talk."

His voice did not waver—nor did Temuchin's sword come one centimeter more out of the loops. The warlord had a massive strength and resiliency, but Kerk was an unmoving boulder. He neither moved nor showed any sign of strain, but the veins stood out on Temuchin's forehead. The silent struggle continued for ten, fifteen seconds, until Temuchin suffused red under the darkness of his skin, every muscle of his body rock hard with the effort of his exertions.

When it appeared that human muscle and sinew could stand no more, Kerk smiled. Just the barest turning up of the corners of his mouth, visible only to Temuchin and Jason, who stood close by. Then, slowly and steadily, the warlord's arm was forced down until his sword was secure in its loops and could go no farther.

"I did not come here to fight you," Kerk said in a barely audible voice. "The young men may wrestle with each other. We are leaders who talk."

He released his grip so suddenly that Temuchin swayed with the reaction, as his tensed muscles no longer had anything to battle against. The decision was his once again, and the intelligent man was warring in his body against the brute reactions of the born barbarian.

For long seconds this silent impasse continued, then Temuchin began to chuckle, the laughter rising quickly to a full-throated roar. He threw his head back and laughed defiance of the universe, then swung his arm and clapped Kerk on the shoulder with a blow that would have stunned a *morope* or killed a lesser man. Kerk just swayed slightly and returned the smile.

"You are a man I might like!" Temuchin shouted. "If I do not kill you first. Come into my *camach.*" He turned away and Kerk went with him. They passed Jason without deigning to notice him. Jason rolled his eyes upward, happy to see that the skies had not fallen nor the sun gone nova, then turned and followed them.

"Stay here," Temuchin ordered when they reached the *camach*, spearing Jason with a look of cold fury as though he alone were responsible for the ill events. Temuchin waved the guards to position, then followed Kerk inside. Jason did not complain. He preferred waiting here in the wind, chill as it was, to witnessing the confrontation in the tent. If Temuchin were killed, how would they escape? Fatigue and pain were beginning to creep back, and he swayed in the wind and wondered if he could risk a quick stab with his medikit. The answer was obviously no, so he swayed and waited.

Angry voices sounded loudly inside and Jason cringed and waited for the end. Nothing happened. He swayed again and decided that it would be easier to sit down, so he dropped. The ground was chill against his bottom. The voices rose once more inside, then were followed by an ominous silence. Jason noticed that even the guards were exchanging concerned glances.

There was a sharp ripping sound and they jumped and turned, raising their lances. Kerk had opened the entrance flap by pulling on it—hard. But he had neglected to unlace it first. The thick leather thongs were snapped, or torn loose from their heavy supports, and the supporting iron rod was bent at a sharp angle. Kerk apparently noticed none of this. He stalked by the guards, nodded at Jason, and kept on walking. Jason had a quick look at Temuchin's face, swollen with anger, in the opening. This glimpse was enough. He turned and hurried after Kerk.

"What happened in there?" he asked.

"Nothing. We just talked and felt each other out and neither of us would give way. He would not answer my questions so I did not bother to answer his. It is a draw—for the moment."

Jason was worried. "You should have waited until I returned. Why did you come like this?" He knew the answer even as he asked, and Kerk confirmed it.

"Why shouldn't we? Pyrrans do not enjoy sitting on a mountain and acting as jailers. We came to see for ourselves. There was some fighting on the way here and the morale has improved."

"I'm sure of that," Jason said fervently, and wished he were laying down back in his *camach*.

12

Back they came from the land of wetness,
Back they came, with thumbs in bunches,
Telling tales of the glorious killing
In the lands below the clifftops.

Though the wind hissed around the *camach* and occasionally blew a scattering of fine snowflakes in through the smokehole, the interior was warm and comfortable. The atomic heater generated enough BTU's to defeat all the drafts and leaks, while the strong drink Kerk had brought sat in Jason's stomach far better than the vile *achadh*. Rhes had supplied a case of meal packs and Meta was opening them. The rest of the Pyrrans were setting up their *camachs* nearby or were unobtrusively on guard near the entrance. For a rare instance, in the heart of the barbarian camp, they were free from observation and safe from sudden violence.

"Pig," Meta said when Jason reached for a steaming and nose-captivating meal pack, "you've already had one."

"First one was for me. This one's for my shattered tissues and drained blood." While he chewed a warming and succulent mouthful, he pointed at Kerk's helm. "I see that you joined the eagle clan all right, but where did you get so many skulls? They sure impressed the locals. I didn't know there were that many eagles on the entire planet."

"There probably aren't," Kerk said, running his finger over the hook-beaked and eyeless skull. "We managed to shoot this one and make a mould. All of the others are plastic castings. Now tell us what these plans are that you have formulated, because, as enjoyable as this childish masquerade is, we want an end to it. And a beginning to the mining operation."

"Patience," Jason said. "This operation is going to have to take a little time, but I guarantee that there will be plenty of fighting so it will have its high spots. Let me fill in some of the things I have discovered since I talked to you last.

'Temuchin has most of the plains tribes behind him, at least all of the ones that count. He is a damn intelligent man and a shrewd leader. He intuitively knows most of the military-textbook axioms. Keep the troops occupied, that's a basic one. As soon as they chased the first expedition away, he talked around among the clans and found the one or two tribes that the majority were feuding with. They wiped these out and split up the loot. This has been the process ever since. You're either with him or against him, and no one is neutral. All this in spite of the nomads' natural tendency to align and realign and go their own way. The few leaders who have tried to get out from under the new regime have met such violent deaths that all the others are very impressed."

Kerk shook his head. "If he has united all of these people, then there is nothing we can do."

"Kill him?" Meta suggested.

"See what a few weeks among the barbarians will do for a girl?" Jason said. "I can't say that I'm not tempted. The alliance would fall apart—but we would be back to square one. If we tried to open the mines, some other leader would appear and the attacks would start again. No, we have to do better than that. If it is possible, I would like to take over his organization and turn it to our own ends. And, Kerk, you're not quite right. He has not united all the tribes, just the strongest ones on the plains. There are a number of smaller ones around the edges that he is not bothering about; they pose no threat. But there are a lot of hairy-necked mountain tribes in the north who pride themselves on their independence, most of them from the weasel clan. They fight each other, but they will work together against any threat from the outside. Temuchin is that threat—and that will be our big chance to take over."

"How?" Rhes asked.

"By being better at the job than he is. By covering ourselves with glory and doing better than he does in the mountain campaign. And arranging it so that he makes a couple of mistakes. If we work it right, we should come back from the campaign with Kerk either in the highest councils or an equal of Temuchin. This is a rough society and nobody cares how great you were last year, but what you have done for them lately. A real barnyard pecking order is in operation, and we are going to arrange it so that Kerk is top pecker. All of us except Rhes, that is."

"Why not me?" Rhes asked.

"You are going to organize the second part of the plan. We never paid much attention to the lowlands, below the cliffs, because there are no heavy metal deposits. However, there appears to be a fairly advanced agrarian culture at work down there. Temuchin found a way of sending down a raiding party, an expedition I do not wish to try again, to get some gunpowder. I'm sure he wants to use it against the hill tribes, an ace in the hole to assure victory. Those mountain passes must be hard to attack. I helped Temuchin bring the gunpowder back—and kept my eyes open at the same time. Aside from the gunpowder, I saw flintlocks, cannon, military uniforms and bags of flour. That's strong evidence."

"Evidence of what?" Kerk was irritated. He preferred to work with simpler, more familiar chains of logic.

"Isn't it obvious? Proof that a fairly advanced culture is in operation here. Chemistry, single-crop culture, central government, taxes, forging, large casting, weaving, dyeing . . ."

"How do you know all that?" Meta asked, astonished.

"I'll tell you tonight, dear, when we're alone. It would just appear like bragging now. But I know that my conclusions are correct. There is a rising middle class down there in the lowlands, and I'll wager that the bankers and the merchants are rising the fastest. Rhes is going to buy his way in. As an agrarian himself, he has the right background for the job. Look at this, the key to his success."

He took a small metal disk from his pouch and tossed it into the air, then handed it to Rhes. "What is it?" Rhes asked.

"Money. Coin of the lower realm. I took it from one of the dead soldiers. This is the axle on which the commercial world rotates, or is the lubrication on the axle, or whatever other metaphor you prefer. We can analyze this and forge up a batch that will not only be as good, but will be richer and better than the original. You'll take them to buy yourself in, set up shop as a merchant and get ready for the next move.''

Rhes looked at the coin distastefully. ''And now I'm supposed to play this wide-mouthed question game like everyone else here and ask you what is next move?''

''Correct. You catch on quick. When Jason talks, everyone listens.''

''You talk too much,'' Meta said primly.

''Agreed, but it's my only vice. The next move will be to unite the tribes here, with Kerk in control or close to it, to welcome Rhes when he sails north with his trade goods. This continent may be bisected by a cliff that normally prevents contact between the nomads and the lowlanders, but you can't convince me that I won't find a place somewhere here in the north where it might be possible to land a ship or small boats. One little bit of beach is all we need. I'm sure that seagoing contact has been ruled out in the past because it takes an advanced technology to make floating ships out of iron. Hide- and bone-framed coracles are a possibility, but I doubt if the nomads have ever even considered the possibility of traveling on water. The lowlanders must surely have ships, but there is nothing up here to tempt them into exploration. Quite the opposite, if anything. But we're going to change all that. Under Kerk's leadership the tribes will give a peaceful welcome to traders from the south. Trade will enter the picture and a new era will begin. For a few tired furs, the tribesmen will be able to gather the products of civilization and will be seduced. Maybe we can hook them on tobacco, booze or glass beads. There must be something they like that the lowlands can supply. And this will be the thin end of the wedge. First a landing on the beach with trade goods, then a few tents to keep the snow off. Then a permanent settlement. Then a trading center and market—right over the spot where our mine is going to be. The next step should be obvious.''

There was plenty of discussion, but only about the details. No one could fault Jason's plan; in fact, they rather approved of it. It sounded simple and workable, and assigned parts to all of them that they enjoyed playing. All except Meta, that is. She had had enough of dung fires and menial manual labor to last for the rest of her life. But she was too good a Pyrran to complain about her assignment, so she remained silent.

It was very late before the meeting broke up; the boy, Grif, had been asleep for hours. The atomic heater had been turned off and locked away, but the aura of its warmth remained. Jason collapsed into the fur sleeping bag and let out an exhausted sigh. Meta rolled over and put her chin against his chest.

"What is going to happen after we win?" she asked.

"Don't know," Jason said tiredly, letting his hand run through her short-cropped hair. "Haven't thought about it. Get the job done first."

"I've thought about it. It should mean the end of the fighting for us, forever I mean. If we stay here and build a new city. What will you do then?"

"Hadn't thought," he said blurredly, holding her close and enjoying the sensation.

"I think I would like to stop fighting. I think there must be other things to do with a person's life. Did you notice that all the women here take care of their own children, instead of putting them into the nursery and never seeing them again as on Pyrrus? I think that might be a nice thing."

Jason jerked his hand away from her hair as from molten metal and his eyes sprang wide open. Dimly, in the far distance, he could hear the harsh ringing of wedding bells, a sound he had fled from more than once in his life, a sound that brought out an instant running reflex.

"Well," he said with what he hoped was due deliberation, "that sort of thing might be nice for *barbarian* women, but it certainly isn't the sort of rate to be wished on an intelligent, civilized girl." He waited tensely for an answer, until he realized from the evenness of her breathing that she had fallen asleep. That took care of that, at least for the time being.

Then he held the solid warmth of her body in his arms and he wondered what exactly it was he was running from and, while he wondered, the drugs and exhaustion hit and he fell asleep.

In the morning the new campaign began. Temuchin had issued his orders and the march got under way at dawn, with a freezing, bonechilling wind sweeping down from the mountains in the north. The *camachs,* the *escungs,* even carrier *moropes* were left behind. Every warrior brought his own weapons and rations, and was expected to take care of himself and his mount. At first the movement was very unimpressive, a scattering of soldiers working their way through the *camachs,* among the shouting women and the ragged children running in the dust. Then two men joined together, and a third, until an entire squad rode together, the riders bobbing up and down in response to the undulating motion of their mounts.

Jason rode next to Kerk, with the 94 Pyrran warriors following in a double column. He turned in his saddle to look at them. The women could not ride with them, and eight men had gone to the lowlands with Rhes, while the remainder were on guard duty at the ship. That left 96 men in all to accomplish the mission—to gain control of the barbarian army and this occupied portion of the planet. On the surface it looked impossible, but the bearing of the tiny Pyrran force did not reflect that. They were solemn and ready to take on anything that came their way. It gave Jason an immense feeling of security to have them riding behind him.

Once clear of the campsite, they could see other columns of men paralleling their course across the rolling sweep of the steppe. Messengers had gone out to all the tribes camped along the river to tell them that they were to ride today. The horde was gathering. From all sides they came, drifting toward the line of march, until there were riding men visible on all sides, clear to the horizon. There was a marked sense of organization now, with different clans falling in behind their captains and forming into squadrons. In the distance Jason saw the black banners of Temuchin's household guards and pointed them out to Kerk.

"Temuchin has two *moropes* loaded with our gunpowder bombs, and he wants me to ride with him to supervise the operation. He pointedly did *not* mention the rest of the Pyrrans, but we're all going to stay with him whether he likes it or not. He needs me for the gunpowder—and I ride with my tribe. It's a winning argument that I'm sure he can't beat."

"Then we shall put it to the test," Kerk said, spurring his beast into a gallop. The Pyrran column sliced through the galloping horde toward their leader.

They swung in from the right flank until they were riding level with Temuchin's men, then slacked back to the same pace. Jason started forward, ready with his foolproof arguments, but found them unnecessary. Temuchin took one slow, cold look at the Pyrrans, then turned his eyes forward again. He was like a chess master who sees a mate 12 moves ahead and resigns without playing the game out. Jason's arguments were obvious to him and he did not bother to listen to them.

"Examine the lashings on the gunpowder bombs," he ordered. "They are your responsibility."

From his vantage point near the warlord, Jason witnessed the smooth organization of the barbarian army and began to realize that Temuchin must be a military genius. Illiterate and untutored, with no authorities to rely on, he had reinvented all of the basic principles of army maneuvers and large-scale warfare. His captains were more than just leaders of independent commands. They acted as a staff, taking messages and relaying orders on their own initiative. A simple system of horn signals and arm motions controlled the troops, so that the thousands of men formed a flexible and dangerous weapon.

Also an intensely rugged one. When all the troops had joined up, Temuchin formed them into a kilometer-wide line and advanced on the entire front at once. Without stopping. The advance, which had begun before dawn, continued into the early afternoon without a halt for any reason. The rested and well-fed *moropes* did not like the continuous ride, but they were capable of it when goaded on by the spurs. They shrieked protest, but the advance went on. The endless jogging did not seem to bother the nomads, who had been in the saddle almost since birth, but Jason, in spite of his recent riding experience, was soon battered and sore. If the ride was affecting the Pyrrans in any way, it was not noticeable.

Squadrons of riders scouted out ahead of the main company of troops, and by late afternoon the invading army came across their handiwork. Slaughtered nomads, first a single rider, his blood mixed with that of his butchered *morope*, then a family unit that had been unlucky enough to cross the path of the army. The *escungs* and folded *camachs* were still smoldering, surrounded by a ghastly array of dead bodies. Men, women and children, even the *moropes* and flocks, had been brutally slain. Temuchin fought total war and where he had passed nothing remained alive. He was brutally pragmatic in his thinking. War is fought to be won. Anything that assures victory is sensible. It is sensible to make a three-day ride in a single day if it means the enemy can be surprised. It is sensible to kill everyone you meet so that no alarm can be given, just as it is sensible to destroy all their goods so your warriors will not be burdened by booty.

The truth of Temuchin's tactics was proved when, just before dark, the racing army swooped down upon a large-sized village of the weasel clan in the foothills of the mountains.

As the great line of riders topped the last ridge, the alarm was given in the camp, but it was too late for escape. The ends of the line swung in and met behind the camp, though it looked as though some hard-ridden *moropes* had slipped through before the forces joined. Sloppy, Jason thought, surprised that Temuchin had not done a better job.

After this it was just slaughter. First by overwhelming flights of arrows that drove back and decimated the defenders, then by a lance charge at full gallop. Jason hung back, not out of cowardice, but from simple hatred of the bloodshed. The Pyrrans attacked with the rest. Through constant practice they were all now proficient with the short bow, though they still could not fire as fast as the nomads, but it was in shock tactics that they proved what they could do. If they had any qualms about killing the nomad tribe, they did not show it. They struck like lightning and tore through the defenders and overrode them. With their speed and weight they did not parry or attempt to defend themselves. Instead, they hit like battering rams, slashed, killed and kept on without slowing. Jason could not join them in this. He remained with the two disgruntled men who had been detailed to guard the gunpowder bombs, picking out chords on his lute as he composed a new song to describe this great occasion. It was dark before the pillage was over and Jason rode slowly into the ravished encampment. He met a rider who was searching for him.

"Temuchin would see you. Come now," the man ordered. Jason was too tired and sickened to think of any sharp comebacks.

They made their way through the conquered encampment, with their *moropes* stepping carefully over the sprawled and piled corpses. Jason kept his eyes straight ahead, but could not close his nose to the slaughterhouse stench. Surprisingly, very few of the *camachs* had been damaged or burned, and Temuchin was holding an officers' council in the largest of them. It had undoubtedly belonged to the former leader of the clan; in fact, the chieftain himself lay gutted, dead and unnoticed, against the far side of the tent. All of the officers were assembled—though Kerk was not present—when Jason entered.

"We begin," Temuchin said, and squatted cross-legged on a fur robe. The others waited until he sat, then did the same. "Here is the plan. What we did today was nothing, but it is the beginning. To the east of this place is a very large encampment of the weasel tribes, and tomorrow we march to attack this place. I want your men to think we go to this camp, and I want those who watch from the hills to think the same. Some were permitted to escape to observe our movements."

That for my theory about sloppy soldiering, Jason thought, should have known better. Temuchin must have this campaign planned down to the last arrowhead.

"Today your men have ridden hard and fought well. Tonight the soldiers not on guard will drink the *achadh* they find here and eat the food and will be very late arising in the morning. We will take the undamaged *camachs* and destroy the rest. It will be a short day and we will camp early. The *camachs* will be set up, many cooking fires lit and kept burning, while patrols will sweep as far as the foothills so that the watchers will not get too close."

"And it is all a trick," Ahankk said, grinning behind his hand. "We will not attack to the east after all?!"

"You are correct." The warlord had their complete attention, the officers leaning forward unconsciously so as not to miss a word. "As soon as it is dark, the horde will ride west, a day's and a night's ride should bring us to The Slash, the valley that leads to the weasel's heartland. We will attack the defenders, with the gunpowder bombs against their forts, and seize control before reinforcements can arrive."

"Bad fighting there," one of the officers grumbled, fingering an old wound. "Nothing there to fight for."

"No, nothing *there,* you brainless fool," Temuchin said in such a cold and angry tone that the man recoiled, "nothing at all. But it is the gateway to their homeland. A few hundred can stop an army in The Slash, but once we are through they are lost. We will destroy their tribes one by one until the weasel clan will be only a memory for the jongleurs to sing about. Now issue your orders and sleep. Tomorrow night the long ride and the attack begins."

As the others filed out, Temuchin took Jason by the arm.

"The gunpowder bombs," he said. "They will blow up each time they are used?"

"Of course," Jason answered, with far more enthusiasm than he felt. "You have my word on that."

It wasn't the bombs that were worrying him—he had already taken precautions to assure satisfactory explosions—but the prospect of another nonstop ride even longer than the first. The nomads would do it, there was no doubt about that, and the Pyrrans could make it as well. But could he?

The night air was bitterly cold when he emerged from the heat of the *camach.* His breath made a sudden silver fog against the stars before it vanished. The plains were still, cut through by the occasional snort of a tired *morope* or the drunken shouts of the soldiers.

Yes, he would make the ride all right. He might have to be tied to the saddle and hopped up with drugs, but he was going to make it. What really concerned him was the shape he would arrive in at the other end of the ride. This did not bear thinking about.

13

"Hold on for just a short while longer. The Slash is in sight ahead," Kerk shouted.

Jason nodded, then realized that his head was bobbing continuously with the *morope's* canter and his nodding was indistinguishable from this motion. He tried to answer, but started coughing at the cracked dryness of his throat, filled and caked with the dust stirred up by the running animals. In the end he released his cramped grip on the saddle pommel long enough to wave, then clutched at it again. The army rode on.

It was a nightmare journey. It had started soon after dark on the previous night, when company after company of riders had slipped away to the west. After the first few hours, fatigue and pain had blended together for Jason into a misty unreality that, with the darkness and the countless rows of running shapes, soon resembled a dream more than reality. A particularly loathsome dream. They had galloped, without stopping, until dawn, when Temuchin had permitted a short halt to feed and water the *moropes* for the balance of the journey. This stop may have helped their mounts, but it had almost finished Jason.

Instead of dismounting, he had fallen from his *morope*, and when he tried to stand, his legs had failed him. Kerk had dragged him to his feet and walked him in a circle while another Pyrran cared for both their mounts. Feeling had finally returned to his numb legs and with it excruciating pain. His thighs were soaked with blood where the continual friction of the saddle had chafed away the skin. He had permitted himself a light injection of painkiller and some stimulant, then the ride had begun again. One fact he knew and hated was that he had to be sparing with the drugs. When this ride was over, the real battle would begin, and that would be the time when he would need all of his wits and strength. So the strongest drugs would have to be saved until then.

In an inverse way he could be proud of himself. More than one rider and *morope* had been lost during this insane ride, and he, t off-worlder who had never seen one of the creatures until a few months ago, was still going on. Barely. Some of the mounts had stumbled and fallen. Other riders had apparently gone to sleep or passed out, had slipped from their saddles and been trampled. It was certain death to drop beneath those running claws.

If The Slash was up ahead, the time had finally come to utilize the drugs he had been hoarding. Squinting against the late-afternoon sun and the blinding clouds of dust, he saw a dark cut against the gray white of the mountains ahead. The Slash. The valley they hoped to capture that would lead them to certain victory. Right now the drugs were more important than any number of victories. He dialed the medikit with clumsy fingers and jammed it against the heel of his hand.

As the drugs cleared the haze of fatigue and drew numbing layers over the pain, Jason realized that Temuchin was insane.

"He's calling for a charge!" Jason shouted across to Kerk as the signal horns sounded on all sides. "After all this riding . . ."

"Of course," Kerk said. "It is the correct way."

The correct way. It wins wars and kills men. An angry *morope*, squealing at the pain of ruthlessly applied spurs, reared up and threw its rider under the running feet of the others. This was not the only death. Still, the attack was pressed home.

Across the plains the army swept and into the mouth of the valley. Picked bowmen dismounted and clambered along the walls of The Slash to add their fire to the attack of the solid column streaming by below them. The leaders vanished into the valley and still others followed. A cloud of dust obscured the entrance. The Pyrrans pressed forward to the attack with the others while Jason turned off and headed for Temuchin's standard as he had been ordered. The personal guardsmen opened to let him through.

Temuchin took a report from a rider, then turned to Jason. "Get your bombs," he ordered.

"Why?" Jason asked, then hurried on as the light of instant anger burst in the other man's eyes. "What do you want me to do with them? Order, great Temuchin, and I shall obey. Only please give me some idea what you want me for."

The anger vanished as quickly as it had come. "The battle has gone as did all the others," the warlord said. "We have taken them by surprise and only the normal garrison is here. The lower redoubts have been taken and we now press on the higher ones. These are rockwalled and set into the cliff. Arrows cannot reach the defenders. They must be attacked on foot, slowly, from behind shields, if we are not to lose half an army. They cannot be stormed. Each time before it has been this way. One by one we take the redoubts and work our way up The Slash. Before we reach the other end the reinforcements have arrived and further battle is useless. But this time it will be different."

"I can just guess. You think that a gunpowder bomb in each position would take the fight out of the defenders and speed the attack?"

"You speak correctly."

"Then here I go, the First Felician Grenadiers to the attack. I will want some of my people to help me. They can throw farther and better than I can."

"The order will be issued."

By the time Jason had found the pack animals and unloaded the first of the bombs, the Pyrrans had arrived—Kerk and two others, sweaty and dusty from the fight, with that look of grim pleasure Pyrrans have only during battle.

"Ready to throw some bombs?" Jason asked Kerk.

"Of course. What is the mechanism?"

"Improved. I had a feeling that excuses are not much good with Temuchin and I wanted grenades that would go off every time." He held up one of the pot-bombs and pointed to the cloth wick. "There's gunpowder in these things all right, but mostly for the smoke and the stink. The wick is a dummy. You'll have to light it. I've made punk pots from grass for this, but that is just for effect. Let the wick smolder a bit, then pull up on it sharply. There is a microgrenade embedded in each one of these things, with the cloth wick tied to the trip pin. After you pull, you have three seconds to toss and duck."

Taking a flint and steel from his wallet, Jason bent over the pot of shredded punk and began to scratch away industriously. As the sparks smoldered and died, he looked out of the corners of his eyes to be sure he wasn't observed, then quickly actuated the lighter he had palmed. The tongue of flame flicked out and fired the punk.

"Here you are," he said, handing the smoldering pot to Kerk. "I suggest you carry this and throw the grenades, as you can undoubtedly toss them farther than I can."

"Farther and much more accurately."

"Yes, there is that, too. I and the others will carry the bombs for you and act as guards in case of a counterattack. Here we go."

They left their mounts and proceeded on foot into The Slash. The attacking troops were still moving up, so they worked their way along the sloping wall of the valley to avoid being trampled. As they went farther in, they met the first debris of battle—wounded soldiers who had crawled to the side out of the path of the still attacking army. The ones who had not made it were just red smears in the dust below. There were occasional dead *moropes* as well, their massive bodies standing up like bloodstained boulders. Now The Slash narrowed and the walls grew steeper. They found themselves following a goat path, their hands pressed against the stone for support. In this manner they reached the first redoubt. This was a crude but effective wall of piled rocks that fortified a narrow ledge. Jason clambered up the boulders to peer inside. He would need some idea of how these things were built up in order to blow them down. The defenders, stocky men in dusty furs, each with a weasel's skull lashed above his forehead, lay where they had fallen. Their bodies bristled with arrows; their thumbs were missing. Hard-carapaced death beetles had appeared out of the ground and were already at work.

'If they're all like this, we won't have any trouble,'' Jason said, sliding down to rejoin the others. "The boulders are just piled up, with no sign of any mortar. A grenade, if it doesn't knock out all the soldiers, should blow a gap in the wall big enough to let Temuchin's lads through.''

"You are optimistic,'' Kerk said, taking the lead again. "These are merely outposts. The main defenses must lie ahead.''

"Well, that's better than being pessimistic. I'm trying to talk myself into believing I'll live through this barbarian war and actually be warm again some time.''

It was no longer possible to walk on the valley side and they had to drop down and push their way through the soldiers. As the rock walls became more vertical, The Slash narrowed, and Jason could appreciate the difficulties of capturing it when it was stoutly defended. All of the *moropes* had been sent back and the attackers were now on foot. An arrow cracked into the stone above Jason's head and clattered down at their feet.

"We're at the front lines,'' Jason said. "Hold the advance here while I take a look.'' He pulled himself up the sloping side of one of the massive boulders that filled the gorge and, with his helm pulled low, slowly raised his head above the top. An arrow instantly clanged off of it and he quickly tilted his head forward until he was peering through the merest slit between the helm and the stone.

The advance had stopped ahead, where two redoubts, on opposite sides of The Slash, could sweep the entire floor of the valley with their accurate arrow fire. The defenders were firing from slits between the rocks and were almost impregnable to any return fire. Temuchin's forces were suffering losses in order to take the defended points the hard way. Protected slightly by their shields, moving in quick rushes from boulder to boulder, they crept forward. And died.

"The range is about 40 meters," Jason said, sliding back to the ground. "Do you think you can toss one of these things that far?"

Kerk bounced the homemade bomb on the palm of his broad hand and estimated its weight. "Easily," he said. "Let me look first so I will know what the distance is." He moved up to the position Jason had vacated, took one look, then dropped back down.

"That defended position is bigger than the others. It will take at least two bombs. I will light this one, hand you the smudge pot, then step out and throw the bomb. In the meantime you will have lit a second one—do not arm it—which you will give to me as soon as I have thrown the first. Is that clear?"

"Crystalline. Here we go."

Jason slipped off the sling of bombs and kept only one in his hand. The nearby soldiers (they had all heard about the gunpowder experiments) were watching closely. Kerk lit the false fuse, blew it into smoking life, then stepped out from the shelter of the rock. Jason hurriedly lit the bomb he carried and stood ready to pass it on.

With infuriating calm Kerk drew his arm back as one arrow zinged close by him and another shattered on his breastplate. Then he lowered the bomb, wet his finger and raised it to check the direction of the wind. Jason hopped from one foot to the other and clamped his teeth tightly together to stop from shouting at the Pyrran to throw.

More arrows arrived before Kerk was satisfied with the wind and drew his arm back again. Jason saw his thumb and index finger give the smoldering fuse a quick tug before, with a single contraction of all his muscles, he threw the bomb. It was a good, classic grenade throw, straight-armed and overhand, sending the bomb on a high arc toward the defended position. Jason reached out and slapped the second bomb into Kerk's waiting hand. This one followed the first so closely that both were in the air at the same time.

Kerk stood where he was and Jason, dismaying his own cowardly survival instincts, remained exposed as well, watching the two black spots soar high and down behind the wall.

There was an instant of waiting—then the entire stone-walled position leaped out into the air and crashed down in fragments below. Jason had a quick vision of bodies tossed high before he dodged behind the boulder to avoid the chunks of falling rock.

"Very satisfactory," Kerk said, pressed against the stone face close to Jason while stone shards rattled down around them.

"I hope the others are all this easy."

Of course, they weren't. The watchful defenders saw quickly enough that one man, throwing something, was responsible for the disaster, and the next time Kerk emerged he had to withdraw swiftly as a solid flight of arrows smashed down on his position.

"This is going to take some planning," Kerk said, automatically snuffing out the sputtering fuse.

"Are you afraid? Why do you stop?" an angry voice asked, and Kerk wheeled around to face Temuchin, who had come up to the front under the protective shields of his personal guard.

"Caution wins battles, fear loses them. I shall win this battle for you." Kerk's voice was as coldly angry as the warlord's.

"Is it caution or cowardice that keeps you behind this boulder after I have ordered you to destroy the redoubts?"

"Is it caution or cowardice that puts you here beside me instead of leading your men into battle?"

Temuchin made an animal-like noise deep in his throat and pulled out his sword. Kerk raised the gunpowder bomb, apparently eager to stuff it down the other's throat. Jason drew in a deep breath and stepped between the two furious men.

"The death of either of you would aid the enemy," he said, facing Temuchin for he was fairly sure that Kerk would not strike him from behind. "The sun is already behind the hills, and if the redoubts are not knocked out by dark, it may be too late. Their reinforcements could arrive during the night and that would be the end of this campaign."

Temuchin swung his sword back to cut Jason out of the way, while Kerk clutched his arm to pull him aside, his fingers steel clamps penetrating to the bone. Jason controlled the impulse to howl with pain and said, "Order the rest of the Pyrrans here and have them, and other soldiers, throw rocks at the defended points. They won't do much harm—but the bowmen will not be able to pick out the real bomb throwers." The sword hesitated, the grinding fingers relaxed the slightest amount—and Jason hurried on.

"It is sure death for one man to stand up to the concentrated fire. But if we can divide the fire, we can march up this valley just as fast as we can walk and clean them out. We'll be past the defenses by dark."

For one instant Temuchin's attention wavered back to his army and the darkening sky—and the tension was broken. Winning this battle was the only important thing, and personal intrigues would have to wait. He began to issue orders, unaware of the sword still grasped in his hand. Kerk's taloned grip finally relaxed and Jason stretched his bruised muscles.

The advance could not be stopped now. Stone-throwing figures bobbed up on all sides, and the baffled enemy had no way of telling which one was the lightning hurler. While the nomads just lobbed their stones and darted back to safety, the Pyrrans, with years of grenade-throwing experience, took careful aim and planted their small boulders behind the barricaded walls, breaking more than one skull in the process. They marched forward relentlessly and, one by one, the resisting strong points were demolished.

"We're coming to the end!" Jason shouted, pounding Kerk on the shoulder to get his attention and pointing ahead.

At this place The Slash was less than a hundred meters wide, pinched in by two tall spires of solid rock that rose straight up from the valley floor. Through this narrow gap could be seen the red of the sunset sky—and the plain beyond. The almost vertical walls ended at the spires. Once the horde passed them, it could not be stopped.

As Jason and Kerk pushed forward with a fresh supply of bombs, they realized that most of the soldiers were running back toward them. From up ahead came the shrill rise and fall of the iron horns.

"What is happening?" Kerk asked, grabbing one of the running men. "What do the horns mean?"

"Retreat!" the man said, pointing upward. "Look at that." He pulled free and was gone.

A large boulder bounced down among the fleeing soldiers, squashing one of them like an insect. Jason and Kerk looked up and saw men clambering on the valley's rim high above. They were clearly outlined against the sky, heaving and pulling at a rounded pile.

"On the other side, too!" Jason called out. "They've got boulders heaped up on both sides, ready to be rolled down on our heads. Pull back!" Reluctantly they retreated as more of the stones rumbled down.

Only the fact that this last-resort weapon had never been used before saved the attacking forces. The rocks and boulders had been piled higher generation after generation, until the supporting props were wedged firmly against the cliff edge. Warriors with long rods pushed at them, but they would not budge. Finally, one brave, or foolhardy, tribesman swung down on a rope and hammered the supports where they sank into the stone. He must have succeeded because in an eyeblink he was gone, swept away by the falling boulders that, for a fleeting instant, appeared to hang suspended in the air before they fell. A short while after this the supports on the opposite cliff gave way as well.

Jason and Kerk ran with the others.

The loss of life was not great, for most of the men had been warned in time. In addition, the narrowness of The Slash at this point acted as a choke, piling up the falling stone behind the gateway higher and higher.

When the last boulder had rattled into silence, The Slash was walled shut, completely plugged by the barrier of rock.

The campaign was obviously lost.

14

"I do not like it," Kerk said. "I do not think that it can be done."

"Kindly keep your doubts to yourself," Jason whispered as they came up to Temuchin. "I'll have enough of a job selling him this in any case. If you can't help, at least stand there and nod your head once in a while as if you agreed with me."

"Madness," Kerk grumbled.

"Greetings, oh warlord," Jason intoned. "I have come bringing aid that will turn this moment of disaster into victory."

If Temuchin heard, he gave no sign. He sat on a boulder with his hands over the pommel of his sword, which stood upright on the ground before him, looking straight ahead at the sealed pass that had stopped his dream of conquest. The last rays of the setting sun lit up the sheer, vertical faces of the towers of rock that formed the gate.

"The pass is now a trap," Jason said. "If we try to climb the rubble blocking it, or clear it away, we will be shot down by the men concealed behind it. Long before we can have forced passage, the reinforcements will have arrived. However, there is one thing that can be done. If we were to stand on the top of the higher spire of rock, on the left there, we could drop the gunpowder bombs down on the enemy, keeping them at bay until your soldiers had climbed the rockfall."

Temuchin's eyes went slowly up the smooth fall of rock to the summit high above. "That stone can not be climbed," he said without turning his head.

Kerk nodded and opened his mouth to agree, then made an oofing sound instead as Jason planted an elbow in the pit of his stomach.

"You are right. Most men cannot climb that rock. But we Pyrrans are mountain men and can climb that tower with ease. Do we have your permission?"

The warlord turned deliberately and examined Jason as though he were more than a little mad. "Begin then. I will watch."

"It must be done during daylight. We will need to see in order to throw the bombs. Then there is special equipment in our saddlebags that we must make ready. Therefore the climb will begin at dawn and by afternoon The Slash will be yours."

They could feel Temuchin's eyes burning into their backs as they returned to the others. Kerk was baffled.

"What equipment are you talking about? None of this makes sense."

"Only because you have never been exposed to accepted rock-climbing techniques. The piece of equipment I will need first is your radio, because I have to call the ship and have the other equipment made. If they work hard, it can be done and delivered before dawn. See that our men set up camp as far from the others as possible. We want to be able to slip away without being noticed."

While the others unrolled the fur sleeping bags and dug the fire pits, Jason used the radio. The *moropes* were arranged in a rough circle while he crouched in the center behind the concealing bulk of their bodies. The duty officer aboard the *Pugnacious* sent a messenger to awaken and call in all the men, then copied down Jason's instructions. There were no complaints or excuses as a war emergency is a normal part of Pyrran life, and delivery of the equipment was promised for well before dawn. Jason listened to a repeat of his instructions, then signed off. He ate some of the hot stew and left orders to be awakened when the completion call came through. It had been a long day, he was on the verge of exhaustion, and tomorrow promised to be even worse. Settling down in his sleeping bag, boots and all, he pulled a flap of fur over his face to keep the ice from forming in his nostrils and fell instantly to sleep.

"Go away," he muttered, and tried to pull away from the clutching hand that was crushing his already well crushed arm.

"Get up," Kerk said. "The call came through ten minutes ago. The launch is leaving now with the cargo and we must ride to meet it. The *moropes* are already saddled." Jason groaned at the thought and sat up. All of the heat was instantly sucked from his body and he began to shiver.

"M-medikit-t," he rattled. "Give me a good jolt of stimulants and painkillers because I have a feeling that it is going to be a very long day."

"Wait here," Kerk said. "I will meet the launch myself."

"I would like to, but I can't. I have to check the items before the launch returns to the ship. Everything must be perfect."

They carried him to his *morope* and put him into the saddle. Kerk took his reins and led the beast while Jason dozed, clutching the pommel so he would not fall. They trotted through the predawn darkness and, by the time they had reached the appointed spot, the medication had taken hold and Jason felt remotely human.

"The launch is touching down," Kerk said, holding the radio to his ear. There was the faintest rumble on the eastern horizon, a sound that would never be heard back at the camp.

"Do you have the flashlight?" Jason asked.

"Of course, wasn't that part of the instructions?" Jason could imagine the big man scowling into the darkness. It was inconceivable for a Pyrran to forget instructions. "It has a photon store of 18,000 lumen-hours, and at full output can put out 1,200 LF."

"Throttle it down, we don't need a tenth of that. The verticapsule is phototropic and has been set to home on any light source twice as radiant as the brightest star—"

"Capsule launched, on this radio bearing, distance approximately ten kilometers."

"Right. It does about 120 an hour wide open so you can turn the light on now on the same bearing. Give it something to look for."

"Wait, the pilot's saying something. Take the light."

Jason took the finger-sized tube and switched it on, turning the intensity ring until a narrow beam of light spiked away into the darkness. He pointed it in the direction of the grounded launch.

"The pilot reports that they had some trouble making a stain take on the nylon rope. It's on now, but they can't guarantee that it will be waterproof, and it is very blotchy."

"The blotchier the better. Just as long as it resembles leather from a distance. And I'm not expecting any rain. Did you hear that?"

A rising hum sounded from the sky and they could make out a faint red light dropping down toward them. A moment later the beam glinted from the silvery hull of the verticapsule and Jason turned down the light's intensity. There was a faint whistle of jets as the meter-long shape came into sight, dropping straight down, slowing as its radar altimeter sensed the ground. When it was low enough, Kerk reached up and threw the landing switch, and it settled with a dying hum to the ground. Jason flipped open the cargo hatch and drew out the coil of brown rope.

"Perfect," he said, handing it to Kerk. He burrowed deeper and produced a steel hammer that had been hand-forged from a single lump of metal. It balanced nicely in his palm: the leather wrappings on the handle gave it a good grip. It had been acid-etched and rubbed with dirt to simulate age.

"What is this?" Kerk asked, pulling a metal spike out of the compartment and turning it over in the light.

"A piton, a solid one. Half of them should be like that, and half with clips—like this one." He held up a similar spike that had a hole drilled in its broad end through which a ringlike clip had been passed.

"These things mean nothing to me," Kerk said.

"They don't have to." Jason emptied the cargo compartment while he spoke. "I'm climbing the spire and I know how to use them. I only wish that I could take along some of the more modern climbing equipment, but that would give me away at once. If we had any in the ship, which we don't. There are explosive piton setters that will drive a spike into the hardest rock, and instant-adhesive pitons that set in less than a second and the join is tougher than the rock around it. But I'm not using any of them. But I have had this rope wrapped around one of those monofilaments of grown ceramic fiber, the ones we use instead of barbed wire. With a breaking strength of more than 2,000 kilos. But what I have here will get me up the spire. I'll just climb until I run out of handholds, then I'll stop and drive in a piton and climb on it. For overhangs, or any other place where I need a rope, I use the ones with the rings. And these are for use close to the ground." He held up a crude-looking piton marred by hand-forged hammer blows and pitted with age. "All of these are made from bar-steel stock, which is a little rare in this part of the world. So the ones Temuchin and his men will see have been made into artificial antiques. Everything's here. You can tell the launch to take the verticapsule back."

The jets blew sand in their faces as the capsule rose and vanished. Jason held the light while Kerk tied the plaited leather rope to the end of the stained nylon line, then stowed this in the backpack, along with the rest of the equipment that Jason would use during the climb. Behind them, as they rode back to the encampment, the first light of dawn touched the horizon.

When the Pyrrans marched up The Slash, they saw that a desperate battle had been fought during the night. The dam of rubble and rock still sealed the neck of the valley—but now it was sprinkled darkly with corpses. Soldiers slept on the ground, out of bowshot of the enemy above, many of them wounded. A bloodstained nomad, with the totem of the lizard clan on his helm, sat impassively while a fellow clansman cut at the bone shaft of the arrow that had penetrated his arm.

"What happened here?" Jason asked him.

"We attacked at night," the wounded soldier said. "We could not be quiet because the rocks slipped and rolled away while we climbed, and many were hurt in this way. When we were close to the top, the weasels threw bundles of burning grass on our heads and they were above us on the clifftop in the darkness. We could not fight back and only those who were not high on the rocks lived to come down again. It was very bad."

"But very good for us," Kerk said as they moved on. "Temuchin will have lost prestige with this defeat, and we will gain it when we climb the rock. If we can—"

"Don't start the doubting act again," Jason said. "Just stand by at the base here and pretend that you know exactly what is going on."

Jason took off his heavy outer clothing and shivered. Well, he would warm up quickly enough as soon as he started his ascent. From below the tower looked as unclimbable as the side of a spaceship. He was tying the piton hammer's thong around his waist when Ahankk walked up, his face working as he tried both to sneer and to look dubious at the same time.

"I have been told, jongleur, that you are so stupid you think you can climb straight up rock."

"That is not all you have been told," Jason said, slipping his arms through the pack straps and settling the pack on his back. "Lord Temuchin told you to come here to see what happens. So get comfortable and rest your legs for the moment when you must run to your master with the glad news of my success."

Kerk looked up dubiously at the vertical face of rock, then down at Jason. "Let me climb," he said. "I am stronger than you and in far better condition."

"That you are," Jason agreed. "And as soon as I get to the top, I'll throw down the rope and you can climb up with all the bombs.

But you can't go first. Rock climbing is a skilled sport, and you are not going to learn it in a few minutes. Thanks for the offer, but I'm the only one who can do this job. So here we go. I would appreciate a lift so I can get a grip on that small ledge right over your head."

There was no nonsense about climbing up onto the Pyrran's shoulders. Kerk just bent and seized Jason by the ankles and lifted him straight up into the air. Jason walked his hands up the stone face as he rose and grabbed onto the narrow ledge while Kerk steadied his feet. Then his toes scrabbled and caught on a protruding hump and the climb had begun.

Jason was at least ten meters above the ground before he had to drive his first piton. A good bit of ledge, wide enough to lie down on, was well beyond the reach of his outstretched fingertips. The rock surface here was interlaced with cracks, so he picked a transverse one at the right height before him. The first piton was one of the disguised ones; he jammed it into the crack. Four sharp blows with the hammer wedged it in solidly. Slowly and carefully—it had been a good ten years since he had done any real climbing—he stepped out and eased his weight onto the piton. It held. He straightened his leg, sliding up the rough surface of the rock until he could reach the ledge. Then he pulled himself up to a sitting position and, breathing heavily, looked down at the upturned faces below. All of the soldiers were looking at him now, and even Temuchin had appeared to watch the climb. The enemy was surely taking an interest in what was happening, but the swell of the rock face cut them off from sight and arrow-shot. They could come to the edge of the canyon's wall, but they could not reach him unless they climbed the tower as well.

The rock was cold and he had better keep moving.

There was no way to estimate the height accurately, but he thought he must now be at least as high as the rim of the canyon. He had his toes jammed into a wide crack and was trying to drive a piton at an awkward angle off to one side when he heard the shouting below.

He bent as much as he could and called down, "What? I can't hear what you are saying." As he did this an arrow cracked into the rock at the place where his head had been and spun away and fell.

Jason almost fell after it, keeping his grip only by a convulsive clutch at the ribbed surface of the rock. When he turned his head, he saw a weasel tribesman hanging from a leather strap that was tied tightly about his body. He had a second arrow notched and ready to fire. The men holding the other end of the strap were out of sight on the rim of The Slash, but by lowering the bowman below the bulging outcropping they had put him within bowshot of Jason.

The warrior carefully drew the arrow back to the point of his jaw and took aim. The hammer was tied by its thong to Jason's wrist so he would not lose it, but he still clutched the piton in his left hand. With a reflexive motion, he hurled it at the bowman. The blunt end caught him in the shoulder. It did not injure him, but it deflected his aim enough so that the second arrow missed as well. He pulled a third from his belt and notched it to the bowstring.

Down below the soldiers were also shooting their bows, but the range was long and the overhead aim difficult. One arrow, almost spent, sank into the bowman's thigh, but he ignored it.

Jason let go of the hammer and took out a piton. It was tempered steel, well weighted and needle sharp. And he had had one try already so he knew the range. Taking the pointed end in his fingertips he drew well back beyond his head, then threw it with all the strength of his arm.

The point caught the bowman in the side of the neck and sank deep. He let go of his bow, scratched for the weapon with his fingers, shuddered and died. His body vanished from sight as the others pulled him up.

Someone had quieted the men below and he heard Kerk's voice cutting through the sudden silence.

"Hold on and brace yourself!" he shouted.

Jason looked down slowly and saw that the Pyrran had moved back from the base of the cliff and was holding one of their bombs, bent over and lighting it. Frantically, Jason kicked his toes in farther and, making fists of both hands, he jammed them deep into a vertical crack in the stone face.

Below him, the soldiers retreated from the base of the cliff. The foreshortened figure of Kerk reached back and back, until his knuckles appeared to be touching the ground. Then, in a single, spasmodic contraction of all his muscles, he hurled the bomb almost straight up into the air.

For a heart-stopping instant Jason thought it was coming right at him—then he realized it was going off to one side. It seemed to slow as it reached the summit of its arc, before it disappeared behind the curve of rock. Jason pushed hard against the cold stone.

The boom of the explosion was transmitted to him through the stone, a shuddering vibration. Fragments of rock and bodies blew out into space behind him and he knew his flank was safe. Kerk would be ready if the same trick were tried again. Yet there was still a feeling of unease.

"Kerk!" Jason shouted. "The piton!" He spoke in Pyrran.

"What happened to the piton I dropped? If Temuchin should see it . . ."

One glimpse would be enough to reveal that they were offworlders. The nomads were familiar enough with the appearance of alien artifacts.

One, two thudding heartbeats of time Jason waited before Kerk called back to him.

"All . . . right . . . I saw it drop . . . picked it up while they were all looking at you. Are you hurt?"

"Fine," Jason whispered, then drew a deep breath. "Fine!" he shouted. "I'm going on now."

After this it was just work. Twice Jason had to sling a loop of rope through the carabiner of a piton and sit in it to rest. His strength was giving out and he had used the most potent stimulants in the medikit by the time he reached the foot of a chimney thating it as the saliva chilled and froze. He brushed the ice from his palms and took off the pack. The less weight, the better; even the hammer had to be left behind now. He piled the discarded items at the foot of the chimney and slung the coil of rope around his neck so that it rested on his chest.

Wedging his back against one wall he walked up the other until his body was parallel to the ground, held up by the friction of his shoulders and his feet. He pushed higher with his arms, then walked upward with his feet. Centimeter by centimeter he worked his way up the chimney.

Before he reached the top he knew he would not make it.

Yet, at the same time, he knew he had to make it. Going back down would be just as hard as keeping on upward. And if he fell, he would break at least an arm or a leg at the foot of the chimney. Where he would simply lie and die of thirst. There was no chance of anyone else's getting up here to help him. It would be better to keep on.

With infinite slowness the sky appeared above, closer and closer, and slower and slower as the strength ebbed from his limbs.

When he finally reached the spot where his toes were actually at the lip of the rock, he had no strength left to pull himself over the edge. For a few seconds he rested, took a deep breath and straightened his legs. He twisted as he did so and clutched at the crumbling edge of rock. For a moment of time he hung there, neither falling nor able to pull himself out of the chimney. Then, ever so slowly, he pulled and scraped with bloody fingertips until he dragged himself out and lay exhausted on the tilted summit of the pinnacle.

The top was amazingly small; he saw that as he lay gasping for air. No bigger than a large-sized bed. When he was able to, he crawled to the edge and waved at the waiting men below. They saw him and a ragged and spontaneous cheer went up.

Was there anything to cheer about? He went to the far side and looked, moving back as the waiting bowmen on the clifftop below fired at him. Only two arrows rose high enough to hit him, but these were badly aimed. He looked again and saw the enemy position spread out like a model below him. Everything was visible and within easy range, both the men on the rim of The Slash and the rows of bowmen protecting the top of the rockslide.

He had done it.

"Good man, Jason," he said aloud. "You're a credit to any world."

Sitting cross-legged, he made a large loop in the end of the line and passed it around the summit of the rock itself, making an immovable anchor. Then he let the leather-tipped end over the edge and paid it out slowly, until a signaling tug told him that it had reached the ground. He shortened the rope with a quickly knotted sheepshank and gave the agreed upon signal—three tugs on the line—to show that it was secured. Then he sat down to wait.

Only when the rope began to jerk violently and stand out from the cliff did he get up. Kerk was right below, looking unwinded and fresh, with an immense load of bombs slung on his back. He had taken the rope in both hands and walked straight up the face of the cliff.

"Can you reach down to help me over the edge of the cliff?" Kerk asked.

"Absolutely. Just don't squeeze or break anything."

Jason lay face down, with the rock rim in his armpit, and reached over. Kerk let go with one hand and they seized each other's wrists in an acrobat's hold. Jason did not try to pull—he probably could not have lifted Kerk's weight if he had tried—but instead he spread-eagled and anchored himself as well as he could against the stone. Kerk pulled himself up, threw an arm over the edge, then heaved his body over.

"Very good," he said, looking down at the enemy below. "They do not stand a chance. I have extra microgrenades that we can use. Shall we begin?"

"You're letting me throw out the first bomb of the season? How nice."

As the explosions roared and rumbled into a continuous thunder, Temuchin's army shouted a victorious echo and started up the rocky slope. The battle was decided and would soon be won, and after it, the war would be won as well.

Jason sat down and watched Kerk happily bombing the natives below.

This part of the plan was complete. If the next step worked as well, the Pyrrans would have their mines and their planet. *Their* last battle would be won.

Jason sincerely hoped so. He was getting very tired.

15

> Strike like lightning, magic thunder
> Slew the weasels, cleansed the mountains.
> Piled high, the thumbs of conquest
> Reached above a tall man's head.
> Then the word of strangers coming
> To his land reached Lord Temuchin.
> With sword and bow and fearless army
> Rode he out to slay invaders . . .
> *from* THE SONG OF TEMUCHIN

Jason dinAlt reined his *morope* to a stop at the top of the broad slope and searched for a path down through the tumbled boulders. The wind, damp and cold, funneled up through this single gap in the high cliffs, struck him full in the face. Far below, the ocean was gray steel, flecked with the spray-blown tops of waves. The sky was dark, cloud-covered from horizon to horizon, and somewhere out at sea thunder rumbled heavily.

A faintly marked path was visible, threading down the rock-covered slope; Jason spurred his mount forward. Once he had started down he saw that the path was well-worn and old. The nomads must come here regularly, for salt perhaps. An aerial survey from the spaceship had shown that this was the only spot for thousands of kilometers where there was a break in the palisade of up on the shore with yellow cloth tents set up beside them. Farther out in the bay a squat two-master, with a smoke-stained funnel aft, lay with furled sails, swinging at anchor. Jason's approach was seen and, from the knot of men around the boats, a tall figure emerged and strode purposefully across the sand. Jason halted the *morope* and slid down to meet him.

"That's a great outfit you're wearing, Rhes," he said as he shook the other man's hand.

"No more exotic than yours," the Pyrran said, smiling and running his fingers through the purple ruffles that covered his chest. He wore crotch-high boots of yellow suede and a polished helmet with a golden spike. It was most impressive. "This is what the well-dressed Master Merchant of Ammh wears," he added.

"From the reports I hear that you made out very well in the lowlands."

"I've never enjoyed myself more. Ammh is basically an agrarian society that is working very hard to enter a primitive machine age. The classes are completely separate, with the merchant and the military at the top, along with a small priest class to keep the peasants quiet. I had the capital to enter the merchant class and I made the most of it. The operation is going so well that it is self-financing now. I have a warehouse in Camar, the seaport closest to the barrier mountains, and I have just been waiting for the word to sail north. Would you care for a glass of wine?"

"And some food. Trot out your best for me."

They had reached the open-sided tent which contained a trestle table loaded with bottles and cuts of smoked meat. Rhes picked up a long-necked green bottle and handed it to Jason. "Try this," he said. "A six-year-old vintage, very good. I'll get a knife to cut the seal."

"Don't bother," Jason said, cracking the neck off the bottle with a sharp blow against the edge of the table. He drank deeply from the golden wine that bubbled out, then wiped his mouth on the back of his sleeve. "I'm a barbarian, remember? This will convince your guards of my roughshod character." He nodded toward the soldiers who stood about, frowning and fingering their weapons.

"You've developed some vile habits," Rhes said, wiping the

broken neck of the bottle with a cloth before he poured a glassful for himself. "What's the plan?"

Jason chewed hungrily at a fatty chop. "Temuchin is on the way here with an army. Not a big one—most of the tribes went home after the weasels were wiped out. But all of them first swore fealty to him and agreed to join him whenever he ordered. When he heard about your landing here, he called in the nearest tribes and started his march. He's about a day away now, but Kerk and the Pyrrans are camped right across his trail. We should join up tonight. I rode on here alone just to check the setup before contact is made."

"Does everything meet your approval?"

"Just about. I would keep your armed thugs close by, but don't make it look so obvious. Let a couple of them lounge around and stuff the rest into a tent. Do you have the trade goods we talked about?"

'Everything. Knives, steel arrowheads, wooden shafts for arrows, iron pots, plus a lot more. Sugar, salt, some spices. They should find something they like out of this lot."

"That's our hope." Jason looked unhappily at the empty bottle, then tossed it away.

"Would you like another one?" Rhes asked.

"Yes, but I'm not going to take it. No contact with the enemy— not yet. I'll get back to the camp so I can be there when we have the meet with Temuchin. This is the one that counts. We have to get the tribes on our side, start peaceful trade and squeeze the warlord out into the cold. Keep a bottle on ice until I get back."

By the time Jason's mount had climbed up to the high plains again the sky was lower and darker, and the wind threw a fine shrapnel of sleet against the back of his neck. He crouched low and used his spurs to move the *morope* at its best speed. By late afternoon he came up to the Pyrran camp just as they were starting to move out.

"You're just in time," Kerk said, riding over to join him. "I have the ship's launch up high in a satellite orbit, tracking Temuchin's force. Earlier this afternoon he turned off the direct route to the beach and headed for Hell's Doorway. He'll probably stop there for the night."

"I never thought of him as being much of a religious man."

"I am sure that he isn't," Kerk said. "But he is a good enough leader to keep his men happy. This pit, or whatever it is, appears to be one of the few holy places they have. Supposed to be a backdoor leading directly to hell. Temuchin will make a sacrifice there."

"It's as good a place as any to meet him. Let's ride."

The dark afternoon blended imperceptibly into evening as the sky pressed down and the wind hurled granular blizzard snow at them. It collected in the folds of their clothing and on the *moropes'* fur until they were all streaked and coated with it. It was almost fully dark before they came to the *camachs* of Temuchin's followers. There were welcome shouts of greetings from all sides as they rode toward the large *camach* where the chieftains were meeting. Kerk and Jason dismounted and pushed by the guards at the entrance flap. The circle of men turned to look as they came in. Temuchin glared pure hatred at them.

"Who is this that dares come uninvited to Temuchin's meeting of his captains?"

Kerk drew himself up and gave as well as he had received. "Who is this Temuchin who would bar Kerk of the Pyrrans, conqueror of The Slash, from a meeting of the chiefs of the plains?"

The battle was joined and everyone there knew it. The absolute silence was broken only by the rustle of wind-driven snow against the outside of the *camach*.

Temuchin was the first warlord to have brought all of the tribes together under one banner. Yet he ruled nothing without the agreement of his tribal chieftains. Some of them were already displeased with the severity of his orders and would have preferred a new warlord—or no warlord at all. They followed the contest with close attention.

"You fought well at The Slash," Temuchin said. "As did all here. We greet you and you may now leave. What we do here today does not concern that battle nor does it concern you."

"Why?" Kerk asked with icy calmness, seating himself at the same time. "What are you trying to conceal from me?"

"You accuse me . . ." Temuchin was white with anger, his hand on his sword.

"I accuse no one." Kerk yawned broadly. "You seem to accuse yourself. You meet in secret, you refuse a chieftain entrance, you attempt insult rather than speaking the truth. I ask you again what you conceal?"

"It is a matter of small importance. Some lowlanders have arrived on our shores, to invade, to build cities. We will destroy them."

"Why? They are harmless traders," Kerk said.

"Why?" Temuchin was burning with anger now and could not stand still; he paced back and forth. "Have you never heard of

'The Song of the Freemen'?''

"As well as you have—or better. The song says to destroy the buildings of those who will trap us. Are there buildings to be destroyed?"

"No, but they will come next. Already the lowlanders have put up tents—"

One of the chieftains broke in, singing a line from "The Song of the Freemen":

"Knowing no home, other than our tents."

Temuchin controlled his rage and ignored the interruption. The words of the song were against him, but he knew where the truth lay.

"These traders are like the point of the sword that makes but a scratch. They are in tents and they trade today—but soon they will be ashore with bigger tents, then buildings in order to trade better. First the tip of the sword, then the entire blade to run us through and destroy us. They must be wiped out now."

What Temuchin said was absolutely true. It was very important that the other chieftains should not realize that. Kerk was silent for an instant and Jason stepped into the gap.

" 'The Song of Freemen' must be our guide in this matter. This is the song that tells us—"

"Why are you here, jongleur?" Temuchin said in a voice of stern command. "I see no other jongleurs or common soldiers. You may leave."

Jason opened his mouth, but could think of nothing to say. Temuchin was unarguably right. Jason, he thought, you should have kept your big mouth shut. He bowed to the warlord, and as he did he whispered to Kerk:

"I'll be close by and I'll listen in on the dentiphone. If I can think of anything that will help, I will tell you."

Kerk did not turn around, but he murmured agreement and his voice was transmitted clearly to the tiny radio in Jason's mouth. After this, there was nothing Jason could do except leave.

Bad luck. He had hoped to be in on the showdown. As he pushed through the flap, one of the guards stationed there bent to lace it behind him. The other one dropped his lance.

Jason looked at it surprised, even as the man reached out with both hands and grabbed him by the wrists. What was this?! Jason twisted upward with his forearms, against the other's thumbs, to break the simple hold, while at the same time aiming a knee at the man's groin as a note of disapproval. But before he could free himself or connect, the guard behind him slipped a leather strap over his head and jerked it tight about his throat.

Jason could neither fight nor cry out. He writhed and struggled ineffectively as he quickly slipped into black unconsciousness.

16

Someone was grinding snow into Jason's face, forcing it into his nostrils and mouth, effectively dragging him back to consciousness. He coughed and spluttered, pushing himself away from the offending hands. When he had wiped the snow from his eyes, he looked around, blinking, trying to place himself.

He was kneeling between two of Temuchin's men. Their swords were drawn and ready, and one of them held a guttering torch. It illuminated a small patch of drifted snow and the black lip of a chasm. Red-lit snowflakes rushed by him and vanished into this pit of darkness.

"Do you know this man?" a voice asked, and Jason recognized it as Temuchin's. Two men appeared out of the night and stood before him.

"I do, great Lord Temuchin," the second man said. "It is the other-world man from the great flying thing, the one who was captured and escaped."

Jason looked closer at the muffled face and, as the torch flared up, he recognized the sharp nose and sadistic smile of Oraiel, the jongleur.

"I never saw this person before. He is a liar," Jason said, ignoring the hoarseness of his voice and the pain in his throat when he spoke.

"I remember him when he was captured, great lord, and later he attacked and beat me. You saw him yourself there."

"Yes, I did." Temuchin stepped forward and looked down at Jason's upturned face, his own cold and impassive. "Of course. He is the one. That is why he looked familiar."

"What are these lies . . ." Jason said, struggling to his feet.

409

Temuchin seized him by the forearms in an implacable grip, pushing him backward until his heels were on the crumbling edge of the abyss.

"Tell the truth now, whoever you are. You stand at the edge of Hell's Doorway and in one moment you shall be hurled down it. You cannot escape. But I might let you go if you tell me the truth."

As he talked, Temuchin bent Jason's body back, farther and farther over the blackness, until only the grip on his wrists prevented him from falling. Jason could not see the warlord's face: it was a black outline against the torches. Yet he knew there was no hope of mercy there. This was the end. The best he could do now was to protect the Pyrrans.

"Release me and I shall tell you the truth. I am from another world. I came here alone to help you. I found the jongleur Jason, and he was dying, so I took his name. He had been gone from his people many years and they no longer remembered him. And I have helped you. Release me and I will help you more."

A weak voice, filled with static, buzzed in his head. "Jason, is that you? Kerk here. Where are you?" The dentiphone was still operating—he had a chance.

"Why are you here?" Temuchin asked. "Are you helping the lowlanders to bring their cities to our lands?"

"Release me. Do not drop me now into Hell's Doorway and I will tell you."

Temuchin hesitated a long moment before he spoke again.

"You are a liar. Everything you say is a lie. I do not know what to believe." His head turned and for an instant the torchlight lit the humorless smile on his lips.

"I release you," he said, and opened his hands.

Jason clawed at empty air, tried to twist so he could clutch at the cliff's edge, but he could do nothing. He fell into the blackness.

A rush of air.

A blow on his shoulder, his back. Then he was scraping along the side of the cliff, struggling to keep his face and hands away from the abrasive dirt and stone. The cliffside tore at the leather of his garments as he plummeted down the outward-slanting surface.

Then it ended and he fell free in the blackness once again. Falling for an unmeasurable moment of time, seconds or minutes—forever—until a crushing impact enfolded him.

He did not die, and that surprised him very much. He wiped something from his face and realized that it was snow. A snowbank, a drift, here at the bottom of Hell's Doorway. A snowbank in hell and he had fallen into it.

"Where there's life, there's still hope, Jason," he told himself unconvincingly. What hope was there at the bottom of this inaccessible pit? Kerk and the Pyrrans would get him out, that was a morale-building hope. Yet, even as he thought this, his tongue contacted a jagged end of metal in his mouth. With restored fear he groped out the crushed remains of the dentiphone. Some time during the fall, he had unknowingly ground it between his teeth and destroyed it.

"You're on your own again, Jason," he said aloud, and did not enjoy in the slightest the tiny sound of his voice in the immense blackness. What were his assets? He floundered about in the drift until he could reach back for his medikit. It was gone. Well, his wallet was still on his belt, though his knife was gone from his boot. His fingers searched through the assorted junk in the wallet until they touched an unfamiliar tube. What? The photon-store flashlight, of course. Dropped in here and forgotten since the night they had picked up the climbing equipment.

But was it broken? The way his luck was running it probably was. He switched it on and groaned aloud when nothing happened. Then he turned the intensity ring and the brilliant beam slashed through the darkness. Light! Even though his situation was not materially changed, Jason felt a lift in his morale. He broadened the beam and flashed it around his prison. The air was still and the snowflakes fell silently through the light and vanished. Snow covered the flat valley floor below and piled in drifts against the walls. Black rock rose up on both sides, pushed out above his head where a ledge of rock projected. The sky was invisible, cut off by the jutting rock. He must have slid down that rocky angle and been shot off like a projectile into this snowbank. Pure chance had saved him.

There was a moaning cry and something black plunged down from above and through the beam of light, striking the valley bottom no more than ten meters from Jason.

The vertical rocks there were coated with only a thin layer of snow and the man had struck full across them. His eyes were open and staring, a trickle of blood ran from the gaping mouth. It was his betrayer, the jongleur Oraiel.

"What's this? Temuchin eliminating eyewitnesses? That's not like him." The mouth still gaped open but Oraiel had finished forever with speaking.

Jason floundered out of his drift and started across the floor of the narrow valley. The ground was smooth in the center, smooth and very flat. He did not consider why until there was an ominous creaking beneath his feet. Even as he tried to throw himself backward the ice broke, splintering and cracking in every direction, and he fell into the dark waters beneath.

The sudden shock of the frigid water almost drove the air from his lungs, but he clamped his mouth shut, sinking his teeth hard into his lower lip. At the same time his fingers tightened convulsively on the flashlight. Without this he would not be able to find the opening in the ice again.

Almost at the same instant his feet touched the rocky bottom, the water was not deep, and he kicked upward. The light shone on a mirror above as he rose and his hand went out to press, palm to palm, against his imaged hand. It was ice, solid and unbroken above him. Only when he felt his fingers being dragged across its surface did he realize that he was being pulled swiftly along by a current. The hole in the ice must already be far behind him.

If Jason dinAlt had been prone to despair, this was the moment when he would have died. Trapped beneath the ice at the bottom of this inaccessible valley, this was indeed the time to give up. He never considered it. He held the burning lungful of air; he tried to swim to the side where he could get some footing, perhaps press up through the ice; he waved the light upward looking for a break.

The current was too swift. It threw him numbingly against the rocks, then hurtled him back into the swift-flowing current. He pointed down stream and kicked to stay in the center, looking down at the smooth rocks that flew by an arm's length beneath his face.

The water was cold; it numbed his skin and carried him along with it. But it was the fire in his lungs that could not be ignored. Logically he knew that he had enough oxygen in his body cells and his bloodstream to live for many minutes. The breathing reflex in his chest was not interested in logic. *Dying!* it screamed. *Air, breathe,* until he could deny it no longer. Numbly he drifted upward to the mirrored surface and broke through into blackness and sucked in a shuddering, lifegiving breath.

It took a long time for the reality of what had occurred to penetrate his numbed senses. He dragged himself to a dark, stony shore and lay half in and half out of the water like some form of beached marine life. Moving seemed completely out of the question, but as the shuddering cold bit deep he realized it was either that or die here. And where was *here?* With pained slowness he pulled himself clear of the water and moved the light up the rocky wall, across the rock above and back down the rock to the water again. No snow? The meaning of this forced through his chilled and sluggish synapses.

"A cave."

It was obvious enough by hindsight. The narrow valley, Hell's Doorway, must have been cut by water, slowly eroded out through the centuries by the small stream. It had no visible outlet because it plunged underground—and it had taken him with it. That meant he wasn't finished yet. The water had to have an outlet, and if it did he would find it. For a moment he considered the fact that it might sink lower and lower into the rock strata and vanish, but he swiftly rejected this defeatist idea.

"Carry on!" he shouted aloud as he stumbled to his feet, and the echoes called back "On . . . on . . . on. . . ."

"Good idea, on, onwards. Just what I shall do."

He shivered and squelched forward through the fine sand at the edge of the water, and the next thing he saw were the footprints emerging from the stream and going on ahead of him.

Was someone else here?! The footprints were sharp and clear, obviously recently made. There must be an entrance to these caverns that was well known. All he had to do was follow the footprints and he would be out. And as long as he kept walking he would not freeze in his sodden clothing. The cave air was cool, but not so cold as the plateau outside.

When the trail left the sand beside the stream and ventured into an adjoining cavern, it became more difficult to follow, but not impossible. Small stalagmites growing from the limestone floor had been kicked down, and there were occasional marks gouged into the soft stone of the walls. The tunnels branched and one went back to the water where it ended abruptly at a rocky bank. The shore was gone and the water filled the cave here, coming close to the smooth ceiling. Jason retraced his steps and picked up the trail again at the next branch.

It was a long walk.

Jason rested once and fell asleep without realizing it. He awoke, shivering uncontrollably, and forced himself to go on. As far as he knew, the watch concealed in his belt buckle was still operating, but he never looked at it. Somehow the measuring of time could not be considered in these endless, timeless caverns.

Walking down one of them, no different from all the others, he found the man he had been following. He was sleeping on the cave floor ahead, a barbarian, in furs very much like Jason's.

"Hello," he called in the in-between tongue, then fell silent as he came closer. The sleep was for eternity and the man had been dead a very long time. Years, centuries perhaps, in these dry, cold, and bacteria-free caverns. There was no way to tell. His flesh and skin were brown and mummified, leather lips shriveled back from yellow teeth. One outstretched hand lay, pointing ahead, a knife just beyond the splayed fingers. When Jason picked it up, he saw that it was tarnished only by the thinnest patina of rust.

What Jason did next was not easy, but it was essential for survival. With careful motions he removed the fur outer garments from the corpse. It crackled and rustled when he was forced to move the stiff limbs, but made no other protest. When he had the furs, he moved farther down the cavern, stripped himself bare and donned the dry clothes. There was no repugnance; this was survival.

He stretched his own clothes out to dry, bunched the fur under his head, turned the light to a dim yellow glow—he could not bear the thought of total darkness—and fell instantly into a troubled sleep.

17

"They say that if everything is the same for a long time, you can't tell how long the time is because everything is the same. So I wonder how long I have been down here." He trudged a few steps more and considered it. "A long time, I guess."

The cavern branched ahead and he made a careful mark with the knife, at shoulder height, before taking the right-hand turning. This tunnel dead-ended at the water, a familiar occurrence, and he knelt and drank his stomach full before turning back. At the junction he scratched the slash that meant "water" and turned down the other branch.

"One thousand eight hundred and three . . . one thousand eight hundred and four . . ." He had to count every third step of his left foot now because the number was so large. It was also meaningless, but it gave him something to say and he found the sound of his voice to be less trying than the everlasting silence.

At least his stomach had stopped hurting. The rumblings and cramps had been very annoying in the beginning, but that had passed. There was always enough water to drink, and he should have thought of measuring the time by the number of notches he took in his belt.

"I've seen you before, you evil crossway you." He spat dryly in the direction of the three marks on the wall at the junction. Then he scratched a fourth below them with the knife. He would not be coming back here again. Now he knew the right sequence of turns to take in the maze ahead.

He hoped.

"Cuglio, he only has one sphere. . . . Fletter has two but very queer. . . . Harmill . . ." He pondered as he marched. Just what was it that Harmill had? It escaped him now. He had been singing all the old marching songs that he remembered, but for some reason he was beginning to forget the words.

Some reason! Hah. He laughed dirtily at himself. The reason was obvious. He was getting very hungry and very tired. A human body can live a long time with water and without food. But how long can it go on walking?

"Time to rest?" he asked himself.

"Time to rest," he answered himself.

In a little while. This tunnel was slanted downward and there was the smell of water ahead. He was getting very good with his nose lately. Many times there was sand next to the water on which he could sleep, and this was far better than the bare rock. There was very little flesh over his bones now and they pressed through and hurt.

Good. There was sand here, a luxurious, wide band of it. The water was wider and must be deeper, almost a pool. It still tasted the same. He squirmed out a hollow in the unmarked sand, turned the flashlight out, put it into his pouch and went to sleep.

He used to leave it on when he slept, but this did not seem to make any difference any more.

As always, he slept briefly, woke up, then slept again. But there was something wrong. With his eyes open he lay staring up into the velvety darkness. Then he turned to look at the water.

Far out. Deep down. Faint, ever so faint, was a shimmer of blue light.

For a long time he lay there thinking about it. He was tired and weak, starved, probably feverish. Which meant he was probably imagining it. The dying man's fantasy, the mirage for the thirsty. He closed his eyes and dozed, yet when he looked again the light was still there. What could it mean?

"I should do something about this," he said, and turned his

flashlight on. In the greater light the glow in the water was gone. He
stood the flashlight up in the sand and took out his knife. The tip was
still sharp. He raked it along the inside of his arm, drawing a shallow
slice that oozed thick drops of blood.

"That hurts!" he said, then, "That's better."

The sudden pain had jarred him from his lethargy, released
adrenalin into his bloodstream and forced him into unaccustomed
alertness.

"If there's light down there, it must be an exit to the outside. It
has to be. And if it is, it may be my only chance to get out of this
trap. Now. While I still think I can make it."

After that, he shut up and took breath after breath, filling his
lungs again and again until his head began to swim with hyperventi-
lation. Then, with a last breath, he turned the light to full intensity
and put the end in his mouth so that he could direct it forward by
tilting his head. One, two, hands together and dive.

The water was a cold shock, but he had expected that. He dove
deep and swam as hard as he could toward the spot where he had
seen the light. The water was wonderfully transparent. Rock, just
solid rock on the other side of the pool. Perhaps lower then. The
water soaked into his clothes and helped pull him down, almost to
the bottom, where a ledge cut across the pool. Below it, the current
quickened and moved outward. Headfirst, pushing against the rock
above, he went under, bumped along a short channel and was in the
clear again.

Above him now was more light, far above, inaccessible. He
kicked and stroked but it seemed to come no closer. The flashlight
fell from his mouth and spun down to oblivion. Higher, higher.
Though he was going toward the light, it seemed to be getting
darker. In a panic he thrashed his arms, although they seemed to be
pushing against mercury or some medium far thicker than water.
One hand struck something hard and round. He seized it and pulled
and his head was thrust above the surface of the water.

For the first minute all he could do was hang from the tree root
and suck in great, rasping breaths of air. When his head began to
clear, he saw that he was at the edge of a pond almost completely
surrounded by trees and undergrowth. Behind him the pool ended at
the base of a towering cliff that stretched upward until it vanished in
the haze and clouds above. This was the outlet of the underground
stream from the plateau.

He was in the lowlands.

Pulling himself out of the water was an effort, and when he was
out, he just lay on the grass and steamed until some small fraction of

his strength had returned. The sight of some berries on the nearby bushes finally stirred him into motion. There were not many of them, which was probably for the best, for even these few caused racking stomach pains after he had wolfed them down. He lay on the grass then, his face stained with purple juice, and wondered what to do next. He slept, without wanting to, and when he awoke, his head was clearer.

"Defense. Every man's hand turned against the other. The first local who sees me will probably try to brain me just to get these antique furs that I'm wearing. Defense."

His knife had vanished along with his flashlight, so a sharp fragment of split rock had to do. A straight sapling was raw material and he worried it off close to the ground with the chip of stone. Taking off the branches was easier, and within the hour he had a rough but usable quarterstaff. It served first as a walking stick as he hobbled eastward on a forest path that appeared to go in the right direction.

Toward evening, when his head was starting to swim again, he met a stranger on the path. A tall, erect man in semimilitary uniform, armed with a bow and a very efficient-looking halberd. The man snapped some questions at Jason in an unknown language, in answer to which Jason simply shrugged and made mumbling noises. He tried to appear innocent and weak, which was easy enough to do. With his drawn skin, tangled beard and filthy furs, he certainly couldn't have looked very ominous or appetizing. The stranger must have thought so too, for he did not use his bow and came forward with his halberd only indifferently at the defense.

Jason knew that he had only one good—or halfhearted—blow in him, and he had to make it count. This efficient looking young man would eat him alive if he missed.

"Umble, umble," Jason muttered, and shrank back, both hands on the length of stick.

"Frmblebrmble!" the man said, shaking his halberd menacingly as he came close.

Jason pushed down with his right hand, pivoting the quarterstaff with his left so that the end whipped up. Then he lunged it forward into the other's midriff in the region of the solar plexus ganglion. The stranger let out a single, mighty whoosh of air and folded, unmoving to the ground.

"My fortunes change!" Jason chortled as he fell on the other's bulging purse. Food perhaps? Saliva dampened his mouth as he tore it open.

18

Rhes was in his inner office, finishing up with his bookkeeping, when he heard the loud shouts in the courtyard. It sounded as though someone were trying to force his way in. He ignored it; the other two Pyrrans had gone, and he had a lot of work to finish up before he left. His guard, Riclan, was a good man and knew how to take care of himself. He would turn any unwanted visitors away. The shouting stopped suddenly, and a moment later there was a noise that sounded suspiciously like Riclan's armor and weapons falling onto the cobbles.

For two days Rhes had not slept, and there was still much to be done before he went away for good. His temper was therefore not of the best. It is very unhealthy to be around a Pyrran when he feels this way. When the door opened, he stood prepared to destroy the interloper. Preferably with his bare hands so that he could hear the bones crunch. A man with an ugly black beard, wearing the uniform of a freelance soldier, entered, and Rhes flexed his fingers and stepped forward.

"What's the trouble? You look ready to kill me," the soldier said in fluent Pyrran.

"Jason!" Rhes was across the room and pounding his friend on the back with excitement.

"Easy," Jason said, escaping the embrace and dropping onto the couch. "A Pyrran greeting can maim, and I haven't been feeling that good lately."

"We thought you were dead! What happened?"

"I'll be happy to explain, but would prefer to do it over food and drink. And I would like to hear a report myself. The last time I heard about Felicitian politics was just before I was pushed off a cliff. How does the trade go?"

"It doesn't," Rhes said glumly, taking meat and bread from a locker and fishing a cobwebbed bottle of wine from its straw bed. "After you were killed—or we thought you were killed—everything came to pieces. Kerk heard you on his dentiphone a almost destroyed his *morope* getting there. But he was too late—you had gone over the edge of Hell's Doorway. There was some jongleur who had betrayed you, and he tried to accuse Kerk of being an off-worlder as well. Kerk kicked him off the cliff before he could say very much. Temuchin was apparently just as angry as Kerk and the whole thing almost blew up right there. But you were gone and that was that. Kerk felt the most he could do for you was to try and complete your plans.''

''Did you?''

''I'm sorry to report that we failed. Temuchin convinced most of the tribal leaders that they should fight, not trade. Kerk aided us, but it was a lost cause. I eventually had to retreat back here. I'm closing out this operation, leaving it in good enough shape for my assistants to carry on, and the Pyrran 'tribe' is on its way back to the ship. This plan is over, and if we can't come up with another one, we have agreed to return to Pyrrus.''

''You can't!'' Jason said in the loudest mumble he could manage around the mouthful of food.

''We have no choice. Now tell me, please, how did you get here? We had men down in Hell's Doorway later the same night. They found no trace of you at all, though there were plenty of other corpses and skeletons. They thought you must have gone through the ice and that your body had been swept away.''

''Indeed swept away, but not as a body. I hit a snowbank when I landed and I would have been waiting for you, cold but alive, if I had not fallen through the ice as you guessed. The stream leads to a series of caverns. I had a light and more patience than I realized. It was nasty, but I finally came out below the cliffs in this country. I knocked a number of citizens on the head and had an adventurous trip to reach you here.''

''A lucky arrival. Tomorrow would have been too late. The ship's launch is to pick me up just after dark and I have a ten-kilometer row to reach the rendezvous point.''

''Well, you've got a second oar now. I'm ready to go anytime after I get this food and drink under my belt.''

''I'll radio about your arrival so that word can be relayed to Kerk and the others.''

They left quietly in one of Rhes's own boats and reached the rocky offshore islet before the sun touched the horizon. Rhes chopped a hole in the boat's planking and they put in some heavy rocks. It sank nicely, and after that, all they could do was wait and admire the guano deposits and listen to the cries of the disturbed seabirds until the launch picked them up.

The flight was a brief one after the pilot, Clon, had nodded recognition at Jason—which was about all the enthusiastic Pyrran welcome he expected. At the grounded *Felicity*, the off watch was asleep, and the on watch, at their duty stations, so Jason saw no one. He preferred it this way because he was still tired from his journey. The Pyrran tribesmen were to arrive some time the following day and socializing could wait until then.

His cabin was just as he had left it, with the expensive library leering at him metallically from one corner. What had ever prompted him to buy it in the first place? A complete waste of money. He kicked at it as he passed, but his foot only skidded off the polished metal ovoid.

"Useless," he said, and stabbed the *on* button. "What good are you, after all?"

"Is that a question?" the library intoned. "If so, restate and indicate the precise meaning of 'good' in this context."

"Big mouth. All talk now—but where were you when I needed you?"

"I am where I am placed. I answer whatever questions are asked of me. Your question is therefore meaningless."

"Don't insult your superiors, machine. That is an order."

"Yes, sir."

"That's better. I maketh and I can breaketh just as well."

Jason dialed a strong drink from the wall dispenser and flopped into the armchair. The library flickered its little lights and hummed electronically to itself. He drank deep, then addressed the machine.

"I'll bet you don't think much of my plan to lick the natives and open the mine?"

"I do not know your plan; therefore I cannot give a judged opinion."

"Well, I'm not asking you. I bet you think that you could think a better plan yourself?"

"In which area do you wish a plan?"

"In the area of changing a culture, that's where. But I'm not asking."

"Culture-changing references will be found under 'history' and 'anthropology.' If you are not asking, I withdraw the reference."

Jason sipped and brooded, and finally spoke.

"Well, I am asking. Tell me about cultures."

Jason pressed the *off* button and settled back in his chair. The lights went out on the library and the hum faded into silence.

So it could be done after all. The answer had been right there the history books all the time, if he had only had the brains to look. There were no excuses for the stupidity of his actions. He should have consulted the library but he had not. Yet—it still might be possible to make amends.

"Why not?!"

He paced the room, hitting his fist into the palm of his hand. The pieces might still be put back together if he played it right. He doubted if he could convince the Pyrrans that the new plan would succeed, or even that it was a good idea. They would probably be completely against it. Then he would have to work without them. He looked at his watch. The launch was not due to leave for the first pickup of Kerk and the others for at least another hour. Time enough to get ready. Write a friendly note to Meta and be deliberately vague about his plans. Then have Clon drop him off near Temuchin's camp. The unimaginative pilot would do as he was told without asking questions.

Yes, it could be done, and by the stars he was going to do it.

19

Lord was he of all the mountains,
Ruled the plains and all the valleys.
Nothing passed without his knowledge.
Many died with his displeasure.

Temuchin sprang suddenly into the *camach*, his drawn sword ready in his hand.

"Reveal yourself!" he cried. "My guard lies outside, struck down. Reveal yourself, spy, so that I may kill you."

A hooded figure stepped from the darkness into the flickering light of the oil lamp and Temuchin raised his sword. Jason threw back the fur so his face could be seen.

"You!" Temuchin said in a hollow voice, and the sword slipped from his fingers to the ground. "You cannot be here. I killed you with these hands. Are you ghost or demon?"

"I have returned to help you, Temuchin. To open an entire new world to your conquest."

"A demon, that you must be, and instead of dying, you returned home through Hell's Doorway and gained new strength. A demon of a thousand guises—that explains how you could trick and betray so many people. The jongleur thought you were an off-worlder. The Pyrrans thought you were one of their tribe. I thought you a loyal comrade who would help me."

"That's a fine theory. You believe what you want. Then listen to what I have to tell you."

"*No!* If I listen, I am damned." He grabbed up the sword. Jason talked fast before he had to battle for his life.

"There are caves opening from the valley you call Hell's Doorway. They don't go to hell—but they lead down to the lowlands. I went there and returned by boat to tell you this. I can show you the way. You can lead an army through those caves and invade the lowlands. You rule here now—and you can rule there as well. A new continent to conquer. And you are the only man who could possibly do it."

Temuchin lowered the sword slowly and his eyes blazed in the firelight. When he spoke, his voice was hushed, as though he were speaking only to himself.

"You must be a demon, and I cannot kill that which is already dead. I could drive you from me, but I cannot drive your words from my head. You know, as no living man knows, that I am empty. I rule these plains and that is the end of it. What pleasure in ruling? No wars, no conquests, no joy of seeing one's enemy fall and marching on. Alone, by day and night I have dreamed about those rich meadows and towns below the cliffs. How even gunpowder and great armies could not stand against my warriors. How we would surprise them, flank them, besiege their cities. Conquer."

"Yes, you could have all that, Temuchin. Lord of all this world."

In the silence the lamp sputtered, tossing shadows of the two men to and fro. When Temuchin spoke again, there was resolve in his voice.

"I will have that, even though I know the price. You want me demon, to take me to your hell below the mountains. But you shall not have me until I have conquered all."

"I'm no demon, Temuchin."

"Do not mock me. I know the truth. What the jongleurs sing is true, though I never believed it before. You have tempted me, have accepted, I am damned. Tell me the hour and manner of my death.''

"I can't tell you that."

"Of course not. You are bound as I am bound."

"I didn't mean it that way."

"I know how it was meant. By accepting all, I lose all. There is no other way. But I will have it like that. I will win first. That is true, demon, you will allow that?"

"Of course, you will win, and—"

"Tell me no more. I have changed my mind. I do not wish to know the manner of my end." He shook his shoulders as though to remove some unseen weight, then thrust his sword back into the slings at his waist.

"All right, believe what you will. Just give me some good men and I'll open up the passage to the lowlands. A rope ladder will get us into the valley. I'll mark the route and take them through the caves to prove that it can be done. Then the next time we do it, the army will follow. Will they go—down there?"

Temuchin laughed. "They have sworn to follow me to hell if I order it and now so they will. They will follow."

"Good. Shall we shake on that?"

"Of course! I will take the world and win eternity in hell, so I have no fear of your cold flesh now, my demon."

He crushed Jason's hand in his and, despite himself, Jason could not help but admire the giant courage of the man.

20

"Let me talk to him, please," Meta asked.

Kerk waved her away and clutched the microphone, almost swallowing it in his giant hand.

"Listen to me now, Jason," he said coldly. "None of us is with you in this adventure. You will not explain your purpose and you will gain nothing except destruction. If Temuchin controls the lowlands, too, we will never replace him and open the mines. Rhes has returned to Ammh and is organizing resistance to your invasion. Some here have voted to join him. I am going to ask you for the last time. Stop what you are doing before it is too late.''

When Jason's voice sounded from the radio, it had a curious flat quality, whether the fault of the transmission or that of the speaker it was hard to say.

''Kerk, I hear what you say and, believe me, I understand it. But it is too late now to turn back. Most of the army has gone through the caves and we've captured a number of *moropes* from the villages. Nothing I say could stop Temuchin now. This thing will have to be seen through to its conclusion. The lowlanders may win, though I doubt it. Temuchin is going to rule, above and below the cliffs, and in the end this will all be for the best.''

''No!'' Meta shouted, pulling at the microphone. ''Jason, listen to me. You cannot do this. You came to us and helped us, and we believed in you. You showed us that life is not only kill and be killed. We know now that the war on Pyrrus was wrong because you showed us, and we only came to this planet because you asked us to. Now it seems, I think, it is as though you were betraying us. You have tried to teach us how not to kill and, believe me, we have tried to learn. Yet what you are doing now is worse than anything we ever did on Pyrrus. There, at least, we were fighting for our lives. You don't have that excuse. You have shown that monster, Temuchin, a way to make new wars and to kill more people. How can you justify that?''

Static rustled hoarsely in the speaker while they waited the long moments for Jason to speak. When he did he sounded suddenly very tired.

''Meta . . . I'm sorry. I wish I could tell you, but it is too late. They're looking for me and I have to hide this radio before they get here. What I'm doing is right. Try to believe that. Someone a long time ago said that you cannot make an omelet without breaking eggs. Meaning you cannot bring about social change without hurting someone. People are being hurt and are dying because of me and don't think I'm not aware of it. But . . . listen, I can't talk any more. They're right outside.'' His voice dropped to a whisper. ''Meta, if I never see you again, just remember one thing. It's an old-fashioned word, but it is in a lot of languages. The library can translate it for you and give you the meaning.

''This is better by radio. I doubt if I could say it right to your face. You're stronger than I am, Meta, and your reflexes are a lot better but you are still a woman. And, hell, I want to say that I . . . love you. Good luck. Signing off.''

The speaker clicked and the room was silent.

"What was that word he used?" Kerk asked.

"I think I know," she answered, and she turned her face away so he could not see it.

"Hello, control!" a voice shouted. "Radio room here. A sub-space message coming in from Pyrrus with an emergency classification."

"Put it through," Kerk ordered.

There was the rustle of interstellar static, then the familiar drumbeat warble of the jump-space carrier wave. Superimposed on top of it was the quick, worried voice of a Pyrran.

"Attention, all stations within zeta radius. Emergency message for planet Felicity, ship's receiver *Pugnacious*, code Ama Rona Pi, 290-633-087. Message follows. Kerk, anyone there. Trouble hit. All the quadrants. We've shortened the perimeter, abandoned most of the city. Don't know if we can hold. Brucco says this is something new and that conventional weapons won't stop it. We can use the fire power of your ship. If you can return, come at once. Message ends."

The radio room had put the sub-space message through to all compartments of the ship and, in the horrified silence that followed its ending, running footsteps sounded from both connecting passageways. As the first men burst in, Kerk came to life and shouted his commands.

"All men to stations. We blast as soon as we're secured. Call in the outside guards. Release all the prisoners. We're leaving."

There was absolutely no doubt about that. It was inconceivable that any Pyrran could have acted otherwise. Their home, their city, was on the verge of destruction, perhaps already gone. They ran to their posts.

"Rhes," Meta said. "He's with the army. How can we reach him?"

Kerk thought for a moment, then shook his head. "We cannot, that is the only answer. We'll leave the launch for him on the same island where we make the contacts. Record a broadcast telling him what has happened and set it on automatic to broadcast every hour. When he gets back to a radio, he will pick it up. The launch will be locked so no one else can get in. There is medicine in it, even a jump-space communicator. He will be all right."

"He won't like it."

"It's the best we can do. Now we have to ready for blast off."

They worked as a team driven by a common urge. Back. Return to Pyrrus. Their city was in danger. The ship lifted at 17G's, and

Meta would have used more power if the structure of the ship could have withstood it. Their course through jump-space was the quickest and the most dangerous that could be computed. There were no complaints about the time the journey took: they accepted this period with stoic resignation. But weapons were readied and there was little or no conversation. Each Pyrran held, locked within him, the knowledge that their world and their life faced extinction, and these things cannot be discussed.

Hours before the *Pugnacious* was scheduled to break out of jump-space, every man and woman aboard was armed and waiting. Even nine-year-old Grif was there, a Pyrran like all the others.

From the eye-hurting otherness of jump-space to the black of interstellar space to the high atmosphere of Pyrrus the ship sped. Downward in a screaming ballistic orbit, where the hull heated to just below its melting point and the coolers labored against the overtaxing load. Their bodies reacted, sweat dripped from their faces and soaked their clothes, but the Pyrrans were unaware of the heat. The picture from the bow pickup was put on every screen in the ship. Jungle flashed by, then a high column of smoke climbed up on the distant horizon. Diving swiftly, like a striking bird of prey, the ship swooped down.

The jungle now occupied the city. A circular mound, covered with plants and tough growth, was the only trace of the once impregnable perimeter wall. As they came low, they could see thornlike creepers bursting through the windows of the buildings. Animals moved slowly through the streets that had once been crowded with people, while a clawhawk perched on the tower of the central warehouse, the masonry crumbling under its weight.

As they flew on, they could see that the smoke was coming from the crushed ruin of their spaceship. It appeared to have been caught on the ground at the spaceport and was held down by a now blackened net of giant vines.

There were no signs of activity anywhere in the ruined city. Just the beasts and plants of deathworld, now strangely quiet and sluggish with their enemy gone, the motivations of hatred that had enraged them for so long now vanished. They stirred and reared when the ship passed over, quickened to life again as the raw emotions of the surviving Pyrrans impressed upon them.

"They can't all be dead," Teca said in a choked voice. "Keep looking."

"I am quartering the entire area," Meta told him.

Kerk found the destruction almost impossible to look at, and when he spoke, his voice was low, as though he were talking only to himself.

"We knew that it had to end like this—sometime. We faced that and tried to make a new start on a new planet. But, knowing something will happen and seeing it before your eyes, those are two different things. We ate there, in that . . . ruin, slept in that one. Our friends and comrades were here, our entire life. And now it is gone."

"Go down!" Clon said, thinking nothing, feeling hatred. "Attack. We can still fight."

"There is nothing left to fight for," Teca told him, speaking with an immense weariness. "As Kerk said, it is gone."

A hull pickup detected the sound of gunfire, and they rocketed toward it with momentary hope. But it was just an automatic gun still actuating itself in a repeating pattern. Soon it would be out of ammunition and would be still like the rest of the ruined city.

The radio light had been blinking for some time before someone noticed it. The call was on the wavelength of Rhes's headquarters, not the one the city had used. Kerk reached over slowly and switched the set to receive.

"Naxa here, can you hear me? Come in, *Pugnacious.*"

"Kerk here. We are over the city. We are . . . too late. Can you give me a report?"

"Too late by days," Naxa snorted. "They wouldn't listen to us. We said we could get them out, give them a place to go to, but they wouldn't listen. Just like they wanted to die in the city. Once the perimeter went down, the survivors holed up in one of the buildings and it sounded like everything on this planet hit them at once. We couldn't take it, standing by I mean. Everyone volunteered. We took the best men and all the armored ground cars from the mine. Went in there. Got out the kids, they made the kids go, some of the women. The wounded, just the ones who were unconscious. The rest stayed. We just got out before the end. Don't ask me what it was like. Then it was all over, the fighting, and after a bit everything quieted down like you see it now. Whole planet quieted down. When we could, me and some of the other talkers went to see. Had to climb a mountain of bodies of every creature born. Found the right spot. The ones that stayed behind, they're all dead. Died fighting. Only thing we could bring back then was a bunch of records that Brucco left."

"They would not have had it any other way," Kerk said. "Let us know where the survivors are and we will go there at once."

Naxa gave the coordinates and said, "What're you going to do now?"

"We'll contact you again. Over and out."

"What *are* we going to do now?" Teca asked. "There's nothing left for us here."

"There's nothing for us on Felicity either. As long as Temuchin rules, we cannot open the mines," Kerk answered.

"Go back. Kill Temuchin," Teca said, his power holster humming. He wanted revenge, to kill something.

"We can't do that," Kerk said. Patiently, because he knew the torture the man was feeling. "We will discuss this later. We must first see to the survivors."

"We have lost everywhere," Meta said, voicing the words that everyone was thinking.

Silence followed.

21

The four guards ran into the room half carrying Jason, then hurled him to the floor. He rolled over and got to his knees.

"Get out," Temuchin ordered his men, and kicked Jason hard on the side of his head, knocking him down again. When Jason sat up, there was a livid bruise covering the side of his face.

"I suppose that there is a reason for this," he said quietly.

Temuchin opened and closed his great hands in fury, but said nothing. He stamped the length of the ornate room, his trailing prickspurs scratching deep gouges in the inlaid marble of the floor. At the far end he stood for a moment, looking out of the high windows and across the city below. Then he reached up suddenly and pulled at the tapestry drapes, tearing them down in a sudden spasm of effort. The iron bar that supported them fell as well, but he caught it before it touched the floor and hurled it through the many-paned window. There was the crashing fall of breaking glass far below.

"I have lost!" he shouted, almost an animal howl of pain.

"You've won," Jason told him. "Why are you doing this?"

"Let us not pretend any more," Temuchin answered, turning to face him, a frozen calm replacing the anger. "You knew what would happen."

"I knew that you would win—and you have. The armies fell before you and the people fled. Your horde has overrun the land and your captains rule in every city. While you rule here in Eolasair, lord of the entire world."

"Do not play with me, demon. I knew this would happen. I just did not think that it would happen so quickly. You could have allowed me more time."

"Why?" Jason asked, climbing to his feet. Now that Temuchin had realized the truth, there was no longer any point in concealment. "You said that by accepting you would lose."

"I did. Of course." Temuchin straightened his back and looked unseeingly out the window. "I just had not realized how much I would lose. I was a fool. I thought that only my own life was at stake. I did not realize that my people, our life, would die as well." He turned on Jason. "Give it back to them. Take me, but let them return."

"I cannot."

"You will not!" Temuchin shouted, rushing on Jason, grabbing him up by the neck and shaking him like an empty goatskin. "Change it—I command you." He loosened his grip slightly so that Jason could gasp in air and speak.

"I cannot—and I would not even if I could. In winning, you lost, and that is just the way I want it. The life you knew has ended and I would not have it any other way."

"You knew this all along," Temuchin said almost gently, releasing his grasp. "This was my fate and you knew it. You let it happen. Why?"

"For a number of reasons."

"Tell me one."

"Mankind can do very well without your way of life. We have had enough killing and bloody murder in our history. Live your life out, Temuchin, and die peacefully. You are the last of your kind and the galaxy will be a better place for your ending."

"Is that the only reason?"

"There are others. I want the off-worlders to dig their mines on your plains. They can do that now."

"In winning I lost. There must be a word for this kind of happening."

"There is. It was a 'Pyrrhic victory.' I wish I could say that I am sorry for you, but I'm not. You're a tiger in a pit, Temuchin. I can admire your muscles and your temper and I know that you used to be lord of the jungle. But now I'm glad that you are trapped." Without looking toward the door, Jason took a short step in its direction.

"There is no escape, demon," Temuchin said.

"Why? I cannot harm you—or help you any more."

"Nor can I kill you. A demon, being dead already, cannot be killed. But the human flesh you wear can be tortured. That I shall do. Your torture will last as long as I live. This is a small return for all that I have lost—but it is all that I have to offer. We have much to look forward to, demon . . ."

Jason did not hear the rest as he bolted through the door, head down and running as fast as he could. The two guards at the far end of the hall heard his pounding feet and turned, lowering their spears. He did not slow or attempt to avoid them, but fell instead and slid, feet first, under their spears and cannoning into them. They fell in a tangle and, for one instant, Jason was held by the arm. But he chopped with the edge of his hand, breaking the restraining wrist, and was free. Scrambling to his feet, he hurled himself down the stairwell, jumping eight, ten steps at a time, risking a fall with every leap. Then he hit the ground floor and ran through the unguarded front entrance into the courtyard.

"Seize him!" Temuchin shouted from above. "I want him brought to me."

Jason pelted toward the nearest entrance, veering off as it filled suddenly with guards. There were armed men everywhere, at every exit. He ran toward the wall. It was high and topped with gilded spearheads, but he had to get over it. Footsteps sounded loudly behind him as he sprang upward, his fingers closing over the edge of the wall. Good! He heaved himself up, to throw his legs over, climb between the spearheads and drop to the other side to vanish into the city.

The hands locked about his ankle, the weight holding him back. He kicked and felt his boot crush a face, but he could not free himself. Then other hands caught his flailing leg and still more, pulling him back down into the courtyard.

"Bring him to me," Temuchin's voice sounded over the crowd of men. "Bring him to me. He is mine."

22

Rhes was waiting, a tiny figure beside the launch as the *Pugnacious* dropped down from the sky. It was a full-jet, 20G landing. Meta was not wasting any time. Rhes picked his way through the fused and smoking sand as the port opened to receive him.

"Tell us everything quickly," Meta said.

"There's little enough to tell. Temuchin won his war, as we knew he would, taking every city with one blow after another. The people here, even the armies, could not stand against him. I fled after the last battle, with all the others, for I did not wish to see my thumbs hanging from some barbarian banner. That was when I got your message. You must tell me what happened on Pyrrus."

"The end," Kerk said. "The city, everyone there, is gone."

Rhes knew that there were no words that he could say. He was silent a moment; then Meta caught his eye and he continued.

"Jason has—or had—a radio, and soon after I reached the launch, I picked up a message from him. I could not answer him and his message was never completed. I did not have the recorder on, but I can remember it clearly enough. He said that the mines could be opened soon, that we had won. The Pyrrans have won, that is exactly what he said. He started to add something else, but the broadcast was suddenly broken off. That must have been when they came for him. I have heard more about it since that time."

"What do you mean?" Meta asked quickly.

"Temuchin has made his capital in Eolasair, the largest city in Ammh. He has Jason there in . . . in a cage, hung in front of the palace. He was first tortured; now he is being starved to death."

"Why? For what reason?"

"It is a nomad belief that a demon in human form cannot be killed. He is immune to normal weapons. But if he is starved long enough, the human disguise will wither and the demon's original form will be revealed. I don't know if Temuchin believes this nonsense or not, but this is just what he is doing. Jason has been hanging in that cage for over fifteen days now."

431

"We must go to him," Meta said, leaping to her feet. "We must free him."

"We will do that," Kerk told her. "But we must do it the right way. Rhes, can you get us clothes and *moropes?*"

"Of course. How many will you need?"

"We cannot force our way in, not against the ruler of an entire planet. Just two of us will go. You will come to show the way. I will go to see what can be done."

"And I will come, too," Meta said, and Kerk nodded agreement.

"The three of us then. At once. We don't know how long he can live under these conditions."

"They give him a cup of water every day," Rhes said, avoiding Meta's eyes. "Take the ship up. I'll show you which way to go. It does not matter any more if the people in the city here know we are from off-planet."

This was before noon. By drugging the *moropes* and loading them into the cargo bay, a good deal of riding time was saved. The city of Eolasair was built on a river among rolling hills, with a forest nearby. They landed the ship as close as they could without being seen and had the *moropes* on the way as soon as they were revived. By later afternoon they entered the city, and Rhes threw a boy a small coin to show them the way to the palace. He wore his merchant's clotnes, and Kerk had put on his full armor and weapons. Meta, veiled as was the local custom, clutched her hands tightly on the saddle as they forced their way through the crowded streets.

Only before the palace was there empty space. The courtyard was floored with gold-veined marble, polished and shining. A squad of troops guarded it, their bearded nomad faces incongruous above the looted armor. But their weapons were in order and they were as deadly as they had been on the high plains. Worse, perhaps, their tempers were not improved by the warm climate.

A chain had been passed between the tops of two of the tall columns that flanked the courtyard and from it, hanging a good two meters above the ground, was suspended a cage of thick bars. It had no door and had been built around the prisoner.

"Jason!" Meta said, looking up at the slumped figure. He did not move and there was no way of telling if he was alive or dead.

"I will take care of this," Kerk said, and jumped from his *morope.*

"Wait!" Rhes called after him. "What are you going to do? Getting yourself killed won't help Jason."

Kerk was not listening. He had lost too much and felt too much pain recently to be in a reasoning mood. Now all of his hatred was turned against one man, and he could not be stopped.

"Temuchin!" he roared. "Come out of your gilt hiding place. Come on, you coward, and face me, Kerk of Pyrrus! Show yourself—*coward!*"

Ahankk, who was the guard officer, came running with his sword drawn, but Kerk backhanded him offhandedly, his attention still fixed on the palace. Ahankk dropped and rolled over and over and remained there, unconscious or dead. Surely dead, with his head at an angle like that.

"Temuchin, coward, come out!" Kerk shouted again. When the stunned soldiers touched their weapons, he turned on them, snarling.

"Dogs—would you attack me? A high chief, Kerk of Pyrrus, victor of The Slash?" They fell back before his burning anger, and he turned to the palace as the front entrance was thrown wide. Temuchin strode out.

"You dare too much," he said, his cold anger matching that of Kerk's.

"You dare," Kerk told him. "You break tribal law. You take a man of my tribe and torture him for no reason. You are a coward, Temuchin, and I name you that before your men."

Temuchin's sword flashed in the sunlight as he drew it, a fine-tempered length of razor-sharp steel.

"You have said enough, Pyrran. I could have you killed on the spot, but I want that pleasure for myself. I wanted to kill you the moment I first saw you—and I should have. Because of you and this creature which calls itself Jason, I have lost everything."

"You have lost nothing—yet," Kerk answered and his sword pointed straight at the warlord's throat. "But now you lose your life, for I shall kill you."

Temuchin brought his sword down in a blow that would have cut a man in two—but it rang off Kerk's blade. They battled then, furiously, with no science and no art—barbarian sword fight, just slash and parry, with eventual victory going to the strongest.

The clang of their steel rang in the silence of the courtyard, the only other sound being the rasping of their breath as they fought. Neither would give way, and they were well matched. Kerk was the older man, but he was the stronger. Temuchin had a lifetime of sword fighting and battles behind him and was absolutely without fear.

It went on like that, a rapid exchange that was broken suddenly by a sharp twang as Temuchin's sword snapped in two. He threw

himself backward, out of the way of Kerk's slash, so that instead of
gutting him it cut a red gash in his thigh, a minor wound. He
sprawled at full length, blood slowly seeping into the golden silk he
wore, as Kerk raised his sword in both hands for the last, unavoid-
able blow.

"Archers!" Temuchin shouted. He would not submit to death
this easily.

Kerk laughed and hurled his sword away. "You do not escape
that easily, ruling coward. I prefer to kill you with my bare hands."

Temuchin shouted wordless hatred and sprang to his feet. They
leaped at each other with the passion of animals and closed in
struggling combat.

There were no blows exchanged. Instead, Kerk closed his great
hands around the other's neck and tightened. Temuchin clutched his
opponent in the same way, but the muscles in Kerk's neck were
steel ropes: he could not affect them. Kerk tightened his grip.

For the first time Temuchin showed some emotion other than
unthinking anger. His eyes widened and he writhed in the clutch of
the closing fingers. He pulled at Kerk's wrists, but to no avail. The
Pyrran's grip tightened like that of a machine, and just as implac-
ably.

Temuchin twisted about, got his hand in the back of his belt and
pulled out a dagger.

"Kerk! He has a knife!" Rhes shouted, as Temuchin whipped it
around and plunged it full into Kerk's side under the lower edge of
his breastplate.

His hand came away and the hilt of the dagger remained there.

Kerk bellowed in anger—but he did not release his grip. Instead,
he moved his thumbs up under Temuchin's chin and pushed back.
For a long moment the warlord writhed, his boot tips almost free of
the ground and his eyes starting from their sockets.

Then there was a sharp snap and his body went limp.

Kerk released his grip and the great Temuchin, First Lord of the
high plateau and of the lowlands, fell in a dead huddle at his feet.

Meta rushed up to him, the red stain spreading on his side.

"Leave it," Kerk ordered. "It plugs the hole. Mostly in the
muscle, and if it has punctured some guts, we can sew it up later.
Get Jason down."

The guards made no motion to interfere when Rhes pulled away
one of their halberds and, hooking it in the bottom of the cage,
pulled it crashing to the ground. Jason rolled limply with the impact.
His eyes were set in black hollows and his skin was drawn tautly

over the bone of his face. Through his rags of clothing red burns and scars could be seen on his skin.

"Is he . . . ?" Meta said, but could not go on. Rhes clutched two of the bars, tensed his muscles, and slowly bent apart the thick metal to make an opening.

Jason opened one bloodshot eye and looked up at them.

"Took your time about getting here," he said, and let it drop shut again.

23

"No more right now," Jason said, waving away the glass and straw that Meta held out to him. He sat up on his bunk aboard the *Pugnacious,* washed, medicated, his wounds dressed, and with a glucose drip plugged into his arm. Kerk sat across from him, a bulge on one side where he had been bandaged. Teca had taken out a bit of punctured intestine and tied up a few blood vessels. Kerk preferred to ignore it completely.

"Tell us," he said. "I've plugged this microphone into the annunciator system, and everyone is waiting to hear. To be frank, we still don't know what happened—other than the fact that both you and Temuchin think that each lost by winning. It is very strange."

Meta leaned over and touched Jason's forehead with a folded cloth. He smiled and put his fingers against her wrist before he spoke.

"It was history. I went to the library to find out the answer, later than I should have—but not too late, after all. The library read a lot of books to me and very quickly convinced me that a culture cannot be changed from the outside. It can be suppressed or destroyed—but it cannot be changed. And that's just what we were trying to do. Have you ever heard of the Goths and the Hunnish tribes of Old Earth?"

They shook their heads no and this time he accepted the drink to dampen his throat.

"These were a bunch of backwoods barbarians who lived in the forest, enjoyed drinking, killing and their own brand of independence, and fought the Roman legions every time they came along. The tribes were always beaten—and do you think they learned a lesson from it? Of course not. They just gathered up the survivors and went deeper in the woods to fight another day, their culture and their hatred intact. Their culture was changed only when they *won*. Eventually they moved in on the Romans, captured Rome and learned all the joys of civilized life. They weren't barbarians any more. The ancient Chinese used to work the same trick for centuries. They weren't very good fighters, but they were great absorbers. They were overrun and licked time and time again—and sucked the victors down into their own culture and life.

"I learned this lesson and just arranged things so that it would happen here as well. Temuchin was an ambitious man and could not resist the temptation of new worlds to conquer. So he invaded the lowlands when I showed him the way."

"And by winning, he lost," Kerk said.

"Exactly. The world is his now. He has captured the cities and he wants their wealth. So he has to occupy them to obtain it. His best officers become administrators of the new realm and wallow in unaccustomed luxury. They like it here. They might even stay. They are still nomads at heart—but what about the next generation? If Temuchin and his chiefs are living in cities and enjoying the sybaritic pleasures thereof, how can he expect to enforce the no cities law back on the plateau? It begins to look sort of foolish after a while. Any decent barbarian isn't going to stay up there in the cold when he can come down here and share the loot. Wine is stronger than *achadh* and they even have some distilleries here. The nomad way of life is doomed. Temuchin realized that, though he could not put it into words. He just knew that, by winning, he had left behind and destroyed the way of life that had enabled him to win in the first place. That's why he called me a demon and strung me up."

"Poor Temuchin," Meta said, with sudden insight. "His ambition doomed him and he finally realized it. Though he was the conqueror, he was the one who lost the most."

"His way of life and his life itself," Jason said. "He was a great man."

Kerk grunted. "Don't tell me that you're sorry I killed him?"

"Not at all. He attained everything he ever wanted; then he died. Not many men can say that."

"Turn off the annunciator," Meta said. "And you may go, Kerk."

The big Pyrran opened his mouth to protest, then smiled instead, and turned and went out.

"What are you going to do now?" Meta asked as soon as the door was closed.

"Sleep for a month, eat steaks and grow strong."

"I do not mean that. I mean where will you go? Will you stay here with us?"

She was working hard to express her emotions, using a vocabulary that was not suited for this form of communication. He did not make it any easier for her.

"Does that matter to you?"

"It matters, in a way that is very new." Her forehead creased and she almost stammered with the effort to put her feelings into words. "When I am with you, I want to tell you different things. Do you know what is the nicest thing that we can say in Pyrran?" He shook his head. We say, "You fight very well.' That is not what I want to say to you."

Jason spoke nine languages and he knew exactly what it was he wanted to say, but he would not. Or could not. He turned away instead.

"No, look at me," Meta said, taking his head in both hands and gently turning his face toward hers. Her actions said more than any words could and he was ashamed of his inability to speak. Yet he still remained silent.

"I have looked up the word 'love,' just as you told me to do. At first it was not clear because it was only words. But when I thought about you, the meaning became clear at once."

Their faces were close, her wide clear eyes looking unflinchingly into his.

"I love you," she said. "I think that I will always love you. You must never leave me."

The direct simplicity of her emotions rose like a flooded river against the shored-up dikes of his conditioned defenses, the mechanisms that he had built up through the years. He was a loner. No one was on his side. I'm all right, Jack. Take a woman, leave a woman. The universe helps those who help themselves. I can take care of myself and . . . I . . . don't . . . need . . . anyone. . . .

"Dear stars above, how I do love you, too," he said, pulling her to him, his face pressing into her neck and hair.

"You will never leave me again," she said.

"And you will never leave me again. There, the shortest and best marriage ceremony on record. May you break my arm if I ever look at another girl."

"Please. Do not talk about violence now."

"I apologize. That was the old unreconstructed me talking. I think that we must both bring gentleness into our lives. That is what you, I and our pack of growling Pyrrans need the most. That's what we all need. Not humility, no one needs that. Just a little civilizing. I think that we can survive with it now. The mines should be opening here soon, and the way the tribes are moving to the lowlands, it looks like you Pyrrans will have the plateau to yourselves."

"Yes, that will be good. It can be our new world." She hesitated a moment as she weighed his words. "We Pyrrans will stay here— but what about you? I would not like to leave my people again, but I will go if you go."

"You won't have to. I'm staying right here. I'm a member of the tribe—remember? Pyrrans are rude, opinionated and irascible, we know that. But I am, too. So perhaps I've found a home at last."

"With me, always with me."

"Of course."

After this there was no more that could be said.

EXCITING SCIENCE FICTION BESTSELLERS!